Birmingham Rose

&

Where Earth Meets Sky

ANNIE MURRAY was born in Berkshire and read English at St John's College, Oxford. Her first Birmingham novel, *Birmingham Rose*, hit *The Times* bestseller list when it was published in 1995. She has subsequently written thirteen other successful novels, including, most recently, *A Hopscotch Summer* and *Soldier Girl*. Annie Murray has four children and lives in Reading.

ANNIE MURRAY

Birmingham Rose
&
Where Earth Meets Sky

PAN BOOKS

Birmingham Rose first published 1995 Pan Books
Where Earth Meets Sky first published 2007 by Pan Books

This omnibus first published 2011 by Pan Books
an imprint of Pan Macmillan, a division of Macmillan Publishers Limited
Pan Macmillan, 20 New Wharf Road, London N1 9RR
Basingstoke and Oxford
Associated companies throughout the world
www.panmacmillan.com

ISBN 978-0-330-54566-2

1 3 5 7 9 8 6 4 2

A CIP catalogue record for this book is available from
the British Library.

Typeset by SetSystems Ltd, Saffron Walden, Essex
Printed in the UK by CPI Mackays, Chatham ME5 8TD

Birmingham Rose

For John

ACKNOWLEDGEMENTS

With special thanks to: Carl Chinn, Tom Golding, Barbara Martin, Pat Oakes, Betty O'Brien, A. M. O'Meara, George and Jackie Summers and Eric Taylor.

PART ONE

BIRMINGHAM
1931–1940

One

June 1931

'Look at this Ronald!'

Catherine leaned closer to the window. Water was streaming off the glass outside. It was the height of the storm, the heaviest Birmingham had seen for twenty years.

'How dreadful – we must do something for her!'

There was silence from the other side of the room. The only noise came from the rain, a constant solid sound as if there were not individual drops but a torrent poured from some great vat in the sky.

Catherine, still holding the spoon she had been using for the tea, tapped it against the window. Ronald, who had been sighing over the latest unemployment figures in *The Times*, finally flung down his newspaper in irritation.

'*Look*,' she insisted. 'That poor little girl.'

Across the street a tiny figure huddled low against the garden wall of a house. Petals of mock orange and yellow roses lay in a sodden covering over the ground. She was squatting sideways, pressed hard against the bricks as if blown there helplessly like a moth by the strength of the wind and beating rain. The arm closest to the wall was stretched out straight as if to stop her from toppling over; her left arm clutched something white close to her body.

'Poor little mite,' Catherine said. 'She can only be about six. Well, she can't stay out there in this. I'm going to fetch her.' Without stopping for a coat or hat she ran through the darkened hall and unlocked the front door.

'Do you think you should?' Her husband followed her. 'You could catch a chill. And the wind's quite dreadful.'

'Don't be ridiculous Ronald. What is the matter with you?'

The door she was opening was flung out of her hand as she spoke and she had to push all her weight on it to clip it shut. She ran down the short path, steadying herself against the wind. In seconds her white blouse was soaked and clinging, her pink flesh showing through.

From the sitting-room window Ronald Harper-Watt watched with a mixture of pride and exasperation as his impetuous wife ran down the path. Oh Catherine, he thought. Here I am always sitting thinking about doing things and you just get on and do them.

Out in the road the only sounds were the uneven roar of the wind, the swish of the rain and water gurgling along the cobbled gutters. Catherine saw a chimney pot hurled down from one of the nearby houses.

Heavens, she thought, there'll be roofs off next.

She expected to find the girl tearful and distressed. Not wanting to spend time comforting her and getting even more drenched, she lifted her up by the waist and twisted her round into her arms.

'Come on – I'll look after you little one,' she said. 'Let's go and get into the dry, shall we?'

4

While she was mainly concentrating on getting back into the house, and taking in as she went the fact that the guttering at one end of the vicarage was wobbling precariously, Catherine was conscious that two dark and quite tearless eyes were watching her face intently. She bent forward, holding the skinny child close to her, and reached the shelter of the front hall gasping. Her light brown hair with blond lights in it had been teased out of its pins by the exhilarating wind and rain and was uncoiling down her back.

Her straight green skirt and the girl's thin cotton dress and bloomers dripped on to the patterned tiles in the hall. Catherine stood smiling at the little girl who had, it seemed, been blown to their door. The child stood staring back with a penetrating, solemn gaze.

'Ronald?' Catherine called out.

To her amazement he was already half-way down the stairs with large white towels. 'The guttering's coming down,' she told him.

Catherine took the girl's free hand as she was still holding tightly on to the white thing with the other. 'Come on, let's get those clothes off you and get you dry. One of my girls is a bit older than you so I'll find you something you can wear. Now, what's that you've got under your arm?'

The child held out the object which turned out to be an enamel dish. Her brown eyes were taking in everything hungrily from under her sodden black fringe. Her hair seemed to be cropped in a rough pudding-basin shape round her head.

'What's your name, my dear?' Catherine asked her as they climbed the stairs.

'Rose – ma'am,' she added. She was looking at the deep red staircarpet in wonder.

5

'And where do you live, Rose?'

'Number five, court eleven, Catherine Street,' she gabbled out.

'Catherine? Well, you won't have any problem remembering my name – it's the same as your street.' She called over the banisters to her husband: 'Catherine Street. That's a way from here isn't it?'

'The only Catherine Street I can think of is about two or three miles away. It's in the Birch Street area. Not this parish, certainly. Probably St Joseph's.' One of the slum parishes, he thought. I wonder why she's strayed away from home – a runaway perhaps? Again he felt a sense of hopelessness overcome him. Recently it seemed that Catherine had a far greater instinct for dealing with people than he did, he who had once felt this was his gift.

As they crossed the landing upstairs the sound of children's voices could be heard chanting loudly in one of the bedrooms: 'Rain, rain, go away, come again another day!'

'Now Rose, what are you doing this far from home?' Catherine asked as she knelt rubbing the little body with her towel. The child's skin, spotted with bug bites, seemed to cover only jutting bones. Rose reminded her of a tiny kitten or a newborn foal, all bony knees and staring eyes.

'Been to me sister's,' Rose said. 'She's expecting, so Mom gave me the custard and raspberry leaves to take over. It's our Marj's first babby you see.'

'I see,' Catherine said doubtfully. 'So your sister – Marj – does she live here in Moseley?'

'Oh no! She lives up Sparkbrook with her husband Fred. Mom says the babby's coming in November. And she says if she takes the raspberry tea it'll stop her coming on so bad with the pains.'

Catherine smiled at this grown-up knowledge, thinking of the patched, infantile dress lying on the floor beside them.

'So you're going to be a little aunt then?'

'Yes. And Marj wants me to sleep over her place sometimes after the babby's born. I'm not sure I want to though, 'cos it'll be blarting half the night and our Marj is bad-tempered enough as it is.'

Struck by the amount of talking this little person suddenly seemed capable of, Catherine asked her how old she was.

'Nine. Ten next January,' she replied promptly.

'You're nine?' Catherine managed to prevent herself from speaking the rest of her astonishment – how small you are, you poor child, how undernourished – and just said, 'Gracious, you're the same age as my Diana.'

She pulled one of her daughter's old dresses over Rose's dark head, wondering whether the child had lice, though she couldn't see any obvious signs of them. The frock hung limply on her, well down below her knees.

'Will that do you?'

Rose nodded solemnly.

'Now, you just stay there a minute and you can meet my children.'

Rose was left standing in the high-ceilinged room. Without moving her feet she looked up and round, twisting her body to see the soft, comfortable-looking bed with its eiderdown well plumped up, the black and white wooden rocking horse in one corner, the shelf full of books on the top of which stood small china ornaments, hedgehogs, squirrels and cats. What caught

7

Rose's eye particularly in all this splendour was a large black elephant, the top of its head and ears decorated with tiny pieces of mirror glass and beads. She was still staring at it when she heard Catherine say, 'Rose? This is Diana, and these two are William and Judith.'

A girl with light brown curls bouncing round her cheeks ran into the room and then stopped and stared at her. Outside the door, held back by their mother, Rose had a brief glimpse of an older boy who had the same broad face and grey eyes as his father, and a little girl with dark brown hair down her back who was trying hard to see into the room.

For a moment Diana stood staring at Rose, and Rose gazed back at her, looking at the pretty cotton print dress and white cardigan the girl had on. Then Diana said, 'You're not really nine are you? You're too small.'

'I am,' Rose said. 'And me brother Sam's ten, and me sister Grace is eight, and me brother—'

'Goodness, how many brothers and sisters have you got?' Diana wanted to know.

'Er . . .' Rose thought for a moment. 'There's Albert and Marj – but they're off married so they don't live at me mom's any more. And then there's Sam, and me and Grace and George. And me mom's expecting. So's me sister Marj.'

'Gosh,' Diana said. 'Well I suppose you can't help being small. Come on, I'll show you my room.'

'Where d'you get that elephant?' Rose asked, going over to it. She thought it was one of the loveliest things she'd ever seen.

'Daddy brought it back from India,' Diana said. 'Here . . .' She pulled out some books from the shelves. 'Come and sit on the bed and I'll show you these.' Rose obediently sat down, one hand stroking the soft bed-

8

covers. 'Now, let's have a look at these. I'm going to be a teacher when I grow up. What are you going to be?'

'I dunno.' Rose had never once thought about it. 'Where's India?'

'It's . . .' Diana ran to the bookshelf again and came back holding a tiny globe on a stand, which swivelled around when she touched it. 'There. And England's here. Daddy's a vicar, in case you didn't know. He worked with a missionary in Madras, before he met Mummy. India's part of the British Empire.'

Rose wasn't sure what a missionary was. 'Do they have elephants like that then?'

'They have real elephants and tigers and snakes. Daddy brought back lots of things. Here, if you want an elephant, I've got a little one.' She jumped off the bed, opened a couple of drawers, rummaged around and came back with a smaller elephant, about two inches high.

'I'm afraid some of the bits of glass have got lost. But you can have it – there.'

Rose looked at her, her eyes stretched wide in amazement. 'Won't your dad belt you for giving it away? You could pawn that.'

Diana laughed. 'We don't go to the pawn shop. That's only for poor people. Are you very poor?'

This was another thing Rose had not thought about before. Most people in Catherine Street seemed to live like her mom and dad. She knew there were houses where rich people lived because her mom used to go charring for them. Otherwise the only people everyone talked about were the king and queen. Grace was forever on about them.

'I dunno,' she said again. 'Are you very rich?'

'Not very, I don't think. But Mummy's daddy has a

9

lot of money. Daddy gets a bit cross about it sometimes but I don't know why because it means we can have a lot more things. Anyway, they won't mind about the elephant. You keep it.'

Catherine called them down for tea a few minutes later and as they went Rose said, 'What's your other name? Isn't your mom called Mrs Something?'

'It's Harper-Watt. But just call her Catherine – she'll laugh otherwise. She's like that.'

Rose sat in the big front sitting room with the family, drinking tea and eating sponge cake with strawberry jam inside and gazing round her. On either side of the fireplace, where there was a vase of dried flowers standing in the grate because it was summer, were rows and rows of books. They were arranged on shelves reaching almost to the ceiling and they had grey, red and brown spines with faded gold lettering. There were never any books in Rose's house. Everyone thought reading anything except the *Gazette* or the *Sports Argus* was a bit barmy unless you had to do it. But Rose liked reading at school and her favourite teacher, Miss Whiteley, said she was coming on a treat.

Catherine poured tea out of the silver teapot and Rose saw that all the cups matched. At home there were never enough to go round and none of them had the same pattern. Little Judith stared at her so much that she kept missing her mouth with the cake and dropping lots of crumbs. Catherine told her to watch what she was doing. William pretended to ignore Rose, but kept staring at her when he thought she was looking somewhere else. Rose wanted to make a face at him but she thought she'd better not.

'So, Rose,' the great big vicar said to her gently. 'Did you get lost on the way home from your sister's?

Moseley isn't really on the way to Catherine Street, is it?'

'No, I wasn't lost. I just wanted a walk round. Sometimes,' she announced, 'I like to have a bit of peace.'

The two adults smiled at each other, both hearing the echo of Rose's mother who presumably often needed to make the same claim.

'Well, I'm not sure if you've had that exactly,' said Mr Vicar, as Rose called him to herself. 'But we shall have to get you home soon, or your poor mother will be worried stiff. I'll walk that way with you myself. The rain is easing off now.' Partly he wanted to make up for his lack of initiative earlier.

By the time they had finished tea, the sun had come out and the heaviest clouds seemed pushed away by its warm arms. The air grew hot and heavy with moisture.

'You can keep the dress,' Catherine said and, seeing Rose's eyes full of happiness at the thought, continued, 'and please come and see us again if you're out for a bit of peace, won't you?'

'*Can* she?' Diana asked, jumping up and down. 'I like Rose. Go on, say you will, Rose.'

Diana demanded to be allowed to walk home with Rose too. The gutters were still running with water and there were puddles all over the pavement. As they walked, trying to keep their feet from getting too soaked, they saw broken tiles, glass and pieces of branch and twigs with leaves on. At one point a large tree had been torn up and was lying across the pavement.

'I do hope people haven't been injured,' Ronald said. 'Thank heavens it didn't happen yesterday when the shops were open.'

As he spoke, he noticed that Diana had taken Rose's

11

hand. He smiled, moved by the sight. All her mother's warmth, he thought. And once more he felt his own inadequacy.

His despondency deepened as they walked towards the middle of the city, the seething, smoking core which circled the Bull Ring, the market at its heart. The houses here were smaller and meaner, crammed back to back in street after grimy street, with factories and mills and small workshops. Those living in their two or three bug-ridden rooms lacked space and light, and their children lived – and often died – in squalid shadowy courts covered with refuse and filth, knowing little of any other street, any other life or possibility of improvement. At least this was his impression that day of this part of the city of which he in fact, to his shame, knew little.

And what about Rose, this curious little person who had suddenly been flung to their door? He watched her as she walked in front of him with his daughter, the two of them chattering as if they had known each other for months. She was hungry for something, knew there was more than her own life was showing her. Surely, he thought, I can learn from this child. He found this more cheering than all his sterile prayers of recent weeks.

Catherine Street was a row of three-storey houses, crushed together, their bricks darkened by the sooty air. The street stood on a rise above the great belly of the city. Walking down it you could see the reddish grey roofs, closely packed, and the church spires and factory chimneys poking up above them. For miles around you could make out the long, pointed spire of St Martin's Church in the Bull Ring.

'I'll go now, ta,' Rose said suddenly, and she started to run off down the slanting road.

'But I was going to explain to your mother!' Ronald's voice boomed along the street so people turned to look.

Diana ran after her. 'Are we going to be friends or not?' she demanded.

'If you want,' Rose said. 'I mean yes – please. You'd best not come to our house though. Better go now.'

Diana went back to her father and they watched Rose's small form skipping down the street, the long dress flapping round her legs.

Ronald noticed that the sky was beginning to darken again. He steered Diana round to walk home, taking a last glance back at Rose.

'Extraordinary child,' he said.

Two

Carrying her old dress and enamel dish, Rose ran down
Catherine Street. She thought she might go off pop, her
head was so full of all the things she had seen that
afternoon: the dress and the elephant in her pocket and
Diana. But going off pop was just what she wasn't going
to do.

I'm not telling no one about what's happened, she
said to herself. Not Geraldine, not even our Grace. I'm
going to keep it all to myself. She watched the cotton
dress with its tiny pink roses flying up and down in
front of her as her feet took her fast along the familiar
blue bricks of the pavement.

I bet when Diana got this it was *new*, Rose thought.
She began to skip so that the roses lifted even higher.

Then she saw her father. As she reached the entrance
to their court she thought he must have seen her – the
smile, the running and skipping and the new dress. She
stopped abruptly and began to walk, holding the enamel
dish against her stomach as if it was a teddy bear, her
old dress rolled up and hidden inside it. She hoped he
wouldn't ask any questions.

Ever since she was a tiny child Rose had had secrets.
They were often very small ones, and quite unnoticeable
to anyone else: a rounded pebble hidden under a leaf by
the wall of the brewhouse or a word of praise at school
from Miss Whiteley. It might be what she had seen on

one of her walks – often not far, but alone – to neighbouring streets. She felt as if she, Rose Lucas, was the first person in the world ever to see them.

At the sight of her father, though, she felt as if everything she had been thinking must be clear from her face, every detail of it. But as he dragged his large frame towards her, his laborious gait managed on one leg and one rough wooden crutch, his eyes watching the path in front of him, she realized he had not even looked up. When he did notice her he said gruffly, 'All right Gracie?'

'I'm *Rose*,' she said angrily, and instead of walking in with him she left him to struggle home by himself and ran ahead into the yard. Couldn't he even get her name right?

The sky was half covered by piled grey clouds. A peculiar harsh light was shining down catching one side of the court, the wet bricks and the small windows on which soot and grime accumulated again as fast as they were washed down. The other side, the wall where the tap for the yard was fixed, lay in deep shadow.

Her brother George, who was three, was standing dressed only in a grubby vest, chewing on a hard finger of bread crust mingled with snot from his nose and stamping his bare feet in the puddles. His bottom was naked and his little peter wiggled about with each stamp. Freddie and Daisy Pye from number six were standing with him on their bandy legs. All the family except Mr Pye had rickets.

When George saw Rose he beamed all over his grubby face and ran towards her with his arms out, saying, 'Rose. Pick me up! Nurse me, Rose!'

Rose got a bit fed up with George's endless hunger

15

to be picked up. No one had the time, that was the trouble.

'Look at the state of you!' she said. 'I can't pick you up now. You'll have to wait.' The little boy went back to his puddles, wiping his nose with the back of his hand. Rose disappeared into the house. She shot across the downstairs room where her mother stood slicing bread and went dashing up the stairs.

'Rose!' Her mother stood at the foot of the stairs, bread knife in hand. 'Where've you been?'

Rose paused for a second to make up her mind whether her mother was really angry. She decided things didn't sound too serious and carried on climbing the bare boards of the stairs, remembering the banisters at the vicarage, the pedestal at the bottom shaped into a huge shiny acorn.

'Got caught out in the rain, didn't I?' she called back. 'Down in a mo.'

'You haven't been at Marj's all this time – I know you,' her mother shouted. 'And where the hell did you get that dress?'

Rose climbed up to the room at the top of the house where she and Grace shared one single bed and Sam and George shared the other. She wanted to hide the elephant before anyone else saw it. She'd have to think up an explanation for the dress, but they needn't find out about all that had happened that afternoon. Not yet anyway.

She had tried hiding things up there before, but it wasn't much good. There was only the black iron rim of the bedstead under the mattress and you could hardly fit anything in there. And if she put it under the blanket Grace was bound to find it.

The Lucases' furniture had dwindled over the years.

This was all part of the change, the decline from 'before' when Sid and Dora lived in a house with two proper rooms downstairs, where they had their first two children. Before, when Sid had been a promising apprentice engineer, until he had come home in 1917 without one leg and the lower part of his left arm, and also missing some less tangible part of himself, perished in the scarred pastures of Flanders. All, in fact, before Rose was born. Albert, the oldest child, could just remember his father before the war. As a six-year-old he had taken weeks to accept that the maimed and haunted figure who appeared one day in a greatcoat at their door was the same man.

Rose moved the chest of drawers a fraction from the wall and hid the elephant behind it. That would do for now. She'd find somewhere better later.

Downstairs, her mother had disappeared and her father was easing himself awkwardly on to one of the family's two easy chairs. He propped the crutch against the wall beside him. Grace was sitting bent over a steaming bowl of water, her head covered by a strip of sacking. She was wheezing heavily. Rose realized she was trying to stave off one of her asthma attacks. We're in for a bad night then, Rose thought, not feeling very amiable about it. She felt irritable being back here with pee in a bucket in the bedroom after the new things she'd seen in the afternoon.

'Get me some tea,' Sid demanded, pushing the muddy shoe off his one foot and putting it against the fender to dry. Rose went to the hob and found there was freshly brewed tea in the pot. A tin of condensed milk was waiting with the bread on the table. She sugared the tea and passed it over without speaking. Sid gave a grunt of thanks.

'Where's Mom gone?' she asked.

'The lav – sick,' Grace gasped tetchily from under the sacking, as if she'd already answered the question once. She pointed in the direction of the four toilets at the end of the yard, shared by the six houses. 'Rose,' she whispered. 'I need a drink.'

'What did your last slave die of?' Rose snapped and then, realizing how unkind she was being, poured out more tea and placed it on the floor by her sister.

Grace peered up through her wispy fringe. 'Ta.'

'You bad again?'

'S'getting better now.' She looked up with a pink, damp face and tried to smile. She took in a deep breath so that her shoulders pulled back and her lungs whispered the air in.

Rose looked at her and then moved her gaze to their father, raising her eyebrows at Grace as she tried to gauge what mood he was in. Sid was sitting silently with his copy of the *Gazette*. There often seemed to be some intense emotion caged up in him which couldn't find a way out. When it did, they were terrified of him. Their mother took the worst of it: the lashings with his tongue and the force of his fist. Sometimes he left the house abruptly, saying nothing, and went off pulling himself round the streets for an hour or two, trying to repress the violence inside him which he so loathed. Sometimes he came back easier in himself. Other times the mood had deepened so the children hardly dared open their mouths.

It was hard to read his mood now, but Grace pulled down the corners of her mouth and rolled her eyes as if to say, 'Better watch our step.'

Through the window Rose saw her mother's thin figure walking across the yard, in her faded brown and white dress. Her arms were folded and pressed into her middle and she was holding herself rather bent forward as she did when she felt ill. Rain was falling again, and hurriedly she went to the tap across from the house and swallowed a few mouthfuls of water before coming inside.

Rose waited for her mother to start on her, but Dora sat down at the table as if drained of any strength. She was working four nights a week and in the second month of another pregnancy. She felt constantly faint and sick.

'Get me a cup of tea, Rose,' she said weakly. 'I want you carding tonight. Sam's at the Pyes and Grace ain't up to it, but you can get on with some of it or we'll never get them back.'

Rose groaned inside at the thought of another evening of work. To make ends meet they took in work from local factories. Rose had spent many evenings of her childhood sewing pearl buttons on to cards in the precise stitches expected by the factory until her eyes stung and watered under the gaslight. This time it was safety pins – fixing them on to cards for the shops. They'd get tuppence ha'penny a gross, and that, as Dora was forever pointing out, was worth a bag of sugar.

'Why can't Sam come back from the Pyes and do some too?' Rose asked. 'He always gets out of it.'

She saw her father's dark eyes swivel away from his paper. 'Don't give your mother lip like that,' he said. 'That's no work for a lad anyhow.'

Dora, sipping the tea with dry lips, waved her other hand at Rose to shut her up. 'Anyroad, they're feeding him, so that's one less of us. Aaah – that's better.' The colour was coming back into her cheeks. She sat nibbling half-heartedly at a piece of bread. She was already a slim woman, and every pregnancy, each baby carried and suckled shrank her thinner and made her look more gaunt and bony. In the overcast light of the evening her cheekbones were emphasized by the shadows beneath them and the skin under her eyes showed blue half-moons of exhaustion.

'Was Marj all right then?' she asked. 'Did you make sure she's taking the raspberry leaf? Which reminds me ...' Dora got up and went to the kettle to prepare her own dose of the brew. Rose thought it smelt horrible, all sour. But Dora had an almost religious faith in herbs and drank it through every pregnancy.

She didn't tell Dora that Marj had said in her most petulant voice, 'She needn't think I'm drinking this muck,' and had thrown the leaves out straight away.

'She's showing a lot,' Rose said. 'She says she's already sick of carrying that belly around.'

'Huh,' Dora said. 'She's only just bloomin' started. Wait till she's at it with a crowd of other babbies running round her. Then she'll find out what it's all about.'

As soon as they'd eaten their bread with a scraping of jam and Sid had shuffled off across the yard to the Catherine Arms, Dora rounded on Rose. 'Right,' she said, emptying the pile of tiny silver safety pins on to the worn American cloth. 'Where've you been all afternoon? Where d'you get that dress from? And where's my bowl?'

'It's upstairs.' In her hurry she'd left it on the bed with her dress. 'I'll get it.' She stood up to go to the stairs.

'Oh no you don't.' Dora grabbed her arm. 'Sit down. Come on, let's hear it. You go off with a bowl of custard and come swanning back in a new dress. What's been going on?'

Rose sat down again. 'I had a soaking,' she explained. 'Right to the skin. And the wind was so strong I nearly went flat on my face. You saw what it were like! This lady saw me from her house and took me in to dry out. She put the dress on me and she said I could keep it.'

'What lady? Where've you been wandering off to this time?' Dora tapped her finger hard on the table. 'Where was this house? Up Sparkbrook?'

'It might've been Sparkbrook,' Rose said, reluctant to give away even the vaguest details. 'Or it might've been a bit further out.'

'And you don't know where of course?'

'I was ever so wet,' Rose said, staring hard at the pins on the table.

Dora couldn't help smiling at her daughter, knowing she wasn't going to get the full story. 'You're the bleedin' end sometimes, Rose, you really are,' she said. 'Come on – get cracking on these or we'll be here all night.'

They sat pushing the thin wire of the pins through their cards. Dora was still feeling sick, even having eaten the small amount of food. She looked across at Rose's dark hair, the same wavy black as her father's, bent over the pile of pins next to Grace, whose hair was a lighter brown, more like Dora's own.

Her pregnancy with Rose had been the third after the war. First there had been the twins – remembering now sent a sharp twisting pain through her. They were born too early. The little mites, only the size of kittens, had barely snuffled their way into life before dying within hours of each other: two boys, Sid and Percy.

21

Next there'd been Sam, a huge, healthy baby who she'd thought would split her right apart as his head forced out of her.

And then Rose. All her babies had been born at home except Rose. Always was a wanderer, Dora thought.

She had been working in that big house in Sparkhill. Albert and Marjorie were ten and eight then and at school so she had to leave Sam with a neighbour.

That morning as she set out to walk to work the sky was low and grey over the rooftops and the ground coated with frost. It looked as if it was going to snow and Dora pulled her coat round her belly as well as she could. She'd felt very down in the mouth that morning, which made her think the baby wouldn't come for a few days yet. Usually, right at the end she felt a mysterious surge of energy and well-being, even when she was quite run down in herself.

Maybe I just can't feel lively any more, she thought. Too many things have happened to us. P'raps I'm just too old.

At twenty-eight sometimes she felt aged and slow, as if everything had been torn and sucked out of her. Today the lower part of her body felt taut and heavy as she walked.

She went down the Ladypool Road, where the smell of fresh bread mingled with the usual road smell of horse manure. People were just coming out on to the streets to walk to work or give shop windows a polish. A delivery boy from the baker's shop whisked past on his bicycle, pushing down hard with his legs on the pedals.

Even now, five years after Sid had come home, she could feel tears suddenly in her eyes at the sight of a young man doing so carelessly all the things her husband was no longer capable of. It reminded her with a deep ache of the whole young man, full of dreams of what he was going to achieve, whom she had kissed goodbye and cried for early in 1915.

Sid had not come back to the home he left before the war. Instead he had returned to find his wife living in one of the courts of back-to-back houses which sprawled in a ring round the centre of Birmingham. He came back to a woman who had struggled to keep herself and her children on whatever the shortages of the war would allow, who had worked in factories churning out munitions to fuel the war and who had, with hardly a break, been working in factories ever since. He had watched her age, get thinner, lose her teeth. She snapped more and swore more and her laughter – once loud, generous laughter – came harder now and more rarely.

That change of address on Dora's letters had not prepared Sid Lucas for the losses he had to face on every side when he came home – of not only his limbs, but his livelihood, his dignity and of the way he and Dora had been together before. Before.

Sometimes, when she was at her lowest, when Sid had been silent for days or sweated and sobbed in her arms at night, she wondered if it wouldn't have been better if the mud and water of Passchendaele hadn't buried him completely instead of leaving her with half a person.

Work that morning turned out to be even heavier than usual. Dora did all the routine dusting and polishing with Mrs Stubbs, the elderly woman who worked mornings there.

Then Mrs Stubbs said, 'Right, I'd best go and do that

silver she's on about in the pantry. You can go out and shake the rugs.'

Dora looked at Mrs Stubbs' plain, rather stupid face and wondered whether she was being spiteful. She decided she was just thoughtless, but the advanced state of Dora's pregnancy should have been obvious to anyone.

'Couldn't we do them together?' she suggested.

'I'll come and give you a hand if it gets too much for you,' Mrs Stubbs said serenely and limped off to polish the silver.

Dora dragged the two large rugs through the hall to the bricked area out behind the house which faced on to a large garden. It was beautiful in the summer. The brewhouse was tucked in at right angles to one end of the building and she and Mrs Stubbs heated the water for the wash there each Monday. The bread oven was in there too, so it was often a warm place to be. Dora was glad that the small building jutting out protected her from the main stab of the cold wind.

She picked up one end of the first rug, unrolled it and started to shake so it rippled heavily along the blue bricks of the terrace, giving off great wafts of dust. Dora's arms immediately felt exhausted, as if the carpet was made of lead. She rested between the vigorous shakes, her heart thumping harder and harder. She grew hot and faint.

The pains began suddenly and very strongly. After the first couple of harsh, breathtaking contractions she stood bending forward, her hands pressing on her knees, taking in gasps of air.

My God, she thought. How'm I ever going to get back? I've got to get home!

It felt so urgent, so far advanced, that she knew already that she'd never make it back – not on foot.

She waited for a lull and then stepped over to the brewhouse. It was a bit warmer inside and rather dark. There was nothing to sit on except the scrubbed quarry tiles. Dora squatted down with her back to the stone sink. It was very quiet apart from the faint scratch of winter jasmine and rose thorns against the window. Dora knew she should get help, that she needed a midwife, but between the contractions she had no strength and couldn't raise the energy to move again.

'Please God,' she prayed. 'Don't let anything be wrong with this babby – not with me all on my own. Just help me – please, please!'

She loosened her clothes and took off her bloomers. They were wet like her legs and the back of her dress, where the warm force of her waters breaking had soaked her. A couple of times she had to pull herself up to vomit into the greyish yellow basin. Her face was shiny with sweat.

'God,' she cried, the words coming out hoarsely. 'Oh God, God!'

She knew the baby was not long from being born. As she sobbed and panted through the next contraction she heard Mrs Stubbs' voice outside, 'Dora? Dora? Where are you? I thought you was getting started out here at least.'

In a moment her head poked round the brewhouse door and she saw Dora kneeling, her eyes stretched wide with pain.

'Gorblimey – Dora!' she shrieked. 'You can't have a babby in here. This is where we bake the bread!'

And then, seeing Dora's wet face, her hair hanging in

25

lank brown strings and her clothes all undone, she came closer and said, 'You poor little sod. There ain't time to get a midwife now. It's all right, I'll help you. I've had a few myself in my time.'

She went to the door saying, 'It's all right, I'm not going to leave you. Back in a tick.' A moment later she reappeared with a ball of string, the big kitchen scissors and a towel. She knelt down and pulled one of Dora's arms over her shoulder. 'Go on – you're all right, you're all right,' she kept saying as the young woman writhed and screamed beside her. And then: 'Sssh – keep it down a bit for God's sake.'

Soon the little girl's head bulbed out from her body as Dora cried out for the last time. The pink slithery body followed, and Mrs Stubbs tied the cord and they wrapped her in the old strip of clean towel. Finally, Mrs Stubbs went off to fetch help.

'I'm going to call her Rose,' Dora said when the midwife arrived. 'I mean, if I'd been any further outside I'd've been in the blooming garden, wouldn't I!'

As they sat carding the pins in the unsteady light, Dora suddenly said, 'You're a funny kid you know. Go on – get off to bed. That's enough for tonight.'

Grace was already asleep when Rose lay down beside her in bed that night, listening to the soft rain against the windows. Something scuttled across the floor in the corner of the room.

She thought about Diana and her house and of how one day she wanted to have carpets and comfortable beds and shelves and shelves of books.

During the night she half woke, hearing sounds from the bedroom below, the painful, incoherent cries that her father made sometimes in his sleep. The shouts grew louder, until she heard him cry out, 'No. NO – over here!' and some more words she couldn't hear. Then her mother's voice over his, comforting him until his sounds stopped with hers and they could all sleep.

Three

Her first thought when she woke the next morning was Diana. How soon could she go back there? After all, they had asked her – twice. Rose was just resolving to go as soon as possible when she realized she must have woken extra early in her excitement.

Usually on school days Mom called up the stairs, 'Come on – get yourselves down here. No messing about. You'll be eating your breakfast on the way, else!' But even George was still half asleep. Rose could hear voices outside and she pushed the blanket back and went to the window, pushing it open a crack.

The sun was shining, lighting up one corner of the yard, and the ground was still very wet. Smells of sodden dirt and rotting vegetable peelings wafted through the window, though they didn't overcome the stink of the pee bucket. Rose had a quick peep behind the chest of drawers to check that yes, the elephant was still there and she hadn't dreamed it.

It was wash day. When Rose and the others got downstairs, Dora was hurriedly bundling up all her washing, though she looked pale and was bent over with nausea. She pointed at the table with her free arm. 'There's tea and you'll have to take your slice with you.'

Rose, Sam and Grace hurriedly drank down some stewed tea and left the house. George was standing rather forlornly by the washhouse with his slice, watching Gladys Pye rocking on to each of her bowed legs in turn as she pulled out the heavy mangle. Rose, feeling suddenly sorry for George, went and gave him a cuddle. The little boy's face shone with delight.

They called for Geraldine Donaghue and her brother Jo and the five of them set out, walking to the church school along the sunny street still littered with the debris of the storm.

'Our dad says the roof's gone off Woodgates,' Jo said.

Rose wasn't listening. She was picturing herself one day walking to the school as a teacher who'd stand up grandly in front of the class. She'd wear clothes just like Miss Whiteley's, a straight grey skirt and a white blouse with a frill down the front, and a little fob watch like hers pinned on to it. She'd be very calm, she'd know ever such a lot and all the children would love her.

'What are you going to be when you grow up?' she asked Geraldine, trying to sound like Diana.

Geraldine peered at her, bemused. 'You all right?' she asked. 'What's the big idea?'

'What are you going to be when you grow up?' Sam mimicked her. 'Getting big ideas, Rose? It'll be the factory or the big house for us. What else is there?' Sam scuffed his already well-worn shoes along the pavement. 'We're not exactly going to be King and Queen of England, are we?'

'I want to be a teacher,' Rose said.

Sam snorted with laughter and Geraldine looked horrified.

'You don't want to be like Miss Smart, do you?' she asked. Miss Smart was a sour woman, given to almost savage outbursts of temper. It was whispered that she'd been jilted on the eve of her wedding a few years before.

'No,' Rose said. 'But Miss Whiteley's nice, isn't she? And she knows about ever such a lot of things.'

Geraldine looked puzzled. 'What d'you want to do that for? I'd never do that. I'd like to be a singer or one of them dancers they have on at the Hip.' She preened and posed in her skimpy dress along the pavement as if it was the stage of the Hippodrome.

'Geraldine!' her brother said. 'Everyone's looking.'

'You're both daft,' Sam said. 'Dream away. I'm going to be Rudolph Valentino. But it's only dreams. People like us don't ever do anything different, do we?'

This dampened Rose's enthusiasm straight away.

'Who d'you know who's ever been anything special then?' Sam continued.

'Mom says Dad was doing all right before he went to the war,' Rose said.

'It was still the factory though. And nothing's the same now, is it? That's what Albert says.' Sam always looked to his older brother, whom they scarcely ever saw, as the source of all information and authority. 'Anyhow, you have to stay on at school to be anything special, and there's fat chance of that.'

Rose felt very down in the dumps after that. Was Diana going to stay on at school? No one she knew in the court had carried on after they were fourteen. She'd never questioned it before, how you couldn't do anything much with your life unless you had money.

Rose knew that some time during the morning her mom would bundle up Sid's Sunday suit and shoes and they'd be down to the pawnbroker's at the end of the street until Friday when she got her money from the factory. Sid joked grimly sometimes that they ought to get 2d extra for the shoes because he only ever wore the one. Rose wondered if her mother was going to pawn her new dress.

That day she stared adoringly at Miss Whiteley as she stood in front of them next to the blackboard, the portrait of the king behind her head. She imagined Diana standing there with her curls tied back, telling them all about rivers and jungles and the kings and queens in history books. And then she tried to put herself in the same position, as she had on her walk to school before all the things Sam had said. All she could think of now were the thick darns on the elbows of her cardigan and her faded old clothes and the way she spoke, which was different from Diana.

I could never be like Diana, she thought.

As she turned from chalking up some names on the blackboard, Sarah Whiteley noticed Rose at her wooden desk wiping her eyes with the back of her hand and sniffing.

'Are you feeling unwell, Rose?' she asked kindly.

'No, Miss Whiteley,' the girl said quietly, and she blushed such an embarrassed pink that the teacher decided not to pursue it just then.

When school finished Miss Whiteley said to her, 'Rose, would you come here a minute?'

Geraldine whispered to her, 'You're for it now. I'll wait for you outside.'

'No, you go home,' Rose replied. 'And take Grace with you or Mom'll be on at me.'

She stood solemnly by her teacher's desk when all the others had made their way noisily out of the room. She could hear them laughing and yelling as they trailed off down the street.

'Are you all right, my dear?' Miss Whiteley asked,

sitting behind her big table at the end of the classroom. 'It's all right, don't look so worried, you're not here to be punished. I saw you crying earlier. Is everything all right at home?'

'Yes, Miss Whiteley,' Rose said.

The teacher looked at the serious brown eyes which were gazing apprehensively at her and she smiled suddenly. She had a soft spot for Rose.

'Are you happy at school?' She was sensitive enough to realize that something was going on inside Rose, and she also knew that whatever her disadvantages in life, this was a child with potential.

Rose just said yes again. She liked Miss Whiteley and trusted her, but standing alone in front of her she felt small and shy. She kept her eyes on the scuffed wooden boards of the classroom floor and her even more scuffed boots.

Sarah Whiteley decided to try once more. She came out from behind the desk and brought her chair up to sit next to the child.

Rose looked into Miss Whiteley's lovely plain face with her round pink cheeks, quite unlike Miss Smart's angular, rather pretty face, which was so often full of spite and irritation. Miss Whiteley seemed to give off comfort, like someone handing out buns.

'What if I wanted to be a teacher?' Rose blurted out. ''Cos Sam says people like us don't do things like that and it's daft of me to think of it. Only my friend Diana's going to be a teacher.' And without expecting to she found she was telling Miss Whiteley all about the storm and Diana and how different her family were from Rose's own.

Sarah Whiteley was startled. This was not what she had expected at all. She'd thought perhaps things were

32

especially difficult for Rose's family, as they so often were in the homes of the children she taught. She had met Dora Lucas a number of times and had taken a liking to her. She'd found her brisk, with the kind of hardness of someone who has no energy left to spare for niceties. But she isn't rough, Sarah thought. Just worn down. And again, Sarah had perceived intelligence. She hadn't met Rose's father, but she knew he had been injured in the war and could not get work.

With these thoughts in mind she struggled for words to answer Rose's eager questions. She wanted to be positive and realistic at the same time and the combination was not easy.

'Whether you could be a teacher is not an easy question to answer. I think you're a clever girl and you do well in your lessons. But I expect you'll have to leave school to go to work soon, won't you?'

Rose nodded miserably.

'But perhaps what you can aim to do is get the best work you can. If you do well at school we might be able to find you something in an office, and you never know what opportunities might come your way. And there are such things as evening classes where you can further your education if you have the means when you're older. But you'll have to be very determined. Do you think you're very determined?'

'I dunno,' Rose said. 'But I don't want to be like my mom, always sick with having babbies.'

Sarah Whiteley felt tears slide into her own eyes at the thought of women like Dora Lucas with their relentless lives of childbirth and worry.

Rose noticed her emotion and was alarmed. Blimey, what had she done to upset her?

But all her teacher said, quietly, as if to herself, was,

'Well, I suppose if you want to do anything else with your life it doesn't really do to have children.' Then she smiled and looked at Rose. 'Cheer up. You don't need to worry about it yet, do you? And you never know what might happen.'

She stood up and said, 'Come along, your mother will be getting worried. Shall I walk a little of the way with you?'

Delighted, Rose felt her dark little hand being taken by Miss Whiteley's soft pink one. The woman strolled along beside her, pointing out things on the way – a police car, a magpie, white clouds all piled up to one side of the sky – until they reached Catherine Street. Miss Whiteley leaned down and, to Rose's astonishment, kissed her cheek before she said goodbye. Rose couldn't remember the last time anyone had given her a kiss. The walk had made the afternoon feel very warm and special.

But when she got home her mother was tense and furious and snapping at everyone in sight. She'd hung her sheets across the yard as usual and the younger Pye and Donaghue children had been running muddy hands all through them and flicking water up from the puddles. She'd had to rinse and mangle the lot again, and as a result was behindhand with everything else.

'Don't tread on the floor!' she shouted unreasonably as Rose stepped into the house. 'Where the hell have you been? No – don't tell me. Just get scraping these.' She pointed to a pile of carrots. Grace, confined to a sheet of newspaper on the damp floor, had already started on the potatoes.

Dora bustled about rearranging washing on the backs of chairs and over the frames of the mirror and their two pictures: one of Sid's mom and dad and one of the king and queen.

'I'll make sure those little bleeders don't get at it this time,' she said. 'Come on, set to it, Rose, and stop dreaming.'

Rose picked up the peeling knife in silence and mulled over what Miss Whiteley had said. All I can do, she thought, is try as hard as I can. Try and try and try.

That night, when she and Grace and the boys were in bed, Rose heard sounds coming from down in her mom and dad's room. It wasn't the strange, rhythmic noise she sometimes heard, with her mother gasping, and at the end of it a cry from her father as if he'd stubbed his toe on the leg of the bed. This time she knew it would end differently, because he'd been down the Catherine after raising a few coppers selling kindling.

Sid turned to look at his wife as he undressed in their room on the middle floor. She was lying on her back, her face grey with fatigue. He could see clearly the lines that had appeared and deepened between her brows and round her mouth and he felt a moment of tenderness watching her there. Now she was able to rest she looked a little more like the lovely girl he'd courted and married, with her sheet of chestnut brown hair, thicker then and glossy, which he'd smoothed over his face during their lovemaking like a silk scarf.

Remembering this, he wanted her. She'd be out working the next four nights and he'd have to sleep alone. He always felt sorry for himself when she was away at night. It seemed to reinforce his sense of helplessness.

'Dora?' He pulled himself over to her on the bed and leaned on his good arm. Suddenly he felt nervous, and then angry because of it. She was his wife, wasn't she? He shouldn't have to beg any favours.

'Come on,' he said. He put his mouth to hers, feeling how rough and dry her lips were. He felt himself harden gradually. In the old days he had only to look at her. This was the one thing he had left – that he could make her produce children.

When she felt him moving against her, a wave of despair came over Dora. How could he do this when he knew she'd be up all the next night? But she always felt guilty when she refused him. It was the only thing which made him happy for a short time.

'I need some sleep,' she said without opening her eyes. 'I'm on again tomorrow night. Some of us have to work, you know,' she finished, rather spitefully.

He always took rebuffs badly. 'That's right – and I'm no bloody good for nothing, am I?' he shouted, sitting up again. 'Your bleeding cripple of a husband. That's what everyone says about me, ain't it?'

'I didn't say that – just don't keep on. Get into bed and let me sleep.'

'Open your eyes.' His voice was still loud and full of hurt and anger. 'At least open your bloody eyes, woman!'

Dora dragged her eyes open and half sat up. She pulled back the covers and patted the bed. 'Just come and lie down, Sid, please.'

Sid could feel the great dark surge which sometimes forced its way through him, a violence of anger and despair which he could not put into words. He ached to spend himself in his wife, to feel her body moving under him.

'Dora, please. Do it for me tonight.'

'NO!' Dora shouted.

Then Rose heard her mother's screams as he hit her twice, three times, giving her the bruised cheek and cut lip which would be there for all to see in the morning.

'You selfish bitch!' she heard.

Rose screwed up her eyes tight and pushed her fingers into her ears. But she could still hear the next part – what always came next. The worst part. Her father's remorse, the sobs which burst from his body alongside her mother's own crying, and eventually Dora's voice trying to calm his anguish.

Rose slipped out of bed and fetched the little elephant from its hiding place. She lay stroking it in the dark.

'Try,' she said to herself. 'Try and try and try.'

Four

January 1935

Dora Lucas was sitting at her table with a cup of mint tea in front of her. Often now, when she had a spare moment she sat, her eyes not fixed on anything, her limbs slack and her mind numb.

She was forty-one and exhausted, like an old woman, yet she was soon to give birth again. Her belly already felt tight and heavy with the child which nudged insistently under her ribcage so that she had to keep straightening her spine to ease the discomfort.

Beside her, three-year-old Violet was clattering pebbles on the tiled floor, involved in her game and singing quite tunefully.

'Do it a bit quieter, can't you?' Dora snapped at her, without really having intended to. Weariness and irritation seemed to be all she could manage.

The others would soon be home from school. And Sam – bless him – from work. After the four grimmest and most despairing years of Dora's life they at last had a regular wage coming into the house. How she would have got by without the neighbours she'd never know – Theresa and Gladys especially. The final humiliation had come when they had been forced to go on the Parish. First there was the gruelling session in front of the board. Dora's innards turned just thinking about it. She'd remember the cold, gimlet-eyed woman there till her dying day. The board, which executed the Means Test, decided whether she was worthy of their meagre allowance of food and coal.

Sam, Rose and Grace had become familiar, sad little figures outside factories as far away as Cheapside and Moseley Street, greeting the men who came off shift with persistent cries of 'Have you got a piece for us?' They'd run after the men until they handed over any leftover portions of bread from their lunches.

On Saturday nights they would hang about in Smithfield and the Market Hall until the stallholders were packing up, and then walk home exhausted, carrying a piece of knockdown meat and bags of bruised fruit and veg. Rose would fall asleep with her head full of visions of pyramids of apples and oranges lit by the the naphtha flares which hissed next to the stalls.

The shame and desperation of those years had nearly finished Dora. When Violet was born she had haemorrhaged so badly that she'd been ill for weeks and had had to give up her night job in the metal stamping factory. They'd had Sickness Benefit, and by the time that finished she was pregnant again, but she miscarried in the third month. Again she was left weak and drained.

Dora had been desperate not to get pregnant again. She tried to fight Sid in bed, and kick him off. But even with only one arm he was stronger. He begged her and then slapped her about, and most often now pushed into her with a force which frightened her and left her sore, sometimes bleeding, and with an overwhelming sense of shame as if she had done something wrong. When she had the strength, she crept out in the dark afterwards and fetched a pail of cold water to wash herself with.

As soon as she realized she was carrying this child, for the first time in her life she tried to abort it. She had tried castor oil and Penny Royal syrup and even water which she'd boiled pennies in. She had trembled at the sin she was committing – however ineffective it proved – but even more at the thought of what Sid would do to her if he ever found out. His one remaining source of power was his and Dora's fertility.

'Think yourself lucky,' he said to her one night in an ugly mood. He was lying on the bed naked from the waist down, his member lolling to one side on its nest of dark hair. 'I saw a fella in the army with it all blown away. Where would that leave you, eh?'

She had been brought too low to feel anything for Sid now. Even pity had been drained out of her. Now when his dreams drove him to cry out in the night she turned away and pushed her fingers into her ears. She had pity now only for her children, and admiration for their pluck and spirit.

She leaned back into her chair, folding her arms over her swollen stomach and thinking of her kids one by one.

There was Albert, over in Erdington, whom she hardly ever saw, and Marj, rather smug with her two kids in Sparkbrook. She realized that these two, who could just remember the life before the war, despised what their parents had become. If that was their attitude they could keep away.

As for Sam, he was a good solid lad. She knew he'd stick by her and look after her. Sticking by people was one of the codes by which Dora lived. Disloyalty figured high on her list of human failures, along with thieving and cruelty to children. She felt Sam had inherited that loyalty from her.

'Don't worry, Mom,' he'd kept saying, while he was waiting out his last year at school. 'I'll get myself a job soon. I'll look after you.' It was a promise he'd kept. He was bringing in ten bob a week which was a start and they made up the rest with odds and sods.

Then there were the two girls. Dora smiled at the thought of Grace. She was so transparent and shared things with her mother. She used to climb on Dora's knee and show her the latest picture she'd found of her great passion – the royal family. She was straightforward somehow. Like herself, Dora thought.

But Rose was more of a mystery. Dora had never worked out why that posh vicar's daughter Diana wanted to be so friendly with her. She must have had pals with knobs on up at her public school, but she and Rose were still as thick as anything. And she didn't even seem to mind coming and slumming it down Catherine Street now and then. It was the neighbours who acted suspicious and said, 'What's she doing down here again?'

Dora couldn't help liking Diana, even if she hadn't been sure at first what she was after. Her mother's family were something titled, it was said, and she'd married beneath her. But Diana didn't put on airs. She always said 'Mrs Lucas' so politely. And she was such a pretty lass with all that curly hair round her face. But Rose went up to the vicarage more often than Diana came down here. Rose didn't want the neighbours gossiping about her or Geraldine Donaghue deliberately messing up Diana's dress out of envy.

Rose worried Dora though. She knew her daughter's contact with the Harper-Watts had shown her a kind of life that would never be within her grasp.

'Don't get big ideas, will you?' she warned sometimes.

Sid put it more brutally. 'You needn't bring her round here and get all toffee-nosed. You was born a slum kid and you'll die a slum kid so you needn't go expecting any different.'

It was already getting quite dark. The lamplighter would soon be out on the streets. Dora was about to stir herself when she heard the girls outside, and George came crashing into the house shouting, 'Rose's had the cane! Rose's had the cane!'

As was her way, she didn't ask questions immediately but pulled herself to her feet and lit the lamp. Then she turned to her daughters. Rose was still the taller of the two and bone thin, with long black hair down her back. Her face was puffed up from crying and her cheeks streaked and red. Grace, who was wheezing heavily, also looked tearful. Instinctively, Dora moved across to boil some water for her.

'What's been going on?' she demanded.

'It's that Miss Smart,' Rose burst out, her voice high with tears and anger. 'She's a wicked, horrible bitch, she is.'

'Rose!' Dora started. But then, seeing how distressed she was, said, 'Turn round.'

Rose turned, and very tentatively pulled her ripped bloomers down to show her bare bottom. It was raw and red with stripes of blood and vivid purple welts, so many that they had all merged together in a hot, angry mass.

'God Almighty,' Dora gasped. 'What the hell has she done? What brought all that on?'

It had been the last lesson, Rose explained. They'd been sitting in the classroom, and she was next to the heavy green curtain that separated her class from Grace's. She knew Grace wasn't feeling too good that day. The weather was damp and cold which always brought on the asthma. She'd been struggling to get her breath even on the way to school. A day in the building, heated by the one feeble stove, had not helped.

As Rose sat through her arithmetic lesson, Miss Smart was teaching Grace in the next section of the room. Suddenly she became aware of Miss Smart's usually abrupt and tetchy voice saying quite clearly, 'Pull yourself together! I've had quite enough of your malingering.'

'I can't help it, Miss Smart,' she heard Grace trying to protest. 'It's me chest. I've got—'

'Be quiet,' Miss Smart shouted. 'You make that horrible noise once more and you'll feel the cane across your behind. I'm not putting up with any more of your excuses.'

Through the curtain Rose could hear Grace's wheezing becoming louder and more agitated. She could picture Miss Smart's angry, spiteful face as she stood over her sister, and suddenly she felt all restraint leave her.

She glanced up at Miss Phipps to check she wasn't looking. Then she lifted up the bottom of the heavy curtain, pushed her way underneath it and ran to Grace, flinging an arm round her frightened sister's shoulders.

'You cruel bitch!' she shouted at Miss Smart. Her

voice sounded surprisingly strong. 'Why don't you pick on someone your own size? Just because you can't keep a bloke for five minutes doesn't mean you have to take it out on my sister. She's got a bad chest, as you ought to know bleeding well by now!'

Grace's face almost mirrored her teacher's in its look of horror. Miss Smart grabbed Rose by the wrist and hauled her through the classroom with astonishing strength, bashing Rose's legs and hips against the desks.

'Come here you uppity little scum,' she hissed, her teeth locked together as though she was trying to hold back some of her rage. 'You'll be out of this school as soon as breathe after what you've just said to me.' The woman's body was quivering all over. 'But now I'm going to give you something you should have been given a long time ago.'

Grace watched, terrified, as Miss Smart grabbed Rose again by the shoulders and forced her round so she was facing the window. She pulled Rose's skirt up and yanked on her bloomers so that the entire class heard them tear.

'Bend over and empty the wastepaper basket,' Miss Smart shouted, only just able to get the words out.

Rose knew the drill. She turned the basket over, tipping out scraps of paper and some balls of fluff, and leaned down on the dusty weave of the base.

Miss Smart thrashed her with the cane as no child in the school had ever been thrashed before. She lost all control as her voice screamed out her frustration and loathing. 'D'you think I like standing here day after day looking at your ugly – ignorant – faces? I hate it. I hate it – do you hear? You stupid – scummy little – slum kids . . . You'll never – do anything – or be anything. I could be married and out of this cesspit by now, but I'm stuck here forever. Stuck – stuck – stuck!'

Rose's whimpering broke into screams as Miss Smart brought the thin cane down and broke the skin. The lashes shot through her, making her feel weak in the legs and dizzy. She was aware only of the pain and of the saliva gathering in her mouth.

'Helena! Helena Smart – what in God's name are you doing?' It was a deep voice, from the large body of Miss Phipps, who had been teaching arithmetic next door. The beating stopped abruptly as Miss Phipps grabbed the younger teacher's arms and took the bloodstained cane from her trembling hand.

Rose slowly turned the waste basket over and retched miserably into it. She heard Grace's loud breathing beside her.

'Rose? Rose – are you all right?' Grace was crying. A thin trickle of vomit began to ooze out through the wicker and across the floor.

Miss Phipps was holding Miss Smart by one of her wrists. The younger woman was sobbing uncontrollably. 'I'll see you later,' Miss Phipps said in a low voice. 'For now I think you'd be wisest to get out of my sight.'

They all watched Miss Smart, her head sunk down and her shoulders heaving as she left the room.

Miss Phipps came over to Rose. 'Go home and get your mother to dress those cuts,' she said gently. 'Grace, you go with her.'

Rose tried to straighten up. Her behind and the lower part of her back were a tight wall of pain.

Miss Phipps guessed what was painting the worried expression on the girl's face even through her obvious distress. 'It's all right,' she assured her kindly. 'You'll be coming back to school again.'

As Rose was finishing off her story, Sid lurched into the house on his crutch, slamming the door as he always did. Dora tensed.

He looked round the room. Grace was sitting at the table with George, breathing noisily over a bowl while Dora held her hair back. Rose was standing holding a cup with a face as long as Livery Street and not a sign of his tea on the go.

'What's going on?' His voice was ugly.

'Rose got caned down at the school for sticking up for our Grace,' Dora said. 'Her behind's red raw with it.'

Sid looked at Rose's tearstained face. It was rare for him to see Rose crying. She was a proud cow, in front of him anyway. Strong, independent Rose. Rose, who had all the aspirations he had had and probably even more, going about with that kid from up the vicarage. He felt a moment of identity with her, but he pushed it aside. For once she wasn't giving him that serious, knowing look of hers, that seemed to say, 'Sod you, Dad. I'm going to get out of here and do something with my life.'

He began to enjoy her humiliation. 'I s'pose you asked for it,' he said. 'You're a cheeky little bugger.'

'I didn't ask for it!' Rose shouted. She felt like someone with nothing to lose. 'She was carrying on at our Grace and I stuck up for her. Like Mom could do with someone to stick up for her when you're down there knocking her about of a night. I've listened to you since I were a babby with your bullying and your carrying on, and your – *crying*.' Rose spat the word out with all the contempt she felt. 'You're disgusting, Dad. So don't go telling me I asked for it.'

She stood unflinching as Sid lurched over and hit her round the head with both sides of his thick hand again and again.

'Stop it!' Dora screamed. Grace and George sat quite still as if paralysed with fright. 'Don't you dare hit her! Don't you ever hit my kids.' Her voice dropped to a snarl. 'I've put up with you knocking me about, but don't you ever lay a finger on my kids again or I swear I'll lay you out for good.' She was looking round wildly for something to use as a weapon when Rose simply took a step backwards and Sid lost his balance, falling to the floor heavily, on his side.

With all the dignity she could summon Rose stood over him. 'I shouldn't bother getting up, Dad.' She left Grace and George gawping and went to her room.

Rose lay with her stomach flat against the bed in the dusk light of the attic.

Dora was bathing the sores on her daughter's behind with warm water and dabbing iodine on the cuts. One side of Rose's face was swollen and shiny and beginning to darken into bruises. Sid's outburst, as much as the treatment she had had from Miss Smart, had created a bond between the mother and daughter stronger than any that had existed before.

'I hate him,' Rose said, banging her fists on the thin mattress, and wincing whenever Dora touched her. 'I hate, hate, *hate* him. He ought to want better than he's had for his kids. He's never cared about us.'

Dora sighed. Rose became aware that her mother was

stroking her hair with a new gentleness that she was unused to. She kept very still in case any movement made Dora stop.

'If it were a few year ago I'd've said that's not the truth.' Dora paused for a moment, breathless with the baby pushing up her lungs. 'Now I just don't know. He's turned sour on everything and there's no getting near him. And you can't blame him when you stop to think about it. But that don't make it any easier for the rest of us. There've been times . . .' She stopped.

As if reading her mind, Rose said, 'You'd have been just as well off without him, wouldn't you?'

'No,' Dora said briskly. 'That's not my way. You make your bed and you lie on it, and that's that, whatever happens after.'

Rose turned her head to look at her mother. In the poor light from the window she could see the outline of her scrawny neck and her thinning hair which looked lanker and more faded every year. Her skin was pasty and tired-looking. She thought of Catherine Harper-Watt's rosy complexion and her thick, healthy hair. She started to cry again because her mother's life seemed so sad, such a waste.

Dora, not knowing the real reason for Rose's sobs, stroked her back in a way that surprised both of them. 'Ssssh,' she said. 'You'll feel better soon, don't you worry. Hang on a minute – I'll go and get you another nice cup of tea.'

Five

A month later Rose and Diana were walking to the Bull Ring. As soon as Diana had called in for her at Catherine Street Rose grabbed her coat and was off.

'Better get her out of here before she catches anything, hadn't you?' Geraldine called out spitefully as the two of them sped out of the court. They were followed a short distance by George, who was becoming a right tearaway, and Violet, lisping, 'Thweets, Diana – bring us back some thweets!'

The two girls soon left them behind. Rose was never comfortable when Diana came to her house and it didn't happen very often. She couldn't help feeling ashamed of the cramped, filthy conditions they lived in. Whenever Diana came the smells drifting from the toilets in the yard always came over stronger than usual.

Diana was always very polite. Rose had never seen her bat an eyelid at the newspaper instead of a cloth on the table or the cockroaches scuttling busily about on the floor and walls, their antennae twitching. She'd only once jumped and squeaked when one landed clumsily on a slice of bread she was eating. Dora had nearly turned herself inside out apologizing.

'Don't you hate coming to our house?' Rose asked her. 'Why would you want to, with us being so rough and ready?' She felt humbled by Diana's tolerance, whereas if her friend had been haughty or critical Rose would have leapt like a wildcat to defend her family and how they were forced to live.

'Come on,' Rose said as they scurried towards town. 'It isn't half a relief to get out, I can tell you. My mom's been on at me all morning: "Rose – blacklead the grate; Rose – Violet's gone and wet the floor, get down and wipe it up will you, Rose; Rose – go and get us some fish and chips for our lunch!" Anyone'd think there was no one else in the house 'cept me.'

It always took the two girls a while to get used to being together.

'We could go on the tram,' Diana suggested breathlessly as they rushed along.

'You mad?' Rose looked shocked. 'What d'you want to go wasting money on that for? It's not much of a walk.'

'All right.' Diana smiled. 'I'll treat you to a cup of tea then.'

'You don't know you're born, you don't.' But Rose was delighted. It was a huge treat to go to Charlie Miles' in the Market Hall or one of the places in the Bull Ring market and sit drinking tea like two grown-up ladies.

'Eh, I haven't told you,' Rose said as they turned into Bradford Street. 'Mrs Smith from number three – you know, Mrs Cut Above – they had to take her to the hospital a couple of days ago. They found her swigging back a bottle of bleach at her kitchen table. Her sons walked in and saved her, before she could take' – Rose struggled to remember the right words – 'the whole lethal dose. That's what everyone said. She had to go and have her stomach pumped out. They put a great thick rubber tube in your mouth and pour water into it till you bring it all back. Mrs Pye told us 'cos it happened the once to her brother.'

'Gosh, how horrible!' Diana said. 'Is she all right?'

'She's home now. She had a bit of a go at Geraldine's mom this morning. Called her an Irish trollop, so I think she's back to her usual.'

Diana stored up this information to tell her father, who waited for the latest instalment of life in Catherine Street with great interest and shook his head in a concerned sort of way whenever she told him anything.

The long street swept them downhill towards the bustling heart of Brum. On either side of them loomed the tall, soot-coated sides of factories from which came all kinds of sounds of hammering and drilling, and the churning of machinery and shouting filled the air round them.

'Let's see if we can spot Sam,' Rose said.

They stopped by the grating over the basement factory where Sam had found his first job. The firm produced galvanized buckets and baths, and all day the sounds of banging and clanging went on as if they were fastening on manacles in hell.

'It's so noisy!' Diana exclaimed.

'Hell of a row, isn't it?' Rose peered down, trying to spot her brother's brown hair and pale, stolid face, but she couldn't see him.

'C'mon Di,' she said, straightening up again. 'Let's get to Jamaica Row for the cag-mag and then we can go over to the Market Hall.'

Bradford Street was crowded with horses and carts and motor vehicles, some stopping for pick-ups or deliveries outside the factories or moving to and from Smithfield, the main meat market at the lower end of the street. You could see the sides of meat hanging up there as you went past. In the road, piles of horse manure steamed in the cold.

Carrying the bag of cag-mag, the cheapest off-cuts of meat, the girls gradually pushed their way through the chaos of the Saturday afternoon crowds into Spiceal Street, past the slim spire of St Martin's and into the Bull Ring.

Diana took hold of Rose's sleeve. 'Better not lose you,' she said. 'Go on – you lead the way.'

Rose felt the usual excitement that welled up once she was inside the market. There was so much to look at. She could hear a band playing, and the delicious smell of roasting meat wafted from the eating houses across from the stalls. Their windows were lit and the glass all steamed up, so you could only see hazy figures moving about inside or sitting at the tables. Outside one a sign said, 'Beef & 2 veg. 11d.'

The market was packed with people swarming around the stalls, which were heaped with fruit, vegetables and flowers. The vendors were competing to see who could shout the loudest to sell their wares.

'Only a penny the cabbage!'

'Get your oranges here – fresh juicy oranges!'

They got tangled up in a knot of people all standing round some attraction. It was the strong man. He had been tied up tightly in his chains and a sack dropped over his head. They could see him struggling inside like an animal in a snare.

'He always gets out, you know,' some know-it-all in the crowd was saying.

'There's got to be a trick in it somewhere. I don't believe in all this rigmarole,' another voice said.

But mostly people stood gasping with admiration watching the man emerge, panting and red in the face as he tore the sack off his head, his face and bare arms shining with sweat.

When Rose looked at Diana she saw that her friend's cheeks had turned quite white and she was taking in fast, shallow breaths.

'I could never do that, never. I can't bear anything over my head. It makes me want to scream and kick.'

'Come on. Forget it,' Rose said, pulling her away. 'Let's go and find something a bit more cheerful for you.'

Round the statue of Nelson in the middle of the market was the place where people always arranged to meet. Probably because they knew this, the Sally Army had set up with their brass band and tambourines. In the background somewhere a man's voice was shouting, 'He who is without sin – he, and only he – shall cast the first stone!'

From the other side of the statue Rose heard the music which she always enjoyed most in the market.

'Come on.' She took Diana's arm. 'If this don't cheer you up then nothing will.'

It was the accordion players. There were two of them, trying hard to compete with the Sally Army, and by the look of things succeeding. The men had a certain snappiness of style even in their old black trousers and jackets, and their black hair shone with oil even in the grey winter light. One of them had a moustache. As they played they both tapped their feet and the one with the moustache sang to some of the numbers.

'Can you hear what he's saying?' Rose shouted in Diana's ear.

'No,' she shouted back. 'It's Italian. They're from Italy.'

'You know bloomin' everything, don't you?' Rose bawled back at her with a grin.

The two girls stood for quite a time watching the

players. Rose thought nothing could ever make her feel so happy as the sound of those dancing tunes. They stood there so long that in the end the one with the moustache danced over to them, inclining first one shoulder and then the other as his fingers carried on playing with astonishing ease and speed. Rose saw the hairs of his moustache, and his shining brown eyes. He sang a long note on some word that sounded like 'maree'. Rose and Diana put their hands up to their mouths and moved away giggling.

They were carried along by the crowd, smelling potatoes baking on a cart and crushed cabbage leaves under their feet and cigarette smoke which seemed stronger on the cold air. There were hundreds of stalls in the Market Hall, selling everything under the sun. They liked to go and see the great crabs and lobsters, bright and astonishing in their shells, and all the piles of toffee and peanut brittle.

'Oh look,' Diana said. She pointed to a big banner. 'It's a hundred this week!'

'Market Hall Centenary Celebrations', the sign read. 'February 11–18', and on each side in bigger print, '1835–1935'.

But it was Diana's turn to see her friend turn pale and serious. At the foot of the steps, leaning against the brick banister, was a man. His face was dark with several days of stubble, and round his neck, hanging from a length of cord, hung a cut-out tray made of cardboard. On it lay a few boxes of Swan Vesta matches. Rose stared at his face, tears stinging her eyes at the despair she saw written in every sag of his rough cheeks. His clothes hung limply, one sleeve of his greatcoat pinned away at the back. Many a night that coat had provided an extra cover on Rose and Grace's bed. The rough, familiar crutch stood against the wall beside him.

Rose stood watching her father, the tears running slowly down her cheeks. Bruises from the beating round the head that he had given her were only just fading. But now, seeing him here away from home, she pitied him for what he so obviously was – a wreck of a man. Her pity was partly for the squalor, the monotony of his life, but mostly it was for the way he had been broken by things too terrible to tell of, that only spoke themselves night after night in his dreams.

'Rose, what's the matter?'

'Nothing.' Rose turned away quickly, realizing he might see them.

'Come on. You were grinning like a Cheshire cat just a minute ago. What's up?'

'I'm not going to turn round again in case he sees,' Rose said sniffing. 'But look, by the steps. It's my dad.'

Diana turned her head and saw Sid's desolate figure. Then she took Rose's hand, and her friend felt a coin being pressed into it.

'Let's go and get the poor old sod a cup of tea.' The two girls smiled at each other, Rose more in surprise at Diana's unaccustomed language than because she thought it was a particularly good idea.

She approached him with the tea, feeling nervous and awkward, and handed it to him saying, 'Here y'are, Dad. You must be cold.'

Sid roused himself, looked at her without any apparent surprise and said, 'Aar. Thanks Gracie.'

'I'm ROSE,' she yelled at him. 'You silly old sod.' And she pulled Diana away, the moment of pity swept away by her anger.

Diana followed her as she stamped her way across the Bull Ring in her worn-out boots. 'Hey, Rose,' she said, running behind to catch up. 'You didn't have to go and tell him what I said about him to his face!'

Rose turned, for a moment still annoyed, and then burst out laughing. The two of them linked arms and moments later Rose was crying with laughter instead of vexation.

'Well, that's the last time I try and do anything for him,' she said defiantly. 'Now, how about that cup of tea we was going to have ourselves?'

Six

Dora's labour pains began in the middle of a cold night in March.

She called up the stairs, 'Sam, Sam! Go and fetch Old Joan – the babby's coming!' Sam shot out of bed and down to the outside door.

Rose scurried around. Her heart seemed more awake than her head and it was beating noisily. As she threw slack on the fire, which had almost gone out, Grace and the other children trooped in and Grace started to get them all organized.

'You come and sit here George, and Vi can sit on my lap. You can see all my pictures. Now, this one's Queen Mary in the royal box at Ascot . . .'

'Oh, not again,' George groaned.

Sid was still asleep and Dora said she couldn't see much use in waking him. She and Rose prepared Rose and Grace's bed in the attic together. They stripped off the bedclothes so the sheets wouldn't spoil, tucked the crackly newspaper round the mattress and spread sheets of it out on the floor.

'This one's a boy,' Dora said as she finally pulled herself up on to the bed. She looked exhausted already.

'How d'you know?'

'I just do,' she said, leaning her head back against the wall so the tendons stood out in her scrawny neck. 'I always know, by the end.'

Rose suddenly felt shy, helping her mother with something so intimate. Before, she'd always been whisked off out of the way like the younger ones, and Old Lady Gooch or Gladys Pye called in to help.

Dora watched her daughter's brisk, practical movements and her serious face as she tucked the paper in neatly round the mattress. She knew Rose had recently started to come on of a month and had therefore become a woman.

'D'you want to stay and help with this one?' she asked. 'I think you're old enough. And Mrs Freeman'll need someone to give her a hand.'

Rose nodded. 'All right then.'

The labour progressed swiftly. Old Joan, who was not in fact very old but enormously fat, puffed and panted around almost as much as Dora. She pushed Sam off downstairs saying, 'This ain't no place for a lad. Go and make us all a cuppa tea, eh?'

'Just help yourself, won't you?' Dora said sarcastically. She knew she needed this woman, and she didn't want to fork out for the doctor as well. But the midwife was notorious for being lazy and sponging off people. She also laid out the dead on occasion and it was rumoured that things had gone missing from the rooms where the bodies were lying.

Rose at first found the sound of her mother's cries frightening. She started to sweat and she felt sick. She had only heard this from at least one floor away before. But between each bout of grunting and moaning Dora got back to normal and said, 'It's all right Rose. The babby'll not be long now.'

Rose ran up and down with water and cloths and alternated between her horrified fascination with the shadowy glimpses she kept getting of her mother's private parts and with the great coils of fat embedded round Joan Freeman's neck and arms and waist. Every inch of her looked as if she was padded with lard.

Joan seemed completely unmoved by what Dora was going through. She sat down on the edge of the boys' bed, her huge lap spreading across much of it. She drew her knitting out of her bag and sat in the candlelight with her head resting on her chins, pulling the brown wool round her stubby fingers.

'Ain't you got any more light than this?' she said to Rose. 'I can hardly see what I'm doing.'

Rose swallowed down her retort that she wasn't being paid to sit and do her knitting and went downstairs to find the small paraffin lamp that they hardly ever used.

'How's she getting on?' Grace whispered. She was very pale with circles under her eyes. Violet had fallen asleep on her lap.

'All right,' Rose said, feeling a bit superior. 'Shouldn't be long now.'

When she was half-way up to the attic she wished more than ever that she could retreat back down again. She heard her mother's cries, louder and more anguished than they had been so far. She had to force herself to climb the rest of the stairs.

'Please don't let me ever, ever have to do that,' she whispered to herself. 'I'll work as hard as I can, I'll get the best job I can. But don't let me have to have babbies!'

When she reached the top the light showed her Dora kneeling now on the bed on all fours like a dog. Her head was hanging down between her shoulders and she was panting and gasping. When she heard Rose she lifted her head. Her face was soaked with sweat. Joan was still knitting complacently on the other bed.

'There's something wrong,' Dora moaned.

Rose hung the lamp on a hook on the wall and went to bathe Dora's face, her hands trembling. Her mother's nightshirt had ridden right up at the back so her behind and legs were on view and she could see her great swollen belly and her breasts dangling beneath her as she knelt on the bed. Rose felt sweat break out all over her again as well.

'The babby – should be – coming down, but he's not – budging,' Dora panted, starting to cry in desperation, moving her body restlessly on the bed. Rose made helpless movements with her hands.

'You'll be all right,' Joan said, switching needles to begin on a new row. 'Just give him a good push.'

Dora heaved again. 'Help me – oh God, help me!'

Unable to do anything to help, Rose felt like crying herself. In the end she went to stand in front of Joan.

'Look, you old cow,' she shouted as Dora writhed on the bed beside them. 'You're s'posed to be here to help, not knit jumpers for the whole British bleeding army.'

The midwife waddled over to Dora in the shadowy light and said, 'You'll have to watch this one, Dora. She's got too much of a gob on her.'

'And you've got too big an arse on you,' Rose retorted. She was suddenly feeling exhausted.

'It's stuck,' Dora screamed. 'It won't come. Get it out, for God's sake. It's killing me.'

'You ought to get a doctor,' Rose hissed at Joan. 'You're not up to this.'

'Cheeky little sod,' Joan said. 'I've done hundreds of these.'

She bent down behind Dora, breathing heavily. Rose watched, horrified, as she pushed two of her thick, lardy fingers into her mother. Dora groaned, and Rose saw frothy saliva dripping from her mouth on to the crumpled newspaper. She was making whimpering animal sounds that turned Rose's stomach.

'The babby's ready all right,' Joan said. 'Must have an arm caught awkward.' And with no warning she forced her entire hand up inside Dora and began to manipulate the baby inside her, trying to free it. Dora's screams rose to a single high-pitched shriek like a creature caught in the iron teeth of a trap. Joan pulled her hand out, slimy with blood, and Rose squeezed her eyes tight and pushed her fingers into her ears, unable to stand it any longer.

When she opened her eyes a moment later, Dora was still screaming, but now it was more of a yell.

'Now you've woken up you can come here and give me a hand,' Joan said.

Still sick and dizzy, Rose just managed to peer under her mother, who was squatting again. Bulging out from her she could see the top of a little head covered in dark, wet hair.

'I can't – I CAN'T!' Dora shrieked.

'Just push,' Joan shouted down her ear. 'One more'll do it.'

With an almighty cry, Dora pushed the child's head out and Rose saw the blood spurt from her ragged vagina. Another push and the little body slithered out covered in blood and a white pasty substance. Dora collapsed forwards on to the bed.

'What is it?' Rose said, all her faintness of a moment before quite forgotten.

Joan's meaty hands picked up the little body and turned it to tie the cord.

'It's a boy, Mom!' Rose said, as Joan wrapped him in an old white cloth. 'You were right.'

'Told you,' Dora said faintly. 'Give him here.' She held out her arms, the palms of her hands grey with newspaper print, and took the little boy to her. 'Go on,' she said. 'You can go and tell your dad he's got another son. And Rose,' she said, as the girl headed for the stairs, 'thanks, our kid.'

Rose wasn't at home when it happened.

George ran across the court in his bare feet as if his breeches were on fire.

'Mom, Mom! Come quick!'

'What?' Dora's heart started pounding as she pulled off her apron. '*What*? Tell me.'

'It's our Violet,' George panted. 'She's gone under a horse.'

Dora was out of the court in front of him and into the street. At the top of Catherine Street by the main road she could see a small crowd of people and she tore along the pavement towards them.

Silently they let her through as if she were royalty. She heard someone say, 'It's the child's mother, the poor cow.'

A man was standing in front of his cart holding the bridle of a heavy black horse. Dora always remembered from that day the smell of the sweating animal, its damp heaving flanks in the sunlight and the stunned expression on the man's ill-shaven face.

At his feet lay the shape of her child. Even in the few moments since it had happened someone had run into their house and brought out an old torn net curtain and laid it over Violet, covering her completely.

Dora saw the ghostly features of her little girl's face through the two layers of net and the blood soaking into the slippery material. 'What d'you go and cover her face for?' she shouted.

She knelt down quickly and pulled back the soft curtain. Her face was expressionless as a stone as she saw the deep wound in Violet's skull and the shards of bone sticking out at grotesque angles. She was dead. Clearly, from the second that the horse's hoof had smashed into the right side of her head she had had no chance of being anything else.

The man with the cart was distraught. 'I hadn't a chance, Missis. She was just there, under the horse. I never even saw her till it were too late.'

Dora nodded at him numbly. She felt no anger towards him. At this moment she felt nothing. She had no idea why Violet had been there when she should have been in the yard. Gladys Pye appeared and led her home. Someone else carried the child's body back to the house.

When Sid came home he stood looking down at her as she sat unmoving at the table. He put his face close up to hers, his breath stinking of beer.

'Can't even look out for your own kid now, can you?'

Three days later Rose was banging hard on the door of the vicarage.

When Catherine opened the door and saw the girl's pinched face and the look of desperation in her eyes she immediately led her inside and sat down with her.

Ronald arrived as well, back from conducting a baptism service.

'It's me mom,' Rose said, starting to cry as the words came out of her mouth. All the anguish of the past days started to pour out of her. 'Our Violet was killed by a horse on Wednesday.'

Catherine and Ronald looked at each other, appalled, but something stopped Catherine from following her instinct to put her arms round the girl. Rose was a warm person, but there was still a self-contained, dignified core to her that they'd seen in the small child they had carried in from the rain.

'I'm so sorry,' Ronald said. He knelt down beside her. Catherine watched, fascinated. For once she couldn't think what to do and Ronald, gentle and sympathetic, knew instinctively.

'But it's my mom,' Rose repeated. 'She hasn't said a word since Wednesday when it happened. She just sits there as if something's gone – you know – in her head. My dad's blamed her for Violet going. She ran out of the court when she wasn't s'posed to, on some prank or other. Dad says her getting killed's all Mom's fault. But she won't say nothing. She'll hardly move or eat or anything.'

She cried harsh, frightened tears.

Ronald suddenly stood up as if something had been decided. 'I'll come down and see her,' he said.

'*You?*' Rose and Catherine spoke exactly together.

'Yes, I,' he said and smiled wryly at their astonishment. 'After all, I'm supposed to be a messenger of the Good News, remember. And I presume you came to us for some sort of help, Rose? Well, this is the best I can do.'

Rose, who was suddenly terrified that Sid might be in when they got home, had no idea how much inner turmoil the vicar was experiencing as once again they walked together along the road towards town and Catherine Street. Rose's head reached above his elbow now, but she still had to make little skips to keep up with his long strides.

Ronald knew this was going to be a decisive morning in his life. He had realized gradually over the past years that he was in the wrong place. That his work in his present parish was not where his heart lay. He had encouraged Rose to tell him more and more about her life in the courtyards, of the conditions they lived in. Now he was going to visit the kind of place which drew him. Of course he could have chosen to walk round the Birch Street area at any time, but something had inhibited him. He would have been merely a voyeur. Now he had a real reason to go.

When George opened the door, Dora saw Rose standing outside with an enormous man, his dark clothes topped by a dog collar. She knew at once who he must be. At any other time she would have felt like giving Rose a good hiding for bringing him at all, let alone with no chance to get the place spick and span first. But at this moment she couldn't have cared less.

Dora stood up silently. She looked more gaunt and pale than ever. Ronald saw just how small were the houses in which so many large families had to live, how mean and cramped.

'Mom,' Rose said. 'This is the Reverend, Diana's dad. I told him about our Violet and he wanted to come and see you himself.'

Dora looked at this stranger whose head nearly

touched the ceiling, and uttered her first words for days. 'You'd better make a cuppa tea, Rose,' she said. 'Kettle's boiled.' And then to Ronald: 'Have a seat.'

Ronald sat down on a wooden chair at the table, carefully avoiding a blob of congealed porridge on the side of it. 'I don't want to intrude.'

He felt foolish as he spoke, knowing that apart from death itself and the Means Testers from the Parish he was the greatest intrusion they'd had for years. He could hear the baby crying upstairs.

Dora folded her arms across herself as if to hide her breasts. 'Go and get him, Rose. I'll have to feed the babby, if you'll excuse me,' she said to Ronald in a flat, lifeless voice.

Rose carried Harry down. He was a bonny four-month-old who looked as if he'd taken all the nourishment from his mother. He was beginning to look rather like Sam.

'Now,' Dora said decisively to Rose. 'You can take this lot outside and leave us.'

She sat down with Harry on her lap, covering herself modestly with an old cardigan as she fed him. Rose, bemused, shoved Grace and George out of the door.

When the children had closed the door behind them Ronald said, 'I'm so sorry to hear about little Violet, Mrs Lucas.'

The moment he spoke he saw her eyes fill with tears. 'All I can think of is how all her life I've been that worried by everything I've hardly had a kind word to spare for her.'

She felt very shy, sitting feeding her child and blarting in front of this huge, educated stranger. But she could also feel an enormous sympathy emanating from Ronald Harper-Watt. And he had two things that she needed: distance from her own situation, so she could talk to him, and time. His job allowed him the opportunity to sit and listen.

'You're a good mother, Mrs Lucas,' Ronald said gently. 'You mustn't think otherwise. Rose often talks about you – fondly.' He'd noticed that more and more recently. 'And it's easy to tell you always do the best you can for your children. I know things haven't been easy for you. I'm sure Violet knew you cared for her very much.'

Dora looked up at him, at his wide, handsome face, the brown hair swept back from his face and his kind, grey eyes. He was the first truly gentle man she could remember meeting.

She began to talk. She had sat in her house for three days feeling she was losing her mind. She had been afraid to speak for fear of what might come out – mad, raving gibberish so that she'd have to be locked away and never let out again.

For about twenty minutes Ronald didn't speak at all. He sat listening attentively, watching Dora as she talked while the baby sucked and sucked at her breast.

She told him everything, from the early, happy days of her marriage to the present, how her once loving husband forced himself on her several times every month and she had almost no feeling left for him in her heart. She spared nothing, talking entirely out of her own need as if it was her last chance.

Finally she stopped and prepared more tea, laying Harry down on a chair. He had fallen asleep with a streak of milk still wet on one plump cheek.

'So that's my life, Mr Harper-Watt,' Dora said, pouring more water into the pot. 'Not much to show for it, is there? Sorry you had to listen to it all, but it's been a relief to have a talk.'

'No.' Ronald sat forward to emphasize what he wanted to say. 'You don't realize. It's been a privilege.'

She noticed suddenly that his large hands were trembling, and she felt disarmed by it.

'In fact,' he went on, 'you've probably helped me more than I could ever help you. You see, I've been feeling very – out of place, shall we say? – in my work. I'm thinking of moving to work in a parish such as your own – like St Joseph's.'

Dora stared at him. 'You're coming to St Joseph's?'

'Well, no. But I'd like a parish near the middle of the – a – city. In places which aren't quite so . . .' He was lost for tactful words.

'In the slums, you mean. Well, if you're asking me, I'd say do it. I'll be frank with you, Mr Harper-Watt. I'm not a churchgoer myself, but I've been to more than the odd wedding and funeral at St Joseph's and that Reverend Gasbag, or whatever he calls himself, he ain't living in the same world as the rest of us. We could do with someone a bit more human like you.'

Ronald sat back, feeling he'd received a great compliment.

'And by the way.' Now Dora had found her tongue again she couldn't seem to stop using it. 'I've never thanked you and your wife for all your kindness to my Rose. You've done a lot for her. And your Diana's a good kid. I thought it wasn't on at first, them two being pals, but now I'm glad it's happened.' And she almost smiled.

'We think Rose is a marvellous girl,' Ronald said, sipping his cup of extremely sweet tea, and to his surprise enjoying it. 'We're all very fond of her. She's a bright child, you know. Given the right opportunities she could go far.'

Even as he spoke, Ronald realized that he was talking out of a different world. Opportunities were not things that had arisen much in Dora's life. She just nodded at him.

When he got up to leave they shook hands, warmly.

'Thank you for talking to me,' he said. 'And for the advice.'

'It were good of you to come,' Dora said bravely. 'I know I can't sit moping here forever. Life has to go on, and I've got my young genius to look out for!'

In silence Rose watched his tall figure walk across the court. Just before disappearing through the entry he turned and waved to her. At that moment she really thought he must be an angel.

Seven

July 1936

'I've got a job!'

They were Rose's first words as soon as Diana opened the door.

'Jolly well done.' Diana beamed at her. 'I'm so glad.'

Catherine came into the hall to add her congratulations, looking as stately as ever. She was wearing a cool, cream dress that flattered her curves and her thick hair was pinned up in a fashionable style round her head.

'Come and have a glass of home-made lemon,' she said to Rose. 'We were just sitting outside.'

They went out to the back of the house where there was a blue-brick terrace facing the old walled garden. Tendrils of wisteria hung down from the house and the garden felt warm and languid as bees buzzed round the hollyhocks and tiny yellow roses climbing the garden wall.

Judith looked up from the book she was reading on her lap. She was quite unlike Diana and William, with a smaller frame and dark hair and eyes. 'Hello Rose,' she said. 'I suppose you're all going to talk now.' She slipped off the chair and went to lie with the book on her stomach on the grass.

'Come on, tell us about the job,' Diana said as she sat down. 'Was it the first one?'

'Yes,' Rose said proudly. 'My first interview. It's at Lazenby's Butcher's Remnants Company near the market. They deal with all the bits of the animals that people don't want to eat. The whole name of the firm is Lazenby's Butcher's Remnants Co. and then in brackets, Skin, Hide, Fat, Wool etc.,' she recited proudly.

'Goodness, that sounds a bit gruesome,' Catherine said. She was afraid Rose had jumped impulsively into the first job that would employ her simply because she was so anxious not to go into service or on to the factory floor. Which was in fact not far from the truth.

'It does stink round there a bit,' Rose admitted. 'But I'm their new office girl. I start on Monday. And the offices are ever so nice. They're upstairs above the yard.' She was all puffed up with pride.

'So what did you have to do?' Diana asked, dipping shortbread into her glass. She saw Catherine frown at her.

'There was two lads up for the job as well,' Rose said, starting to enjoy herself. 'And Mr Lazenby – that's the gaffer of course – he said we had to show him how we could read and write. So I said to him, "I bet I can read and write better than either of them two." And he made us write a few things down, addresses and that. And then we had to read him a bit out of a book.'

Rose had stood and read as well as she possibly could, remembering not to drop her aitches, which she could do when she thought about it, and trying to put expression in her voice.

'And when I'd finished,' she giggled, 'Mr Lazenby said to me, "It's all right, we're not here to put on a

Shakespeare play, you know. We just want a kid for round the office."'

But one of the boys had scarcely been able to read and write at all and the other, who seemed to be terrified of Rose, had read slowly, stumbling over the words. And Rose knew she had left school with an excellent reference from Miss Whiteley.

'So he said the job was mine!' she said. She didn't tell them the last part, that Mr Lazenby had said, 'Right. You can start Monday. You'll be getting eight and six a week.'

'Excuse me,' Rose said politely. 'But I thought it was ten shillings you was offering.'

'Oh yes.' Mr Lazenby stretched his jowly face into a smile. 'But you're a lass. We've only ever taken on boys before.'

Rose was a bit put out, but eight and six seemed a good amount to be taking home. Besides, she was proud to be the first girl that Lazenby's had ever employed.

'And I was thinking,' she chattered on, not noticing in her excitement that the others were very subdued. 'Just because I've left school doesn't mean I can't go on learning. You can teach me about all the things you're learning at school, can't you?' At this moment, Rose felt she could do anything.

Diana was looking lovely in a pale blue dress, her wavy hair tied up in a bouncy ponytail. Her skin was tanned from playing tennis and sitting out in the garden. But Rose suddenly noticed her miserable expression. Emerging from her own preoccupations she looked across at Catherine and saw she too had a solemn face.

'What's the matter?' She tried joking: 'If I ever saw two people looking as if they've lost tuppence and found a farthing, you're the ones!'

72

'Rose,' Catherine said, smiling kindly at her. She held her glass on the wood of the tabletop and slowly circled it round. 'Don't think we're not delighted that you've found a job – and so quickly. It's marvellous news. It's just that we have some news as well, and we're not sure yet whether it's good news or not.'

'You may not be sure,' Diana said, scowling. 'But I am.'

'Well go on – what is it?' Rose spread her long dark fingers on top of the table as if preparing herself for a shock.

Gently Catherine explained that Ronald had been looking for a new kind of job, and that as the diocese had not been able to place him in Birmingham he had accepted a post in Manchester.

'Manchester?' Rose was completely knocked for six. It might as well have been Australia. She wasn't even precisely sure where Manchester was. 'But what about your school, Di? And your pals? I'll never see you again if you all go up there.'

Rose's eyes filled with tears, and Diana was already crying.

'It's really rotten,' she sobbed angrily. 'Daddy decides he wants a different job and the rest of us have to change everything.'

'Look darling,' Catherine said to her outraged daughter. 'I know you think it's not what you want, but you won't know until you've gone and tried it. And when you've settled in, I'm quite sure you'll make friends every bit as good as you've got here.'

She wasn't aware of the appalling tactlessness of her last remark and its effect on their visitor.

But Diana said, 'It'll be beastly. And I'll never find another friend like Rose. How can you even think it?'

She got up and put her slim arm round Rose's shoulders. Rose's lips were trembling with the effort of not crying.

'Oh, goodness, Rose,' Catherine corrected herself, horrified. 'I didn't mean – oh my poor child, I'm so sorry. How awfully rude of me. But Diana will be able to come down on the train in the holidays and visit.'

'What, and sleep at our house?' Rose asked, her voice heavy with sarcasm.

Catherine chose to ignore the girl's tone, knowing she was upset. 'Not necessarily. There are other friends of ours whom she could stay with.'

Rose stared into her lap. A tight, mutinous feeling was rising up inside her. She wanted to scream and throw all the glasses off the table. Horrible things were happening again that she couldn't do anything about, just as she thought she was beginning to get somewhere. Her joy at having found her job was for the moment completely wiped away.

'Listen girls,' Catherine said, looking at the two sullen and tearful faces in front of her. She leaned one of her plump elbows on the table. 'I know it's bad news and none of us is pleased about it. Judith and William are upset as well. But we've all got to make the best of it. And it's not happening for a couple of months yet, so let's all be brave and enjoy the time we have got here together, shall we?'

Catherine changed the subject, talking about the civil war that was breaking out in Spain, and how she felt that Mr Stanley Baldwin was not doing any better than the Labour Prime Minister Ramsay MacDonald had at tackling the problem of people out of work. Both the girls realized she was trying to say how small their problem was compared to some of the big things going on in the world. But of course that didn't make them feel any better. Already it felt as if things were not the same. And Rose had a feeling that now they never would be.

It took the employees at Lazenby's a few weeks to get used to having a girl in the office. There was Miss Peters of course, but she was old enough to be most people's mother, if not grandmother.

Rose became a familiar figure, running errands to and from the traders on the balcony of the huge meat market, delivering statements and cheques and invoices. At first they ribbed her because she was a girl, but after a few weeks she often heard, 'Hello Rose! All right Rose!' from the lads as she made her way round between the office and the trading area.

One part of the job she didn't like was running messages down to the yard at the back of Lazenby's. She found she was surprisingly squeamish about what went on down there. She'd already seen the slaughter yard at Camp Hill. Groups of kids often gathered there to watch when they did the killing early in the morning and she'd been dragged along once by Sam. The dogs chivvied the cows or sheep a dozen at a time into the pen which was open for all to see behind a fence of palings. The slaughterers caught the animals one by one as they shrieked, sweating in terror and running at the fence trying to escape. They drove a sharp stick like a poker into their heads through whichever orifice they could reach to penetrate the brain of the flailing, screaming animal. In through the eyes or ears until the damage inflicted on them reached their whole bodies and they writhed and twitched and finally lay still.

In the yard of Lazenby's they dealt with everything

leftover that could be sold. When Rose went down there the first time the stench turned her stomach. Slightly sweet and putrid, it was a smell she never got used to. The brick floor of the yard was covered with piles of cow hides which had to be examined to see if they had been holed by warble fly. Then they were rubbed over with salt and stacked in piles graded according to size. Sheep fleeces were dealt with in the same way.

Each time she went down there she had to contain her revulsion for the place and put up with the constant gibing of the yard men. The first time she stepped out into the yard they all straightened up from what they were doing and stood staring at her in their rubber boots and aprons, giving each other mischievous grins and making smart-alec comments. One of them was hideously disfigured. His head and neck ran into each other and a goitre was slung like a squashed pig's bladder right round to the back. A cluster of bristles sprouted out of his nose.

'What're you doing here then?' one of them called to her. 'Come to do a turn for us, have you?'

'I've got a note for Mr Freeman actually,' Rose said timidly. They were gawping like idiots as she stood in the navy skirt and soft pink blouse that Catherine and Diana had bought for her – new! – as a present for starting work.

'Ew – ectually!' they mimicked.

Rose slowly walked across the yard where there were small pieces of gristle and fat and furry bits stuck on to and in between the bricks. She slipped and nearly fell on a lump of something yellow and greasy.

'Watch your step,' they sniggered.

'This is where we keep some of the, er – accessories of the job,' the goitre man said mockingly.

The smells and the fatty lumps on the ground and the great mauve bulge on the man's neck were already getting all mixed up in her mind. He took her forearm with his huge hairy hand and led her towards a row of bunkers at one side of the yard. Inside two of them she could see roughly picked bones piled all together, and in the other, glutinous mounds of fat. Shiny green flies were buzzing round greedily.

'And this one's where we keep the salt for the hides.'

Rose could hear the goitre man's heavy breathing as he stood beside her. She looked into the end bunker at the off-white heap of salt. Immediately she became aware that the pile was moving. It was a mass of maggots rubbing ceaselessly against each other's bodies and between the large granules of salt.

Rose knew what the man wanted. She wouldn't give him the satisfaction of looking squeamish, even though the sight sickened her. 'Well, thanks for the guided tour,' she said pertly, keeping her face quite calm. 'Now, which of you gentlemen is Mr Freeman?'

The man pointed his thick arm, letting go of Rose with the other. 'Him over there.'

As Rose made to walk off he said, 'Oi, just a minute. What part of town d'you come from then?'

'Birch Street, near by there,' Rose said.

'So you are one of us then. You look a bit poshed up in them clothes, that's all.'

In the office, though, it was different altogether. There were three main rooms where they worked. Mr Lazenby's office was up at the far end, shut off from the main workroom. You didn't go into Mr Lazenby's without permission and he sat with the door shut.

Rose sometimes knocked and crept in with messages. But she found Mr Lazenby disconcerting, although he was always polite to her, and even seemed to take an interest in her. He sat at his desk with its scratched leather top, all his things arranged on it extremely neatly: the blotter, penholder and account books or whatever he was dealing with. He was in his early fifties with a balding crown and soft, loose-looking cheeks. Rose expected them to slither down off his face at any moment. He had watery blue eyes and a rounded shiny nose. His manner was always quiet and courteous and he often asked how she was settling in with the firm and whether there were any problems.

Once, when she had come in with a message from the meat market, he thanked her and then said, 'Now, you just come round here a minute. I'll show you a picture of my kids. My youngest daughter is about your age.'

Rose walked obediently round the desk and leaned forward a little to look at the photograph. She suddenly felt Mr Lazenby's breath close to her ear and jumped back abruptly.

'It's all right,' he said. 'Don't be nervous, my dear.' And he put his arm round her waist for a moment in a fatherly sort of way to reassure her.

The photograph was another of the items placed neatly on his desk.

'There, you see,' he said. 'My two sons and my little girl.'

Three faces smiled rather stiffly out of the grey photograph. They all looked very well dressed and one of the boys closely resembled Mr Lazenby.

'Thank you,' said Rose, blushing. Mr Lazenby was staring at her and she didn't like being this close to him. He always smelt rather stale and sweaty. 'It's very nice of you to show me.'

'You're a good lass,' he said as she escaped out of the door, her feet sounding too loud on the lino floor.

At the other end of the long office space there was a storeroom for stationery, next to the stairs, and the office in between was where Rose spent most of her time. She dealt with the post and record cards and the stencilling machine. In the same office Miss Peters did the main secretarial work, and Michael Gillespie, the clerk, kept the books.

Michael was seventeen. He towered over Rose, his black hair slicked back very smartly and his blue eyes full of warmth and fun. To Rose, Michael might have been a whole generation older than herself. He seemed so grown-up and knowing about the world, and he was already learning a proper skill which he could take on to other firms.

'I don't want to be stuck as an office dogsbody for the rest of my life,' he told her. Rose could hear the very slight Irish intonation in his voice even though he'd been born and brought up in Birmingham. 'There's all the world waiting out there ...' He moved one of his strong fingers along the frayed edge of a ledger with a grin on his face, pretending it was a plane taking off. 'Lazenby's is just my runway to greater things.'

'What greater things?' Rose asked curiously, franking a pile of letters that Miss Peters had completed.

'Well now, little Rosie, let me see.' Michael sat back in the chair with the air of a tycoon surveying his latest acquisition. 'There's all sorts of things. One of these days I'm going to be running my own business. With a big office. And I'll be able to sit at my desk and send someone running for cups of tea. And I'll tell you what: you and Miss Peters can come and work for me!' He sat forward again, laughing loudly. 'What do you say, Miss Peters?'

'I can hardly wait,' Miss Peters said, looking across at him over her round, black-rimmed spectacles. 'Rose, are those letters going out this week – this month even?'

Rose smiled wryly at Michael, who jumped up and went to lean impishly over the back of Miss Peters' black Remington typewriter.

'You know what a wonderful woman you are, don't you?' He smiled appealingly, bending his head down towards her. 'So efficient, so correct, such a sense of humour. You're an example to us all.' He sensed that Miss Peters was coming round to his charm in her prickly way. 'Sure,' he said, bouncing back to his desk. 'I'd have you to work for me any time!'

Miss Peters made noises of exasperation and gestured at Rose to get off to the post. She ran down the stairs, laughing.

Rose was happy. She treasured the thought of Dora's proud face as she set off, all dressed up on her first morning, and then when Rose had brought home her first wages. Even the pain of saying goodbye to Diana the week before seemed lightened by the fun she had in the office.

She had been at work on the day they actually left, so they said their goodbyes on the Sunday before. Ronald and Catherine had both embraced Rose as well as Diana, and even William shook her by the hand, rather stiffly, and said, 'I hope we shall see you again, Rose.'

'You'd blooming better,' Rose said, being all joky so she didn't start crying. 'I'll expect you down here to see me as soon as you can, Di.'

'Oh, I shall come, I shall. But you must write to me very, very often. I shall miss you so much.'

They'd given each other a long big hug. They didn't want to let go, and promised each other all kinds of things: above all, letters. And Rose had waved goodbye as she started for home, choked with sadness. When she reached her house she cried and cried.

Later she told Geraldine Donaghue that Diana had left. The girl's face lit up maliciously. The two had spent a lot of time together at school, but Geraldine had always remained jealous of Diana, knowing that she and Rose shared something very special.

'Going to lower yourself to speak to the rest of us now are you?' Geraldine said.

'I've always spoken to you,' Rose said impatiently. 'You know that very well. And if you hadn't always been so green round the gills about Diana we could've been better friends all the time.'

'Hark at her,' Geraldine said. 'Miss High and Mighty.'

Rose knew Geraldine was sore because she hated her boring factory job, and her dad had been laid off again. She knew the Donaghues were struggling, and none of it did much to improve Theresa Donaghue's temper.

But Rose was not very bothered about Geraldine. She had only to be in Michael's cheeky, vivacious company for a few minutes and she felt renewed and lively herself. She had been attracted to him from the first day there, though she was not thinking about courting. She knew Michael was a regular on the Stratford Road monkey-run and had had a succession of dates. She was very childlike and innocent still about relations between men and women, although she knew that sometimes she was flirting with him. Mainly he provided a figure for her to look up to, who had an infectious kind of drive and wanted to put a lot into his life and get a lot out of it. He made her feel more alive.

'You're a funny kid,' he said to her one day as they

were working together. Miss Peters, despite her crustiness, was very tolerant of their conversation so long as she knew the work would be done.

Michael looked appraisingly at Rose. 'You come down here from Birch Street all dressed up in nice clothes that would set anyone back a bit. And sometimes you talk common like the rest of us, and other times you can turn it on and put on your aitches and sound quite posh. What's your secret, eh, little Rosie?' He grinned at her. 'Are you a foundling from Buckingham Palace or something?'

'That'd be telling, wouldn't it?' she said rather pertly, and she knew once again that there was a mild flirtation going on between them.

She had come to Lazenby's with enormous hopes, to learn, as a way of getting experience for better things and eventually moving on.

But not yet, she thought. I'll stay and enjoy it while it lasts.

Eight

The summer ended. Rose walked to work on fine days in the rich slanting light of autumn. When it grew colder she put on Diana's coat – one of a number of pieces of clothing that the family had left for her – and walked more briskly.

Though still small and thin Rose was not as painfully bony as she had been during the poorest days of her childhood. She was of a different build from Dora, more rounded, and her breasts had begun to fill out. With her dark wavy hair cut to the level of her chin and softly brushed back from her face and wearing Diana's well-cut clothes she looked surprisingly elegant for someone so young. Her brown eyes shone with vigour and intelligence.

Twice every day she passed builders working on a nearby warehouse whose scaffold extended out across the pavement so she had to skirt round piles of bricks and a cement mixer. The lads working on the site, their boots dusted grey, gave appreciative whistles as she walked by.

It didn't take her long to notice that one of the young brickies had taken quite a shine to her. As the days passed he seemed to be waiting for her, watching quietly. He wasn't one of the whistlers. He was a thin, pale lad with spiky brown hair that looked as if no amount of Bryl or any other creem would force it to lie flat.

Then he began to smile at her and say hello whenever she walked by. Once, when she had almost passed them, she heard the others egging him on, 'Go on – go and ask her name!'

Suddenly the nervous boy was beside her. 'Er . . .' The words stumbled out clumsily. 'I just wondered – I mean – what's your name?'

'Rose,' she replied, amused. 'And what's yours?'

'Alfie,' he said. 'That is – Alfred – Meredith.'

'Oh,' Rose said. 'Hello then, Alfie.'

Alfie seemed to be quite struck dumb and as Rose was still hurrying on down the road he said, 'Tara then.'

'Tara,' Rose said smiling, attaching no real importance to the meeting.

She was still smiling when she reached Lazenby's and walked into the office. Michael was already sitting behind his desk and he looked up and grinned when he saw her. 'All right, little Rosie?' he said. 'Don't you look a picture this morning? Had some good news or what?'

'Yes I have.' She took her camel coat off and hung it up. 'A letter from Diana.'

Rose had gradually told Michael about Diana and her own hopes to get on and do something with her life. She was rather afraid at first that he'd laugh at her and tell her she'd not got a hope. Sometimes she couldn't make Michael out. He could be as kind and generous as anyone she'd ever met – even Diana – and innocent as she was, she realized that the hunger for life they both shared resulted in an electric kind of attraction between them. But there was also a wild streak in him. She knew he was already beginning to drink heavily, and he had come into the office a number of times with his face cut and bruised from fights.

When she told him her greatest ambition was to become a teacher of young children he looked at her and gave a low whistle.

'Well,' he said. 'You're quite a girl, aren't you? Can't quite see you as one of them blue-stocking women though – let alone how you're going to get there. But good luck to you all the same.'

She knew it was not an ambition he could really understand, but she was grateful to him for not making fun of her.

And hearing from Diana was always encouraging.

'I can't wait until Christmas when I come down to see you,' Diana wrote.

I miss you and Birmingham so much. My school is all right I suppose, but I haven't really made any friends properly yet. The school is rather a long way from where we live, as we knew it would be. So William, Judith and I all have to go to school on the bus every day. Mummy says it's good for us! But I don't like Manchester as much as Birmingham.

She told Rose that her father was enjoying his new job and Catherine was getting stuck into things as ever.

Missing you ever such a lot. With love from your good friend,
Diana. xxx

Things were looking less cheerful for Dora. She was pregnant again. At nearly forty-three she'd hoped this kind of sickness was something she'd seen the back of. And this time it came with an intensity and violence that she recognized from nearly twenty years earlier. It could mean only one thing.

'It's twins, I'm sure of it,' she wailed to Rose and Grace as they helped her back up the stairs to bed. 'I've only been sick this bad with babbies once before and that was with Sid and Percy. What the hell am I going to do? Twins at my age!'

'It might not be twins, Mom,' Grace tried to reassure her as they helped her on to the bed, so weak from the incessant retching that she could barely stand. 'It might just be your age making it worse.'

'Ooh,' Dora groaned. 'I feel as if someone's trampled all over me ribcage.'

'Look Mom,' Rose said. 'There's no need to worry. You don't have to do anything. The money's coming in from me and Sam and our Grace'll be out at work next year when the babby's born. We'll do everything round the house. You just take care of yourself for a change.'

'What about Sid's dinner today? You know how he carries on . . .'

'Let him get it his bloody self for once,' Rose snapped, exasperated that her father's needs were as usual the thing that overrode everything else.

Grace shushed her. 'It's all right, Mom,' she said to Dora. 'I've got a few minutes before I go to school. I'll sort out something to keep him quiet. You just have a sleep and you'll feel better. Rose – you'd better get off to work or you'll be late.'

Rose could feel her sister's stoical calmness beginning to pervade the room. She realized it would be better if she went. She left Grace methodically tidying her father's things in the bedroom and tucking the covers round Dora so that only her grey face, creased in discomfort, was visible.

It was the first time Dora had been able to take to bed during a pregnancy. The sickness left her weak and wretched, and it was several weeks before she was able to be up once the worst was over.

The day had begun well. It was a frosty November morning. The builders on Rose's walk to Lazenby's had almost finished their work, and this fact had stirred Alfie Meredith to new realms of courage. He thought Rose was the best-looking girl he'd ever seen. He longed to ask her out and spent almost all his time rehearsing what he might say. Rose, though she smiled and waved at him, never gave him a thought the rest of the time.

When Alfie approached her that morning, Rose turned to him with her usual smile and said, 'All right, Alfie? Job's about done, isn't it? I s'pose you'll be moving on soon?'

'Yes,' he said, walking alongside her. 'That's it – yes. Er, Rose. Just stop a tick will you?'

She stopped and waited, looking at him.

'I wanted to ask you ...' He ran his sandy hand through the already wayward hair and it stuck up even more. 'Would you think of coming out with me – on a date like?'

Rose decided in a split second what approach to take to this. She wasn't keen on the idea of walking out with Alfie, though flattered by the question. She decided to let him down gently by keeping up a joking banter. She started to walk on again slowly.

'Well – I'm not sure about that,' she said. 'I'd have to think about it, wouldn't I?'

Alfie immediately took this as a refusal. He ran after her awkwardly in his cement-caked trousers. 'Well tell me your address then – or I might not see you again. We finish here today, see.'

'Court eleven, Catherine Street,' Rose called over her shoulder to him. 'Got to go or I'll be late. Tara, Alfie.'

It was a tiring day. She ran back and forth to the markets with messages amid the seething activity in the echoing building hung with the skinned sides of animals. There were so many invoices and bills to be sorted out that she was not much in the office until the afternoon. When she finally came back the short distance up Bradford Street and along the side street to Lazenby's she saw that the lights were on and the place looked quite warm and inviting.

Upstairs Mr Lazenby was standing in the main office with Jo Perks from the meat market. Miss Peters had already left, her desk cleared and immaculate. Michael still seemed to be concentrating at his desk.

'Hello stranger,' he said, looking up. 'They've certainly kept you on the go today haven't they?' He closed the ledger and tidied a few sheets of paper. 'Well – that's me done. I'm off to the Adam and Eve for a quick one.' Rose smiled as he smoothed back his shiny black hair and put his jacket on. She knew it would be more than a quick one. 'Tara. See you in the morning, kid!'

'Bye,' Rose said, smiling after him. She watched him walk jauntily to the top of the stairs. Just before he disappeared down them he turned and raised his thumb to her with a smile, and she grinned and waved at him.

Jo Perks and Mr Lazenby were standing sorting through a pile of slinks – the hides of unborn calves which Lazenby's also purchased from the markets. They went to make fancy wallets and purses.

Rose looked at her table to see if there were any jobs

that needed doing, and then began to get ready to leave. Her feet were very chilled and tired and she thought longingly of soaking them in a pail of hot water when she got home.

But as she made to go Mr Lazenby called over to her. 'Rose – if you wouldn't mind hanging on a minute till I've finished with Mr Perks. I've got a couple of things need sorting out.'

Rose nodded and waited as Mr Lazenby showed out the dapper figure of Jo Perks, carrying a couple of the rolled-up slinks that hadn't come up to scratch.

'Come here a minute, Rose,' Mr Lazenby said in his polite but brisk business voice.

He stood back to let her into his office, where the light was already on, making it look completely dark outside. He closed the door behind them.

With rather odd enthusiasm he said, 'I tell you what. Since we're out of hours, you sit in the boss's seat. Go on, for a bit of a joke like. Yes, that's right my dear. Go along and sit yourself down!'

Rose walked round to the big chair behind Mr Lazenby's desk. It had wooden arms and a shiny leather seat. She looked uncertainly at Mr Lazenby, who stood the other side of the desk. His worn black jacket was unbuttoned and as he leaned down to rest his weight on his hands on the desk, the flaps of the jacket swung outwards making him look enormously wide.

Rose began to wonder if he'd been drinking. She'd never seen Mr Lazenby looking so animated. But he was normally a very abstemious man – known for it in fact. His soft cheeks had more colour in them than usual and he kept tapping his fingers restlessly on the top of the desk.

'There are a couple of invoices I'll need first thing,'

he said once Rose was seated on the slippery chair, which smelt rather sweaty, like Mr Lazenby. 'Since you're so good at writing, you can write these ones out yourself. How about that?' he said.

He opened one of the desk drawers and produced a wodge of forms, then handed Rose a pen. 'This one's for Clark's, so write in the name up there – you know how to do it,' he said, pointing with a grubby finger. He gave her details of the address and Rose slowly wrote them on the invoice sheet in her very neatest handwriting. Mr Lazenby watched over her shoulder.

'Very good,' he said, and Rose jumped because the voice sounded so close to her.

'Now – the next bit,' he said.

Rose sat with her heart beating fast. She was beginning to sweat under her arms. She didn't know what Mr Lazenby was up to but he was making her most uneasy. She just wanted to get the job done and go home.

As she was listing the items on the form she suddenly felt Mr Lazenby's hands moving round her and cupping her breasts. She gasped out of shock and discomfort because he was pressing her quite hard. She sat quite still, completely unable to think what to do. What on earth had come over him? This was a mistake – a terrible mistake. Mr Lazenby must realize it in a minute and stop touching her. She thought her heart was going to burst it was beating so loud, and her hands had gone clammy.

'Stand up,' Mr Lazenby ordered. His voice sounded polite still, but had a hard, unfamiliar edge to it. He pulled her up by moving his hands under her arms and he steered her away from the chair. Rose obeyed, bewildered. She was very afraid, but she couldn't think what else to do. The building around them had gone quiet.

After that, quite silently except for his breathing, which sounded loud and fast, he pulled her against him. She was still facing the desk, the impassive blotter, the penholder and the set, smiling faces of his children. He moved up and down against her buttocks, fitting himself close to her.

He began grabbing at her clothes, the green cardigan and soft white blouse. He lost patience with the buttons and she heard the blouse tear apart at the front. The image of Miss Smart's face as she had ripped Rose's bloomers that day filled her mind for a second. At least then she had understood what was happening.

'Stop it, Mr Lazenby – please,' she begged, her voice turning high like a little girl's. 'I don't like this. Please stop and let me go home.'

She turned her head and felt a plunging sensation of revulsion at the sight of him behind her. He didn't look like Mr Lazenby any more. His eyes were half closed and seemed to be rolled up into the lids so he looked all peculiar, as if he were in a trance. And his tongue was sticking stiffly out of his mouth towards her ear.

'What are you doing?' she shouted. 'Help me some-body – please. Please!'

She tried to get his hands off her, but as if prompted by her cries, Mr Lazenby shoved her to the floor, cold against her breasts and stomach as she writhed and kicked. She felt his knee in her back pinning her to the floor, and twisting round she saw he had unbuttoned his trousers and was rubbing himself with his hand, fast up and down. He pulled off her underwear and stock-ings, pausing to caress himself with one hand as he did so. She knew she didn't have the strength to get away from him. She put her arms flat on the floor and laid her head down so she didn't have to see his face with its self-absorbed expression or his horrifying, swollen member.

He pushed her skirt up and made her move her legs apart. She had never taken her clothes off in front of a man before, not even a doctor. She pressed her eyes shut at the shame of it. Tears squeezed from her lids on to the floor. She thought at least she hadn't got her monthly to add to the humiliation. She knew that what Mr Lazenby was doing must be what she had heard her father do so often to her mother, but it didn't prepare her any better for what happened next.

He gradually forced one of his fingers up inside her so that she squirmed and cried out in shock and pain.

'Oh . . .' Mr Lazenby gave a low groan. 'Young, tight.'

They were the only words he spoke until he'd finished. Quickly he climbed on her and forced hard up into her from behind and she screamed and then whimpered at his repeated movements. Each time he pushed into her she felt a terrible stab of pain somewhere deep in her guts. Her hipbones and ribs were grinding hard against the floor with the weight of him on top of her and she was finding it hard to breathe. She lifted her head, sobbing and trying to take in gasps of air so her mouth dried out. It took some time before he managed to finish, and he came at last with a loud, relieved cry.

When he had stumbled off her he buttoned himself up again and watched as she slowly pulled herself off the floor and found her clothes. The wet ran down her legs as she stood up and her tears wouldn't stop coming. She didn't look at Mr Lazenby when she was clothed again. She began to walk mechanically to the door.

Mr Lazenby gave a little cough. 'Er – Rose, just a minute,' he said.

She forced herself to look round and saw he was bringing his wallet out of his jacket.

'I've been thinking. You've done your best since you've been here,' he said in his normal courteous voice. 'But I'm not sure this is really a job for a lass. I've decided to let you go and get a lad in like we've always had. It'll be for the best I think.'

He was holding out a pound note to her.

'Here – take a couple of weeks' pay. And if you need a decent reference you can rely on me, you know that.'

He came a little closer, holding the money out as if he was trying to tempt a dangerous animal. Rose quickly snatched the note, backing away from him again.

He unlocked the door and she went slowly down the stairs and out into the freezing evening, holding in her hand a larger sum of money than she'd ever earned at once before.

Nine

12 May 1937

Coronation day. All over the nation there were excited preparations to celebrate the crowning of a new king – George VI. Red, white and blue bunting rippled and flapped along Catherine Street in the bright spring morning. Union Jacks billowed out from the sills of some of the houses, and as it was a day off work for everyone, the road was more full of people than usual. Already the inhabitants of the street were setting up trestle tables along the pavements, to be laid later with white cloths and heaped with plates of food for the street's celebration party. George and his little band of followers were tearing in and out of the courts in their draggle-arsed shorts, pretending to be aeroplanes with a lot of roaring sound effects and getting under every-body's feet.

In Court 11 most of the women were inside hastily icing platefuls of tiny sponge cakes and slicing bread for the little triangular sandwiches which would grace the tables later on. Old Lady Gooch declared, breathing heavily as she went to inspect what was happening in each house, that she'd made a 'rich fruit Dundee – one of me best'. Her large bloodshot eyes ran over every contribution to make sure everyone was doing their whack and that there'd be enough to go round in the afternoon. She was still wearing her working clothes. The dressing up would come later and the pawn shops had been rifled for suitable clothes, some of which had not seen the light of day for months or longer.

The happiest person in the court that day was Grace Lucas. Not only was she to leave school that summer, but she was ecstatic that there was another coronation so soon after the last. Now she'd got over her grief at the death of her beloved King George V and the startling abdication of his successor Edward VIII, she was ready to throw herself wholeheartedly into the occasion. She had trimmed the edges of her frock by hand with strips of red, white and blue, and decorated a straw hat in the same colours with elaborate ribbons and bows. With it pulled on over her straggly brown hair, her pale, sweet face was almost pretty. Even Sid had noticed and commented that he'd never seen her looking such a 'fine lass' before.

'Rose – you can't miss coming this afternoon,' Grace entreated her sister, who was scraping the last hardening crust of white icing out of a mixing bowl. 'It wouldn't be the same without you. You're not thinking of the neighbours are you?'

'Bit late for that isn't it?' Rose said sourly. 'I'm just not in the mood, that's all, and I need a rest. I cleaned that blooming pub from top to bottom yesterday and I could do with a lie down. I don't feel right.'

Grace's and Dora's eyes met and Grace shrugged. She couldn't get close to Rose any more. She felt like crying when she looked at her older sister standing by the table. She was wearing an old dress of Dora's which they'd shortened together and tucked up at its wide, loose waist. Her belly was straining forward with the unmistakable curve of pregnancy. She was having to lean more than usual towards the table to accommodate the shape of the child. Her hair was hanging limply down her back and around her face. Grace couldn't help thinking – with the realization of how aware Rose must be of it too – that she looked just like a miniature, black-haired version of her mother.

'Leave her,' Dora said rather irritably. She was tired, being now seven months pregnant herself, as well as having had to deal with all the goings-on over Rose.

'I'm going to go and see how they're getting on outside,' Grace said a bit huffily. Her mother and sister had an understanding nowadays that she definitely was not part of.

She went out into the street to look up and down at all the busy preparations. She saw someone coming towards her along the street and for a few seconds she couldn't place who it was. Then she was back across the court to the house as fast as she could move.

'Rose!' she shrieked. 'He's here again!'

Rose looked up lifelessly. 'Who?'

'That bloke – Alfie – the one who come before. He's got flowers this time.'

'Oh no,' Rose said. Dora and Grace could both hear the panic in her voice. 'Don't let him see me, for God's sake.' She was wiping her hands so hurriedly that she fumbled and dropped the cloth. 'Go and tell him I'm not here again. Tell him I've gone away or something.' And she was off upstairs.

Grace managed to reach Alfie as he was coming into the court. 'You looking for Rose again?' she asked, thinking what kind eyes he had and how funny his hair looked all sticking up like that.

'Is she here?' Grace could hear the combined hope

and nervousness in his voice. 'I'd really like to see her – if she'll let me.'

At that moment young Harry waddled up and stood staring at this strange man who had appeared. He had wide blue eyes and a fat tummy. And he had nits and was forever scratching busily at his head.

'E-yo,' he said to Alfie.

'Hello.' Alfie smiled down at him. 'Doing all right, are you?'

'That's our Harry,' Grace told him.

'Nice kid,' Alfie said. 'Anyway, is Rose in today?'

'Rose . . .' Harry said, turning towards the house, and Grace could tell he was about to point at it. Hurriedly she grabbed his hands and picked him up, wishing someone would pursue her with flowers and obvious admiration, because she'd make better use of it than Rose.

'Rose ain't here,' she told him. 'She's gone away for a bit – to stay with Mom's sister down Alcester way. She won't be around for . . . well, we don't know how long really.' She didn't like lying to him, but she felt it would save both his feelings and Rose's.

'Oh,' Alfie said despondently. 'Only I was hoping – you know, as it's a holiday today . . .'

'Well I'll let her know you've been round – when I, er, write,' Grace said. 'It was nice of you to call.'

'Here,' Alfie said, holding out the bunch of pink and white flowers to her. 'You might as well take these anyway. You have them, or give them to your mom.'

As he turned to go he pointed at number five. 'That your house then, is it?'

'Yes,' Grace said shyly. 'That's us – number five.'

'Tara then.'

Glancing up at the dark windows, Alfie felt sure he

caught a glimpse of a pale face edged with black hair, before it ducked down below the sill.

He walked away angrily. What's got into her? he thought. I s'pose she thinks I'm not good enough for her or something.

There had been a number of changes in Court 11 during the past six months.

First, Rose had been faced with telling Dora she had lost her job. When her daughter walked in that November evening, Dora had only to look at her to realize something had happened. Normally she came in from work tired, but quite animated, and often full of stories of things that had happened during the day. But that night she was quite silent, as if something had been tied up tight inside her.

'Had a bad day?' Sam casually asked Rose as he polished his boots. 'Aren't you going to tell us what wonder boy's been up to today?' Sam got a bit browned off with Rose's adoration of Michael Gillespie.

Rose didn't answer him. She took off her coat and hung it up behind the door and then went to go upstairs.

'Grub's ready so don't go disappearing again,' Grace said. 'You're late enough as it is.'

Rose ignored her.

'Did you hear your sister?' Sid shouted after her, throwing the newspaper down. 'We've all been waiting for you as it is. You ought to be thankful our Grace lets you off so much of the work around here, you uppity little cow.'

Dora and the others held their breath as they waited for the explosion from Rose which would set off another of the increasingly bitter fights between them.

Grace had had to intervene to pacify Sid on a number of occasions when Dora wasn't up to it.

But Rose just said, 'I'm not hungry,' and went to her room.

She sat painfully on the bed, feeling the damp still on her clothes. Her mouth twisted for a moment with revulsion. Then she lay down, curling herself on the mattress like an unborn child. The pain throbbed inside her. She pressed her hand on her bruised private parts, and clamped her legs tight together with her hand still between them, trying to dull the ache of it. What she wanted overwhelmingly was to wash every part of her over and over, but she knew there was no chance of that with all the family sitting round down there. She screwed her eyes tight shut and wished she could fall down, down somewhere very dark and safe where she could be held and comforted. No tears came to begin washing away the shame and despair she felt.

And as she lay there she was overcome with loathing for herself. All the smells of Lazenby's seemed to seep out from her clothes and her body. She smelt the foul stink of the hides, the bunkers of bones and rancid fat in the yard. She saw the maggots squirming among the grains of salt, the frantic greed of the flies; she saw the discoloured bulging shape of the goitre man's neck and the soft, floppy cheeks of Mr Lazenby. She could see him kneeling with that horrible, trance-like expression on his face, his trousers unbuttoned and his hand busy on his penis.

She rushed over to the bucket in the corner of the room and retched over it, feeling the muscles in her bruised stomach heave painfully. She didn't hear Grace coming up the stairs.

'Are you bad, Rose?' she asked sympathetically. 'You

should've said instead of just going off. I could've brought you a cuppa tea. Dad just thought you was being awkward.'

'I'll be all right,' Rose said weakly, and she sounded so wretched that Grace said, 'I'll get our mom.'

Dora slowly climbed the stairs holding a candle stuck on to a saucer. She wasn't feeling too good herself.

'What's up with you then, miss?' she demanded roughly, sitting down on the bed, panting from the climb.

Rose had only intended to break the news that she'd lost her job, but when she began talking the tears started pouring down her cheeks again. She had to tell Dora what had happened. She couldn't hold back.

The second she heard what Rose had to say, Dora was on her feet. With more energy than she'd summoned for weeks she slapped Rose hard on each cheek.

'What did you do?' Dora shouted at her, before remembering that on no account must Sid or the neighbours overhear this conversation. 'You must've encouraged him,' she hissed at Rose. She stood with her hands clamped to her waist, her elbows at sharp, hostile angles. Her shadow in the candlelight looked huge and menacing. 'Going off to a place like that in all them clothes of Diana's. You must've given him ideas, you silly little cow.'

'I didn't!' Rose wailed. 'I didn't know what to give him ideas about, did I? He just went for me – held me down on the floor!'

Dora stood over her, her mind trying to take in the implications of what had happened. Then, as if bracing herself, she said in a matter-of-fact voice, 'We'll just have to wait and see if you're having a babby. If not, then there's no harm done. You can go and find another job.'

'A babby?' Rose sat up, horrified. The thought hadn't occurred to her.

'If you didn't know where they come from before, you do now,' Dora said drily. 'God help you if your dad finds out. I'll tell you one thing though. Whatever he says I'll stick by you. You'll not be sent out on the streets like some. But you'd better start praying hard, Rose, that there ain't no babby come out of this. Because you're going to need all the help you can get.'

She gave Rose's quivering body a rough pat. 'When your dad's off to the Catherine again I'll send Grace up with a pail of water for you. We'll just tell her you're a bit feverish. It'll have to be cold though – I can't spare the slack for the fire this time of night. But if you want to wash a man off you that bad you won't be bothered how cold the water is.'

'So you're nothing but a bloody little tart after all!' Sid's harsh voice ran through the house. 'Even that Geraldine Donaghue ain't poking out at the front and she's been working down the factory. But you've been nothing but cowing trouble ever since you learned to open your gob.'

Rose noticed again the perverse triumph that came over him when he saw her put down. But she rode her father's attacks more easily than anyone's. She was used to them. And as she had promised, Dora stood like an immovable wall between him and Rose as he ranted at both of them. But even his insults felt as if they were true, she was in such an emotional state.

It was telling Grace and Sam that came hardest. One afternoon they went with George and Harry to Calthorpe Park. The two young boys ran on ahead as soon as they were released into the green space, little Harry trying to keep up with his nine-year-old brother. Sam, Rose and Grace walked behind, keeping them both in sight.

'How could you, Rose?' Sam demanded, rigid with indignation. He immediately fell into what Rose was beginning to recognize as his role of responsible citizen. His shoulders were pulled back and he clasped his hands behind his back, walking along with a rather ponderous stride. For a split second Rose wanted to giggle hysterically. She had only got as far as telling him that in five months' time she'd be having a baby.

'How could you lower yourself like that?' Sam lectured. Beside her, Rose sensed, Grace had gone rigid with distress, but would not of course be judging her. Not Grace.

'I've always had my suspicions about that Michael Gillespie bloke,' Sam went on. 'Always sounded like trouble to me. You shouldn't be taken in by things that glitter, Rose. All that glitters is not gold, you know. And where is he now you're carrying his child? That's what I'd like to know.'

'It wasn't Michael!' Rose cried, bursting into tears. She was completely horrified that that should be Sam's first thought. Sobbing, she told him who the child's father was.

'You must've given him some encouragement,' Sam said. 'That Mr Lazenby sounded like a respectable feller. You said yourself he lives in a road in Edgbaston, not a street like the likes of us round the Birch. You should be ashamed of yourself.'

'Of course I'm ashamed of myself,' Rose sobbed brokenly beside him. 'D'you think I've felt anything but ashamed since the day it happened?'

'Sssh, for goodness sake,' Sam urged her. 'People're staring at you.'

Grace put her arm round Rose's shoulder and with the other pointed across the park to the two boys. 'Go and get them, Sam,' she said icily to her brother. 'And take your time.'

The two sisters sat down on one of the benches. Rose, beyond caring that she had chosen to tell them in such a public place, leaned on Grace's skinny shoulder and cried and cried. From the evening she had left Lazenby's she had felt only a leaden depression so that some days she could hardly drag herself around. But now the pain released itself from the deepest part of her. The tears wouldn't stop coming, and Grace stroked her hair gently. Sitting there so close, as Rose finally grew quieter, her body still shuddering from the sobs, she could hear the pull of her sister's lungs.

'Why didn't you tell me sis?' Grace asked her. 'I'd never've blamed you, you know. This is the worst thing that could happen to anyone and I know you're not the type to go looking for it.'

'I couldn't.' Rose gulped. 'I mean, I had to tell Mom – about why I'd lost my job at Lazenby's and everything. But telling the rest of you – it made it real somehow. And I didn't know about the babby at first. If there'd been no babby I could've tried to put it out of my mind and just got on with it. But now ...' She began to cry again, weakly. 'I can't do anything ever again, can I, except be like Mom and have kids trailing after me. Oh Grace – sometimes I could just finish myself, I really could.'

'You mustn't think that!' Grace gripped Rose's shoulders with surprising strength. 'Don't you ever think anything of the sort.' She was crying herself now, and the two of them sat there frozen on the bench on that icy March day as Sam stood in the distance with his back to them, staring across the park.

Little Harry toddled up and stood there gazing worriedly at them, so the two girls picked him up and cuddled him to reassure him.

'Can you feel the babby?' Grace asked timidly.

'I think so. Just a bit of a bubbly feeling at the moment, like wind!' Rose said. She was grateful to Grace for being so matter of fact and kind. She only wished Sam could find it in himself to overcome his principles and be good to her.

'Are you afraid it'll look like him?'

Rose thought about it for a moment. 'It's a funny thing – it doesn't seem to be anything to do with him somehow. As if the two things don't tie up. It's my babby.' Suddenly she was speaking in a surprised, wondering tone. 'Mine. I'm the one stuck with it inside me. As for him, I hope he falls under a bleeding bus. This babby's nothing to do with him.'

They sat in silence for a while. A touch of warmth from the sun came and went as small clouds passed over its face. They watched families out walking in the park, some of the mothers pushing heavy black prams. It was as if Rose's fate was being paraded in front of them.

Finally Sam headed towards them with George in tow and fell self-consciously into step next to Rose.

'I've been thinking,' he announced as they walked to the edge of the park. 'I won't say anything else, but I'll say this. I may not like what's happened or how you've behaved.' Suddenly he sounded rather bashful.

'But you're my sister and I'll stand by you. The neighbours'll no doubt have their say and none of us'll like it. But you can count on me, Rose.'

'I'm glad you said that,' Grace said, and Rose was surprised to hear the strong edge of anger in her voice. 'You've been a right preaching old gasbag lately and we're all getting blooming weary of it. If you hadn't said you'd stand by our Rose, I'm not sure as I'd've had much to say to you again, whether you're my brother or not.'

Rather stiffly, Sam linked his arm through Rose's, and they walked home close together along the cold streets.

The gossip threaded round Court 11 in a matter of an hour or so. There were two events competing for attention. Number two, otherwise known as Moonstruck House, was again standing empty. Like so many of the former tenants in that house, the Donaghues had vanished, lock, stock and barrel in the night and no one knew where to. Things had been bad for a while, but whether they'd sit it out or do a moonlight to dodge the landlord was anybody's guess. Now the front door was swinging open and there were still a few things left inside from the hurry in which they'd had to load up the cart.

But even this piece of gossip paled when Gladys Pye put it around that Dora Lucas had told her Rose was expecting. Dora made a shrewd choice in telling Gladys first. While Dora knew Gladys would tell everyone the news as fast as breathe, she was also Dora's friend. They had helped each other at the birth of their children and shared their worries day after day. Gladys, while full of twittering speculation with the other women in the court, would in the end come down on Dora's side.

'So who's the father?' Gladys whispered. The two women were standing in the brewhouse.

'I'd rather not say,' Dora hissed back. 'It were a case of him forcing himself on her. There ain't no airy-fairy feelings on her side, you know. She's been bad ever since.'

Gladys saw Dora's eyes fill with tears, and she made sympathetic noises. 'And Sid . . . ?' Gladys looked the picture of concern. She was a tiny woman, made even smaller by the bent bones in her legs.

Dora shrugged in reply to the question. 'I stick by my own,' she said. 'He can moan and mither as much as he likes, but Rose is staying home and we've got to make the best of it. But I've hardly had a decent night since it happened, I can tell you.'

Gladys tut-tutted, saying, 'As if there ain't enough to worry about. I saw you was looking anyhow lately, but I thought it was just the babby.'

'Babbies,' Dora corrected her.

Gladys gasped. 'No! You sure?'

'Sure as I've ever been,' Dora said. 'And I can feel them both now. But I always know, and I'm just as sure our Rose is carrying a lad.'

When Old Lady Gooch heard the news from Gladys she said, 'Well I never. That'll take the little madam down a peg. Strutting about here with her airs and graces. Now she'll find out a thing or two. I should send her off to the Church Army. She'd soon find out what happens to girls who ain't careful with themselves.'

*

On the afternoon of the coronation, Rose lay on her back in the bedroom, seeing little white clouds move across the pale blue sky outside the window. She could hear the excited hubbub from the street as the party got into full swing. All the kids would be sitting along the tables with the grown-ups standing round, everyone in little hats and all enjoying the food and the rare day's holiday. She knew this was a day of all days for Grace, who would be almost counting the minutes until the evening paper came out carrying the pictures. And then tuppence for the *Weekly Illustrated* on Saturday. A breeze blew through the open window and she heard snatches of a band playing somewhere.

Wish I was like you, Grace, she thought. Grace, who could live off other people's exciting lives and not expect to have much excitement in her own.

Rose lay, not wanting to sleep but feeling tired and muzzy. The further the pregnancy progressed the more remote she felt from her life as it had been. Even her sense of despair, which had been most acute when she first knew she was to have a child, had dulled. She felt she was living in a kind of trance which would only end with the birth.

How could she have had dreams of becoming a teacher, of being a friend, let alone equal to someone like Diana? How could she keep in contact with her now? She wasn't even equal to Geraldine who had, after all, held down her job. And when she thought of Michael Gillespie, sometimes she wept with shame. What would he say if he knew what state she was in?

She put her hand on her belly and felt the light twitching of the child inside her. She had no bad feelings towards it. It just seemed unreal and, as she'd told

Grace, not part of Mr Lazenby at all. But its presence, its inexorable growth in there, and the certainty that one day she must experience what her mother had gone through, frightened her. She felt so helpless.

'You were a stupid little fool,' she said to herself. 'Thought you could do great things with your life, didn't you? Do better than your mom?'

She listened bitterly as a loud cheer rose from the street, and another and another.

Ten

There was a moment of complete silence as the three women waited. Then a snuffle and a cough, and finally the baby let out its first anxious cry.

'He's all right!' Gladys cried. She was tying the cord as the baby lay between Rose's legs. 'You may've got here a bit too soon, my lad, but you're going to be all right!'

Dora was sitting next to the head of the bed, suckling one of the twins. The other lay asleep in a drawer on the floor. They had been born only three weeks earlier and Dora's face sagged with exhaustion.

'Well – you've done it,' she said to her daughter, suddenly feeling choked with emotion. 'So now you know.'

Rose lay back, hot and worn out. The labour had come on early and had been painful but not too prolonged.

'Reckon you didn't have it too bad,' Gladys said. 'Specially for a first. No need to've had old Joan in after all, was there?'

Despite Dora's pleas, Rose had flatly refused to have 'that old cow' anywhere near her.

She lay looking at her tiny son lying curled in her arms. His hair was very pale, even though still damp from the dunking Gladys had given him. He turned his wrinkled little face and began to snuffle at Rose's body.

'He knows what he wants, anyroad,' Dora said. 'Give him a bit of titty, Rose.'

Rose was startled by the force with which the tiny baby sucked at her, and the pain which gripped her innards as he did so.

She looked down at his face. His eyes were tightly closed and he was already completely absorbed in feeding. 'I'm going to call him Joseph,' she said. 'He looks like a Joseph.'

It took several days before she began to feel much for the child. He was very small, with the tiniest limbs Dora said she'd ever seen on a baby. Rose gradually understood just how much her life was tied to him, so that his slightest sound would set her heart pounding and wake her from sleep or make her leave whatever she was doing to attend to him. It was his fair hair and skin that at first had made him seem such a stranger. She had never seen a baby with such fair hair in the family, and it took some getting used to. But by the end of the first week she could look at him and find tears running down her cheeks at the realization of how beautiful he was, how small and helpless.

'Let me nurse him,' Grace would say, when she was home. 'He's a lovely babby, Rose.' And sometimes Rose felt reluctant to hand him over, but Grace would take him and cuddle him close, singing softly to him until he cried to go back to his mother.

With three babies in the house, Dora and Rose were both sleeping downstairs on makeshift beds on the floor. One night as they were getting settled down, Sid came in and lurched awkwardly over to Rose. She looked up warily at him.

'It's all right, I'm not going to bite you,' he said

roughly. And then out of his pocket he pulled a small wooden object. 'I made this for the kid,' he said. 'Here. Come on – take it.'

Rose found she was holding a little wooden horse, rather rough and misshapen, but still obviously a horse, with a little spot of black paint on each side for its eyes.

'Here Joseph, this is for you,' she said to him. His blue eyes were open, staring over at the gaslight on the wall. 'Your grandad's made you a little horse. Are you going to say ta?' It was a relief having Joseph between her and Sid, to use the child as a way of communicating with him. Since Joseph was born he had been gentler with her, as if he could cope with her now she was doing what a woman was intended to do.

'Thanks Dad,' Rose said, feeling unexpected tears fill her eyes.

'No need to make a fuss,' Sid said awkwardly, going to the stairs.

Mother and daughter spent most of the night up and down feeding the babies. If it wasn't one it was another.

'I've had enough of this,' Dora said one night. It was well into the small hours and she was sick with fatigue. 'These two babbies are going to have to do everything at the same time or they're going to finish me.'

The boy, Billy, was yelling loudly for food. Dora woke the little girl, Susan, and latched the two of them on, stuffing a couple of pillows under her arms for support.

'Pour me a drop of milk, will you Rose?' she said. 'I could do with something on my stomach.'

Joseph was asleep, so Rose got up and handed her mother a cup of milk in the candlelight. 'I hope he's all right,' Rose said, frowning down at Joseph where he lay tucked up on the floor. One of his hands was clenched in a tiny fist next to his cheek. 'He's not feeding as well as he was.'

'Can't say the same of these two,' Dora said wearily.

'Here,' Rose went over to her. 'Give one over here. Joseph's not interested yet and I've got enough spare.'

She took Susan off her mother and held the unfamiliar body of the little girl. Even being a twin she felt rounder and heavier than Joseph. Having been able to rest more than she had during any other pregnancy, Dora had carried the two of them almost to term. They were good-sized babies. Rose sighed and looked over at her little son.

'Be right as rain in the morning,' Dora said. 'He's just tired I s'pect.'

By the end of the night they managed to get some sleep. Rose lay down next to Joseph with her nose against his soft scalp, hearing his quick little breaths. Now her life before him seemed even more like a dream. The days and nights felt almost indistinguishable with the round of feeding and changing his napkins and waiting for him to sleep. Joseph had happened to her, and he was not just a part of her life – everything she did was connected inextricably with this tiny person next to her.

Rose was dreaming. Dreams came rarely with all the broken nights, but this one burst in on her, vivid and clear.

She was with Diana on the tram which ran south along the Bristol Road out as far as the Lickey Hills. They had done that ride together a few times, Diana treating her at weekends. The tram lurched along the tracks down the middle of the road with the hedges separating them from the traffic on either side. When they had travelled that way in reality the tram had been crowded full of people, but in her dream it was empty. She and Diana had seats right at the back, looking down the deserted carriage. When they swayed through Bournbrook the tram passed the red bricks of the university, its pointed clock tower standing tall and elegant above the buildings around it.

'I'm going to go there,' Rose said. And then suddenly she was chanting,

Pussy cat, pussy cat, where have you been?
I've been up to London to visit the Queen . . .

And Diana sat beside her, her pink cheeks streaming with tears. 'I don't want you to go, Rose,' she begged. 'Stay and be my friend, Rose. Please stay.'

And then they were both crying and holding on to each other and the tram rolled downhill, down and down, and they didn't know or care where it was going any more.

Rose woke, tears wet on her cheeks. Diana had felt so close to her again, and she knew with a physical ache how much she missed her and how ashamed she felt. All the letters Diana had sent, full of hurt, begging Rose to write and not to forget her, were upstairs, lying unanswered in a cardboard box beside the little wooden elephant which had put the seal on their friendship. How could she reply to those letters now?

As she lay wretched in the grey dawn light, one of the twins started stirring and began to cry. She saw Dora pull herself up off the floor, still stunned by tiredness.

Perhaps Joseph would eat a little better this morning? During his first week he had thrived, but over the last

113

fortnight he had sucked at her breast for a time and then given up to lie listlessly, as if the effort was too much.

She turned to him to enjoy lying with him while he was still asleep, trying to forget the memory of Diana's distraught face in her dream. Very gently she stroked Joseph's soft baby head with one of her dark fingers. His skin was so much paler than hers! He felt cold and anxiously she searched out his hands. They were chilled.

'Come here,' she whispered, and turned him to cuddle and warm him.

His tiny body was stiff. Looking at his face, she saw his lips were still and blue.

Rose jumped up as if she'd been bitten, her lungs constricting so she could hardly breathe. 'Mom!' she gasped. 'Something's wrong with him. Quick – come here!'

Dora hastily put Billy down and rushed over. She picked Joseph up and Rose saw her face tighten. She listened to his chest and rubbed him vigorously. Then she put her mouth over his tiny one, breathing into him again and again to rouse him. Finally, with her head down, she laid him on Rose's bed, instinctively drawing the covers over him. Very slowly she turned to her daughter, who was standing still as a rock beside her.

'There's nothing else I can do, Rose,' she told her. 'He's gone.'

A man had died in a neighbouring court and Dora arranged for Joseph to be carried on the hearse the next day. When the horse clattered to a standstill outside, Rose was still holding the little body to her as if her arms would be fixed forever in that position, even after he was taken away from her.

'For God's sake get him off her,' Sid said to Dora upstairs as they readied themselves for the funeral. 'I can't stand to see it any longer.'

'D'you think I'm enjoying it?' Dora snapped. 'She's just parting with the child in her own time.' She remembered how her own dead children – the twins, Violet – had been snatched speedily away from her by everyone around, who thought it for the best.

Downstairs, Marj had arrived from Sparkbrook, dolled up in a smart black dress with a full skirt and a hat with a wide sloping brim. 'Make us a cuppa tea, Grace,' she said, sitting herself down with exaggerated relief. 'I'm worn out already after carting all the way over here.'

Sam turned his head in surprise as Grace replied, 'There might be a drop left in the pot, and if there is you can get it yourself.'

Marj pulled herself to her feet, murmuring huffily about what a welcome she got in her own home now-adays.

'You've not been so keen to look on us as your family when it didn't suit you,' Grace replied.

'Now, now,' Sam said. 'That's enough of that.' He looked at Rose. She didn't seem to be listening to the conversation at all. She sat with her eyes fixed on her little son, as if she was intensely afraid that she would forget what he looked like.

Grace went up to her timidly. 'They're here, Rose,' she said. 'The undertaker wants to know if he can take him.'

For the last time Rose slowly kissed the boy's cold cheek. She ran her finger along the line of the tiny nose and soft lips.

'I'll take him,' she said, and the others moved back to let her through.

She walked outside and handed him over to be laid in a small box that Sam had nailed together for him. The undertaker placed it on the step of the hearse, close by his feet.

A crowd was gathering in the street. The coffin lying on the hearse was draped with a Union Jack; the dead man had served in the war. As the horse began to move off, Sid solemnly saluted it, standing as straight and upright as he could manage.

The children started spitting on the ground and chanting,

> Catch your collar, never swaller
> In case you catch a fever;
> Not for you, not for me,
> And not for any of my family.

Rose stood tearless and in silence. She thought of all the times as a child that she had joined in the superstitious rhyming. And what good had it done her? Every step the horse took seemed to tear her further apart.

Suddenly she heard Marj's voice in her ear. 'It's all for the best you know, Rose,' she said in a knowing whisper, as if imparting a morsel of gossip. 'You'll get over it soon enough. And who really wants a babby at your age? Now you can get back on with your life, can't you?'

Marj would not easily forget the look of bitter hatred that her young sister turned on her that morning, or the adult hardness that she suddenly saw in her brown eyes.

A very thin, subdued Rose Lucas went back to her charring job at the Dog and Partridge. She could easily fit back into all her old clothes, although she felt like an impostor wearing them.

She started work at nine in the morning, walking into the smell of stale beer and smoke. When she got home she helped Dora, handing over all her meagre wages. She shopped and cooked, gave a hand with George and Harry and, as she had continued to do since Joseph died, she helped to feed the twins. They were the main comfort in her life. Her body was still poised to do all the things for which nature had prepared it. At least she could sleep next to Billy or Susan, cuddling up to them, and hold and feed them.

'She's lost her spirit, Mom,' Grace said one day. 'She could get herself a better job again now. She don't want to be charring all her life. I mean I knew I was going into service, but our Rose always had her eye on something better, didn't she?'

Dora sighed. 'It's early days yet,' she said. 'Give her time.'

Grace tried getting through to Rose, but never felt she got very far.

'I'm earning a wage, aren't I?' Rose would say woodenly. 'What more's anyone s'posed to want? What's the use of having dreams of doing something else? It'll only bring trouble.'

And in her head a voice kept saying: I'm not worth it. I'm cheap and dirty. I'm a slum kid with a dead bastard baby.

Grace looked at her reproachfully. 'You're still cleverer than me,' she said. 'You could do better for yourself.'

Rose just shrugged.

As autumn came round again, Alfie appeared once more in Catherine Street. He'd tried going out with other girls, but none of them could erase the image in his mind of the dark, vivacious girl he'd seen the autumn before walking to work. He had to speak with her, and he decided to give her the benefit of the doubt. Maybe she had another sister and it was her he thought he'd glimpsed looking out of the upper window that day?

He came on a grey Saturday afternoon, with rusty leaves whirling along the pavement.

This time it was George who saw him and came running into the house as Alfie approached, slamming the door behind him. 'It's that Alfie again – the bloke that's after Rose.'

Rose automatically fled to the stairs.

'Mom,' Grace said. 'Ask him in. He seems a good bloke, I reckon. I'll go up and talk her round.'

She found Rose sitting nervously on the bed. 'What're you doing hiding up here?' Grace demanded.

'Well, I can't let him see me, can I?' Rose replied with nervous irritation.

'Why not? You're not expecting any more are you? If you straighten yourself out a bit and put a decent frock on you'd look a picture again. He's all right that Alfie. So why keep yourself hidden away? If I had him following me around I'd jump at the chance. You could do a lot worse.'

Rose sat thinking for a moment. Grace's last words had hit home. What was she really hiding for now? Waiting for a prince to come along? Grace was right. She could do worse, and she wasn't likely to do any better.

'Tell him I'll be down in a minute.'

Grace gave a little skip and ran smiling downstairs. She found Dora handing Alfie a cup of tea. He was talking rather bashfully to her.

A few moments passed before Alfie finally saw the thin, beautiful girl he remembered emerging slowly, almost reluctantly, from the stairs. She'd brushed out her hair and pinned it back loosely so that it waved softly round her face, and she had on a cream dress of Diana's with a pattern of navy dots on it and a swinging skirt.

She came towards him and gave him a rather stiff smile. 'Hello Alfie,' she said.

Eleven

1 September 1939

The long line of children standing in pairs snaked along from the gates of the railway station and curved around the wall outside. They stood in almost eerie silence as the teachers counted and recounted them to make sure there was no one missing. In one hand they each clutched a bag of the most basic belongings; round every neck was tied a piece of string to which a large luggage label had been tied bearing its owner's name. The children waited to be loaded on to the carriages which would take them to places which few of them had even dreamed of. Many of them had scarcely travelled any distance from the streets where they had grown up.

Rose stood near George, anxiously watching his tight-lipped, mutinous face. She was glad that Alfie stood reassuringly beside her. He was seeing off his younger brother and sister, Tom and Bessie, both still at school.

'Some of them think it's just a spree,' he said. 'Look at their faces.'

'Not George,' Rose said. 'He's played hell over being sent off. It's a good job they only announced it yesterday.'

The van had come round the day before, the big rectangular loudspeakers like wide, merciless mouths crackling out the announcement. All children of school age were to be evacuated to places of safety, away from the centres most likely to be bombed, when – and it now seemed to be when and not just if – war broke out.

Immediately the mothers in the court banded together for mutual advice and support, on what would ordinarily have been a beautiful late summer day.

'Not the kids!' Dora cried. 'They can't split up families like that. How do we know where they're sending them? We'll never have a wink of sleep worrying.'

'What if Adolf Hitler starts throwing bombs down on us?' Mabel demanded grimly, leaning her meaty arm up against the brewhouse wall. 'Then you'd be bad with worrying about them all being killed in their beds. It's for the best, you know.'

'There's not going to be bombs, surely?' Gladys asked, puckering up her face in concern.

'Don't kid yourself,' Mabel said. 'What about Czechoslovakia last year?'

'And now they're after Poland,' Mabel went on. 'Things ain't going to get any better I don't reckon, so you might just as well get used to the idea.'

The rest of that day the families could think of nothing else. For the first time in years Dora turned to her husband for advice when he came in. 'What're we going to do?'

'Asking me are you, all of a sudden?' he said sourly, swinging his good arm back and forth to relieve the muscles after supporting himself on the crutch. 'If they say send them, then do it. They're best well out of it.' He sat down heavily. 'We should've finished them off properly the first time round, when we had the bloody chance.'

'I'm NOT GOING!' George shouted.

Sid took off his cap and flung it over on to the table. 'If we say you're going then you'll go!'

'What about Harry?' Dora said. She turned to put the kettle on, trying to steady herself. 'I can't send him away – or the twins. Not that young.'

'Couldn't Edna have Harry for a bit?' Rose suggested. 'After all, most of hers are grown up and gone now. We'll club together for some money for the fare.'

Dora's sister in Alcester seemed, out of the few choices, the most reassuring one. Dora got Rose to write to her straight away.

'But the twins stay with me,' Dora said. 'And that's that.'

They'd got George ready the next morning. He soon realized there was no point in arguing. Dora tidied him up to go down to the school, tugging his collar straight and giving his face a wipe.

'Go on,' she said to him, rather roughly, to stop herself blarting there on the step. 'Don't give anyone any lip and make sure you write and tell us how you're getting on.'

As soon as he was out of the court, walking with bravado beside Rose, Dora sank down at the table, laid her head on it and wept.

Now George stood at the station in front of the two Meredith kids, all with their little paper parcels of 'iron rations': a small can of corned beef, a packet of biscuits, a pound of sugar, a tin of evaporated milk, a quarter of tea and – George's eyes had lit up for the only time that day – a half-pound block of Cadbury's chocolate.

'Still warm from the factory,' one of the teachers joked.

As the kids piled into the railway carriages, Rose tried to give George a goodbye hug, but he pushed her away with his wiry arms. 'Don't go getting all soppy, Rose.'

And Rose, like her mom, held back her tears until they'd waved goodbye to the children, all crowded up by the windows of the train, some looking excited, others forlorn and bewildered. The train gave a loud shriek and puffed out of the station, the smoke and smuts rising in clouds to the wide arching roof. Rose waved her hanky at the little dot she thought was George until the train was out of sight, and then used it to wipe her eyes.

'They'll be well looked after, you be sure,' Alfie said. 'And he's got Tom and Bessie for company. He's a tough lad your George. He'll be all right.'

'It's so horrible not knowing what's going to happen,' Rose said as they walked out of New Street Station. 'I know it's an awful thing to say, but if there's going to be a war, I wish they'd just get on and get it over.'

'Some of the lads got their call-up papers today,' Alfie said.

Rose went quiet. Alfie and Sam were both nineteen and had not yet been called, but the shadow of war, of families being split up even further, hung over all of them.

'Come on,' Alfie said. 'It's no use getting all down in the mouth. I'll take you for a cuppa. Lyons or the Kardomah?'

'Whatever you like,' Rose said. She always let Alfie make the decisions.

'The Kardomah then.'

He took her arm and led her along New Street. It was as busy as ever with trams and buses and people shopping or standing at bus stops. But there was a different atmosphere. The news from Europe was on everyone's lips. Everything felt precious, Rose thought. As if the threat from Germany had made the things they had always known sparkle and shine.

Along the street they could see preparations going on in the offices and shops for blacking out the windows – assistants trying the large black rectangles for size against the panes of glass. And already groups of people were filling sandbags and stacking them against the sides of buildings. They heard the raucous news-vendors' voices shouting, 'Germans overrun Poland! Get your *Mail* here!'

'Blimey,' Alfie said. 'He really means it, doesn't he?'

Rose felt her stomach tighten with a mixture of dread and excitement.

'I should get back to work,' she said, as she and Alfie found a table in the Kardomah amid the comforting smells of roasted coffee and warm rolls.

'They gave you the morning to send off the kids, didn't they?' Alfie said. 'Come on – have a cuppa tea and calm down. The Co-op'll survive for half a day without you!' He grinned and, leaning across the table, chucked her lightly under the chin. 'That's my girl.'

Rose smiled back dutifully and sipped the tea he'd bought for her.

Alfie sat back in his seat, looking at her. As usual he felt pleased with himself for just being with Rose. Even though he'd been walking out with her for almost two years now he still couldn't believe his luck, that this beautiful girl wanted to be with him. He'd heard some gossip about her of course, but that was all in the past and he preferred not to know about it. He was going to believe the best of her. And she seemed to have quietened down since he'd first seen her, which was no bad thing. Who wanted a loud mouth on a woman? She was his girl and he was dead chuffed with her.

Alfie himself had filled out over the past two years. His hair was just as unruly above his pale face, but he looked less lanky and more substantial. His shoulders had grown broader and stronger from his heavy work. And the fact that he'd been luckier than many in the trade and had been in work more than out of it had done wonders for his sense of himself. His blue eyes looked directly at people now and he was much less hesitant when he spoke – especially with Rose on his arm. What a picture she was in that red frock she had on! Soon, when he'd maybe managed to save a bit, he planned to make her his wife.

Alfred and Rose Meredith, he thought. That sounded truly grand.

Rose stood preparing butter in the Co-op that afternoon dipping the wooden pats in the jug of cold water and teasing the yellowish lumps into shape. She was partly mesmerized by the movement of her hands and by the rhythmic click and whirr as the money cup shot along its overhead wire to the little cash office at the back of the shop.

'Come on, Rose, wake up! We need three pound of sugar over here!' the woman in charge of her called over. 'I dunno what's got into that girl today.'

Without speaking, Rose moved over and began to shovel out the sugar into the blue paper bags. Then she went back to sort out the butter and bacon again.

What had got into her was that she had, for the first time since Joseph's death, begun to allow herself to think properly. It was not something she decided to do; the thoughts just seemed to come upon her, long-buried feelings nudging for her attention.

She had been grateful in one way for the problems in Europe, for the looming war. Since they had waited tensely through the last threat, the crisis in Czechoslovakia the year before, it had all helped to take her mind off her own sorrows. And, she thought, it's brought me closer to Alfie – hasn't it?

They had things in common to talk about now, important things. Before he had talked about football or the latest murder trial.

'Have you heard about the one they're doing at the Old Bailey this week?' would have been the conversation before. Then he'd give her a long and gruesome description of the crime.

They'd shared a lot of experiences over the past months: the flicks and walks and family meals. Changing jobs. But had they shared the experience of falling in love? The question wouldn't leave her alone that afternoon, try as she might to put it out of her mind. Was what she felt for Alfie what people would call love?

From that day when he had turned up again in Catherine Street, she had tried to close her mind to everything that had gone before – to Joseph, Diana, Michael and everything about Lazenby's. To her dreams. She tried to be someone with no past. From now on she was going to be sensible and down to earth and take whatever came along.

He's made me feel better, there's no doubt, she thought. He's kind and generous and he loves me. What more could I want from anyone? I've already got more than me mom.

When she first went out with him she had felt relieved and grateful. Here was someone who wanted her and thought highly of her – she who at fifteen felt so old and soiled and washed up. And she was especially grateful to him for not probing into her past. He was prepared to accept her just as she was.

Those feelings she had had for Michael, the electric excitement in his presence – that was all airy-fairy nonsense, not real life. What she had with Alfie was real, like married people had if they were lucky.

She knew one day he'd ask her to marry him. That was another thing she'd tried not to think about. As long as they stayed as they were she didn't have to decide or face up to things. But the threat of war was overturning everything. For a moment she had an overwhelming feeling of panic. All her life – forever – spent with Alfie. Nothing else? Then she pushed the feelings away.

What's got into me? she thought. He'd make a good husband and he wouldn't knock me about. That's what matters.

Of course it made sense to marry Alfie, she said to herself. Perfect sense.

In early December the government extended the call-up age to men between the ages of nineteen and forty-one. Both Alfie and Sam received their papers almost immediately.

'At least I'm sure of a job now!' Sam joked. 'So you can keep the wireless.'

After they'd heard the soft voice of Prime Minister Neville Chamberlain crackling out of the Pyes' old wireless set, Sam had rashly gone out and bought one for their own house, with its battery and accumulator. Now, at almost every news bulletin, some member of the family was listening in.

When the broadcast finished that Sunday morning, the distant voice informing them that 'consequently we are now at war with Germany', Sid had pulled himself up abruptly and left the house.

Grace watched him out of the window. 'What's got into him?' she said.

'Leave him,' Dora said.

Out in the brewhouse, Sid Lucas stood propped on his crutch next to the old stone sink, his whole body trembling. The build-up to another war had set his fragile nerves on edge. Breathing in shuddering gulps of air, he tried to steady the emotions aroused by memories of the last war that suddenly sprawled out in front of him like fresh corpses. After the war to end all wars, here it was beginning all over again.

Dora looked out and saw the shadow of her husband's hunched figure. She could guess what was going on in his mind, but she had her children to think of now, their survival and their future. That was what mattered.

It was Grace who slipped outside and went to him. As she walked quietly into the brewhouse she knew immediately that her father was weeping. All through her childhood she had heard this sound through the floorboards from her parents' room, but she had never seen him with tears on his face before.

'Dad . . . ?' She went and put her work-roughened

hand on his heaving shoulder. He didn't throw it off. He didn't move or turn to her.

'I'll be all right, Gracie.'

'It's the war, isn't it?'

He nodded. After a moment, he said, 'I'm fit for nothing. The last war saw to that.'

'Don't say that,' Grace said. She took his arm. 'Come on. I'll leave you if that's what you want, but it's best you come in. We've all got to stick together now there's a war on, haven't we?'

Sid took out his grubby handkerchief and wiped his eyes in a way that made Grace's own fill with tears. At that moment he looked so much like a child.

'Come on now, Dad. Come in and have a cuppa tea.'

The evening before Alfie was due to leave, he and Rose walked slowly back from town in the blackout darkness that had overtaken the city. They had been to the flicks at the Scala and then Alfie had treated them to a hot pork sandwich from the Market Hall, so despite the freezing evening they felt quite warm and well fed.

Now and then people loomed up out of the cold, foggy darkness, close enough to touch almost before you could see them. A few were carrying small torches so you could make out little lines of light moving towards you.

'I can't get used to the dark,' Rose said. 'If it wasn't for this mist you could see the stars.'

'I s'pose it's a bit daft making you walk instead of catching the tram,' Alfie said. 'But then we'd have got there too quick. I wanted to spend all the time I could with you.'

Rose felt her stomach plunge at the thought that Alfie would be gone the next afternoon. She kept forgetting, and then something reminded her again, like the muffled lights on the few cars that passed them, which gave you a tiny glimpse of something before the darkness fell back over everything again.

'It feels like the end of the world,' Rose said.

Alfie grinned in the darkness. His Rose said the queerest things at times.

'Nah,' he said. 'We'll show that Adolf Hitler feller in no time. They'll get us all trained up and it'll be time to go home again. The lights'll be back on and we'll be right as rain, you'll see.'

Rose said nothing, wondering how much Alfie believed of what he was saying.

He peered at her, trying to make out her expression. 'You're not scared, are you? Here, stop a tick.'

Alfie pulled her arm and guided her over to the dark factory wall. He pulled her close to him. She looked up, just able to see his eyes and the outline of his angular face.

'I'll miss you,' he said. 'You know how much I love you, don't you?'

She looked guiltily up at him. 'Yes. Of course I know.'

She knew he was waiting for her to tell him the same, how she would long for him to be there, how she couldn't live without him. But the words wouldn't come. It would be stepping over a cliff if she said more than she meant tonight of all nights, when things were so serious. Once the words were spoken, she could not take them back.

Alfie leaned forwards and began to kiss her. She felt his soft, familiar lips on her mouth, and all the warmth and sincerity going into that kiss. She kissed him back, trying to summon up all her gratitude to him. She had got over his touching her reminding her every time of Mr Lazenby. Alfie had always been very gentle and never demanded anything more of her. She didn't feel revolted by him. She didn't feel – the thought came to her like a cold shock – anything. And inside, her heart was pounding with a sense of panic she could not explain even to herself.

'Rose – I wasn't going to ask you yet. I'd planned to save it. But now things are different – you know ...' He stumbled over the words, unused to expressing his feelings. 'What I mean is, would you – will you marry me, Rose? We could have a wedding when I come home next. There's bound to be some leave in a few weeks around Christmas, and it'd give you time to get sorted out a bit ...' he babbled on nervously.

Rose felt an almost unbearable sense of tension inside her, as all the feelings she'd been keeping at bay for the past months flooded into her in conflict and confusion. Should she be content, accept what was being offered by a good, kind man whom she could at least like? Or should she listen to that part of her which as a young girl had clamoured for fulfilment?

In utter vexation with herself she dissolved into tears.

'Hey, Rose,' Alfie said tenderly, holding her again. 'There ... don't upset yourself. I know I'm asking a bit sudden like, what with going away in the morning. But I've put a lot of thought into our future, you know.'

'I know,' Rose said sobbing. 'You're so good to me. I don't deserve it.'

Alfie stroked the soft, dark head that was pressed against his chest.

'What d'you mean? How can you say that? My God,

131

you're the most fantastic girl I've ever seen in my life, and it was a miracle when you said you'd come out with me. And now you're saying you don't deserve me?' He laughed. 'You're a case, Rose Lucas, you really are.'

Rose calmed herself and stood sniffing and wiping her face. After a few moments she said with unexpected resolve, 'We'll have to ask my dad.'

'Right,' Alfie said, and she could hear the jubilation in his voice, so at odds with the flat sense of inevitability she was feeling herself. 'It's not too late. I'll come and ask him now.'

'No. You can't.'

Rose and Alfie looked at each other, dumbfounded.

'But—' Alfie said.

'But nothing. You heard what I said.'

'What the hell's got into you, Sid?' Dora gasped. 'You've always said Alfie were a good lad!'

'And we're promised to one another,' Alfie said, his voice starting to tremble.

'You can promise what you like,' Sid shouted, slamming his newspaper down on the table and standing up. 'But you're not marrying my daughter one day and going off to get yourself blown to buggery the next.'

'But—' Alfie said again.

'Look at me!' Sid's voice rang round the walls of the small room. 'D'you want to give your wife a husband in a state like this, who can't keep his family and's no bloody good to anyone? Do you? I'm not making one of my kids a war widow or marrying her off to a wreck like me, so you can forget it.'

Rose and Dora stared at him, both rooted to the

132

spot. Sid seemed bigger and broader than they'd ever seen him. And Rose was aware, while feeling sorry and angry on Alfie's behalf, of a warm sense of relief spreading through her.

'Get married after the war's over if you come back in one piece,' Sid was saying more quietly. 'But don't ruin her life by rushing into things 'cos you think you're going to be a hero. There ain't no heroes in a war, lad – only blokes getting killed all around you.'

There seemed no more to be said. Alfie whispered to Rose, 'I'll come round and say goodbye tomorrow if I can.'

And she watched him walk, crestfallen, out into the darkness.

There was silence except for the clock ticking on the mantelpiece and Dora's coughing. Rose was still standing where she had been since they started talking, and Sid sank down into the chair again.

'Anyroad,' he said, looking up at her with defiant eyes. 'You didn't really want to marry him, did you?'

Twelve

May 1940

Rose sat, bleary-eyed, drinking a very welcome mug of tea as Winston Churchill's gruff voice growled at them out of the wireless.

'I speak to you for the first time as Prime Minister in a solemn hour for the life of our country, of our Empire, of our Allies, and above all, of the cause of freedom . . .'

'Well – he sounds as if he might know what he's on about. Not like the last one,' Jean said, stirring sugar into her tea.

Rose was sitting in her brother Albert's house in Erdington with her sister-in-law Jean, a plump, rather plaintive woman whom Rose was quite glad she only saw for limited parts of the day. Jean was about to give her full opinion of Neville Chamberlain, but Rose raised her hand to quieten her.

'Ssh. Let's hear the end of it.'

'Today is Trinity Sunday,' the voice was saying. 'Centuries ago, words were written to be a call and a spur to the faithful servants of truth and justice: "Arm yourselves and be ye men of valour, and be in readiness for the conflict, for it is better to perish in battle than to look upon the outrage of our nation and our altar."'

'Ah,' Jean said, shifting her wide hips on the chair.

'Ain't that nice? He can string together a good lot of words, can't he?'

Rose had felt a thrill, a sensation which raised goose-pimples on her flesh on hearing the commanding speech. With all the grimness, the increasingly terrible news which greeted them daily from Europe, she had been unprepared for the exhilaration she felt at the challenges with which war had presented her.

At least I'm doing something, she thought. She felt free for the first time in years. She pitied Jean, and all the other women left to fend for themselves with nothing changed in their lives except for more struggles to feed their families, and more worries to carry in their minds about their loved ones. Rose smiled across at Jean. Her sister-in-law, with her long blond hair tumbling untidily over the crumpled blouse she was wearing, smiled back, rather startled.

'You heard from Teddy?' Rose asked her, reminding herself that Jean, like Dora, was going through the hell of being separated from one of her children. Teddy, who was seven, had been evacuated out of the city.

'I just can't stop fretting about him,' Jean said. 'He says he's all right, but I don't know if it's true, do I? And after what happened to your George I can't sleep nights thinking about it.'

'Oh, I s'pect he's all right,' Rose said, laying one of her slim hands over Jean's plump one. 'Not much chance of the same thing happening to both of them, is there?'

January had been one of the coldest anyone could remember, the city clogged up with deep snow so the traffic could barely pass along the streets. It was a strange time. It felt as if everything had frozen up: the arteries of the city, the food supplies, which began to be officially rationed, and even the war itself. It had not begun to affect Britain with the intensity anyone had expected. The strange blanket of quietness brought to the streets by the snow, and the houses muffled at night by the white blanket outside and the blackout coverings inside, all added to the air of peculiar unreality.

Rose stayed at home through the winter. She saw Alfie briefly at Christmas. He had long got over the shock of Sid's outburst and was all for looking on the bright side.

'We're engaged anyroad, aren't we?' he said.

He chatted on about army life and the pals he'd made, and while Rose enjoyed his company and was glad to see him looking so full of it all, she felt even more distanced from him.

Sometimes she popped over to Small Heath to see Mrs Meredith, who always gave a gasp of delight when she opened the door, crying, 'Rose, come on in, bab! I was just making a little cake, so you can take a few slices back with you!' She always tried to feed Rose up like a turkey cock on whatever she had to hand, and always seemed to remain astonishingly cheerful.

The same was not true of Dora. Rose had been worried about her all winter. When the weather hardened against them, Dora's chest became infected and her lungs ached agonizingly as she coughed, bringing up terrible amounts of green phlegm. Rose and Grace nursed her as best they could, though Grace wasn't at her best either during the cold, with her asthma.

Christmas had been difficult. Edna managed to get over from Alcester with Harry. They put up a little tree and did their best to make it a jolly day, especially for the little boy's sake and for the twins. Dora burst into tears at the sight of him when they arrived and wouldn't let him out of her sight, holding and stroking his plump, healthy-looking limbs in a way which Rose never remembered seeing her do with any of them before.

'I can't let you take him again,' she said to Edna. 'I know you've looked after him as if he were your own, but I'll not part with him again. Not unless things start to get bad.'

Edna nodded, understanding how she felt.

But the worst was that they hadn't heard from George at all since the middle of October. He'd written three sentences saying he was with a family in Wales and he was all right. Then they'd had an equally brief note from a Mrs Beamish saying that George had moved from her care to work on a farm near by. Dora looked lined and tattered with worry.

'He's probably living the life of Riley,' Grace said, without much conviction. 'He said he was all right, didn't he?' They all tried to blame his silence on the bad weather.

As usual it was the neighbourliness in the court which helped them all pull through. They compared the best ways to make the food rations go far as possible. Mabel's corned beef hash was voted one of the best dishes.

'I fried the potatoes,' she told everyone darkly. Though quite what in she wasn't prepared to say.

When the snow came, everyone who was around came out into the court and built a snowman for the little kids who were left and Gladys and Mabel built a fire outside from an old door out of Moonstruck House, which was now in bad repair and boarded up. Everyone chipped in a lump of coal and they managed to bake a few potatoes for the kiddies. The twins, Billy and Susan, both stood wide-eyed and pink-nosed by the fire, cramming the warm potatoes into their mouths. Rose had dressed them up in so many clothes to come out that they looked quite rotund.

'All right, you two?' she said, smiling at them. She leaned down and gave them each a kiss on their round, cold cheeks. They both nodded, mouths full. Rose looked wistfully at their lovely trusting little faces, and stood with a hand on each of their shoulders, wishing she could hold them forever and protect them from all harm.

Afterwards they all had a snowball fight. It was a memory Rose knew she would treasure forever. She remembered Dora's face smiling at the window, still not recovered enough to be out in it, but cheered by the sight. And Old Lady Gooch trotting with her swaying gait across the yard in pursuit of Gladys Pye, gleeful as a twelve-year-old, with a huge ball of snow ready in one hand. Soon Gladys was flat on her back on the snow, helpless with laughter.

'I can't get up!' she shouted, trying to get her bandy legs in a position so she could stand up. 'God Almighty, look at the state of me – I'm caked in it!' And she collapsed into more helpless giggles.

As darkness fell, everyone was getting cold, and they all went in for a hot drink feeling more cheerful than they had for months.

By the time spring came and the snow turned grey and slushy in the streets and gradually disappeared, Hitler had progressed across Europe. Czechoslovakia, Poland, and now Norway and Denmark had fallen, and the forces of evil and destruction were pushing up against France, the Netherlands and onwards as if this was their destiny.

One evening in April, Rose and Grace sat in their bedroom talking. It was a rare moment of leisure shared together, and they were taking it in turns to brush each other's hair as they had when they were little girls. Through the window Grace saw Sid come shuffling in across the yard.

'Dad's back.'

Rose began to sing softly: 'The day thou gavest Lord is ended,' and both of them fell back giggling on the bed. It was a relief to get rid of some of the tension they all felt.

'You are terrible,' Grace said, wiping her eyes.

'Well,' Rose started to unpin Grace's brown hair. 'He always seems to be on at me.'

'You always answer back.'

'I can't help it. I know he's got some good in him really, and a lot of what's happened hasn't been his fault, but I just wish we'd had the chance to see him before and know what he was like.'

'I think you're quite alike. He was stubborn and determined to get on in them days. Like you are.'

'Like I *was*,' Rose corrected her. She stopped brushing and sighed. 'I don't know what's happened to me,' she said, hesitating to say what she was thinking.

'You mean you don't want to do all them things you used to talk about when we was at school?'

'Yes. Well, no. It's just ...' She sat down next to Grace and spoke very seriously. 'When Alfie was here and we were together and everything, I felt as if I was in a kind of dream all the time. I didn't have to think for myself, and after all that happened with Joseph and

Lazenby's I was glad not to have to. You know what blokes are like – they always think they have to do all the thinking for you. So I just let him. It was easy. Nice in a way. Like having a rest.' She smiled rather wistfully at Grace who watched her sister's brown, troubled eyes, rather puzzled at what she was getting at.

'You miss him, don't you?' she said, thinking this was the right response.

'I miss his company,' Rose said carefully. 'And I want the best for him of course, for him to be safe wherever he is. But now he's gone – I don't know.' She looked at her sister.

Grace saw that her eyes had the life back in them that always made Rose so striking as a child.

'I feel as if I've just woken up or something,' Rose said. 'Now that I can't just lean on him. I know it's an awful thing to say with the war and everything but I suddenly feel happier than I have in years.'

'But you do love him, don't you?' Grace asked, bewildered. She longed to have a young man of her own to walk out with.

Rose looked away, down at the floorboards. 'I like him of course. But I can't honestly say I know whether I love him or not.'

Grace made tut-tutting noises. 'You don't half get yourself into some messes, you do.'

Rose was silent, trying to think of some way in which she could express the overwhelming sense of restlessness she had felt since Alfie left. The past, before Joseph, had welled up, and she found herself thinking about Diana and the Harper-Watts with an aching sorrow for what she had lost.

Suddenly she said, 'You know those women we saw in town today?'

140

'The recruitment lot you mean?'

As they'd walked along Colmore Row, a long line of women had marched past, many of them carrying placards which urged: 'We have the Work – We want the Women!'

They were employed by many of the industries round the city. Some of them were wearing dresses and skirts, but a large number of them had on baggy dungarees in dark, heavy materials. Rose had been startled at the sight of them, but also warmed and excited. How strong and capable they looked! She had always known women who worked in factories, of course – Dora had for years. But she could never remember seeing them marching together like this, looking as if they really belonged in the world.

'I want to do something for the war effort, something really useful. I've been thinking about it all day. There's that new place they're recruiting for – the Nuffield over near Albert's place. They need a lot more workers. I thought what with Albert being away and Jean on her own with the kids, she'd be glad of a bit of company. And I could do war work in the factory.'

'I'll miss you,' Grace said.

Rose laughed. 'I was only talking. I haven't done anything about it yet!'

'No – but I know you when you've decided on something. And Mom was only saying the other day how sorry she feels for Jean. She'll let you go as long as you come home now and then.'

'Course I will,' Rose said. She began to feel excited.

Suddenly they heard a shriek from down below, then Dora's voice yelling up the stairs, 'Rose! Grace! Get down here quick! Quick!'

'What's got into her?' Grace said as they clattered

141

down the stairs into the dusk light of the kitchen. They found Sid and Dora both standing by the Morrison shelter, the top of which was laid up for tea.

Warming his hands by the stove was George.

Both the girls fell on him, trying to hug and kiss him. 'George! Where've you been?'

'How on earth did you get here?'

Their delight soon wavered and turned to concern. George pushed them off roughly. As they looked at him properly they started to take in the state he was in. He'd always been a skinny kid, but now he looked gaunt and hollow round the eyes. His legs, poking out of a filthy, torn pair of shorts that they'd never seen before, were stick thin, making his knees look pathetically bony. His skin was grey and shadowy with deeply ingrained grime and his hair, dull with filth, was sticking out in tufts all round his head. But the worst was his eyes. The expression in them was blank and hard, making him seem a person quite strange and alien to them.

As she stood looking at him, Dora burst into tears.

'What's happened to you?' She went to him and squatted down, putting her hands on his shoulders.

George pushed her away as if she were some kind of monster. 'I want some grub,' he said. 'NOW.'

'Don't talk to your mother ...' Sid started to say, but Dora gestured at him impatiently to be quiet. Sid himself looked shocked at the sight of his son.

'I'll get you some broth. And here's some bread to be going on with,' Dora said gently, slicing a huge chunk off the loaf. 'And you can tell us in your own time.'

'Fat lot you care,' George snarled. 'You'd have left me there to rot – the whole effing lot of you.'

'George!' Dora cried, her cheeks still wet. 'Oh

142

George, that's not true. It wasn't like that. They told us you had to go. Because of the bombs. And we was told you were all having a marvellous time. I didn't want you to go.'

George gave her a look of complete contempt and then started on the soup. He ate like a starved animal. He flung chunks of bread into the bowl and pulled them out soaked in soup, cramming them into his mouth apparently quite unbothered by how hot they were. The family were silenced by the sight. Rose felt her insides tighten with anger and sorrow. George only paused to scratch his head every now and then with soupy fingers. They could see the nits moving between his clogged hairs.

When he'd finished he pushed back his chair and said, 'Now I need some kip.'

'Leave him for now,' Dora said as he went upstairs. In the short time since George had returned, her face seemed to have fallen into even heavier, darker lines. 'I s'pect he'll talk to us after he's had a sleep.' And her face crumpled in distress again, her lips pulled back as she cried, showing the dark gaps between her remaining teeth. 'I only wanted to do the best for him!' she cried. 'I knew it was wrong to send kids away to strangers.'

When she crept up later to look at her own little stranger of a son, he had thrown himself just as he was on his old bed and pulled the blanket over him. In the candlelight she watched him for a few moments as he slept. His frail body was never still. His eyes and his arms twitched about and he kept moving his head, painful whimpering noises breaking out of him.

What his life had been over the past seven months emerged only gradually as he began to adjust slowly to being at home again.

So far as they could gather, the first month hadn't been too bad. The Beamish family who had picked him out originally had been quite decent. They lived in a village near Llanelli in South Wales and regarded taking in evacuees as their contribution to the war effort. Unfortunately, in their enthusiasm they had taken in three at once, including George. As they already had four children of their own, they quickly realized that introducing into the family three city kids with their strange ways was too much. The children of the house had rebelled and turned against the newcomers, and in particular they disliked George, the only boy of the three.

Eventually George was told that they were going to pass him on to a Mr Evans who owned a farm some distance away from the village, who wanted a boy old enough to lend a hand on the farm.

George had not felt at ease in the first house, but at least there had been company and, as he said, 'They gave you as much grub as they could spare.' Now his problems really began. Mr Evans was a short, burly man with a gingery-coloured beard who lived alone on the farm. He had no idea about children and no ambition to learn. George had spent most of the past six months almost entirely alone, except for the surly, religious-minded Mr Evans, a few chickens, a dog and fields full of sheep.

He had not been allowed in the house except for his meals which Mr Evans supplied when he remembered – at best once a day. In the evening he usually brought him into the cold, stone-flagged kitchen for some kind of soup or stew. The rest of the day he went without. In the beginning, as it was the end of September, George had found a few blackberries. As the winter drew in there was nothing. He slept in the barn where Mr Evans had supplied him with one filthy blanket stinking of dogs. During the day he had to help on the farm – herding and feeding sheep when there was work to be done, and being sent round with the dog to catch rats.

George woke in the morning often before it was light, to a hard prod from the farmer's boot and a gruff 'Get up now', which was often Mr Evans' longest utterance of the day. He communicated more readily with a cuff or a kick, as if George was just another of the sheep or dogs from the farm.

Once the snow came, George lived wrapped permanently in the stinking blanket and an old pair of boots of Mr Evans' that he wore over his own shoes. The snow cut the farm off from everywhere, so there were no letters, there was no one to talk to, not a word of kindness or of even the most basic communication. He lived like the animals: waking, sleeping, eating only when given the chance.

Some time after the thaw came he walked away from the farm one night and reached Llanelli by the morning. From there he jumped trains to Birmingham. He hid his wiry, emaciated body in any cranny necessary to escape the guards on the train, sometimes ducking and dodging as they moved along between carriages. And a couple of days later he was home. They may have abandoned him, but where else did he have to go?

His one remaining, overriding emotion was that of anger towards his family. They had sent him away to this place, left him for months now without a word of contact, as if they didn't care whether he was dead or alive. And for that he would never forgive them.

Thirteen

Rose moved to Erdington at the end of April and was taken on the night shift at the new 'shadow' factory, as the extra factories built to extend wartime production were called, at Castle Bromwich, right on Birmingham's northern edge. They taught her to use a rivet gun for attaching the metal plates which made up the wings of the Spitfires.

When she first walked through the gates of the huge works she felt so frightened that she nearly turned back and went home again. The rows of long production sheds where they turned out the Spitfires and Lancasters stretched further than she could see. There were people walking about briskly in overalls, all looking as if they knew exactly where they were going.

Workers were needed from any possible source, and Rose found herself working among a wider mix of people than she'd ever been with in her life before. Alongside her stood a girl called Maureen from Londonderry. They worked just far enough apart for there to be little opportunity to chat, but the two of them often sat together in the canteen at break times and became quite friendly. Maureen came from the Catholic side of Derry, and like Rose was from a large family.

'I'd most likely have come to England anyways, even without the war,' Maureen told her. 'But now they're

146

giving out jobs like First Communion cards, I thought I'd take the chance while it was offered.'

Maureen was a thin, anaemic-looking girl with terrible spots. She was kind and soft-spoken and Rose found her easy enough company. She was also very homesick, and spoke with special affection for the baby of the family, her four-year-old sister Josie.

'It's not the same without little ones about,' Maureen said. 'I'd give anything to see her.'

One day when she was sitting under the bright lights of the canteen with Maureen, Rose noticed the man with one arm.

'Hang on a tick,' she said. 'I'm going to have a word with him.'

The man was older than many of the employees, and when she got up close to him, Rose saw that on one side of his face the skin was shiny and puckered up as if from a severe burn.

'Excuse me,' she said. 'I hope you won't think me rude for asking . . .'

The man turned and smiled with the half of his face that worked. He had one vivacious blue eye; the other was missing. The injured side of his face remained still, as if dead.

'What's up love?' he asked.

'It's just when I saw you I thought of my dad. He's without one arm and a leg from the last war and he hasn't been in work for years.'

'Well now's his chance,' the man said chirpily. 'Doesn't he know they'll take anyone on nowadays? They've found me a little job I can do with one arm – with the petrol tanks. If your dad asks, you can bet they'll find him something – even if they turn him upside down and sweep the floor with his head!' He gave a long chesty laugh and Rose couldn't help joining in.

Within a week Sid was taken on by the Birmingham Small Arms Company, which in peacetime manufactured bicycles and motorcycles. It had reverted to turning out bombs, rockets and guns and all the ammunition needed to feed them. They found him a job packing bullets.

The day he left the house in dungarees to catch a bus to a proper job for the first time in over twenty years, Dora watched him as he pulled himself on his crutch out of Court 11. She reflected with some pride and more bitterness on the irony that her husband, who had been so shattered by the last war, might only begin to feel useful to anyone again now there was a second one in progress.

At the end of May, France fell to the Germans, and a huge flotilla of British boats evacuated all the troops they could transport from the French coast at Dunkerque.

On 2 July, Hitler ordered the invasion of Britain.

'The Battle of France is over. I expect that the Battle of Britain is about to begin,' Churchill told the House of Commons. 'The whole fury and might of the enemy must very soon be turned on us.'

And the country waited, as if holding its breath for a long descent into deep, dark water.

One night, at the beginning of August, the first bombs to fall on Birmingham dropped on Erdington, in the streets around Albert and Jean's house.

When she came in from work the next morning, Rose found Jean in a proper state. She was sitting on the old sofa in her dressing gown, with a tearstained face, and clutching Amy and Mary close to her as if she'd never let them go.

'Thank God you're all right,' Rose said, putting her bag down and running to her sister-in-law. 'You poor things, you must have had an awful night. We heard them come down. We were all in the shelters as well.'

Jean sat and sobbed helplessly. The Anderson shelter down the garden had a puddle right along the middle and it had grown even damper with the condensation from their breath. It had been horrible sitting there all night, cold and scared stiff.

'I wish Albert was here,' she cried. 'He'd know what to do. I hate being here without him. I can't stand it. And he might never come back!'

'Look,' Rose said firmly, wishing Albert had married someone with a bit more to her. 'You should try and keep things normal for the kids' sake. Get them dressed and send them out to play.'

'No!' Jean protested. 'I'm not letting them out of my sight – either of them. Them planes could come back any time!' Her face was getting puffed up with tears.

Rose sighed. 'Look. Get the kids dressed. Then you give me the ration books and I'll take them down the shops. That'll give you a bit of time to pull yourself together and get some things done, won't it?'

On the streets and in the shops everyone was saying 'Wasn't it awful?'

'We're not going to stand for that,' Rose heard a woman say as they queued in the butcher's. 'Coming over here and knocking people's houses down. Who does he think he is?'

They were comments that would recur many times as the bombing intensified. The raids became so much heavier and more frequent that the journey to work in the evening was often hazardous. And then in the morning Rose travelled home, her stomach churning with worry that Jean's house might not be still standing, and wondering about Dora and the others in Catherine Street.

Every time she got the chance, Rose caught a bus over there. One afternoon in late August Dora's first words were, 'Have you heard – the Market Hall's gone up?'

'What?' Rose said, stunned. It seemed impossible that a building she'd known and loved all her life should have been hit.

'The middle of town's a right mess,' Dora said, brewing up tea for Rose. She was delighted to see her, though less likely to show it. 'Didn't you see it when you came across? I took the kids in this morning. The Market Hall's a shell. The roof's gone – the lot. And what a stink! All burnt and musty. And there was flaming rabbits and guinea pigs running about all over the place.' She sat down, laughing slightly hysterically. 'I know I shouldn't laugh, but I saw this great fat bloke chasing his rabbits all round the churchyard ...' She sobered up suddenly. 'And there was Union Jacks all stuck in the mess – that's the British for you.'

Rose could see Dora was in a state and trying not to show it. 'How's everyone?'

'All right.'

Rose looked at the worn face in front of her. Dora didn't look well. She had never really thrown off her cough from last winter and the strain showed in every line of her face.

'I hope you're looking after yourself,' Rose said.

'I'll do.' There was a pause. 'Could do without spending the night in this thing though.' She patted the Morrison shelter.

'What about Dad?'

'Oh, he's all right. Better than the rest of us as a matter of fact. He's palled up with some bloke from the BSA who's got an allotment over that way. Your dad helps out how he can. Digging for Victory and that.' Dora smiled, reluctantly. 'Gives me a bit of peace any-road. I even heard him whistling the other evening. No, he's not the problem . . .'

Rose saw her mother's face cloud over again. 'George?'

'He's started thieving. I found him with a clock this morning and he wouldn't say where he got it. Next thing is he's sold it and put the money in his pocket. I reckon it came from one of the houses that got it last night. I'm ashamed of him – I really am. But it don't seem no good saying anything.'

'I wish I could do more to help,' Rose said.

'You're doing what you can. And it can't be a picnic for Jean over there either.'

As autumn came, Dora was taken ill again. Grace gave up work to be with her and take care of the family. The bombing began in real earnest in November. On the fourteenth the centre of Coventry was burned to the ground, and it seemed only a matter of time before the attention of the German Luftwaffe would be turned more fully on Birmingham.

A few days later it began. Night after night the waves of bombers came over, dark, malevolent shadows in the sky. All night searchlights criss-crossed the darkened buildings and the ack-ack guns rattled out their fire.

Across the city fires burned and the water supply

was disrupted. In the quiet mornings, after the all clear had sounded, exhausted people emerged blinking and sick with nerves out of the shelters or from under their staircases to the smell of damp, charred masonry, wet plaster and the sour smell of the incendiaries.

One morning, after another heavy raid, Grace arrived just as Rose was about to go to bed.

'What's happened?' Rose shouted down the stairs, seeing Jean letting Grace in. She was down in an instant. 'What're you doing here? What's wrong?'

'It's Mom,' Grace said. She looked pale and exhausted. 'She's been taken very bad. We had to get the doctor in after the all clear. He says it's pneumonia.'

'Oh my God,' Rose said. She just stared at Grace, stupid with tiredness.

'I can look after her,' Grace assured her hurriedly. 'Only she's fretting about the kids. It was so bad last night she wants Harry and the twins over at Edna's till it's all over. She's sure Edna'll have them.'

Rose felt a momentary pang at the thought of Billy and Susan being sent away, but she knew it was for the best. 'What about George?'

Grace gave her a look which implied how stupid the question was. 'I need you to come and stay over a night at Mom's while I take them over. It'll be too much to do it in a day.'

Rose thought for a second. 'I can get Maureen to swap with me for tomorrow. She'll do anything for kids. I'll get over early. Do me a favour and don't go till I've had a chance to see them.'

Grace nodded, knowing Rose felt they were almost her own. 'Make sure you're over sharpish though.'

*

As Rose made her way home the next day she was horrified at the extent of the damage wreaked on the city. She sat in her old grey coat, looking out of the window of the bus. Some of the solid edges that had outlined her existence were gone. It was shocking, impossible, as if the very foundations of life were shuddering underneath her.

Two of the houses at the end of Catherine Street were down. The house next to them had been shattered in half, some of it still intact, with a chest of drawers with clothes spilling out and a picture still untouched on the inside wall. It seemed indecent: the details of the private parts of people's lives hanging there on display.

Grace hadn't told her how bad it was. She must have wanted to avoid worrying her any more.

She gave the little ones as cheerful a send-off as she could. Dora was upstairs in bed and had already said her goodbyes.

'Why do we have to go?' Susan raised her dark eyes to Rose with a puzzled frown.

'Well, it's because of all the big bangs you keep hearing in the night,' Rose told her.

'We don't like the bangs,' Billy whispered.

'No. Well, it'll be quieter at Auntie Edna's. And there's a lot more space to run about. And Harry'll look after you – won't you?'

Harry nodded, holding on to a very old rag doll that had been Violet's.

'I tell you what,' Rose said. 'I've got something for you two to look after for me.'

She ran upstairs, and when she came down after a few minutes she put into Susan's hand a small wooden elephant and into Billy's the roughly carved little wooden horse. Both of them beamed with delight.

'I'll put him in bed when we get there, 'cos he'll be tired,' Susan said solemnly.

'That's right. You look after them for me until I see you – all right?'

Rose found Dora in a bad state. She was very weak and her breathing through her one good lung was laboured and noisy. She had a high fever and was drifting in and out of consciousness. Rose sat beside her most of the day, offering her sips of water, bathing the hot, sallow skin of her face and rubbing camphorated oil on her chest. When Rose became so tired she could no longer stay upright, she lay and slept beside her.

In the early evening, when Dora opened her eyes and seemed fully conscious for the first time, Rose said, 'They've gone off all right.'

Her mother nodded and whispered, 'Best out of it.' Then she said, 'Grace is a good girl.'

Rose smiled.

'And so are you,' Dora went on in her rasping voice.

'Don't talk if it hurts, Mom.'

'No – I wanted to say—' Dora went on, and then started coughing, her body curling in pain as she held her side tightly. It was some time before she had enough breath to speak again.

'You've had some bad things happen to you – before you should have—'

'Don't, Mom—'

'No . . .' She stopped to get her breath. 'It's as rough as it gets losing a babby. And your friend – Diana . . .' She saw Rose look at the floor. It was the first time anyone else had mentioned Diana, and hearing her name suddenly was more painful than she expected. 'All I was going to say was – I'm proud of you – how you've come through it. Alfie'll make you a good husband. And you can have some more of your own kiddies then.'

For a moment Rose couldn't think of anything to say, she was so moved by the fact that her mother understood how bad she still felt about Diana. And at the same time she realized with a wave of guilt how seldom she worried about Alfie.

She just said, 'Thanks Mom. Shall I get you some camomile tea now?'

As she was preparing the hot drink, George came back into the house carrying a bag of trinkets which he'd rifled out of another of the houses bombed the night before. He laid them out quite brazenly on top of the shelter.

'You ought to be ashamed of yourself,' Rose said.

'Oh yeah? How's that?' he said, insolently. His little pinched face was hard and bitter.

'Look,' Rose said, infuriated, her hands on her hips. Small as she was, she looked forbidding in her anger, her slim curving figure outlined by the red dress. 'I know you think you're a special case and everyone's got to apologize to you for the rest of your life. But you're not. Mom sent you away because she wanted the best for you, and there's no excuse for you acting like a thieving litle urchin and taking advantage of other people.'

'Aw, sod off,' George said.

Rose marched up to him and gave his face a sharp slap. She turned, shaking with anger, to begin preparing their rations of food for the evening meal.

'You're a selfish little bugger,' she shouted after him as he went out of the door.

He left the door swinging open so that the forbidden light streamed into the yard. Rose went and slammed it shut.

'We'll have the ARP lot round carrying on next,' she muttered to herself. Despite her anger she saw in her mind George as a tiny child forever running to her to be picked up. She felt sorry for being so hard on him. But all their nerves were on edge and he'd become so distant and infuriating.

Soon Sid came in with a cabbage and a handful of carrots in a bag dangling from his crutch. 'You can throw these in the pot,' he said proudly. 'How's your mother?'

'She's just had some tea,' Rose told him. 'She's about the same, I think.' She took the cabbage and started to clean it up. 'How's it at the BSA?'

'Hell of a mess up there,' Sid said, easing his coat off. 'The whole of the new building went up. Awful lot of blokes went with it. We're carrying on the best we can.'

While she finished preparing the meal, Sid went round the house and checked it was properly blacked out. She heard his voice upstairs as he said a few words to her mother. It was odd getting used to seeing him differently. Now he was someone with things to do, with a role. Like a proper dad, she thought.

When he came down, she said, 'How do we get Mom into the shelter?'

'She won't come,' Sid said flatly.

'Is that what she said?'

'She didn't need to say. She hasn't been in there since she was taken bad.'

Rose gaped at him. 'You mean ...? Well, who's looked after her?'

'Our Grace has stayed up with her. Your mother told her to go down and leave her, but Grace wouldn't hear of it.'

'Grace? You mean all these nights they've been bombing the guts out of us those two have both been . . .' She pointed towards the ceiling. Sid nodded. 'Why didn't you make them come down?'

'Don't you think I've tried?' His voice was loud with guilt and worry. 'She just won't hear of it.'

'Good God,' Rose said. 'Our Grace is tougher than you'd think. Well' – she looked defiantly at Sid – 'if she can put up with it, so can I.'

Sid shook his head. 'I thought you might've been the one that'd talk her down. I just wish there was something I—'

'It's all right. Save your breath,' Rose said irritably, and then added more gently, 'It only takes one to see to her, doesn't it?'

Her father sat down, quiet for a moment. Then he said, 'Grace is very like your mother used to be. She was always one for looking after people.'

'Good job really, wasn't it?' Rose retorted. She was finding being alone with her father for the first time in years strange and uncomfortable. She suddenly realized that Dora had always stood between them so they had seldom talked to one another without someone else to mediate.

'You can be a hard bitch, you can,' Sid said matter-of-factly. He stared at the plates Rose was laying on top of the shelter as he spoke. 'Whatever you think, I do love that woman up there.'

Rose turned away, knowing that whatever tender feelings she'd ever had towards her father, or might

157

have now, she was damned if she'd ever be able to show him.

The raids began early that night. Rose spent part of those long hours lying in Sid's place in the bed beside Dora's restless, feverish body. The rest of the time she sat up or stood by the window, frozen in spite of the blanket wrapped round her.

The seemingly endless groups of planes droned past overhead, ack-ack defences hammered at them, and finally there came the crump of bombs landing at a distance or a much louder explosion if they were nearer. Then the planes roared away again. She peeped out from behind the blackout curtains and saw the searchlights moving over the city and the sky orange from the reflected light of the burning buildings. She thought she could smell smoke, but wasn't certain if it was her imagination.

She thought of Jo Pye out there helping to put out the fires, and Gladys and the kids all crushed into their shelter.

I should have volunteered for the ARP or something like that, she thought. Where I could have been out helping people.

Suddenly there was a huge explosion, so close that the house shook and the windows rattled. Rose found that she was lying flat on the floorboards without having thought about it.

Dora stirred. 'Grace . . . ?'

Rose crawled shakily over to the bed. 'It's me – Rose.'

'Oh. What was that?' Dora sounded very drowsy.

'Don't know. Wasn't us, anyway!' It could only have been a street or two away though, she thought. Astonishing that the glass was still in the window. Good job they'd taped it across. If she hadn't had her mother to look after she felt she would have panicked, her nerves were stretched so taut.

'D'you want a drink?' she whispered.

Dora accepted a few sips of water, with Rose supporting her arm. She was so frail, her face and limbs pared right down to the bones. Feeling the ghostliness of her mother's body, Rose knew that she didn't have much time left to her.

'D'you remember those nights we spent together up with the babbies?' she asked Dora.

Her mother nodded her head very slightly. 'It weren't right – you losing yours like that.'

'I miss him still – terrible sometimes.'

'Course you do – mine too – it never goes.' The coughing took her over again, and the attack seemed to go on for a long time. Rose was quite oblivious now to what was going on outside. Dora seemed to doze off again when the coughing eased up, but suddenly she said, 'You'll always have Billy and Susan.'

Rose knew she was saying, look after them, keep an eye on them for me. She reached out and took her mother's hand gently in her own.

'Sod them out there,' she said. 'I'm coming in to lie down.'

When she returned wearily to work the following night she noticed that the space beside her where Maureen usually worked had been filled by another girl, whom she'd never seen before.

'You done a swap have you?' she said, puzzled. 'What's happened to Maureen?'

The girl said she didn't know because she'd been asked to move over from another block. Rose saw Madge, an older woman who worked in a position near by, moving quickly over to her.

'You'll have to know, Rose,' she said. 'Maureen was killed last night on the way to work. One came down when she was going for the bus. House came down on her. She never stood a chance.'

Hurriedly someone fetched a chair for Rose, who had turned a sick-looking white in the face.

'You all right love?' Madge asked. 'I never meant to give you such a shock. Only I didn't think you two that close.'

Rose sat under the remorseless lights of the vast factory, her mind a collage of confused thoughts. Maureen walking out for her bus from her lonely digs, the bomb coming down like a great slug in the darkness, and a small Irish girl called Josie, little Josie whom Maureen adored and whose heart would break.

A fortnight later, on a frozen, gusty December afternoon, Rose, looking pale and exhausted, stood between her father and sister at Dora's funeral. They walked back from the graveside under an iron sky, between the leafless trees, Sid, Rose, Grace and George. They hadn't called the little ones back. With Sam away, this, for now, was the family.

But as the wind murmured in between the skinny branches of the trees that bleak afternoon, Rose glanced back to the spot from where they had walked. And she knew that the centre of the family, the person who had kept them together, now lay buried beneath the fast-freezing ground.

PART TWO

ITALY
1943–1945

Fourteen

March 1941, Berkshire

The truck swayed along the narrow country lanes, its huge khaki bulk looking out of place between hawthorn hedges and elms. From the half-open back of the truck women's faces looked out at the early spring countryside and they waved at people they passed. They all held on to anything they could to keep from falling on top of one another. Deeper inside the truck, where it was almost too dark to see, someone was singing 'My Bonny Lies Over the Ocean' in a loud, tuneless voice.

'So this is the British army,' a voice piped up over towards the daylight end. 'You can see why they call them cattle trucks, can't you! I say – you've got your foot on my case. Move it, would you? There's a dear. Mustn't have my things crushed before we've even started.'

'You won't be needing crêpe de Chine where we're going!' someone shouted over the growling engine, and the others round her tittered. The voice had come from a large woman with peroxide blond hair. 'And stop that bleedin' racket, will you?' she yelled down at the singer. 'Me head's thumping something awful already.'

Rose, who was standing near her towards the back, silently agreed. As the afternoon had worn on a tight band of pain had stretched between her temples so she felt almost unable to think, exhausted as she was from all the newness and strain of the journey further away from home than she'd ever been before. She could hardly feel her feet in her old down-at-heel shoes and she was hungry. The few sandwiches Grace had packed for her were long gone. The day seemed to be going on forever.

'Here . . .' She realized the blonde was speaking to her through the gloom of the truck. 'You deaf or something? I said pass us me bag will you? Yeah. That one.'

Rose bent down unsteadily and got hold of the heavy carpet bag. She pushed it to the other woman along the floor of the truck.

'Ta. Where'd you come from then?'

'Birmingham.'

'Ooh ar!' the blonde squawked. 'Yow'm a Brummoy then – orroight are yer!' she mocked.

'That's all right with you is it?' Rose snapped at her. She couldn't place the woman's own accent.

'Now girls,' a voice called from the light end. 'No point in being cattish. We've all got to get along and live together. There's a war on, remember.'

The blonde said, 'Oooh, yes. I'd almost forgot!' and rolled her eyes round in such a comical way that Rose couldn't help grinning.

'What's your name then?'

'Rose. What's yours?'

'Gloria. From Deptford. That's London to you. This is a lark innit?' Gloria stood with her solid legs braced apart as far as space would allow. 'Could do without the old school tie brigade though.'

While they had waited for their transport at Didcot

Station surrounded by piles of army supplies, the women had gathered instinctively into two groups. The old school tie group, as Gloria called them, looked much better dressed and cared for, and one of them even had a fur collar on her coat. From the loud conversations in their posh accents, Rose gathered that several of them were bound eventually for the élite Intelligence Corps. There was a rather mousy, timid-looking girl with reddish brown hair who Rose noticed because she seemed to be constantly on the point of bursting into tears. She didn't seem to be sure which group she belonged in, and hung around the posher ones as if hoping to be taken under their wing. The second group, which Rose and Gloria had fallen into, looked scruffier, mostly togged up in second- or third-hand clothes and lumpish old coats. Gloria seemed the most brashly confident. A couple of them looked pale and unhealthy and terrified. One clearly had nits, so everyone shrank back from her.

The journey from the station to the camp was roughly four miles.

'I say – I think we're here!' someone soon called out. Others pushed towards the back end to get their first sight of the camp where they were to spend their first three weeks of initial training. Rose could see nothing at all.

'Golly, sentry boxes,' one of the posh girls said. 'Those chaps look jolly cold, don't they?'

'Look at all that barbed wire. Makes it look frightfully serious, doesn't it?'

'Let's hope they'll let us have a cup of tea now. I'm quite parched.'

The truck stopped abruptly at the reception hut and they scrambled out with their bags, those from the dark inside screwing up their eyes as they reached the day-light. The March afternoon had turned damp and windy. They all looked round at the camp which extended along the edge of the Berkshire Downs. There were row upon row of Nissen huts with corrugated-iron roofs, and round the camp stretched the spiky border of the barbed wire. It was a bleak scene, with no trees and few bushes between the huts, and the rounded greyish hills curving away beyond. Rose experienced the same feeling as on her first day at Castle Bromwich, an urge to turn round and run home. But home was much further away now, and there wasn't much to run back there for.

After they had filed into the reception hut they were each given a printed postcard to fill in saying they had arrived safely and where they were. Rose addressed hers to Grace.

A brisk officer with an Eton crop introduced herself to them as Lieutenant Waters. 'I'd like to welcome you to the Auxiliary Territorial Service. I know everything must seem very new and strange to you now, and I'm sure you're all rather tired and cold. But you will get used to us and our ways here and, before long, our ways will of course become your ways.'

She went on to say that they were part of Platoon 4, and that later that day they would be issued with ATS uniform, of which, she assured them, they would become very proud after a few weeks. Rose listened rather blankly, sitting on a hard wooden bench beside the girl with nits, who kept fiddling with her head.

Then a plump woman in uniform came in and announced herself their corporal.

'Right!' she shouted at them. 'Outside in threes!'

Carrying their cases, they slouched and stumbled out of the hut into the cold and stood in rough lines, three abreast.

'Let's see you begin on some marching,' the corporal yelled. 'When I say march you lead with your left foot. Ready? Right – march! Left, right, left, right, left . . . left . . . left . . .'

And the line of women, tall and short, plump and skinny, in as great a variety of clothes, tried to discipline their tired legs and march, heavy cases swaying in hands, to their huts. Rose heard Gloria give a snort of laughter at the sight.

Hut J, into which Rose was ordered, housed twelve women in beds with black iron frames, six down each side. Along the middle of the floor ran a very shiny strip of brown lino, and in the centre of the hut stood a stove, its rather rusty pipe angling up and out through the roof. It was not lit at the moment and the hut, with its drab greenish walls, felt cold and cheerless.

Rose sat down, slipped her shoes off and rubbed her slim, icy feet. She closed her eyes for a moment, wishing she could lie down on the bed and sleep straight away. She opened them again at the sound of a voice next to her.

'Gawd! This is the first time I've ever had a whole bed to meself.'

A skinny girl with a pale, rather rat-like face, her lank greasy hair held back by a couple of kirby grips, was unpacking her things on the next bed. 'How about you?' she asked Rose.

'Me too,' Rose said wearily. She was tired and didn't feel like talking. The girl had an accent rather like Gloria's. Her name was Tilly and she came from Canning Town.

Rose realized she meant London as well. Between all her actions Tilly kept biting furiously at her rough nails.

Rose got up slowly from the bed and started to open her case. As she glanced down the long room she saw that Gloria was up the far end, and she recognized the mousy girl who'd been hovering round the posh group at the station.

Standing by the bed on the other side of her was a girl with wavy brown hair and round, healthy-looking cheeks. For a second Rose was startled by how much she reminded her of Diana.

The girl smiled at her. 'You look done in,' she said. 'Come a long way?'

'From Birmingham,' Rose replied. 'It's felt like a hell of a long day.'

'Yes, I'm lucky. My people only live over near Oxford, so it hasn't been too much of a chore for me. My name's Muriel, by the way.'

Rose warmed to Muriel. She was well spoken, but without a trace of the stand-offishness she'd sensed in some of the others.

'We'll be able to help each other out, won't we?' Muriel said. 'Did you know that these funny mattress things are called biscuits? Odd, isn't it?'

Rose saw that the mattress on the iron frame was made up of three thin sections: – the 'biscuits'. They also had two sheets each and four blankets.

Suddenly there was a to-do at the other end of the hut. The mouse was in tears.

'What's up with her?' Tilly asked, with more curiosity than concern. 'Can't see there's much to have a crying match about. S'like a boarding house here I reckon!'

The mouse, whose name turned out to be Gwen, had

promised to write to her mother the instant she set foot in the camp and had just realized she had lost her writing paper.

'Oh for heaven's sake, wrap up,' Gloria said to her. 'Someone'll give you a bit of paper. And you've already sent her one of them cards, so what're you fussing about?'

'But the card didn't *say* anything,' Gwen sniffed. 'And Mummy worries so. She's a widow, you see.'

Rose thought for a moment of Sid, and of Grace left to look after them all. She thanked her stars Sid had the BSA job to keep him occupied. And Grace had told her that in a few weeks when she had reached eighteen she was going to volunteer at a first aid post. 'That way I can stay home with Dad and George and still do something useful,' she'd said stoically.

Now Rose wished overwhelmingly that her sister was there with her. It would be so good to see a familiar face.

Muriel found Gwen a sheet of paper and an envelope, but the moment she sat down to write they were all ordered out again. The rest of the afternoon and evening was spent rushing from one thing to the next: getting fitted into their stiff khaki uniforms and peaked caps, pulling at skirts and tunics to make them fit over hips and busts, and collecting a huge mound of kit: steel helmet, greatcoat, groundsheet, respirator ... And clothes and more clothes, the shirts and slacks and gloves and everything you could think of except, for some reason, handkerchiefs. There were shrieks of laughter at the sight of the heavy underwear and thick khaki stockings.

'Cor – look at them passion killers!' Gloria cackled, waving a pair of stockings round her head.

Then there was bed making and a quick meal of

169

poached egg on toast in the Naafi canteen and, finally, bed.

Rose lay under the sheet and heavy army blankets. A couple of girls were crying. It was very dark in the hut, but Rose guessed from the direction of the sound that one was Gwen. She wondered if she ought to get out and try to comfort her, but she couldn't think of anything to say and wasn't sure Gwen would want her.

The hot cup of tea she'd drunk earlier had begun to ease her headache, but she could still feel her heart thumping too fast. Unable to sleep in this strange new place, she thought over the peculiar day she'd had and back to one event in particular.

That morning when she had left Catherine Street, she told Grace she'd rather say her goodbyes at number five. 'I'd sooner think of you here when I'm gone,' she said. 'And you've got enough on your plate without traipsing into town with me.'

Grace had fussed around her like their mother would have done, and Rose couldn't help thinking how much her sister looked like Dora now that her face had become thinner. The two of them packed up Rose's few things in a small, decrepit suitcase.

'I'll miss you like anything,' Grace said shyly, with tears in her eyes.

'D'you think I'm deserting you?' Rose asked. She had felt many pangs of guilt at going off and leaving Grace at home.

'We'll be all right,' Grace said. 'I've got used to you being over at Jean's, and if you was here with Dad the pair of you'd do nothing but fall out anyhow. It's best this way – specially with Alfie being stuck out there and everything.' Grace still persisted in her fantasy that Rose was pining dreadfully for Alfie.

Sid had said a gruff goodbye to Rose before he left in the morning. 'I don't s'pose they let you lasses get anywhere near the action like the blokes. Just make sure you don't give 'em lip and you'll be all right.'

George just said, 'Tara,' as if Rose was off down the shops for the morning.

'You'll let me know how Billy and Susan are, won't you?' Rose begged Grace. 'And Harry of course,' she added quickly. 'It's going to be the worst thing, not having any kids around.'

The sisters embraced. The strong grip of their arms round each other said everything. Neither was the sort to make a fuss. Rose walked away from Court 11, past the bomb rubble at the end of Catherine Street.

Sitting on the bus into town, she began to feel this was actually real. She was really going to leave Birmingham for the first time. Her stomach churned with nerves and excitement. It was a bright, blustery morning and she stared hard out of the window as if trying to remember every stone of her city: the dark factories, Smithfield, St Martin's, and all the other less obvious places that were so much part of her. She couldn't imagine anywhere different. Leaving it all was terrifying now she was actually facing it. But this was what she had always wanted, wasn't it? To see something of what was outside? The war had at least given her that chance. She sat hugging the small, battered weekend case on her knees, the one familiar object in a world that was shifting all around her.

New Street Station was seething with people, many of them service personnel in their blue or khaki uniforms. Rose wondered if there were others going to the same place as her. Trains were constantly moving in and out with a great clamour of engines and whistles blowing. The air was full of sharp smells of soot and cinders and acrid whorls of smoke from cigarettes.

Rose picked her way along the crowded platform, saying 'excuse me' and 'sorry' until she was somewhere near the middle. According to the long fingers of the clock there were still twenty minutes until her train to Oxford was due to leave. She wondered whether to go back and try to get a quick cup of tea.

A train slid slowly into the station from Rose's right. She stood on tiptoe to watch. It was a grand sight as it hissed finally to a halt, steam clouding up to the steel beams of the roof. The doors opened and people clambered out on to the already packed platform. Rose, like everyone else, shuffled back to give them room.

She was standing like that, deciding against the tea, when she heard the voice: a strong, well-spoken woman's voice but containing a waver of uncertainty.

'It is, surely – is it? Rose? Rose Lucas?'

Rose turned and found herself face to face with a smartly turned out WAAF officer, her fair, wavy hair fastened back stylishly under the grey-blue cap. Her vivacious face wore an apprehensive smile. In the five years since she had seen her, Diana had matured into a beautiful, poised young woman.

'It is you, isn't it?' Diana exclaimed.

The two of them eased further back into the crowd to let the other passengers past and someone behind said, 'Here – watch who you're pushing, will you?'

Diana made a helpless gesture as if unsure where to begin the conversation. 'Well. Where are you off to?'

'The army. ATS,' Rose managed to gasp out. Her heart was beating breathtakingly fast. She was amazed how Diana could begin chatting as if they'd only seen each other the week before. But then that was her upbringing – politeness, social graces.

'Good for you,' Diana said. 'I'm a WAAF – well, as you can see . . .' And she giggled, looking down at her uniform. For the first time Rose realized that Diana was as nervous as herself. 'I'm just off home on leave. Mummy and Daddy will be thrilled I've seen you!'

Rose found herself unable to speak. Lying remembering it now, she thought of all the things she should have said. She should have asked after Catherine and Ronald, said how pleased she was, *something* at least. But she had felt so scruffy and ignorant and overpoweringly awkward, and those feelings were made worse by the memory of how much the two of them had shared and of the way she had cut Diana off so abruptly.

Diana quietened suddenly and looked serious. 'Listen. I'm going to have to be off shortly – train to catch. But Rose, I . . .' She struggled for the right words. 'What happened to you? We were all so worried about you and it made me so unhappy. I couldn't understand why you didn't answer my letters.'

Seeing the tears in her old friend's eyes Rose realized that she was, beneath all the jolliness of her class and of service life, still the same, kind girl she had known.

'I couldn't . . .' Rose's face felt hot and red and she knew that if she tried to explain here she would be unable to stop crying. 'I wanted to tell you,' she stumbled on. 'But you'd have hated me if you'd known . . .'

The sight of Diana's blue eyes so full of concern made Rose feel even more emotional. 'Look. You'll miss your train. Give me your address. I'll write. There's no time now and I'd just make a fool of myself. But I'd like to tell you . . .'

Diana handed her a slip of paper with her WAAF address on it. They reached out and awkwardly gripped each other's hands. And then she was gone, vanished among the other drably clad bodies. Rose was left feeling weak-kneed and suspecting it had all been a daydream.

She tossed and fidgeted on the hard bed. What am I going to say to her when I write? she wondered. More than ever, Diana had seemed to come from a different world. But the only thing to do was to tell her everything, truthfully. She owed Diana that. To finish things off. But as she drifted off to sleep, she couldn't help wondering whether this might also be the beginning of something new in a friendship that had never truly died.

Fifteen

'Oh, these confounded blisters!' Muriel groaned, gingerly trying to squeeze her feet into her slippers.

They were all in Hut J because it was domestic night. Each Wednesday of the three weeks in camp they were expected to scrub the hut and catch up on any cleaning or mending chores. Some of the girls were crowded round the stove, which was lit only in the evenings.

Squatting in front of the glowing coals with her legs apart in a silky confection of a nightie was Gloria. She was holding out a large pair of scissors on which was stabbed a slice of bread she was toasting. Rose, Tilly and a couple of others were sitting round in stiff blue and white striped army pyjamas. Muriel was wearing her own floral cotton nightie, and Gwen sat swamped by a pair of pale pink winceyette pyjamas. Both she and Tilly were dabbing at their feet with blobs of cotton wool.

'Our feet'll be in ribbons by the end of this,' Gwen moaned.

All of them had sore feet but they also had pink, healthier-looking cheeks than when they'd arrived, after the new experience of half an hour's vigorous PT every morning. They tucked into the toast with increased appetites from all the fresh air.

In between the gripes about blisters and arms throbbing from the inoculations they'd had, Gloria was regaling them with tales of her men. She apparently had several in tow at once. To prove the point she'd pinned four photos on the wall behind her bed, and went through a half-joking ritual of kissing them all at length before she settled down to sleep.

'That one's Bob,' she told them, pointing out a dark, moustachioed figure. 'He's my favourite really. It was him who give me this.' She flounced round in front of them in the shimmering, peach-coloured folds of cloth.

'Under the counter stuff,' Tilly said knowingly. 'Has to be. How'd he get it otherwise with rationing on?'

Gloria stood magnificently above her, curling a lock of her pale hair round a finger. 'I'll have you know,' she said disdainfully, 'that my Bob actually owns the factory where they used to make these here gowns.'

Gloria turned to Rose, who was sitting with her army jacket in her lap, lighting matches to burn off the pinkish film which covered the buttons. It was something they all did to make the jackets look more presentable.

'You're a looker,' Gloria said. 'Why ain't we seen any pictures of your bloke? Or ain't you interested in fellers?'

'I'm – sort of engaged to someone,' Rose told them hesitantly, still not feeling sure it was really true.

Muriel and Gwen both said, 'Ah, how lovely.'

'Where is he then?' Tilly asked. 'He in the army too?'

'Yes, but he's in Germany.'

There were noises of horror from the others.

'Picked him up, did they?' Gloria asked, more gently. 'Is he in a Kraut prison camp?'

Rose nodded. 'I just had one of them cards, a couple of months ago. You know, name, in good health and all that. The camp's called Felsig. I think they picked him up in France.'

The others sat silent for a moment.

'That must be terrible,' Muriel said.

'Yeah,' Gloria joined in, trying to cheer things up. 'But at least you know where he is and that he's alive. Eh,' she nudged Rose playfully with her elbow, 'he won't be getting up to much mischief in one of them camps!' She gave her loud laugh. 'So in the meantime you can have some fun, can't you? I mean being engaged ain't the same as being married, is it?' She laughed again. 'I'll tell you one thing. I'll give this army lark a chance, and if I don't like it I'll be over the men's quarters right quick, getting meself a Paragraph 11!'

Paragraph 11, in army regulations, provided a let-out clause for women who were having babies. The others laughed, rather uneasily, at the thought of Gloria going brazenly over to the men's side of the camp to help herself to a pregnancy.

'That's awful,' Gwen said, blushing.

'Oh, ta very much.' Gloria was unruffled. 'I can't see any point in not having a good time when you can – specially with a war on. And I don't know why you're looking so bug-eyed about it. You only joined up to get away from that bleedin' mother of yours, didn't you?'

Gwen leapt to her feet, her face instantly a hot red. 'That's not true!' she cried. 'How could you say something so awful?' And she ran sobbing over to her bed and lay down on it, curled up tight.

Rose put her jacket down. 'I thought I had a gob on me till I met you,' she said matter-of-factly to Gloria, and went to sit on Gwen's bed. The other girl wouldn't say anything, but gripped Rose's hand.

177

'Time for bed, methinks,' Muriel said, with all the authority of a boarding school prefect, which until a few months before was what she had been.

Gloria grinned, making a thumbs up sign at Muriel and winking at the others. 'Definitely officer material there!' she said.

Every morning they were up at six-thirty and ready for PT by seven. This was made even more of an agony for the first few days by pain in their arms from the injections. Rose felt as if the scab was lifting up and down every time she swung her arm in the freezing air.

Compulsory inoculations had only been one part of the medical when they'd first arrived. They had also had to go through the dreaded 'free from infection' inspection.

'Oh my Gawd,' Gloria had said as they queued up. She seemed genuinely rattled by it. 'It's the bugs, babies and scabies job isn't it? Do we really have to take our bits off in front of that lot?'

They all stood in line outside the chilly medical hut. Weak sunshine lit the grey camp buildings and a damp wind swept across the downs. Their grumpy corporal kept shouting 'NO TALKING!' and refused to answer any questions.

All of them were anxious. Most had never taken off their clothes even in front of their closest family before. When they had filed inside and Rose was stripped down to her vest and pants, she found herself trembling, and not just with cold. The stale, sweaty smell of some of the girls reminded her sickeningly of Mr Lazenby. She saw with enormous relief that the medical officer was a woman.

She listened to Rose's heart, poked about in her hair and felt along her spine. She pulled out the elastic of her knickers to have a quick, impassive glance down them, and then it was over and Rose was pronounced nit-free and fit for duty.

'It's nothing much,' Rose whispered to Gwen, who was standing outside looking pale with fright.

Every day there came another trial: kit inspection. Beds had to be 'barracked' – arranged with the sheets and blankets folded in a very particular way – and then all of the kit had to be laid out in precise order and immaculately folded. Woe betide you if any of it was missing and could not be excused as being in the laundry.

And then drill. They stood in lines, an extraordinarily unformed-looking bunch in the first few days, as one of the male NCOs bawled relentlessly at them.

'Right, you lousy shower. Let's see some discipline around here! You've got to learn in three weeks what we normally take three months of army life to pick up, and I'm damned if any of you are going to let me down! Right. Chests foward, shoulders back, bottoms in. Atten-*shun*!'

Gradually, as the days of marching and saluting and manoeuvring back and forth went by, their bodies creaked and cranked into familiarity with it. They began to look as if they might belong in the army.

After lunch, for which they lined up in the canteen, men and women bantering together, they sat down for a bewildering assortment of lectures and films. One talk on army regiments or history might be closely followed by a luridly educational film about VD or how a baby is born. This was a mixed camp in a mixed army and they were expected to take all this in their stride, but there was many a green, shocked face after they'd seen the festering genitals in the VD film.

And then came the fatigues or camp chores; scrubbing floors, washing dishes or spud bashing.

One afternoon Rose was standing in the canteen hut with Gloria. They both had their khaki sleeves rolled up so they could dip their hands into the freezing, muddy water.

'You know, gypsy Rose,' Gloria teased. 'I can never make you out. What d'you really make of the army?'

Rose was silent for a moment, working on the cold, earthy skin of a potato. She turned her strong gaze on Gloria.

'I don't like being pushed around, except when I can really see the point of it. I mean I'll do what they say if it's right – for the war effort like. And I've always wanted to get away, see a bit more of life than just Brum. I miss home of course, but my mom's died anyhow and I can't stick living with my dad.'

Gloria seemed in an unusually solemn mood. 'Seems like everyone's running away from something when you come down to it, doesn't it?' She grinned. 'Quiet here though, isn't it? We hardly had a wink of sleep back in Deptford. They was bombing the balls off of us.'

Rose pulled back a wavy strand of hair with cold, wet fingers. 'Is that why you joined up then?'

'Not just,' Gloria said briskly. 'They got me brother. He was a rear gunner in the RAF. Went through all the Battle of Britain, right till the end. Then he went out one day and they lost him over the Channel. We was close, me and Jo. It was only me he told how scared he was – brown trousers, the lot – you know. When he went I thought, I'm not going to just sit here with them

180

dropping this bloody lot on us night after night. I'm going to get the buggers.'

Rose still found Gloria an unlikely addition to the army with her peroxide hair, her curl papers and slinky nighties. 'D'you think you'll stick it?'

'Oh, I'll stick it,' Gloria said grimly. 'I'll stick it if it kills me.'

'So all that you said about Paragraph 11 – you was joking?'

Gloria gaped at her in astonishment. 'Course I was bleeding joking! What d'you take me for?' With a broad grin on her pink face she picked up a wet potato and lobbed it over in Rose's direction. 'The very idea, you cheeky bugger!'

It was two weeks before Rose found an opportunity to write to Diana. She sat under the stark light in the hut with her pillow propped against the black iron bedhead. She wanted the letter to be warm and friendly. It was easier to write than she'd feared. Away in this place that was so different from home and Birmingham life, she felt almost as if those terrible years had happened to someone else. She wrote about Lazenby's and, as clearly but briefly as she could, about what Mr Lazenby had done to her.

Yet when she described Joseph's short, fragile life, tears began to pour down her face and on to the paper. It brought back vividly what she tried to keep from her mind: the feel of his soft, downy head, and the tiny frozen hands she'd found that terrible morning. She knew with renewed clarity that that day would be the worst of her life – far worse than the day Mr Lazenby assaulted her and worse than anything she might face in the future.

'I wish now I'd told you, Diana,' she wrote.

Now I think back I know you'd have understood – and your mom and dad. But at the time I wasn't thinking straight. I just felt dirty and ashamed all the time and I couldn't see how you'd want to be friends with me again. I hope you can forgive me. I know you'd never get yourself in a mess like that – much too clever, you are! And I want you to know I never stopped thinking about you and wondering how you was getting on. And your family too. They were all so kind to me. Please remember me to them.

I'd like to see you again some time. Maybe in more cheerful days after this war's over?

She signed the letter,

With kind thoughts from your friend,
Rose.

After that, when she'd wiped her face, she dashed off a quick note home. She usually found herself talking in her mind to Grace as she wrote.

'I miss you ever such a lot,' she finished off. 'When I come home next I want to see you in your nurse's uniform!

'Love to all – Rose. xxxx'

She heard the door open, and glanced up to see Gwen come in looking wet, dishevelled and flustered. She sat down miserably on the edge of her bed without even taking her coat off. After a moment Rose realized she was crying. She put her writing things down and went rather timidly to sit beside her.

'What's up with you?' she asked.

Gwen looked up, startled and rather uneasy. She hadn't even noticed Rose when she came into the hut, and she wished that if anyone had to be there, it had been Muriel.

'You'll think I'm so stupid.'

'Why should I?' Rose asked, genuinely surprised.

'You give the impression of being, well, not exactly worldly, but of knowing a lot about life.'

'Me?' Rose couldn't help bursting into laughter. 'Gwen, you do know this is the first time I've ever set foot out of Birmingham, don't you? Come on – out with it.' She patted Gwen's shoulder.

Gwen mopped her eyes with a delicate lacy handkerchief. 'I went to the Naafi tonight. And one of the chaps – it doesn't matter who – kept making up to me all evening. He seemed quite nice, but then he asked me to go outside with him. It's raining, so it wasn't very pleasant, but he didn't seem to care. He pushed me up against the ablutions hut and started ...' She paused, her head down, ashamed. 'He kept pawing at me. And then he grabbed hold of me and started sticking his horrible tobaccoey tongue in my mouth. It was disgusting. So I just pushed him off.' Her voice had gone high and plaintive with emotion again. 'I mean it was all wrong! D'you think there's something the matter with him, Rose? Or with me?'

Having so recently revived the memory in her letter to Diana of how she'd had to find out about sex herself, Rose felt her heart go out to Gwen. 'Look,' she said gently. 'I know it seems a bit funny if you've not done it before, but that's just a way of kissing.'

'*Kissing!*' Gwen squeaked. 'That's not kissing. It's . . . it's – insanitary!'

Rose looked at Gwen's distraught face in silence for a moment, trying to work out how to phrase what she knew she had to say next.

'You know that film we saw last week, about the babby being born?' she said. Gwen nodded, eyes wide. 'You don't know how it got in there in the first place, do you?'

'Well, Mummy said they just get sort of planted there . . .' Gwen trailed off. 'No, I don't. She told me I didn't need to know anything about "that" until I'm married. And she said even then I'd be luckier not to find out. She's very protective.'

Rose sighed, and then, as carefully and clearly as she could, so that Gwen could be left in no doubt what she was talking about, she explained. She watched Gwen's expression change from astonishment to disbelief and horror, and then to a stunned gratitude.

'So when they call us ATS "officers' groundsheets", that's what they . . . ?'

Rose nodded.

'And that's what Gloria meant about Paragraph 11,' she said slowly, her horrified expression returning. 'That she'd actually . . . ?'

'It's all right,' Rose reassured her with a wry smile. 'From what I hear in this place she wouldn't be the first to try that way out. But I'm sure she was only joking – honest.'

By the end of the final week of basic training, they had been drilled and barracked and bumpered into something that not only resembled army discipline, but was also becoming second nature. Now it was time to be assigned a trade. They all sat through aptitude tests and interviews designed to help the army allot each of them a suitable job. Rose found most of the tests less formidable than she'd feared.

During the interview with Lieutenant Waters, the question Rose remembered despite her nerves was when the woman, sitting behind her desk, asked in a crisp voice, 'You're from Birmingham, aren't you, Private Lucas? What was your father's occupation before the war?'

'Well, he was an engineer—' Rose began to tell her.

'Ah,' the officer said, jotting something down. 'At last, some mechanical potential.'

Rose didn't have the heart or opportunity to tell her that Sid hadn't worked as an engineer since before the last war.

When she came out of the interview she met Muriel outside.

'So – what was the verdict?' Muriel asked her.

A broad smile spread across Rose's face. 'Driver. I'm off to start at Camberley next week.'

She felt not only pleased and excited but flattered too. She, little Rose Lucas, being able to drive Jeeps and trucks about!

She walked to lunch with Muriel in the moist April wind, across the open area where they did their square bashing, saluting a male officer they passed on the way.

'Gloria's furious,' Muriel said. 'They've told her she's got to be a cook!'

'Gloria?' Rose exploded into laughter. 'Oh my God, heaven help the poor sods who have to eat her cooking! What's yours then?' she asked Muriel.

'Oh, admin. Predictable, I suppose. I've done a certain

amount of helping out in my father's firm. Gwen's doing something similar – or is it wireless operations? And Tilly'll be on the telephones I think.'

So the five of them from Hut J who had been thrown so incongruously together were now to be scattered again.

At the end of the three weeks they waited with all the others for their transport back to Didcot to begin on their new careers. They looked a very different collection of women from those who had arrived, all setting off to equip themselves with skills that a few weeks ago they would scarcely have dreamed of. Except for Gloria, who was vowing furiously that every meal she cooked would be sabotaged until they let her do something else.

'Burnt sodding porridge – that's what they'll get!' she yelled out of the back of the truck.

They parted with more emotion than they would ever have thought possible for such a mixed group of strangers within the space of three weeks.

Sixteen

November 1943, at sea

The merchant ship *Donata Castle* slid slowly away from Southampton in a grey choppy sea and under a heavy winter sky.

Those who stood at the quayside saw that the decks were lined from bow to stern with the drab khaki colours of army personnel. Among them, for the moment cordoned off in their own separate section, were three hundred women of the British ATS.

It was a solemn hour for all those on the ship. They knew neither when they would be returning home, nor where the *Donata Castle* was bound. The land receded behind the stern, becoming less distinct until it shrank to a soft line on the horizon like a land in a dream. Then it was gone.

As if released, everyone began to move away from the rails of the ship. They had really left England now, so it was time to look forward instead of back. They needed some immediate purpose, and most made their way towards cabins and berths to sort out the rest of their belongings.

A slim, pale young woman with reddish brown hair and a rather perturbed expression was one of the last to turn away from the rail. As she did so, her eye was caught by another of the khaki-clad figures walking away from her on the gently swaying deck. A short young woman, dark hair curled round her ATS cap, a neat but somehow intensely purposeful walk . . .

'I say – Rose!'

The young woman turned, brown eyes searching out the voice. Then her serious face was suddenly smiling broadly. 'Gwen!'

They gave each other a strong hug, something unthinkable in their early army days.

'I didn't see you when we came on board,' Gwen exclaimed.

'I was late.' Rose was looking Gwen up and down. 'Well – you're a sight more pleased with yourself than when I last saw you!' She laughed. 'I thought there wasn't anyone I knew on board here. I *am* pleased to see you.'

'Oh, me too,' Gwen assured her. 'And I can't get over the sight of you. You look marvellous!'

It was true. The reliable army food and plentiful amounts of fresh air that Rose had had access to for the past two and a half years had improved her looks no end. She had gained weight, so that her cheeks were no longer gaunt, and her complexion a healthy pink. Her petite figure was now curvaceous instead of skinny, her rounded breasts and hips filling her uniform.

'Fancy you signing up for abroad!' Rose said, remembering the anxious girl she had first known at the Berkshire training camp. 'What about your mom? She must've had a fit.'

Gwen's expression suddenly turned stiff and obstinate. She glared back at Rose with blue eyes that held a new conviction. 'Mummy is having to fend for herself,' she said abruptly. For a second she wavered and looked appealingly at Rose. 'You must think me terribly hard-hearted, but it's taken the war to make me see just how much my mother ruled my life.' She smiled. 'Come on. Let's go and get a cup of tea and have a good old chat. I want to know all about where you've been.'

They climbed down to the makeshift canteen and sat together with mugs of tea next to a porthole where the dark slant of the sea kept appearing as the ship rocked back and forth.

For a couple of minutes neither of them knew where to begin. It was less painful to look to the future, with all its uncertainties, than to look back on the past couple of years of the war.

They had been two of the grimmest years anyone could remember. At home there had been the separation and uncertainty over loved ones, the privations of shorter and shorter rations, bitterly cold winters, and of course the bombing, things precious and familiar being destroyed all around. Across the world, what Churchill had in 1940 called 'the foulest and most soul-destroying tyranny' had swept on relentlessly. Those years had brought defeats on the eastern front in Russia, the Japanese advance through Malaya into Singapore, and the failed invasion of the Allied forces at Dieppe as they tried to get a foot-hold in occupied Europe.

Then, when things could not have looked bleaker, there was at last one overwhelmingly hopeful piece of news. General Montgomery and the Eighth Army had fought against German commander Rommel's forces in the deserts of North Africa. And they had triumphed at El Alamein in northern Egypt. There was a sense that the tide had turned. British and American forces had landed first in Sicily, then Italy. The balance of the war had shifted, but many of the memories Rose and Gwen

189

looked back on now were associated with the darkest days of 1941 and 1942.

'Do you really drive those fearful trucks?' Gwen giggled. 'Silly question, I know. Girls do it all the time. But it looks so difficult.'

'You just learn it like any of the jobs,' Rose replied. 'But it was hard at first, I can tell you. When we got to Camberley, at the start I'd be at it day and night. When I wasn't driving I was dreaming about it. I'd wake up with the sheets all tied up round my legs with trying to double-declutch in my sleep!'

At first she had been astonished at the responsibilities that the army seemed willing to entrust to her. She had learned to drive anything: army pick-up trucks, fifteen-hundredweight Bedford wagons, and the huge canvas-covered three-ton trucks. It seemed absolutely normal now that she should.

'So where were your postings?' Gwen wanted to know.

'Oh, all over – all HAA Batteries. First it was Lancashire, Widnes. I was driving the supplies, messages. At one place I even had to empty the lavs, oh my God! You needed to be patriotic to put up with Lancashire that winter. It were enough to freeze the balls off a brass monkey! In the March I went down near Winchester for a few months. And then it was Essex for the rest of the time. Tillingham Marshes, another ack-ack battery, trying to get the planes before they got to London.

'Then they asked me if I wanted my name down for abroad, so I thought, what the heck? I'm not at home anyway and I feel like a cuckoo in the nest when I'm back there. So I might just as well be even further away.'

'My feelings exactly,' Gwen agreed.

She told Rose that she had been sent to Sussex

originally to do clerical work. But she had found it very tedious and had proved lucky in applying for a change.

'Once I'd managed to break away from home I thought I might as well go the whole hog! So I applied to train in Signals and as they were short at the time they agreed to let me go. I'm Royal Corps of Signals now.'

'By the way,' Gwen said, after Rose had fetched more of the warming tea. 'I heard news of a couple of the others we were with. Tilly got pregnant fairly early on and was released after the six months. And Gloria didn't last long as a cook – surprise, surprise. She served up such unspeakable food that they let her change after a couple of weeks. She's on a predictor at one of the ack-ack batteries somewhere round London.'

Rose grinned. 'Good for her. So she's getting the buggers after all.'

When Rose went back to her four-berth cabin, she found to her relief that she was alone. Wearily she sat down on her lower berth, leaning well forward so as not to bang her head on the one above. She rested her elbows on her khaki skirt and rubbed her eyes. The journey to Southampton after a couple of days of leave in Birmingham had been a strain. There had been several delays and she had wondered if she was going to miss embarkation.

The two days she had spent in Catherine Street had not been easy. She felt so changed, so enlarged by her experiences. The army had become her life for the time being. It was closer, more immediate and exciting, and in many ways easier.

She had been greeted like a hero by the neighbours,

and she'd managed a reasonably cheery visit to Mrs Meredith, who was as delighted as if she was a physical extension of Alfie himself. Even Sid had seemed openly proud of her. Grace cooked the best meals she could manage on the rations, and the great treat for Rose was that they managed to get Edna over for twenty-four hours with Harry and the twins.

Billy and Susan had grown into robustly healthy-looking six-year-olds who were faring well on fresh eggs, country air and Edna's kindness. Rose hadn't seen them for two years, and she knew they could scarcely remember who she was. She couldn't help crying when they left, especially when Susan, forgetting Rose was her sister, said, 'Bye bye, Auntie Rose – it were ever so nice to meet you!'

'I wish I wasn't missing them growing up,' Rose said wistfully to Grace afterwards. 'They'll be so used to Edna when the war's over that they won't want to come home!'

Grace frowned. 'That's the best thing really, isn't it? No good having people swanning in and out of their lives. They want someone who's always about.'

Rose swallowed the reproach in silence, hurt but knowing she was right.

Grace was also growing in confidence. She had trained as a nursing auxiliary and worked several nights a week at the first aid post in the local baths. Rose knew without seeing her working how good she'd be at it. She was outwardly just as kind and warm a person as she'd always been, but Rose knew there was a new distance between them. They could not at present share the kind of closeness achieved by living with each other and sharing the same concerns.

George was still causing them worry, going off for

several days at a time, although he always came back, and Grace told Rose she'd learned to live with it.

Being back in Catherine Street also brought back sharply Rose's grief at Dora's death and the huge gap it had left in her life. She could sense her father's loneliness even though he seldom spoke. Away in the army the loss felt less real.

With all the shadows of the pre-war years crouching round the house, and her feeling of being an outsider in her own family, she was glad to leave again, even with the sadness of not knowing when she would be back.

She sighed, sitting there in the half-light of the cabin. Other reminders of the past were tucked into her kit-bag. She drew out two more of the standard cards which she had received from Alfie. He was still in Felsig POW camp, apparently in good health. There were no other details. Rose stared for a long time at the two cards. They seemed to bear no relation at all to the Alfie she had known four years ago in Birmingham. She tried to picture his pale face, his kind expression, which she could only remember rather sketchily. She wondered in what ways the war would have changed him, as it had changed her. And suddenly she wished, for the first time in months, that she could see him. At least then maybe she could make up her mind how she felt about him. She still told people she was engaged. Partly because strictly speaking she was, and also because it was useful to avoid getting involved with all the forces men from whom she was constantly receiving attention and offers. Little of it was welcome. After Mr Lazenby she still found it hard to trust men, or even like most of them.

She had trusted Alfie. Memories of the good times they had had together filled her mind. It was not easy, after all that had happened since, to remember the passive, dependent state she had fallen into when she was with him. She felt anything but passive and dependent now.

She put the cards aside and took out the other envelope that she was still carrying with her. Inside there was one letter on thin, wafer-like blue paper, and the beginning of another on a thicker, cream-coloured sheet. Rose lay down on her side, resting on one arm, and read them both again.

The blue paper letter gave only the central WAAF mailing address and the date: 2 September 1941.

Dear Rose Lucas,

I hope you won't mind my writing to you, but I felt it right that I should, and am sorry not to have done so sooner.

I'm afraid that what I have to tell you will come as a terrible shock. I am writing as a friend of Diana Harper-Watt. We were fellow WAAFs and mostly recently I have been posted with her. Diana was killed last month when she was travelling up to London from our base. The train received a direct hit before it pulled into Waterloo and only about half the passengers aboard survived.

Diana's mother has requested that as a close friend I look through her things down here to see if there was anything that needed tying up. In the course of doing so I found your letter dated 30 March this year, and also the enclosed letter that Diana had obviously started to write in reply. Knowing that you were also a friend, may I send my condolences for the sorrow we all share at her

death? She was a marvellous person. I'm sure I don't
need to tell you.

    With my kindest regards to you and apologies for
bearing such ill news,
Celia Ravenscroft.

Diana's own letter consisted of only a few lines.

My dear Rose,
    Thank you so much for writing to me. I shall
truly treasure that letter. My apologies that I've
taken so long to reply – WAAF life is so hectically
busy. I'm sure you know from your own service
life. Your letter made me feel so, so sad, I can't tell
you

It broke off there as if she had been called away. And
that was all. It was so tantalizing, this minute taste of
her thoughts. If she had finished the letter, at least Rose
would have had a fuller picture of her, of the person she
had become. The letter and their brief meeting gave her
just enough to know that things could heal. 'My dear
Rose', she read over and over again. 'My dear Rose'.
She had long ago written a brief note of condolence to
Ronald and Catherine and had received a brief, though
warm letter in reply. She knew her own letter explaining
herself would have reached them among Diana's possessions.

    She read the letters again, and then climbed back up
to the deck with them in her hand. The ship was
travelling at a steady speed now, and she stood looking
out over the water with the rush of the cold wind
against her cheeks. Standing by the rail, she thought of

the first time she had seen Diana in her bedroom at the vicarage. Her beautiful, curly-haired, generous friend who had accepted her immediately and without hesitation. And of that last time, her blue eyes hurt and questioning, on New Street Station. And she remembered for a moment Diana's face that day when she saw the strong man in his chains struggling to loose himself inside the heavy sack. She closed her eyes against the pain of it, hoping fervently that Diana's death had been instant, that she had not lingered there, trapped and suffocating in the railway carriage.

She wanted to open her mouth and scream and scream into the wind. Instead she tore the letters into tiny cream and blue pieces. When she opened her hands the wind whisked the light fragments away instantly towards the stern of the ship.

'They've taken the ropes down between the quarters,' an excited voice announced at the door of Rose's cabin. 'Now we'll see some fun!'

They were a week into the voyage and until this point the male and female troops had been kept firmly apart. The ropes across the passages separating the two were guarded at night, and fraternizing was strictly forbidden.

Now everything suddenly became more relaxed. The sky was a pale, clear blue and, though not hot, the sun was shining and it was a great deal warmer than it had been in England. The sea had turned a rich green-blue, its surface ruffled by a strong breeze. Conditions for the voyage so far had been perfect. Now they were allowed the run of the ship, and romances started to blossom in every nook and cranny. Promises were made, weddings planned, and it all felt like a fantastic holiday reprieve after the dark winter of war they had left behind.

But of course the war was never far away.

'I wonder where we're going,' Gwen kept saying as she and Rose paced restlessly up and down that morning. They spent most of their time on the ship together.

'I think it's Australia,' Rose said. 'I mean they've given us all that lightweight uniform, haven't they? Must be somewhere hot, wherever it is.'

'It could be quite a number of places, couldn't it?' Gwen said, staring rather absently out over the endless water. 'But it's awfully unsettling not knowing.'

They were to find out sooner than they realized. Just as Gwen, screwing up her blue eyes, had said to Rose, 'I say – it's not my imagination, is it? That is land over there?' an order came that they were all to assemble on the deck where Rose and Gwen were already standing.

When the three hundred women were standing smartly to attention in the bright sunlight, their new Company Sergeant Major Marjorie Keaton told them she had an important announcement to make. She was a tall, thin, pleasant-faced woman with large teeth that made her look as if she was permanently on the verge of smiling.

'Some of you may already have noticed that we're sailing pretty close to land,' she shouted, trying to make her voice carry as far as possible. 'I am now authorized to tell you where we are to be posted. Later today we shall pass through the Straits of Gibraltar – between the coast of Spain and the north coast of Africa,' she explained carefully to those whose geography was not what it might be. Three hundred pairs of eyes gazed at her intently.

'We shall then enter the Mediterranean. From there,

if conditions stay as they are, it will take us approximately six days to reach our destination. The ship will dock at Naples. The orders for our company are that we staff the new Allied Forces Headquarters which have been transferred to Caserta, seventeen miles to the north of Naples.' They all saw her smile. 'Evidently our work is to be housed in a royal palace. That'll make a change for some of us, won't it?'

A wave of appreciative murmurs and laughs passed through the crowd.

Then CSM Keaton's face grew solemn again. 'Enjoy the rest of the voyage,' she said. 'There will be a great deal of work to do when we arrive. Every effort will be needed in order to help the progress of our forces northwards.'

The women's assembly broke up, all chattering excitedly as they moved off to different parts of the ship.

'So much for Australia!' Gwen teased.

'Italy?' Rose seemed completely bemused by the news. 'We're really going to be living in Italy? I hardly know a thing about the place. Doesn't seem real, does it?'

That afternoon, the ship slowly negotiated the Straits of Gibraltar. People lined the rails of the decks pointing out the famous Rock, monkeys and all. And there were constant cat-calls from the men to the ATS on board: 'Come over here!' 'Give us a kiss girls!' 'Go on – get your knees brown!'

As soon as they were through the straits they all noticed a number of small boats peeling off from the Spanish coast and homing in on the *Donata Castle* before she had a chance to pick up speed again. As they drew in closer everyone leaned over the rails to watch, and started cheering and whistling when they realized what was going on. In the painted boats dark Spanish men stood up unsteadily, their legs braced against the sea's movement.

'Stockings!' they shouted up in accents which sounded strange to English ears. 'You buy stockings – silk, nylon – very good?'

Silver coins, half-crowns and shillings, started to rain down from the *Donata Castle*. The Spaniards passed up the stockings on long thin poles. There were squeals of excitement from some of the ATS on board as the goods were examined for their colour, length and lack of holes.

'Here – let me treat you to a pair, may I?'

Rose and Gwen turned to find out who the rather smarmy voice belonged to. A strongly built, red-haired fellow was standing behind them smiling. Openly he looked the two of them over and targeted Rose as the more obvious looker of the two with those sultry dark eyes.

'Let me buy you some of the merchandise they're offering?'

Rose returned his stare quite indifferently and said abruptly, 'No thanks.' She turned back to watch the noisy, hectic scene on the water below.

The man smiled knowingly at Gwen and winked at her. 'Well, what about you?'

Gwen, flattered by the attention and rather embarrassed by Rose's lack of grace, nodded, smiling and blushing.

'My name's Brian by the way,' the young man said. He pushed between them and called out, 'I say – over here!'

One of the vivid blue and red boats sped over on the bright water, the boatman rowing eagerly.

Brian tossed a half-crown down and the boatman

reached up, trying to snatch it from the air. When he'd passed the nylons up on the pole he made off again at high speed.

'Well, that is kind of you,' Gwen said, beaming at him.

She held up the stockings to admire them, and Rose turned to watch. She saw Gwen's smile drop into an expression of horror and embarrassment. The stockings only had one foot between them.

Brian grabbed hold of the one and a half nylon legs he had just bought, shouting, 'Of all the damned cheek! Come back here, you thieving, cheating . . .'

He disappeared along the deck yelling helplessly down at the boatmen between everyone else's shoulders. If he had been listening, he would have heard Rose's unrestrained cackles of laughter.

Gwen, one hand clapped over her mouth, started to giggle too.

'Oh – his face!' Rose cried, straightening up and wiping her eyes. 'I'll never forget it as long as I live!'

When they had stopped laughing, Gwen said to Rose, 'You don't like men very much, do you?'

'Oh – some of them are all right.' Rose's black eyebrows pulled into a slight frown. 'I just can't stand the ones who think they can buy a favour before they even know your flaming name.'

Rose sensed they were approaching land even before she was out of bed. It was only five-thirty in the morning, but she found she was completely awake, her heart pounding, and she knew she would get no more sleep.

When she'd dressed, very quietly so as not to disturb

the other three in the cabin, she went outside into the bright, chilly morning.

There it was, nearer even than she had expected. The curve of the bay was blurred as yet, so that she could not make out any clear details. She could only form an impression of the brightness of it, the buildings near the top of the slice of land must be dazzling white. She stared, quite mesmerized, as the *Donata Castle* inched nearer and nearer.

There were only a couple of other people out on the deck at that hour. She noticed a young private standing not far away, staring with fascinated attention in the same direction as herself. She was struck by the concentrated look of interest on his face as he gazed towards the land, unaware of her watching him. She saw that his short hair, just showing round the edges of his army beret, was very light brown, almost blond. He was slim, not especially muscular in build, and he stood gracefully resting his weight on one foot as he leaned on the rail.

He turned suddenly and saw Rose watching him. Without smiling or changing his expression, he walked slowly along the deck and stood beside her.

'Incredibly beautiful, isn't it?' he said. He had a soft voice, his accent southern, she thought, and quite well spoken.

'I've never seen anything like it,' Rose said. She spoke quietly and rather correctly, affected by his serious presence.

He turned and pointed back to one of the open arms of the bay. 'That's Vesuvius,' he told her, indicating the grey, cone-shaped mountain rising up from the sea. 'The volcano. Quite spectacular. I hadn't realized just how near it would be.'

'How did you know about that?' she asked.

'I've done a bit of reading, that's all. I've always been fascinated by volcanoes. I didn't know we'd end up here of course.'

For the next hour the two of them stood side by side, almost entirely in silence, watching the lines of Naples slowly grow clearer. The city seemed to tumble down to the sea in layers, made up of a hotch-potch of terraces, with houses and trees stepped at different levels down the cliff. The vivid blue sea lapped at its feet and, above, a few puffs of white cloud were the only marks on the sky.

The white brilliance gradually turned to more ambiguous greys and yellows. They could see trees, and roads like nail scratches zig-zagging down the steep cliff. Gradually, drawing into the port, the briny sea smell became obscured by the stench of sewage. Any illusion that they were entering a shining, pearl-like city melted away rapidly as the *Donata Castle* nosed towards the remnants of the heavily bombed port area of Naples.

Seventeen

'Blimey – what a pong!'

'See Naples and die, smell Naples and you *will* die. Not far wrong!'

'What the hell must it be like in August?'

Kit-bags slung on shoulders, they all made their way down the plank walkway from the *Donata Castle*, a long stream of khaki-coloured movement in the warm air of what was now almost midday in Naples. They walked briskly away from the sea to the trucks which were waiting to transport them to their new billets. Everyone was glad to be back on land.

Around them the stench suggested a city festering like a corpse left for days in the sun. The Allied bombing of the port area, before the Germans had finally given up the city in September, had wrecked the sewers and cut off the mains water supply. The two hundred thousand already impoverished Neapolitans the bombing had left without homes were camping out where they could among the rubble of bricks and unrecovered bodies. It was a city stinking not only of charred wood and sewage, but also of disease, starvation and death.

It was early enough in the day for the transport to take them straight to Caserta.

'You ought to be driving us,' Gwen teased Rose as they climbed up into one of the trucks. Rose didn't reply.

'By the way, who was that feller I saw you with this morning?' Gwen chatted on in the back of the truck. 'He looked awfully nice, I thought.'

For a moment Rose stared blankly at her. 'Oh – you mean when we were coming in? I never asked his name.'

'You're hopeless,' Gwen told her.

Rose wasn't in the mood for talking. She had made sure they had been almost the last to get into the truck so as to be near the back. She didn't want to miss a single opportunity to take in this new place.

As the trucks rumbled further into the city, Rose saw people in the streets, some shouting and waving, standing in front of the rubble or the dusty husks of houses. Some were hawking a selection of their possessions on the pavements. Dark-eyed, scrawny children, wearing only the filthiest remnants of clothes, ran after them for a few yards yelling things they couldn't hear. Faces looked pinched and pallid even under the dark skin. In contrast, the Allied servicemen on the streets, who came from many different countries, looked well fed and full of muscular energy.

There was little traffic. The Neapolitans had been starved of petrol along with everything else, and the trucks passed only some bony mules pulling carts and a couple of very decrepit old cars with patches riveted on to the tyres.

There was a lot to take in at once, but one detail which didn't escape anyone's notice was that across the entrance to each side street off the main road was strung a wire bearing a bold army sign: 'OFF LIMITS – OUT OF BOUNDS. VD AREA'.

'That inspires no end of confidence, doesn't it?' someone said.

Most of the comments were adverse.

'Of course, they don't live, in places like this,' a voice said close to Rose. 'They merely exist.'

Rose turned and saw a fair, milky-skinned face, freckled and healthy-looking. She shouted over the noise of the truck, 'What part are you from then?'

'Me? Oh – Buckinghamshire,' the young woman shrilled.

'And you know all about being poor, obviously,' Rose bawled back at her. Even under those conditions the sarcasm communicated itself quite clearly.

The young woman looked very taken aback. Rose felt Gwen nudge her hard with her elbow. 'D'you have to be so damn prickly all the time?' she yelled in Rose's ear.

Her touchiness was part of a more complicated emotion. Almost from the moment she had caught sight of the Italian coastline, and with increasing force since they had docked, she had felt drawn to the place. As she looked out at the old, splendid buildings of central Naples and saw at the same time the plight of its people, a powerful sense of kinship came over her. These hungry, downcast Neapolitans seemed, astonishingly, part of her. She didn't even know yet whether she liked the place. All she could be sure of, instinctively, was that she was meant to be here.

As they reached the northern edge of the city Rose caught sight of a huge cemetery which overlooked the Bay of Naples, containing some graves the size of small stone houses. Then they were away on the road north to Caserta. They passed small villages with crumbling tile roofs, fields showing a down of tiny green growth surrounded by fig trees and vines which had fingered across and clung on to the trunks.

It was slow going. There had been rain in recent days

and the road suface was covered with a slippery layer of mud. The journey took over an hour and a half, and on the way they saw several Jeeps overturned in the ditches by the side of the road.

'Goodness, someone needs driving lessons!' Gwen shouted when they'd passed the third Jeep.

'They're all American ones!' Rose called back with a grin. Now out of the city, she was exhilarated by the new countryside, which even in winter looked so much lusher than England, with the dark shape of Vesuvius behind them pushing steam clouds into the sky.

Caserta was a small town of faded red roofs and cream and yellow paint peeling from the fronts of old buildings. Rose took in the wooden shutters on the windows, the tiny wrought-iron balconies, the slim square tower of a church. But the town itself seemed completely dwarfed in size and significance when they caught sight of the palace. There were gasps of astonishment from those who could see out.

'Is that where we're going to live?' Rose asked.

'I don't think so,' Gwen said. 'That's the head-quarters, I think, where we'll work. We're going to our billets now.'

It was during their first viewing of the inside of the eighteenth-century palace the next day that they were to discover the full extent of its majesty. The vast central block of rooms was the royal apartments. It was poss-ible to walk through those for a long time without finding a room that looked in the least commonplace. Every floor and doorway was a work of art in different colours and textures of Carrara marble; the ceilings soared above, resplendent with gold and rich-coloured oil paintings and intricate designs of paintwork and stucco. Each room was different, and each magnificently designed. At first the sight was impressive and awe-inspiring. But after walking round for any length of time it cloyed and overwhelmed.

'It's like hogging a whole plate of cream cakes all at once, isn't it?' Gwen commented wearily. 'Rather indecent really.'

'Out the back's the best bit,' Rose agreed. 'Now that is beautiful.'

From the back entrance to the palace an enormous landscaped garden extended as far as the eye could make out any detail. A narrow road ran straight through it, thinning to a pencil width as it climbed the tree-covered mountain in the far distance.

The real glory of the garden lay in the fact that from a far point up the mountain water rushed in cascades over the rocks. The water was channelled into a long line of stone tanks, from where it fell splashing into a green pool. Watching over this stood a semicircle of stone statues. As a recreation ground for the huge number of forces people who were to be living in the area it could not have looked better.

Their billet, a mile from the palace, had previously been a hospital. It was a stark white building, housing groups of sixteen of them in blocks which each extended off a long central corridor. Rose and Gwen made sure they took beds in the same block, along with the young freckled blonde Rose'd had words with in the truck.

She latched on to them straight away. 'My name's Wilhelmina,' she announced.

Rose grimaced and said, 'Oh my God,' flinging her kit-bag on the bed.

'Is she always so rude?' Wilhelmina asked Gwen.

Rose grinned repentantly. 'Only when there's an R in the month. But for heaven's sake, we can't carry on calling you Wilhel— whatever it is. What in God's name did they call you that for?'

'Most people call me Willy,' the girl said apologetically.

'And what's your name?' Gwen asked the solidly built young woman who had taken the bed on the other side of her. She had dark brown, rather greasy hair, cut in an abrupt bob round the bottom of her ears.

'I'm Madge,' she said gruffly. 'And before you ask, I'm a driver, and I come from Leeds.'

'Rose is a driver.' Gwen pointed her out.

Madge put her hands on her broad waistline and stared at Rose. 'Where you from, then?'

When Rose told her, she said, 'You look all right. At least you're not from down south – well, not quite, anyway.'

'Glad I qualify for the human race,' Rose quipped. She took to Madge straight away with her straight talking. Eyeing her up and down she asked, 'Do they use you to jack up the trucks when a wheel needs changing? You could do it with one hand I should think!'

Gwen and Willy looked anxiously at Madge to see how she'd take this. She gave a great snort of laughter. 'They just call me in when the blokes can't get their nuts undone!'

Everyone else joined in the shrieks of laughter.

After they had returned to their unpacking there was a sudden squeak from Willy. 'This is blood here – look!'

They went over to where she was kneeling by the

bed, peering anxiously at some reddish brown stains on the wall. 'Doesn't that look like blood to you?'

'It does rather,' Gwen said. 'Goodness, what a thought!'

'Well, what do you expect in a hospital?' Madge said. 'That's why the beds still feel warm.' She gave her great bellow of laughter again. 'Don't worry. I think some American WACs have stayed here already. You won't catch anything!'

Life soon began to settle into a routine. Rose was assigned a three-ton truck and was soon occupied in taking people from their billets to the palace for work and back, bringing in the loads of rations from the Divisional Headquarters and transporting the laundry and all the other requirements of the huge community they lived in. It was often her job to carry the German prisoners from the POW camp near by to the compound where they worked. And there were nurses to transport to the hospital, lifts to be given to officers in pick-up trucks, and messages to be relayed. All day she was in and out of some vehicle or other, refuelling them, sometimes repairing them, but, more often than not, on the move.

She wouldn't have changed her job with anyone in the service. At the beginning of the day she climbed up on to the hard bench seat of her truck to handle the big steering wheel, with a load of passengers in the canvas-covered area behind. The seats in the trucks were high, but she still needed to add a firm cushion to give her a good view out. Even though most of the journeys were fairly short, she was exhilarated seeing this new place, the villages around Caserta strung together by muddy tracks, the ragged *contadini* working the fields, mules pulling carts and hens bustling in consternation across the road in front of the truck.

Though it was winter the weather was better by far than it would be at home. The cool, often sunny days were more like an English spring, so there was not the struggle to wield a spanner with hands she could barely move for the cold. She felt no envy at all of Gwen, who spent her shifts on duty receiving the coded messages from her wireless set deep in the cavernous basement area of the palace.

'It's odd, isn't it,' Willy said to Rose and Madge one day, 'how whenever we go out anywhere for fun we have to be chaperoned to the hilt, yet you two go driving off all over the place on your own.'

'Typical army logic I'd say,' Gwen commented.

At Christmas they did the best they could to brighten up their sleeping block. They hung home-made coloured paper streamers across the bare white walls and brought in cuttings of greenery from outside to decorate the corners and windows. Some of the German POWs had also made little wooden Christmas trees which they put on the windowsills. The place still looked pretty bleak, but the decorations did something to soften the hard angles of the room.

'I think it's going to be a good Christmas,' Gwen said the day before Christmas Eve as they were all getting ready for bed. She sat down on her bed beside Rose's. 'In fact, I have to admit I much prefer Christmas in the army to being at home.'

'It's not the same without the kids around,' Rose said sadly. 'That's what I really miss. But they're not even at home any more.'

Gwen reached over and took Rose's hand. 'Come on – let's try and be cheerful,' she said. 'I know it's not the New Year yet, but let's talk about resolutions. What great things are you going to do in 1944?'

Rose, her chin set in her determined way, and just waiting for Willy's look of bewilderment, said, 'I'm going to learn to speak Italian.'

Eighteen

By the beginning of January 1944 the Germans had established a defensive line across the shin of Italy known as the Gustav Line. At its central point was the Benedictine monastery set in craggy isolation on the peak of a high mountain called Monte Cassino. The Allied troops, made up of British, American and many other nationalities, found themselves unable to progress further north. They were enduring a gruelling winter camped out among the sharp ridges and muddy gullies of the Abruzzi Mountains.

In the middle of the month the Allies, convinced that the Germans had taken possession of the monastery as an observation post, began to bombard Monte Cassino. It was the beginning of a long, mainly futile and mutually destructive battle. And on 22 January, Allied forces landed on the coast at Anzio, a point north of the Gustav Line, as a way of trying to break the stalemate. However, instead of moving immediately north from there, they delayed, became trapped by German forces, and were once again unable to make progress. The destruction of Monte Cassino continued.

In Caserta, in the Allied-occupied south, things remained relatively peaceful. It was possible to work each day at the royal palace and almost forget that there was a war going on.

One morning in late January, a REME engineer,

Tony Schaffer, was walking across the open area at the front of the palace, enjoying the feel of the sun through his cotton shirt. He noticed a three-ton army truck pull up in front of the building. The small figure of Rose Lucas jumped from the cab. Tony smiled and headed over to her. She flexed her legs, stiff after sitting for several hours, and reached up into the cab for her canvas bag.

'Hello Rose,' Tony said. 'Buzzing about as usual?'

She turned to look at him and a smile transformed her thoughtful face. 'Hello Tony. Yes, I've been trying to keep the army fed again.'

Since she had been in Caserta she had a number of times run into this young man with whom she'd had her first sight of Naples on the *Donata Castle*.

'I'm just off for a cuppa,' she said. 'You got time for one?'

The more Rose saw of Tony, the more she liked him. Her automatic caution in relating to men had been allayed by his own obvious shyness. He wasn't one of those cocky sods, she thought. He didn't put any pressure on you. He wasn't like some of the other blokes who wanted to kiss you the minute they'd said hello, if not before. He seemed to want friendship, and he was interesting to talk to.

They strolled down the curving path to the palace which ran along the front of one of the stable buildings. Rose was telling Tony about where she'd been. He liked the directness of her conversation, the spontaneity which had not been curbed by too much education, but which made her seem to him somehow vulnerable. He felt very protective towards Rose, unlike a number of other chaps around who were put off by the sharpness of her tongue.

213

'You really enjoy your job, don't you?' he said. 'It's good to hear someone who's not constantly full of complaints. That's the trouble with institutional life – the way it leads to this constant carping about everything.'

'I do like it,' Rose agreed, thinking suddenly what a solid person Tony was. He reminded her with a pang of Sam, though he was less stodgy. 'I never thought I'd do something like this,' she went on. 'I mean what other job gives you the chance to—?'

She stopped talking abruptly, with a gasp that made Tony look round, concerned that she was in pain.

'What's the matter?' he asked. She didn't answer.

In front of them, a tall figure had turned out of one of the stable doorways close to the palace and was walking towards them. He was dark-haired, with wide, muscular shoulders which looked constrained by the khaki tunic top. Rose noticed he was walking with a slight limp as he came forward whistling 'Run Rabbit Run' with extra flourishes and patting his breast pocket as if in search of cigarettes. Despite the limp, she would have recognized the jaunty, slightly bow-legged gait anywhere.

As he reached them he nodded, interrupting the whistling to say 'Morning', and was clearly going to carry on past.

'Michael?'

He stopped and turned, clearly not having any idea who she was.

'Michael Gillespie.' It was not even a question. She knew it was him.

He stared at her. 'You sound like another Brummy but who the—?'

Rose said just one word: 'Lazenby's.'

She saw Michael register the word. Then he slowly pointed a finger at her, still unable to believe it. 'Jesus – if it's not little Rosie!'

And to her astonishment he came forward and picked her up easily by the waist, swinging her round and laughing, and Rose laughed with him, completely delighted to see him.

'Oh, Michael,' she said breathlessly as he finally put her down. 'You always were a mad sod!'

Suddenly she remembered Tony and introduced him. The two men nodded at each other. Tony muttered, 'Pleased to meet you,' and Michael said, 'All right Tony?' and they all stood together in the bright morning sunlight.

'Well,' Michael laughed. 'Lazenby's. That's real old times now, isn't it?' His memories gradually began to come back to him. 'You did a bunk from Lazenby's, didn't you? What got into you? Old Lazenby came in blinding away one morning, saying you'd gone off without a please or a thank you and he'd have to get someone else.'

'Did he?' Rose said drily. 'Well it wasn't quite like that. Let's just say me number came up. Anyhow – what on earth are you doing here? Got time for a cuppa?'

'No – 'fraid not. I'm late already. I'm after having a bath – the first in a long while I can tell you. And now I'm clean and fit, and this is sound again' – he stamped his left foot – 'I've got to rejoin my unit pronto. I've had sick leave. Smashed me ankle up jumping off a wagon soon after we got here. Not much of a war wound eh?'

'What division are you?' Tony asked him.

'Infantry,' Michael said. 'One of the poor buggers

215

who goes up front and cops all the shit – 'scuse me, Rosie. These bust-up bones down here have got me out of quite a bit of it so far. There's no putting it off now though.'

'You're not going to Cassino are you?' Rose asked, horrified.

'Not Cassino, no. Further east along the front somewhere. Dodging the mines.'

Rose's eyes showed her dismay, so that Michael bent down and kissed her on the cheek. 'You're a sight for sore eyes,' he said. 'Look at you in that uniform – you're a picture. I've got to go now, but don't you worry, Rosie. I'll see you in Corporation Street when it's all over!'

And he backed away, clowning around and singing 'We'll meet again, don't know where, don't know when!' with a flourish of his arm, and then he was gone.

'Mad sod,' Rose said again, and realized suddenly that she had tears in her eyes.

'Are you all right?' Tony asked. 'You look a bit shaky. I take it Michael is an old flame of yours?'

'Oh.' Rose was startled. 'No. No – not really. I worked with him. It's just – things keep happening like that. Bits of the past and bits of home blowing in when you're somewhere else and not expecting it.'

As they sat drinking a cup of tea Rose found herself telling Tony about Lazenby's and Michael and the sort of work she had done there. She didn't explain why she'd left. Tony sat listening, his grey eyes attentive, his large hands curved round his mug.

'Sorry,' she said after a while. 'I'm running on again.'

Tony smiled. Rose liked the way his wide mouth with its generous lips made his smile look completely wholehearted.

'That's all right,' he said. 'I was enjoying hearing about it. Your life's been so different from mine.'

Tony had already told her that he came from a village in Sussex and that his father had died when he was five. He and his brother and sister had been brought up by their mother. Tony had been an apprentice engineer when the war started.

'You've had a decent education, haven't you?' she asked him.

'Well – we had a good local school,' he agreed. 'I think I educated myself really. I was the sort of child who sat reading *Encyclopaedia Britannica* and filled my mind up with a whole collection of apparently useless snippets of information. It's surprising how often they come in handy though.'

'We never had books in our house, except a few a friend lent me now and then. I remember reading *Treasure Island* out in the lav to get a bit of peace. Someone always came knocking on the door sooner or later though. I thought I was going to surprise them all and become a teacher. Some hope.'

'But just because you haven't had all the chances doesn't mean ...' Tony saw Rose was watching him very seriously as if hungering to be given assurance. 'I mean intelligence just shines out of you. Look – there are a lot of well-educated ATS here, but how many of them are taking the trouble to try and learn Italian like you?'

Rose shook her head. 'I dunno. I don't understand a lot of the people here. We've been given the chance of a lifetime really, haven't we? To come and live in this country, which is fascinating – to me anyway. And all most of them can think about is the next social and what bloke they can get hold of ... It's not the only thing is it? They all live as if they're still in England. I mean, what the hell's the point of that? We'll be back there sooner or later and none of them'll be any the wiser.'

'Oh, I agree – although my goodness, it can be a harsh place.' Into his mind flashed the uncomfortable image of a warehouse in Naples where a misguided friend had taken him a couple of weeks before. All around inside, women waited impassively to give their bodies there and then to any man, in return for tins of army rations. The men had queued awkwardly at the door. Ashamed and revolted, Tony had put down some food and left. He didn't feel he could tell Rose about this so he just said, 'You need to be careful.'

'Yes, but I want to see a lot more,' she said. 'More of Naples for a start. Get to know people. I've found someone to help with the Italian already.'

She told Tony she had got to know an old woman across the other side of Caserta who did tailoring.

'She's called Signora Mandetta. She's making me a skirt at the moment – you know, she's only got that black stuff like the old ladies wear. Anyway, she said she'd help with my Italian. I think she likes the company, so I pop down whenever I get the chance.' Rose sighed as they stepped out into the sunshine. 'Touble is, to get anywhere much there's all this ruddy chaperone lark.'

'Well . . .' Tony looked at her shyly. 'Would I do?'

Suddenly Rose felt full of confusion. She had seen Tony as a friend. Was he now asking her on a date? What did he expect from her?

'I . . .' she stumbled over the words and then decided to cope with anything that happened when the time came. 'Thank you. That'd be very nice.'

'Right,' Tony told her. 'If you want to see Naples, there's going to be transport over on Friday evening. Let's go, shall we?'

Rose nodded, excited, noticing with relief that unlike most people he didn't refer to the leisure transport as 'passion wagons'.

It took them just over an hour to reach Naples. The sun was setting over the bay as they wound through the evening clamour of the city's streets. The uncertain light, and the familiar stench, to which was added a smokiness as evening fires were lit among the rubble, made them hurry towards the familiarity of the Naafi to spend the evening drinking and dancing.

Even over that short distance they were surrounded by a gaggle of children, their hair caked in filth, most wearing the meagrest of rags. The boys gave out gruff adult cries, 'Ey – ey!' they shouted, bony hands prodding at the well-fed foreigners, fingers snapping for attention. They wanted food, cigarettes, anything that was on offer.

'You come!' one of them shouted at Tony. 'My sister pretty! *Mia sorella molto bella* – ey, jig a jig!'

Some members of the party, in slight panic, threw cigarettes and coins. The children scrambled for them like wrangling birds.

'My God – they're starving!' Rose said, horrified, once they had entered the relative comfort of the club. She had been moved almost to tears by the sight of them.

One curly-haired boy who could only have been two or three had stood silently, his huge brown eyes staring, his small hand stretched out to them. He had been covered from head to foot in filth. 'Oh, I wish I could've taken that little one back with me and looked after him!' she said.

Tony smiled at her. 'There must be thousands out there like him,' he told her. 'You can't feed them all. Let's just try and enjoy the evening, shall we?'

Rose was beginning to look disgruntled. 'We're not going to see a lot of Naples sat in here, are we? Home from bleeding home again.'

Couples sat round the tables laughing and drinking. A band was playing songs of home: 'The Lambeth Walk', 'There'll Be Bluebirds Over' and, as ever, 'In the Mood'.

As Rose sat beside Tony they were joined by another fair-haired lad who Tony introduced as Alex. He was a fellow engineer and the two of them were soon chatting beside her. Opposite them, a chap called Stan from Huddersfield was trying to entertain everyone by telling jokes. The ATS girl with him kept snuggling up like a kitten, resting her head on his shoulder, giggling. After a quarter of an hour of this Rose could have happily socked the pair of them.

Lightly she nudged Tony, who turned a little apologetically from his conversation with Alex.

'I'm just going to find the Ladies,' she murmured.

She walked towards the front entrance where there was a small reception desk, as if to enquire. Then, casually glancing back towards the table to check none of them was watching her, she walked to the door. A moment later she was standing alone out on the street.

Nineteen

of it seemed to be going up, and it disclosed one of those little interior courtyards so rare and so precious in summer...

She knew she needed to move fast. Her eyes adjusted quickly to the dark of the unlit city. Now that the Germans had moved out of Naples it was their turn to bomb it, so the inhabitants were still constrained by a curfew and blackout. When she reached the end of the street the Piazza Municipio opened out in front of her. In the gloom a huge building loomed up, round, dark turrets at its corners, and she remembered having driven past it. It was the Castel Nuovo.

She made the mistake of stopping for a moment to get her bearings. The sea was a whisper to her left. From somewhere else she could hear a wheezing, squeaking sound as if someone was playing a very old and asthmatic concertina. She heard carts go by, creaking to the exhausted clop-clop of the mules' hoofs, and a number of shadowy figures passed her in the darkness, some of them in uniform.

And then she felt a hand grip her. She jumped, giving a loud gasp, feeling bony fingers clasping her lower arm. She turned to see a minute old lady standing beside her whose body was bent forward so that her shoulders were rounded into a grotesque hump and she had to twist her head round to look up. Her mouth appeared like a terrible empty hole in the darkness and Rose could make no sense of the cracked whimpering noises she was making. In revulsion and panic of which she was immediately ashamed, she jerked her arm down to rid herself of the goblin-like figure beside her and walked away very fast. She began to hear other voices calling out to her from people she could barely see.

Rose knew she had no definite way of finding her way back once she left the main square. But she had been taken over by her old drive to press on and explore, and it would not let her turn away. She turned her back on the sea, her stomach churning with fear and exhilaration, and walked quickly towards the dark, mouth-like openings of the side streets. She could just make out a pale OFF LIMITS sign over her head, suspended in the smoky air. She felt as if she was watching herself from the outside and was not really responsible for what she was doing: an ignorant, reckless foreign woman heading into the blackness of the slum streets; and thought, I must be off my head.

And then she was inside, or that was how it seemed: that these streets were the real heart of the city. It was even darker here, the sides of the buildings looming on either side of her very close together, so that looking up she could just make out a ribbon of sky above her head between them. There were a couple of stars showing their minute clear light. Around her the shadows were thick and menacing. She had no idea whether anyone was watching her, but ahead she could see a faint flickering light which must have come from a candle burning in one of the *bassi*. Further along the street she became aware of an orange glow playing on the outlines of the buildings. She could hear voices, women shouting, and somewhere a man was singing.

There was no chance of walking very fast. There was too little light and the thick paving slabs underfoot were littered with rubble from the destruction wrought by the bombing and such rubbish as the Neapolitans could spare lay rotting and urine-soaked on the street. Among the stones and chunks of wood, Rose felt her foot slide on something rounded and yielding and nearly cried out in revulsion.

As she moved along, now and then she felt hands clutching at her. She held her bag clutched tightly to her chest, cursing herself for bringing it. She pushed people away with a roughness born of fear and panic. She was beginning to realize just how foolish she had been to come.

I'll just go a bit further and then I'll get myself out of here, she said to herself. She was breathless with fright.

As she drew nearer the glow of the fire she saw that it was burning in the shell of what had once been a tall building like the rest around them. Some lower sections of the outer wall were still standing. Inside was a chaos of stone and timber with beams jutting across at odd angles to the floor and heaps of rubble. In a space among the obviously dangerous ruin, what looked like two or three families were clustered round the darting flames. The stench of drains was even worse here. She watched the circle of people crowded round the fire over which a large cooking pot was balanced on a make-shift support.

She stopped for a few seconds, only to find herself surrounded by clamouring children. The shadows of the fire wavered over their faces, and Rose felt herself unable to move from fear and helplessness.

'I haven't got anything for you,' she shouted. 'Go away – leave me alone. *Va te!*' Adults, attracted by the noise, were joining the children. She was crowded in by stinking bodies, all shouting and groping at her, moving in like vultures.

'Leave me alone,' she cried again. 'Let me go!'

Only once before had she felt such fear: that November evening in Mr Lazenby's office. But here she was also aware that she could disappear and never be seen again in this dark, fetid warren. An image pressed on her mind of the crowd carving her up and roasting pieces of her on sticks by the fire.

She tried to back away from them, hitting out in panic at the grabbing fingers. Someone wrenched her bag out of her hands and made off fast into the darkness. She found herself pressed up against the crumbling stones of the building opposite the fire. In despair she clamped her arms across her chest and shut her eyes tight.

She sensed a ripple of movement and the clamour around her quietened. She opened her eyes just as strong, male fingers gripped one of her upper arms and another hand reached roughly round her back and wrapped tightly over her mouth so that she had no chance to make a sound. The man shouted a few rough words to the people around who stepped back to let them through. Without loosening his hold on her, the man half dragged her along the street and round a corner.

They stopped, and still gripped by one arm, she heard him opening a lock. In the dim light she could make out a huge wooden gateway. Then a small door set into it swung open and she was pushed over the step and inside. She heard the dull slam of the door behind her and his key turning again in the lock.

He released her slowly, and she could hear him

breathing heavily beside her. He stood in silence for a moment, and then uttered one angry word: '*Pazza!*'

Madwoman.

From then on it was like a dream. Rose realized they were standing in the entrance to an inner courtyard. There was a scratching sound as the man lit a match. He handed her a thick, white candle.

'Follow me.' Bending down to pick up a bundle wrapped in newspaper which had been lying by the outer door, he walked across the courtyard.

They came to a doorway which led to a flight of stone stairs. At each level the side of the building that looked over the courtyard was partly open to the air through high, rounded arches like huge windows without glass, with a low protective rail to stop anyone walking off the edge. In some of the arches Rose saw the wilted shapes of plants in heavy pots.

On each floor, doors opened off the stairway. She followed the young man's legs in their dark trousers, bewildered, but sensing that he meant her no harm. They climbed three floors and then he turned off and walked to one of the doors. As she held the fat candle near the wall, Rose saw that on the greyish green of the plaster were painted in rough white letters the words IL RIFUGIO. The man knocked briskly three times on the door.

'Where are we?' Rose asked timidly, praying that her Italian might be good enough to understand at least some of the answer.

The man turned and she saw his face properly for the first time, a smooth, surprisingly aristocratic face with a long aquiline nose and thin lips. His curly hair was clipped neatly round his head and he had large eyes which he kept directed at the door as if he was listening.

'Don't worry,' she thought he said to her, rather absently. 'I'll take you back.'

Then they heard a woman's voice calling softly through the door. 'Francesco?'

Impatiently he replied '*Si, si,*' and they heard the door being unlocked inside. A young woman with a round, gentle face and black hair curling over her shoulders was looking out at them with anxious eyes. 'Thank God,' she said. And then, 'Who's this?'

As they went inside Rose heard Francesco explaining how he had found her in the next street. He unwrapped the parcel he was carrying and showed the young woman what was inside, though Rose couldn't see what it was. The two of them conversed in the sort of quiet voices Dora had used when there was a baby asleep near by. She noticed that Francesco had seemed more relaxed the moment he was inside the place.

Rose looked round her as they talked. They were standing in a sizeable square hallway off which led four doors. On three of the walls there was nothing but bare, crumbling paintwork. Against the fourth stood a small shrine where a tiny candle burned in front of a statue of the Madonna, casting shadows over her gaudy face and robes. Around it hung carefully placed strands of flowers and leaves.

The young woman moved closer to Rose. 'Who are you?' she asked cautiously. 'Are you American?'

'No,' Rose said. '*Un'inglese.* English. A soldier.' She tried to explain that she had been lost, and the young woman smiled suddenly.

'You have learned Italian?'

Rose nodded. 'A little.'

One of the doors in front of them opened and Rose found to her further confusion that she was suddenly

226

face to face with a short, plump nun, her heavy black clothes reaching to the floor. Cradled in her arms was a young child. The nun smiled, a rather odd gnome-like smile as she had a bad squint in one eye, and her expression suggested someone without all their mental faculties.

'She needs water, Margherita,' she said in a high, lisping voice.

The younger woman disappeared, returning a few seconds later with a small china cup and put it to the child's lips.

Rose felt herself drawn towards them. She could see the child's black curls resting on the nun's arm. She reached out and stroked the dark mop of hair. It felt stringy with dirt. She knew all their eyes were on her.

'You like children?' Margherita asked her softly.

Rose nodded. Margherita looked questioningly for a second at Francesco, who gave a slight nod.

'Then come.' She beckoned Rose forward. 'I will show you.'

Still holding the candle, Rose followed her to the door from where she had seen the nun appear. She came with them now, the scrawny child in her arms. They walked through the dark doorway into a long room which must have extended along the back of the building. There was one other candle in the room. Beside this other fragile light a second nun was sitting on the floor, her face in shadow.

After a moment, Rose took in that the little bundles of rags of varying sizes in rows along the floor were the bodies of children. There must have been twenty or thirty of them. She became aware of the sound of their breathing as they lay in exhausted sleep. Despite the size of the room she could smell the dirt on their bodies, and realized that the pungent stench of excrement was coming from a tin pail which stood near the door.

Looking first at the others for permission, Rose walked slowly along between the sleeping children. Some of them lay on mattresses which appeared to be stuffed with something coarse like straw. Others had only an arm crooked under their heads for a pillow. A few of them twitched and stirred in their sleep. They reminded Rose of George, how he had slept without really resting when he came back from his months in Wales.

Her mind was alive with questions about these people. As she drew near the seated nun, she saw that she was watching over a young girl. The nun's face was pale and thin, with prominent cheekbones, and she looked up at Rose through thick black-rimmed spectacles.

Seeing the tenderness in Rose's eyes as she looked at the girl she said in a whisper, 'This is Maria Grazia.'

Rose smiled and nodded, looking at the little girl lying asleep on her side, her face half hidden by long, straight hair. She had to struggle to understand the next part of what the woman said.

'*E gravida*,' she said sorrowfully. '*E ha solo dodici anni.*'

Rose frowned. The girl was only twelve. She had understood that. The nun made a graceful gesture, a curving movement out from her stomach.

Rose gasped, pointing at the girl's belly. '*Un bambino?*'

The nun nodded, watching the horrified pity spread over the stranger's face. 'Her father is dead,' she explained. The woman spoke so fast that Rose could understand only snatches of what she said. She gathered that the girl's mother had also recently died and that to

228

survive she had 'pleased' the soldiers. 'All these children,' the nun went on, 'they have seen terrible things. Some of their families are so poor they even try to sell them.' Gesturing round the room she indicated that though they could only take in a few, they tried to create a home for them.

Rose was aware as she listened that Francesco and Margherita were watching her and discussing something in low, urgent voices. They beckoned her to come out of the room with them. Rose noticed that Margherita looked almost excited, as if in anticipation.

Now she spoke slowly and carefully. 'What is your work in the army?'

Rose couldn't think of the word and mimed turning a steering wheel and changing gear. She saw the two of them exchange glances.

'I see by the way you look at the children that you have a special feeling for them. We have decided to ask you if you can help us.'

The dreamlike peculiarity of Rose's evening was increasing even further. 'I don't understand.'

Francesco made as if to answer, but Margherita gestured at him to be quiet.

'We need help here from wherever we can find it,' she said, still speaking slowly. 'Our refuge is linked with the Church, but it's not official.' Seeing Rose frown she said, 'Francesco and I were members of Catholic Action when we were students. We are also anti-Fascists. The Fascists banned Catholic Action, a long time ago, from any sort of involvement which was not Church-related. We stayed in Catholic Action but we carried on our other activities outside. You understand?'

Rose nodded. She had picked up most of it.

'Now that Mussolini has gone things have become a

little easier.' Margherita continued. 'But our bishop has confused feelings about us. We are loyal Catholics, but we are also seen as troublemakers . . .'

'You mean the Church supported Mussolini?'

Margherita sighed. 'At first, no. Later – yes. Mussolini did deals with the Church, offered bribes . . . presents for them,' she explained. 'Anyway, because of who we are we cannot get official support from the Church for our orphanage. Not in the form of money. This building belongs to the Church. We do not have to pay rent. And the sisters, Magdalena and Assunta, help us with the work. And candles.' Her mouth curved into a wry smile. 'A lot of candles! But we have to feed the children from the black market like everyone else. There is hardly any water. Sometimes it is dangerous because people try to steal from us. They are hungry too, of course.'

Rose was struggling to keep up with her. 'I'd like to help,' she said, cursing her slowness in the language. 'I like children. What do you want?'

'Anything you can bring,' Margherita told her. 'Food, soap, blankets, clothes. We can use anything or we can sell it. I know you cannot come here often. But you come how and when you can. We cannot give you anything in return.'

'Yes,' Rose smiled, 'I think you can. A refuge, perhaps.'

And the two women laughed for the first time. Rose had taken to Margherita straight away. She felt that they could be friends.

'I will come,' Rose said. 'I promise. But you must show me the way back. My friends will be worried.'

'What were you looking for here?' Margherita asked.

'I wanted to see Naples,' Rose said. 'Even at night!'

Francesco indicated that he was ready to leave and Rose went out with him. 'You were very foolish to walk here alone. It is dangerous for us, but even more so for you.'

As they walked down the stairs again they heard hasty footsteps coming towards them and a man appeared, with something stuffed under his jacket. He looked startled as he saw them.

'Evening Enrico,' Francesco said. 'What's that? Bread? Rosa, this is Enrico – he is a magician. He finds bread from the stones.'

The man was staring with wide eyes at Rose and she saw sweat on his pallid skin even though it was a cool night. He had brown hair and a thin, stubbly face.

'This is Rosa,' Francesco said. 'An English soldier. She is going to help us.'

The man gave her a long, intense stare, fearful or hostile she was not sure, and then ran on up the stairs.

'He does not speak,' Francesco explained to her. 'We know almost nothing about him except that he has shown he can be trusted. We think perhaps he is a little—' Francesco tapped a finger against his head. 'But he has connections and from somewhere he brings us food.'

He walked with her, back to the edge of the dark square, from where she said she could find her way.

'When you come again, you will remember,' he said. 'We are in the street next to Via degli Spagnoli. You will help us?' For the first time he smiled, rather appealingly.

'Oh yes,' Rose said. 'I will.'

'Good. Then you will need this. It's for the outer gate.' She felt a large key being pressed into her hand.

Then he turned to go, saying *'Arrivederla.'* And disappeared into the darkness.

'Where the hell have you been?'

Tony was standing outside the club, rigid with anxiety and anger. 'God knows what might have happened to you!'

'Why?' Rose asked stupidly. She had just returned as if from another existence and didn't have her wits about her. She'd only just remembered that she was without her bag. Fortunately there had not been much in it.

'Why?' Tony shouted, and then lowered his voice to an infuriated whisper, not wanting anyone else to hear. There was no one standing near them. 'You walk out and disappear for almost an hour and a half and you ask me why I'm worried! For God's sake, I thought you had a brain, woman. And besides,' he added rather petulantly, 'you've made me look a proper fool.'

Rose was astonished at the strength of his anger. He was usually so gentle and soft-spoken. She looked at his thin face and felt sorry she had let him down so badly.

'I'm terribly sorry,' she said, reaching out to touch his arm. Instantly he pulled away from her. 'I just wanted to have a look round the place. It was so boring in there and—'

'Oh – I apologize for being boring. I was under the impression you liked my company until now.'

'I do, Tony. But you were talking to Alex and that Stan was carrying on and getting on my nerves. I never meant to stay out for so long – honestly I didn't. I don't know what came over me.'

She was very surprised to find it was now only ten-twenty. It felt as if she had been away for hours, and she realized that it had not even crossed her mind to worry about being stranded here if they'd left without her. The passion wagons were due to start back for Caserta at eleven.

The two of them walked a short distance down the slightly misty street.

'Look,' she appealed to him again, glancing at his dejected face. 'It was stupid of me. I'm sorry. But I'm all right – see?' She did a mock curtsey to try and make him laugh. 'I just didn't think you'd be that bothered.'

'Well you were wrong then, weren't you?' he said grimly. Rose realized to her consternation that the young man beside her was not far from tears. 'Just because I don't—' he stopped abruptly.

Rose stepped closer and went to touch him on the shoulder, moved by the emotion she seemed to have aroused.

'Don't,' he said savagely. He turned to her, his white face looking strained, the lick of fair hair falling down over his forehead. 'It'll be wrong. We'll just get each other all wrong.' He stood in silence for a moment, hands thrust down hard into his trouser pockets, looking away from her. A few people passed – the shadowy figures of other servicemen, some with women on their arms, laughing and necking together after an evening's drinking.

In the end he said almost formally, 'I just want you to know I do have feelings for you, Rose. That's all.'

'Well, I'm fond of you too,' she said helplessly, thinking how strange he was.

'Come on,' he said impatiently, as if unsatisfied by what had been said. 'Let's go and have a last drink before it's time to go back.'

Twenty

March 1944

By the third week in March, Rose had only managed
one brief visit to Il Rifugio. She felt she had failed them
badly. The first time she had tried to go back, in
February, she had only managed to get together a few
bars of army soap, some cigarettes and a few tins of
food. She had a lot to learn. Naïvely, as she realized
afterwards, she had packed the supplies into her army
bag, which was instantly recognizable even though she
was dressed in mufti herself.

After the truck from Caserta had dropped them off
and she and Tony had parted, Rose walked quickly into
Via degli Spagnoli looking around her anxiously. She
had just begun to take in the full destitution of the place
in daylight when she felt a hand hard on her shoulder.
Thinking it was someone begging for food she tried to
shake the grasping fingers off.

'And where do you think you're off to?' an English
voice said sternly.

She turned to find herself staring into the mocking
eyes of a Red Cap, the Military Police. She couldn't
think of anything to say.

'Open the bag,' he ordered from under a little ginger
moustache.

'You from the Midlands?' Rose appealed to him as she unfastened the bag. She thought she heard a familiar ring to his accent.

'Coventry,' he snapped. 'Though I hardly see that's any concern of yours.' He took a notebook from his breast pocket and bent over to look into the bag.

'What have we here? Army soap, army rations – cigarettes. Hmm. I see. Got your legs under the table in one of the *bassi* have you? My God – I thought it was only the chaps who played at that sort of game. You want to watch you're not rounded up with all the other prostitutes in the VD wagons.'

'I beg your pardon!' Rose shouted at him, absolutely livid. 'Don't be so bloody rude! Who d'you think you are talking to me like that? You and your poxy little notebook.'

The young man glared at her, infuriated.

'And a fishwife to boot,' he said. 'Now, let's see: being found in an area designated out of bounds to service personnel, unauthorized use of army property . . .'

'But that's all *my* stuff,' Rose argued. 'It's none of your business what I do with it!' She was wild with frustration.

'. . . and insubordination to a senior officer.'

'You're only a ruddy corporal!'

'Which makes me senior to you, doesn't it, *Private* Lucas?'

As a result her leave was cancelled, she was ordered to return to Caserta immediately, and spent a substantial part of the day waiting for transport. As well as that, she was confined strictly to the limits of her working area for a fortnight.

'Well, what were you doing in Naples?' Madge asked,

standing by her bed and attempting to squeeze her large waistline into a non-uniform skirt. 'I should've thought you'd have had more sense. Anything for a quiet life, I say.'

'Oh, I was just nosing around.' Rose bent to undo the laces of her heavy black shoes, evading Madge's curious eyes. If that was army rules, she thought, then they were made to be broken.

As soon as the fortnight was up, Rose went to Signora Mandetta in Caserta, who had made her a skirt. The widow sat at her old sewing table, her gnarled hands working on the intricate seams of a wedding dress.

'I need to look like an Italian,' Rose said.

Signora Mandetta smiled indulgently at her. She was a woman of about sixty with faded hair and a large wart on her left cheek. But her eyes were like those of a seventeen-year-old – a little watery, but still dancing with life.

'Rosa ...' She held out her hands, palms up, and shrugged as if to underline Rose's eccentricity. 'You already look like an Italian – your hair, your eyes ... Tell me the truth. Your father – he is really a Neapolitan?'

Rose laughed, enjoying the signora's teasing. 'Not wearing these clothes I don't,' she said, pointing at the khaki. 'I need to look really Italian. I want black clothes made of old material.' Her Italian was coming more easily now through use at every possible opportunity.

The signora narrowed her eyes with shrewd curiosity. 'You have a boyfriend? An Italian *amante*?'

'No.' Rose wondered how she could possibly explain. It might be easier if Signora Mandetta thought she was disguising herself to meet a lover. She giggled with as much coyness as she could manage. 'Well . . . it's a secret. You'll make me the clothes?'

'Of course. Whatever you want.'

'Marvellous. *Grazie*. Now look what I've brought.'

She often brought a cake or two from the Naafi with her and shared a snack with the signora. This time it was a couple of rock cakes. Signora Mandetta chewed on hers thoughtfully, pouring out tiny tumblers of rough red wine.

'Better if they leave them for the rocks next time,' she commented.

Rose grinned. 'Next time I'll bring doughnuts.'

Within a few days the signora had produced a black outfit for Rose, cobbled together out of some other old clothes. To top it off she offered her a threadbare cardigan and some worn black mules of her own for which Rose paid as well.

'These look just right,' Rose told her as she tried them on.

Signora Mandetta cackled unrestrainedly when she saw Rose in her 'new' clothes. 'Now you just need a fat belly on you to look like a true Italian signora with at least four children!' she cried, wiping her eyes. 'Holy Mother, what a transformation. I only hope he doesn't go off you, *mia cara*!'

When the leave day finally came round Rose brushed a drop of olive oil through her hair. She also bought herself a couple of string bags in which she carried the objects, well wrapped, that she was going to take into Il Rifugio. She changed in the Ladies at one of the Naafi clubs, slipped out the back entrance and walked briskly across the square towards the Via Toledo.

The black market was flourishing on almost every street corner, and she identified with some amusement the array of army goods laid out to be sold on the streets. The food, cigarettes, soap and many other objects which were spirited away from the docks with the collusion, quite often, of army officials and sold openly to the locals. Rose approached one of the little makeshift stalls and bought another handful of packets of cigarettes so that Francesco or Margherita could sell them and buy something they really needed.

Then she made her way through the filth of the Via degli Spagnoli, startling fat green flies with her feet as she walked. She let herself quickly into Il Rifugio. Francesco and Margherita greeted her with admiring hilarity.

'You should have been a spy,' Margherita cried, kissing her with real warmth. 'Oh, look at this! Soap, Francesco, and meat. When can you come again?'

'Soon,' she told them. 'At the beginning of April I get two days. Can I stay here and help you? I will try to bring more things with me.'

'Come when you can. Stay as long as you like,' Francesco said with a shrug. Then he grinned at her. 'You're welcome – *pazza*!'

She spent a few hours there that day, talking with Francesco and Margherita and playing with some of the children. The oldest of them, Margherita told her, was fifteen and the youngest only just over a year old. The routine seemed surprisingly relaxed, and they sat outside in the late afternoon after feeding the children and giving a few of them as much of a wash as was possible with the limited supplies of water which had to be fetched from a pipe outside. Some of the children played out in the courtyard, watched by a couple of the elderly tenants occupying lower rooms in the building. Sometimes they sat out and talked to the children, but mostly they kept to themselves.

Rose picked out the figure of Maria Grazia trailing round the courtyard, her pregnant belly protruding from her pitiful, stick-thin body. She had long straggling hair, and deep-set, myopic-looking eyes which held a sad, dreamy expression. She and another little girl were playing with a filthy cloth doll.

'What will happen to her?' Rose asked Margherita, who had sat down wearily on a stool beside her in the courtyard.

'She will stay here. We can help her care for the baby.'

'But after . . . ?'

Margherita shrugged. 'What will happen to any of them? We shall have to see what God intends for them.'

Rose was silenced by this. Her practical upbringing had not accustomed her to leaving things up to God to decide.

After a while Francesco came out, stretching and yawning from a long siesta. He sat beside them on the ground in the pale afternoon light, his arms round his legs.

Margherita smiled and rumpled his curly hair with her hand. 'My husband would sleep all day if there was not work to be done,' she said affectionately.

'Husband?' Rose said, wondering if she had heard right. 'I didn't know you were . . .'

Both of them laughed, so much that Rose wondered whether she had said something hilarious in Italian by mistake. They laughed even more at her astonished face.

'You are not a Catholic, are you?' Margherita gasped out eventually. 'You think the Church would even give us candles for this place if we weren't married? Can you imagine the bishop, Francesco!'

That afternoon Rose learned as much as she could about everyone at Il Rifugio. Margherita told her that Francesco came from a wealthy Neapolitan family who had a large house at Vomero, the affluent suburb high up on the cliff overlooking the bay. He was evidently something of a rebel. When Italy entered the war he had been completing his studies in political history at Naples University. His family knew where he was but left him to follow what they saw as his bizarre inclinations.

'He calls you mad,' she said, 'but the family think he is truly . . .' She tapped her head with one finger. 'For them, madness is to live here and to identify with the poor. To make their troubles one's own.'

Francesco silently shook his head as if what he was hearing made him sound too heroic. 'But,' he said, jumping up suddenly, 'I have not given away all my possessions to the poor. Let's have some music.'

In a moment he was back with an old wind-up gramophone which he set down on the pale paving slabs. He wound the small machine and fed it with his thick records, songs in Italian and French, most of which were strange to Rose.

'The soul must have music,' Francesco pronounced, in the solemn manner which made Rose unsure whether he was taking the micky out of himself. 'I will sell my body to feed the poor, but not my gramophone.' He saw Rose looking at him rather quizzically and laughed. 'She takes me very seriously this Englishwoman.'

While the tinny sound of the music played across the courtyard, Rose asked Margherita whether the two of them had married as students.

'No, only when we came here,' she said. She told

240

Rose that her family came from a village near Torre del Greco, and that she had met Francesco while studying literature. 'My family are much poorer than his,' she said. 'We got married very quietly.'

'But you're happy, I can see that.' Rose was impressed by the pair of them, by the degree of freedom they seemed to have with each other along with a respect and commitment matched only by their devotion to Il Rifugio.

The two nuns, Assunta and Magdalena, had also made her very welcome during the visit. Magdalena, for all her soulful appearance, proved to be a very down-to-earth woman in her thirties, who could always be relied upon to get things done.

Assunta, who tended the shrine in the hallway as lovingly as if it were another of the children, spent her life waiting for miracles to happen. All her conversation that day while they were preparing food for the community was of the flying monk at Pomigliano. He was said not only to have demonstrated the stigmata, bleeding from hands and feet, but also to have left the ground and soared up to rescue an Italian pilot from a burning plane. Assunta was completely convinced of the truth of this. But for Rose, who nodded politely as she listened, hearing these bizarre claims from Assunta's pallid, cross-eyed face made them seem only more barmy than they would have done otherwise. The children, however, seemed to adore her, and whenever she was not busy with some task she sat cradling one of the younger ones in her plump arms.

The only discomforting presence was the brooding Enrico, who stood at the edge of rooms, silent, always watching. Then he would disappear without even indicating to anyone that he was going. Rose could not quite make out what was odd about him but he made her feel very ill at ease.

The day passed far too quickly, but seeing the children, getting to recognize some of them and realizing at the mealtimes just how little food they had to live on was a spur to her to think up more ways in which she could help.

'You see the problems?' Margherita had said to her while they were eating, all sitting round on the floor of the long room where Rose had first seen them asleep. 'We can manage to feed them – just. But it means we spend so much time finding food. We have so little time to give them any teaching or the love they need.'

Rose looked round at all the dark faces, wolfing down the tiny portions of sloppy army meat and vegetables that she had brought in tins, mixed with macaroni. She would have liked to put her arms round every one of them, dirty and ragged as they were. She felt as if she had found herself a family in Italy. And she was damned if she was going to let them go hungry.

As spring progressed the temperatures grew quite hot. The country was at its most beautiful, with oranges and lemons hanging heavy on the trees. During off-duty periods the men and women stationed at Caserta spent more of their time outside in the grounds of the palace. The last long tank into which the cascades fell was large enough to land a light aircraft on. It was certainly big enough for a swimming pool and already people were making use of it.

One evening Rose and Tony were strolling towards the cascades in the uncertain light of dusk.

'I always forget what a long way it is,' Tony said. 'It must be a couple of miles I suppose.'

Rose just said, 'Umm.'

Tony turned to look at her. Her thoughts were obviously elsewhere. For a moment he enjoyed looking at her face, the soft line of the cheeks and her dark, pensive eyes.

'Sorry,' she said suddenly. 'I was just wondering if there's going to be any more bombing tonight.'

A couple of nights ago they had heard heavy raids on Naples and, knowing that most of the raids were concentrated on the port area and Il Rifugio was not very far from the sea, Rose was concerned. Her mind was constantly occupied with thoughts of how she could help them further. It had ocurred to her that Bill, Gwen's young man who worked in supplies, might be prepared to help. Most likely not. He seemed a bit of a stuffed shirt. Because what was she really thinking of? Stealing from the army? On a large scale? The thought frightened her. Of course odd things were going missing all the time – but more than that . . .

'That Virgin parade in the town,' she said to Tony suddenly. 'Those costumes the girls were wearing. A lot of that was army mozzie nets wasn't it?'

'Certainly looked like it,' Tony said, bemused.

Rose snorted with laughter at the memory. 'Virgin parade!' she said with her deep chuckle. 'God Almighty, have you ever seen anything like it?'

The young women in the town's parade had been wearing an astonishing collection of clothes, many trimmed with netting dyed in dazzling colours. They marched through the streets of Caserta to display their chaste beauty.

But as these 'virgins' passed, voices of Allied soldiers had piped up in the crowd, 'Eh – that's Rita (or Theresa or Maria); I was with her last night!' which caused raucous outbursts of laughter all round.

Seeing Tony look rather embarrassed at her forth-rightness she asked, 'D'you think it's wrong to steal from the army?'

'I suppose it's wrong to steal from anywhere really. But you can't help thinking when you see some of the poverty around this place that we probably wouldn't miss a bit. Why – thinking of joining the black market?'

Rose laughed rather nervously. 'When d'you think I'm going to find time to do that?'

They passed the rows of tanks until they were at the bottom of the cascades, where white water rushed down over the stones. It was possible to scramble up the rocks alongside the water, but on the hillside round behind the cascades, pathways had been cut on both sides, zig-zagging up steeply until they rejoined at the top. Up there, where the water gushed out of the ground, the spring was covered by a great rock, carved round and hollow inside like a shell, so that it made a small cave.

Rose suddenly felt full of energy and mischief. 'Tell you what, I'll race you to the top. You go that way and I'll go up here. Go on, I dare you!'

'Are you joking?' he asked. Clearly, this time it was his mind that had been elsewhere.

'No, course not. Come on.'

Tony roused himself. 'All right then. You're on.'

They set off, each taking a path on opposite sides of the cascades. Immediately she lost sight of him and stared up the path, Rose began to feel frightened. There was a gate behind the cascades which opened on to the rest of the mountainside. There was no knowing who might be wandering about up there, and the darkness was falling fast. But she enjoyed the sense of danger, scrambling up in the half-light smelling the sweet scents of herbs and plants by the path. All her senses were alert and her body felt strong and capable.

She reached the top a fraction later than Tony, her lungs heaving, and stopped beside him panting and laughing.

'Oh, thank God!' she gasped. 'I thought I was going to get caught by bandits down there and never make it to the top!'

Tony laughed, leaning over to get his breath back. She could see the sheen on his honey-coloured hair in the last of the light.

There was something about the scented warmth of the air, the loneliness of the place, that allowed feelings to come to the surface. Rose knew she was not in love with Tony. She had not come out of herself as far as that yet. But she was aware from the evening they went to Naples together, as well as from many small acts of kindness and affection, that Tony cared for her. And she felt that, given time, she could love him. His very reticence had broken through her fear and mistrust. But there was never more from him. Never a touch, any other sign, except for his quivering emotion when she had disappeared in Naples. What was it? Was he afraid of her? She felt very strongly that she needed to understand.

Tony straightened up and saw her dark eyes watching him. It was a look he had never seen on her face before. Whether serious or full of fun, he knew that Rose had strong defences, usually showed you herself only at one remove from what she was feeling. Now her expression was disarmingly naked. Even in the half-light he could read bewilderment, sadness and a kind of hunger. It was a moment he had feared would come.

'Shall we go up on top?' he asked softly. A short flight of steps led up to the flat top of the rock, which gave a marvellous view of the palace, the town and over to Naples and Vesuvius. Tony let her climb up first and they stood together in the light breeze looking at the gleaming ribbon of water below, and the sky still rimmed with light. Over the volcano the light deepened to a pink incandescence.

The pressure for one of them to speak increased every moment. Rose struggled to find words that would not sound complaining or critical.

'Tony, can I ask you something?'

'Of course.' He didn't turn to look at her. 'I think I can guess.'

'Can you?' This confused her even further. 'I just feel muddled up about ... well, how to feel about you. I feel a lot for you, as a friend, but—' She broke off, feeling that each of her words sounded more clumsy and unfortunate than the last. 'When we're together we're not like – well, like a man and a woman can be. Oh dear. I can't say this properly. I'm sorry. You must think I'm ever so forward.'

'You mean I don't hold you or try to kiss you?'

'Well I don't mean you should,' Rose said hastily. 'I mean I don't want ... mostly I don't want men touching me.' She could feel her cheeks burning with shame and embarrassment in talking like this, but she knew Tony well enough to be certain she could confide in him.

'Because you're supposed to be engaged?'

'No. Not really. That's what I tell people. I mean I *am* – supposed to be. But it's not that.'

Taking a deep breath she told him quickly about Mr Lazenby and Joseph. When she'd finished she saw he had turned and was watching her, his sensitive face full of emotion.

'My poor Rose.' He stepped close to her and took one of her hands in his and stroked it. His hand was very warm and reassuring and surprisingly soft.

'You really pick your men,' he said, and she was startled by what sounded like anger in his voice.

'What's the matter?' she asked, her own voice turning high and tearful. 'I just don't understand you.' She felt tears running down her cheeks. 'I don't know how to feel about you!'

And then to her distress she realized that he too was weeping.

'Tony,' she cried. 'What is it?' She moved forward to comfort him. To her surprise he accepted, and for the first time they held each other. She felt his slight body in her arms, smelt the familiar salty smell of him, and she could feel his heart beating against her.

'Please tell me what's the matter.'

'I'm afraid to.'

He was silent again and she reached up and stroked his face with her hand. He removed her arms until he had hold of her hand again and wiped his eyes. He led her to the low parapet which ringed the rock and they sat down, leaning against it.

'Rose – I want you to know that I feel a great deal for you. Much more than I ever believed I could—' He broke off abruptly. 'You're a marvellous person, so bright, so full of life. I can't express very well what you mean to me. But I can't . . .' He stopped again as if he simply could not bring the words out of him.

'You can't love me?'

247

'I do love you. That's what I'm trying to say.' His voice grew louder with frustration. 'But not ... You have to understand. I can't love women. Not like a man is supposed to love a woman.'

He loosed her hand and lowered his head nearer his bent-up knees as if to shelter from a blow.

'You mean ... ?'

'I mean that, sexually, I love other men. Only men.' He spoke very deliberately and slowly. 'Ever since I can remember, Rose.' He paused. 'I'm sorry.'

She was silent. Eventually he looked up, interpreting her silence as disgust or disapproval.

'You won't tell anyone. Please?' She shook her head. 'Rose, I'm so sorry if you feel I've been deceiving you. I do love you, in a way which is very important. But I can't make love to you. It's not in my nature.'

'It's all right.' She looked up at him and he saw how powerful her gaze was even in the poor light. 'I'm just trying to think about it. It's the first time I've ever known anyone ...'

'Homosexual?'

'Yes.' She could feel herself, like a sea anemone that had begun to reach out slowly and tentatively towards love, touched by something unexpected and shrinking back. But her thoughts were more objective. Those very occasional knowing looks when she was young, hushed talk of 'queers'. How different it was when it was real. When it was someone you ... liked.

'I'm glad you told me. I wanted to understand, and now I do. You got me confused, and the reason I liked you to start with was that you left me alone – you know – like that. But now I know where we stand I won't do anything stupid. We can be friends without spoiling it, can't we?'

Tony watched her. 'I don't disgust you?'

Rose considered this for a moment.

'The father of my son disgusted me. What he did to me had nothing to do with love or kindness or anything good. I know you better than that. No – you don't disgust me.'

The conversation stopped and started with patches of thoughtful silence.

'D'you have anyone. A bloke, I mean?' she asked after a while.

'I think perhaps, yes. It looks like it. You don't know him. He's an American. His name is Lewis.'

'And you care about him too?'

'I don't know him as well as you. But we have certain things in common.'

'Like both going for other blokes.' Rose cursed herself immediately for her sarcasm.

'You're right to be angry.'

'I'm not angry. I'm sorry. Anyway . . .' She hesitated. 'I've just thought. You can help me out.'

'Me? Of course. How?'

Suddenly excited, she confided to him her discovery of Il Rifugio. 'It's perfect,' she said. 'If you don't want people to know about you and Lewis, you can carry on letting them think you're going about with me. If you're my chaperone to Naples on leave weekends, you can meet Lewis and that way I'll get left alone as well and I can go and help with these kids!'

Tony burst out laughing in pure astonishment. 'My God, Rose Lucas, you're one of the most extraordinary people I've ever met! You mean to say you've been wandering about in the slums of Naples dressed up as an Italian because you've fallen in love with an orphanage?'

She nodded happily. 'That's where I was, that night

I went off. I'm sorry I didn't tell you before, but it all seemed like a dream at the time. And I hadn't realized I was going to get so involved. But you should see the kids, Tony. They're poor little mites who've been left on the streets by their families. Some of their moms and dads are dead, but not all. Some of them were even sold into prostitution. I want to find ways of getting more food for them. We've got more than enough here and there must be some way . . .'

'So that's what that was all about. Now wait a minute. Just wait a minute. Are you talking about diverting army supplies? Because if you are, you could get yourself into one hell of a lot of trouble.'

Rose looked down at the ground, away from him. 'I don't know what I'm talking about really. I haven't thought it through enough. But it's not right that they're hungry and that Margherita and Francesco have such a struggle. It's not the kids' fault there's a war.' She was becoming quite emotional, trying to convince him.

Tony sighed. 'You're right, of course. Relative morals, I suppose. You can count on me to help – I think. And yes, the Naples weekends are a grand idea.' He touched her shoulder gently. 'You must believe that I wish with all my heart I could marry you, Rose, if things were different.'

She reached up and stroked the hand on her shoulder and they sat in comfortable silence.

As they did so they became aware of a strange sound, a distant roaring as if a massive beast was roaming somewhere in the sky behind them.

'What the hell . . . ?' Rose said.

Tony was on his feet instantly, looking back towards Naples. 'Good Lord!' he cried. 'Look! She's going up!'

The sky round the volcano had turned blood red, and from the top of the crater they could see what looked like great clumps of fire being hurled into the air, with giant orange sparks, as Vesuvius spat fury and venom out into the night sky. From lower down the sides trickled bright streams of lava, bleeding down the volcano's flanks from points like giant stab wounds.

There was nothing they could do except stand watching in petrified silence. A massive belly of cloud had gathered over the volcano, the eruption a low, growling roar beneath it. Every now and then they heard a louder sound, like a great hoarse voice, and a pillar of fire shot up from inside the cone, hurling itself up towards the cloud and the terrible sky.

They watched for a long time as the night air around them grew colder. It reminded Rose of the nights of the Birmingham blitz: such complete helplessness when faced with destruction all around.

'Will Naples be all right?' she asked, and Tony knew immediately whom she was most afraid for.

'It's quite a way round the bay, so it should be. But God help all those towns and villages underneath it.'

After a while he said, 'It's enough to make you want to pray, isn't it?'

And Rose nodded. Prayer did not come naturally to her, but she was praying with her whole heart tonight.

Twenty-One

By the time she returned to Il Rifugio in April – this time for a whole precious weekend – the force of the eruption had abated. While it was going at full strength, the sky had stayed grey and soupy for days, and soft grey ash fell to a depth of at least half an inch for miles around. Walking through the streets of Naples, Rose saw that even the graffiti of the multitude of political parties, and the large black letters proclaiming 'DUCE! DUCE' (now often crossed out with blacker paint), were dusted over by a layer of ash which clung to the crevices in the walls.

Naples, now convalescing from its days and nights of fear and prayer, had been spared the full destruction of the volcano. Many of the population were convinced this was due to the beneficence of their patron San Gennaro, who had watched over them for fourteen centuries since his martyrdom in Pozzuoli, just along the coast. His protection had, however, been of no help whatever to the inhabitants of the towns and villages strung along the fringe of coast between Vesuvius and the sea, many of which had been engulfed once more by the lava.

Francesco opened the door to her, and she saw at once the strain and exhaustion plain in every line of his face.

'Are you all right?' she asked anxiously. 'You look terrible.'

252

'It has been a terrible time.'

Rose searched around with her eyes. 'Where's Margherita?'

Francesco pulled one of his hands through his unruly curls. 'She's gone to visit her father. He had found a place to stay. He was away from home when the eruption started. Her mother and sister – both gone.' He made a wiping motion with his right hand, his face full of pain and bewilderment. 'The house was destroyed.'

'You're saying that . . . ?'

'Now she has only her father and one sister. She has two older brothers who are in the army.'

In English, Rose said, 'My God. How terrible.'

She wanted to comfort Francesco somehow, but felt shy of him. After all she barely knew him. If Margherita herself had been there it might have come more naturally.

They were still standing in the gloom of the hall, Rose holding her two parcels of rations. From the big room, where Magdalena and Assunta were keeping the children occupied, came the sound of singing.

Francesco seemed to rouse himself. 'There is something else I need to tell you. Another person has come to live here. A friend of ours called Paulo Falcone. We were at the university together. He is a bit older because he was a medical student. He arrived two days ago from Rome – God knows how, across the lines. He says he has been with a group in the resistance, but he will not talk to me any more about it. Perhaps if Margherita were here . . .' His expression seemed to sink further into tiredness and pain. 'I am telling you to warn you that he is not easy to be with at the moment.' He pointed to the small room to the left of the big room, where they stored and prepared food for the community. 'He is sleeping in there now, but we can go in. He won't wake.'

Francesco suddenly reached out and touched her hand in an unexpected gesture of gratitude. 'I'm glad that you have come, Rosa.'

She smiled sadly at him, picking up the parcels which she had put down while he was speaking. 'I hope I can relieve you all a little. You must be so tired.'

They carried the food parcels to the storeroom. Rose felt how small and inadequate they were. How could she do better?

She could hear the man's deep breathing from where he lay in shadow under the window on two poor straw mattresses laid end to end. He was lying very straight as if sleep were a duty rather than a relief. She went and looked down at him, intrigued to encounter another of their educated friends. The young man was sleeping with a slight frown on his face. He looked well built, though thin, but his naturally rounded jawline had prevented his face from turning gaunt. The closed eyes were fringed by long dark lashes, and his black wavy hair had grown untidily down to his shoulders. The lower part of his face was shadowed by several days of stubble. It was hard to picture him as a doctor, reassuring and authoritative, perhaps smartly dressed. He lay vulnerable as a child battered by the hurts of the day before. Rose surprised herself with an impulse to reach down and stroke his brow, to smooth the perturbed expression off his face, but she held back.

'Come,' Francesco whispered, surprised by her attention to the stranger. 'Let's go.'

She went and joined Magdalena and Assunta, who greeted her with delighted though tired smiles. On seeing her arrive, one of the boys, a three-year-old waif called Emilio, ran to Rose crying, '*Bacio! Bacio!*'

She knelt down to take his small form in her arms, giving him the kiss he wanted so badly. She sat with him on one knee, and on the other a younger girl who sidled up to her shyly. She pressed her face against Emilio's, and against the plumper cheeks of the little girl, enjoying the feel of cuddling children again. Emilio turned and put his skinny arms round her neck.

Magdalena finished off the session by saying the Angelus with the children, and then it was time to prepare something to eat.

'Let me help tonight,' Rose offered. 'You should all sleep. I do little enough here. I'll sit up to watch the children.' They took it in turns to perform this vigil, partly to comfort any children who woke up disturbed in the night, and also to make quite sure no one else found their way into the building.

Magdalena nodded in response to Rose. 'It is good that *il dottore* Falcone has come,' she said. 'He can help us with Maria Grazia. That child needs every help we can give her.'

It was not until they were settling the children down for the night that the doctor woke up. He stumbled out from the small room carrying a cup of water in one hand, his expression entirely bewildered, as if he had woken to find himself in another country. The eyes which looked round at them were large, dark, fringed by the long lashes Rose had noticed as he slept. She saw his gaze settle curiously on her and linger there for a moment.

'So Falcone – you feel better?' Francesco called to him.

Falcone nodded absently. Now he was standing, Rose could see he was a powerfully built man, though, like almost all Neapolitans she had seen, too thin for his build. His dark grey trousers and green shirt were dirty and extremely worn. The shirt had only two or three buttons remaining near the bottom, so that it fell open in a V, showing the dark, curly hair of his chest. He stood watching them all from the doorway as they settled the children, covering them with a strange array of old curtains, army blankets, tablecloths – anything they had managed to get hold of.

Some of them wanted comforting before they could sleep, and when they were all settled Assunta stayed in the room for a while, sitting in a ring of candlelight with her rosary beads held between her fingers.

The others went quietly into the room opposite the kitchen storeroom, where there was a thin rug on the floor and an assortment of old chairs.

'Rosa has brought some English tea,' Francesco announced, perking up for a moment. 'The life-blood of the British army.'

'I'd better make it then, hadn't I?' she laughed. 'Goodness knows what you might do to it!'

As she stood in the dim light of the kitchen, waiting for the flame from the gas cylinder to heat the water, she heard knocking on the outside door. She realized Francesco was letting Enrico in and she felt immediately uneasy. He sloped in behind her, laying a number of wrapped loaves of bread on the table. She jumped slightly when she turned and found him watching her, his pointed features accentuated by the candlelight.

'Good evening,' she said coolly.

Enrico nodded, still staring hard at her, and for a

moment she thought he was about to speak. But he turned and went out of the room again.

The place seemed strange and empty without Margherita. Rose sat drinking the black tea with the strange assortment of people who were left: Magdalena and Francesco both seemed stunned by exhaustion, Enrico, whose eyes carefully watched everyone else, and the troubled figure of Falcone, who despite Francesco's attempts to rouse him was often wrapped in his own thoughts.

'Should I take Assunta some tea?' Rose asked.

'No, leave her. She is saying her rosary every night. For the liquefaction,' Magdalena said, yawning, her eyes straining to keep open behind her spectacles.

'The what?'

Francesco explained. 'It is a miracle which shows us that there will be good fortune for our city. The blood of San Gennaro which is kept in a phial in the Duomo liquifies. Assunta is very worried that too many bad things are happening. The war, the eruption. She's frightened that there will be no liquefaction this May, so she's saying a special rosary every evening.'

Rose nodded solemnly, glad that she had managed to bite back the words, 'Thank God for that – I thought it might be something really important.'

After a moment Magdalena said, 'What are we going to do about Maria Grazia? Margherita thinks she should be taken to the cemetery before the child is born and I think she is right. She should be able to see her mother's grave. Her mind has nothing to settle on.'

'But when?' Francesco asked wearily. 'We have so little time and transport is impossible. It would take us all day to walk up there. I don't even know when Margherita is going to come back.'

At the thought of Margherita they fell silent again, so Rose took her opportunity. 'I've been thinking,' she started timidly, gathering courage when she saw they were all paying attention. 'I don't come here very often, and when I do I bring very little with me. You asked me for help, and I think I have disappointed you. I should be able to do more. After all, I'm a driver. I could transport almost anything, except I don't know how to get hold of it. I can't think who to ask.'

Francesco nodded. 'It's always a question of making the right connections.'

Suddenly, to everyone's amazement, a voice said, 'Why the bleeding hell didn't you say you was a driver before?'

Everyone looked round for the owner of this English voice. Enrico.

'If you've got a truck,' he went on, addressing Rose, 'then that's all I need. I can get the rest of the gear. Blimey – I've been trying to get hold of a driver who can shift the stuff free for months but no one'd cough.'

'What did he say?' Magdalena pulled on Rose's sleeve impatiently. 'He's English too? Who is he?'

Falcone and Francesco were both looking astonished. Especially when Rose burst out laughing.

'So that's why you've been giving me those queer looks every time I've seen you! You're a deserter, aren't you? D'you think I was going to blow the whistle on you or something?' She laughed again. 'We all thought you had a screw loose!' The others watched, totally bemused. 'Enrico, my foot,' she said. 'What's your real name then – Fred?'

'No. Henry,' he said, looking rather sheepish. 'I'm from Bromley. Couldn't stick the army. When they moved on through here I just stayed. There's quite a few of us in Naples you know. Scared the arse off me – all them mines every time you moved a foot forward. I can fight a better war helping to feed these kids than anything I could ever do with that lot. But I couldn't work you out at first. I had to size you up and make sure you wasn't trouble.'

'So – come on, then. How d'you get hold of the food?'

'Easy. The depot. When they've taken the stuff in from the docks it all goes into the warehouse. I've got a couple of mates there. They can make a packet selling the stuff, but they'll give me the odd load free – in a good cause.' Henry winked at her. 'Anyhow, I've managed to get hold of a bit of petrol, which makes a good price, so they don't do it all out of love. Problem is, I've never had proper transport. If you can get yourself over here a night or two in the month, we can get these kids fed up like turkey cocks.'

'Excuse me.' Magdalena gripped Rose's arm, no longer able to contain herself. 'Please – what is he saying?'

Rose explained. 'Don't you speak Italian?' she asked Henry.

'Nope. But I can tell what they're going on about as long as it ain't too involved.'

Rose could feel her breathing going shallow from excitement and anxiety. In Italian she asked, 'D'you think it's right that I take my truck and steal for you from the army?'

There was silence for a moment, and then Francesco said, 'Of course. Already we eat their food, their bread. You know, even the fish in the city's aquarium have been eaten by now. What choice do we have?'

Suddenly they were all startled by Falcone's voice,

low, but full of conviction. 'We have to do what is good for the children,' he said. 'What use are the laws of peace during a war? Our Lord tells us to feed the hungry, so that is what we must do, even if we have to take a little from the rich.'

'You sound like another Lupo,' Francesco teased, referring to the Robin Hood figure of Domenico Lupo who travelled in the south with a small gang of bandits, raiding the army and the black market to feed the poor of his people. 'You'll have us holding up trains next.'

Falcone said nothing, but sat staring at the ground between his knees.

Henry pressed Rose further. 'We'll have to be on the spot about times and meeting places. No hanging about. It's a risky business. So – d'you think you're up to it?'

Rose took in a deep, fearful breath. 'I'll have to find a way, won't I?' she said.

Twenty-Two

It was a night Rose would remember all her life. The sisters and Francesco gratefully accepted the chance of rest and soon all of them were fast asleep. She sat up watching the children with Falcone.

At first it looked like being a long, hard night. Rose was very unsure of this silent, scruffy man who sat leaning against one side of the doorframe smoking cheap cigarettes. For a while she busied herself by walking round the room with a candle to check on each of the sleeping children. As she turned at the far end of the long room and her huge shadow leapt up the wall behind her, she realized that he was watching her. When their eyes met he moved his solemn gaze to the wall opposite him.

When she had exhausted all the activity she could think of, Rose offered to make tea. She sat tensely on the floor at the other side of the door, drinking the watery brew, unsure whether to try to talk to him.

Eventually she said, 'You are an old friend of Francesco and Margherita?'

He pulled the cigarette out from between his lips and said, not ungraciously, 'Yes. We studied together.' Then he added, 'That seems a very long time ago.'

After another silence he said, 'You are English. You do not look English. Why are you here?'

'I wanted to help.'

Suddenly he turned his whole head to examine her fully. Shyly, she turned also and looked into his large brown eyes with a hint of challenge in her own. But in his she read sorrow and vulnerability. Francesco had hinted that Falcone was holding back a weight of feeling that he could not communicate and in that moment she knew it was so. That exchange of glances between them after such brief conversation seemed to carry an intimacy which went a great deal further than their words.

But they could not find any more to say, and Rose began to resign herself to the fact that the rest of the night would be like this.

After about half an hour they heard the sound of planes overhead, followed by a number of bangs. Rose saw Falcone jump, shocked out of his thoughts. Several of the children began to cry. Glad of some diversion to keep her mind off the bombing, Rose went round whispering comforting words to the little ones who, only half awake, were only too happy to sink back into sleep again.

There was another wave of explosions from outside, evidently from the port, as the Germans sought out Allied supply ships. As she sat holding her breath it brought back vividly to Rose the night she had spent watching over her mother while the blitz raged outside.

She heard another shrill voice calling 'Rosa! Rosa!' It was Emilio. She went to sit beside him. To lull him to sleep she sang 'Golden Slumbers' in English because she didn't know any lullabies in Italian.

There was one more wave of bombing and then it seemed to go quiet. A brief raid, thank heaven. Rose stayed by Emilio, humming to him and rocking her slender body in time with the tune until she began to feel quite sleepy herself and closed her eyes.

A shadow moved in front of the candle. When she opened her eyes, Falcone was squatting down opposite her looking at Emilio. Curious, she watched him. As he gazed into the child's face she saw in his expression an extraordinary sympathy and tenderness. Emilio, barely awake, smiled up at both of them and she saw Falcone smile for the first time, lighting up the dark eyes with a warm, mischievous light. Emotions she could barely identify stirred in her.

He said softly to her, 'You must love children very much. You could be resting in comfort away from all this.'

As she looked up at him she too felt trusting as a child, and spoke without hesitation. 'My own little son died when he was three weeks old. I never saw him at this age. If he was alive now he would be seven this year.'

Falcone looked a little puzzled. 'You have a husband?'

She shook her head. 'I was raped. By the man who employed me.'

How strange that she should make this confession to this stranger whom she had sat with for only a couple of hours. That she should feel able to trust him as much as anyone in her life before.

Falcone said sadly, 'That is a terrible thing. And to suffer the death of your child as well. Now I understand why you long to be with children.'

'I don't usually tell people,' she said. 'I felt you wouldn't judge me.'

He let out a sharp rush of breath as if she had said something outrageous. 'I am not fit to judge anyone.'

Suddenly he sat down facing her and scanned her face. 'You do not look English,' he said again. 'Perhaps your face does not look quite Italian, but your colouring, the clothes – one could almost think ... You are very beautiful.'

Rose smiled, looking away from him to deflect the compliment. 'Your name – does it mean, like the bird? Is it the same?' she asked.

'Yes, *falcone*, the bird with the sharp, vicious beak. I hoped that I wasn't like this bird but I'm not sure what my nature is any more.' His face took on the sad, troubled expression it had worn for most of the evening.

'Why are you here?' she asked gently.

He replied slowly, as if he had not spoken the words before but had been thinking for a long time how to say them. 'I'm here to wait for the end of the war. Until it's finished I have to be like someone without a real home. A wandering soul.' Seeing Rose frown at this rather abstract notion he went on, 'As soon as the war's over I shall enter the seminary of San Domenico Maggiore. I'm going to be a priest.'

'A priest?' Rose cried, then lowered her voice again, looking round to see if she had disturbed any of the children. 'But you can't do that. You're a doctor.'

'I was a doctor.' His voice was bitter. 'Actually I only practised for a short time after I qualified. I don't have a lot of experience.'

'But being a doctor is one of the most important things you could do,' Rose argued. 'Honestly, you people with an education don't know you're born. All that work to become a doctor and you want to give it up and be a priest? You must be mad.'

Falcone didn't rise to her anger. 'You didn't have an education?'

'Not much, no. It was what I wanted, badly. To be a teacher. But ...' She shrugged. 'Dreams.'

'I would've thought you were educated. You're a very intelligent woman. And you speak my language well.'

'Thanks.'

'You're right though. It's a great privilege to have an education. But you see, to be a doctor – a doctor is supposed to have reverence for life, to cherish and preserve life.' Falcone cupped his hands as if holding up a large and delicate egg shell. 'And I'm tainted. This war has given me a feeling of guilt, of loathing. Whatever I try to do for the best, I'm pursued by death, by destruction. You see?'

He saw that Rose's eyes were full of sympathy and interest. He knew she would not condemn him, that he could lay on her the weight that was pulling his mind down, sometimes it seemed, towards madness.

Rose indicated that they should move back to the door so as not to disturb the children. She fetched them each half a cup of water, and they sat each side of the door again, surrounded by their shadows and the sleeping children.

'When Italy became involved in the war I was still finishing my studies,' he began. 'I felt it right to stay because I was doing something dedicated to giving life instead of working to destroy it.'

'Didn't you have to join up?' Rose asked. She had wondered the same thing about Francesco.

Falcone smiled wryly. 'The Italian army does not even have enough socks to go round. We steal them from the dead when they have finished with them. No – not everyone joined the army.

'When I finished it was 1941. By then we were occupied by Germany. Things were very hard. Naples was growing hungrier by the day. I went home to my family in Cellina, north of Caivano and Acerra, not all that far from Caserta. My father was the town's doctor. Perhaps I would've simply taken over his role. Who knows? For about eighteen months I helped him in the practice. It wasn't difficult work. I enjoyed it, using the skills I had been trained in. Even under occupation a job like that brings a lot of satisfaction.

'Then everything changed. It was December forty-two. I had been out on a late call and I was still in bed. That was why my father was the one to open the door. The body of a German soldier had been found in a side street off the main square. He'd been stabbed in the night and bled to death there. Naturally no one would admit to such a crime. When the Germans found out they had to have their revenge. To teach us Italians a lesson. They are a people who carry out vengeance with mathematical precision. For each German, the life of ten Italians. The ten most prominent men in the town. The mayor, Signor Pacelli, the postmaster – and of course they came to the house of the doctor. They took my father.

'The same morning, they made them stand—' Falcone made a slow pointing gesture with his finger. 'A line of them against the wall of the post office. They made sure there was a big crowd to watch the spectacle. They didn't even blindfold them. I stood there in the piazza as they shot my father. One moment he stood, looking so old suddenly, so frail. He was looking for me, I could tell. But his eyes did not find me among the crowd before the guns went off. And then they were all on the ground. The wall of the post office is broken open with holes. We were allowed to take them for burial.'

Falcone paused for a moment to light another cigarette. Rose sat very still, not wanting to interrupt now that his story had begun to flow out of him.

'For a time I stayed at home alone. My mother died when I was a small boy, and my sisters and brother are all married and live elsewhere. I tried to keep the practice going, and for some time I succeeded. But all the time I was corrupted inside by anger and guilt. If it had been me who opened the door that morning my father wouldn't have died. It would have been me. For the first time in my life I experienced the power of real hatred. I'd felt it touch me when our country was invaded. I'd known disgust and loathing against the Fascists. But nothing which approached this bitter need for action, as if I was possessed. It lay inside my intestines like a poisonous snake. I wanted to join the resistance, to fight back, but there was no organized resistance in the south. Nothing that I could find.

'It was when they threw out Mussolini in July last year. The army was taken over by General Badoglio. All through the winter before there had been signs that Fascism was collapsing. There were even strikes, up in the north – Milano, FIAT at Torino, many other factories. This was unheard of under Mussolini – people like that speaking with their own voice. Such signs gave me hope that it was possible to achieve changes by direct, personal action. So I left Cellina and went to Rome.

'At first I suppose I was filled with an enormous kind of joy, of euphoria at being able to join the resistance at last. I made contact with the Gappisti – GAP is Gruppi di Azione Patriottica. The groups work in many cities to subvert German and Fascist operations. They – we – planted bombs. We attacked columns of soldiers on the move. Assassinated prominent German officers. We attacked the prison, Regina Coeli, the opera house when it was full of German soldiers . . . One of the first actions I was involved in was to plant a bomb in a petrol depot for German trucks. Everything went up – the drums on the trucks, the storage depot itself. What a feeling that was! We destroyed more than two thousand gallons of their gasoline that afternoon.

'The life we lived was very hard. For those of us without many contacts there was nowhere to sleep except in stone cellars with their cold, hard floors. Often we shared them with prisoners who were trying to escape, English, Canadians, Poles. And we became sick living like this. But the extraordinary thing was that the atmosphere among the people was such as I had never met before. The unity of feeling against the Germans. I was brought up in my faith to believe that people are unified by the love of God. But I discovered there how strongly people are brought together by hatred.

'I lived this life of destruction for eight months. Then, only a few weeks ago, I was ordered to be involved in an ambush against a column of German forces. They weren't just an arbitrary collection of soldiers. We'd heard they were training on the streets of Rome specifically to search out and destroy partisan cells both in and around the city. Our attack was to show that we were not prepared to be intimidated. It was really just a statement, of course. Already they had executed more than half the partisans in Rome.

'The plan was to ambush the column as they passed down the Via Rasella. It's a narrow street with a tunnel at the end. It would be hard for them to turn back or escape. I wasn't one of the key operators. There were members of GAP with much greater nerve and skill. But I was involved as surely as one brick holds up the others in a wall. My job was to watch the column approaching along the route and to signal to Pietro, the next in the chain along the way. In the Via Rasella, one of our women was waiting to give the signal to a man called Bentivegna who was disguised as a rubbish collector. His cart was loaded with explosives. Others were ready to throw mortar bombs.

'We all waited. How can I tell you how it felt that day? It was as if my body was pumped full of electricity. One touch and I would explode. The Germans were over an hour late. We were wondering whether to give up the attempt, all terrified that the police would search Bentivegna's cart. Then they came at last, marching perfectly – beautifully, though it is horrible to say it – the way German soldiers do. The attack went according to plan. The mortar bombs went off, Bentivegna lit the fuse, and we all began to run towards the Via Nazionale.'

Falcone stopped talking for a few seconds. Rose looked at him and saw him take several deep breaths.

'The whole place was in chaos. The bombs blew thirty-three of them to pieces and wounded a great many others. The Germans were there within minutes and we heard gunfire in the streets. While we were escaping, scuttling like rats to our cellars where we hid, the SS were rounding up civilians, door to door, dragging out anyone they could find and loading them on to their trucks.

'The mathematics was the same. That night they took at least three hundred and thirty people – from the gaols, ones they had pulled out of their homes – almost anyone to make up the numbers. Ten Romans for every German soldier.'

His breathing became shallow as he talked, and he was having difficulty taking the air in.

'The orders came direct from the Führer. They drove

them to the catacombs, the Ardeatine caves. You must have heard of them. The German soldiers who took them had been drinking. They were blind with drink, taking it like an anaesthetic. Blind enough to lead the prisoners inside, five at a time. They had lit torches so that the shadows shuddered in the caves. Then they made the people kneel and shot them in the back of the neck. It went on until dawn. The last ones had to climb over the dead to be shot. Then they sealed up the cave and blew it up inside.'

Falcone's shoulders were heaving so violently that Rose thought he might vomit. His strong frame was shaking with the horror of those memories. Through chattering teeth he said, 'It was inaccurate. The German commander was very angry. They shot five too many.'

Rose fetched a blanket and wrapped it around his shoulders. He trembled under it as if he had a fever. She handed him some water, and when his hands were shaking too much to take the cup from her, she raised it to his lips herself, so moved she could not speak.

When he was a little calmer he said, 'I haven't talked about it before. It's made it come alive again.'

'Could you not tell Francesco?'

Falcone shook his head. 'Francesco was part of my life when I was a different person. I did not know what destruction I was capable of. I can't bring myself to speak of it to him, or Margherita, though she is so kind, so well-meaning. Although they work in this place and it's hard, their lives have been smooth until now. They haven't even known the suffering that you've known. I find I can talk to you.'

'I think Margherita is suffering now.'

'Of course,' Falcone corrected himself.

Their eyes met again with the peculiar tenderness

which communicated itself between them, the more so after their shared confidences.

'I knew I should have to tell someone, or such memories would corrupt me even more.'

Though it was the small hours of the morning they continued to talk for the rest of the night. When Falcone had recovered he seemed eager to listen. In those hours Rose talked more than she had ever done, disclosed more about herself than she ever had to anyone in her life. She found herself telling him about her family, about Diana, about Lazenby's, and finally about Alfie. And Falcone talked more about his father, of his rather distant respect for him, and of the little he could remember of his mother. He tried to explain his motives for entering the priesthood, a point on which they could not even begin to agree.

'To be a priest is the highest service you can give to God,' he told her. 'If you were a Catholic you would understand.'

'Just because I'm not a Catholic doesn't mean I'm stupid,' Rose replied heatedly. 'I just can't see the good of you wasting all you've learned by going off and saying prayers all day.'

'I feel strongly that my life has become corrupted. As a priest I can dedicate my life to the truth. To repentance. Perhaps even to holiness.'

'But why not as a doctor?'

'This is my calling now,' he told her. 'I feel sure of it.'

After they had talked and argued through the night, the light gradually seeped over the city as dawn broke. They saw daylight round the edges of the shutters, and after a time, Magdalena appeared looking surprisingly fresh and rested.

'I will sit until they wake,' she said. 'You go and sleep.'

Falcone thanked her. 'But first I want to go out and see what damage they did last night.' He looked at Rose. 'Do you want to come?'

Early morning light washed over the weary, battered city. Already, as they set out through the smoky air towards the sea, people were coming in the opposite direction carrying pails of shellfish which they could try to sell for a few lire. Voices echoed through the streets and children squatted to relieve themselves among the refuse. They crossed the Via Speranzella and headed for the square. One of the narrow side streets behind the Via Toledo was completely blocked by rubble where buildings had collapsed, making it impossible to pass or even see much light along it. People were digging frantically among the rubble looking for loved ones. Somewhere a dog was howling.

The dead were already being laid in rows away from the rubble, to be loaded on to carts. Among them were several children, and into their cold arms the survivors had thrust huge, pink plastic dolls, their gaudy splendour probably far superior to any toy the children had possessed when alive.

Falcone gently steered Rose by the elbow back in the direction of Il Rifugio. 'It was a mistake to come,' he said. 'There's only so much any of us can do, and the authorities are doing their work. We should sleep.'

'I don't want to sleep,' Rose protested. 'I haven't come here to sleep.'

'Sleep!' Falcone commanded as they climbed the stairs. 'We don't want any martyrs here. You must sleep!'

Twenty-Three

'Who d'you think you are, Gracie Fields?' Madge demanded, astonished.

Rose had walked into the dormitory singing. All the ATS girls were getting ready for an Easter dance to be held in the ballroom at the palace. The contrast of all this colourful gaiety with the doleful Italian Holy Week was striking.

'She's in lo-ove!' Willy sang as she rubbed cream into her already perfect skin. 'I never thought I'd see you looking this half soaked over a man, Rose!'

'That Tony's obviously doing something for you that no one else can,' Madge teased.

Gwen, looking up from flattening out the skirt of her floral dress, said with a bright smile, 'Are you two really getting serious? I'm so happy for you. I've never felt so good in my life as I have since I met Bill. It's marvellous, isn't it?'

Rose just smiled and unfastened her uniform belt.

'Oh heavens, why are you always so flipping secretive?' Willy asked, frustrated.

Rose looked round at them all, bewildered. Was it so obvious? Had she changed so much that they could read it in her face? 'There's not a lot to say really,' she told her inquisitive room mates. 'Tony and I are just very good pals that's all.'

She knew she had changed. She also knew that she

was in love with Paulo Falcone. It was as if the feelings that Tony had stirred in her had found their completion in him. She did not think what this might mean for the future. Falcone determined to become a priest and herself engaged to Alfie. It made no sense. While the war, the agonizing crawl of the Allies towards Rome continued, it was not possible to contemplate the future. For the moment the newness of her experience of passion – of her excitement at the thought of seeing him, of the way they could confide in each other, and the expression in his eyes when they rested on her – these were enough. She was also rather enjoying the way Gwen, Madge and Willy were all jumping to the wrong conclusions.

The dance was already warming up when they arrived at the palace ballroom. Rose walked in beside Willy, who was wearing a shimmering emerald green strapless evening dress, her blond hair fastened immaculately on her head. Willy always looked very pure, freshly washed, every line neat and crisp. Beside her Rose felt dark and rather gypsyish. Willy was immediately surrounded and taken off by a circle of admirers.

Tony was waiting by the door for Rose. 'I say – what a stunning dress,' he told her. 'Is that one of the signora's creations?'

Rose nodded, smiling, and Tony was startled by the ecstatic glow of her face. The plain, close-fitting black dress she was wearing was not cut from expensive cloth, but Signora Mandetta had tailored it perfectly to the shape of Rose's curving figure. She had brushed her hair up into a simple knot at the back, and the smooth, unfussy style emphasized her large brown eyes and the fine shape of her face.

She danced with Tony for as much of the evening as she could, though other partners frequently tried to cut in and split them up. Rose's radiant looks and Tony's admiring, affectionate expression gave all the impression of two people who were strongly attracted and perhaps falling deeply in love.

The ballroom was huge, its beautiful floor inlaid with brown and white Carrara marble, the walls and ceiling encrusted with rich gold ornamentation, and warmly lit by lamps suspended from wall brackets and crystal chandeliers which hung on long chains from the ceiling. The centre of the ceiling was covered by a vast mural of what looked like courtiers, dressed in rich reds, blues and greens. At one end of the room was a low, red-carpeted dais on which a low gold throne upholstered in maroon cloth usually stood. Tonight it had been shifted to one side to make room for the band.

'You're not really the impoverished little child you've told me about, are you?' Tony teased Rose as they danced, holding each other lightly. 'You're really an Italian contessa in disguise.'

'Oh, if only!' Rose laughed. 'You don't reckon I'd be driving for the British army if I was do you?' Her eyes wore a mischievous expression. 'How's Lewis?'

'For heaven's sake keep your voice down. He's fine, thank you, since you ask. And we're all right too – together I mean – if that was your next question. We haven't fallen out or anything.'

'Good,' Rose replied, rather taken aback by his flustered response.

During the next dance she could not resist murmuring to him in a low voice, 'It's tonight, by the way.'

'What is?'

'The first drop.'

Tony nearly stopped dancing altogether on hearing this. 'You're going to Naples – tonight?'

She nodded serenely back at him, as if they were talking about a day's pleasure trip to Sorrento or Capri.

'I'm driving the midnight shift over. Then I'm off. Sorry to desert you.'

'But what about the truck? You'll be so late back.'

'Oh, I've got it OK'd – special delivery. They don't ask too many questions as long as it's back for work the next morning.'

'I'm coming with you,' he said heatedly. 'You can't go wandering round the countryside at night on your own. Let alone in Naples. God knows what might happen.'

'No you're not, Tony,' Rose said, still smiling, and rather enjoying the sense of danger inherent in discussing her plans while surrounded by all these people. 'Henry and his mates are meeting me. And then Francesco, or someone else from the refuge.'

To his puzzlement, Tony was sure he noticed a blush seep across her cheeks.

'They'll carry the stuff in. I've got to do this on my own.'

At half past eleven Rose said goodbye to him and slipped out of the ballroom to go and change. Twenty minutes later she had signed the truck out of the compound for the shift drive and was on her way to the palace again carrying a group of signallers and other administrators.

'Thanks Rose!' they called as they jumped out. 'Sorry you're missing the dance.'

She backed the truck up and then drove along the

sweeping curve at the front of the palace. Turning into Caserta, she took the road for Naples.

Henry had briefed her that afternoon a fortnight ago at Il Rifugio. He had given her details for 'the drop' as he insisted on calling it. He gave her a plan of where to find the supply depot in Naples.

As she sat in the cab her mind ran over the instructions again. From the yard behind the depot to the Via Toledo and as near as she could get to the Via degli Spagnoli. Her mind kept leaping forward to delivering what she had picked up. Who would come to help fetch it in? And what if the truck was raided while they were doing it? Who would come to help? Would Falcone come? Would she see him? She forced her thoughts back to concentrate on the driving.

She left the sleeping town of Caserta and headed out across country. It was a dark night with no moon, and the lights of the truck were half muffled by blackout shields throwing the light down on to the road. It was fairly warm, and she was not chilled by the air rushing past the open sides of the cab. She drew a couple of squares of chocolate out of her bag and sat chewing them. Cadbury's, all the way from Birmingham. It was so dark that the truck created its own little world of light and she could not see anything other than the road immediately ahead.

During the journey to Naples she passed only a couple of *contadini* who were trudging wearily along at the side of the road, another with a mule and cart and, at one terrifying moment, an army Jeep coming towards her. But as it rushed past she realized it was an American one. They pipped their horn briefly and sped on towards Caserta.

Approaching the outskirts of Naples, she pulled up for a moment to study the map again. Following the northern road from Caserta into the city she memorized the main junctions of the first part of the journey. It was not too complicated, though it was an area she was not familiar with. She looked at her watch. A little after one o'clock. She had got there even faster than she expected. So long as she didn't get lost she should arrive just about on time. Suddenly aware of all the darkness around her now she was not moving, she hurriedly pushed down on the clutch and pulled the long gear lever into first.

The road came into the city from the north-east, and she found herself muttering the directions out loud as she went along, very nervous now, every fibre of her body awake and alert. She could already smell the city, that fetid, urine-soaked smell. Supposing she got lost and let them all down?

'Turn into the Via don Bosco,' she told herself. And then she kept saying 'don Bosco, don Bosco' until she had found the turning and was looking out for the next one. She had to take a turn off to the left, which seemed an impossible task in a strange street with no lights. A church on the corner, Henry had said. Not a big one – need to keep your eyes peeled. Once along that road she should find herself eventually in the Piazza Nazionale. After driving in frustration down several streets which might or might not have been a continuation of the same one, she saw the square open out in front of her. It was already one-fifteen. A few more turnings and she would be there.

Finally, after ten minutes, she had located the depot, and drove quickly round into the street behind. At once the doors of the yard swung open and she reversed inside.

'Get your engine off quick,' Henry hissed at her as she slowly negotiated the space between the high gates. He flashed a torch into the cab. 'There could be trouble. We've had wire cutters out here. I've only just managed to get shot of them.'

'Wire cutters?' Rose turned off the engine as they swung the gates shut behind her, and in the darkness and sudden quiet she realized how hard her heart was pounding. She sat taking long, deep breaths.

'They nick the telephone lines to sell the copper wire. Anyway – you all right?' Henry suddenly appeared beside her with the torch. 'Any problems?'

'No, not really. It was a hell of a lot harder than I thought in this pitch black though.'

'Better get cracking then. Open up will you? Johnny's started bringing the stuff through. Best not to use the torch unless you really have to.'

By the time Rose had got out and unfastened the tarpaulin at the back, Henry was already on his way over with the first load from the gate at the back of the yard.

'What's in there?' Rose asked.

'Christ alone knows,' Henry said, grunting as he hauled it up into the truck. 'They'll have to sort that out when we get it there. Imagine Margherita's face when she sees this lot though, eh?'

For half an hour the two men ran back and forth with boxes, and threw in a few extras like blankets and mattresses for good measure. Rose found herself smiling at each new item that was brought across. How good all this would be for the children – for everyone at Il Rifugio!

When the floor of the truck was covered inside and part of it stacked up at the sides as well, Henry told her to close up again. He called Johnny to come and lock the gates behind them, and jumped into the cab beside her.

'Let's go then.'

As soon as they reached the arranged place on the Via Toledo, where they could not take the truck any further into the narrow streets, Francesco melted out of the shadows and came towards them.

'Any trouble?' he asked anxiously.

Rose and Henry reassured him.

'Now we've got to be quick,' Henry said. 'You stay with the truck, Rose, and we'll make sure there's always someone else here too. Take this.' She found a rifle being thrust into her hands. 'Chances are most people are asleep, but you never know. I'll take a few bits over and bring Falcone and Magdalena back with me. The others are staying with the kids.'

'How's Margherita?' Rose asked Francesco.

'Back with us at least. What else can we do but carry on?'

Rose nodded, and they stood in silence until the others came back. As they emerged from the complete darkness of the side street Rose could feel her heart beating faster. First she saw Magdalena. Falcone was behind her. When he came up close to the truck she saw that his hair was shorter, clipped round into his neck.

Dark though it was, she easily caught his smile and it lifted her, filling her with happiness. He looked slightly amused to see her wearing army trousers and tunic but with her hair still arranged as it had been for the dance.

'*Buona sera*,' he said softly, and she smiled back and said good evening to him and Magdalena.

After that, one of them always stayed while the other three carried the supplies back to the courtyard at Il Rifugio.

Only once, briefly, were she and Falcone left together.

'Are things going well for you?' Rose asked.

'Il Rifugio is a very peaceful place to live – even with all the children. You understand what I mean? It's one of the few places to make something good out of this war.'

'Yes, I suppose that's true. In England I felt I was doing something. Everywhere was under threat, you see. But when I came here, at first the army seemed so peaceful – such an unreal life. I suppose I'm fighting the war through the children.'

'You've done well tonight. It will make Margherita very happy.'

'We've done it together. I'm surprised. I thought there would be trouble of some kind.'

Falcone smiled in the darkness. 'So perhaps God is on our side after all. When are you coming next?'

'I have a weekend. May the sixth and seventh.'

'You know the sixth is the day of the liquefaction, at the Duomo?'

'That business Assunta was on about?'

'The blood of San Gennaro. Why don't you come with me? You'll learn a lot about Naples. Make sure you dress like an Italian.'

Rose agreed happily as the others came into view from across the road.

'Rosa?' Francesco approached her. 'Margherita sends her love and says thank you a thousand times for all this. But she has another request. We need help to take Maria Grazia to the cemetery. Since Margherita has lost her own mother she feels . . .' He didn't need to finish the sentence.

'Of course,' Rose said. 'But it might have to be at night.'

'OK, if it has to be. The child will be born in June, so we have some time.'

'We'll arrange it,' Rose said. 'I'd better go. See you all in a fortnight.'

Magdalena gave her a kiss before she climbed up into the cab, and Falcone took her hand for a second.

She started up the great growling engine, which sounded horribly loud in the street, and waved as she moved off.

'*Ciao!*' she called through the window. She could just see them all waving.

During the drive back along the deserted road she was fully awake and elated. It had worked! She had really managed to bring in something they needed. It made her feel more a part of the place. And he had been proud of her – that was what seemed to matter most of all. She shivered, half with cold, half with excitement.

Soon after four-thirty she was undressed and in bed.

Twenty-Four

As usual they were discussing and arguing almost from the moment they were together. Rose drove the truck through the darkened city on the way to the cemetery. Beside her in the cab, Falcone sat with Maria Grazia on his lap. And in the back was Henry, who had volunteered to stay and guard the truck.

'But how can you say that?' Rose demanded, her hands tight on the wheel. 'Which way now?'

'Left,' Falcone instructed. 'And it's not me that says it. The Church teaches that it's wrong ever to destroy life.'

Rose snorted. Sod the Church, she found herself thinking, but fortunately could not have said it in Italian even if she'd wanted to. Maria Grazia, about whom the conversation had started, sat holding a bunch of flowers and looking dreamily out at the shrouded streets. Occasionally she stared wonderingly up into Falcone's face. He had been looking after the health of all the children in Il Rifugio, and hers in particular. She seemed to have formed a strong bond with him.

'But what have they done to stop all this destruction?' Rose asked. 'What about Cellina? What about what happened in Rome?'

'You don't have to remind me,' Falcone said bitterly.

'OK, but apart from the war, how many women have you seen die from having too many children? You're a doctor. You know what happens. My mother's life was destroyed by having too many kids.'

'But it is against nature to prevent it. Against God.'

Rose was growing ever more exasperated. 'If your God says you should spend your life miserable, and exhausted and sick even if you can do something about it, then I don't think much of him.'

Falcone was silent.

'After all, it's not the effing Pope who has all the babies, is it?' Rose muttered in English. She often felt frustrated in Italian because she spoke more slowly and correctly. It didn't feel natural.

'What did you say?'

'I just mean, what have all these rules to do with real people?'

'It's an ideal we're supposed to try to live up to, however miserably we fail because we are human.'

'You're so sure about it, aren't you?'

Falcone gave her a surprised look. 'It's all I have left. I don't really know if I'm sure about anything any more.'

It had been the same when she went with him to the liquefaction. She had come to Naples with Tony that morning.

Summer had truly begun. The fields were full of ripening plants with chaotic vines twining along the edges. In Naples blinds were being pulled down over windows, and the street hawkers stood with newspapers draped over their heads.

'You sure you'll be all right?' Tony asked. He was going to meet Lewis.

'Perfectly, ta. Once I've changed out of this garb

anyway. Go on. Have a good weekend.' They kissed each other on the cheek.

By the time Rose and Falcone arrived at the cathedral in the muggy late afternoon, there was a tense, hysterical atmosphere and Rose noticed the Military Police were gathering at the edge of the crowd.

'Do I look Italian enough?' she murmured, half joking, to Falcone.

'Everyone will think we are husband and wife,' he replied mischievously and, to her embarrassment, Rose blushed.

'But you won't be allowed a wife if you're going to be a priest.'

'True. So you see, priests don't have everything their way.'

They stood among the garlic-fed, sweating throng, Rose sickened by the stench of unwashed bodies. A few yards away, an old woman collapsed and Rose watched, helpless, as she disappeared under the feet of the overwrought crowd.

'She'll be killed!' she shouted to Falcone, pointing to where the woman had fallen.

They tried to elbow their way towards her. They had nearly reached her, when two men lifted out her body, the face still and dry as parchment.

'*Morte! Morte!*' they yelled. Most of the faces did not even turn to look, their eyes fixed in rapt expectation on the Duomo.

'Perhaps she died as she fell,' Falcone said.

'This crowd's enough to finish anyone off,' Rose called back. She felt shaky at the way death was taken so lightly.

At the edge of the crowd someone had started smashing

shop windows and the police moved in, arms swimming through the bodies. Several people seemed to be in a trance-like state, rushing here and there where space permitted and shouting out in strange, high voices. Rose saw a crinkled old man shrieking in a shrill, unearthly tone. A yellowish froth spewed from his mouth.

She indicated to Falcone that she had something to say and he bent his ear close to her mouth. For a second she longed to kiss his dark, stubbly cheek.

'This is horrible!' she said. 'Why do people believe in this?'

'In what?'

'In this saint who's supposed to stop the lava flowing and keep everyone safe.' He hadn't saved them from the bombs after all, she thought. 'And all these great big churches. Why don't they use the money to help poor people?'

Falcone bent close to her and said, 'If there weren't any churches there'd be nowhere better for the poor to go. People need somewhere to shelter their dreams, their hopes. These people have been through so much. First the Germans, now the British and Americans. At least the Church is something constant for them to hold on to.'

'I can see that,' she yelled back. 'But why not give them something better to believe in than a little bottle of blood?'

'Sssh!' Falcone said urgently. 'Not here of all places. You'll get us lynched. This is the Neapolitan way. Just watch and see, OK?'

She heard the defensive note in his voice and was ashamed of sounding so critical. After all, she loved the place, but she also wanted to understand.

It was impossible to see any of the ritual. Only the earliest and most privileged had a place inside the Duomo. The crowds in the streets could do nothing but wait for the news.

Bursts of shouting could be heard near the doors of the cathedral. Sometimes a surge ran through the crowd, a powerful ripple forcing them towards the building, crushing the people in front. Sharp elbows dug into Rose. With each terrifying sweep forward she was afraid she too would trip and be swept underfoot. Then everyone would fall into a doom-filled silence again. The liquefaction was a long time coming.

Soon after eight a cry went up. The miracle had taken place! Slowly, reluctantly, as they heard later. But it had happened. A collective sigh almost like a breeze passed through the crowd before voices all around them, cracked and hoarse from thirst and tension, were raised in jubilation and relief.

Rose turned, smiling, to Falcone, and saw to her surprise that he was standing with his eyes closed. She bit back what she was going to say, not wanting to intrude.

The rejoicing of the crowd was in the end fairly muted, and soon everyone began to move away.

'Let me take your arm,' Falcone said rather formally as they set off. 'Otherwise you may get lost.'

Rose linked her arm through his dark-skinned one, intensely conscious of every contact of her flesh with his. She looked up at his thoughtful face, which wore an expression of slight puzzlement.

'So are we safe for another year?' she asked as they walked slowly down the Via Tribunali.

'Only until September,' he replied, looking down at

her with smiling eyes. 'The liquefaction happens twice every year.'

'Oh, blimey,' Rose said. In English.

'Don't fall asleep for God's sake,' she hissed at Henry as they climbed out at the cemetery gates. 'It's more than my life's worth.'

'Trust me. Anyway, you're not going to be that long, are you?'

It was a clear night, with a few wisps of cloud covering the stars. The thin slice of moon gave little light. Crickets were loud in the scrubby vegetation as the three of them slipped away from the truck which Rose had parked in the dense shadows outside the main cemetery entrance. Maria Grazia walked between them, holding tightly on to Falcone with one hand, and on to her flowers with the other, her back very straight to balance the weight of her pregnancy. The main iron gates were chained and padlocked, but to one side of them a stiff-hinged wooden door in the wall was left open for late visitors.

Inside the cemetery, Rose became aware of huge shapes around them, the towering old mausoleums of the wealthy with their roofs and doors and plaques. For a few seconds Falcone switched on the torch Henry had given them, and shadows leapt and shuddered up their walls. Rose saw that many of the graves were decorated with pictures of the dead and bright sprays of red and white gladioli.

'Better switch it off,' she suggested. 'The shadows are horrible.'

'Don't be afraid,' he said, extinguishing the torch. 'We'll be all right. We need to go down.'

'Is it far?' Maria Grazia asked in a trembling voice. 'I don't like it here.'

'No, not far, *piccola*,' Falcone said tenderly. 'Come on – you're safe.'

They headed down the hillside, along the terraces lined with graves and vaults. Rose's heart was pounding in her chest. She was trying to keep her thoughts away from ghosts and the stories she had heard about Italian burial traditions. Sometimes bodies were unearthed after being buried for a year. The bones were scraped, then laid in much smaller boxes which were stacked in a chancel house.

She had asked Falcone about it, horrified. 'They don't really do they?'

'It does happen here, but more further south. You have to understand – this isn't a big country and there are a lot of people. In many parts the ground is made of solid rock, so it's difficult to find places for burial. You have to find a way to deal with it. You see?'

She had been amazed by his acceptance of such macabre practices.

'That's why many cemeteries have wall graves, built above ground. It's all to save space.'

Rose had seen them, the coffins inserted into slots in a stone structure like a giant chest of drawers.

She sensed Maria Grazia shivering beside her, so she took off her jacket and wrapped it around the child. They walked on slowly, the sound of their feet crunching on dry earth.

Suddenly they all stopped. There was a strange, unearthly sound in front of them, a high moaning, growing louder, making the hairs rise on the back of their necks.

'My God,' Rose said. She wondered for a second if it

was a cat, but the sound was too loud and full. Maria Grazia turned to Falcone and buried her head against him.

Then they heard another noise, a low grunting, rhythmic and urgent. After a few seconds both cries began to die down together. Rose's eyes met Falcone's as the intimacy of what was happening so close by dawned on them both.

Falcone looked away quickly and bent to cuddle Maria Grazia in the darkness. 'It's all right,' he soothed. 'It's nothing to be afraid of.'

Without looking at Rose, he said, 'Lovers meet here during the day. I had not expected them to be here at night too.'

As they continued down the path in silence, Rose was seized by an overwhelming desire to giggle. Tight bubbles of hysterical laughter were welling up inside. She could see herself from the outside, a stranger in a foreign cemetery at two o'clock in the morning, with a prospective priest and a pregnant twelve-year-old, listening to the coupling of complete strangers in the dark. Who would believe her if she told them? A loud snort of laughter escaped and Falcone turned in bewilderment.

'Are you all right?'

Rose began laughing then, and couldn't stop. Maria Grazia, quite unused to people roaring with laughter around her, started to giggle at the sight, and eventually, completely astonished, Falcone joined in as well.

Gradually they got themselves back under control. Falcone reached out and put his arm lightly round Rose's shoulders. 'You crazy woman. Do you English always act like this when things are horrible? I haven't laughed so much since – well, I can't remember.' Quickly he removed his arm. 'Come on – we must go.'

Further on the path became much rougher and more stony under foot. Small pebbles rolled away as they walked.

'This must be the oldest part of the place,' Falcone said. 'I'm lost.'

He switched on the torch and shone it in front of them. The sight that met their eyes instantly wiped away any last traces of laughter. At this side of the cemetery some of the oldest wall graves had been built against the rocky side of the hill. With age and erosion, and perhaps from earth tremors in this turbulent area, most of the graves had collapsed. Among the rubble they could clearly make out the broken shapes of coffins. From some, the shrunken bodies had slid out, white, petrified figures, tossed carelessly about among the ruins. Rose would take away the memory of perfectly preserved fingerbones at the end of an arm, pointing up from behind a slab of stone, the hand bent forward at the wrist as if the person behind was relaxing in a bath.

Maria Grazia screamed and rushed in to Falcone's arms. She had seen the dead before many times, but never in these conditions.

'D'you still want to find your mother's resting place?' Falcone asked her gently. 'Or would you like to go home?'

'I want to see it,' she said, sniffing. 'I want to know where my mother is lying.'

'It must be that way,' Falcone said, pointing.

Once they reached the lowest level it was not difficult to find. All signs of attempts at individual Christian burials came to an end, and in front of them, as Falcone flashed the torch around, was a large area where the ground had been disturbed and refilled to cover one of a number of mass graves. The bombing, the typhus epidemic, the general ill health of the population meant that death carts trawled the streets as if in a medieval plague, and none but the wealthy could hope for a gravestone above their heads. Maria Grazia's mother had been poor. It was a bleak, sad sight. Flowers and trinkets had been scattered among the stones on the rough soil. Otherwise the graves lay unmarked and indistinguishable from each other.

Maria Grazia stood staring at the place. Falcone laid the torch down on the ground.

'Find a spot for your flowers,' he said, putting an arm round her shoulders. 'You can make it hers. You are very near her.'

The child walked miserably forward, a skinny, pathetic sight with her bulging belly, and her half-crushed blossoms.

She found a place where there were no other flowers, and knelt on the dry earth to place them. After a few moments she threw herself forward on to the ground, weeping. Then she sat back on her knees, rocking slowly in what seemed to be prayer.

Rose moved as if to go and comfort her but Falcone stopped her. 'Leave her,' he said. 'It's good for her to do this.'

They stood watching her, and Rose felt tears come to her eyes at the thought of her own mother, and the freezing day on which they had buried her. How long ago it all seemed: England, her family, everything, as if it had happened in another life.

She knew that Falcone's eyes were on her, and she turned to look at him as they stood in the shadow behind the torchlight. He moved awkwardly towards her. Then his arms were round her, drawing her to him, and they embraced, his lips seeking out hers. All the tenderness and longing they had seen in each other's eyes were expressed in that kiss. Falcone stroked Rose's hair, and then her face, with wonder, and she leaned against him, filled by emotions she had never known before. For the first time she knew what it was to respond to a kiss, to long for the other person.

She did not know how long they stood in each other's arms. It was only when Maria Grazia finally stood up and walked slowly away from the grave that they parted. Falcone picked up the torch and they went to meet her. Supporting her between them, they began the climb back to the gate.

'Thank Christ for that!' Henry exclaimed as soon as he saw them. 'You've been gone blooming ages. What the hell've you been doing?'

'It took us a bit of time to find her,' Rose told him vaguely. She had a strange, dreamy sensation of complete happiness, as if nothing mattered, neither the truck, nor getting back to Caserta, nor being exhausted the next day. Everything she needed was here.

They drove back to the city in silence, except for Falcone's directions. She wondered whether he was thinking, as she was, of the night's strange, conflicting moods. He sat beside her, his hand laid on the head of the young mother who had fallen asleep across his lap.

Twenty-Five

On 4 June, two days before the D-Day landings on the coast of France, General Mark Clark led the tanks and trucks of the Allied Forces along the sweeping, majestic roads into Rome. For many of the troops there was an awesome sense that they were moving along the paths of history. But when they reached Rome there was no decisive battle to determine which occupying force should control the fate of Italy. The Germans immediately shifted north to consolidate another line straddling the country's knee. It felt as if the slow crawl up this long, spiny country would never come to an end.

A week after that, another small but momentous event took place at Il Rifugio. Maria Grazia gave birth to a son, a tiny, fragile creature with only enough strength to snuffle into life. The birth was hard and Falcone was forced to call upon another doctor for help to be sure of saving the child. But enter life he did, and he clung to it. Maria Grazia called him Mauro.

Rose first saw him when he was ten days old, and was entranced by his crinkly perfection.

'He's so beautiful,' she said, smiling tearfully down at Maria Grazia as she let her hold him. 'Isn't it an amazing thing?'

The young girl stared blankly at her. She was very pale, and now she no longer carried the weight of the child it was clear how thin she was. Every effort was being made by Margherita, Falcone and the others to feed her up so she could nourish the child with her barely formed breasts. Thanks to Rose and Henry's monthly 'drops', which had so far gone miraculously well, the children were all thriving, except for two boys who had fallen ill and been removed to the hospital for fear of infecting the others.

If it had not been for Falcone distancing himself from her, Rose would have spent the summer in a haze of happiness. How many times during those weeks did she regret that kiss! Such a small thing, that moment of intimacy, but it changed everything. It had brought into the open the powerful current between her and Falcone which, once acknowledged, could not be ignored.

But wasn't she committed, at least verbally, to Alfie Meredith? It would soon be five years since she had, in a backhand sort of way, agreed to become his wife, a man from a different life, imprisoned in a country she had never seen.

She had tried to abide by her promise, but her feelings for Falcone overpowered everything else. Who was that person who had bound herself to Alfie back in Birmingham? A sad, fragile girl who had no idea of what she was capable. How could she have foreseen meeting Falcone, or the feelings aroused in her by his presence, of wanting to reach out and touch him each time they found themselves close, to stroke his thick black hair or smooth the back of her fingers down his cheek?

She remembered the kiss with longing, but also with a poignant sense of loss. Her own confusion was simple compared with the tension her presence appeared to have set up inside Falcone. He had been so sure where his future lay! Now when she was at Il Rifugio, they were almost never alone, nor did Falcone create opportunities for them to be so as he had before.

They still talked and argued about things, but usually in the presence of Francesco and Margherita, once the children were all asleep. Often they talked about Italian politics. What should happen once the war was over, now that Fascism seemed to be defeated? Magdalena would join in in her deep, animated voice. When Rose and Falcone were alone she found it possible to express her thoughts in a direct way, but she was intimidated by this gathering of educated Italians. She felt truly at home only when they were dealing with the children. Yet she needed more now from Il Rifugio than her work with the children. She needed Falcone. To talk with him, be alone with him, to understand why he was withdrawing from her, shutting her out.

In every other way her life felt charmed. The country came into bloom. Caserta flowered with red and pink geraniums hanging from almost every window and bright blooms of bougainvillea stained every wall across the town. In the countryside oranges and lemons hung ripe on the trees and the vines were heavy with grapes. The heat of the sun softened the road surface, giving it a spongy feel, and the air blowing in at the sides of the trucks was warm and caressing.

Behind the palace the long sweep of grass turned brown and wiry, and the tanks below the cascades gave off a slightly stagnant smell. The ATS pulled up their light cotton frocks on the grass to sun themselves during their hours off duty. Rose found that she had formed an easy, if not intimate camaraderie with Willy, Madge and, of course, Gwen.

As the temperature rose, Naples steamed and came alive with fat green flies which shimmered in dark clouds and settled on anything damp, heading for the face, mouth and armpits.

'It's beyond me why you spend your weekends over there when you could get out to Amalfi or Capri,' Tony said to Rose. 'God, the stink of the place! Lewis and I get out as fast as we can. Anyway, I thought you were mad keen to see the country round here?'

'But you've never been to Il Rifugio,' Rose retorted indignantly. 'And it's much cleaner there than you'd think. The two nuns spend half their lives cleaning up.' But he did have a point. There were so many places she still hadn't seen.

One Sunday afternoon, Rose was sitting in the courtyard with Mauro in her lap while Maria Grazia slept. The baby's tiny hand gripped her little finger as he lay half asleep. Rose smiled down at him. She'd found a spot in the shade on the warm stone flags, her back against the wall, and she could smell the pungent leaves of a geranium plant growing in a pot near by.

She looked up, to see Falcone watching her. He was standing, his hands in the pockets of his blue dungarees, leaning against one of the pillars of the arched entrance to the staircase. He had been talking with Francesco. Now he stared at her in silence, and she saw in his face such a depth of longing and bewilderment that she had to turn her face back towards Mauro.

Falcone pushed himself away from the pillar and turned to walk inside.

'What's eating him?' Francesco asked.

'He's in love with Rosa,' Margherita said without looking up from her sewing at Rose, who started, but kept her eyes on Mauro.

'He's *what*?' Francesco exploded. 'He can't be! He's going to the seminary.'

Magdalena snorted, pushing her veil back over her shoulders. 'Can't be? What nonsense you do talk.'

'Of course he's in love. It stands out a mile,' Margherita told him.

'I haven't noticed anything,' Francesco said rather petulantly.

'What do you expect?' Magdalena was scornful. 'You're a man.'

'Rosa?' Francesco leaned down to see her expression. 'Is this true?'

Slowly she raised her head, her cheeks burning red. There was no need for her to reply.

'And you love him?'

'Of course she does,' Margherita said, biting off a piece of thread. 'It's obvious.'

'So what's going on?' Francesco had the air of someone who has had a fast one pulled on him in a card game. 'You don't speak to each other any more. Falcone is like a mule with a sore bottom. What is the matter with you both?'

'Falcone is trying to decide his vocation,' Magdalena explained, in the kind of patient tone she usually reserved for Assunta and the children. 'Not everyone gets a visit from an angel to tell them which way to go.'

'Do you think he will be a priest?' Rose asked. 'It's all very strange to me.'

'Only God can tell us that,' Magdalena said, smiling at her.

'He's no priest,' Margherita said firmly. 'Two heads

298

on the pillow. That's his vocation, and deep down he knows it really.'

'He won't even speak to me,' Rose said. It was a relief to confide in the others. 'I don't understand him. I never even see him alone any more.'

'Go now,' Margherita told her. 'Assunta is asleep. He's alone up there.'

Rose stood up and laid Mauro in Magdalena's arms.

The others watched as Rose and Falcone crossed the courtyard together and unlocked the gate. Out in the baking streets the stalls were closed down and the usual clamour was muted by the routine of the Sunday siesta.

Not speaking, they walked down to the small strip of parched parkland which edged the Mediterranean at Santa Lucia. Scrubby pine trees offered a meagre shade, and they chose a spot to sit away from the sea, where there were no bodies snoring in the heat. Through the trees they could see the white glare of light on the water, and make out the hazy, grey shape of Vesuvius, quiet now, in the distance across the bay.

Falcone said, 'It's my fault. I'm sorry. When you're not here I begin to believe that I know what I'm supposed to do with my life. As soon as I see you again, I'm thrown into confusion.'

'Sometimes, the way you look at me,' Rose said haltingly, 'I begin to think you hate me, that I'm nothing but trouble in your life.'

'You know I don't hate you.'

'But it would be better for you if I did not come here – to Il Rifugio?'

Falcone sat leaning his elbows on his raised knees, his head between his tanned hands, staring out to sea.

He shook his head. 'No. That's not true either. You know as well as I do that you're far more help to them than I can ever be.' He picked up a small, dry twig and threw it hard towards the sea. 'I couldn't even manage to deliver Maria Grazia's baby safely on my own. I'm no great asset to them. It's not you that's at fault, Rosa. It's me. I told you: everywhere I go I bring hurt and destruction. I thought things were clear. God's call felt ... strong, pure. I don't know if you can understand that. And sometimes I can feel it. But when I am near you I don't know which is the right path for me. In the meantime I just bring you pain.'

In the silence that followed, Rose found herself crying. They were mostly tears of frustration, at not knowing how to console him since she was the source of his conflict. She wanted to take him in her arms and hold him, but she knew that for him it would be like being embraced by a thorn bush.

'Rosa?' Falcone said in distress. 'Please. Please don't.' He made helpless gestures with his arms and laid one of them briefly round her shoulders before withdrawing it again. 'Please don't cry, dearest Rosa. It's better for you if you're not near me – I'm so confused, I only hurt you. That night in the cemetery, I allowed my feelings for you to – to sweep me along. I shouldn't have. It was wrong.'

His words only made Rose weep even more. Why was it wrong? Why?

He stood up suddenly. 'When the war's over you'll go back to England and marry your English husband. Think only of that and forget me. Please.'

He turned from her, aghast at himself, and walked away from Santa Lucia and back towards the Via Toledo. When he crossed the courtyard of Il Rifugio alone, only half an hour after they had left, the others exchanged sad, puzzled glances.

Rose sat for a long time under the dry, bleached pine trees, crying for both his anguish and her own.

She tried to bring down her protective shutters as she had done in the past, to stop any expression of her feelings for him, even to herself. As the autumn came and began to turn to winter, and the fields faded to blander colours once more, she carried on with the drops. She spent her leave weekends at Il Rifugio, but as far as possible she avoided contact with Falcone. It wasn't difficult. They were polite to each other when they had to work together. Rose talked to him briskly and brightly, almost as if he was a new arrival in the place whom she barely knew.

'Could you go and fetch a bucket of water please?' she might ask, or, 'Margherita says she needs you to look at one of the children upstairs.' And Falcone would nod respectfully as if she were in charge and do as she asked.

She stayed just as committed to the place, but her mind began to hunger to see more of the country around. She mentioned the fact to Margherita and Francesco, and they encouraged her to go.

'Perhaps Falcone could take you?' Francesco suggested.

Margherita looked at him as if he were a half-wit.

'I can easily find a chaperone from the army, thank you,' Rose said rather bitterly.

'I'll take a weekend to go some time,' she said to Margherita later on. 'But I'd like to come here for Christmas. Is that all right?'

Margherita gave her tired smile. 'You know you don't have to ask. Just come when you can.'

As it turned out, she did not spend Christmas at Il Rifugio. One evening in November Gwen came rushing into the dormitory as most of them were preparing for bed. She looked as if she was about to explode with excitement. 'Bill's just asked me to marry him.'

'And . . . ?' Rose said.

'I've said I will.'

'Course you have!' Madge dashed up to supply one of her bear hugs. 'As if you'd have turned him down. We'd've all lynched you after the amount we've heard about your Bill this year!'

All of them went to add their congratulations. Willy had tears in her eyes. 'Oh, it's so romantic,' she cried. 'Are you going to get married at the palace?'

'Yes,' Gwen told them. 'We've fixed it for Christmas Eve. We thought it would be an awfully nice time, when everyone's feeling festive anyway. Goodness knows if we'll be ready by then though.'

'What's the problem?' Madge asked. 'All you need is a bloke and a dress, isn't it?'

Gwen laughed, looking really pretty. 'Yes, I suppose you're right. But where shall I get a dress from?'

'Ah – I can help you there,' Rose said. She knew Signora Mandetta would be pleased to have the work, though she would have been more delighted had it been Rose's own wedding dress.

When the fuss had died down, Gwen came and sat on Rose's bed.

'I'm so happy for you,' Rose told her. 'Bill seems a good bloke.'

'Thank you,' Gwen said, smiling again. 'He is, really.' She was watching Rose, her auburn hair curling round her face. 'I wanted to ask if you'd be my bridesmaid. I'd be ever so pleased if you would.'

'Of course,' Rose said. 'I'd be honoured.' She leaned over and gave Gwen a hug. 'I'm really chuffed.'

'I'm not going to tell Mummy,' Gwen told her, looking serious suddenly. 'Not until it's all over and settled.'

'Oh, blimey,' Rose said. 'Don't you think you should? She could hold it against you for the rest of your life.'

'She'll do that whether I tell her now or later.'

Gwen became Mrs William Charles Crowther in the little blue-walled chapel in the palace, with her ATS friends standing round. They had gone to great lengths to get hold of flowers to decorate the place, which already had its share of marble and ornate white inlay against the blue ceiling.

Signora Mandetta had made Gwen a beautiful satin dress which hung in soft folds round her hips and swept the floor behind her, decorated with tiny mother-of-pearl seeds. For Rose she had chosen a dress in a pale blue material, and both of them held simple bunches of white lilies.

'It's funny, isn't it?' Rose said to her, before they set off to the palace in a specially decorated army Jeep. 'I can't help thinking about the first time I saw you, at Didcot Station that day when we'd joined up. I'd never have dreamed I'd be doing this with you.'

Gwen looked solemn for a moment. 'Sometimes it makes me go cold thinking about how my life would have turned out if I hadn't joined up.' Suddenly she stepped forward and put her arms round Rose. 'I'm so happy,' she said. 'And you've been a real brick the way you've helped with everything.' She looked into Rose's face. 'Maybe it'll be you and Tony next. Maybe our wedding'll give him a push in the right direction.'

Rose smiled back, impishly. 'Stranger things have happened, I s'pose.'

Standing with Gwen as she and Bill made their vows, Rose was glad of Tony's solid presence behind her. Everything went smoothly, and when she danced with Tony at the little celebration afterwards, Rose realized she felt almost light-hearted, glad of a break from Il Rifugio and from Naples.

'I was thinking of going to see Capri on my next leave weekend,' she told Tony. 'Any chance of you sparing some time to show me around?'

Twenty-Six

April 1945

The letter from Grace arrived two days before Rose's weekend leave. It was the second that fortnight, which was unusual for Grace who never wrote more often than every month or so, and only a brief note when she did. In the first letter she had announced her engagement to a GI called Joe Landers. He had just been posted and she was missing him. Just like Grace not even to mention him until she really had something to say.

The second letter was only a couple of sentences: 'We had a telegram today. Sam's been killed. Thought you'd want to know straight away. Love, Grace.'

Rose re-read the skeleton of a letter, trying to take in the reality of it. She knew its brevity stemmed from Grace's shock and grief, and also from the fact she didn't know any more than that. After all, what else was there to say? But Rose longed for detail. Where was he? How had he died? Suddenly the reality of home poured in on her, of life back in the greyness of England, stuck there, waiting for news. In Italy it had all receded from her mind as if Catherine Street was an old film she had seen years ago and half forgotten. Home. The place she would go back to when this was all over, with no Dora, no Sam. No reliable, pedantic Sam.

Over the next two days she thought more about her elder brother than she had in the whole of the war. Memories of their childhood kept forcing themselves into her mind: of playing marbles with him out in the yard; of Sam rescuing her little cloth doll when one of the Pye children threw it over the wall into the next court. Sam going out to start his first job; his stiff loyalty when he found out she was pregnant.

The next weekend she had planned to go to Sorrento with Gwen and Bill and a friend of Bill's. They'd made up a foursome on the previous leave to see Positano and Amalfi. Tony had taken her to Capri for one weekend, and she had revelled in the rich blue of the sea, the sparkling beauty of the island with its bright white villas and cobbled squares where people lingered and drank and talked, even in winter, as if there was no war anywhere in the world.

Rose had only been to Naples for the weekend once since November. She could not face spending her days so close to Falcone while they were so remote from each other. Now she felt a strong need to talk to Margherita, whom she saw as her closest friend in Italy. Several times Margherita had confided in her, breaking down and pouring out her worries about her father, living in a new place surrounded by strangers. Rose knew Margherita was the one person she could allow to see her feelings.

Without mentioning Sam, she told Gwen she would be going off with Tony for the weekend after all. Gwen smiled knowingly at her.

'What is it?' Margherita asked as soon as Rose set foot through the door. She was sitting pounding at some piece of cloth in a bucket of water, her eyes ringed with tiredness. A circle of children stood watching.

Rose burst into tears for the first time. She started to shake and sob. 'My brother is dead.'

Margherita stood up and led her into the little sitting room, indicating to the children that they should not follow. She put her arms round Rose and let her cry for as long as she needed to, as Rose had done for her a number of times in the past. She stroked Rose's hair as she sat beside her, her kind eyes solemnly watching her friend's face.

Then Rose, still shaking, but quieter, was able to tell the little she knew. 'I don't even know where he was – what country,' she said. 'I know we'll find out in the end. But it seems terrible to die so far from home.'

Margherita nodded, understanding.

'I feel so guilty,' Rose said, starting to cry again. 'I've hardly given my family a thought since coming out here. I've been so wrapped up in the army and this place – you've all been like my family. It's suddenly come home to me all they've been through, and I've been no help at all.'

Margherita sighed sadly. 'I know,' she said. 'Believe me, I have those feelings too. When the eruption came and I lost my mother, that was when I realized I had hardly seen them since the war began. The children had taken all my time. Francesco and I were always so busy, so involved with each other and this place. My family only lived across the bay, and still I did nothing for them. Now I shall never see my mother again. Every day my heart aches when I think of it.'

Holding Margherita around her waist, Rose felt how thin she had become. When they let each other go, she realized they were not alone. Falcone was standing in the doorway, his face full of concern and at the same time surprise at seeing Rose there at all.

'What's happened?'

'Rosa's brother has been killed,' Margherita told him. 'Somewhere,' she added. '*Qualche parte.*' The words hung woefully in the air.

'I'm so sorry, Rosa,' Falcone began.

'You need some time,' Margherita interrupted. 'You shouldn't be working here this weekend, Rosa.'

Rose started to argue, but Margherita silenced her.

'You must go somewhere else, somewhere more peaceful and pleasant. Falcone – you take her.'

'But . . . I—' Falcone started to say.

'You are the person we can spare most easily,' Margherita continued ruthlessly. 'Take her. Look after her.' She sighed, tilting her head on one side with a certain impatience. 'Forget your own struggles for a bit, eh?'

'No!' Rose cried immediately. 'No. I'll stay here. It will do me good to be working.' A few months ago nothing would have filled her with greater delight than the idea of two days alone with Falcone, but now, the thought of him being forced to take her away for a weekend against his will filled her with panic. 'If I'm busy I won't have to think,' she protested.

'Go,' Margherita said. It was an order. 'You need to think.'

Rose had never heard her so steely and commanding before. It seemed as if she and Falcone would be thrown out bodily if they refused to go. They looked at each other warily for a moment. It was the first time their eyes had met for a very long time. Rose went and picked up her bag.

*

'Where are we going?' she asked as they stepped out into the warm spring air of the streets. The hawkers were in full throat on the pavements.

'I know a peaceful place I can take you. I used to go with my father. We had holidays there when he needed a rest. You'll like it.'

'I'm sorry you have to do this.'

'You don't have to be sorry,' he said stiffly. 'Margherita's right. I've been too wrapped up in myself. I need to do my duty by other people.'

Quelled by the coldness of the word 'duty', Rose fell silent again. They walked along the majestic Corso Umberto and into the Piazza Garibaldi where they could catch a train. Rose felt her spirits plummeting. The easy friendship, the fire of discussion between them, the tenderness – all this had vanished. Now they were like wooden puppets with each other. She felt despairing at the thought of the cold, awkward weekend ahead.

They took a train for Sorrento. Falcone had money and they each paid for their own ticket. He also bought a newspaper. They sat opposite one another, and throughout the entire journey Falcone read the newspaper. Rose often glanced across at his solemn face, the brown eyes moving in concentration across the print. A stranger's face, she thought. Had she loved him? Who was he? Where was the vulnerable, complex man she had given her heart to?

Determinedly she looked away from him out of the window. She wanted to see more of Italy, didn't she? But she could have been seeing this same place so much more cheerfully with Gwen. She stared out at the louring shape of Vesuvius. The lava fields from the eruption lay greyish mauve, spongy-looking, and cool now. Villages, orange groves and vineyards pushed defiantly right to the edges of them. On her side of the train she caught glimpses of the sea, the morning sunlight wrinkling in its deep blue surface. How these sights would have exhilarated her had her mood not been so sad.

The train climbed high along the verdant cliffside, and Rose smelt the pine trees. For a time they looked right across the sea, and then gradually rolled down into Sorrento.

Everyone climbed out at the small station. Immediately the place felt different from Naples. Quieter, with almost a holiday feel. Rose was terrified of meeting any service people who might recognize her, and she was relieved to get away from the station. Walking with Falcone and dressed in her black clothes she was certainly not conspicuously British.

'We have a way to go,' Falcone told her. 'I hope you're not too tired? My friends live on the hillside outside the town.'

'I'm all right,' Rose said, though in truth she felt dragged down and exhausted.

Falcone led her along the cobbled streets, usually walking slightly ahead of her, though she was unsure whether this was through impatience to get there or because her presence was unbearable. As they left the town and toiled uphill, past rough cottages with flowers bright at the windows, the stones burning hot under their feet, she became convinced it was because he could not stand to be near her. That long walk in the heat, bothered by flies, seeing his back in front of her, was the lowest point she could remember since being in Italy. With her head aching and her hand sweaty on the handle of her bag, she could only think about what she had lost and this terrible silence that had grown up between them.

For the first time she found herself thinking, 'I wish I could just go home. Get away and forget it all.' Hot tears stung her eyes and she wiped them away crossly. She was not going to let him, an alien creature, as she thought of Falcone now, see her cry again. At that moment she hated him.

Falcone stopped finally at what seemed to be the end of the road, at a large house, its front covered in pink, crumbling plaster and shaded by two eucalyptus trees. As he went to knock at the door they heard a dog give a moaning bark somewhere behind the house, and two white geese waddled out from among the weeds and stood muttering at them.

Rose put her bag down and wiped the sweat from her forehead. There was a slight breeze up there and, suddenly refreshed, she looked around her. Not far from the house, where the road petered out, a stepped path built from huge, pale stones wound upwards between the trees which covered the higher slopes of the mountain. She longed to walk there and lose herself among the trees, to escape from Falcone and these people she now had to meet.

The door opened and a voice cried, 'Paulo! Is it you, really? How marvellous. Welcome, welcome . . .'

An elderly man, with steely grey hair and a stubbly little moustache, opened his arms wide in greeting. His face was deeply lined and tanned the colour of strong tea.

'Who's this?'

'This is Rosa, Signore Finzi,' Falcone said loudly. 'Rose Lucas. She is English.'

'*Un'inglese?*' Signore Finzi looked puzzled, staring at

Rose, who suddenly found herself blushing at the thought of all the questions that must be going through the old man's mind.

Falcone explained briefly what they were doing there, and their host offered condolences while leading them inside to a large cool kitchen.

'Clara, Clara! Look who's come to visit us!'

No sooner had Clara Finzi set eyes on Falcone than he was clasped tightly in her plump arms amid loud expressions of delight, and wasn't he thin and where had he been all this time and, finally, tears, which she mopped from her round, soft-looking cheeks. His father, his father. It would seem like the old days young Paulo being here – but holy Mother, how it made her think of Doctor Falcone . . . What a terrible, terrible thing . . .'

As soon as Rose was introduced as a friend she also found herself crushed against the signora's bosom, and kisses landing on her cheeks from lips with a hint of moustache above them.

'Fetch wine, Angelo – and water,' the signora commanded at the top of her voice. Rose had quickly grasped that Signore Finzi's hearing had almost gone. They sat down at the scrubbed wooden table. On a side table the signora had been cutting long strips of tagliatelle. Her husband sat down with them having brought the drinks and the signora talked and talked while she carried on preparing the food.

'You have come right in time for a meal!' she exclaimed. 'It's so long since anyone has been to stay here. We have the rooms ready, but not even the soldiers come. They don't know we are here, of course, and they want the sea, the bars, the shops. Nothing is like it was in the old days. And we make no money.' She stopped to take a swig of the wine. 'But now I have someone to cook for,' she added, almost like a threat.

'We must drink to your father,' she said to Falcone. Looking at Rose she added, 'Ah – *il dottore* Falcone. What a gentleman. What a doctor!' Her tears started to flow again. 'Of all the places he could have stayed, he came again and again to our poor house. Every year, with his children. From when this one was a small boy. Look – I have a photograph.'

Rose glanced nervously at Falcone, but saw nothing but affection and amusement in his eyes. He had relaxed suddenly, and looked younger, as if revisiting this place of his childhood had stripped some of the troubled lines from his face.

The signora swung herself back to the table after taking a small photograph from a shelf of the dresser.

'There. You remember?'

She held out the picture between Rose and Falcone. Rose saw a tall, thin man with a serious but gentle face, standing rather formally beside two boys. Behind them was the Finzis' house. The three of them were dressed in dark trousers and jackets. The taller of the two boys next to him closely resembled his father, the face thin and hair lighter than his younger brother's. Clearly the smaller of the two was Falcone, even if Rose had not known he was the youngest. Darker and stockier than his brother, he stared out of the photograph with the mischievous expression she recognized and those long-lashed eyes.

Without thinking she turned and smiled at him. 'You've hardly changed at all.'

'It's true, he hasn't,' Angelo Finzi said. 'He was always like his mother, God rest her.'

To Rose's surprise Falcone returned her smile, the

warmth suddenly back in his eyes. The Finzis exchanged glances.

Signora Finzi put in front of them bowls of delicious tagliatelle with *pomodoro al sugo* and an egg on top, which they both ate hungrily. All the while the signora talked and reminisced and lamented the war, and the tragic murder of *il dottore*, so that neither Angelo Finzi, who sat nodding at what he could hear, nor Rose and Falcone were required to say anything at all. They sat eating beside each other in what now felt a more comfortable silence.

'You need to rest now,' Clara Finzi instructed them.

She led them upstairs and into a small passageway at the top from which led several doors. The first she opened was for Rose. It was a simple, white room, very cool, in the middle of which a huge wooden-framed bed took up most of the space. Wooden shutters were closed at the windows, and when she pushed them open, letting in warmer air and languid flies, she realized the room looked over the back of the house. The Finzis had a small plot of land which stretched out to the point where the trees took over. They cultivated it intensively, and among all the rows of growing vegetables and tomato plants, chickens and geese ran here and there. Rose could still hear the dog, but it was not in sight.

She breathed in the warm air, her headache easing off a little now they were out of the direct heat, and turned to the whitewashed room behind her. Over the bed hung a small wooden crucifix. There was a chair and a rough chest of drawers with a deep porcelain bowl resting on top. That was all.

Well fed and tired enough now for all thoughts to be blocked out, she lay down gratefully on the firm, white bed.

314

Twenty-Seven

When she awoke, the only sound was the clucking of chickens below the window. She had left the shutters open and the light had grown softer, with the gentle, pinkish tinge of late afternoon. Her watch said four-thirty. Slowly she drank the cup of water by her bed and stood up, stretching her limbs.

There were no signs of life in the rest of the house when she left the room, so she let herself out of the front door. She would walk. It would be good to be alone, really alone for a time. Army life meant always being with other people.

The air outside was caressingly warm, full of the scents of herbs and gorse, and from somewhere the smell of frying onions. Rose turned towards the path which led up the hillside and began to climb, still feeling rather muzzy from her sleep. Every few yards along the sloping path there was a deep step, and she could feel the muscles in her legs pulling hard as she climbed between the greyish olive trees, with salamanders scuttling away from the path and the loud, abrasive rhythm of the crickets and cicadas.

She soon realized this was more than a convenient path up the side of the hill. In fact there were no other houses up there that she could see, nowhere for the path to lead. But at every other bend in the route as she made her way up was a little brick shrine, about waist height.

Bending to look inside she found that set into each brick column was a roughly painted picture, each bearing a number. The pictures were the same as she had seen on the walls of the austere Naples churches, the fourteen Stations of the Cross. Jesus receives the Cross, Veronica wipes Jesus' face, Jesus is nailed to the Cross. On the sills of some of the shrines she saw the remains of candle stubs and wilted flowers, perhaps left over from the Easter procession.

It felt appropriate that she should have come walking here to think about Sam. Sam, who had had his own beliefs, in his way, even if he would have staunchly disapproved of the colourful Catholic imagery in this thread of shared belief she was following up between the trees. She tried to concentrate on Sam, to talk to him.

She sat down on one of the cold steps, suddenly overcome by a great welling up of feeling. Hot tears ran down her cheeks.

'I'll miss you. I'll miss you so much.'

Putting her hands over her face she wept for a few minutes, picturing the old, hard life in Birmingham, the way it had all been swept away by the war, changing and displacing all of them. Killing them, one way or another. None of it would ever be the same again. This thought was reinforced by the sight of the worn black skirt pulled tight over her strong tanned legs. It seemed such an alien thing. Who was she now? Who was Rose Lucas? Alone in a far-away country, dressed in strange, foreign clothes, giving her heart to a man who could not love her back. She remembered the smile Falcone had given her as they looked at the photograph together, and it made her cry again. It felt so cruel, that glimpse of how things could have been.

Angrily she stood up and walked on up the hill, trying to work the pain out of herself by physical exertion. She passed the final three stages of the pilgrimage without stopping to look at them, her legs aching.

At the top there was a small stone chapel. Outside stood a pale, bland-faced statue of Mary. The path led on upwards behind the chapel, but it looked less well tended.

She pushed open the door of the chapel quietly. It was gloomy inside, but her attention was drawn straight away to a raised altar where stood a Madonna quite different from the lifeless image depicted outside. She was dressed in heavy blue velvet, and at her breast was pinned a large metal heart, pierced through with a bristling collection of pins, large and thick like nails. One of her arms was outstretched, and her mouth was open as if she was constantly crying out, her grey eyes staring across the chapel in anguish. This was no serene plaster statue, but a woman who had watched her son die a most terrible death and had been powerless to stop it.

In front of her lay all kinds of tributes: garlands of flowers and sacred hearts, offerings of money and rosary beads. And more personal objects: the army cap of someone else's son, a ring and some bracelets, a pair of thick black-rimmed spectacles. Had she been able to save the kin of others when she had failed so completely with her own?

Rose stood staring at her for several minutes. As if sharing the grief of the woman in front of her, she thought of all the people she had lost, Falcone among them. Try as she might to think of anyone but him, he was rarely out of her mind. She remembered that first night when they had talked all through the hours of

317

darkness with the children sleeping round them, how there had been that new sense of herself moving out to him from her very centre, which she later recognized as love.

She turned to look at the rest of the chapel, and jumped violently. As if her thoughts had spirited him to the place, there he was, kneeling at the back of the rows of chairs, looking across at her.

'I'm sorry,' he said gently, standing up. 'Didn't you know I was here?'

'No. I thought I was on my own. Have you been here all the time?'

'I've been here nearly an hour,' he said, walking towards her. 'It's a very peaceful place, isn't it? My father used to come here often and sometimes I came with him.'

He stood beside her, looking up at the statue.

'You know she shares in all our sorrows?' he said. 'When I came and prayed here as a boy I used to remember all my father's patients, those who were suffering great pain, and the ones who had died. It was as if I could commit them all to her.'

'And now?'

Falcone shook his head sadly. 'Now I wonder if even she can comfort all the suffering in the world.'

As they walked out into the early evening light he said, 'The path doesn't end here. Come, I'll show you, it's lovely. No one comes up here except on feast days. There's just an old man who looks after the olive groves.'

Rose climbed beside him. The stones here were further apart, with tufts of wiry grass and weeds poking up between them. Falcone did not rush on ahead as he had earlier, but walked beside her, quite unlike his harsh self at midday.

'Were you thinking about your brother?' Rose noticed with bewilderment that he sounded rather nervous.

'Yes. I was thinking about all my family. How the war has changed everyone. Taken away so much of what was there before. And the way everyone has become someone else.'

'Do you think the people we were are still some-where inside us?' he asked, in that way she remembered, as if he really needed her opinion. 'That one day we can be reunited with ourselves again?'

'Not the same,' she insisted. 'I know I'll never be the same after being here.' After you, she added in her thoughts.

When they had climbed a little higher the path forked, one branch continuing upwards, obscured by the vegetation around it. The other, which Falcone took, led into a clearing. There was a flat area like a ledge that had been cut into the hill to make a semicircular space, the long, straight side of it against the body of the hill. In the middle of that line stood one more statue, this time of the risen Christ, its stone stained by green lichen. Through the trees he looked out over the town, his arm raised in benediction.

'It's beautiful.' Rose walked to the edge of the clearing. The air was hazy, but the faded terracotta roofs of the town were easily visible below. She stood trying to absorb herself in the sight, but she was acutely aware that Falcone was watching her. Her body tingled under his gaze. Her heart was beating hard. She knew that something had changed, that the charged atmosphere which had existed between them before had returned, but she did not know how to react, or what to do with the turmoil of feelings inside her.

When she realized that he had come to stand just behind her she said, 'You were very angry with me this morning, weren't you?'

She heard him make a low sound, as if in pain, and turned round quickly to look at him. She was moved by the look of sorrow and desire she recognized in his eyes.

'If you knew,' he said. He looked down at the ground, unable to face her.

'Every step of the way up here as you walked behind me, all I could think of was that you were there, as if your shape was burning into my back, and I couldn't look at you. The train was torture, pretending to read that newspaper when I could only think that you were there, a few feet away from me. I knew if I was alone with you again it would be like this. If I'd looked at you or touched you I would have—' He shrugged helplessly. 'I want you so much. I can't help it.'

Each could feel the other trembling as they moved into each other's arms. They kissed again and again, faces, lips, necks, in a great hurry as if at any second the experience might be snatched away. Rose made little whimpering sounds, almost of distress, at the strength of the emotions he aroused in her.

It did not occur to her to hold back from him. They clung together, exploring each other's bodies with their hands. Slowly, Falcone unbuttoned the black blouse Rose was wearing, uncovering her breasts, cupped in a black cotton bra. His hands were trembling so much as he tried to undo it that she reached round and unfastened the hooks herself. She pulled the little garment out through one sleeve, freeing her breasts with their dark, generous nipples, already peaking at his slight touch.

'You're so, so beautiful,' he said. As his hands moved over her breasts, stroking her, he heard her give a sharp intake of breath at the intense pleasure of it. Never had she been touched like this before. Alfie had not had the imagination to give her more than a clumsy squeeze through her clothes. But this, this stroking, his taking her nipple between finger and thumb sent waves of desire through her body such as she had never even begun to experience before. Her legs were trembling, and the lower part of her body had come alive. She felt a sharp, warm sensation of need rising in her.

'Don't stop,' she said. 'I couldn't bear it if you stopped touching me.'

Quickly they looked round for the softest part of the dry, stony ground. There was not one patch which appeared better than any other, so they knelt down together anyway, unfastening clothes, and they were in each other's arms again, with Falcone's shirt spread out beneath them.

It was awkward, their lovemaking that first time, their unfamiliarity with each other's bodies, the hard ground, but they barely noticed the discomforts of it. At the height of it she called out some words in English and burst into tears at the release. He held her tenderly until both of them quietened, stroking her wet face. He stayed inside her for a long time afterwards.

'I love you,' she whispered into the silence. 'I love you so much.'

She heard his voice, felt his warm breath on her neck. 'And I love you.'

*

He came to her that night, after they had eaten with the Finzis and talked long into the evening over fish and bread and glasses of wine until the old man fell asleep in his chair, snoring softly, his whiskery mouth hanging open.

As she let Falcone into her dark room, their lips were on each other before either of them had even spoken, their bodies already tight with wanting each other.

'I can't see you,' Falcone whispered. 'I want to see you naked – every part of you. Is there a candle in here?'

'I'll open the shutters,' Rose replied, shivering slightly. 'There's a moon tonight.'

Laughing as quietly as they could manage, they released the shutters, both saying 'Ssshh' with childlike exaggeration as one of the slatted wooden blinds banged too loudly against the frame.

'Well *he* won't hear us anyway,' Rose whispered.

'No. But the signora, she's always had ears like a cat.'

To Falcone's amusement Rose was still wearing her striped army-issue pyjamas, not having bothered to get any others. Smiling down at her he unbuttoned the jacket. The solemn, concentrated expression in his eyes made her want to take him to her straight away, but she stood still. He pulled the top away from her breasts and pushed it off down her arms. He slid his hands gently inside the top of her trousers and eased them down over her hips until she could step out of them. She stood naked in front of him, her black hair falling in soft waves over her shoulders, her eyes wide and vulnerable, looking up at him.

For a moment he didn't move to touch her, but stood gazing at her, the moonlight casting deep shadows on her small, curving body, the strong hips and slight curve of her stomach, her full breasts. How many times he had tried to imagine her like this, unclothed, ready for him.

He moved towards her but she raised a hand. 'Wait a minute.'

He had changed into a very worn cotton shirt and frayed shorts. She pulled the shirt off and ran her hands through the black curling hair on his chest, feeling the powerful beating of his heart, aware of his wide brown eyes watching her, a little shy at her taking control. His body was slim but muscular, and she stroked him tenderly across his shoulders, down over his chest and belly. She brought her hands slowly along the soft hair of his thighs, feeling him shudder and flex his legs slightly in anticipation. When he was naked, hard and ready for her, she took him between her hands, caressing him until he gasped and moved to stop her.

'No – wait. Not yet, please.'

And then he was touching her all over, his lips kissing her mouth, her breasts and limbs and then, laying her on the bed, exploring between her legs until she was whimpering with amazed desire, aching to have him inside her. At last she pulled him close, guiding him into her. They both cried out with relief and pleasure and both came almost instantly, first he, then she, and she began to make such a noise that Falcone lovingly laid one hand over her mouth until they both lay back laughing, quietly but slightly hysterically, in each other's arms.

They stayed like that for a time, talking drowsily, sleeping at last on the hard bed. Later in the night Rose woke to feel Falcone's hands moving over her body. The moon had moved and it was darker, but they made love under the covers, more slowly this time, with less urgency, an experience more of touch than sight, both taking longer to climax, but still moved to tears by each other's pleasure.

When she awoke, Rose expected to find him gone. But as the lemon morning light bathed the room through the open shutters, she realized he was beside her still. His face and hair looked very dark against the coarse white linen of the pillow. He was lying with his head resting on his bent arm and she saw his smiling, long-lashed eyes watching her.

Rose half sat up, startled. 'You shouldn't be here! What if they—?'

'They get up very early. I can hear them outside. Don't worry.'

He stroked her hair and kissed her. Then, as they embraced, he pulled her over on top of him, moving against her. The feel of her immediately hardened him, and he lifted her until he could enter her. She sat, both of them moving together gently, his hands stroking her breasts.

'You are a miracle,' he said, rising under her like water until she felt herself come alive again with the tingling at her breasts and his reaching deep into her.

'It feels very good, like this,' she told him. 'I can feel you so far inside me.'

He smiled. 'Good,' he said, 'good.'

She saw his eyes half close as the power of the sensations overcame him, and once more they moved together until they were lost in each other, and every other thought or feeling was taken from them.

Twenty-Eight

May 1945

It was over!

On 2 May the German forces in Italy made their official surrender, and the fortunes of Europe had fallen to the Allies. After the long stalemate in the Italian campaign, events had suddenly speeded up during April in a landslide of activity. The Allied Forces finally crossed the enormous span of the River Po, which had long proved such an obstacle, and pushed across the northern plains to the French border. It was a time of sudden reversals, of power overthrown. Mussolini and his mistress, Claretta Petacci, were seized by a colonel in the partisan army in a farmhouse at Dongo on Lake Como to which they had retreated in hiding. The two of them were shot and hung ignominiously by the feet for all to see outside a garage in the Piazzale Loreto in Milan. And on 30 April Hitler and his mistress Eva Braun committed suicide.

The Victory in Europe celebrations were set for 8 May. Caserta was taken over by an air of fiesta and celebration, although the work of administering the army still had to go on. The war was over! They would be going home! Sooner or later they would be back in Blighty with familiar people and places around them.

Home, far away and long unseen, was enhanced in the memory and seemed the very sweetest place to be.

But among all the dances, the hugs and kisses and drinking and singing, there were deeply mixed feelings. Some ugly scenes broke out when British soldiers exulted in their victory by taunting the local Italians, whom they saw as defeated. Fights broke out, and at least one Italian in the area was stabbed to death. As it began to sink in that returning home was not just a dream which might be realized some time in the future, memories grew sharper, less softened by nostalgia.

'I'm longing to set up a home with Bill,' Gwen confided to Rose as they walked round the palace grounds. 'Make a real cosy nest, have lots of children. But in some ways I dread going so much. I'll have to face Mummy, and she's going to expect us to live as close to her as possible and I know she'll never leave us alone.'

'Go and live near Bill's family then,' Rose suggested. 'His dad's not too well, is he? That's a good enough reason I'd've said.'

'Not good enough for Mummy,' Gwen said grimly. 'If I go and live in Bromley she'll never speak to me again. Are you looking forward to going back?'

'No,' Rose said bleakly.

Earlier in the war she had longed to see Grace and the twins and Harry – even George. But so much time had passed that although she did want to see them they felt like strangers. How could she leave Italy now, when the person she loved most in all the world was here? Her mind was already working on how she could arrange to stay. The thought of making her life here with Falcone was the only future she could imagine.

'You and Tony haven't ... I mean – is there any chance?'

Rose looked at her, frowning for a moment as if puzzled. Then she registered what Gwen was saying. 'Tony? You mean us getting married? No. Tony and me have never been anything but good pals. That's all.'

Gwen sighed sympathetically. 'I'll miss you such a lot, you know, Rose. You've been ever so good for me. Don't know what I'll do without you in fact.'

Rose smiled, her dark eyes warm and suddenly amused. 'We've all been good for each other, when you think of it. Look at that toffee-nosed Willy for a start. She's almost human nowadays!' They laughed together. 'Anyway, come on. We're not leaving yet. Knowing the army, it'll take them months to get round to demobbing us.'

Rose went to Naples a week later. The truck carrying them there could not move fast enough for her. She was almost frantic with anticipation at seeing Falcone, of feeling him close to her again. In her mind a plan had been forming over the past days. It was exciting, frightening, but right. She knew it was what she must do. This was home, the place she wanted to give her life to. When her number came up for demobilization she would not leave. She was going to stay on. Whatever else mattered in her life, there was nothing so important as being here with Falcone.

As they reached the city and rumbled over the cobbles, the usual stench hitting them, she felt like putting out her hand to stroke the faces of the dusty, weary-looking buildings. They had become familiar to her and she knew she was meant to remain here among them.

Napoli, she said in her mind. Napoli, Napoli. My home, God help me. And she smiled so broadly that the barrel-chested corporal opposite her in the truck might have mistaken it for a come-on had her mind not been so obviously elsewhere.

She half walked, half ran to Il Rifugio through the squalor of the back streets. She had not bothered to put on her old black clothes this time, and she had gathered quite a bunch of poking, nudging children around her by the time she reached the rough wooden entrance. She opened the gate with her key and locked them all out behind her. She ran up the stone stairs, her heart pounding, and hammered on the door. Next to her on the wall, more faded now, were the rough letters she had first seen: IL RIFUGIO.

Margherita opened the door. Rose saw her look of pleased recognition tighten into one of sorrow, fear almost. Without speaking she took Rose's hand and led her inside, not even kissing her, and she shooed away the children with unusual sharpness. Rose felt her insides turn with dread.

'What?' she gasped. 'What is it? Where is everyone? Where is he?'

'Rosa,' Margherita said gently. She led her to a chair in the little side room and made her sit down.

She went over to the old table and opened the drawer. For a second she hesitated before turning to Rose with an envelope in her hand. Rose saw that she had tears in her eyes.

'He left this,' Margherita said. 'Rosa, I've never seen him more distressed, more frightened of himself.'

Numb, not understanding, Rose took the army-issue envelope and opened it, her hands beginning to shake. She realized as she read the short letter, written in bold, black ink, that she had never seen his handwriting before. '*Mia carissima Rosa*,' it began. 'My dearest Rose,

What can I write to you that will ever make you understand what I have done? In my mind I can see your eyes filled with nothing but pain and I know that I, and only I, am the cause of it.

As you read this you'll know I am thinking of you, as I begin life in the seminary of San Domenico Maggiore, because I can think of nothing else until I can be sure you have left Naples and I know there is no chance of us meeting again.

Now that the war is over, I know that you will go back to your country, my beautiful English friend, for your life is there. I know that this is what you have to do, that our days together here during the war have been a time like no other that we shall never have again. I have asked myself a thousand times if we could make a life together, but I know that your home is really in England, and that my certainty that I must try this vocation would stand between us. Please know that you take my heart with you. I am following God's call, but believe me, it's a road of thorns.

I don't have the words to ask you to forgive or to understand. I know only one thing. That I love no other human being as I love you.

Please accept this ring as a bond, a memory of a time like no other. Forgive me. Go well, my love. Paulo Falcone.

Slowly Rose tipped the envelope and shook it, and into her hand fell a slim, silver-coloured ring. She recognized it as one of the many hammered out and sold as souvenirs in the area after the eruption. Into its rim was engraved 'NAPLES '44'.

For a few seconds she sat staring dumbly at the letter, at the ring, both of which seemed to bear no relation to him, to the man she loved. Then, leaping up, she exclaimed wildly to Margherita, 'Where is he? Where is San Domenico Maggiore? It's on the way to the Duomo, isn't it? I remember. I can walk. I must go.'

Solemnly Margherita held her back, taking her firmly by the shoulders, almost shaking her to make her stand still.

She looked hard into Rose's distraught face, willing her to accept, to understand. 'No,' she said. 'It's no good, Rosa. Even if you go they'll never let you see him when he's just entered. It's the rule.'

She watched her friend's face, so alight with love and anticipation when she arrived, as it crumpled finally into shock and grief. For a long time she held Rose in her arms that afternoon as her heartbreaking sobs filled the room, the sound of a woman beyond hope and beyond comfort.

PART THREE

HOME

1947–1957

Twenty-Nine

May 1947

Gradually she came to, feeling sick and muzzy, and opened her eyes, becoming aware of the white room. She saw the edge of a long blue and white curtain hanging beside her, and, above, a light with a white institutional shade over it like a stiff little hat. Wherever was she? She tried to move, and felt a sharp, tearing pain across her stomach which made her sink back on to the bed again.

After a moment a face appeared, smiling down at her. A young woman with blond hair pinned back under a starched white cap.

'What happened?' Rose demanded. 'What's wrong?'

'Wrong? Nothing at all,' the nurse said soothingly. 'You've got a lovely little daughter, Mrs Meredith. Just over seven pounds. You needed a bit of help with her, that's all. Anyway, now you're awake I'll bring her to you. Your husband's waiting outside.'

Soon Alfie walked into the ward following the nurse who was carrying their tiny child wrapped in a white cellular blanket. Alfie was grinning broadly. Rose felt the blanket bundle in her arms and saw the baby's small squashed face, her eyes closed and a shadow of brown hair on her head.

'There,' Alfie said, as if he'd given birth to the child all by himself. 'Meet Hilda Grace. Our firstborn. Ain't she grand, eh?'

Hilda. Rose tried to smile back at him. So he had named her already, before she, Rose, had even come round. They had argued for months about the name. Rose had wanted Diana if it was a girl ('That's a toff's name,' Alfie had said), or Dora, or Margaret. Hilda was Alfie's mother's name. Though she was fond of Mrs Meredith, Rose thoroughly disliked the name. But it had been said. Once a new baby had been greeted by its name it seemed too late to go back on it.

She looked down at this child, whose birth she could not remember and whose name she had not spoken, with a strong sense of unreality. She was lovely, it was true, healthy and wholesome. But even at a few hours old, so obviously Alfie's child – his colouring, his narrow eyes. What connection did she have with her mother?

Alfie's face wore a delighted, triumphant grin as he watched Rose suckling their daughter, oblivious to the hard, angry expression on her face.

'Ah, Mrs Meredith. You're back with us I see.' A doctor with dark, bushy hair was striding towards the bed, white coat gusting out behind him. 'Feeling all right? Your baby was breech I'm afraid. Feet first, in other words, and very awkwardly positioned. So we had to whip her out by Caesarean section. All's looking good now though, as I can see.' He spoke very fast.

'Just have a quick glance at you.' He pulled the curtain across briskly on one side and gestured at Alfie to move out.

When he'd checked her wound and opened the curtains again, the doctor suddenly turned with a smile.

'By the way, do you speak Spanish by any chance? Or Italian?'

Bewildered, Rose said, 'Italian. Well I did. In the war.'

'I've been hearing about you from my staff,' the doctor told her with an amused grin. 'Believe me, you haven't lost your touch. You caused quite a stir – chatting away nineteen to the dozen in Italian as you came round from the anaesthetic.'

'Oh my God!' Rose was suddenly delighted, and smiled back at him. Then she saw Alfie scowling beside her. He didn't like hearing anything about Italy, about her war. He was jealous of it in ways he didn't really seem able to explain.

Cautiously she asked, 'What did I say?'

'No idea,' the doctor said. 'Afraid none of us speak the lingo. I was out east myself. Picked up a smattering of Hindustani. You must have worked hard at it. Apparently it was quite impressive.'

When Rose was finally left alone and Hilda had been taken back to the nursery, she lay drowsily in bed, trying to take in the existence of her daughter. It all seemed very new and strange. Her body, having recovered sensation, felt battered and sore from the operation, and her breasts tingled with the forgotten pains of feeding. She had not yet experienced much in the way of any stirring of love for her child. But those feelings would come, she hoped with all her heart. That little girl had to be the centre of her life, for what else was there? A baby. A child. Was it not, if she was honest, mainly so that she could have children that she had agreed to change her name from Lucas to Meredith?

*

Hilda was crying. Again. All afternoon, on and off, she had screamed and cried until Rose, after trying to work out what it was that was distressing her, had now reached the point where she could scarcely bring herself to care. The sound set all her nerves on edge again. Tutting with infuriation, she picked the baby up and started suckling her in the hope that it would put her back to sleep.

As she was gently laying the child in her wooden cot, she heard the slam of the back door.

'Got the dinner ready?' Alfie shouted. Holding her breath, she heard him drop his heavy boots on to the floor one by one. Then she heard him rattling the lid of the big stewpot, the contents of which had been simmering for over an hour, the smell of gravy and vegetables filling the little prefab house.

'Smells a bit of all right,' he called out.

Hilda stirred in her cot and let out a loud, cracked-sounding wail.

Alfie padded through in his dusty socks, daubs of greyish cement stuck round the ankles. 'Hello. All right, love?'

'You've woken her up again!' Rose snapped at him. 'D'you have to shout about the place every time you come in?'

She had meant it to be different. She was going to try much harder today: smile at him when he came in; make life sweeter between them.

Alfie shrugged. 'Can't have your whole life ruled by a babby. They have to fit in with everyone else. That's family, ain't it?'

He came over to try and cajole her, putting his arm round her shoulders as she picked up Hilda, who was showing no sign of wanting to go back to sleep. Rose flinched at his touch.

'Can't you get changed first? You're filthy dirty.'

'Oh, a dirty frock won't hurt. Not when you hear what I've got to tell you. Got some news. I've got a new job. Bigger firm – not just houses like MacMahon's is, so we shouldn't get buggered about so much. All that on, off, on, off with the government. Don't know if you're coming or going. And it's fifteen bob a week more. How about that?'

'Oh, good,' Rose said, trying to sound enthusiastic.

Alfie kissed her. 'I knew you'd be pleased,' he said. He unfastened his trousers and slipped them down as he sat on the bed. 'You'll see,' he said. 'Half this blooming city needs rebuilding. I'll have me own little firm one day.'

She tried to arrange her face into a tired smile. 'I 'spect you will.'

His shoulders flexed back allowing his work shirt to slide off and revealing his very white, though quite muscular torso. Fishy white, Rose thought, staring at his back. Alfie turned to look at her, deliberately, she suspected, not putting his clean shirt on straight away. Did he really imagine the sight of him would excite her, with a restless baby in her arms?

'We're going places, you and me, Rosie,' Alfie said, his grey eyes showing his habitual optimism. 'We're going to give our kiddies the best you can get.'

Hilda was now looking up at Rose with eyes that were the image of her father's, and though her face was flushed she was quiet, as if listening to them both. Rose stepped over the pile of filthy clothes her husband had left lying carelessly on the floor and went towards the kitchen.

'Spuds should be ready by now.'

She laid her wakeful four-month-old down to kick on a blanket in the little living room next to the kitchen. Then she went through and strained the potatoes and mashed them without any milk. After all, there was gravy. Something was always in short supply it seemed, and at the moment it was milk. As she pushed the masher through the potatoes, Hilda began to cry again.

Rose stood still, closing her eyes. The cries grew louder and more agitated until Hilda sounded as if the whole universe must be collapsing around her. Rose slammed the lid on the potatoes and marched into the living room.

'What d'you want?' she demanded roughly. Hilda was already in such a state that sweat glistened on her pink skin. Sometimes she screamed for so long and so vigorously that her fine brown hair became drenched and stringy.

Rose picked her up.

'Why can't you just be quiet?' she shouted. 'For God's sake stop this sodding racket. There's nothing to scream about.'

'Don't talk to her like that.' Alfie came in behind her, still smoothing Brylcreem into his wayward hair. 'Here – give her to me. That's no way to talk to a babby.'

'Well, *you*'d soon yell at her if you had it all day!' Rose screeched at him. 'You can't even stand five minutes of it when it's your precious sleep she's breaking into!'

It was true. Alfie would mumble drowsily, 'Can't you do something with her?' as Rose hurried out of bed in the night. She felt permanently tired and foggy in the head. The days seemed to swim around her, shapeless, busy, but tedious. She had no spare energy to do

338

anything but care for Hilda's needs, and for Alfie's, and to take a quick nap in the odd half-hours that Hilda slept during the day.

Mrs Meredith, on her occasional visits from Small Heath to see her granddaughter, was kind and fussing and full of unwanted advice.

'If you have a happy mother, you get a happy child,' she told Rose one day, her plump little frame perched on one of their two old chairs. Rose, hollow-eyed, sat staring at her, hardly listening.

'Your job is to pull yourself together and look a bit more cheerful,' she said. 'Then the babby'll soon perk up, you'll see if she don't.'

Rose did feel everything was all her fault. She had selfishly had a child by a man she didn't really love and everyone was suffering.

Now Alfie was walking round the little square of garden in the late afternoon sun, with Hilda in his arms. Rose sat down and burst into tears. She cried a lot nowadays, and Alfie, at first sympathetic, was growing rather impatient.

'What's up with you?' he'd ask. 'You've got a nice home, and a bonny babby. What more can I give you?'

Then he'd assume that protective, fatherly air which made her want to scream with frustration. But she could not break through it without saying things which would have been far crueller than he deserved.

After a while he came in with Hilda dozing in his arms, went through and laid her in her cot. He kissed Rose on the cheek. 'Come on Rosie, that's me girl. Let's see a smile out of you, eh?'

Rose turned her mouth up into a guilty smile.

'That's more like it,' Alfie said. 'Now – how about some of that stew?'

The stew had cooked too long and the carrots were mushy, but Alfie shovelled the food down without comment. Rose watched him gratefully. He was as uncritical over her cooking as he was over housework, not seeming to notice whether she'd done much or not.

'So,' she said. 'How did you get this job then?'

Alfie looked at her with a rather sheepish expression on his pale face. 'It was just – well, a bloke Eddie knows.'

Rose rolled her eyes upwards. 'Might've known he must've had something to do with it.'

'Look, he's all right. I keep telling you.' Alfie forked his last mouthful of potato into his mouth. 'He's on the level, honest he is. He just has the contacts, that's all.'

'Alfie,' Rose said emphatically, 'Eddie is as on the level as Dr Crippen. He's a horrible bloke. Why did you have to pal up with him of all people?'

Alfie looked across the table at his wife's thin, tired face. A little frown line was beginning to form between her dark eyebrows. He loved Rose, proudly and loyally, and knew that he always would. But he couldn't hide from himself the fact that she'd changed, that his affection for her was stronger than hers for him. He could live with that, provided she was there for him. What was harder was this sharpness, the way she was so critical of people. She hadn't been like that before the war. Tart as an acid drop now.

'If I get this job, money and all, I don't s'pose you'll want to moan about that, will you?' he said, sarcastically.

Rose looked at him in silence, refusing to be drawn. 'If you want the job, then you'll do it. Not up to me, is it?'

'No,' Alfie agreed. 'It isn't.'

As she was pouring the boiling water into the teapot after their meal, Rose heard a hasty tap on the glass of the back door. She opened it into the dusk, the air still warm.

Grace was standing on the step, her hand still raised to knock. 'There's trouble,' she said grimly. 'It's George. He's been arrested.'

Rose gasped. 'What the hell for?'

'There was a big job last week. One of the warehouses over Bordesley way. They had parts in there for one of the bigger firms. I don't know if it was the Austin or what. But it was done over. They shifted a whole load of stuff and one of the blokes had a gun on him. George was in on it.'

'No!' Rose protested. 'He wouldn't. Even George wouldn't go that far, surely.'

'Oh wake up, Rose,' Grace snapped. 'George is as crooked as a bent half-crown – has been for years. I always hoped the army'd straighten him out, but he's come back even worse. Since he's been with that spiv Ronnie Grables he's turned professional. He'll have been in on it, no two ways.'

Rose banged the teapot down hard on the wooden surface. 'Silly little sod,' she said. 'What the bloody hell's the matter with him?'

As they carried the tea through she said to Alfie, 'I suppose you heard all that?'

'All right, Gracie? Yes, I heard. It don't surprise me. He's been heading that way for a long time I reckon.'

'Did they come round to the house to pick him up?' Rose asked as they all sat in front of their cups.

Grace shook her head. 'No, thank God. They found

him with Ronnie somewhere.' She was silent for a moment. 'Anyway, it'll be the magistrates next week, and then we'll see, won't we?'

Rose sighed. 'He was such a nice little kid.'

Grace shrugged. 'Weren't we all?'

The war had changed Grace in a number of ways. Though still only twenty-four, the skin stretched over her bony face looked aged, with the kind of lifeless greyness Rose had noticed in most of the people who had stayed in the city during the war. The sweetness which had marked her out in her teens had turned sour. Perhaps we'll just be bitter now, Rose thought, for the rest of our lives, over what we've lost. And as for George, his own bitterness, his damage, had begun even earlier in the war.

Alfie pushed back his chair. 'I'll just go and have a walk in the garden before the light's all gone.'

Rose smiled gratefully at him, knowing he was leaving them alone for a talk.

The two sisters sat on despondently at the table.

'If he goes to prison,' Rose said, 'we'll have lost him, sort of, won't we?'

Grace looked dispassionately at her. 'We lost him years ago.'

'But he's our brother. We can't just turn away from him for all he's done. We've got to stand by him.'

'No,' Grace said. 'He ain't our brother. Say what you like, but it's his choosing. We've all done our best. I stood by him for years while you were off in the army and I've had enough of it. He's made his choice in life and he can go to hell his own way.'

Rose was startled. Was this Grace, idealistic, sweet Grace? 'Well what choices are *you* going to make then?' she challenged her.

'I'm going to train to be a nurse if they'll have me. A proper one. If I'm going to have to work for the rest of my life then I might as well do a job worth doing.'

'Does that mean you'll be living in, at the hospital?'

'How else am I going to get out? Dad can take care of himself when he needs to. You got out – everyone else has, one way or another. Why shouldn't I?'

'No—' Rose held her hands up as if to protect herself from this onslaught of resentment. 'You've got me wrong. I'm not getting at you. I think you're right. I've always felt bad that you've been the one left taking all the flak. I think it's just the right thing for you. In fact I . . .' Suddenly all the frustration of her own life bubbled up. 'I wish I could get a job. I wish I could get out and do anything except being stuck here all day long. Hilda just screams and I can't get anything else done. And Alfie—' She bit back the words. She could not let the truth out, even if they both knew it. Alfie bores me. I have no feelings for him. I should never have married someone so dull and calm, so kind, so limited . . .

Grace watched her sister with anger and disgust written plain on her face, as if she had sucked all the angry, guilty thoughts out of Rose's mind.

'You're a silly cow, d'you know that? Never satisfied, are you? Always have to be off wanting something else than what you've got. D'you know what I'd give to have a kind husband and a home of my own and a babby daughter? You can't see yourself for looking, Rose, and if you don't pull yourself together and act a bit more like a proper wife you're going to lose what you have got!'

Thirty

Grace had not heard that Joe was dead until weeks after the war ended. A letter arrived one morning on thin, crackly blue air-mail paper from a neighbour in Peoria, Illinois, who had been drafted at the same time as Joe. Only then, once he was back in mid-western America late in the summer of 1945, had he thought to write. Grace's hopes of a reunion with the only man she had ever given her heart to were cut to nothing.

It had happened only shortly before Rose arrived home to find what was left of her family still in Catherine Street, shrunken by loss and grief. She felt that she added nothing to it except her own restlessness, her own loss and mourning.

Since she had been one of the first group, with Gwen, to be posted at Caserta, she was also among the first batch to be sent home. Those final three months, before they began their journey across Europe, should have been the sweetest in Italy. The atmosphere had become more relaxed, and there was more opportunity for 'jangling off' on excursions all round the area. For Rose and many others there was a poignant sense of making the most of the warmth and the languorous beauty of the country before the goodbyes began and they all had to head back into new, possibly more difficult lives.

When Rose went for the last time to Il Rifugio, steeling herself to say goodbye to Margherita and Francesco, she found the place depleted. Apart from the one great absence in the house which made it so painful to her, Henry was gone too. He had hot-footed it out of Naples as soon as the war was over.

'I'm sorry our home has come to be such a sad place for you,' Margherita told her. 'Please don't forget us. You have been a very good friend – to me especially.'

On the very few occasions that she had seen them since May, Rose could never hold herself back from asking, 'Have you heard from him? Have you seen him?'

'Not a word,' Francesco told her each time. 'Truly. If we had I would tell you straight away. You must understand. They have to adjust to a new way, their lives are so disciplined . . .'

She had still been unable to believe it completely; to accept that he would not change his mind as he had done so often before; that he could transfer such feelings of passion into a way of life that she could not begin to understand. Some time before she left, she still hoped he would come back to her.

'I wish I could be angry with Falcone,' she said to Margherita.

'It's true he treated you badly,' her friend said. 'Though he did not mean harm, I'm sure.' Margherita always tried to be fair on the motives of others. 'But no one could blame you for being angry.'

'I'm not, though,' Rose said flatly. 'I just feel . . .' She searched round for the right word and settled for the simplest: '*Triste.*' Sad. A deep, deep sadness which never seemed to leave her, which Gwen and the others attributed to her 'failed' relationship with Tony.

'What will you do, Margherita?' Rose asked. 'Will you stay here?'

'Of course.' Margherita looked as calm and steady as ever. 'And perhaps now the war is over we can persuade the Church to give us some proper backing. After all, there is no British army for us to live off now.'

'Well, God help you,' Rose said, without irony.

The two women stood with their arms round each other for a long time before Rose left. Magdalena and Assunta and Francesco all came and embraced her, Assunta with tears running down her kindly, cock-eyed face. When Rose handed back her key and heard the wooden door slam behind her for the last time, she held in her hands a beautiful, poignant present from Francesco: the copy of his favourite French song that they had listened to so often, *'J'attendrai – le jour et la nuit j'attendrai toujours –* I will wait . . .'

The journey to England took them several days on trains with hard, slatted wooden seats. Rose and Gwen travelled together, exclaiming when at last they saw the Channel and the white cliffs of Dover, which they seemed to have left a whole lifetime ago, and at how lush and neat and altogether more cosy the English landscape looked than anything they had seen during their years away.

'I say – it all looks bigger, doesn't it?' Gwen exclaimed as they gazed out at the Kentish orchards, and the elder and hawthorn along the railway tracks. 'I suppose we did leave in the middle of winter, but even so, everything seems to have shot up.'

Rose nodded silently. She felt disorientated and strange, as if returning to another foreign country, not her own. The feeling took quite some time to wear off.

Once she and Gwen had been to the army clearing

house and were released from the ATS, they said their farewells in central London before catching trains for their different parts of the country.

'You'd better write!' Gwen said.

Rose nodded. 'Of course.' She had already made Tony the same promise.

On her journey out of Euston in a hot, smoke-filled railway carriage bound for the Midlands, she pulled from her bag the letter each of them had been given from the Senior Controller of the ATS.

'As you say goodbye to service life,' it began, 'I am writing to thank you in the name of the Auxiliary Territorial Service for the loyal and devoted service you have given to your King and Country.'

Rose looked up for a moment, glancing at the drab outskirts of north London which were beginning to give way to countryside. The man in the seat next to her glanced curiously at her letter.

'You will be called upon,' she read, 'to make further efforts in the service of your country, and I know that you will make them with the same generosity which has always marked the work of the ATS. Goodbye and the best of luck.'

The train was crowded and a number of those on board were men and women obviously as freshly demobbed as she was. But even amid the hum of conversation and jokes and scraping of matches to light cigarettes, she felt a kind of solitude descend upon her. The letter made the army seem official and impersonal again. There was a sense of it all falling away from her, the experiences of the past four years beginning to recede, dream-like. Now she needed to reshape herself, though how, as yet, she didn't know. She thought of Gwen heading towards her mother's home to wait until

Bill was released. What would her reception be? And her own? How would it feel to walk into Court 11, Catherine Street, again?

Birmingham came as a shock to her. Although she had been there during the worst of the bombing, the city had somehow reformed itself in her mind while she was away. She had tended to remember it still complete, with the Market Hall standing and the rows of terraced houses undamaged. But now she saw afresh the jagged gaps which the war had left in the city: the bombsites between the houses, a few levelled off, but many still with rubble in place. Young lads took them over as playgrounds, still plundering shrapnel, and thistles and purple fireweed pushed up between the timbers and bricks.

As she stepped in her solid service shoes across the dirty blue bricks of Court 11, she was struck for the first time by just how small were the houses in which thousands like her had spent their years growing up. She put her hand up automatically to knock at the door, forgetting for a moment that this was where she now belonged. This was life now and she had nothing else. She was home.

Only Sid was in. He was sitting at the old table, a paper open in front of him. He looked up as she opened the door, seeing for a moment a beautiful, neatly dressed stranger in khaki, her hair still arranged carefully under the ATS cap as if she was afraid to take it off.

He looked blankly at her for a moment.

'Rose?'

He pulled himself up, then waited at a loss as she closed the door and came in to stand the other side of the table, putting her bag down on its newspaper surface.

'All right are you?' he said eventually.

Rose could tell he was finding it difficult to think of anything to say, and she was faced with the same problem. She felt tears slide into her eyes. Nothing had changed, although everything had. Sid's face looked thinner, haggard and unshaven.

'You still at the BSA, Dad?' she asked finally, looking for a point of contact.

He shook his head, and she saw how many grey hairs there were among the black. He was fifty-four and he looked an old man.

'They let me go,' he said. 'Back to making bikes now the war's over.'

'Oh. I'm sorry,' she said.

Sid shrugged and then frowned, his pallid skin wrinkling as if he was trying to remember something. 'Where've you come from then?'

'Italy. Near Naples.'

Sid nodded slowly, bemused. 'Have a good journey then, did you?'

Rose knew at that moment that it would be quite pointless trying to talk to anyone at home about her years out of England. It was too far away, too removed from their own experience.

She nodded. 'Got cheap tickets on the train – cut rate if you've just been demobbed.'

She looked around. So far as she could remember, the room was exactly the same as when she had left, almost eerily so.

'Where's Grace?' she asked.

'Up Willett's. She's got a job. On the bedsteads like.'

After a moment he said, 'Fancy making us a cuppa tea?'

And that was that. His sole interest in her war.

The distance was there with Grace too, though the two of them embraced and laughed and looked at each other with tearful eyes when she came in from work. Rose was shocked by Grace's thin, careworn appearance. She felt there ought to be years' worth of things to say, that they should be making up for lost time, yet no one could think what to say.

'How are the twins?' Rose asked eagerly when the two of them were peeling and cutting up vegetables together late that afternoon. 'Have you seen them?'

'Oh, they're full of the joys,' Grace said. 'And Harry. All at school near Edna's. To tell you the truth, she can't bear the thought of parting with them. I asked her if she wanted to send them back here now it's all over. But as she says, they've been there nearly all their lives.'

'I'll have to go over,' Rose said. More people, she felt, who would be lost to her.

As the days and weeks passed after her homecoming, Rose fast began to resent the narrowness of the life she had been thrown back into, and her own lack of independence. How restless she felt! How could she ever settle down to this drab existence of rationing and dreariness after her time in Italy?

It was 'Where've you been? Make sure you're in by ten. Who've you been with?' From Sid, from Grace. Not that she went out much anyway. But Grace had got into the habit of questioning her as if she was her mother. She had completely taken over the role of woman of the house.

Everything seemed shrunken and oppressive. Even the clothes Rose had left behind when she joined up no longer fitted her new, rounder figure. Number five was like a doll's house, while Rose felt like a giant who had been out striding across the world. Why couldn't they realize that after these four years she was now an adult who could run her life without being questioned all the time?

Once more, when there were important considerations like the family's mourning for Sam and Grace's personal grief over Joe, Rose found herself cast in the role of the restless, selfish one, always looking over the wall for fresher, greener grass.

After a month at home she found herself a job as a delivery driver for Snell's grocery store in Balsall Heath. Of course it had none of the excitement of her Italian driving, but at least it got her out and about and brought another wage into the house.

She would never forget her sister's face that day. Usually when Rose reached the house after Grace she found her sister's skinny form bustling round, tidying, handwashing, the evening meal already in hand.

Opening the door, Rose thought for a few seconds that there was no one in. She put down the few groceries she had bought on the way home – Typhoo and milk and Rinso. A ray of late afternoon autumn sunshine had managed to reach its way through the normally dark court windows and lay in a bright slanting shape on the tabletop. Rose was already adjusting her mind to doing the evening meal herself when she saw her sister sitting there, to her right, the horsehair chair swivelled towards the window which looked over the court.

Grace didn't turn to look at her. Rose watched for a couple of seconds, seeing her cheeks drained of any colour, and the tight compression of her lips. She was taking in quick, shallow breaths.

'Are you all right?' Rose asked anxiously. 'Got an attack coming on?'

She stepped closer. Still Grace didn't move. Then Rose saw the letter in her lap, the thin blue paper.

'What's happened?' she asked gently, kneeling down by the arm of the chair, her heart thudding.

Without turning her head, Grace said, 'It's from Joe's mom.'

Rose frowned. Grace knew he was dead. What more could be wrong? 'Poor woman – she must be in a right state.'

'No.' Grace's head whipped round suddenly. 'She ain't in a state. She's got nothing to be in a state about.' Her voice suddenly rose to a piercing shriek. 'Because he's not dead! He's not bloody dead! And he's getting married next month!'

She got up suddenly and moved agitatedly round the room, as if she couldn't think what to do with her body. She picked up the bread knife.

'I could stick this in me!' she screamed at Rose. 'He's stuck enough knives in me to make me feel as if I'm bleeding to death!'

And then the sobs broke out of her. Rose took the knife from her, and drew her shaking sister into her arms.

'I don't understand,' she said softly, after she had let Grace have a good cry.

'That bloke who wrote to me,' Grace gasped out, her head pressed hard against Rose's shoulder. 'He must've known Joe was still alive. They were pals. They live in the same town. Joe must've told him to say he was dead – just to get rid of me.'

'Oh my God.' Rose suddenly saw it as clearly as Grace had done. 'What a bastard.'

'All he's put me through,' Grace went on in her distraught voice. 'Thinking he'd been killed, when all the time . . . He could've had the guts to write and say we was finished.'

'Men have a queer way of going about things,' Rose said drily.

She led Grace back to the chair to sit down, and knelt beside her, holding her and letting her cry, as Margherita had done for her only a few months ago. For days and weeks afterwards she comforted her sister through the shock of this betrayal and, perhaps Grace's most hurtful realization, that at least if he had been truly dead, she could still have carried on believing that he loved her.

During her first weeks at home, Rose had to try to adjust to all the details of living back in an England freshly recovering from war.

Closest to home were the changes which had taken place in the court. The only familiar faces left were the Pye family and Mabel Gooch's household. The two sisters from number four had both died during the war, one quickly succeeding the other, and the house was now occupied by an old couple. Moonstruck House still had occasional tenants, who never stayed long, probably more because of its atrocious state of repair than any other kind of blight on the place. And there was a new family at number three.

Apart from learning the names of the new neighbours, she found she had to carry an identity card, use a ration book and clothing coupons still and register with the grocer and the butcher. There was the damp, drizzly weather and the worn, grey people around her, many of whom – with some justification she soon realized – gibed at her for being 'well out of it' down there in Italy.

The elections that year also shocked many people by removing Winston Churchill as prime minister and replacing him with Clement Attlee.

'How could they do it to him?' Grace demanded. 'After all he's seen us through. They'll be throwing the king out next.'

Rose, who had looked round at her country with new eyes on her return, had heard all the voices clamouring for change and decided to join them. Things had to be moved on, to be improved after the war, otherwise what was the point of it all? She didn't tell Grace, but her vote had gone to Attlee, and she rather suspected Sid's had as well.

There was talk of all kinds of changes, of visions almost unheard of before the war. Of a 'Welfare State' – better support for the out of work, for big families – even for getting looked after when you were sick. Who would not vote for that?

During all this time when change seemed to be constantly in the air and Rose struggled to endure this regressive state, as it felt to her, of living back at home, she had one more adjustment to make – really the biggest of them all.

When she walked in from work one afternoon, Alfie was waiting for her.

'Look who's here!' Grace said as Rose pushed open the door. There was a note of warning in her voice, Rose realized. 'Don't waste this opportunity,' she was saying. 'Make the most of him. You don't know how lucky you are.'

'Alfie!' Rose cried, more startled than pleased. She had known he must come home soon if he had survived the war, and no one had heard that he hadn't. But she had kept pushing the thought from her mind.

There he was, in his slightly too big demob suit, thin and pale, his hair cropped so short there was not enough of it to stick up in its unruly spikes. He looked older, Rose realized. His jaw was stronger as if his whole face had broadened a little.

'How are you?' she asked, full of confusion. So strange him being there, looking much the same, yet with these small changes which were all that signified nearly six years' absence.

'I'm all right.' Bashful and nervous, his eyes lingered over her wonderingly. How her figure had filled out! His eyes moved hungrily down over her breasts, her curving sides. She was wearing a tight-fitting jumper of moss green, and a straight tweedy skirt cut with all the meagreness of war garments, which she had managed to alter so it fitted her.

'You look a treat,' he said.

Rose blushed. She wasn't ready for this, this directness, this talking as if the war had passed in only a few days and nothing had changed.

'Have a cuppa tea,' Grace said firmly, pouring hastily from the brown teapot. 'He wouldn't have one till you got here, Rose. Come on, sit down both of you.' She handed Sid a cup and then sat at the table with Rose and Alfie. Rose watched her smile at him – about the warmest smile she had seen on Grace's face since she'd arrived home.

'I'm sorry to hear about Sam,' Alfie began awkwardly. 'He were a good bloke.'

Rose and Grace both nodded. 'Thanks,' Rose said. 'Yes, he was.'

'Where was it? Out east somewhere?'

'Burma,' Grace told him.

Again they all nodded sadly, lost for words. They didn't talk about the losses of the war much; everyone bore them privately.

'Grace tells me you was in Italy?' Alfie said. 'What the hell were you doing there?'

'ATS. I was a driver,' Rose said, feeling suddenly prickly. His voice held a slight mockery, as if he didn't believe it. 'Was through most of the war.'

'You mean they let you loose on them trucks!' Alfie chuckled, looking at Grace as if expecting her to confirm the joke. 'God Almighty, what a thought!'

Rose gave him a hard, defiant look. 'So where've you been all the war then? Found a better hole to go to, did you?'

She saw her words had hit home. Alfie turned red and looked down at his tea cup.

'It weren't my fault,' he said. 'That's how it was, going into France. If you'd been there you'd have seen.'

Prisoner of war through the whole thing. It was a hard homecoming. Not much to brag about.

'Sorry,' Rose relented. 'It must have been grim for you.'

'Thought at times we'd be there for the rest of our lives,' he said. 'It was only hearing from people . . .' He turned to look at her with a hurt expression in his eyes. 'You could've written more.'

'I did!' Rose exclaimed guiltily. She knew that her communication with him, especially once she had reached Italy, had been the bare minimum. 'I'm sorry. We were very busy.'

It was hard for her even to look at him. Had his feelings stood still during the war? What else did you have to change them when you were locked up in a prisoner of war camp?

'It was such a long time,' she said wearily.

'Come out with me tonight,' Alfie said suddenly. He wanted to be with her away from the others. Kiss her. Get back on their old footing. After all, she was the girl who had promised to be his wife.

Walks, the flicks, evenings spent at her house or his, with Mrs Meredith fussing adoringly round them both. It was more peaceful at Alfie's. To make ends meet, Mrs Meredith had taken in a lodger, a widow in her fifties, but she kept herself to herself most of the time.

Rose found Alfie easy undemanding company. Gradually she remembered that he had made her laugh sometimes, that he was kind and generous. That he adored her, and being adored was warming in itself, even though the feeling was not mutual and she knew it. During the winter of 1945–6 they met almost daily. Alfie soon found work amidst all the rebuilding of the city. When both had finished for the day they met up, already washed and changed, and spent the evening together. Anything to get out of Catherine Street, with Sid morose, often half drunk, and Grace sad, quiet and dutiful.

'When we're married,' Alfie said one evening, 'you won't have to work any more. Not having my wife working.'

Rose looked round at him startled. It was growing dark and they were walking away from Catherine Street after he'd come to pick her up.

'Oh – and what d'you reckon I'm going to do all day

357

long then?' she said indignantly. He had not even asked her to marry him again yet.

'You'll be looking after the babbies, won't you?' he said, as if it was obvious.

He had voiced something that she had not realized yet in herself. Was this not the one thing left that she really wanted? Babies – children? Passion, locked deep in her as a part of the past, did not seem accessible now. Perhaps it was something you could only have for a short time, a dream time, not part of real life. She didn't see much passion in the tired, struggling people around her.

But babies. Something in her surfaced and said yes. Please. If she could have nothing else out of life now, she could have children. That was what Alfie was offering.

In April 1946, in St Joseph's Church, Birch Street, Rose became Mrs Alfred Meredith.

Thirty-One

Moseley, Birmingham, 1949

'Rose? Coo-eee. Rose!'

Rose's neighbour Joan walked down the side of the little prefab house, pulling her eighteen-month-old son Freddie by the hand. She found Rose pegging washing on the line. As she called out again she saw Rose start violently. She turned, the peg-bag in one hand and the other laid over her heart.

'Oh, Joan. I was miles away. You didn't half make me jump.'

'Well, who did you think it might be – Jack the Ripper?' Joan moved over to the line. 'Here, let's give you a hand with the rest of this lot.'

She was a sturdy woman in her early thirties with heavy arms and legs and long, thick brown hair. She soon had the rest of the washing pegged out. Then the two of them turned to watch Freddie and Hilda, who were both bent over something that had caught their attention at the other end of the garden. Hilda was growing up to look the image of her father, though her hair was more manageable than Alfie's and hung in wispy strands round her head.

'Mom!' Hilda shouted imperiously. 'Come here – look!'

'You'll have to watch her,' Joan said. 'She's turning into a right little madam.' It was said inoffensively and Rose knew it to be true.

'I know. Sometimes I don't know how to deal with her. Mind you,' she laughed, 'that's what they all said about me!'

After a moment Joan said, 'Actually the reason I came over was, I was wondering if you could have Freddie for a bit of today. Dave's off sick like, and he can't stand his noise . . .'

'And you need a break,' Rose finished for her. 'Yes, course I can have him. If you bring a bit of something over for his dinner he can stay all day. Be good for Hilda – she's better when there's company.'

Joan's fleshy face broke into a broad smile. 'Are you sure? Thanks Rose. Oh, what a difference it makes to have good neighbours, eh? Now, if there's anything I can do for you – bits of washing or anything – you just bring it right over.'

'Right,' Rose said. She loathed housework. 'You're on.'

As Joan left, full of gratitude, Rose watched her with an amused expression. She wasn't at all sure she believed the story about Dave being poorly, but it didn't matter. The fact was, Freddie was a good kid but Joan couldn't stand to have him round her. Not day in day out. Any excuse and she brought him over to Rose. And she wasn't the only one. 'Oh, I 'spect Rose'll have him' was a common refrain among her neighbours with small children.

One way or another, most days the house was full of them, sometimes with their mothers, but more often without. In fine weather there were often five or six, with Hilda playing Queen Bee at the centre of it all, bossy, perverse, but generally easier to handle when there were other kids about.

'I don't know how you manage it,' the other women would say gratefully as she ran her unofficial little nursery. 'You're a godsend!' And they repaid her with admiration, company and small offerings they could spare out of their rations. They took in her washing and ironing, and sometimes even offered to clean her house – all of which seemed less fraught than spending their time in the company of their offspring.

This was how Rose filled her days. Alfie wouldn't allow her to work, so she managed in her own way to do what she loved best, caring for small children.

Rose used everything she could get her hands on for those kids. Alfie didn't mind how she occupied them, so long as the mess was all cleared up by the time he came home. Often the mothers didn't come to collect their children until the afternoon, and they'd stop and have a cuppa, sometimes bringing their own tea. They sat round as their little ones told them in shrill, excited voices all they had done during the morning.

'We helped Rose in the kitchen!'

'She gave us a apple and toffees!'

'I sat on the potty!'

And Rose smiled delightedly at them all, at their enjoyment of coming to her house.

'When you going to have another then?' Joan asked when she came round later that afternoon. 'Hilda's two now, ain't she? Don't want to have too big a gap.'

'When it comes, I 'spose,' Rose called through from the kitchen. She was mopping Hilda's cotton dress where she'd spilled her drink down it. 'Can't have one any sooner than that, can I?'

'You do remember what you have to do, don't you?'

another of the women teased. 'They don't just grow inside by magic after the first one, you know!'

'You try telling my old man that!' Rose quipped back, going back to join them in the living room.

It was partly a joke. But after the women had left, Rose's emotions were stirred up by this conversation, leaving her unsettled and sad. There was much less lovemaking between her and Alfie than there had been in their early days of marriage and it was nearly always at his demand. Although she wasn't sorry he left her alone more nowadays, she did wonder why it was taking her so long to conceive another child. Was there something wrong? She had taken the risk with Falcone but there had been no baby then either. Often she wished there had been. Perhaps she wasn't able to bear many children?

She thought she had put behind her all those painful feelings of longing and restlessness which had plagued her after the war. She had even managed to quell her frustration at being married to Alfie, burying her desire for a wider, more challenging life by putting all her energy into her most lasting and satisfying love – small children. If this was her life, then she must make the best of it. Look at George, locked away for what might be as much as five years. And Grace, who had been denied the opportunity to achieve even her modest aspirations. She had not been accepted for training by any of the local hospitals, and was still at home, still taking jobs in factories and keeping house for Sid. Wasn't she, Rose, lucky? She should strive to return Alfie's kindness and affection and build a life which was good for both of them and for Hilda.

She had made an enormous effort to create this new

life, like a person who has had a couple of limbs amputated and must adjust to new ways of living.

'It's good to see you looking happier,' Alfie had said to her recently. 'All that looking back to the war – don't do anyone any good, you know.'

She knew he resented her war, even though she had told him only the barest details of her life in the ATS. His own had been so limited, so unheroic. She tried for her own peace of mind to block out her memories. It was another country, another time. Over.

She submitted dutifully to Alfie whenever he turned to her in bed. She had almost forgotten the feelings her body was capable of. Alfie was quickly aroused and very soon satisfied. Invariably he mounted her almost immediately after a kiss and a quick feel of her breasts and he would enter her, almost unable to wait until he was inside, and then it was over. Rose patiently held his slim, pale shoulders time after time as he murmured 'Oh, Rosie, Rosie' into her left ear, feeling nothing except his moist, softening member withdrawing from her. He expected nothing more, and seemed never to notice that she got as much excitement from peeling potatoes as from his lovemaking. He was content. He had a good, pretty wife whom other men envied him for. She never complained, so she must be all right. He was not aware there could be anything more and Rose had shut out any expectation that there might be.

But if she could not even have more children . . . She began to shake, her body letting out the tension that her mind had been keeping so tightly under control. She sat in the little living room as Hilda sat watching her with wide, frightened eyes. Finally, the tears came and Hilda began to cry too.

Rose picked her up and cuddled her. 'It's all right love, don't you worry. Mommy's just feeling a bit poorly, that's all.' She felt steadied by the child's warm body.

Could there ever really be love between a man and a woman? Mr Lazenby, Alfie – both used her in their way. And what about Tony? That was unreasonable, she knew, but in her state such terrible thoughts came. Worst of all, the one she tried to keep furthest from her mind persisted. What about Falcone? Had his words, his confusion, the looks of tenderness and desire that she had from him all been his way of using her? Of getting what he wanted and then dropping her for a 'higher calling'? Had she been deluded even when she responded to a man with every fibre of herself? All these doubts stabbed into her mind.

Though she had tried to avoid thinking of Italy, and especially of Il Rifugio, she knew that what sustained her and kept her feeling worth something was the knowledge that she could truly love and be loved in return. If no one else ever showed her that, then Falcone had done so. Try as she might to forget Italy and him, the thoughts still came to her from time to time.

Sometimes she dreamed of him, seeing his dark, serious eyes close to hers. In some of the dreams he was telling her how much he loved her. She saw herself back in the Finzis' house with the moon slanting through the windows on to their naked bodies. Or in Il Rifugio, making love with him on the thin straw pallets where she had first seen him sleeping. In other dreams he kept telling her over and over again that he had to leave her. He was cold and distant, cruel even. She would repeat the feeling of desolation of returning to Il Rifugio to find him gone. Sometimes she would wake crying, finding Alfie stirring next to her. The depth of her disappointment that he was not Falcone made her weep even more – harsh, quiet tears that she could never share with him.

A few weeks earlier she had had a letter from Gwen. She and Bill had compromised between their two sets of parents and settled in a small village in Berkshire. Bill was working in a bank in the nearby town.

'We're not very far from where we all started out together!' Gwen had told her. She already had a son and a daughter, Edward and Elizabeth, and was expecting her third child.

'I must say, I'm awfully happy,' Gwen wrote. 'Bill is a good husband and father and provides wonderful protection against Mummy when necessary! I should so love you to see E and E and to meet Alfie and your little Hilda. Perhaps we shall all be able to meet up one day?'

Gwen had apparently found a settled, serene sort of happiness with someone she loved. It was possible. But Rose knew she did not love Alfie.

As she sat that afternoon, holding a now rather drowsy Hilda and looking blankly over the child's shoulder, she knew starkly that though she had settled for what she could get, for filling her life with children, it was not and never could be enough.

She had to believe in her love for Falcone and his for her, even knowing she would never see him again. Without that life seemed worth nothing.

Thirty-Two

Rose was hanging decorations on a little Christmas tree when she heard the banging on the door. With her were Hilda and Freddie and another little girl, all squabbling eagerly over the few baubles and the home-made foil stars.

'Hey! Anyone in?' a voice shouted.

She went to the door. Outside stood two men, struggling to support Alfie between them, his arms pinned over their shoulders and his body sagging between.

'About time,' one of the men said. 'He's a dead weight.'

Rose looked at them all, dumbfounded. Alfie's head was lolling to the right and his eyes rolling strangely from side to side like those of an idiot.

'Move out the road,' the older of the two men grunted at her. 'Let's get him on the bed. Silly bugger's got himself properly tanked up. Been a right game getting him over here on the bus, I can tell you.'

They hoisted Alfie into the bedroom and half laid, half threw him on to the pink-candlewick-covered bed. His eyes rolled upwards and then he closed them.

'He looks terrible,' Rose said. The sight of him really disturbed her. She stood close to the door holding back the three curious children. 'What's got into him? He's not a big drinker.'

'Oh, he'll be right as rain by tomorrow. Must've been

putting it away while no one was looking. He'll have one hell of a head on him in the morning!' The younger man laughed knowingly.

The other, more serious, said to Rose, 'You'd better tell him, though, one more do like this and he'll be out of a job. He's lucky they're not putting the boot behind him today like. He'll have to watch himself.'

Still startled, Rose watched them go as they called out cheerfully, 'Tara, Alfie. See you in the morning.'

'Save it till Christmas next time, mate!'

Rose sat the children down in the next room with a beaker of rosehip syrup and a biscuit each, and came back in to her husband. He was lying with his eyes closed, but when he felt her unfastening his boots and pulling them off, he opened them.

'Rose?' he murmured indistinctly. 'I feel terrible.'

'Well, what were you thinking of?' she asked him. She knelt down by the head of the bed. 'No wonder. You're not used to more than the odd pint.'

'No.' Alfie's voice sounded thick and strange; out of his control. 'I told them – I kept saying . . . I haven't had a drop. Nothing.'

Rose frowned. 'What d'you mean? Look, you don't have to make a big secret of it. Was it something the others gave you? Whisky?'

'No,' he slurred back. 'I told you . . . nothing. I don't know. I'm scared, Rose.'

Suddenly very alarmed, she bent close to him and smelt his breath. There was not a trace of alcohol on it. She stood up quickly. 'I'll get a doctor.'

By that evening Alfie was in Selly Oak Hospital. Rose left Hilda with Joan and went in to see him. She found him lying in a long ward with rows of beds along each side, his face almost as white as the stiff pillow case and his eyes closed. Rose stood for a moment looking down at him. His hair was sticking up on top of his head and still looked greyed from the dust at work. His neck was bent rather awkwardly to one side as if he had a crick in it, and the shape of his body underneath the thin covers looked slight suddenly, and vulnerable.

'Alfie?' she said softly. On the floor by the bed she put the little bag of his possessions she'd brought in: pyjamas, shaving brush and razor, and the day's paper, thinking he'd have been feeling better.

His eyes opened slowly, trying to focus. He also seemed to be trying to smile.

'How you feeling?'

'Bad,' he said. 'Never ... had anything ... like this ... before.'

She reached under the covers suddenly, surprising them both by taking his hand, feeling compassionate and protective towards him as she would have done towards a child.

'They'll look after you,' she told him. 'Soon see you better.'

Alfie nodded slowly and his eyes closed again. 'Sleepy,' he managed to say.

Rose sat by him until he was deeply asleep and then went to speak to the matron, a tall, well-spoken woman with a sheaf of papers in her hand. She had a brisk, forbidding air which suggested she might be kind so long as you submitted to her totally.

'My husband, Alfred Meredith,' Rose said, rather timidly. 'Do you know what's wrong with him?'

'Mr Meredith,' the woman said, her grey eyes scanning the ward for inspiration. 'Ah yes, the *ataxia* – new admission. No. Too early to say I'm afraid. Could be something quite simple but you never know. Might be a few days before we're sure.' She made as if to walk off.

'But how long will he be here – please?' Rose called after her. The woman seemed more intimidating than any officers she had come across in the ATS.

'Oh, I couldn't possibly say,' Matron replied. She noted something down on one of the papers she was holding. 'Let's wait and see what they say in the morning, shall we?'

Rose walked desolately out of the echoing hospital building to catch the bus home. Seeing Alfie lying there had come as a terrible shock to her. He looked so broken and helpless. Though she did not love him with anything approaching passion, she knew that it mattered to her a great deal what happened to him. She relied on him, on him being there with her, on his bland optimism and steady kindness. She had simply grown used to him. And he was Hilda's father. She was really frightened.

Before she reached the bus stop she changed her mind. Hilda would be asleep by now at Joan's. It was already dark. Instead, she made her way to Catherine Street. She felt completely churned up inside and she needed to see them, to tell them what had happened. Grace may have hardened herself to many of the problems of others, but she could always summon up sympathy for anyone who was sick.

Rose knocked on the door of number five. Outwardly the house looked much better than it had in the old days. The back-to-back terraces in Catherine Street were among a number that had been 'soled and heeled' by the council, who could not keep up with the demand to build new houses and had decided to patch up some of the ones they already had. New roofs, windows and doors had made the whole place look smarter. The front door was painted a cheerful sky blue.

'What you doing here?' Grace asked when she opened the door.

Rose walked in amid the smell of meat cooking and the gaslight which seemed so much dimmer than the electric they had out in the prefabs. She noticed there were no signs of Christmas about the house.

'Where's Hilda?' Grace demanded anxiously.

As Rose sat down, Grace stood by the table, hands on hips. She was dressed in a drab brown skirt and fawn blouse, on top a flowery apron which Rose realized with a pang had been cut down from an old dress of Dora's. Grace's hair was fastened up in an old scarf, the end tucked in at the front, to keep her hair out of the way while she was working.

'Hilda's with Joan,' Rose said. 'I've been with Alfie. He's in Selly Oak. Been taken bad.'

Grace automatically reached out and poured Rose a cup of tea. 'In hospital? What's up with him?'

'They don't know.' Rose began to cry at last, the worry and shock of the afternoon finally released.

Grace leaned close to her sister's dark head and put an arm round her shoulder. Rose got a whiff of the sweaty smell from under her arms, sharp, but somehow comforting.

'They brought him home at dinnertime. Looked as though he'd had a skinful. He was all over the place – eyes rolling, could hardly get a word out of his mouth, the lot. And he hadn't touched a drop.'

Grace looked quizzically at her. 'You sure he's not just having you on? After all, what with Christmas coming up – you know what they're like.'

'No,' Rose sobbed. 'He hardly drinks ever. He'd never lead us on and make us think he was bad when he wasn't.' She looked into Grace's concerned eyes. 'When you were nursing, d'you remember seeing anyone like that – like Alfie is now?'

Grace shook her head. 'I've seen blokes in a proper state – shocked and that. But not like you said. Never heard of that.' She patted Rose's arm with sudden kindness and Rose could hear the wartime nurse coming out in her. 'Anyhow, the doctors do all they can, so there's no point in fretting all night about it. You should get back to Hilda before she thinks she's lost both of you.'

As she spoke, the door opened and Sid pulled himself into the room. His hair, so dark when he was a young man, was now a powdery grey.

'Dinner ready?' he asked Grace, and she got up to spoon out the meat and vegetables.

'Alfie's in Selly Oak Hospital,' Rose told him, and tried to explain what was wrong. She wished overwhelmingly that Dora was there for her to turn to.

'Oh ar,' Sid said. Then through a mouthful of swede he commented dispassionately, 'Blooming shame. I always thought he looked a weak little runt though.'

Rose stood up abruptly. 'Time I was going,' she said bitterly. She put her coat on. 'Tara Dad. I see you're much as usual.'

Sid raised one hand as a goodbye, but Grace followed Rose out into the yard.

'It's no good expecting anything from him,' she said, with more gentleness than Rose had heard from her for a long time. 'He lives in his own little world now and the rest of us might just as well not be here.' She touched Rose awkwardly on the shoulder. 'If you need anything, come to me, all right?'

Rose smiled at her. 'Still here, aren't you – after all this time. Running about after everyone.'

Grace shrugged rather evasively. 'Looks like that's what I'm good for, don't it? Now remember what I said. Just ask for help if you need it.'

Humbled, Rose kissed her quickly on her rough cheek. 'That's nice of you,' she said. 'Ta.'

Alfie spent Christmas 1949 in hospital. Hilda kept saying, 'Where's my dad?' Rose brought her in to be with Alfie for a short time, walking into the warm ward from the icy air outside. When Hilda saw him she ran to him, dressed in her little red coat and black boots, her hair tied up in two pigtails.

'Hello little monkey,' Alfie said as Hilda hurled herself at him. He was propped up on several thick pillows. His voice sounded stronger now and his words were easier to understand.

'Not on the bed, please,' a nurse said as she walked past. 'I know it's Christmas, but we still have to keep the rules.'

'She's a real daddy's girl,' Rose told her apologetically. 'Been missing him like anything.' She lifted Hilda down on to her lap. The nurse walked off in her heavy black shoes, smiling.

'How are you?' Rose asked. 'You look a bit better today.'

'I feel better,' Alfie said. He was even wearing one of the coloured hats they'd all been given to jolly things along for Christmas, and the soft orange tissue paper kept slipping off his clumps of hair. 'It's wearing off a bit. My hands felt all queer, sort of numb. Scared me, I can tell you.'

372

His pale face suddenly lit up with an adoring smile. 'It's lovely to see you, Rosie. Give us a kiss, will you?'

She stood up and leaned forwards to kiss him. Affectionately she straightened the orange crown. 'I'll have to bring some Brylcreem in,' she joked.

But Alfie was staring at her with a seriousness which silenced her. 'I love you,' he said. 'You know that, don't you? I should tell you more often. Only when you're always about I forget ... But, if anything was to happen ... ?'

'I know,' Rose said. She couldn't look at him straight, and felt her cheeks turning red. Hilda was pulling at her skirt, impatient at this conversation which took the attention away from her.

'You'll be home soon though, won't you?' Rose said brightly.

They didn't tell her then. It was a couple of days later. A condition affecting the nerves, the doctor with the grey hair and distant eyes said. Very hard to predict how it would progress. Some patients lived normal lives for years. Attacks and remissions, that was the pattern. Sometimes he'd be perfectly all right, sometimes not.

'Does he know?' Rose asked. Her eyes rested on the doctor's dark blue tie.

Looking out of the window beyond her, he said, 'He's known for a little while. He's had the chance to think about it. Said he'd rather I told his, er, family myself.'

'What about work?' Rose asked. 'Will he be able to carry on?'

'Your husband's a builder I see.' The doctor made a

373

sharp, regretful intake of breath. 'Very difficult. Building's not a good job to be in with his condition. Any work off the ground, on scaffolding for instance, could cost him his life if he had another of these attacks. You must impress that upon him strongly, Mrs Meredith. He can't afford to be careless with himself.'

'Course I'm going back to work!' Alfie said. It was January, snowy, and thick fog covered the city, so dense that the traffic was having trouble passing along the streets. 'I feel fine. Don't s'pose they'll be doing a lot today anyway, but I've told them I'll show me face and see what's cooking. Don't you worry, Rosie,' he said, seeing her anxious expression. She was standing at the door with Hilda in her arms. 'I'll keep me feet on the ground. After all, someone's got to be the breadwinner round here!'

After he'd kissed them both they watched him, Hilda waving as he walked away, fast disappearing into the fog.

Two months later Alfie collapsed again. This time he was at home, and the attack seemed even more severe. Rose was terrified by the fear and distress on his ashen face. A pattern emerged. Hospital, a recovery period, a time when he felt weaker perhaps, but more or less normal, and then another attack. By the late summer of 1950 he was barely recovering between each one. His legs, from which he was gradually losing all sensation, finally became paralysed. He could do very little without help. Alfie had become a permanent invalid.

Thirty-Three

'This house is all pongy!'

Little Hilda, only a few months off her fourth birthday, sniffed distastefully as she eyed up the place that was to be her new home. She had grown into a pale, rather scrawny child, her brown hair scraped back into a high ponytail, the end of which did not even reach as far down as the back of her neck.

'Moonstruck House.' Mabel Gooch's gruff voice came from the edge of the room, where her barrel-shaped body was leaning up against the doorframe. Mabel, still the matriarch of Court 11, had aged from a woman with a strong, handsome face into one who looked almost masculine, with a hint of a moustache gathering on her top lip. 'Bet you never thought you'd end up here, eh, Rose?' There was a strong hint of satisfaction in her voice. But then she added, 'Still, it's good to know there's someone decent living here for a change. God knows, we've had some rum'uns in here, I can tell you.'

'It'll have to do us,' Rose replied flatly. 'I can't keep up the rent where we are.'

Like number five, Moonstruck House had been soled and heeled. All the windows were in, the doorframes

375

had been replaced and the roof fixed. But on the inside it was a different matter. The smell of damp was unmistakable and there was mould growing all along the walls under the windows. In the downstairs room there was still some paper on the walls – a yellowish colour with clusters of dull pink flowers and a border of green cheese-plant leaves a few inches from the ceiling. A few sections of it near the floor had been ripped off upwards, and in other places the corners were curling back.

Upstairs, both rooms showed the barest traces of paper. Otherwise it was bare plaster, some of which had fallen or been gouged out in places where through the holes you could see the bare brick. In the second-floor room the floorboards opened up suddenly to the stairwell which plunged down in a corner. It was bleaker than number five had ever been.

'Never had anyone in long enough to take a pride in it. But you could soon cheer it up, give it a lick of distemper.'

Rose nodded absently. Mabel noticed how painfully thin she had become again. Even her pre-war clothes hung on her now and her eyes seemed more prominent in her face.

'He'll have to have a bed downstairs,' Rose was saying. She was grateful to Mabel for sticking around to talk things through. 'I can't get him up the stairs of a night. And anyway,' she added resignedly, 'it's hard to get him out of bed in the first place nowadays.'

'Like that is it?' Mabel shook her head sympathetically. She felt suddenly rather maternal towards Rose. 'Well, you'll have to make it as easy on you as you can. You working and night school and that. Don't worry' – she patted Rose's shoulder with her thick hand – 'we'll see you through. Your mother would've done the same for any of us.'

There were tears of gratitude in Rose's eyes as she turned to her old neighbour. 'Yes,' she said. 'I know she would.'

They did fix Alfie up with a bed downstairs, along the wall away from the front window. Rose put up some net to stop people gawping in. The Pyes lent her a hand one weekend in filling in the worst holes in the walls and giving the place a couple of coats of whitewash upstairs. Rose scrubbed down all the floorboards with disinfectant and laid down what she had in the way of old peg rugs and little off-cuts of carpet they had acquired in Moseley.

Alfie half sat, half lay watching her one Sunday morning as she attempted energetically to carry on turning the place into somewhere they could call a home. It was cold and she had built a fire and was sweeping up the scullery.

'You should get out of bed,' she told him patiently. 'You know what the nurse said about you getting sore if you lie about all day.'

Alfie looked up at her languidly. 'It's so cold,' he protested, in the strange, slurred voice he spoke in now. 'And you've got too much to do already, Rosie.'

'I can do that later,' Rose said, growing impatient. 'Come on – let's get you up.'

Hilda appeared from upstairs as Rose was preparing a bowl of warm water to wash her husband. 'What can I do?' she whined.

'D'you want to come and help me give your dad a wash?' Hilda had grown very used to seeing her father's body since he had been ill. His place at the centre of all that was going on made his a very public illness.

'No,' Hilda said, sitting on the bottom step of the stairs and kicking at the wood with her heels. 'S'boring. And smelly.'

'Well go out and play then,' Rose said, trying the temperature of the water in the bowl.

'Don't want to.' Hilda's face twisted into the expression of stubborn sulkiness she often wore nowadays. 'You're just trying to get rid of me.'

'Yes,' Rose snapped. 'I am. Sitting around moaning at me. Now do as you're told and get out there with the others.'

'Me dad'd never be so horrible to me,' she said snidely as she pulled her old coat on.

Silently Rose began soaping Alfie's scrawny white arms. He had lost all the muscle tone that his building work had given him, and the translucent skin seemed to cover bone and little else. His arms had become stiff and awkward, and she had to lean on them to bend them. She washed under his arms, the light brown wiry hair turning white with soap. She'd tucked a towel under his shoulders so as not to wet the sheets. Gently she wiped his face, and then slid her hands flat under him to turn him so that she could wash his back. The nurses had showed her how – the lifting and bed baths. How to position a little container between his legs to catch the urine which dribbled from him beyond his control.

When she had turned him back over and was washing his chest she realized he was watching her, and that tears were rolling down his cheeks. She stopped what she was doing and stroked his hair which was rather greasy and needed cutting.

'What's the matter?' she asked softly.

'I'm sorry, Rose.' The sobs shook his body, his thin, gentle face growing pink and streaked with the tears. 'You shouldn't be having to do all this.'

'Ssshh,' she said, trying to soothe him, tears of sorrow and pity filling her own eyes. 'Don't say that. I've told you. I'm your wife, aren't I? Who else should be looking after you?'

'But living back here.' Alfie's voice came out horribly slurred from the disease and his distress. 'It was the last thing you wanted. I was going to do so much for you, Rosie, give you so much. I'm sorry . . .'

In the early days, when she had first begun caring for him, he had wept like this often, full of remorse, frustration and fear as to what was going to happen to the family. He had worried how they would live on sickness benefit alone. About how Rose would manage, and what would happen to Hilda. And in sheer horror at what was happening to his body. Worst of all had been the times when, at first, he had still wanted to make love to her.

'Rosie, come here,' he'd beg, wanting things to be all right, for at least that to be possible between them. She would lie in his arms as he took her breasts in his hands, touching her, kissing her desperately, trying to force some sensation into the limp lower half of his body. Sometimes he would say, as he had never done when he was well, 'Will you help me? Will you touch me?'

Pityingly she had taken him in her hands, trying to kindle him, caressing the soft, small part of him which could feel nothing, and trying, more for his sake than for her own, to arouse him. He would lie watching her with a fixed expression of concentration on his face, longing, willing himself, and it was that desperation she saw in him which made her cry, and his failure and shame which brought on his own tears, so that they would end up lying in distress in each other's arms, in a strange way closer than they had ever been before he was ill.

They no longer attempted lovemaking now. Rose cared for him and he, most of the time, just accepted that this was how it had to be. Seeing him in this broken state she grew to realize how grateful she was to him, and that she did indeed care for him, not as a lover – which she never had and never could – but as a kind, familiar friend, and the way she would care for a child or any sick, fragile creature.

As she dried his tears that cold morning, he appealed to her in a whisper, 'Give us a kiss, will you?'

She bent and kissed his lips, smelling the rather stale, sour smell of him despite the wash. When they had kissed she smiled kindly at him. 'I'll change your sheets again. Come on – let's get you into a chair.'

'I'm sorry,' he said again.

'It's not your fault,' she told him, touching his bony shoulder. 'Look – it's all right.'

In a way it was. Her feelings at that time were so mixed, so mercurial that at times she could barely make up her mind what she felt about anything.

Moving back into Catherine Street had symbolized for her the end of any aspirations of her own. The circle had closed. Now she was back just where she began and could hope for nothing better. But in another way it had been a relief to see the familiar old faces and know she could always rely on them for help. At that moment that was her greatest need.

At other times she was overcome by an extraordinary exhilaration, even through all the tiredness. It was like a resurgence in her of someone entirely forgotten. There was the thrill of risk, and the challenging sense that she was in charge. She could no longer be dependent and passive. She began to experience some of the zest for life she had felt in the army. Now at last she could do something.

'I'm going to have to earn more than the odd bob or two,' she had said to Grace. 'I'll have to learn how to do something. I'm only fit for the factory floor or a shop.'

So she had started the evening classes. She signed on for three evenings a week at Sparkhill Commercial School over on the Stratford Road. English, typing and shorthand, she decided, would stand her in the best stead for the future. Meantime, whatever job she got they would have to make the best of it until she was trained to do something better.

She applied for a job working in the offices of a firm in Burton Street, only a couple of streets away from home: Turner's Metal Smallware.

Since it was so near at hand she was able to run home in the lunch hour and give Alfie a few moments' company as well as hastily making Hilda something to eat. The rest of the day either Mabel or Gladys Pye saw to her and she played with the other kids in the court who were too young for school.

Her duties at Turner's ranged from seeing to the outgoing post, of which there was a great deal to be sealed and stamped on the cranky old franking machine, to helping actually to pack the goods: shining piles of hairgrips and hairpins and metal coathangers and straight pins, which were boxed up and sent out to shops all over the country.

Though the work was often tedious and she felt

guilty leaving Alfie and Hilda, the fact was she had no choice in the matter if they were all to eat. As her mother had done before her, she was going to keep her family, though at the moment the money was never enough. Mrs Meredith helped them out a little when she could, but it was the kindness of the neighbours which really kept them going: Gladys popping in saying, 'Look – we've a couple of portions of stew left over. You have it, Rose. It'll go bad else'; or Mabel coming by with a loaf or a cake or a pat of margarine. Even the neighbours whom she had not known all her life pitched in. Rose sometimes wept at their unquestioning generosity.

Often in the evening, when she had walked the couple of miles to Sparkhill after a hasty bite to eat, she would sit for two hours learning the intricacies of Pitman shorthand, her whole body throbbing with tiredness. Despite that she was one of the best in the class. She practised at every opportunity. Whenever she had to write something down she would think how to do it in shorthand.

'Some people have a natural bent for shorthand,' the tutor told her, smiling. 'And you're certainly one of them.'

Rose beamed with delight at learning something new and being praised for it.

One evening, when she had been going to Sparkhill for a few months, she walked down the front steps of the school with some of the other girls from the class. They were chatting, groaning over their typing speeds on the heavy Underwood machines. It was a warm evening, still light, and the air was soft and still, scented with fading laburnum and lilac. Occasionally a car passed by on the Stratford Road.

'I'm tired,' Rose sighed as they reached the pavement. 'I've a good mind to get on the bus and to hell with it.'

'Money down the drain,' her friends reminded her cheerfully. 'Bus or bread.'

Rose smiled. 'It's a good job you're here to keep me in line. Anyway, by the time I've been into town and out it'll take me just as long. And at least it's still light.'

They said their goodbyes and set out in different directions.

Rose turned, still smiling from the friendly company, to walk towards the side street where she would turn off towards home. She caught a whiff of roses from the gardens and breathed in the scent, so different from the usual smoky smells of the city.

Just before she turned off the Stratford Road, wondering whether Hilda had played Grace up about going to bed, she felt a hand settle firmly on her shoulder. Startled, she turned with a gasp, and behind her she found a handsome, and suddenly familiar face grinning at her.

It was Michael Gillespie.

Thirty-Four

March 1952

Again she woke from a vivid dream, those dreams which came only occasionally now. She realized her face was wet with tears. It had been so vivid.

They were in Il Rifugio, alone in the storeroom where she had first seen Falcone on the maize-straw mattresses. The others may have been around somewhere but the two of them were alone, and knew they would not be disturbed. She did not recall any particular words, or that they had spoken at all. What was most overpowering was the atmosphere of tenderness and passion as they loved one another. She remembered his body, slim and strong and dark, in every detail, as if they had only truly been together the night before. And the look on his face, his delight in her and care for her and her own sense of giving herself unreservedly and with joy.

For a moment she lay wiping her eyes, still completely taken up in the mood of the dream. Then other thoughts forced themselves into her mind, thoughts which filled her with excitement, but at the same time with strong pangs of guilt. Michael. She had agreed to meet Michael tonight. Though her conscience and common sense cried out not to do it, she knew that she would go.

She had seen Michael a number of times, at first only occasionally and seemingly by chance, after their first meeting. Seeing him there had truly delighted her.

'Michael!' she'd cried in wonder. 'You're alive. All this time you've been alive!'

He'd laughed at this, bending his strong body down to give her a kiss on the cheek. 'Oh, I'm alive all right. Even survived the River Po and that's saying something, I can tell you. Sea of corpses it was when we crossed.' His expression lost its exuberance at the memory. 'But that's long in the past, and we both came through it, eh?'

'I was never in much danger down there,' Rose said. 'Hell of a lot quieter than it was here really.' She stood staring at him, amazed at the thought that the last time she had seen him had been outside the stables at Caserta. And it was so precious, that memory, that link with the war. Just those few minutes when they had stood together with Tony. Someone else who would remember him, remember the place.

'You living round here?' Michael asked.

'No. Been to school.' She outlined briefly what she was doing, told him about Alfie and Hilda.

Michael let out a whistle of sympathy. 'That's really rough. You poor kid. I thought you wasn't looking as bonny as when I saw you in Italy. But you always did have guts, I'll say that for you, Rose. Can't see my wife getting out earning a living.'

'You're married then?' They were still standing where he had caught up with her, Michael pressing one of his shiny black shoes up against the wall facing him as they talked. A tram made its way noisily along the road.

'Oh, yes. The wife and I live on down there a way.

385

Edge of Hall Green.' He pointed down the Stratford Road. 'Mary her name is. Good Irish girl. I've a lad too – Joseph. He's two.'

Rose felt a pang at the name Joseph. For a second she calculated how old her own Joseph would have been now. Fourteen this year. A grown lad, perhaps just starting out on a job.

'I've got the bookies down the road,' Michael was saying proudly. 'My own little outfit. Gillespie over the door. Doing well. You know how it is with a growing family. We've another on the way – due in October.'

'I'm glad. It's really good to see you.'

'Listen – come for a drink with me,' Michael urged. He went to put an arm round her shoulders and usher her along. 'Jesus, you're skinny! We can have a quick one in the Mermaid.'

'I can't,' Rose told him regretfully. 'Sorry Michael, I just can't. I've left my husband and kid all day.'

'OK,' Michael said easily, removing his muscular arm from her shoulders. 'Then let me walk you home.'

'Well . . .' Rose hesitated. 'That'd be nice. But what about your wife? Weren't you on your way home?'

Michael made a quick, dismissive gesture. 'Oh – she'll be off to bed any minute. She gets tired, what with the babbies and that. Anyroad, I'm out most nights to tell you the truth. She never kicks up a fuss.'

All the way back to Catherine Street they chatted and reminisced. Michael told her he had met Mary, his wife, three years ago.

'It was one of these Irish dos. Lots of booze and the music going and all the couples dancing and all the old'uns getting sick for the home country. She was fresh over here and she stood out. Really pretty face she had – well, she still has, except she's got a bit of fat on her after having Joseph, of course. But she's a good lass. Looks after me all right.'

'Bet that takes some doing,' Rose teased him. She realized, as ever with Michael, that she had begun to flirt with him. 'Not sure I'd fancy the job myself!'

'Would you not?' Michael sounded mock wounded. 'I'd've said we'd have made a pretty fine team, you and me, Rosie.'

Rose realized he was not entirely joking, and she blushed in the dusk. Guiltily, she knew she had not felt so alive, so stimulated by anyone's sheer presence, in months and months. She steered the conversation on to less personal things.

When they said goodnight at the end of Catherine Street, Michael gave her another kiss on the cheek.

'Come for a drink another time,' he called, turning back towards Sparkhill.

Inside, to her surprise, she found Sid dozing in the chair beside Alfie, who was also asleep. She crept in, and Sid roused himself as she closed the door.

''Bout time,' he said, looking up at her with the bleary eyes of an old man. 'Our Grace has gone home to bed.'

Rose looked at the clock. She had taken half an hour longer than usual to get home. Had she and Michael really spent so much time talking? It had seemed to pass in seconds.

She saw Sid out, giving herself a ticking off when she remembered how much help they were giving her.

She and Michael met for a brief drink some weeks later, but then it was months before she saw him again. There was no English class on the Thursday evening before

387

Christmas, and they arranged to meet then. Rose knew she was deceiving Grace, who would spend the evening with Alfie. But sometimes she thought Grace would be lost now without her role in Rose's house. It had become part of her life. And Rose hungered for company, for interest and someone to have a good talk with.

As she sat opposite Michael in the busy Mermaid pub, she found all her doubts disappearing, and relaxed back into enjoying his company. They made an attractive pair, Michael in what looked like a new dark blue suit, his hair cut perfectly and greased back, and Rose with her long hair curling down prettily over her shoulders. She looked beautiful, especially when animated by her conversation with Michael.

They started talking about general things: Michael's business, the way money was so tight still, and of Michael's satisfaction that Winston Churchill had been re-elected to office in October.

'Now things'll get back to rights again,' he told her, with the almost superstitious regard in which some people still held Churchill. 'All that Labour lot messing about. What we need is a proper government – someone who knows what they're doing. Been like rats from a sinking ship, all these people looking to go abroad to work. What good's that to our country?' He pushed back his stool. 'Another?'

Rose watched him going to the bar. He still walked with the trace of a limp which had stayed with him from his injury in Italy. He was a fine-looking man with strong features and those direct blue eyes, always a hint of mischief in them.

He's a bit of a chancer, she thought. Bet he gives that poor wife of his the runaround. But she couldn't resist being with him this evening. He was a connection with the past, and being able to go out and meet him made her feel she could laugh and be her age again, for a short time at least, instead of driven, worried and overworked.

'I was just thinking,' he said, sitting down with their drinks, a pint for him and port and lemon for her. 'If you're out working all day, who looks after your husband?'

'Neighbours. I moved back to the Birch Street area again when Alfie was taken bad. They all help mind Hilda, my little girl, too. Me and Grace do the shopping between us – I mean, who's got the time to stand in a queue for hours on end? Anyroad, that's all that's left of the family now. My brother George is . . .' Blushing, she looked down at the table. 'He's in Winson Green.'

'Jesus! What for?'

'Burglary. He went bad on us during the war. I was away of course, so I hardly saw it coming. But Grace had him all through. She's done with him. She don't even go and visit.'

'But you do?'

'When I can. Only every month or two, and he's due out soon anyroad. He's my brother. I always had a soft spot for him as a kid. I s'pose it was after the evacuation – he ran away, and he was never the same after he came back. It's as if—' She looked up at Michael, and he saw that tears had filled her brown eyes. Gently he leaned over and laid one of his large hands over hers, which were clasped tensely together on the table.

'It's as if he went off like a pint of milk. You can't get through to him any more. When I go over there' – she grimaced at the thought of the dark stone walls and towers of the prison – 'he sits there, all pinched in the face. All hard-looking. I don't know who he is any more.' Slowly she pulled her hands away.

'I'm sure you're doing the right thing,' Michael told her. 'Though God knows, with all you've got on your plate no one'd think bad of you if you didn't go.' Then he asked gently, 'And your husband – Alfie, isn't it? How much can he do?'

'Nothing.' Rose sounded very matter of fact. 'It's got to him very hard and very fast. He doesn't move out of bed. Can't do anything for himself at all. Someone has to be about all the time.'

She took in Michael's appalled expression, realized that he was reaching for her hands again, but she kept them under the table. At that moment she felt that if he touched her she might just turn into his arms and cry out all the worry and tiredness and frustration of the past months. She longed for such comfort, to be able to lean on someone as solid and kind and reviving as Michael.

'Oh, Rosie,' he said. 'You poor, brave kid.'

She could think of nothing else to say to him, and was relieved when after a few moments he started talking. As she wiped her eyes she realized that her telling him about her own life and worries had released him and he was now able to disclose to her his own.

'When I met Mary, I thought I'd found the best woman ever,' he told her. 'She was pretty and sweet. She looked up to me and I loved her. I really thought the world of her, Rosie . . .' He hesitated, and as she looked across at him she saw confusion in his face.

'But . . . ?' she prompted.

'I don't know if it's having the babbies that's done it. Joseph's a great kid, and now we've got little Geraldine and she's a bonny babby. But Mary, she's got time for nothing else. What with feeding Geraldine at night and both of them on all day. And she frowns all the time.

You may smile, Rosie, but before I'd hardly seen her crease her face in that way. She was the sweetest girl . . . But now she's got a line, as if someone's taken a pencil right down.' He pointed to the little bridge of flesh between his eyebrows. 'She never had that before.'

Rose leaned across the table and pointed at her own face, so that a man at the next-door table watched with a puzzled expression. 'Look – I've got one too. They ought to call it the mother's mark!'

'But I don't get it . . .' Michael trailed off, frowning. 'You've got more worries than she has. She's not got a care in the world. All women have kiddies, but they don't go all mardy on you like Mary. She ain't got time for me, not in any department.'

He sat in gloomy silence for a moment, his deep blue eyes staring unfocusing across the bar. Around them people were laughing and two old men had started singing 'Roll out the Barrel'.

He brought himself up with a jerk. 'Sorry, Rosie. Didn't mean to bring you here and pour out all my troubles. You won't want to come again?'

She knew it was an invitation.

'But don't you think sometimes, looking back to when we was kids at Lazenby's, we were full of all we were going to do. What was it you went on about? Teaching kids, wasn't it? And I was going to run the world, have a big business . . .' He chuckled bitterly. 'And now look at us.'

'But you're doing all right?'

'All right. That's about the sum of it. But I wanted more, much more than that. Maybe that's where I went wrong.'

They talked a little while longer before Rose told him she really had to go in order to get home at the normal time. They walked back together, further into the darkened city, where the points of greatest light and noise were the pubs on corners and down side streets.

'Meet me again, won't you?' he asked as they parted, and she nodded. She knew that this meeting, and the way they had found they could confide in each other, had sealed their need to see each other.

Before she could stop him, he took her in his arms briefly and kissed her hungrily on the lips.

As she walked into Court 11 she tried to push from her mind what had just happened. It was a mistake, the result of an evening of resuming old friendship and sharing emotion. She wouldn't let it happen again.

Quietly she released the catch on the door and pushed it open. For a few seconds she stood startled in the doorway, watching unnoticed before Grace turned, conscious of the draught from the doorway.

Alfie was lying as usual, on one side in the bed. They had to turn him every couple of hours to relieve the pressure on his bedridden body, which opened up his skin into deep sores. Grace was sitting beside him, tenderly holding one of his hands in her own.

Unsettled, and feeling strangely guilty at the apparent intimacy of the scene, Rose moved in briskly, pretending not to have noticed. Alfie's eyes opened and his face lit up as far as it was able into his lopsided smile.

'Everything all right?' she asked. 'Hilda asleep?'

'She's well gone,' Grace told her.

Rose poured some tea for all of them.

'These sores, Rose.' Grace pointed at Alfie. 'They're not getting any better, are they?'

Rose sighed, sipping the warm tea. 'It's a losing battle. I don't know what else we can do.'

The two of them gently turned back Alfie's bedclothes, and he stirred slightly, his eyes closed again. A rank smell emanated from him, a mixture of sweat and urine and the discharge from the sores.

'We'll turn him,' Rose said. 'I'm glad you waited. It's a job on your own.'

They slid their arms under Alfie's inert body, pulling him gently across the bed, and rolled him over on to his other side.

Grace tutted. 'Sheet's wet again. We'll have to change it.'

Manoeuvring Alfie's body from side to side, they pulled out the bottom sheet and smoothed over another one. Washing and more washing. Rose carefully wrapped his reddened heels and elbows in soft cloths to help protect them against the bed's chafing.

They eased Alfie out of his pyjamas. His limbs kept stiffening into muscular spasms, so that for minutes at a time they could not straighten his arms enough to slide on a fresh pyjama jacket.

Before they replaced the trousers, Rose turned her attention to the worst sores at the bottom of his back. On the right side, the top part of his buttock was beginning to break up, the skin all red and cracked, and they were doing all they could to prevent it getting as bad as the other side. On the left a full-blown sore had developed into a discoloured, oozing hole large enough to hold a golf ball. It looked appalling, though Alfie said he was not aware of much pain from it.

Rose carefully pulled off the lint dressing and grimaced. From inside oozed a yellowish grey, foul-smelling liquid. 'We'll have to dress it again,' she said.

The nurse had recommended packing the wound with lint and a concoction of whipped egg whites, something which Rose had a decreasing amount of faith in as a remedy. When they had finished they tucked a bottle between his legs to try and keep the urine off the sheets, and covered him up again.

'D'you want your tea now, Alfie?' Grace asked him gently. Almost imperceptibly he nodded his head.

Rose met Michael on other occasions after that. What was the harm in meeting a friend, she reasoned. Except – and the thoughts hovered around and were pushed to the back of her mind – she couldn't bring herself to tell Grace.

Michael was like a lifeline. How could she give that up when the rest of life, the drab, everyday routine of illness and Turner's and rationing and struggle offered so little?

As she got out of bed that March morning, the dream of Falcone gradually sliding from her mind, she tried to quell her excitement at the thought of meeting Michael in the evening. After all, they were both married people with families meeting for a chinwag. So why should her feelings be so stirred?

Thirty-Five

'I needn't go tonight,' she told Grace, her guilt making her wish that her sister would demand her presence. 'I'll stay if you think you'll need me.'

Alfie had a bad cold which had gone to his chest, and she had been helping Grace to prop him up so that he could cough and clear his lungs.

'No, you're all right. You go,' Grace said, seating herself on the wooden chair beside Alfie's head. 'I can always fetch Gladys in.'

Rose wondered if she was imagining that Grace really preferred it when she was out of the way. Or did she suspect that Rose was not going to a class at all?

'Well, all right,' she agreed. 'I'll get back as early as I can.'

'No need.' Grace pulled some knitting out of an old cloth bag. 'We'll get on fine – won't we, Alfie?'

As she walked into the cosy light of the Mermaid she saw Michael raise an arm to her. He was as usual dressed immaculately. She had never seen him wear anything the least bit worn or shabby. He had on a dark blue suit which emphasized the already powerful outline of his body.

'Sorry I'm late, Michael,' she gasped, sitting down at last with relief on the bench opposite him.

'Oh, no need to apologize.' He got up as she unbuttoned her coat. 'What'll you have?'

Clearly he'd managed to fit in a couple of drinks already. When he came back to their table with the glasses and sat down, Rose immediately sensed a tension between them, something which made her feel self-conscious, and she found it hard to look him in the eyes.

She chatted to him nervously. They must keep things normal and conversational. Within bounds. She must not let him touch her hands across the table as he had done before. Otherwise she could not carry on persuading herself that she was justified in meeting him.

'Your family all right?' she asked. 'How's Mary? And the babby?'

'Mary's getting more sleep nowadays,' Michael told her. He was sitting with a generous tumbler of Scotch in front of him. 'They're all OK. They're doing fine.'

He sounded evasive, as if he didn't want to go into how things were between him and Mary. Rose had begun to realize that Michael only found it possible to confide in her if she first disclosed something about herself or showed emotion in front of him, and she was deliberately keeping that at bay.

Suddenly Michael said, 'I've been meaning to ask you something. About your ... about Alfie.' Rose waited. 'Well, how is he?'

Rose was puzzled. 'Well, he's not too good. He never is of course. But he's got a chill at the moment.'

'I meant ...' Michael looked down at the floor between his legs. 'Is he never going to get right again?'

'No. There's nothing anyone can do for him. No cure. Michael, you know that. I've told you endless times.'

He shook his head sadly. 'I thought – I was just making sure.'

'Anyroad,' Rose went on. 'The next thing is George

is coming out, next week some time. God knows I've wished him out of there often enough, but now he's really coming I don't know what the hell we're going to do with him. I'm scared at the thought, Michael, to tell you the truth.'

'Where's he going to live?'

Rose shrugged again. 'I s'pose he'll have to come home. I mean where else? Grace hasn't said a word about it and Dad might as well have forgotten who he is. We'll just have to see if he can hold down a job.'

'Can he do anything?'

'Thieving. He's good at that.'

Michael laughed, pulling out his cigarettes. Rose felt as if his blue eyes were piercing right through her. 'You only see your family as they are, don't you, Rosie? Not like me. Always wanting to put Mary on a pedestal like a plaster statue.'

'Well, how else?' Rose joined in his laughter and accepted a cigarette. 'Bit late to go making up fairy stories about them, isn't it?'

'Not for me. It's just the way I like to dream about people.' And again the sadness crept back in to his eyes. 'Trouble with statues on pedestals is that one way or another they keep getting knocked off.'

Then he asked, with the kind of intensity she had started to dread from him, 'What about you, Rosie?' He asked the question as if he wanted something from her: some pronouncement or decision. 'What are you going to do?'

'I'm going to look for a new job,' she told him. 'I should be able to get better money now, so I'll be looking around. I've got one place in mind, but really I'm being a bit cheeky. It's in town, with a solicitor. But I might as well have a try.'

Michael was draining his glass as she spoke. He put the glass down excitedly. 'Maybe I could find you something. I'm sure I could.'

Rose decided to treat this as a joke. 'Let me try out my wings first before you rush in to rescue me. But thanks for the offer. Now, let me get the next one in.'

But Michael stubbed out his cigarette with sudden resolve and picked up his coat. 'Come on, Rosie. It's not cold out. I'll take you to see my place. It's only a walk along the road.'

'Your house?' Rose asked, astonished.

'Jesus, no. I'll show you the business.' Seeing her hesitate, he urged her, 'Come on, what's the harm? I'd be proud for you to see it. You'll be home with time to spare.' He took her arm.

It was a cloudy night and mild, with a threat of drizzle. The shop was only a few streets away, and they walked in silence, well apart, as if they were afraid even of their hands touching by accident. It was an apprehensive, embarrassed silence. Rose knew why he was taking her there, and he knew that she knew. It all seemed inevitable after their meetings, but suddenly so very uneasy. Not at all a comfortable progression from confiding friendship to possible lovemaking, but driven, and somehow at odds.

He stopped outside a quite smart-looking shop front and, looking up, she saw 'GILLESPIE'S' in bold dark letters above the window. He didn't go into the darkened betting shop. Instead he led her up a narrow staircase, between walls covered with brown, chipped paint and smelling of stale cigarette smoke and general dirtiness.

'Not too nice, that bit,' he apologized when they reached the top. 'Come on in here. This is my office.'

He produced another key, and she stood waiting behind him, looking at the weave of his suit, depressed by the smelly seediness of the staircase and wondering what to expect from the room on the other side of the door.

'People have to knock to come in here,' he told her proudly.

Once he had pushed the door open and switched on the light she looked round in real surprise.

In contrast to the staircase, the room was freshly decorated in cream paint, and she found her feet suddenly cushioned by what looked like brand new carpet with a crimson background patterned with fashionable skater's trail curves in black and white. All the furniture was brand new as well: a sideboard, its wooden veneer still gleaming with the sheen of newness, and two easy chairs covered in a vivid green woven fabric. In the middle of the room stood an enormous desk behind which Michael evidently presided from a chair covered in bright red and black material.

'Blimey, Michael!' Rose said, laughing. 'This furniture's a bit bright, isn't it?'

Proudly he joined in her laughter. 'Right up to the minute that,' he told her. 'Makes a change from all that blooming depressing brown stuff, doesn't it? Makes me think of nothing but the war that does. Mary still likes it though. So I thought, well, if I have to put up with all that old-fashioned look at home, then I'll have my own little place here where I can do just what I want!'

Although the room did not seem all that warm, Michael took off his coat and hung his jacket over the back of the red chair. Rose watched his broad, muscular frame with some curiosity as he went over to the sideboard and squatted down to open one of the low cupboards. He was really such a stranger to her.

'I'll get us another drink,' he said. 'Will you be having a nip of Scotch? Haven't got much else.'

'Oh – no ta,' Rose replied quickly. She already felt light-headed from the pace he had set drinking in the Mermaid. 'If I have any more I'll get bad.'

Unbuttoning her coat, she walked round Michael's very tidy desk. From one of the frames facing his chair Mary smiled sweetly back at her. Face like an angel, Rose thought. Poor cow. Her wavy hair looked as if it must be a middling brown, and the camera had caught her glancing up, as if it had taken some persuasion to make her look in that direction at all. Round her neck you could just see a small crucifix gleaming at the bottom of the picture.

She's lovely, Michael, Rose wanted to say. She's beautiful. But she couldn't bring herself to speak. To say such things would be to bring Mary into the room between them.

There was a second photograph, evidently more recent, of Mary holding the baby Geraldine, with Joseph leaning into the picture beside her. The little boy's expression was solemn. Geraldine had that startled kind of baby face, all eyes. Michael's eyes. Mary was smiling. Did being married to Michael make her happy, Rose wondered?

She realized Michael was watching her. She glanced up at him. His eyes looked slightly glassy: at once sad and lustful. She pitied him, but with a sense of panic. Everything about this was wrong.

'Come away from the window,' he said. She didn't resist when he took her by the hand and led her to a corner of the room. She wanted, needed him to hold her, to allow herself to feel excited by him. She wanted that dreamlike, swimming feeling which would allow her to make love with him, give herself up to the swell of it and forget everything else.

As soon as he moved against her and they began to kiss, she felt her body come alive with all the sensations she had not known for so long. His hands reached insistently inside her clothing to touch her skin, to close over her breasts, and her eyes closed as she gave way to the pleasure of it.

Michael released her slightly, his eyes half closed. 'God. It's been so long since she's let me.'

Something like icy water sluiced through her mind and she was out of the dream, eyes wide open and seeing herself and Michael with clinical clarity as if from a distance. She was in a room above a betting shop, with a man's body pressed to hers, his black hair close to her cheek. Black hair which could almost have been Falcone's but wasn't. A man who aroused her, filled her with sexual desire, but whom she did not love. She thought of the last time she was forced to the floor by a man in an office where photographs of his family looked on from the desk, and she knew that whatever it was she'd desired of these few minutes, she could only ever see them as cheap afterwards. Soiled and cheap.

Michael felt her stiffen and straighten up, withdrawing from him. She pulled on her blouse, buttoning it over her breasts.

Michael's eyes opened and he made a despairing sound. 'Oh God, Rosie,' he implored her. 'Don't pull out on me now. Please.'

She removed his arms from round her and moved away, rearranging herself. 'It's not that I don't want you. You know that. But I can't do it. I feel as if everyone's here watching us – Mary and Alfie and everyone. I'm sorry, Michael.'

He turned from her abruptly and went to pick up his glass, draining the last gulp from it. He lit a cigarette and sat down on one of the green chairs in silence. She knew he was not going to try to force her.

'I don't go with women, you know,' he said finally. 'That's not the way I was brought up. It's just – you're different Rosie, I can talk to you, and we go back a long way. There was always something there between us, wasn't there?'

'There was. And there is, in a way. But I can't do this. We'd be doing wrong to so many other people.'

There was an awkward silence before Michael spoke. 'What you said, about your husband, him being bad and that. I mean you and him, you don't . . . ?'

'Not any more, no.'

'Then why?'

'He's still my husband. He's had enough bad luck without his wife going bad on him. And there's Mary. I looked at that picture and I thought I'd like her if I met her. That's daft I know, because what difference does it make? But I couldn't do it to her either. Or to myself.'

'But they'd never know. I don't want to hurt anyone either. It's between you and me, Rosie. Even if it's only the once, it's just for us.' His blue eyes suddenly looked very young in their appeal.

'I'm not going to come here any more, Michael.'

'Not come?' He made to stand up and she turned away from him. 'What? Not even for a drink now and then?'

'I can't. If I keep coming it'll always come to this, won't it? Because it's always there between us. Sooner or later I'd give in to you and I'd hate myself for it. And you wouldn't be happy either. Not in the end.'

Michael shook his head. 'You always were more grown-up than me, Rosie. I can't help admiring you for it. Come here, will you? Just for a moment?'

She went to him and they held each other again briefly.

'Go and give Mary some of your time,' she told him as they released each other. 'And your kids. They're what matters. If you stick with them I bet things'll work out.'

Michael kissed her. 'I hope you get that job of yours. I'll miss you.'

She told him she would walk back alone and he let her out of the office and the door on to the street.

She was late home again. Grace was sitting in her usual position by Alfie's bed. The fire had burned down to a glow in the grate, and beside Grace lay a long skein of knitting which she had abandoned out of sleepiness.

She said nothing when Rose came in through the door, but her whole manner spoke of reproach. She bundled her things into the cloth bag and placed it pointedly beside the door. Still in silence the two of them settled Alfie down for the night. Usually they talked and made tea while Alfie dozed, but tonight he lay watching them as they went about their tasks, their eyes not meeting each other's nor a word passing between them.

They re-dressed his sores, though this time the sheets had stayed dry and did not need to be changed. When he started coughing again they supported him between them by his skeletal shoulders and dosed him with linctus, waiting until he was calm again.

Eventually Rose asked Grace, 'D'you want a cuppa?'

'No ta.' Grace took her apron off. 'I'll be glad to get home to my bed. And not before time either.' Rose could hear the anger pressed into her voice.

'By the way. I'm stopping the classes. I'm ready to go for a better job now.'

Normally Grace would have looked pleased for her and asked questions about where and how much. 'That'll be a relief for everyone, won't it?'

Rose sighed. 'I can be home evenings.'

Grace continued to look huffy, busying herself with her bag. 'Well – we'll see about that, won't we?'

Then she was gone.

Rose boiled some water on the gas and made tea. She poured for herself and Alfie and helped him, spooning the sweet liquid into his mouth. Often when she came in he was sleepy and hardly seemed to notice she was there. But tonight he was wide awake, partly perhaps because of his troubled breathing. She knew he was watching her as she moved round, tidying away the cups and getting the room ready for the morning because it was always such a rush.

She went over to him. 'Would you like me to turn you again? Would it help you to breathe better?'

'No. I'm OK.' He carried on staring up at her. His gaze seemed to hold a knowing sort of wisdom which made her feel ashamed. In the end she could bear it no longer.

'What? What, Alfie?'

In his stumbling, slurred way he brought out the words, 'Wanted ... something ... more than ... half alive ... did you?'

She knelt and laid her head down on the bed next to the thin curve of his body. 'I'm sorry,' she whispered. 'I'm so sorry.'

For a moment he managed to stroke her hair before his arm went into spasm again.

'You deserve ... better,' he said. When she looked up at him she saw he was crying too.

'I'm going to be here now,' she told him. 'Evenings and all. I'm going to get a better job and work hard – for all of us. I'll make things better if I can.'

She took one of his stiff hands in her own. 'Grace makes you a better wife than I do, doesn't she?'

She looked into Alfie's wet face, and reached across to wipe away his tears.

'But you're ... the wife ... I want. Always. You know. I love ... you.'

Thirty-Six

George Lucas stood outside the entrance to Winson Green Prison for the first time in over four years and heard the heavy gate shudder behind him. He stood for a moment or two in the overcast March morning, turning his pinched face this way and that, trying to take in the fact that after all these months he could make choices about his own movements. He appeared weighed down by the responsibility of it.

He looked even thinner after his time inside, giving the impression that he had grown taller, like a plant that has bolted up in poor light, and his skin had a yellowish, waxy look. Under his arm he carried a small bundle of the few possessions he had with him when he went into prison, and these he carried wrapped in a strip of white towelling. With his old, threadbare jacket pulled close round him and a crushed-looking brown felt hat pulled over his cropped hair, he began to walk slowly away from the prison in the direction of Birch Street.

The same morning Rose made her way into the middle of Birmingham. She stopped at the entrance to some narrow offices squeezed in near the bottom end of Temple Street. Screwed to the wall beside the heavy wooden door was a brass plaque which read, 'LAURENCE ABEL AND MATTHEW WATERS: SOLICITORS'.

Rose checked there were no stray bits of fluff on the full navy blue skirt she was wearing, and adjusted the collar of her white blouse, relieved they wouldn't be able to see the mend in the right sleeve under her thick navy cardigan. On her head she wore a little felt hat with a narrow brim in a royal blue which looked striking against her jackdaw hair and, to finish off the outfit, some high-heeled black shoes. She wished the shoes had been navy as well, but the neighbours had rallied round to help her out and lend her clothes for her interview and she had had to take what she could get. She peered at her faint reflection in the window of the corridor leading to the office. Nothing seemed to be amiss, so she patted the hat gently and said in a whisper, 'Come on, Rose Meredith. Get yourself in there.'

She was precisely on time. When the door opened she found she was facing a tall blonde woman of about forty with an immaculately made-up face, who looked at her appraisingly and then held out her hand with what Rose could only feel was disdain.

'Good morning. Mrs Meredith?' The 'Mrs' was definitely unenthusiastic. 'I'm Miss Crosby.'

Miss Crosby had a small outer area to work in off which led the two offices of Mr Waters and Mr Abel. Each had a slim wooden sign on his door. Miss Crosby sat down behind her heavy black Olivetti with an affected caress of the back of her skirt. Every hair on her head sat in precisely the right place.

Brassy cow, Rose found herself thinking.

'You have a very satisfactory recommendation from Sparkhill Commercial School,' Miss Crosby said. 'Your shorthand and typing speeds are well within our requirements. Have you kept them up?' she asked suspiciously.

'I've only just left the school.'

The woman's stony blue eyes watched her coldly. 'You've been employed as an invoice typist in the pool of a small firm. Do you really imagine you're capable of taking a job as a personal assistant to a professional solicitor?' She spoke the words 'personal assistant' as if the position was second only to membership of the royal family.

'I think I can do the job,' Rose told her. 'I've got good speeds, I'm well organized and I'm a very good worker.'

'Perhaps I should make it clear what is required here. I have been secretary to Mr Waters, the senior partner, for several years. It is only in the past month that he has gone into partnership with Mr Abel, who has come to join us from Manchester. Mr Waters will be retiring in a couple of years – that's why Mr Abel is now named first in the practice.'

Rose had the definite impression that Miss Crosby's nose had been put out of joint by all these changes.

'Mr Abel needs his own personal assistant, since I am fully occupied with all Mr Waters' affairs. If we were to take you on – and I have my doubts as to whether you'd be up to it, quite honestly, Mrs Meredith – you would be working under me. Is that clear?'

Rose nodded. 'Do I have to be seen by Mr Abel?'

'Oh, that won't be necessary,' Miss Crosby told her briskly. 'Mr Waters and Mr Abel leave all that sort of thing to me.'

Miss Crosby seemed on the point of pronouncing one way or another as to Rose's prospects with Abel and Waters when one of the inner doors opened and an energetic figure bounded out of the office. Rose saw a man with a round, cheerful face wearing a suit which looked good quality but was somehow comically ill-fitting on him, who bustled across the room, a newspaper tucked loosely under one arm.

'No, no, don't get up,' he said. 'I'm Laurence Abel. So, Miss Crosby, is this my new secretary or do you have a whole line of others waiting breathlessly outside?'

'I was just discussing with Mrs Meredith whether she is really suitably qualified for the position.'

Just then their interviewee, who had been looking anxiously up at Mr Abel, let out a loud gasp. Rose's hand rose automatically to her mouth to apologize for the sound.

'What's the matter, Mrs Meredith?' Laurence Abel joked. 'Is my presence too much for you?'

'I'm sorry. It's just – you'll think I'm very odd, but I noticed your newspaper.'

Laurence Abel frowned as if he had forgotten he was carrying the thing. He pulled it out and spread it out on the desk. It was a copy of *Corriera della Sera*.

'It's Italian,' Rose explained unnecessarily.

Miss Crosby was looking at her as if she thought Rose had lost her mind. But she had Laurence Abel's avid attention.

'I used to speak it.' Rose glanced anxiously at Miss Crosby. 'I was there for nearly two years. In the war.'

'Good Lord!' Mr Abel cried. Rose was almost sure his feet left the ground in his enthusiasm. 'How marvellous! You mean you really speak it? Can you remember it?'

Suddenly he launched into a list of questions, mostly in energetic Italian, but with the odd English word thrown in when he got stuck. Having heard Rose's replies he said, 'You're obviously a darn sight better at it than I am. Come on into my office for a minute.'

He led her into what seemed a surprisingly orderly room for so chaotic-looking a character: the walls lined with shelves of all his files and reference books with gold lettering on the spines.

'You know, I really should be working,' Mr Abel said, leaning back at his desk, his podgy stomach pushing out the front of his shirt. 'But I can't throw up an opportunity like this.'

Rose found herself telling him about the ATS and a little about Il Rifugio and her feeling that she belonged in the country.

'I know what you mean about the sense of belonging,' Mr Abel agreed eagerly. 'I had exactly the same feeling. I go back as often as I can. Couldn't do without it.'

'You go back?' Rose was amazed. She never imagined such a thing. Italy was part of the war, not accessible at any other time.

'About once a year. Managed a quick visit before moving down here. It's not quite the other side of the world you know.'

'It is when you've got no money.'

Laurence Abel looked at her in silence for a moment. 'If you came to work here, would you agree on a condition that when we're not actually dictating letters, we'll speak in Italian?'

Rose grinned at this bizarre request. 'That'd be lovely.'

*

She almost danced into number five that evening to tell Grace the news.

'I've got the job!' she cried before she was even properly through the door.

And then stopped abruptly. Grace was standing by the table wearing her apron and a grimmer, angrier expression than Rose could ever remember seeing on her face before. Sid was sitting on the other side of the room by the fire, but was for once intent on what was going on. And at the table sat George, his hat lying in front of him, a cigarette in his mouth, his defiant eyes staring down at the table.

'Oh my God,' Rose said. 'I'd forgotten it was today.'

'That's obvious,' George said bitterly. He pulled the cigarette out of his mouth, wincing as if it tasted bad and held it in one hand, tapping his fingers on the table.

'Well – what's going on?' Rose asked. The atmosphere was pure acid.

'He thinks,' Grace's voice grated out, 'that he's going to come swanning back in here to live as if nothing had happened – and have me waiting on him hand and foot again no doubt. And then' – she leaned down and shouted into George's face – 'I s'pose you'll just be off thieving and getting into more trouble and expecting the rest of us to carry the can for you! No. I'm not having it. I'm not having you back here. You can go where you like, go to hell for all I care, as long as you're not coming in and out of here.'

George sat in silence. He had walked most of the day, with no money for food as he made his way home, putting off going to the old house where he had grown up, skirting round it time and again, until by the afternoon he was so hungry and weary from the unaccustomed exercise that he had finally slunk into the court.

Sid had opened the door and when it dawned on him who had arrived, he said, 'You'd better come in, but I don't know what your sister'll say.' He'd let him have tea and bread and jam and a slice off a leathery bit of leftover beef.

Rose could tell that, for all his toughness, George was upset. She was horrified at what she was hearing from Grace. Grace hadn't been to see him once in prison and was turning him out now as if he was a stranger who meant nothing to her at all.

No one had spoken after Grace, but she leapt to her own defence as if they had, her hands clamped to her waist. 'Say what you like. You come in here and I go – simple as that. You can go rot for all I care.'

George looked over at Sid for some sign of authority, of contradiction, but saw only his father's watery eyes staring defeatedly back at him.

Sid shrugged tiredly. 'You'd better do as she says.' He couldn't have Grace walking out on him, after all.

'George.' Rose spoke more gently and he was struck even at that moment by the difference between his sisters: Rose's animated beauty despite her thinness, compared with Grace's haggard, bitter face.

Rose laid her hand on the back of his chair. 'What are you going to do, George? Find a job and get yourself straightened out or what? You can't go on the way you've been. You don't want to end up back in there, do you?' She looked with pity at the side of her brother's face with his shorn brown hair. He was a sad sight.

'I dunno,' he said. 'What can I do?'

'Never done a straight day's work in your life.'

Grace's voice drilled on into him. 'Come as too much of a shock to you, wouldn't it?'

Rose frowned at her to shut her up. 'Look,' she went on. 'If you'll say you're going to try and find a job, I'll help you. There's a few going round here – and if you promise you're not going to go fooling about looking up all your old pals who're no good for you, I'll have you to live with us. Hilda can move down to sleep with me. You can pay me a bit of rent and I can always do with someone else about to help with Alfie and that. But just you watch yourself.' She wagged a warning finger in front of George's face. 'Any sign of trouble, of anything, and you're out. Right?'

George nodded in silence.

'You'd better get your lodger off home Rose,' Grace told her. 'I'm late with the tea already and what there is is only enough for two.'

George picked up his meagre bundle of possessions and slunk out with Rose across the yard to Moonstruck House. They were both well aware that other eyes were on them from the windows.

'Never thought you'd end up here, Rose,' George said as they went through the door. 'Thought you had ideas well above this place.'

'When did having ideas ever do anyone any good?' She felt completely deflated after her euphoric mood earlier. She turned to Alfie, ignoring George's horrified expression as he set eyes on him.

'You remember my brother George? He's coming to lodge with us for as long as he can keep his nose clean.' Then more kindly she said to George. 'I s'pose you're hungry. I'll get something on in a minute.'

Hilda, who was sitting near her father, gazed at George with interested eyes. She liked men: they picked her up and paid her attention and played games with her. 'Is he a real brother?'

'My brother. Your uncle.'

'This is your kid?' George asked astonished. Though Rose had told him what Hilda was getting up to on her visits, the child had never progressed further than babyhood in his mind.

'This is Hilda.'

Hilda was standing in her little flowery frock, lips pursed ready to give George a kiss. Rose watched her brother's confusion. Any such display of affection was something unusual enough in their family, and to George was a part of life long forgotten. Kissing a child was something he could barely imagine how to do. Slowly he bent down until he was level with Hilda, who popped a kiss on his cheek. As he stood up she rubbed her lips. 'You've got prickly cheeks, like Grandad,' she said. 'But I'm glad you're coming to live with us, Uncle George.'

Thirty-Seven

July 1952

'What're you doing here?'

The moment Rose opened the door of Moonstruck House she felt herself tense up, infuriated. George was supposed to be out at work, at yet another of the jobs she had found for him. Instead, he was just sitting there, smoking.

'I asked you a question.'

'Oh, don't go on. You get to sound like her over there.' He nodded in the direction of number five.

Rose was almost afraid to hear his reasons for being at home at this time. Had she wasted yet more time and energy helping him to find a job which he had either just walked out of or got the sack from for idleness and bad timekeeping?

In the end he said, 'Couldn't stand that bloody place. Got on me nerves. I thought bugger it and came home.'

'Got on your nerves!' Rose flared up at him. 'You're an idle little sod, that's what you are!'

She strode over to him furiously and snatched the cigarette from between his fingers. 'And you can put that bloody fag out and all. This is my house, and if you're living here you do as I say.'

'Leave me alone, can't you?' George snapped back.

Rose went to the window and flung it open, throwing the stub of cigarette, still burning, out on to the ground.

'Uncle George is going to buy me a bicycle,' Hilda chimed in from by the fireplace.

Rose swung round. 'And pigs might fly.'

After George had slammed out of the house, Rose went up to her bedroom. She felt despair wash through her, as strong as any she had experienced since her first days back at home after the war. The summer afternoon air drifted in through the window, and she could hear children shouting and laughing in the courts around them. The long, lonely evening stretched ahead of her.

Tears began to slide down her face. She lay face down on her bed and let them come on like a child. For so long she had been so busy, so driven by all the necessities in her life that there had been no time to think about anything. She found herself remembering her first meeting with Diana, and the dress with the pink sprigs of roses. How much hope she had had in those days!

Even lately she had persisted in believing that if she tried hard enough things would come right in the end. God knows, she had made enough effort with George. She had goaded him on day after day to look for work. And when she could manage to find the time, she walked the streets herself on his behalf, even in her own dinner breaks. Finding him a job was not especially easy, though there was plenty of work to be had. She saw vacancies for toolmakers, die-sinkers, stampers, rivet-makers and a whole host of other skills. But George had no skills.

The only jobs he was able to get were of the most menial; the unskilled, heavy work of stacking and loading and cleaning up after those doing the better-paid jobs. The money was never up to much and George had neither the application nor the staying power to stick to the work. Rose knew, and feared, that he could make easier and quicker money elsewhere.

'Why can't you give it a bit more time?' she'd implore him when feeling more patient. 'Can't you try a bit more than you do?'

Usually he'd just shrug off her questions, her encouragement. Once he turned to her and said, 'Give it a rest will you, Rosie? I'm no good for anything, so just don't keep on.' And she'd seen a wooden, beaten expression in his eyes.

But she had still believed, naïvely, that given a few more chances, a bit of help, he could go back to being someone more like the old, sparky George she had known as a child.

She heard the door downstairs open and voices. It was Grace. Since she had spent so much time looking after Alfie, she still kept up a slightly proprietorial air over his care and was always popping in to check things were being done properly.

'Where's your mother got to?' Rose heard her say to Hilda, before shouting up the stairs.

'Be down in a mo,' Rose called back, trying to make her voice sound normal and not weepy.

Grace stood leaning up against the sink in the little scullery that was still filled with gloom despite the bright sunlight and echoing summer sounds from outside. She had her hair wrapped up in a scarf as usual and wore her shabby brown skirt and flat, sloppy shoes. She looked as if she might be well on in years compared with Rose, who was still smartly dressed from work in her floral skirt and pink blouse, although she had taken off her heels to lie down.

'Coming round to my way of thinking, are you?'

Rose nodded miserably in reply.

'I warned you. You could've saved yourself the bother. You know who's sniffing round here again, don't you? Ronnie Grables.'

Silently Rose got on with peeling potatoes.

'Did you hear me?'

'He wouldn't. Not after all this.' Her secret fears about George seemed to be being confirmed one by one.

Grace let out a harsh, cynical laugh. 'None so blind as them as won't see,' she said. 'How do you know what he'd do? You don't know where he is now or what he's doing, do you?'

That evening she sat down with a new copy of *Corriera della Sera*. Alfie was asleep. Rose looked across at him. His face was moist with perspiration. It seemed so strange, him lying there and her in a tussle with this language she might never have any proper chance to speak again.

Why she carried on with it she wasn't even sure. After her initial enthusiasm at Mr Abel's offer, she had had to ask herself, who was she kidding?

At first she found the reading a terrible struggle. And she felt triumphant when she managed to make sense of short sentences, then longer ones, and gradually whole paragraphs. But tonight she was finding it hard to concentrate. She was very unsettled and anxious. It was partly because of George, of course. He had not come back for the evening meal and was still out somewhere. Doing what? Who with? Her mind followed him anxiously out into the streets.

And there had been an incident at work which had in a strange way brought her a little closer to her odd colleague Ella Crosby, and yet at the same time she felt depressed because of it.

It had dawned on Rose only gradually that Ella Crosby was in love with Mr Waters. At first she thought she was reading the signs wrong. Of course a secretary looked up at her boss with attentiveness when he came in to give her some work. But surely not always with the gaze of hungry pain that Miss Crosby directed at Mr Waters? Say something to me, it seemed to say. Just one extra thing which is not on the subject of work and which shows me you even notice me! But the longer she worked there, Rose found the situation at first unbelievable, then pitiful. She began to warm to Miss Crosby for that, if for no other reason.

That morning the two of them had been working hard at their typewriters with a stack of papers in front of them when Mr Waters' door opened. Miss Crosby and Rose both looked up.

Mr Waters was very tall, almost unhealthily thin-looking, with such sallow, papery skin that when Rose first saw him she had thought immediately of the cemetery at Naples. He was carrying a sheaf of papers in his left hand, and Rose saw Miss Crosby's cheeks turn a deeper red under all the powder as he laid them down rather impatiently in front of her.

'I'm sorry, Miss Crosby,' he said. As always he was polite, but there was a tetchy edge to his voice. 'I'm afraid we really can't send them out like this. They'll all have to be done from scratch. Rather a waste of time, of course. Still, I'll leave them with you. I know you'll do your best.' Without another word, he drifted back into his office again.

And to her horror, Rose saw Miss Crosby bring her hands convulsively up to her face, and she realized the woman was trying to hide approaching tears. She could feel her pain and embarrassment across the room. Rose wondered what to do. She decided to carry on typing for a while to give the woman time to recover.

Eventually, when she could see that Miss Crosby had regained some of her control, she stood up and said carefully, 'Never blooming satisfied, are they? D'you fancy a cup of tea?'

Miss Crosby nodded.

Rose was saddened by this. Did no one ever love the right person, she wondered? Were so many people really doomed to spend their lives longing and wishing and never happy?

She got up to check on Alfie and Hilda and brewed herself a last cup of tea for the night. She felt so tired that she was tempted to stop reading. But if she did stop, then what? On this night in particular she would start thinking and brooding. As she had been reading Italian she would find Falcone insistent in her mind and she did not want her emotions disturbed again.

She was settled in bed beside Hilda's warm body and already drifting off to sleep that night when she was aware of George coming back into the house, his loud, thoughtless tread on the stairs up to the attic. It had not long struck eleven o'clock. Rose closed her eyes and turned to lie with her back against Hilda. Where he had been and what he had been doing were not things she wanted to think about now either.

As the months went by things did not improve. George gave up any pretence that he was going to try and hold down any sort of job and yet Rose could not bring herself to throw him out. He came and went, back to his old pattern of disappearing for days at a time, paying her odds and sods of rent but nothing regular. She never knew where he was and she worried and Hilda sulked and was unsettled. But there was no trouble as such, no police round, nothing that she could actually hold up in front of him. Only the constant anxiety and suspicion which left her feeling worn down and angry.

Alfie's health was an increasing strain. Grace came and helped them often again now, apparently glad to be back in her role as nurse. Alfie went through chest infection after chest infection, his weakened body wracked by terrible coughing. Time and again she got for him the new wonder medicine – antibiotics, which fought off the infection for a time before it returned again, apparently stronger and more tenacious than before. She was mystified by his strength, how he managed to keep going after all these months. For what, she often wondered guiltily. What reason does he have to live any more?

As the autumn wore on and the days closed in, dark, and often foggy and wet, she was finding it hard to hide her strain and exhaustion at work. Her face looked pale and sunken and she was bone thin. Both Laurence Abel and Ella Crosby noticed.

'Is there something worrying you?' Miss Crosby asked one afternoon when Rose was yawning over her typewriter and struggling to keep her head clear. 'You don't seem quite yourself.' She blushed slightly, unaccustomed to trying to extract confidences from others.

It was a relief to tell her.

'It's my husband. He's very bad. I've been up a lot nights.'

'Oh, I'm sorry,' Miss Crosby said rather stiffly. She suddenly felt rather moved by the pale, lovely young woman in front of her. 'If there's anything I can do . . .'

'I don't think so.' Matter-of-factly, Rose added, 'We don't reckon he's got long left. There's not much anyone can do.'

'I didn't realize . . .' Miss Crosby looked genuinely sorry. 'I had no idea it was as bad as that.'

A kind of numbness overcame Rose, as if she could bear feeling no more. She was waiting for Alfie to die. Not because she willed it, but because she knew it must come. It was plain in his face. The nurse who came in tutted and said so in hushed tones as well. And now life was strung between these nights of waiting, watching his struggle with his weak, helpless body.

One December evening when she had finished work, she walked home from the bus stop in a wet dusk. The wheels of cars and buses hissed through the puddles, and she could hear the soft, rhythmic sound of windscreen wipers even over the engines. The red lights of the cars seemed to glow more warmly in the rain.

Inside the house she was slowly peeling off her wet coat when there was a tap on the door, and to her surprise she saw Sid standing there with his cap on, the raindrops shining on his dark, stubbly cheeks.

'Someone to see you,' he said. 'Over at our place. She's been waiting.'

He turned his back and went on his crutch back across the court. Frowning with irritation at him, Rose slid her coat back on again. He could at least have told her who it was.

'Stay with your dad a minute,' she said to Hilda.

She followed Sid across the wet bricks and stepped into number five. She saw someone stand up immediately and move towards her. The face had aged, of course, and looked tighter somehow, but was instantly recognizable.

'Rose – my dear!'

A moment later she was being drawn into the arms of Catherine Harper-Watt.

Thirty-Eight

Rose could hardly take in Catherine's sudden appearance. Here she was, thinner but still beautiful, her thick hair arranged in an elegant chignon and wearing an obviously expensive suit tailored in slate blue and black checks and all nipped in nicely at the waist. She sat on the old wooden chair by the table in Grace's poor kitchen looking quite at ease as she might anywhere, so accustomed was she to mixing with anyone and everyone. Sid and Grace had taken their meal over to eat with Alfie.

Rose began to chop off florets of cauliflower for cauliflower cheese, waiting for the pan of water to boil.

'I know this'll sound rude,' she said. 'I'm ever so pleased to see you. But why are you here tonight suddenly?'

'No, it's a good question.' Catherine remembered that even as a child Rose had always gone straight to the heart of things, no messing about. 'The practical truth is that I'm here in Birmingham because I was sent down to a meeting in the Town Hall. More of my organizing and interfering with other people's lives.' She smiled.

'I have to admit this isn't by any means the first time I've been back, and I've thought of calling in on you. I came this evening to see if anyone could tell me your address, and to my astonishment I find the person I'm

424

talking to is your father! But I'm sorry not to have warned you, Rose dear. I had fully intended to write you a better letter after you wrote to us so kindly during the war. And to have come and looked you up much sooner. But I just – even now it's . . .' She laid the palms of her hands flat on the table in front of her. 'I just couldn't do it.'

Rose put down her colander, realizing with consternation that Catherine's voice was breaking up with tearfulness. She reached out to provide the family comforter. 'Let me get you a cup of tea while we're waiting.'

'I knew I must at some point,' Catherine told her, accepting the cup of strong tea. 'When we moved to Manchester and got settled in, Diana made a lot of friends, of course. She was always that kind of girl – you remember how open and friendly she was. But you know, despite all the differences between you two, I don't think there was ever anyone she cared for as much as she did for you. Perhaps we make very few real friendships in our lifetime. When I think of Diana's childhood now, that's the first thing that comes to my mind – you and her.'

There was a moment of silence. The two women looked at each other across the poorly lit kitchen and Catherine saw that Rose's brown eyes were full of tears.

'It's ten years since she died, and it's taken me all this time. Only . . . I know I've got William and Judith, and they're a great support to me and both doing so well. But losing Diana, losing any child is just . . .'

'I know,' Rose said gently.

'You poor girl, what a time of it you've had. Here am I, carrying on. Of course you know how it feels.'

'You know I met Diana. At New Street Station?'

'She told us. She was so delighted. You see she

thought she'd done something terribly wrong when she didn't hear from you. After she got your letter I remember her saying to me, "If only Rose had told us. Why d'you think she felt she couldn't? I wanted to be her friend whatever." It's all right' – Catherine stood up and took Rose by the shoulders, seeing her really beginning to cry on hearing this – 'she understood. You poor child. You were young and afraid, and so . . .'

'Ignorant,' Rose finished for her, sniffing.

'Well, yes, you were in a way. But so very bright and lively with it.' She embraced Rose briefly, and then the two of them carried the food to the table.

'I haven't talked about Diana,' Rose said as they ate. 'Not for years. There's been no one I could tell. No one round here would want to know anyway.'

'I should have done this years ago!' Catherine said later as she laid down her knife and fork. 'What a chump I've been, thinking it would all be terrible and gloomy. You won't be able to keep me away now, Rose. But for tonight' – she looked at her slender wristwatch – 'before I have to go I want to hear a lot more about you.'

Their shared memories allowed Rose to open up and relax in a way she had not done for years. The Harper-Watts' talent for helping others to confide and Catherine's motherly concern for her made her feel she could say anything.

She told her about Dora's death, about her war and Sam and Grace and Grace's fiancé; about the factory at Castle Bromwich and about the ATS. And to her own relief, pleasure in fact, she told her about Italy and Il Rifugio and the drops, and quite straightforwardly she told her about Falcone. She explained too how things

426

had been since the war, with Alfie and Hilda and her work, and Alfie's illness.

'So at least I've got myself a more decent job,' she finished, 'which means we're doing a bit better now. But Alfie's very bad. No one thinks he's got long, to be honest with you. To tell you the truth, Mrs Harper-Watt—'

'Call me Catherine, please.'

'Well, Catherine then. The one place I always hoped I'd get away from was Catherine Street. I had all these ideas. And here I am. Square one.'

Catherine smiled sadly. 'You had so many dreams, both of you, when you were children.' She watched Rose's face carefully as she asked the next question. 'And this man, this priest. He was something very special to you?'

Rose paused. 'He wasn't a priest then. But yes. Like no one else, ever.'

'Oh Rose!' Rose saw the sympathy in her eyes.

Catherine suddenly started and looked at her watch again. 'Heavens, I shall have to go.' She got up and put on a soft grey wool coat, belting it round the waist. 'The time has gone so quickly,' she said. 'Now listen, my dear. Thank you for feeding me at such short notice. And please thank your family for putting up with this disruption. It was most kind of them all.'

As they stood at the door, she said, 'I'm so glad I came.'

Rose nodded with pleasure, not sure what to say, and Catherine kissed her quickly on the cheek. Smiling, and suddenly elated, Rose watched her smart figure disappear quickly out of the court.

*

Two days later when she arrived back from work she found a long white envelope waiting, addressed in black ink in Catherine's beautiful italic script. Under their Manchester address on the thick, white paper she read,

My dear Rose,

I hope you will not take this amiss. I am not at all sure whether I conveyed to you when we parted on Tuesday just how much our meeting meant to me. You and Diana were so special – but then I think I *have* said all that.

I should be most grateful if you will accept the enclosed. It is not meant to be seen as charity or anything you need take offence at. You'll know I have always had means of my own, and I should love you to think of yourself as something of a daughter who need not feel ashamed of accepting a gift from me. I should like to think that as soon as circumstances allow, you, who were such a dreamer as a child and whose dreams have been so consistently pushed aside by events, might be able to put this little offering towards fulfilling those dreams in some way, whatever that may be. I would gladly give you more if you were not too proud to ask. I can't do anything for Diana, but I have at least found you.

I told Ronald about my visit to you and he was overjoyed (a very Ronald word!) and sends much love to you, as do William and Judith.

I do hope to see you again before long, if you don't mind.

With much gratitude and affection from us both,
Catherine H-W.

Folded in the sheet Rose found ten £10 notes. The moment she had read through the letter and had re-read it in wonder, she pushed both it and the money hurriedly back inside the envelope. Pulling out one of the loose bricks from round the fireplace she arranged the envelope neatly behind and replaced the brick. No one else need see that money just now.

But she thought about it endlessly as she got on with the evening's chores. Dreams? What dreams did she have left that were not buried almost deep enough to have been forgotten? She had no clear idea what she might do with such a sum of money. Except for one thing.

'I'll do something special for Grace,' she thought. Grace, whose life had been so lacking in excitement, who had always stood by her and helped out when she was needed, even if she did have a good moan about it. She'd think of some way, however small, to pay Grace back. She deserved it.

'He ought to be in hospital,' the nurse kept saying, tutting over Alfie. 'He's in a terrible state! Look at those sores, and hark at his chest!'

'We've done the best we can,' Rose told her exhaustedly. 'And he doesn't want to go.' Even Alfie himself had tried to impress this on the nurse in his more lucid moments.

The new doctor who had started coming supported Alfie's wishes, rather to Rose's surprise. 'You know that your husband has not much time left?' she told her gently.

'So everyone keeps saying. To be honest with you

we've all wondered how he's kept going this long with what he's been through.'

As Sid had put it only yesterday, 'You'd never have thought that weak little runt'd have held out like this, would you?'

The past weeks had, of course, prepared Rose. Several times she had walked warily over to Alfie, her own breath stilled in her throat, thinking he'd stopped breathing altogether. But each time there had been a pause and then his loud, laboured breathing had started up again. They could talk very little now. Mostly his eyes were closed, so he did not take in what she or Hilda were doing. But paradoxically her life revolved round him more and more: on his washing and feeding routines, or simply being there as much as possible, even though the nurses were spending more time there during the day, and one neighbour or another was constantly with him.

For the first time she had seriously begun to think how she would feel after he died, and again to her surprise, the thoughts which came filled her with apprehension verging on panic. For what was her life now without Alfie to care for?

Hilda had begun to say to her at night, 'Will Dad still be here in the morning?' The mother of one of her classmates had recently killed herself and it was always on Hilda's mind. And people kept saying Alfie hadn't long.

'I hope so,' Rose would tell her, with decreasing certainty. 'Don't get all worked up about it. Just go and give your dad a kiss, love.'

The night he died, Grace was there as usual. They took it in turns, each sleeping half the night in Rose's bed, and sitting for the remainder downstairs with Alfie. It was agonizing and exhausting. Each of his breaths seemed to demand from him such effort. And his poor, contorted body looked so corrupted by the illness. Occasionally Rose allowed herself to think of him as he was when she had first met him before the war, and she would weep at the sight of him now. He had become such a strange thing in the room, his unconsciousness a mysterious barrier against them all. Was it simply sleep, or had he already begun to leave her behind?

Grace ran up the stairs and pulled on Rose's shoulder, rousing her from a light, confused sleep.

'What? WHAT?' She sat up at once.

'It's just – he's changed. I can't tell you. You'd best come and see.'

The two sisters skimmed down the cold stairs again in their nighties.

Alfie's breathing had grown even louder and more irregular. Watching him from the bottom of the stairs, Rose felt he might rise bodily off the bed in his attempt to capture his next vital lungful. His chest rose and fell, rose and fell, the rasping breaths hauled in and out. Then they stopped.

Hypnotized by the rhythm, for a moment both women carried on staring at him. The silence continued. They looked at each other, unable to move.

Then Rose rushed over to the bed. She took Alfie's emaciated wrist and felt for a pulse. For a few seconds the tips of her fingers felt for the delicate blood vessel. Nothing.

'He's gone,' she said solemnly.

It was Grace who fell to her knees by the bed wailing

431

'Oh Alfie!' and laid her head down on the covers beside him.

The burial took place in the cemetery where they had laid Dora. Unlike the overcast day in 1940 when Rose had stood beside Grace and Sid at that graveside, the day was a crisp, bright one in February, with the old rusty leaves of autumn crackling underfoot. The beauty and calm of the cemetery with its mature trees and sloping green areas dotted with the silent stones moved Rose. Alfie's death and all the suffering of his life weighed heavily on her. She had lost a friend, and the focus of years of care and energy. The future lay blank in front of her. But what felt worst was the knowledge of how little of herself she had really given to him. Everyone kept telling her how marvellous she'd been, what a staunch wife. And it was true that she had served him and cared for him in his physical need. But no more.

After the ceremony, Rose held Hilda's cold little hand in hers, with Grace supporting her on the other side, as they followed the slow progress of Sid and Mrs Meredith along the curving path. George had not made an appearance. Grace's face was as drawn with misery as Hilda's and Rose's own.

'A couple of days more,' she said softly to Rose, 'and he'd have died exactly a year after the old king.' She seemed to find this comforting.

Rose nodded, squeezing her arm. A little further on she said, 'Grace, if he'd asked you – back in the early days – would you have married him?'

Grace kept her eyes down, looking at the dry twigs and pine needles along the path. 'You know I would.

And not just then either. Any time. Right up to the end.'

Then she looked round at Rose with a most wistful smile on her thin face. 'But it was only you he had eyes for. Ever. You know that, Rose.'

And then she stroked her sister's arm as Rose finally began to break into sobs beside her.

Thirty-Nine

August 1953

For months after Alfie's death Rose felt tired to the very core. It seemed a huge task just to get to work in the morning. Through the end of the winter and the lightening days of spring she dragged herself around feeling only half alive, as if Alfie had taken a part of her with him, her own youth seeping away gradually through his illness.

She missed him more than she had ever imagined possible. One thing had been certain, ever since she moved to Moonstruck House: that Alfie would always be there. Whenever she came down in the morning or in from a class or work, there he was, almost as she had left him. Wakeful and watching her, providing as much conversation as he could manage, or dozing, semi-conscious – but there. Now, just as certainly, the room was empty of him.

But like a gift, from somewhere within her, her vitality and zest were returning. She had other things to think about. George for a start. And, with a certainty which increased with each summer day, she knew what she was going to do with her money from Catherine Harper-Watt. One of the things that she had thought most unattainable, that Laurence Abel had talked of yet still sounded like a fantasy, was now within her grasp. Italy. She would go back, and she probably even had enough money to take Hilda.

'It's a barmy thing to do,' she thought to herself, almost giggling with excitement. It was a baking hot Saturday. On the sunny side of Court 11, near the brew-house, Rose was standing bent over an enamel bucket, swilling through some of Hilda's clothes. A few children were listlessly playing marbles in the shade. 'I could do up the house, move out even. I could buy us all new clothes or furniture, or just put it away for a rainy day. But I'm damned if I'm going to!'

Italy was her dream now, and Catherine had pre-scribed the money for a dream. She could go and visit Margherita and Francesco. She still received cards from them at Easter and whenever they had had another child, always with entreaties to visit. It was clear to her that this was what she must do. Just as her idea of what she could do for Grace had come to her with equal force a couple of months earlier.

As June approached, coronation fever had struck the court, the city, the entire country and, of course, Grace, who showed the kind of excitement that only a royal occasion ever brought out in her.

'A queen!' she cried. 'Oh, isn't it going to be lovely to have a queen for a change! Elizabeth the Second. Doris at work says it's going to change everything. Things'll never be the same again. Oooh, what I'd give to live down London!'

For weeks beforehand the talk and activity all centred round bunting and flags and plans for street parties and big celebrations with brass bands and fireworks.

'What if you could go?' Rose said to Grace one day

in May. 'You know, go down and really see it, in London?'

'I'd give my right arm,' Grace replied. 'But we'll hear it all. And we might get a sight of one of them televisions somewhere. And all the pictures'll be in the papers.'

'No,' Rose told her. 'You're to go. Down to London, on the train. It'll be my treat.' She blushed at sounding like Lady Bountiful with her sister. 'Look – you've done nothing but help me over the past few years. I'd like to pay you back a bit. One way I can think of anyway.'

Grace's face had gone pink with excitement. 'But – you can't afford that, can you? It'd mean the price of the train and . . . and new stockings, and . . .'

Rose grinned. 'That's all right. Listen. No one else need know about this, but when Mrs Harper-Watt came she gave me a bit of money. It doesn't matter how much, but take my word for it, it's enough for you to have a new frock and your rail ticket. And I'll stand you taking Doris as well if you like.'

Grace was flabbergasted. 'But why don't *you* come? If you've got enough money for the two of us?'

'I'm not that keen really, you know that. Go on – go with Doris and get into the spirit of it. You'll have much more fun with her.'

So Grace went, feverishly excited and wearing a new peach-coloured frock. She and Doris sat out all night in the Mall with a flask of tea and their sandwiches with all the other thousands of people breathless to catch a glimpse of the new monarch. And she came back brimming full of it all: the procession and the flags and trombones and all the aeroplanes flying over, and how the woman next to them had shared her ham sandwiches with them because they'd run out, and how everyone cheered and cheered when she came out of Westminster Abbey and stood there for hours with their little flags despite all the showers.

So it went on for days and weeks after. Rose was never in any doubt as to whether she'd made the right choice.

Things with George, though, were getting worse and worse, and Grace's excursion brought things to a head.

'So who paid for that, then?' he demanded.

'I did, if you must know.'

'Where d'you get the money from?' he asked in his usual sneering tone.

'Some of us do a job of work if you remember.'

She watched her brother with loathing that day as he sat smoking, as usual. Fag after fag, flicking the ash towards the fireplace and missing half the time. All the sympathy she had mustered for him had evaporated over the past few months. God knows she had tried. But he had given her no respite, and not an ounce of help or sympathy. He sickened her. He couldn't even be bothered to come to her husband's funeral. Things she had hoped never to say tumbled out of her mouth.

'I used to think it might be worth helping you out,' she spat at him as he sat staring indifferently at the floor. 'But you're a useless sod if ever there was one. Other people have problems and get on with their lives, but not you. Poor old George. You sit on your arse and wait for everyone to run round you. And then you turn round and go back to thieving and wasting your stupid, useless life away.'

George's head whipped round savagely. 'Who says I'm thieving?'

'Well, aren't you? You're up to something. Out all

hours and mixing in with God alone knows who. Anyone out at the time of night you come in is up to no good. And you're not stony broke are you? So where's it all coming from if you're not nicking it?'

'Leave me alone, you silly cow!' George yelled at her. 'Stupid nagging bitch. You're all the bloody same!'

Rose watched her brother's face, its expression of pure malice. His grey eyes were the coldest she had seen for a long time. Shuddering, she thought of Mr Lazenby.

'I tried with you,' she said more quietly. 'I'm the only person who's even tried.'

'Only so everyone could tell you how bloody marvellous you are. You thought I'd come in here and be your dogsbody, looking after that cripple of a husband of yours, and your stupid kid. But now people can start doing the running for me for a change.'

'What d'you mean?'

George sat down again, nipping his cigarette nervously between his lips. 'Never you mind – sis,' he said contemptuously. 'You just go on being a good little girl and working for your nice law man. I s'pose he's giving you one, is he?'

'Get out. Take your things and get out of my house.'

George turned to her with mock casualness. 'Going to make me?'

Thinking back over this now as she wrung out the clothes, Rose could feel the rage rising in her again. Things had settled down for the moment, it was true, but sooner or later she was going to have to face up to it. She pegged out the clothes and flung the water down the drain. She had to do something about George. She simply could not stand the sight of him.

*

In September everything changed at work. She reached town rather late that morning, trying to hurry in her tall slim heels through the usual sounds of thumping and drilling and all the dust and mess that signified the resurrection of the city. She hoped Ella Crosby would not notice she was late.

Climbing the stairs up to the Abel and Waters offices, she became aware of more crashing about and shouting from inside. What the hell's going on? she thought, hurrying even more. It sounded as though the offices were being ransacked.

She cautiously pushed the door open and was greeted by an incredible sight. Near his closed office door, as if trying to take refuge from it all, stood Mr Abel.

'No – please!' he cried as if that was the last straw. 'Not the typewriter, please! They're so expensive! Ah Rose – Mrs Meredith. Thank goodness you're here!'

Across the room was strewn what looked like the entire contents of Miss Crosby's desk. There were shorthand pads open and spread over the floor, files and typed letters and crumpled sheets of carbon paper, wodges of new stationery with sheaves of envelopes fanning out across the carpet, and against the wastepaper basket the blotter stood tipped up at an angle. A typewriter ribbon lay unravelled in black coils across the layers of paper.

Ella Crosby still seemed to be searching for things to throw, a snarl of fury trapped for the time being in her throat.

'What's happened?' Rose asked. 'What on earth's going on?'

'It's . . .' Mr Abel tried to explain.

'The stupid, selfish, miserable old—' Ella Crosby finished the sentence with a screech of fury. She thumped her fist down on the desk and the sight was so melodramatic that Rose wondered for a second whether she was putting it all on.

'What the heck have you done?' she demanded of Mr Abel.

'Not me!' Laurence Abel squeaked. 'God in heaven, not me! It's Mr Waters.'

'He's only gone and died, hasn't he?' Ella shouted. 'He's gone and damn well died on us!'

'It was a heart attack,' Laurence Abel explained. 'Last night. Someone found him this morning lying on the floor downstairs.'

Rose walked cautiously over to Ella Crosby, who had sunk down on her chair and was sitting sobbing at the desk.

'Miss Crosby,' she said gently. Somehow she did not dare touch the woman. 'You've had a shock. Why don't you go home and have a bit of a rest? Take the day off?'

Ella Crosby looked round at her slowly, rather stunned. 'But I've made such a terrible mess. I'm so sorry. I should clear it all up at least before I go.'

'No. You're all right, I'll do it,' Rose told her. 'Go on. We'll see you in the morning.'

Slowly Miss Crosby picked herself up, wiping her face with a handkerchief, and went out of the door.

Ella Crosby applied for another job. Laurence Abel was left with the sole running of the practice, and Rose stayed on with him. It took several weeks before things began to settle down.

'I'll be able to pay you a bit more now,' he told her. 'You'll be doing more work for a start.'

'Well, I'm not going to complain about that,' she told him.

'But,' he went on, 'come hell or high water I'm going to take the time off that I'd planned. Complete folly of course in the circumstances, but I can get someone to stand in for me and do at least the basics for a fortnight.'

Rose smiled at him without the sense of wistfulness that she had always felt before whenever he mentioned his trips to Italy. It was her secret. She was going to go as well! It didn't matter how soon, but she was going.

She realized that Laurence Abel was looking at her with unusual intentness.

'I'd have thought you must be in need of a holiday too,' he said. She noticed that his cheeks were turning pinker as he spoke. 'You could – er – come with me. I mean, don't get me wrong, Rose. I know how much it'd mean to you to go. I'd be happy to pay for you.' He laughed nervously.

Rose was so startled she could for a moment think of nothing to say. What was it he was actually asking her? He had been extremely kind and understanding to her during the last weeks of Alfie's life. But now she was back to being a single woman, was he trying to push things further? She wanted to believe the best of him, but she found her old mistrust flaring up again.

She sat staring down at her typewriter, her cheeks burning. She could feel his own discomfort even though she was not looking at him.

'I'm sorry. Don't take that the wrong way, will you? I wasn't expecting ... anything of you. I'd just enjoy the company.'

She wanted to believe him. She looked up shyly at

441

him. 'Thanks. But I couldn't just go, anyway. I've my daughter to think of.'

When Laurence Abel returned from his trip in November, it sharpened even more her own longing to go.

'Hilda,' she couldn't resist saying one night as she pulled the bedclothes up round the little girl, 'how would you fancy coming away on a little trip with me?'

'To Weston?' Hilda asked eagerly, half sitting up.

'No, not Weston. But we might see the sea.'

'Ooh yes!' Hilda said, and wriggled with excitement. Then she wrinkled up her nose. 'Would Uncle George have to come with us?'

Her uncle had been losing his glamour as the months passed and all his promises failed to come true. Since Alfie died, she had clung increasingly to Rose, the one really reliable person she had left, and they had grown much closer.

'No, not Uncle George,' Rose said. 'We don't want him along with us, do we? It'd just be you and me.' With a sudden rush of affection she leaned over and kissed Hilda's warm cheek. 'Now you go to sleep and dream all about it, eh?'

As she made herself a cup of tea she resolved that before she and Hilda went anywhere, she had to get George out. She sat down, kicking off her shoes and stirring sugar into her tea.

She hadn't seen him for two days. Perhaps she could threaten him with the police? Call his bluff? She had absolutely no proof that he was doing anything, but she knew him too well and he had to be up to something. She couldn't just throw him out. She had tried that. She began to think of something that would work.

Money. She could bribe him. She put her cup and saucer down. Give him some cash for a clean pair of heels? Perhaps she could spare some of Catherine's money. That would mean she would have to delay her plans a little, but it would be worth it. She could save the rest up gradually.

She went over to the fireplace and jiggled the loosened brick out of the wall to recount the money.

Her fingernails scratched against the brickwork. For a moment she scrabbled around, not believing it. Where was the envelope? Growing frantic, she slid her hand all round the inside of the cavity. Nothing.

A horrible suspicion filled her mind. Heart thumping hard, she ran up to the attic, to George's room, where she had not ventured for weeks.

The stench of stale cigarette smoke hit her immediately. With trembling hands she held the candle high and looked around. The bed was unmade and the old cupboard door was hanging open. Beside the bed lay the only remains of George to be seen in the room: a white saucer brimming over with cigarette stubs.

A week later a letter arrived from Catherine Harper-Watt. They kept up a regular correspondence, but this letter was different and short. Rose read it through several times, the full implications of it taking time to sink in. Finally she laid it down, shaking with anger and embarrassment.

My dear Rose,
    Just a quick note to let you know that all is well and I am most happy to have been able to help. The fact that you felt able to send your brother here

when he needed assistance is most gratifying to me, and he seemed such an interesting and purposeful young man.

I was able to let him have £50 to help him on his way, and we left him at Piccadilly heading north to his new life feeling we had truly done someone a service. Perhaps this removes a burden from you, and of course of that I am also glad.

We are all well. Judith has announced that she is at last to be married to her teacher friend Robert. How old that makes me feel!

I shall write again, but I just wanted to set your mind at rest.

Loving greetings,
Catherine Harper-Watt.

The winter months passed very slowly. Rose felt as frozen inside as the weather outside. Even work seemed less enjoyable. To her surprise she missed Ella Crosby, and it was lonely sitting in the outer office on her own.

She could not bring herself to write and tell Catherine the truth. For a start it might sound as if she was asking for more money. She had not even told Grace what had happened. Now she did not have Catherine's money as a back-up, she felt compelled to save as much as she could of her wages, scrimping along as a matter of habit.

Laurence Abel was keener than ever to speak Italian whenever possible, and although she went along with it, it only rubbed in the fact that she never seemed to get anywhere in her life.

What she needed to do now, she told herself, was to forget all this foolish hankering for something that was past, and build the best future she could for herself and her daughter. Hilda, after all, was the future.

The bus drew up with its brakes shrieking. Climbing inside Rose realized she had the chance of a seat and squeezed across to sit next to the window. It was a surprisingly warm spring day and the bus felt hot inside. She was on her way home from work, tired and stuffy in the head.

On her lap with her bag was her last newspaper from Laurence Abel, a December copy of *Corriera della Sera*. She knew she was feeling too inert to make any sense out of it at that time in the afternoon, but she opened it up, taking care not to wave it in the face of the man next to her.

The words seemed to shout at her, from a small news item in the middle of the second page. She blinked hard and tried to make sense of it.

'Vatican makes example of rebel priests' was the headline above the words that had drawn her eyes: Paulo Augustino Falcone. Father Paulo Falcone.

Many of the words in the article were unfamiliar to her as she seldom bothered to read stories connected with the Church.

She tore home, the paper not even properly folded in her hands. Once she was sitting down at the table with her dictionary she began to make more sense of it.

Three priests were referred to in the story. All of them had preached or taught on issues of faith or morals in a manner which had come to the displeasured attention of the Sacred Congregation for the Doctrine of the Faith. Rose had no idea what that was so she skipped over it. The story said that the Vatican had decided to clamp down on these three to provide a moral example to the rest of the Catholic community. Consequently, all three had to some degree been silenced by suspension from their duties as priests.

Rose skimmed over the details about the other two.

The most severely reprimanded of the three and also the youngest is Father Paulo Augustino Falcone, ordained three years ago in the Dominican house of San Domenico Maggiore in Naples. His radical views on issues such as poverty and contraception, and his calling to question the obligatory state of celibacy for all priests have resulted in his being banned from teaching, preaching, or celebration of the Mass.

Rose sat staring across the room, only realizing after a moment that Hilda was prodding her arm.

'I'm hungry, Mom. What's for tea?'

In a dreamlike state Rose got up and started spreading margarine on bread, the past still crashing in around her. Just reading his name like that rekindled such strong feelings.

'I said I wanted jam!' Hilda protested, swinging her legs crossly against the chair when the food arrived.

Rose stared, confused, at the slices of bread. Instead of jam she had put margarine on them twice.

He was still there: he was real. And now, after all his agonizing, all those years of training, his commitment to the priesthood was leading him into what, she recognized, devoid as she was of any real understanding of the Catholic faith, must be a good deal of pain and confusion.

'Mom! Listen to me! Can I have some jam? Is there any cake?'

Now she knew with a kind of frightening clarity that whatever it took, whatever the outcome of it, she had to go there. Finish things if necessary. She had to see Falcone again.

Standing by the table with the saucer of strawberry jam in her hand she said to Hilda, 'You know I said – ages back – that we'd be going on a journey? Well, I've been saving, and I'm going to go on saving our money until we've got enough to go – together. What d'you think of that?'

'Smashing,' Hilda said. 'Now please give me some of that jam!'

Forty

September 1954

'You really going tomorrow then?' Grace's voice held a definite tone of disapproval.

Rose was folding clothes into a decrepit old suitcase of Alfie's that had stood for years in her bedroom. 'Looks like it, doesn't it?'

'Beats me why you want to go off over there,' Grace said, shifting her weight to lean up against the doorframe. 'You could've gone anywhere for a break – a week by the sea at Rhyl for a quarter the price. I'd have thought you'd have had enough of over there in the war. They say it's ever so dirty and smelly.'

Rose smiled. 'Do they?'

'And you could've left Hilda with me and our dad. No need to go dragging her along as well.'

'I want her to come,' Rose said. 'She's seven, old enough to see it and remember. And Margherita's got kids. They can all play together.'

'You sure you've got enough money? Is that Mrs Harper-Watt paying for you to go?'

'No,' Rose said briskly, pushing a pair of shoes down into the side of the suitcase. 'She sent me some money for my birthday so I put that in the pot.' She turned to look squarely at Grace. 'The money she gave me after she came that time—'

'How much was it?' It was something Grace had always been dying to know.

'A hundred quid.'

Grace's eyes widened in astonishment. 'Blimey. She must be rolling in it!'

'When I'd taken some out for you and some other bits and bobs, there was still about eighty left. George had it off me.'

'You gave him eighty pound?' Grace screeched at her, standing absolutely upright now.

'Course I didn't. He pinched it, when he went off. And he stopped by in Manchester and conned some more out of her on the way to wherever he's gone.'

Grace stared at her, speechless for almost half a minute. 'Did you tell her?' she managed to say at last.

'No. Couldn't really, could I? It'd have sounded as if I was on the scrounge or something. What we're going away on is what I've saved, bar the ten pound she sent me.'

'He should be strung up.'

'Probably has been by now, for all we know.' Rose shut the case and struggled with the rusty fastenings. 'There – all set. Oooh.' She gave a little jump. 'I can't believe it, Grace. I'm really going – for ten whole days!'

'Nor can I,' Grace said drily, though she was smiling. 'Must be mad.'

With rhythmic, comforting sounds, the Naples train eased its way out through the suburbs of Rome. It was not very crowded and they had seats facing each other. Hilda, exhausted already from the excitement of a very long day – travelling on an aeroplane! – was dozing, her head lolling against the window. Rose felt she could not have slept even if she had been heavily drugged. She watched Hilda, her cheeks soft and lovely in the gentle light of the approaching sunset. Her perverse, self-willed but lovable daughter, here with her in Italy. Bringing these two parts of her life together seemed quite extraordinary.

She turned her attention to the regal Roman buildings outside the window. Even in the suburbs many of the tenements had a grandeur about them, with their flaking paint in yellow or terracotta or pink, and the contrasting greens and blues of the wooden shutters. Rose took in a deep, satisfied breath. This country! Whatever happened while she was here, at this moment she felt deeply content just to see it, to take in all the half-forgotten things that she loved about it. Fig trees and peeling trunks of eucalyptus softening the sides of buildings, the washing strung across narrow side streets glimpsed as the train hurried past; the baskets and buckets hanging outside windows ready to be let down to receive a delivery of bread or groceries. All the different smells that were so peculiarly Italian, the trace of drains and cigarette smoke mixed with the evening air – and she was sure she could smell the *prosciutto* between chunks of white bread that the elderly woman was tucking into on the seat across the passage.

As the light began to fade they passed through miles of fields, with small towns and villages strung along the railway line. Part of the land was fallow now that the summer was closing, and some fields held late crops of hay or spindly maize, with mules and carts still out collecting the dry cobs. On the left ran the line of the mountains, sometimes close enough to see the dark green cover of trees, sometimes smoky grey outlines in the distance, the foothills of the long spine of Italy.

When it was completely dark outside and the lights were on inside the train, Rose pulled Margherita's latest letter out of her bag. It seemed incredible that in a few hours she and Hilda would be sleeping in Francesco and Margherita's flat, and waking with the sun to meet their children.

'*Carissima Rosa*,' Margherita's bold writing looped across the cheap piece of paper.

> We are so happy that you are coming and bringing your daughter with you. How excited we all are about seeing you – it seems now only like a dream!
>
> I hope you will forgive our little place – it is small and cramped with all of us in it, but we can always find the space for such a welcome guest.
>
> Your train will arrive in Naples at about 22.00, and Francesco will be there to meet you, we promise you faithfully. I hope you will recognize each other! Please stand in the area near the ticket office and he will come to find you.
>
> We wait in eager anticipation of your visit – and until then, love and blessings from us all.
> Margherita.

The train began passing between buildings again, some of them higher than any Rose remembered from the war. Like Birmingham, she thought. The war has given us all a new face. As they rattled past tenements and factories still dotted with lights, and junctions with roads where cars, lorries and carts waited facelessly behind the gates, she began to smell the sulphury city smell.

He's out there somewhere, she thought. His city. The train was slowing now from its hectic pace so that the buildings slid past instead of being whisked immediately from view. They were replaced by light and the concrete of railway platforms as they drew to a halt in the great yawning central railway station in Naples.

'Hilda!' She leaned across and shook her gently. 'Come on, love. We're here.'

Francesco spotted her the moment she and Hilda walked out from the railway platform. Before she had even had time to look for him he was beside her.

'Rosa!'

'Francesco! Oh, Hilda, this is Francesco.'

And their arms were round each other, laughing and exclaiming and oblivious to anyone else in the huge, echoing station.

'*Come sta?* Are you well?'

'*Bene – benissimo!*'

'I think you've got a bit fatter, you know.' Rose prodded him playfully. 'It must be married life!' She found herself speaking slowly, feeling her way into the language again.

'But not much, truly. With six children you don't get fat! And you – you look lovely as ever. A little different perhaps . . . ?'

'Older – but then who isn't!'

Francesco bent down and Rose watched as he smiled warmly at Hilda who glanced doubtfully at her mother before smiling back.

'Welcome, *piccola.*' He pinched one of her cheeks affectionately. Unsure, Hilda drew her face away. 'We have a lot of friends at home for you to play with.'

Rose explained this to Hilda in English.

'She'll come round,' she told Francesco. 'By tomorrow night she'll be bossing them all about even if she doesn't speak the same language. Oh – I can't wait to see them all!'

Still laughing and joking, with Francesco carrying her suitcase, they walked out to a side street near the station.

'My brother Carlo lent me his car,' he said, unlocking a shiny red Fiat. 'He works as a salesman,' he said with slight mockery. 'Impoverished school teachers like me don't have cars. In any case, if we did we'd never all fit in it.'

Rose watched him curiously as he settled Hilda on the back seat and stowed her case away. It was true he was not as painfully thin as he had been during the war, but despite her teasing he was still a slim man. And he really did look older, much older. She remembered his pointed, aristocratic face as she had known it before: that aquiline nose and the striking blue eyes. But there was something different now. He looked – she kept glancing at him as he drove them home, struggling for the right word – he looked more *ordinary*. That was it. And did she look so to him? Had she ever seemed extraordinary? Perhaps it had been the war, its romantic element of adversity and drama that had lent them all a touch of romance. Was this how everything would look now she was back? Ordinary? And if so, would that make it any less of a pleasure to be here, now they were all back to everyday life?

'Why did you move to Pozzuoli?' she asked, as Francesco steered the car rather joltingly out west away from Naples to the small town along the coast.

'My job is in Pozzuoli, the school. I try to cram some history into their unwilling heads. And my brother lives there, so we can borrow his car!' he joked. 'No – but it is smaller, and quite cheap. It's OK.'

'And you're happy there?'

'Happy enough,' Francesco said with a shrug. 'Yes, why not happy? It's not a question I often find time to ask myself.'

It was not a long drive and soon they pulled up in a side street outside a pale, four-storey building. It looked pinkish in the streetlight.

'We're on the first floor so it's not too much of a climb,' he told her.

Rose could hear dogs barking and a buzzing sound, something electric. Cats shrank in and out of the shadows.

'Margherita is on tenterhooks to see you. And with any luck all the children should be asleep by now.'

The three of them climbed a dark, rather musty-smelling stone staircase. As they got near the top they heard a door open. Margherita must have been listening for them.

'Francesco?' Rose heard her soft, so familiar voice.

'Yes. We made it,' he called to her.

And there she was, outlined in the dim light from the flat. Rose almost stopped climbing the stairs in astonishment. Was that really Margherita? The figure of the woman standing at the entrance to the flat was plump and thick-limbed, her long hair draped down over her shoulders.

Before she had had time to take in fully the changed appearance of her friend she was at the top and they were embracing and kissing, both with tears of joy on their cheeks.

'At last you are here!' Margherita cried. 'I have been so longing to see you! Come in. Come and have some coffee and we will get you settled in. And you, little Hilda – I have some milk for you, *cara*'.

Francesco disappeared to take the car back to Carlo. Margherita disappeared for a moment and came back cradling a baby who had a shock of thick black hair.

'She is wakeful tonight,' she told Rose. 'This is my little one – Magdalena. She is nearly six months.'

Rose smiled wonderingly at the baby and called Hilda over to admire her too.

'She's lovely, Margherita. Quite beautiful. You have so many children already.'

Margherita smiled with the gentle wistfulness that Rose remembered. She had not really changed so much once they got talking.

'I have been blessed with so many little lives,' she said. Then with a despairing look she passed her free hand down over her waist and right hip. 'But that is why I am so fat. You would have walked past me on the street, eh, wouldn't you? With each one I seem to gain kilos and they never go again. We Italian women are fated this way. Whereas you – you look just the same!'

'Well, I've only had one, haven't I?' Rose laughed.

Margherita led them into a little kitchen with a tiled floor and pale blue walls.

'I am so happy to see you.' Margherita sat suckling the child. 'I really missed you when you left. And you left us so sadly.' She smiled quickly and then switched the conversation.

'Your little girl is lovely. Hilda, you are beautiful! She is the same age as my Marco, so they will be able to play. But of course the older ones will have school tomorrow – and Francesco too! We shall have a nice lot of time together. Come now.' She stood up, fastening her blouse. 'You can have a look at my babies.'

Suddenly extremely weary, Rose followed her along

455

a little passage to the bedrooms. The children had all been moved in together to leave a room for her and Hilda.

As Margherita pushed open a door the light fell on some of the children, some in beds and two on the floor. Rose learned the names of the quiet, sleeping faces.

'Come. We can talk tomorrow.' Margherita leaned over and kissed both of them again. 'Thank you for coming – you have made me so happy.

For two days they did hardly anything but talk. Margherita did not mention Falcone and at first Rose was content to enjoy simply being there. She soon felt at home in the chaotic, ramshackle flat with its crumbling paint and old furniture, shelves and surfaces spilling over with books and papers and children's clothes and drawings and toys. And she helped Margherita with her chores as they got to know one another again.

While the three older children were at school, Hilda settled into playing with the others. Caterina, who was three, looked up to her as if she was some kind of pale English goddess, and they soon found ways of communicating. And little Giovanni followed them about and they fussed over him and chivvied him to join in their games.

Rose learned that Margherita and Francesco were, as he had put it, 'happy enough'. But they were constantly worried about money, like so many of the families around them. Though Margherita clearly had a Neapolitan adoration for all her children, Rose noticed a suppressed kind of restlessness about her.

'How many children d'you think you'll have?' Rose

asked her the second evening. They had spent the day shopping for food and walking in the town and were preparing spaghetti for the evening meal.

'As many as God gives me.'

'You're not serious!'

Margherita looked round at her, and Rose saw a look of desperation in her eyes.

'What else can I do? There's no way of stopping it. The Church tells us that if we limit our relations to the time in the month when it is safe . . .' She sighed. 'For some women that works. For me, it doesn't make any difference. I couldn't easily say this to anyone else, but I wonder sometimes why I studied. Why do they allow us women to have an education if our fate remains the same – to bear child after child and bring them up in poverty because there are too many of them?'

The tears welled up and ran down her cheeks. Rose put her arms round her.

They had barely even mentioned Il Rifugio during those two days. Rose was growing anxious and frustrated. She was eager to reminisce – one of the things she had most looked forward to about coming. In the evenings, once the mayhem of the children had died down for the night, they sat in the stuffy little flat drinking cheap wine and eating bread and late summer fruit, and talking, but they avoided the subject she most longed to discuss. If she asked a question they moved quickly on to something else. Most resolutely they did not talk about Falcone. Up to now she had not been able to bring herself to mention his name either. But to be here so near him, yet as closed off from him as she had been in Birmingham, was agonizing. She found herself constantly watching for his face among the crowded streets, even though they were not in Naples.

By the third morning she was beginning to feel that if she or someone did not mention Falcone soon she would explode. She walked with Margherita down to the little port to go to the fish markets, the stalls strung out along the front next to the sea. Hilda was fascinated by the fish. They strolled along with the vivid blue of the Mediterranean on one side, dotted with sunlight and coloured boats. And on the other, wooden tubs painted pale blue inside seethed with live eels or shellfish like piles of coloured pebbles, or small silver and orange fish flitting about in the shallow water. On the stalls behind lay heaps of prawns, and larger fish, already dead and glassy-eyed on banks of ice. Their smell was pungent on the air, and mixed with that of the sea and the drains.

'Oh look, Mom!' Hilda cried, running to bend over a row of tubs where lobsters tangled their claws together, crammed in in a brick-coloured mass. From a nearby one a number of large octopuses stared out balefully, some of their tentacles slipping experimentally out over the side and curling as they touched the ground. Caterina was chatting excitedly and Giovanni gingerly dipped his fingers in the water.

As they were occupied for the moment, Rose took Margherita's arm. Speaking loudly to be heard over the long, doleful cries of the fish hawkers, she said, 'I've heard what's happened.'

Margherita frowned. 'What?'

'To Falcone.'

Margherita's expression showed first astonishment and then apprehension. 'How did you know?'

'I read it in a newspaper. Why won't you talk about him?'

'We hoped you would think of him as a priest still. That nothing had changed. We wanted to avoid causing you pain – if that's what you would feel after ten years, of course. How could we know what you would feel? You might even have forgotten.'

Rose shook her head impatiently. 'You've seen him recently?'

'Yes, a month or so ago. We didn't tell him you were coming, by the way. He's in a lot of trouble. He began to question what the Church teaches and of course that disturbs a lot of people. He's obviously very unhappy. He loves his faith deeply, but he's so disillusioned, with the priesthood especially. And the hierarchy have come down hard on him. You'd think it might be enough to crush a person.'

Rose hesitated. 'Did he ever mention me – when you saw him after the war?'

'Of course. In the beginning.' She paused. 'I know I never thought he was cut out to be a priest, but that's for God to decide. He's had so much to bear, and whether now you should be part of this . . .'

Rose gripped Margherita's arm again with a determination that clearly communicated itself.

'I have to see him.'

Forty-One

The church of San Domenico Maggiore was a forbidding building of stained, sandy-coloured stone.

Rose stood in the piazza looking at it. That Falcone had worked and studied here for so long was hard for her to imagine – a place which seemed to suggest such rigidity and conviction. She could not reconcile that with the man she had known; so tender and so confused.

Now the prospect of simply walking round the building to the seminary and knocking on the door seemed quite impossible. After all, what if he opened the door? She had been partly prepared for approaching the place by Margherita, who seemed to have decided that if Rose was going to do something of such doubtful wisdom she might as well give her as much help as she could. She had insisted that Rose leave Hilda with her for the day.

'Go to them and ask for Father Falcone,' she told Rose. 'Tell them that you want him to hear your confession. They may try to get you to accept someone else, but you can say you have something particular to ask him. If he's busy you can always go back later, can't you?'

I'll go and have a look at the church first, she said to herself. Get a feel of it.

She walked slowly over to the entrance. She was wearing a pleated skirt in a soft yellow poplin, cream court shoes, and a close-fitting navy blouse. The skirt swished luxuriously round her legs as she walked. She had felt very smart and feminine when she put them on, but now she was unsure of herself. Should she have worn something darker and more staid to come to a place like this?

The inside of the building was almost as austere as its exterior, the floor flagged in black and white marble on which her thin heels seemed to make far too much noise, and a ceiling which was plain except for frescos above the aisle, and even they were in restrained colours. There was very little else in the way of decoration.

She had evidently arrived just at the end of the Mass. As she entered people were beginning to stream out of the building. A few stayed in their places at prayer or moved to the front to light candles. Others stood round in small clusters talking. She watched those who were leaving bow to the altar and cross themselves and she made an attempt to do the same, overcome with a sudden distaste.

Bowing and scraping, she thought.

As she looked up towards the high altar, two figures caught her attention. Long white robes, with black cloaks over them which wafted out behind as they walked, seeming to glide across the floor. For a few dizzying seconds his face was superimposed on each of them. Then she focussed properly. One had white hair and was short and stocky. The other was tall and slim with black hair, but everything else about him was wrong; the nose too long, the eyes, brows, complexion all unknown to her. She stood watching. So this was his life, here, doing this.

Soon she was almost alone in the church, still standing there in the aisle. The younger priest had disappeared. She knew that if she did not act now she might never find the courage again.

She walked up towards the altar. The elderly priest was standing to one side in one of the choir stalls, leafing through a book. His thick, white eyebrows were pulled into a frown.

She wasn't even sure how to address him and when she spoke her voice sounded too loud.

'*Signore? Mi scusi!*'

The priest looked up with an irritated air. 'Yes. What is it?'

'I – I'm looking for Father Falcone.'

He stared at her for a moment, then with startling force he slammed the book closed so that dust flew up from the wooden choir stall. He stepped out and began to walk briskly away.

'Father Falcone is not here.' He spoke over his shoulder with unmistakable dislike.

Rose followed him for a few steps. 'Where is he – please?'

The priest stopped and turned round abruptly, obviously shocked. His first answer should have been enough. She was not supposed to question further.

'Father Falcone is away on retreat – again. Not, as one would expect of a priest in a position as serious as his, in a religious house of prayer, but' – he flicked his right wrist several times, dismissively – 'in some place of his own choosing. Where that may be I have no idea.'

He turned and was gone.

The impact of the old man's bitterness left her reeling and close to tears. Only as she was walking back along the black and white flagstones did she know just how consuming was her need to see Falcone. But she was no closer to finding him.

She sat down on one of the seats at the back of the church. His church, which felt so desolate now she knew he was not here. She stared up at the high altar, shrouded and mysterious at the far end of the church.

'Please. Please help me find him,' she found herself whispering. Perhaps his God would come to her aid?

She thought of him kneeling in here day after day. He was in deeper trouble than she could have imagined. He had felt the need – or been sent – to get away and think about things, and not for the first time by the sound of it. And he had even chosen to go somewhere they would not think of looking.

And then it came to her, making her catch her breath. Of course! If Falcone needed time to think, her instinct told her, she knew the first place he would go. Not even questioning now the need that drove her on to find him, she ran out of the echoing church and across the piazza.

Less than an hour later she was on the train to Sorrento.

She might have revelled in being in Sorrento had things been different, but as it was she hardly took in the town at all. By the time she had walked up the road to the Finzis' house, having several times had to ask the way, it was one o'clock, and though no longer the height of summer it was hot enough to tire her. Her feet were sore from walking in her flimsy, high-heeled shoes.

The bubble of excitement and eagerness which had driven her on in the early part of the day had almost evaporated through weariness and thirst. She felt very nervous. All the things she had planned to say on meeting him again, the scenes she had so often visualized had vanished, and instead she could only think of flat, lifeless things. The day had gone wrong. And she was only guessing that he was here.

When she caught sight of the Finzis' house she slowed down, her heart hammering in her chest. The house had recently been painted in pale green, and the shutters in a darker shade, so that the whole place had a newer, fresher air about it.

What on earth was she doing here? If he really was here, what could she say to him? But to turn back now would be unthinkable.

Without waiting to summon up courage she knocked on the door. There was a pause before it opened and she was facing a middle-aged, heavily built man who stared at her in silence. He was chewing hard on something and clearly in the middle of a meal.

'Yes?' he said eventually.

'I'm sorry to disturb you.' Her heart was sinking. It was all a mistake. The Finzis weren't here any more. 'I am looking for Paulo Falcone – Father Falcone.'

The man nodded. 'Yes,' he said abruptly, showing no surprise. 'Come in.' And she was stepping back into the Finzis' house.

The inside had also been painted, and as she walked through the coolness of the rooms it felt strange, less homely than she remembered. He led her immediately to the kitchen which was little changed from when she had stayed there.

Before she had time to collect her thoughts the man was saying, 'Paulo – someone to see you.'

Not their meeting as she had pictured it at all. She stood in the doorway looking into his face as their eyes met, trying to take in that it was really him. He was sitting at the table, fork in hand, dressed not in the white robes she had seen earlier, but in a shirt and trousers, both black and worn. He looked much the same as she remembered: serious, a little more careworn perhaps. Those large, long-lashed eyes stared back at her, puzzled. Whatever emotions may have been present in him, whether surprise or dismay, did not give themselves away in his face. He put down his fork and pushed the chair back.

'Rosa?' He stood in front of her, apparently unsure what to do. Then convention took over and he held out his hand. Somewhere in her mind she registered how warm it felt. She tried to smile at him, but her lips barely seemed to obey.

'Er – we were eating,' Falcone said, quickly. 'Will you join us and have some food?' He pulled out a chair for her.

'Thank you. That would be very nice.' She imagined him with the worshippers at San Domenico Maggiore, measured and courteous.

He gave her some of the tough bread and a dish of spaghetti with meat and tomatoes.

At the table Rose was shocked to recognize Clara Finzi. She had aged greatly, her once plump cheeks sunken, her eyes watery and holding an absent expression.

'Clara.' Falcone spoke to her loudly. 'This is Rosa – from England. She stayed here once, during the war. When Angelo was still alive. Do you remember?'

He looked at her then. Rose found herself blushing. He remembered. Of course he remembered. And what else could he have said to the old woman, who just nodded, mumbling something indistinct. Clearly Clara did not recognize her.

'I'm sorry,' Falcone said with the same formal politeness. He gestured to the man who had opened the door to her. 'This is Lorenzo Finzi, the eldest son of the family. He has been living here with his mother since Signore Finzi's death.'

'I'm sorry,' she said. 'About Signore Finzi.'

Both men nodded, acknowledging the comment.

'Where are you staying?' Falcone asked her.

'With Francesco and Margherita in Pozzuoli.'

Falcone smiled for the first time. 'And all their lovely family?'

'My daughter is with them.'

He looked attentively at her. 'You're married.' It was not quite a question.

'I'm a widow.'

'Rosa ...' He stopped. 'How did you know I was here?'

'They told me you were on a retreat somewhere, and I thought ...'

'They? Margherita and Francesco?'

'No. A priest. At your church. He didn't seem very happy at me asking.'

'You went to San Domenico?'

She nodded, unable to work out his reaction to this. Was he angry? Had she made things even worse for him? He was shaking his head gently from side to side, whether in amazement or displeasure she could not decide. She felt terribly embarrassed and clumsy, and longed to leave. Even her clothes felt wrong. She was overdressed, a stranger even to herself.

She looked away from Falcone's face, down at his hands, dark against the red and white checks of the tablecloth. They looked so familiar that the sight of them brought a lump to her throat. Those gentle, loving hands. Incredible that the hands of this stranger beside her had once known her so intimately. She was a fool for coming, for reviving the memories. She would go immediately. She could not even finish the food on her plate. If she and Falcone could have anything to say to one another it was quite impossible here.

'I really have to go now.' Getting up nervously she said to Clara and Lorenzo Finzi, 'Thank you both for your hospitality. I'm very grateful.'

Falcone took her to the door. She felt the lump in her throat again as he walked behind her. She could not have imagined a meeting as dreadful as this. She had visualised conversations where he reinforced to her his priestly vocation, and stood up for his decision to leave her so abruptly: perhaps rejected her all over again and with even more force. Anything seemed preferable to this unreadable formality.

'I'm sorry for disturbing you.' She was having difficulty controlling her voice. 'I should not have come here.'

She turned and began to walk away down the road so he would not see her tears.

'Wait!'

Almost angry now, she turned to him.

'I . . . You must understand how surprised I am to see you,' he said lamely, walking to stand closer to her in the dusty road. She stood dumbly in front of him, hardening her feelings. She could not speak.

'I had no idea you were coming, and . . .' He stumbled over the words. 'You look so different.'

He turned aside from her, looking up at the trees on the opposite side of the road. He was breathing in fast, shallow breaths.

'Look . . . I'm sorry. I can't . . . Every time I speak it

condemns me.' He gestured despairingly with his hands. 'Seeing you again ... Could you – would you come back?'

'When?'

'Tomorrow – afternoon? I'll be walking.' He pointed up towards the mountain. 'I often do at that time of day. Lorenzo will not bother us.' He seemed to recover himself a little. 'I'm sorry you have come so far and I am unable to – that I can't be more ... welcoming today.'

In a dignified voice Rose said, 'I'll come tomorrow, if that's what you want?'

He nodded. 'Please, Rosa.'

She turned and walked back down towards the town.

It was a warm, languorous afternoon bathed in rich autumn sunlight which touched the fading leaves with gold. Walking to the house, she saw red blooms still on the geraniums, tiny children watching her from doorways and cats curled sleeping in the sun. She was dressed differently this time, her feet comfortable in flat shoes, feeling the warmth on her arms. She felt strangely calm, as if anything that happened was now up to him. She was here, come what may.

There were no signs of life at the house and she walked past. As she began to climb the first deep step to the Stations of the Cross, the sense of recognition hit her oddly – those stones, so unchanged. At every other twist of the steep path were the stations she remembered; the crudely painted little pictures each protected by its alcove of brick, which also held their tributes of candles and flowers. She looked fondly at them, though their actual meaning was mostly lost on her.

Perhaps she had come too early? They had not agreed on any particular time. She sat down on one of the steps and looked back. The town was just becoming visible through the trees, though they had grown and thickened. She thought back to the last time she had sat up here on one of these steps. She had been thinking of Sam, still soaking in the shock of his death.

She breathed in the smells of the herbs and trees around her. There was a light scuttling sound. A salamander dashed off into the dry grass alongside the path in alarm. Startled, Rose turned her head.

Falcone was standing watching her. He had come down from the chapel where he had spent some of the early part of the afternoon, thinking perhaps to meet her. As he turned the bend in the path he had come upon the sight of that familiar little figure sitting below him. He stopped, narrowing his eyes to make it out more clearly, as if perhaps it might be another dream. She had come to him many times before, dressed in the old black blouse and skirt, her hair taken up in a coil behind her head. It was an image that had haunted him against all the power of his will for the past nine years.

As she turned, she heard his voice saying softly, as if unsure, 'Rosa?'

She stood up and slowly climbed up to join him. When she reached the step on which he was standing she looked up at him solemnly. It was impossible for either of them not to remember their last time together in this place.

Falcone looked back at her, then as if in some way defeated by the sight of her, he directed his gaze away at the ground. But in that brief moment of contact the emotions she had seen in his eyes were all she needed.

Together they turned and began to climb.

'So,' she asked softly, 'why are you here up on this mountain instead of getting on with being a priest?'

'Well.' He sighed heavily. 'I'm in a mess.'

To his amazement, Rose suddenly grinned. 'Are you always in a mess, or is it just whenever I turn up?'

Falcone burst out laughing. The sound startled her. He stopped and leaned up against the rocky wall next to the steps.

'I had almost forgotten,' he said. 'How could I forget – how you . . . ? All the time I'm surrounded by earnest, righteous people telling me I'm mistaken, that I must stop speaking my mind because it will threaten the whole fabric of the Church. And then you come along and blow right through the whole thing! But in answer to your question: since I'm no longer allowed to do any of the things that are normally the framework of my priesthood, they can't think what to do with me. They keep sending me off to "reconsider my position" on various questions. To examine my conscience and so on and so forth. So here I am, trying to do just that.'

'And are you getting anywhere?'

'Oh . . .' Falcone tilted his head back for a moment, wearily, as they walked on. 'No further perhaps than I should have got if I'd taken more notice of you when we used to argue back then.'

He turned to face her. 'I don't want to go over and over it again. It's – oh, it drags you down. Rosa, I'm so sorry about yesterday. Your coming here at this time was so extraordinary that I didn't know how to react. Why did you come?'

'I had to see you.'

They'd reached the little chapel and sat down together on the top step at the entrance, soaked in warm afternoon light.

She felt bold because there was no time not to be, but also because the priest figure had gone, and they could talk as immediately, as honestly as ever.

'I saw what had happened to you in the paper,' she said. 'There's a man I work for at home who gives me Italian newspapers. When I saw your name again, real like that suddenly, I knew I had to come. I don't know if you realize how cruel it was, the way you went and never spoke to me again. Your letter. It left me all ragged at the ends. I could never settle, not really. It never ended for me you see ...' She trailed off, her cheeks burning and suddenly wet with tears. 'I always loved you.'

Falcone was sitting with his face in his hands. She longed to touch him, but hesitated, before gently laying a hand on his shoulder and stroking him.

After a moment, trying to control his voice, he said, 'Oh, Rosa, Rosa. Would you believe me if I tell you that not a day has passed without me thinking of you? Of how I treated you? When I saw Margherita after you'd gone back to England, she let me know very clearly just what I'd done. She was so angry with me. She would never show that she despised someone but she must have despised me then. It was another guilt to add to all the others. But at the time I couldn't – really couldn't think what else to do. I wouldn't have been any good to you, not then. Margherita even told me she didn't think I had a vocation to the priesthood. It's dangerous to say such things of course. I've had to find that out for myself.'

'Without Margherita I think I would have fallen apart.'

'But you married – your English husband? I knew that. When I heard, it made things easier for me in a way. To think that you were really taken from me. That you loved someone else.'

'No,' Rose said bleakly. 'That was my mistake. And I say that more for his sake than mine. I could never give him what he really deserved from me. I had learned what love was before that and I could never forget it. However much I tried not to think of you, you took something from me that I was never able to give again, to him or anyone.'

He turned to look at her and she saw his eyes were full of pain. 'Rosa – come here.'

And they were in each other's arms, he rocking her gently as she laid her wet face against his chest, his own tears falling on her hair.

'I'm so, so sorry,' he said. 'All this time you have felt so much . . . And sitting here now I feel so close to you, as if I saw you only last week.'

'I feel it too,' she said through her tears. 'Paulo – what will happen to you?'

'I think I stopped being a priest in the way they define it a long time ago. When my conscience could no longer stomach some of the teachings, but I was expected to act as if I believed absolutely that they were God's laws. It's a sickening position to be in. Only I hadn't yet found the courage to let go of it. But now . . .'

She turned her face up to his and they looked into each other's eyes before they kissed, at first soft, quick touches of their lips, each still full of wonder at the other's presence.

Their hands began to rediscover each other's bodies. Rose wanted to touch every part of him: the soft curve of skin at the back of his neck, his shoulders, his warm flesh under the rough shirt, and she felt his hands moving hungrily over her hair, down her back and round to her breasts which ached for his touch.

In moments they were taken over by their desire for each other. He lifted her on to his lap and she sat astride him, her skirt riding up round her waist. She could feel his hardness pressing beneath her and his face was taut with the urgency of it.

She took his face between her palms, steadying him. 'I don't want you to regret this.'

'Never. This is not what I regret.'

When he came up into her their cheeks were wet with tears again before either of them had climaxed. Rose held Falcone tightly as he came, his body shuddering, hands gripping her back as if in pain. As she reached the height of her own pleasure she cried out, 'I can't bear it' and heard him making reassuring sounds as if to a child.

They clung to each other for a long time as their breathing slowed, her cheek pressed against his, and he still deep inside her.

Afterwards they sat very close, talking until shadows slipped over them and cooled them as the night drew in and mosquitoes whined round their heads. There was so much to share, to tell of their lives.

When it had grown almost completely dark, Rose got up, stiffly and reluctantly. 'If I don't go now I shan't even catch the last train back.'

It was not easy to move away from this place where the communication had grown up between them again, from roots which had never been destroyed.

'Can you come again?' Falcone asked with sudden awkwardness. 'Bring your daughter so that I can see her?'

'I'll bring her tomorrow. But then you must come and see Francesco and Margherita. They'll think I've deserted them. Are you allowed to?'

Falcone shrugged. 'I suppose so. If not, then it will be just one more transgression to add to all the others.'

They stood at the top, reluctant to take the first step, as if fearful that going back down to the rest of the world might destroy what had happened there that evening.

'Look – I'll have to go.' She could see his eyes watching her, the faint remainder of evening light shining in their dark surface.

'Don't leave me again,' she said.

Falcone moved towards her. 'My love.'

And then they held each other, very gently this time, like old, fragile friends, standing together between the dark shapes of the trees in the scented night air of the mountain.

Margherita and Francesco were both waiting up for her, though it was very late by the time she let herself into the flat. She had long missed the last bus to Pozzuoli and had had to take a taxi.

They were very relieved to see her, and the glow on her face was unmistakable to both of them as she walked in, startled to find them both up. Margherita was watching Rose's face intently and Francesco handed her a glass of wine.

'Well?' he demanded. 'Come on – what happened?'

'Rosa?' Margherita said more cautiously. 'Holy Mother – what have you both got yourselves into this time?'

Rose put her glass down. 'One moment. I just need to go to my room. I'd like you to do something for me.'

She stayed long enough to kiss Hilda and return to them carrying a flat package.

'Francesco, have you still got your record player?'

She smiled when he nodded in reply. 'Play this for me then.'

And she drew out his old gift to her: the long unplayed recording of 'J'attendrai'.

Forty-Two

Italy, June 1957

The voice she could hear shouting somewhere in the house was unmistakable, and though it was impossible to make out a word of what was being said, she smiled to herself in amusement.

It must have been quite a house once, she thought, examining it before going right up close. Certainly more promising than she'd expected when she was travelling out here on the train. All those drab little towns north of Naples! Cellina itself was one such town: small, poor and more or less featureless, except for one redeeming sight, a little church she had caught a glimpse of, with a vivid turquoise dome. Otherwise the place seemed to consist only of that one square, the Piazza Garibaldi, streets of ill-kempt houses and a few dismal shops.

But this house, out towards the more peaceful western edge of the town, reassured her. The doctor's house. It stood detached, and behind it was an orchard, planted with a mixture of citrus and apricot trees. The place was in need of some repair, of course, but these things took time – and money.

What pleased her most about the front of the house was the tiled plaque obviously newly attached to the wall beside the front door. In dark green letters on a cream background it read, 'ORFANOTROFIO DIANA – ORPHANAGE DIANA'.

She banged on the heavy brass door knocker, and as she did so caught sight of a man, stooping under the weight of a heavy box of vegetables, hurrying round the side of the house with an annoyed expression on his face. He flung the box into his little three-wheeler truck, and started up its rough, coughing engine to rev off down the road.

As she watched, the door opened.

He looked different from how she had imagined, more gentle and approachable, and certainly more casual, in his cotton trousers and open-necked shirt. Not at all her image of an Italian doctor. Despite Rose's descriptions she had visualized someone in a suit and perhaps rather aloof. Instead – what warmth in those eyes! Although slightly startled, they already held a welcome.

'Dr Falcone? I'm Catherine Harper-Watt.'

His face creased into a delightful smile. In awkward English he said, 'Of course. We wait for you.' He beckoned in that Italian manner, almost as if shooing her away. 'Please come.'

As she stepped into the house she heard the voice again: 'Paulo – *chi e*? . . . Oh Catherine it *is* you. At last!'

Rose ran forward and the two women flung their arms round each other.

'Oh, I'm so glad you've come to see us!'

'I heard you even before I arrived,' Catherine told her teasingly. 'You seem to be familiar enough with the language to hold your own!'

Rose chuckled, translating what Catherine had said to Falcone.

477

He also laughed, shrugging in mock despair. 'You should tell her that now you've learned to swear in Italian as well there's no stopping you!'

Rose repeated what he said. 'It's just that bloke who comes round delivering the veg. He always tries to palm off all the old frowsty stuff on me. I'm sure it's because he thinks I'm a foreigner and I won't notice. So I gave him what for this time. Anyway, come on through and let's get you settled. I'm dying to hear all the news.'

Falcone took Catherine's bags to her room, and the three of them went through to a huge, white-tiled kitchen at the back of the house. The room was slightly clinical with its grey lino on the floor, and a huge white sink and steel range. But there was a pot simmering on the top of it which was homely, and on the windowsill above the sink stood several flowering plants.

Four children, all between the ages of two and four, were sitting at a large wooden table in the centre, tucking into thick chunks of bread. Watching them was a plump-faced young woman who was sitting with her rounded arms resting on the table. The children fell silent at the sight of Catherine, their brown eyes watching her every move as their little cheeks bulged like hamsters' with the bread.

'So these are part of the family,' Catherine said. 'I shall have to learn all their names.'

'This is Anna Lucia,' Rose said, indicating the young woman, who nodded and smiled back amiably. 'She works here now every day except Sunday. We couldn't do without her.'

Rose placed a bottle and some glasses on the table.

'There are nine children here so far – and Hilda, of course. The older ones are at school and we do the best we can with the rest. There's about room for a couple more.'

Falcone put a hand on Rose's shoulder. 'Shall we take them out for a run about when they've finished? Then you can talk.'

Catherine watched smiling as the little ones all climbed down from the table and followed Falcone and Anna Lucia out of the door.

'You seem to have got yourselves organized quite speedily,' Catherine said, accepting a glass of wine and some of the bread.

Rose looked at her gratefully. 'We couldn't have done it without your help.'

'And the help of some worthy WI women in the Manchester area,' Catherine reminded her. 'They've been quite fired up by the idea of this place. You have a little money from the town now?'

'Yes. That's something. You've come at a good time.' Rose sat down. 'We've just heard that Paulo's registered to practise again, so now he can go back to what he's meant to be doing. It's a bit of a relief too, because the money his father left is all but gone. There've been so many extras to get the place going.'

'And for your wedding.'

Rose laughed. 'That didn't set us back much. It must've been one of the quietest weddings ever to happen in Italy! Which was fine by me and it was all we could afford. And another reason was that even after the dispensation came through so we could get married it took him quite a while to get used to the idea that he wasn't a priest.

'I didn't care what we did so long as I could just get back over here with him. You'd think with all the time since the war that another couple of years wouldn't make much odds, but I've never known two years go so slowly!'

'You were very patient,' Catherine told her. She leaned forward to take off her soft fawn cardigan. 'How beautifully warm it is here! And you're looking positively marvellous, my dear!'

Rose was dressed in a frock in her favourite navy, a colour which always flattered her dark looks, and her hair was taken up in a swinging ponytail. Catherine was noticing for the first time just how beautiful Rose could look. Her face had always been attractive, arresting even, but now, the one ingredient which had been lacking before – the bloom of happiness – had transformed her.

'You must work hard with all these children, but I must say you don't look at all worn down by it.'

'Well, we've got Anna Lucia. And Paulo's been around a lot – though that'll change when he's back to being a doctor. I s'pose it is tough, but I love doing it, that's all. Doing what you like isn't too difficult is it?'

When Catherine had settled into the tiny spare bedroom, Rose showed her round. It was a spacious house, with five bedrooms and plenty of room to accommodate the growing 'family' downstairs.

'The surgery will be here,' Rose said, opening up a room beside the front door. 'It was where Paulo's father worked, so he can soon get it all set up again.'

The room must have been much as the older Dr Falcone had left it, with shelves of books and an old wooden desk with a crucifix hanging behind it. Against the opposite wall stood a high, flat examination bed.

After their little tour she led Catherine out of the

back door of the house. They sat out on a terrace where so much grass had grown up between the stones that they were almost completely hidden. Rose found some old wooden chairs on which there was still some peeling brown paint.

The scents of honeysuckle and other flowers that Catherine could not identify filled the air, and pink bougainvillea burst its colour all over the wall along one side of the garden. On the dry grass under the trees Falcone was entertaining the children by teaching them to turn somersaults, while Anna Lucia stood by giggling.

'He's very good with them.' Catherine watched Rose carefully as she looked over at her husband, happy to see the love so plain in her eyes. She had come to feel as protective towards Rose as if she were her own daughter and she was anxious to see her happy.

'He's so much freer now – laughs more than I've ever known. Hilda loves him, she really does. He's the first proper dad she's ever had. Of course her real father was special to her, but he could never play with her. And she's teaching him English! I think she's picking up Italian quicker though.' She turned to Catherine. 'Tell me how things are at home. Any news?'

'Well, most of it's reasonably good. I stopped by in Birmingham on the way. Grace sends all her love of course, and . . .' She paused. 'I asked her if she'd like to come out and see you both.'

'You mean . . . ?'

Catherine held up a hand, embarrassed. 'I'd love to help. Don't say any more.'

'Oh, thank you!' Rose actually clapped her hands together with delight.

'Paulo!' She shouted across to him. 'Catherine is going to send Grace over to see us!'

He smiled and waved back, and was promptly toppled to the ground by the two four-year-olds who
shrieked with laughter. Rose and Catherine laughed too.

'I can't get over how fast Birmingham is changing,'
Catherine said. 'All those tall buildings going up. Real
skyscrapers. Of course you'll have seen a lot of it, but
the centre of the city seems to be altering almost beyond
recognition. They're going to redo the Bull Ring completely you know.'

'I know.' Rose sighed. 'Sometimes I wonder if I'll
know any of it if I go back. In a way I'm glad not to
see it happening.'

'But the big news is that they're going to demolish
Catherine Street and all the others round it.'

'What? Grace never told me.'

'She's only just heard. Apparently they've got the
choice of moving out somewhere on the edge of the city
or having one of the new flats close by. Grace says she's
determined to stay near the same spot. She thinks the
suburbs will be all kippers and curtains and your father
would embarrass her by still insisting on cutting up his
squares of newspaper for the lavatory. She made me
laugh over it in fact. And he seems prepared to do whatever she wants. To tell you the truth, he barely said a
word the whole time I was there.'

'That's Dad for you,' Rose said. 'Poor old Grace,
though. He always had a soft spot for her and she's
never really had a break from him. I don't s'pose he'd
have lived for long with me even if I had stayed around
to let him. We'd have fought like blooming alley cats.'

'Grace seemed remarkably cheerful, I thought.'

'I don't half miss her,' Rose said thoughtfully. 'Fancy
the old place going, though. I knew they were going to
get round to it some time, but it really will be the end

of an era. Can't picture Grace in a new flat. But then I 'spect she can't picture me over here either.'

'There is one piece of bad news,' Catherine said hesitantly. 'Your brother George has been arrested. In Glasgow.'

'Glasgow?'

'That's where he went, evidently, on your money and mine. Oh yes, Grace wasn't going to let me go without putting me straight about that. For goodness sake, Rose, you should have told me. I wouldn't have been angry. Anyway, for some reason he gave the police the Birmingham address. Perhaps he hasn't got a fixed abode up there.'

'What's he done this time then?'

Catherine shifted her gaze to the ground. 'I'm not certain.'

Rose looked at her closely. 'You *do* know, don't you?'

Catherine gave a painful sigh. 'Well, all right, yes. He's been acting as a pimp. Lining his pockets quite successfully I gather.'

Rose's mouth fell open. 'A pimp? My God. All that time he was with me! To think – what did I have in my house?'

She sat silent, shocked, until Catherine thought of something else.

'A more cheerful piece of news. Grace said she'd heard from Alcester. One of the twins? Apparently she's recently had her first baby. A little boy called Jimmy.'

Rose smiled, shaking her head in wonder. 'Dear little Susan. Fancy.'

They spent an uproarious few hours when the older children arrived back from school. Hilda, a tanned and healthy ten-year-old, was thrilled to find someone else in the house who spoke English, and chatted away non-stop to Catherine.

Once they were all fed and in their beds and Anna Lucia had gone home, Rose cooked a meal for the three of them. They ate in what was still the dining room of the house, with its dark, formal furniture. Rose put candles on the table. A bowl of nectarines and green grapes glistened in the light at the centre of it.

They ate tagliatelle and fried fish, with a salad of huge, succulent tomatoes by the side of it, and drank the rather harsh local red wine.

Catherine watched Rose and Falcone together. She found she liked him immensely. Though most conversation had to take place through Rose, she noticed that he listened attentively when she talked, as if eager to make out her words. Every so often he would join in a joke with them, exploding into wholehearted laughter which transformed his rather serious face. Sometimes when he laughed he would reach over and touch Rose's hand for a second, and Catherine saw her smile back at him, the shadows from the candles moving tenderly over her face.

She asked Falcone, 'How are people reacting to you now that you're back here? They must know you've been a priest?'

'There's been some disapproval, from a few. Those who did not know my family mainly. But the welcome we have had I owe entirely to my father.' He laughed softly. 'It's the reverse of what it says in the Bible – that a prophet is never welcome in his home town.'

'Also you're a doctor and you and your wife are caring for children who would otherwise be destitute?'

'I'm sure that also helps,' he agreed.

'And you have made an old woman from England very happy with your Orfanotrofio Diana,' she told them, slightly self-mocking.

'Old, my foot,' Rose interrupted.

Looking at the two of them and what they were creating here, Catherine knew she had before her a strong couple. She was longing to tell Ronald about them already. It was all so right. So improbable at first sight, but so entirely right.

'I must toast your future,' she said, raising her glass of the inky red wine. 'Here's to the Orfanotrofio Diana – and to you both, with all my heart.'

They raised their glasses.

It was a time of night that Rose always loved, and on this night it was particularly special. When her husband was asleep, his hands resting softly against the curve of her back, she slipped off the huge, lumpy bed and went to sit for a while by the window. She opened the shutters a crack so that she could just see the half-moon casting its light on the trees behind the house.

She was excited and stirred up by all the news from England, and at the same time had a sense of enormous joy in her life. She was becoming certain that she would have another piece of news to tell first Paulo and then Catherine this week: that soon she would be adding another child to the household, a real brother or sister for Hilda after all this time.

She sat for some time with no clear thoughts in her

head, just fragments of the day passing through. Then she went quietly out of the room and through the upper floor of the house, looking in on all the children who lived here in their care. Every bed was full tonight with Catherine sleeping at the end of the corridor.

Finally she climbed back into bed beside Falcone's warm body. Impossible as she knew it to be, she fancied as she lay down that she could feel the child moving inside her.

Where Earth Meets Sky

For Sam, Rachel, Katy and Rose

You're the best.

With lots of love,

Mum

xxxx

My thanks for help in researching this book are due to the National Motor Museum at Beaulieu and Brooklands Museum in Surrey. Also to my mother Jackie Summers for invaluable information, Rajinder Singh for assistance in Ambala and a special thank you to Bill Meyer for the time, expertise and information he shared with me on the way.

'Throughout its history, the car has been a liberator, an agent of freedom. Throughout its history, the car has enabled people to break out of their constraints, to attempt something they could never previously do, to venture somewhere they could never previously go, to support ideas and trends they could never previously endorse.'

L. J. K. Setright

Glossary

anna – 1/16th of a rupee in monetary currency
ayah – nanny
bari hazri – main breakfast
chai – tea (also *char*)
chelo! – go on! get a move on!
chota hazri – 'little breakfast' served around six a.m.
chowkidar – nightwatchman
dal – spiced lentils
dhobi – laundry
dhoti – loose loincloth worn by Hindus
dirzi – tailor
garam chai – hot tea
jhampanis – rickshaw pullers
jao! – go!
limbopani – lemonade
lingam – male fertility symbol (usually Siva's penis)
mali – gardener
pukka – proper, good quality
punkah – fan
punkah-wallah – fan puller
syce – groom
tonga – cart
topi – hat
wallah – man

Chapter One

Birmingham, 1905

'Don't cry over me, Lily, my dear girl! I've had such a very good life – you mustn't grieve.'

'I'm sorry, Mrs Chappell, I can't help it,' Lily sobbed, as she sat beside the dying woman whose motherly kindness she had known during these past, precious years. 'You've been so very good to me!'

She had waited all evening, in an agony of pent-up emotion, for Mrs Chappell's jealous son Horace to allow her to pay her last respects to the woman she loved so much.

'You've been like a daughter, you know that . . .' Mrs Chappell's rasping whisper came to her. The lids flickered over her blue eyes. She was fading fast.

Lily sat in the candlelight beside the big comfortable bed with its silk drapes. She clung desperately to the shrunken hand of this woman into whose household she had arrived as a scullery maid when she was thirteen. In her own grief and loss Maud Chappell had, over the years, grown to depend on Lily as a companion. Mrs Chappell's body had fast become frail with her illness. She did not look any more like the comforting figure who had dressed in pretty, floating clothes, who adored small children, beaming at them with her beautiful, loving eyes. The light of her life was failing and her sons were in the house, waiting. Lily told herself that they were full of pain at losing their mother, that it was their sorrow that made them so harsh, especially Horace, the older brother. They had kept her out of the room all evening, only reluctantly letting her in now it was so late.

'Mother's asking for you,' Horace had said, stiff with resentment. 'You'd better go up.'

Now she was here she sat in dread of them coming to tell her to go again.

'Oh, Mrs Chappell,' she whispered, looking down at the ravaged face, her own tears flowing again. She felt her heart was being torn in two. 'What's going to become of me without you?'

Mrs Chappell was a year off her seventieth birthday, and until her illness had looked younger than her years, with her soft, glowing complexion and cheerful ways. But she was much changed now, months of sickness taking their toll. She lay with her arms straight, outside the covers, her soft brown hair which had so fast turned grey brushed back from her face. She seemed to have slipped far away into sleep, so that Lily thought she might never wake again. But as if a sign had been given, just as the grandfather clock down in the hall was striking eleven with its gentle 'bong', the elderly lady opened her eyes, seeming quite alert, and tried to get up.

'Lily?'

'Yes, dear Mrs Chappell?' Hope surged through her. Perhaps Mrs Chappell was not dying! She seemed so bright suddenly, as if she might sit up and take some broth.

'I'm still at home, then?'

'Yes, you are. You're in your own bed.'

'Bring me the picture, please, my dear. Of my Naomi.'

'It's here – right beside you.'

She lifted the silver-framed photograph from its position on the bedside table and turned it so that Mrs Chappell could see the face of her dead daughter. Naomi, a dark-eyed beauty, had died of a cruel brain fever when she was only seventeen. It was the last portrait taken of her, her shoulders wrapped in a lace shawl and the young face, never now to age, smiling radiantly from behind the glass as it had for over twenty years.

Mrs Chappell reached out as if to embrace the portrait, a gentle smile on her lips.

'My darling . . .' she murmured. And her arms dropped back. She had not the strength.

'I think you'd better fetch my boys,' she whispered. But she clutched at Lily's hand to stop her.

'You'll get a good appointment. You're so sweet, so beautiful. You be happy, my dear love. Bless you.'

By the time Lily had fetched Horace and John Chappell up to their mother's room, she was lying on her pretty, embroidered pillows with her eyes closed and a look of utter peace. She had already left them.

'My mother has left you a small bequest, according to our solicitor,' Horace Chappell told her. His voice was icy cold.

Lily stood before him on the Persian rug in Mr Chappell's old study. Horace had not invited her to sit down.

They're kind really, she made herself believe. Mrs

3

Chappell said so. Since Mr Chappell died only three years ago, Mrs Chappell had relied on her sons, Horace and John, for everything. After all, they have looked after their mother, Lily told herself. And don't they both have wives and families who all look happy and well cared for?

These were the families who, at Mrs Chappell's strict instructions that she should be included, she had followed to the funeral: Horace and his wife and three little girls, and John and his wife and twin sons, alike as two peas. None of them had said a word to her or even acknowledged her existence, but of course they were wrapped in grief and she was only a maid. Why would they have any time for her? It was a beautiful June morning with laburnum and lilac in bloom, just the right kind of day for Mrs Chappell's funeral as she was such a sunny person who loved young life and flowers and pretty things around her. Once the funeral was over, though, they were fast making arrangements to clear and sell the house and seemed to be in a great rush to get it all done and dismiss all their mother's employees.

'Can't get shot of us fast enough, can they?' grumbled Cook, who had worked for Mrs Chappell for more than twenty years.

'I suppose they have a lot of business to sort out – they're very busy men,' Lily replied, knowing it was the sort of thing Mrs Chappell would have said because she always tried to see the best in her sons.

'They just want their hands on the money,' Mary, one of the maids, retorted. 'Since Mr C died she's had no say in anything – not with those two vultures in charge. They couldn't wait to get their father out of the way – no, it's no good arguing, Lily. You're just like Mrs C – you'll see black as white to find the best in someone. You're going to have to toughen up your ideas when you go away from here! They ain't all like her, you know.'

Horace, the older brother, had called her into the study. He had his mother's blue eyes, but instead of her embracing warmth, his looked cool and calculating. There were official-looking documents laid neatly across the desk.

'My mother left us a number of instructions regarding you and your future,' he said. He didn't meet her eye. He had always seemed most uncomfortable in her presence. 'Far too sultry, that's your trouble,' Cook once said. 'You provoke him.'

'You are very fortunate.' He held out an envelope. 'Firstly, this contains references to secure your future. You should be able to attain a very good position.' He cleared his throat, grimacing, and, as if it pained him to speak, said, 'My mother has not left you money. She did not think that would be the best thing for your welfare.' Lily watched him, wondering, after what Mary had said, whether Mrs Chappell had had any money to call her own in any case. 'But she has left you a number of items of jewellery, from her personal effects.' He nodded at a small box, inlaid with ivory, on the desk, then looked sternly at her. 'I believe them to be rather valuable. More than generous, I should say, Miss Horne. And this is where we draw a line. I should like to make clear that after this there is nothing else you can take from this family.'

Lily was stung to the core by this remark.

'I never . . .' she stuttered. 'I never took anything that

was wrong or out of place! She wanted me . . .' The last utterance, the miraculous truth of it, brought her to tears.

'That will be all, Miss Horne.'

With the envelope and box in her hands Lily fumbled her way from the room, hardly able to see through her tears. She was dreadfully hurt by his unjust, jealous remarks, and overcome by Mrs Chappell leaving her anything at all. Her heart ached with longing for her friend.

'What did he say?' Cook and the others were all agog to know. They had been told they would each have a turn to be called in.

'She left me some jewellery!' Lily told them with tears running down her cheeks.

'Well what're you blarting about?' Cook demanded. 'You're a rum 'un, you are.'

'She was so kind!' Lily sobbed. Mrs Chappell had been her saviour and friend; she had raised her up from nothing, from her beginnings as an abandoned urchin off the streets. It felt unbearable that she was gone.

Lily went up to her room at the top of the house and sank down on the edge of her bed. She realized she was still holding the box and envelope. She wanted to look inside in private. Opening the lid of the box she smelled a lovely scent of lavender, and what she saw on the base of the velvet box made her weep all the more. Lying in a pale, glowing coil was Mrs Chappell's skein of tiny seed pearls. Maud Chappell had always said to her, 'You should wear pearls, Lily. They would look marvellous on your skin.' She picked them up, feeling their warm, smooth weight, and held them lovingly to her cheek. '*Oh, thank you . . .*' she whispered. Also in the box were a matching pearl bracelet and a beautiful opal brooch in a silver setting. Lily laid them out and looked at them in awe.

Then she remembered the envelope containing her references and she pulled out an expensive piece of notepaper. She could hardly read the warm, praising words through her tears. '. . . kind and sweet-natured . . . staunchly honest, hard-working . . . it would represent the greatest good fortune to employ her . . .'

Overcome, Lily lay on her side and wept heart-brokenly. What tugged so powerfully at her heart in those moments was not the shower of kind words, or the gift of precious jewellery, but the strength of Mrs Chappell's love and kindness, flowing to her from beyond the grave.

Chapter Two

Later, she got up from the bed and poured water from the pitcher to wash her face, sitting to look in the glass tilted over her little white chest of drawers. Her face was blotchy from weeping and her dark eyes stared mournfully back at her. Mrs Chappell's death had taken away all the safety she had found for the last nine years in her employment and friendship, where she had settled into a household where she knew her place and was treated with ever-increasing kindness.

When she was fifteen, by which time Lily had worked for nearly two years on the lowest rung of the ladder, Mrs Chappell stopped her one day as Lily was passing through the hall carrying a heavy coal scuttle, dressed in her black maid's uniform with a white cap and apron. She was pink-cheeked and strong, in good condition from the physical work demanded in the house.

'My goodness!' Mrs Chappell uttered the words in a shocked tone, as if she had just noticed some terrible fault in the domestic scene. 'Wait, child! Stop and look at me!'

Lily paused, heart pounding. Although she had barely ever had anything to do with Mrs Chappell, by then she knew her employer was usually a gentle lady. What had she done so wrong?

'Come a little closer, dear – er, what is your name again?'

'Lilian Horne.' *I'm in for it now*, Lily thought, keeping her eyes lowered, seeing the lower edge of Mrs Chappell's sage-green skirt and her elegant brown shoes on the polished tiles of the hall.

'Do look at me,' Maud Chappell said softly. 'It's quite all right. You've done nothing wrong. Put the coal down, dear – it looks heavy.'

Lily obeyed and looked blushingly up into her employer's face. Mrs Chappell wore her hair swept up and pinned in a wispy, abstracted style which made her look rather artistic and vague. Wisps of it were forever escaping about her round face. In her eyes, Lily saw kindness, and a great yearning.

'Oh, my dear . . .' Mrs Chappell put a hand to her chest and her eyes suddenly filled with tears. 'So like – in a way. Your lovely dark hair, your shape . . . A kind of essence . . . I'm sorry, dear, you must find me very strange. You'll know we lost our daughter Naomi, bless her heart, oh, eleven years ago now! And when I saw you just then, of course you're different, but you have a look of her . . . Why have I never seen it before?' She sighed, wiping her eyes. 'How lovely, to have you in our house . . .'

And she drifted away, lost in emotion. Lily picked up the coal scuttle, confused, but also surprised to find her own eyes full of tears, her own hunger for a mother and for love answering Mrs Chappell's loss and grief.

That was how it began, her ascent in the house. By the time she was seventeen, the age at which Naomi Chappell lost her life, Lily had risen to be a maid of all work, and then, gradually, into personal maid and companion of Maud Chappell, a woman whose personal warmth covered a great inner loneliness. There was no shortage of money as Mr Chappell owned a string of carriage-building works, and the house in Hall Green, a pleasant suburb of Birmingham, was large and beautifully furnished. But with a mostly absent husband, two sons whose lives had long moved away from her into working the world, and a dead daughter, Mrs Chappell had lost a great deal that was dear to her. She adored young life and waited in hope of grandchildren.

'Before my marriage, I was a trained nanny, you see,' she explained to Lily one day in the flower-scented drawing room. 'I lived with some beautiful families – and some of the dear little ones still write to me, now they're older.' Her eyes filled every time she talked about her charges. 'There's not much I don't know about small children.' She gave a sigh then, also. 'I should have liked more of my own, but it was not to be.'

As time passed, she grew to require more and more of Lily's company.

'You're such an intelligent, gentle girl, and so very lovely. I can teach you, you see, if you like. If you learn about looking after small children, and a little elocution to correct that accent, you could have a very promising future.'

Over the last five years, especially with the arrival of her five grandchildren, who she looked after as often as her daughters-in-law would let her, Mrs Chappell had more than made up for Lily's lost education, and had also taught Lily everything she knew about the care of young children: diet and feeding, how to play with and handle them and all their infant needs of warmth and cleanliness, their training and how to remedy their maladies. Over the years Lily learned all sorts: how to soothe a child's temperature with a wet pack, to put an infant with croup in a mustard bath or induce vomiting with ipecacuanha wine, to paint a tincture of iodine on a patch of ringworm, or treat scabies with Balsam of Peru. Mrs Chappell's training of Lily became a labour of love and Lily was an eager student, thriving as much upon affection as education. She taught her to read and write beautifully, and speak in a more genteel manner, flattening out her Birmingham accent.

'You really are turning into quite a young lady!' she said sometimes, watching her with pride. As Lily grew older and entered her twenties, Mrs Chappell didn't want to let her go to another position in the world. She needed her too much herself. And Lily had no wish to go either, from this home where she was loved and valued, after the cruel beginning life had dealt her.

Mrs Chappell never asked much about Lily's past. Lily was grateful, since she could remember so little and what she could remember, about living with the Hornes, she preferred to push from her memory. Maud Chappell asked only a few gentle questions and Lily told her that Mrs Horne had been good to her, which she had, until she died, leaving Lily at the mercy of her drunken husband and cruel daughters. But she did not want to think of them, of the agony and loneliness of that time. And Mrs Chappell simply saw something in her that it suited both of them to develop. The other maids working in the house at that time had been envious and spiteful about Lily's rise up the ranks.

'You're the favourite all right, ain't you?' they'd say. 'What makes you so blooming special, Miss La-di-dah?'

Apart from Cook, those maids had all gone now, and the new ones coming into the house accepted things as they were. Lily enjoyed their company – Mary and Fanny and Joan – and knew she was going to miss them terribly now the household was all to be broken up.

11

Only Joan, the youngest, was staying in the family, as she was being taken on by Mr John Chappell's wife.

Lily gazed at her own face in the glass now, suddenly deeply confused and frightened. All these years she had had a place. Now she had to go out and face the world alone.

That week, Horace and John Chappell, with the help of the staff who they kept on for the purpose, were clearing the house with great speed. Two of the maids, Mary and Fanny, were paid off immediately, and there were tearful farewells as they left the house for the last time with their modest bags of belongings.

Lily found it heartbreaking, watching her home of so many years being taken to pieces and having no say in the matter. Furniture began to disappear, workmen in overalls came and took away dressers and cupboards, rugs were rolled up and now their feet clumped loudly on the bare floorboards. Mrs Chappell's elegant curtains were taken from the windows in the drawing room. More than once, Lily found Cook weeping into the pastry in the kitchen, and she kept dissolving into tears herself. It wasn't just the house. Although Horace Chappell was unkind, his brother John was a more gentle character, and she was genuinely fond of all their children, whom she had known since they were born. Now she would never see them again!

As her illness progressed, Mrs Chappell had said, 'What you need to do, Lily dear, when I'm gone, is to apply for a position in *The Lady*. You're quite experienced enough to work as a nanny for a family after all I've taught you. You're just the sort of girl a good family would be crying out for.'

Remembering Mrs Chappell's advice, she went in search of a copy of *The Lady*, a genteel women's publication in which were advertised posts for nannies and companions. One hot afternoon she sat out on the terrace at the back of the house, half in the shade of a laburnum, and looked at the positions on offer. She drew a ring round two of them. One was for a family by the name of Clutterbuck, who had just had a baby girl and wanted a nanny very quickly. They lived in Dorset. Lily was not absolutely sure where Dorset was but it seemed a possibility. There was another similar in Scotland, but it was a place she always thought of as dreary and cold. But the third advertisement made her heart pick up speed. A nanny was required by a Mrs Susan Fairford, wife of Captain Charles Fairford of the 12th Royal Lancers, stationed at Ambala, India, for their son, aged two. The address to apply to was in Chislehurst in Kent.

Lily looked up from the magazine and stared unseeingly at the rose beds along the side of the house. India! Her head reeled. She was bewildered, afraid and suddenly full of excitement. India was the other side of the world! It was so different she could barely imagine it, except for other pictures she had seen in books of people riding elephants and one she remembered of a huge, waving grove of something called bamboo. But she was already captivated. She already knew she was going to apply for the position and go far away from this place, now all that had kept her here was gone. She had no one now. For a moment she thought about Mrs Horne. She was the only person she had ever called mother – but she was not her mother. Why had Mrs Horne brought her up in her kindly but rough and ready way? What had happened to her real mother and father?

'They did a flit one night, according to the neighbours,' Mrs Horne had told her. 'Hadn't been there long, in any case. They said she was dark and pretty like a gypsy, and expecting another child. All I know is, there you were playing in the gutter, all alone in just a little camisole, in the pouring rain. But I don't s'pose you'll ever find out now, bab. Best not think about it.'

Lily knew there was no hope of ever finding out about her origins, and it hurt too much, looking back. She had moved too far from Mrs Horne, from growing up in Sparkbrook. She would start again, clean and fresh, and with sudden resolve she hurried up the now uncarpeted stairs to her attic room, sat at her little table and took the references Horace Chappell had handed her out of their thick envelope.

But looking down at the sheets of paper with her name at the top of Mrs Chappell's glowing reference, that desperate, lost feeling washed through her again. Her name, *LILIAN HORNE*, was written in capital letters at the top in Mrs Chappell's immaculate copperplate script.

Little Lilian Horne. Whoever was she? Had she not been playing the part of someone else all these years, someone who Mrs Chappell needed her to be, and whose identity she had now taken on herself?

She stood up and went again to the glass on her chest of drawers and her face stared back at her, strong-featured, with her burning dark eyes, her thick, wavy chestnut hair modestly fastened back and her demure, white-frilled blouse at her neck. It was the look of a respectable young woman, one who was now nicely spoken, genteel. Not an abandoned slum child fit only for the workhouse, the way the two Horne girls had made her feel. They'd always made sure she was a cuckoo in the nest, with their cruel tricks, their slaps and scratches.

'*Not Lilian Horne,*' she whispered. 'I'm not a Horne and I never was.'

She sat at her little table and opened its drawer, where she had some writing paper. Beside it in the drawer were three books. The one on top was a book of wildflowers, sketched by a John Waters. For a moment she picked it up and looked at it.

Lily dipped her pen into the bottle of ink, and began, painstakingly, to copy out the references again, well instructed in mimicking Mrs Chappell's elegant hand. At the top of the page, in large letters, she gave her name: *LILY WATERS.*

Chapter Three

'Miss Waters?'

The maid had shown Lily into the parlour of the Chislehurst house to face a small, plump woman with a harassed expression and faded blond hair curling round the edge of a white bonnet. She found herself appraised by pale blue eyes, but somehow the experience was not as frightening as she expected. The house, though a fair size, was shabbier than the one in Hall Green! And she could hear children's voices, squabbling in the background somewhere.

'My name is Mrs Burton,' the woman said, distractedly. 'I am Mrs Fairford's sister. Please, do take a seat.'

She indicated an upright chair with a slightly moth-eaten seat cover, while she perched on another wooden chair nearby, her feet, in their laced brown boots, barely touching the floor. For a moment they both looked at one another. Mrs Burton seemed at a loss. She was obviously not used to the job in hand.

'Well, you're here, anyway.' There was a pause in which Lily wondered what she was supposed to say, but this was followed by, 'You have come all the way from Birmingham, I take it?'

'Yes, I have.'

The woman pressed the tips of her fingers to her forehead as if to gather her thoughts, then said, 'My sister, Mrs Fairford, has asked me to find a nanny for her son, Cosmo – he's just two years old. If my sister was in the country herself, she would be doing the interviews.'

There was another awkward silence in which it occurred to Lily's interviewer that she might peer at the references provided, holding them as far away from her as her short arms would permit.

'These are very good – *very*!'

'Thank you.'

Mrs Burton rested the paper in her lap and squinted slightly. 'Are you a *proper* nanny?'

'Yes,' Lily said, as Mrs Chappell had told her to, speaking slowly in her best, well-spoken English. 'I've had a very good training and considerable experience of looking after five young ones. I don't think I'd have any problem with one little boy.'

'No, quite. And ... What about India? You did realize you'd have to sail the seas? Live quite the other side of the world!'

'Yes. I should welcome the adventure.'

'Well, Susan hates it!' This seemed to slip out by mistake and the colour rose in Mrs Burton's cheeks. 'Lord, I shouldn't have said that. Most indiscreet of me. But she does. All those diseases. Of course, that was what led to ... Oh, dear me, my mouth does run away so ... She tries to make the best of it, though, dear Susan does. But the poor darling does so need help, what with Isadora being so ...' Once again she stopped. 'Cosmo is not Susan's only child. She has a daughter, who is ... rather difficult. But she would not be your responsibility. Do you think you could adjust and be a help to my poor sister?

'Well, I hope so – very much.'

'Well—' Mrs Burton stood up. 'That's very hopeful.

I'll be letting you know. But I expect you'll take the post? You look the adventurous sort.'

On the long train ride home, Lily already felt she had indeed begun on an adventure, was discovering in herself a taste for it. She kept saying her new name to herself. *Lily Waters*. That's who I am now. It made her feel strong.

Three days later a letter arrived, saying that her interview had been successful and if she was still willing to accept, the family would book her passage on a P&O liner to India.

Chapter Four

Ambala, India, 1905

Lily's first months in India were full of mixed, sometimes overwhelming, emotions.

There was the journey to begin with, exciting, daunting, setting out to the other side of the world with nothing but hope and excitement, a small tin trunk containing her possessions and no clear idea of what she was going to find. The P&O steamer was an adventure in itself. She made friends with another nanny called Jenny, who was blonde and good-humoured and was on her way back out to a family in Poona after delivering one of the children to relatives in England.

As they progressed east, the temperatures gradually rising, the two young women often walked out on the glaring deck to take the breeze blowing from the sea. Jenny, in a big sisterly way, was able to brief Lily about India.

'You get used to it after a while,' she said cheerfully. 'The summer months can be hellish if you don't go up to the hills, of course, though I expect your family will. And there's a lot of social fun – parties and so on – for the adults and children. Just make sure you drink boiled water and wash your hands a lot. Lots of carbolic soap! It's all right out there, really it is. You'll soon settle in.

Beats living in a backstreet in rainy old England, I can tell you.'

The morning the boat gently nosed its way into the harbour at Bombay was one Lily would never forget. She stood on deck beside Jenny, the sun high, the humid heat alleviated by the breeze over the sea. The ship was rolling gently, the sea was a deep, ruffled green, and gradually the land came more clearly into view.

'Dear old Bombay,' Jenny said, shading her eyes with her hand. 'D'you know, I loathed it all when I first came. But it's grown on me. See the coast there – they call that the Ghats, that part rising from the sea – and then the mountains behind.'

Lily thrilled with excitement at the sight of it. The high land in the distance looked a dull sandy colour, stained with patches of verdure lower down. Jenny had said the monsoon rains were not yet over and all the land was bright and green during the rainy season. As they moved closer, she began to see the city, a wide hotch-potch of white buildings, brilliant in the sun. The breeze dropped and gradually smells began to reach her, strange, alluring, sulphurous and scented. She felt the damp, heavy heat wrap round her. By the time they slid into the dock she was sweating profusely, her clothes limp with moisture, but she barely noticed, so enthralled was she by the sight of the bright colours and seething activity on the quay below, the white-uniformed band playing a toe-tapping marching tune and the busy, brown-skinned, *different* people of India.

She said tearful farewells to Jenny at Victoria Terminus in Bombay as they both went to board different trains, Lily north to Delhi, on another leg of her long journey.

'You'll be all right, Lily, dear,' Jenny assured her as

she kissed her goodbye. The two young women had grown very fond of one another. 'You're one of the ones that will feel at home in India – I can tell.'

It was true. Though it was all new and bewildering, beggars and teeming streets and everything strange, the heat, the food, the temples and mosques, yet amid all that she felt immediately happy and at home, as if this was a place where she was somehow born to be.

The long train journey to Ambala Cantonment, across the great Punjab plain north of Delhi, was exhausting, as were the first days of getting used to the town and its ways. It was half native town, half army cantonment, and riding in a *tonga* that first afternoon, along a wide road through the cantonment, she caught sight, with an astonished gasp, of the huge, elegant residence of Captain Charles Fairford, in whose employment and family she had now placed herself.

'So – you are the nanny they've sent?' Susan Fairford held out her hand.

'Yes,' Lily said, shrinking inside. Her employer seemed as remote and frozen as the Antarctic.

Mrs Fairford was petite in stature, with hair of a pale honey colour and a strikingly pretty face, with Cupid's bow lips and wide blue eyes. She was dressed in a beautiful ivory gown with bows and flounces in the long skirt, the whole outfit nipped in tightly at the waist and showing off a slim, well-proportioned figure. As she spoke, Lily saw that she had little white teeth almost like a child's. What was absent was any sense of warmth. The hand that she took to shake in introduction was small and unresponsive, like a dead thing.

'Do sit down.'

They sat opposite one another and Lily waited, hearing the ticking of the small ormolu clock from the mantelpiece. The room was at least pretty and feminine after the opulent, but creepy, hall, a museum to dead creatures whose heads and skins decorated the walls and floor. From the garden came the sounds of crows cawing.

'My sister wrote to tell me that she thought you had sufficient experience as a nanny for my son. She also said that she liked the look of you. Knowing Audrey, I suppose she meant that you are pretty, though whether that is a qualification remains to be seen. I have had to trust my sister, being so far away. I hope she has made a wise choice.'

All this was said in a distant, rather languid tone. Lily began to feel rather like a cow which has been brought from the market by proxy. Her heart sank further, but she told herself not to get upset. She had only just arrived and she had not met the boy yet. He was what mattered!

'Well, I hope you think so,' she murmured. 'I'm looking forward to meeting your children.'

'You only need to concern yourself with one of the children,' Mrs Fairford said sharply. 'I don't know if my sister explained to you that we need a nanny for our son Cosmo, to prepare him for going home to school in England. Our daughter, Isadora, will not be going home. She is not ... She ...'

Lily watched the woman's face. For a moment her composure had slipped and an expression of pained confusion passed over her face.

'Isadora is not fully able to be educated. She has certain – difficulties. Unfortunately she is much attached to her *ayah*, the Indian girl who continues to look after

22

her. We've tried several times to prise her away from the girl, but it's no good.' Now there was bitterness in her voice.

She's jealous, Lily saw. It was a chink in the woman's armour, and even though she found her cold and intimidating, she could see that Mrs Fairford suffered because she thought her daughter loved an Indian girl better than her own mother, that there was much that lay behind this frosty mask.

'Cosmo is to be your charge.' For a second her tone softened a tiny fraction, but immediately grew cool again. 'We don't want him brought up by natives. When he's old enough he'll go home to Eton, like his father, away from this beastly country. He will learn to be an English gentleman. In the meantime we want you to speak with him – in English, of course, always: you must stop his native prattle. Teach him songs and games from home, his letters and numbers and so on. Above all—' suddenly she looked very directly at Lily as she spoke, with a tone of pleading – 'be a friend to him.'

'Yes, Mrs Fairford.' She was not sure what else to say to this odd, naked request. She felt very discouraged by what she had seen so far of this chilly household. What on earth could Captain Fairford be like? She imagined a tight-lipped, forbidding man and wondered if that was the reason why Mrs Fairford seemed so tense and unhappy. Because she could see straight away that she was not looking at a contented woman. She decided to take the woman's plea for her son as a sign of hope.

'When am I to meet your little boy?' she asked.

'He and Isadora are resting at present. I suggest you go and do the same. I'll send one of the servants to bring you to the nursery at teatime.' It was a dismissal.

'Yes, ma'am,' Lily said.

'You may call me Mrs Fairford. I don't enjoy being called "ma'am".'

'Yes, Mrs Fairford.'

Her employer stood up. 'You may go.'

Lily left the room, feeling low and close to tears. Was she wrong to expect Mrs Fairford to ask her a single thing about herself, about her welfare after her long journey, or to give some indication of welcome or gladness?

You've been too used to Mrs Chappell, she told herself as she slipped along the passage to her bedroom. Not everyone's like that. You're going to have to get used to the fact that you're a servant and nothing else.

But as she lay down on her bed, having crawled in under the swathing mosquito net, it was a dispiriting thought, and her heart ached with unshed tears. On the journey to get here she had felt only excitement and expectation, but now she felt chilled and lonely.

Chapter Five

To her surprise she was awoken by a servant in a maroon uniform bringing a cup of very sweet tea which revived her spirits. The sight of his friendly face also made her feel better and he provided a pitcher of warm water with which she washed, then changed her clothes. Some time later the servant returned.

'I am to take you to the nursery – Mrs Fairford sent me to fetch you.'

As she made to leave the room, he added politely, 'Your name is?'

She gave him her name and he said his was Rajinder. His would be the first of many names she had to learn of the family's large retinue of servants.

The nursery consisted of two adjoining rooms, one for each of the children. Mrs Fairford was waiting for her with both the children: Cosmo on the floor, head bent over a box of wooden bricks, and the girl on a big rocking horse at the side of the room. Lily was delighted to see that they had a magnificent array of toys.

Squatting on the floor beside the boy was the young *ayah*, dressed in a deep red sari. Lily was perturbed to see she had a silver ring through her left nostril. Mrs Fairford sat looking very stiff and formal and Lily felt once again intimidated, though at the same time she suddenly saw that their ages were not so very far apart either. Susan Fairford could not have been many years her senior, but it felt as if a great gulf of age and class separated them.

'Ah – Miss Waters,' she said in her clipped, cut-glass voice. 'Your timing is good, at least. These are my children. Isadora, Cosmo – this lady has come to live with us. She has come to be your new nanny, Cosmo, darling!' There was the first real hint of warmth in her voice as she spoke to her little boy.

'Izzy – Isadora! Say hello to Miss Waters.'

The girl stopped rocking for a moment and looked at Lily from beneath a very straight fringe of mole-brown hair. She had a round face with slanting eyes which stared hard at Lily. Then she smiled in a remote, inward-looking way and said something Lily couldn't make any sense of before going back to her rocking.

'In English, please, Izzy,' her mother rebuked her sharply. 'This is the trouble, you see, with children spending all their time with native servants. They pick up all sorts of bad habits.'

Lily glanced at the Indian girl. It seemed very rude of Mrs Fairford to speak like this in front of her, but her face remained expressionless.

'Now – Cosmo, darling,' Mrs Fairford's pretty face softened a fraction. 'Come and meet Miss Waters.'

The boy stood up and came towards them and as he did so, Lily experienced a peculiar pang. Never before had she seen such a beautiful child! He was slender, almost fairy-like, with a head of tumbling, honey-coloured hair. His lavender-blue eyes were widely set and shone with life and energy, with an open affection, utterly winning in its lack of guile. He was wearing a navy and white sailor suit, and his little legs, protruding from the shorts were slim, and fragile-looking.

26

'Oh!' Lily exclaimed, hardly meaning to. 'Hello, Cosmo, dear! Aren't you lovely!'

She squatted down as he came towards her and to her surprise he ran straight into her arms and cuddled her, clinging on like a baby monkey. She found herself laughing and, caught off balance, almost tumbling over.

'My goodness, well, this is a very nice greeting!'

Looking up as she held the slender form of Cosmo Fairford, she caught sight of his mother's face, alight with a kind of wistful joy. The *ayah* was smiling as well and Lily saw that she was young and sweet-faced.

'Nursie nursie!' Cosmo drew back and chanted into her face. 'My nursie nursie!'

'Yes – I'm your nursie,' Lily agreed, a smile of joy on her face. In that moment she had received the warm welcome for which she had yearned.

'Well – he appears to approve of you, at least,' Mrs Fairford said. As she got to her feet she seemed to close down again, becoming cold and withdrawn. 'The children always spend an hour with myself and their father before bed. Otherwise, *Ayah* will be able to tell you about Cosmo's routine and his likes and dislikes.'

She went over to Isadora who looked round at her with a blank expression, then as she went to pat the girl's head, Isadora fought her off, screeching.

'Oh, Isadora, do you *have* to?' Mrs Fairford withdrew, her voice full of weary distaste, as Isadora cried, '*Ayah*! Want *Ayah*!'

The *ayah* seemed to have more success in soothing the child's strange outburst. Lily could see that Mrs Fairford tried not to show the change in her feelings as

27

she parted with her son, but her smile, the softening of her eyes showed the great love she had for him, which broke through her mask of coldness. She kissed his cheek, stroking his hair.

'You talk to Miss Waters about your little Chip-chip, um, darling?' Aside to Lily, ignoring Isadora's screams, she explained, 'He has a favourite chipmunk in the garden. Goodbye, Cosmo, darling – Pater and I will see you later on.' She left the room with a rustling of skirts.

Isadora's tantrum only lasted a few moments, as the *ayah* stroked her head, and arms, soothing her, then hummed a melancholy, high-pitched tune. She looked young, barely eighteen, Lily guessed, but there was something full-figured and mature about her. As she stroked Isadora's head, the silver bangles on her arm gave off musical little jangling sounds. Now her mistress had left she seemed to feel free to speak. She turned and smiled sweetly at Lily.

'*Missy-baba* is getting upset sometime. She like me to sing to her.'

'You're good with her. She likes you,' Lily said, admiringly. It was clear that the girl's mother had little affection for her and no idea how to behave towards her and it seemed very sad. Instead, Isadora had attached herself to this loving young girl who would give her affection.

'She is good girl,' the *ayah* said. She had warm, friendly eyes and Lily smiled back, feeling she had found a friend in this chilly household. 'What is your name?' she enquired shyly.

With a pretty incline of her head, the girl said, 'I am Srimala. You are Miss Waters?'

'Oh, do call me Lily.'

A second later, Cosmo, very emphatically, echoed, 'Lily.'

And the two young women smiled at each other.

When she met Captain Fairford later that day, he came as a surprise. After meeting his wife, she had somehow expected a loud, overbearing man with blond hair like Cosmo's and a stiff, military bearing, like the portraits she had seen hanging in the hall. Instead, when she and the *ayah* took the children down after their tea, she met a lean, slender man with a gentle expression and brown hair, which, though cropped short, threatened to break into curls. He wore a neat little moustache which seemed to smile along with his lips, and his eyes were warm and welcoming.

'How very nice to meet you, Miss Waters.' His tone balanced charm and formality in equal measure.

Her hand was taken in a manly grip for a moment and quickly released, but his eyes lingered on her face with a kind look, so that she was startled to find tears prickling in her eyes. She was tired, she told herself, and more emotional than usual.

'I trust you had a good journey? Quite an experience, first time in India, I should imagine?' His voice was soft and beautifully spoken.

She was nodding a reply, a lump still in her throat at being treated so kindly, but he went on, 'Cosmo, I'm sure, has given you a warm welcome. He likes people, I'm happy to say. Not shy or retiring.'

'He's a lovely boy,' she said carefully.

'Oh yes!' he laughed, bashfully. 'Quite so. Grow up to be a credit, I'm sure. Fine chap . . .'

'Perhaps you'd like to go to your room now,' Mrs Fairford interrupted. 'Your supper will be brought to you.'

Lily nodded obediently. It was a relief to her to learn that, as she fitted neither into the category of family nor one of the large retinue of native servants, she would eat on her own in the evening. At the moment, since she was so used to faring for herself, that felt by far the least nerve-racking solution. That night she was longing to be alone.

One of the servants had brought a tray to her room with chicken stew and vegetables, and afterwards she prepared herself for bed and lay with all the new impressions of the day seething in her mind. She wasn't sure about Susan Fairford at all yet – the woman made her nervous. But the captain was much nicer than she expected, even if she wouldn't have a great deal to do with him. Srimala seemed very easy to get along with. And then there was Cosmo – adorable, loving Cosmo. A smile spread over her face in the darkness. She had done the right thing coming here, she knew.

Chapter Six

Lily found Cosmo blissful from the start. She had never expected to experience such a deep attachment so quickly, but the feeling had been instant and only increased over the following days and weeks. He was quite a precocious child, but much loved and therefore very loving. And he seemed to adore her straight away, unquestioningly, as if she was a gift he had been expecting and longing for.

From that first day he called her nothing but 'Lily', however much they worked for a time on 'Miss Waters'.

'Lily, Lily – come and play!' he cried when she first appeared in the morning. And she found there was nothing she wanted more than to come and play! This instant, loving adoration was something she had never experienced before and she found she could hardly take her eyes off him. Of course he adored Srimala too, since she had cared from him when very young, but he seemed to have a heart that extended wide and fully.

It took her much longer to decide whether or not she liked his mother. One moment Susan Fairford was snobbish and cold; the next she could be vulnerable and, at times, even warm, just in glimpses. One of the first surprises was her coming into the nursery during that first week and saying to Lily, 'I suppose you don't know how to ride a horse?'

'No,' Lily stuttered, astonished. 'I've never even sat on one!'

'Well, I want you to learn,' Susan Fairford announced, perching herself stiffly for a moment on the low wooden nursing chair. A large fly buzzed sleepily across the room. 'We are in the habit of riding in the morning here, but Charles and I don't ride together. He rides with the regiment and I like to take Cozzy out myself – we're teaching him, you see. And I'd like some help.' She swallowed and added, as if the admission pained her, 'And company. Not just natives.'

Lily stared at her. The only horses she had ever seen were the nags which pulled drays on the streets of Birmingham. She hardly knew one end of a horse from another! But she wanted very much to please. And the idea of learning to ride and being able to explore the countryside outside the cantonment seemed immensely exciting.

'I could try,' she said uncertainly.

To her surprise, Susan Fairford softened suddenly.

'Good girl. You can learn quickly, I'm sure. Our *syce* is very good.' Seeing Lily's baffled expression she gave a faint smile. 'That's the groom – he looks after the horses. His name is Arsalan and I must say, for a native he's very able. I'll ask him to teach you on a leading rein until you feel more confident.'

Within days, Lily had her first session seated on a horse, in a pair of riding breeches. Susan Fairford rode side-saddle, clad in a long riding dress, but she said Lily might feel safer straddling the horse and being able to grip on. She had never worn trousers before in her life and the thick breeches made her feel manly but much freer.

The *syce* Arsalan was waiting at the appointed time

32

on the lawn at the back of the house, holding a sleek chestnut horse on a leading rein. Arsalan was a slender man, dressed in loose white trousers and tunic, a bright white cloth coiled with impressive style round his head, with eyes which danced with mischievous warmth. Lily found it impossible to guess his age, but she liked him immediately, even before he had said a word, and she felt her nerves begin to fade.

'Miss Waters?' He gave a little bow from the waist. 'I am here to give you a riding lesson. This is a good, quiet horse. You can ride her solo when you are ready. She will not be giving you any trouble.'

He had a box for her to stand on and he instructed her how to climb on before teaching her how to sit and hold the reins. Although she was very nervous, she instantly liked the feel of sitting on the horse, and the smells of the warm animal and leather rising to meet her. She learned that the horse was called Blaze, because of the white stripe down her nose.

'Now,' Arsalan said, taking the leading rein. 'We are ready to begin walking.'

Patiently, day after day, he taught her to walk, then trot. She started to look forward to her lessons, and as she grew confident, she found it exhilarating. After the first week, though, her leg muscles were so strained that she could hardly walk. When she limped into the nursery one morning with a woebegone expression, Srimala put her hand over her mouth and broke into irrepressible giggles.

'Horse riding is not good for ladies,' she snorted, her eyes dancing with laughter. 'Not riding legs over, like a man!'

Lily sat down, wincing. 'I'm only following orders.' She squeaked with pain as she tried to move a leg again and then started laughing. 'Oh dear! I like it really. I just hope I can get used to it. I don't want to feel like this forever!'

Srimala just giggled more, shaking her head, but then said, mischievously, 'Arsalan says you are very good pupil.' And she realized the servants had been enjoying the progress of her lessons and that she was a bit of a curiosity in the house. 'And that you are very pretty lady.'

Soon, she began to ride with Susan Fairford, Arsalan beside her, while Susan Fairford rode with Cosmo perched on the front of her saddle.

On these excursions, Lily discovered the beauty of the Indian dawn. She would get up in the dark and go outside into the smell of dew on the ground. In the smoky-grey dawn light the trees were like ghosts which became washed in the pink rays of the rising sun. The air filled with smells of flowers and smoke from dung fires and the special aroma of the Indian earth. And she discovered a sense of freedom and space in the immensity of the Indian landscape which lifted her heart into a state of great joy such as she had never experienced before.

Each day they rode for an hour or more, along the road out of the cantonment and into the countryside, all of them silent for long periods, awed by the scene about them. Lily began to get a sense of Ambala as a tiny dot, like a speck of dust in the immensity of India. Her view of it widened, seeing the vivid green fields round the town, the rising sun glinting on streams and paddies and village tanks, the terracotta temples close to the river and the the wayside shrines and circular haystacks at the edges of the fields. She saw that Ambala was simply one of a myriad of settlements on the great Punjab plain stretching north to the mountains, to the snowy Himalaya whose meltwater poured down to become the great Ganges on its way to the Bay of Bengal.

It was the first time she had been out, anywhere, into wide countryside, not hemmed in by streets and buildings, and it made her see things afresh. The cantonment was an inward-looking world with its own bazaar, and rituals of church and flag-waving military parades and parties, striving to keep as separate as possible from the 'native' town: from India itself. This state of affairs was in fact maintained by a stream of Indian workers whose names Lily was gradually beginning to learn. She liked learning these new words, often from Srimala, who laughed unrestrainedly at the way she pronounced them. 'The man with the donkey – he is the *dhobi*, the laundryman,' she instructed. Lily soon came to recognize this man, who peered out through round, pebbly spectacles and carried a flat iron full of heated coals. 'And the *mali* – he is doing the garden.'

The cantonment life seemed to be all-consuming, as if there was nothing else. Yet now, riding through the soft air of these beautiful, roseate dawns, she saw with wonder, with infatuation, that there was so much more; there was all this vast land, and the great arc of the sky, stretching almost unimaginably further than she could see.

During these morning rides, she began to get to know Susan Fairford differently.

Over the weeks Lily had watched the Fairfords and found them confusing. Charles Fairford, when he was at home, behaved like a model husband, ever courteous and charming to his wife, and attentive to his children during his brief times with them. The regiment had a number of animals attached to it as mascots and companions for the men. Some were dogs, but there was also a monkey called Nippy, and sometimes Charles Fairford carried Nippy home on his shoulder to see the children and let them watch his tricks. Lily was as charmed as they were by the tiny brown creature with its shiny, intelligent eyes.

At first Lily envied what seemed to be the idyll of a perfect marriage, lived out in splendour and comfort. But she soon grew to see the loneliness of Susan Fairford's life. Charles was away a great deal. He dined in the Officers' Mess several times a week, leaving Susan to find what friendship she could among the other army wives. Lily saw, and Susan allowed her to see, that Charles was a man married more to the army than to his wife. And though Charles was the picture of strength and health, India did not suit Susan, who was prone to prostrating stomach complaints and fevers which reduced her to a most wretched condition.

She was also forever in a nervous state about the children's health, the hygiene of their clothes and food and who they mixed with, and her anxiety made her constantly irritable. But sometimes, in the gentle light of those morning rides, she relaxed and became more confiding, as if the uncertain light of dawn dissolved also some of the boundaries between mistress and servant. On a horse she became girlish and happy.

Chapter Seven

The burning, muggy months of Indian summer gave way to the pleasant days and chill nights of winter. For Lily, life revolved happily round the little world of the nursery, the children's routine of meals and games and sleep, and its child's rhythm made her feel secure.

One night, towards the end of October, she woke to the sound of knocking.

'Miss Lily!' Srimala hissed through the bedroom door.

Srimala was outside. 'It is Mrs Fairford. She has been taken ill, and is asking for you.'

'For *me*?' Lily said, astonished.

'The captain is not here—'

Captain Fairford had gone up country for a few nights with the regiment and Susan's maid did not sleep in the house but went home to her family every night.

'She has a fever and she wants you to come – quick, hurry!'

The night was cold, and Lily put her dressing gown on and followed Srimala. She had never been in Susan Fairford's bedroom before and she held her gown round her, feeling nervous and as if she were trespassing. A candle was burning on the bedside table and the mosquito nets were lifted back over the bed frame out of the way. Lily could make out the restless form, lying under only a sheet and looking surprisingly small and vulnerable.

With grave eyes, Srimala looked across and beckoned to Lily, who moved nervously, closer to the bed.

'Lily?'

'Yes, Mrs Fairford.'

'Give me a drink of water . . . Please . . . Srimala, you can go.'

Srimala shot an encouraging smile at Lily and disappeared with a gentle clink of bangles.

'You may sit down,' Susan Fairford said, after sipping from the glass of water. As Lily sat on the chair by the bed, she heard Susan murmur, 'I do feel so very unwell.'

Lily was reminded of sitting beside Mrs Chappell's bed in her last weeks.

'Is there anything else you would like?'

Susan was obviously running a high fever. She gave a low moan, her face creasing in distress.

'Oh, I do have such a terrible pain in my head . . . As if it's going to crack open . . . If you could cool my head . . . There, in the drawer – handkerchiefs . . .'

Lily carefully laid a wet handkerchief across Mrs Fairford's forehead, pressing it gently to her temples, the way Mrs Chappell used to ask her to. As she did so, Susan Fairford moaned again.

'Oh, you dear girl . . . Oh, for someone to understand . . .'

She began to sob suddenly, tears rolling out from under her closed lids, her body quivering. Lily was quite unsure what to do, so she took the sodden handkerchief and cooled it again, pressing it gently to her mistress's forehead, wondering what it was that was causing her such distress. But she did not feel it was her place to speak and she stood, gently caressing her temples. She wished Srimala was still there. After a few moments of the shuddering sobbing she said, as she

38

remembered saying to Maud Chappell, 'Is there something else I can do for you?'

'Get me out of this country – that's how you can help!' Susan Fairford cried, in a distraught voice. 'I hate India – it killed my baby and they'll take Cosmo away from me, they'll send him away and there's nothing I can do about it, nothing! Oh God, what can I do? I'm so worthless, sitting about here in pretty clothes doing nothing, being nothing in my life! All I can ever so is sit and watch life go past. And they'll take my beloved little boy away from me and he's all I've got I'll ... I think I'll go mad ... !'

She curled in on herself, on her side like a child, and the sobbing became truly heartbroken, though in between she groaned at the extra pressure her crying was inflicting on her head. The sound of her grief reached down into Lily, touching something in her. When the woman had quietened a little, Lily said to her, 'What do you mean, they'll take him away?'

'To school, of course ...' She spoke slowly, her voice slurred with exhaustion and pain. 'He has to go ... No choice – Fairford family, traditions and so forth. Eton, the army, India ... That's Cosmo's life, whether he likes it, or I like it. Charles won't hear of anything else. Boarding school before they're five, get them out of India to prep school or they go native, send them home ... My family's not of their station ...' Her voice had been hard and bitter as she spoke but now her face contorted and she was crying again. 'And there's Cranbourne, that wretched place. It's only in the family through Charles's mother: her brother inherited the estate and he was far too odd to marry – and Charles's brother William is just like him ... Oh, I don't want Cosmo to go. I can't bear it!'

39

Lily took courage and reached across, taking Susan Fairford's clammy hand in hers as she wept. Feeling the pressure of Lily's hand on hers, she opened her eyes, startled, as if she had almost forgotten she was there.

'Thank you,' she said with such sudden humility that Lily felt tears slide into her own eyes. 'You're a dear. I do believe you are. I do so need someone to be kind to me.'

What about Captain Fairford? Lily thought. He was such a gentle and handsome man and he seemed so kind and polite. Perhaps Mrs Fairford was missing him?

'The captain will be back very soon,' she said, in an attempt to be reassuring.

Susan Fairford opened her eyes again. She looked sad, but also angry. Haltingly, she said, 'The trouble is, you see, Charles was born in India. That makes all the difference. He can't begin to understand how I pine for home, because for him, this is home. But it will never be for me.' Her lips curled in disgust. 'Filthy, stinking place, with all their heathen habits ... D'you know, on winter mornings like now, when we take the horses out, just every so often there's a smell, a whiff of England in winter or spring, that cold air. And just for a second then, I'm back in Sussex, and the orchards, the villages and little churches. I haven't seen it for five years now and I so long to. Sometimes it feels like an illness, like grief ... Can you understand?'

Lily thought about it. Did she know how to feel loss, grief, for a place, or a person? Move on, don't miss anything, anyone, that was her way. After all, who had she ever had in her life who she could really lose or miss? She had barely let herself think of Mrs Chappell or England. She had shut it all away and left with barely a backward glance, had simply transferred herself here. No, to be truthful, she could not really understand.

'I do a bit,' she said, trying to be helpful. 'But I don't have a family at home, you see.'

Susan Fairford's eyelids were drooping with pain and tiredness.

'No?' she said, drifting. 'I suppose I know nothing about you, Lily. You're a strange girl ... But kind. I can see that ...'

Lily sat by her as she drifted off to sleep and stayed with her until the dawn light seeped in at the windows.

Chapter Eight

Ambala, India, 1907

'Ironside? Mr Ironside, the Daimler mechanic? Splendid – it *is* you!'

The round, pink face appeared among the natives who swarmed round Sam the moment he stepped down from the train. Sam was damned glad to see the bloke. He had no idea where to go next or how to deal with all these wogs, not knowing the ropes at all, so he stood looking over their heads and brushing smuts off his sleeve. It wouldn't do to look uncertain of himself.

The fellow was barking commands in Hindustani, shooing all the Indians out of the way, and suddenly the hustle and bustle of coolies and tea vendors shifted away in search of someone else who might be interested. The two of them faced each other in the shade of the platform.

'Corporal Hodgkins – sir.' The fellow clicked his heels and made as if to salute, but as an afterthought, stuck out his hand instead. 'At your service, sir. Welcome to Ambala Cant. The captain sent me to meet you, sir. They're waiting for you at the Fairfords' residence.'

'The car . . . ?'

'Already unloaded, sir, this morning. All ready to go, she is, and looking very nice, if I may say so. Hand me your bag, sir – no, *jao, jao*!' He bawled at another coolie who approached to try and take the luggage. Sam could see the fellow enjoyed shouting about the place like that. 'Let's be going, shall we, sir?' he continued unctuously. 'You'll find it more congenial at the house. Very nice, it is, at the Fairfords'.'

Corporal Hodgkins led the way along the platform, past the whole array of waiting rooms – first, second, third classes, one for ladies with its closed screen doors which immediately made Sam curious about what went on inside, his mind diverting irresistibly to the mysterious bodies of Indian women under those bright, silken clothes which they wore so seductively, and he had to drag himself back to the present. He sized Hodgkins up from behind. Not what you'd think of as a soldier, Sam thought. He reckoned that of the two of them he was the one who looked fitter for soldiering. His frame was trim and muscular. Nothing to be ashamed of there. But following the corporal he saw that the fellow was very robust, despite the schoolboy face. Sam wasn't keen on these army types, expecting them to come on all superior, so he took childish pleasure in seeing that one of Hodgkins's bootlaces had come loose and was trailing in the dust.

As they left the station building, Sam screwed up his eyes against the piercing sunlight. It was February, so the temperatures were pleasant, the sky a wintry blue. At once they were surrounded by more hullaballoo, a teeming crowd of humanity all desperate to scratch a living. Among the crowds he noticed human grotesques from which he averted his eyes – one ghastly figure squatting by the wall with no nose! And all muddled up with them were cows and filthy, skeletal dogs and huge, dusty crows. And the flies and piles of ordure – the

43

stench of the place! God in heaven, what a hole! It was worse even than Delhi, if that were possible. The sights and smells turned his stomach.

But when they reached the goods yard all this was wiped from his mind because, to his astonishment, there was the Daimler! Of course this should not have been any surprise, but it still felt like a miracle.

'Amazing,' he muttered to himself, a delighted grin spreading over his face. 'That anything works in this hellhole!'

He hadn't seen her since the docks when they craned her on to the ship, and hadn't actually seen her taken off when they arrived in Bombay. He'd still been feeling so dicky when they arrived that he hadn't been able to leave the cabin, so a fellow had brought him a docking paper to sign. But now, here she was, paintwork shining, parked up there like a familiar face in all this foreignness, so that he almost wanted to go up and kiss her, as if she was his woman waiting out there for him.

'There we are, sir . . .' For one second he thought Hodgkins was going to salute the car, but he managed to restrain himself. 'I say, the horseless carriage! I'm looking forward to seeing you start her up!'

Sam was looking forward to it too. He knew that car, every inch of her, like he knew Helen's body. He could show Hodgkins a thing or two. While he was getting the starter handle in place, Hodgkins went to put his bag in the back, but the next thing Sam heard was a strained kind of grunt and when he straightened up he couldn't see Hodgkins anywhere.

'Damn and blast it!' came from the rear somewhere.

Hodgkins had sprawled flat on his face in the dirt, and by the time Sam got round to him he was jumping up quick, brushing himself down, putting his *topi* back on straight. The silly bugger had tripped over his own bootlace.

'All right?' Sam asked, keeping his face straight.

'Yes, of course,' Hodgkins snapped, with puce cheeks.

Sam strolled round to the front again, cool as you like, and cranked the handle. The Daimler started up like a dream.

Until then, he hadn't given much thought to meeting Captain Fairford. The journey itself had been adventure enough: the sea voyage through Suez to Bombay, then the long train ride to Delhi, and north-west to Ambala. He'd had no real idea, until then, of the true size of India. He had to hand it to those engineer boys – building railways here was some feat. The few paper inches the journey had traversed on the map translated into hour upon hour of baked country.

In fact, the notion of seeing the Daimler again and delivering her safely hadn't seemed real, but now it felt marvellous to be behind the wheel. With Hodgkins barking out directions, he drove along the edge of the 'native town' to the cantonment, where Captain Fairford would be waiting for his car. Sam's job was to instruct the captain and his staff in driving and maintaining her.

'The native town is pretty much off-limits,' Hodgkins was saying.

'Many motors here?' Sam was having to watch the road carefully, what with all the carts and bicycles, the dogs, children and cows all gawping as they passed and meandering across the dirt road.

'Just a few. Not all as fine as this one though. The captain is very *pukka*.'

At a glance, in the bright sunlight, Sam saw glimpses of side streets, jumbled messes of hovels heaving with dark-skinned people. He shuddered, but he wasn't going to show Hodgkins. He wanted to be seen taking everything in his stride. But it was the smell that was most overpowering. A pall of foul smoke seemed to lie over the native lines, the air tinted brown.

'Dung.' Hodgkins had seen his grimace. 'The fuel they use. Cow dung. The stink gets right into your nostrils until you don't notice. But you don't want to have anything to do with the natives. The only chaps who take themselves off there are after a bit of . . . well, you know . . .' Sam didn't have to turn and look to see the smutty expression on his face. 'A bit of recreation, let's say. By crikey, you'd have to be desperate – that's all I can say. Oh – and for Christ's sake don't go hitting any of the cows. You'll have every Hindu in the neighbourhood down on you in a pack. Sacred, you see, old man. Top of the pecking order, the cow.'

'I see,' Sam said.

'Now – this is the cantonment,' Hodgkins announced proudly.

He hardly needed to say. They were on broader roads, trees on either side, and larger buildings set back from the road. After the glimpses of the native part it seemed very orderly and quiet. There were a few individuals on the road, in khaki drill, and a horse and trap came trotting towards them, with a jingling of bells. A red stone church tower appeared on their left.

'Just down here,' Hodgkins said.

Blimey, Sam thought as they swung into the drive of the dazzling white residence. He was nervous now. There was serious money here. As they turned in, a native child who'd been squatting by the gate leaped up

46

and dashed towards the house on legs thin as hairpins, shouting and waving his arms. He must have been waiting to pass on the news, Sam realized, because a moment later people started to appear and by the time he'd cut the engine off there was quite a crowd gathering outside the arched frontage of the house. In the sudden quiet, the billowing cloud of dust the car had raised blew in a slow swirl across the lawn.

Hodgkins leaped out of the car, looking immensely important and pleased with himself. Sam just had time to take in that the whole household seemed to have come out and there was quite a gaggle of natives, all staring, with a few white faces scattered among them. One figure pushed through the rest and walked smartly towards them. Sam felt himself tighten inside. Captain Fairford. He had to spend the next six weeks or so at the man's side. He braced himself for all the class and army superiority which would come off him like sweat.

At last Hodgkins had a viable reason to salute, which he did with tremulous gusto, heels clicking.

'At ease,' Captain Fairford said. 'Thank you, Hodgkins.'

Hodgkins lowered his arm, took two steps back, tumbled over one of a row of flowerpots neatly arranged along the front edge of the lawn and lurched backwards, ending up flat on his back on the grass. Titters came from the female members of the party. With an effort, Sam kept his face straight.

'Are you all right, Hodgkins?' Captain Fairford, who had been striding towards Sam, diverted for a second.

'Yes, sir. Quite all right, sir.' Once again, Hodgkins scrambled to the vertical, hat in hand, bending to right the pots of fledgling chrysanthemums.

'Splendid.' Captain Fairford held out his hand, eyes

not quite managing to convert their twinkling amusement at Hodgkins's antics into something more formal. 'Captain Fairford, Twelfth Royal Lancers. You're the Daimler mechanic? So glad you've arrived at last. The house has been on tenterhooks.'

The captain was younger than Sam had expected, lightly built with dark brown, wavy hair and a sensitive face that would have seemed more in place on a scholar than a soldier. And he had a modest, neat 'tache, much like Sam's own. There was keen intelligence, shrewdness, and the dark brown eyes, though still tinged with laughter, took Sam in at a glance. However swift the glance and with whatever upper-class etiquette, Sam knew he was being measured up. But he felt himself relax. He liked the look of Fairford, so far.

'Ironside. Motor mechanic.'

'Well – welcome to Ambala.' He looked properly at the car then. 'I *say*,' he breathed.

The captain circled his new acquisition, making admiring noises and firing questions and the rest of the household edged forward. Most of them seemed to be native servants. Among them, though, Sam's attention was caught by a European woman holding a sleepy-looking boy in her arms. She was dark-haired, her features voluptuous and extraordinarily striking. He thought he had never seen a face with so much life in it, the dark eyes seeming to flash with energy as she looked at the car, and yet there was a closedness in her expression which he found immediately intriguing. She held the boy to her very tenderly, his fair curls bright against the dark stuff of her blouse. After a moment Captain Fairford seemed to remember something and looked round.

'Where's Sus— er, Mrs Fairford?'

'She's with *Ayah* and Isadora,' the dark-haired woman said. Her voice was soft and well-spoken.

Captain Fairford nodded, and turned his attention back to the car. The servants were gathered round now, chattering quietly, inquisitive fingers marking the dust on the hot bonnet.

'Well, Ironside,' the captain said, hands on hips. Sam could see the man was excited and he liked him for it. He was a car man, all right. It just got hold of some men and wouldn't let go. 'We must get you a drink, and as soon as you've had a wash and brush up, we'll take her out for a spin.'

'Why not before?' Sam said, holding his gaze. 'Sir.'

A grin spread across Captain Fairford's face. The fact that the establishment where Fairford was educated would have been far superior to Sam's Coventry Board School was of no account in those seconds. They were like two eager lads in a school yard.

'Well, Ironside, if you're game – why not?'

Chapter Nine

Charles Fairford was a gentleman. From the moment Sam arrived in the cantonment the captain went out of his way to put him at his ease, treating him almost like an equal. The same, however, could not be said of his wife.

Sam disliked Susan Fairford on sight, and it was pretty clear she felt the same about him. Of course, he thought, it was hard to tell with these stuck-up little English misses what their actual feelings might be about anything, but she certainly went out of her way to pull rank and put up every social and class barrier she could get away with.

That first afternoon Sam took the captain out for a quick spin. They weren't alone. From the crowd of servants, Charles Fairford called out a tall, thin native fellow. With everyone else watching – that was something Sam was discovering about India, the way everything seemed to be done to an audience – he introduced the fellow as his *syce*, or groom, Arsalan. He had been chosen to learn about a new 'horse power' they were developing in the modern world of industry.

'I want you to teach me, and Arsalan here, everything you know,' Captain Fairford said. 'He's my right-hand man.'

Sam hadn't expected that, not entrusting the Daimler to a native. The chap had probably never learned to read and write, so it seemed a bit rich to expect him to get to grips with the workings of the internal combustion engine! But it wasn't his place to argue. As they got into the car he caught sight of the dark-haired woman carrying the sleeping boy along the veranda. Something about the way she moved drew him and he had to be careful not to stare.

This Arsalan fellow sat up at the back and Sam drove the two of them out along the cantonment roads, which all looked pretty much the same to him. The sun had sunk low as they made their way back and the light turned bronze, then pink.

'I don't think I've ever seen light quite like this before, sir,' Sam said, very taken by it.

'Best time of day in India,' the captain replied. They had to speak up to be heard over the engine but even so, Sam could still hear the fondness in his voice. 'Nothing like the Indian sunset, except the dawn, of course, which is beautiful almost beyond description. Or at least by me.' He gave a chuckle. 'I'm no poet, I do know that.'

'You must miss home though?' Sam said.

'Ah, but this is home. I was born here, you see. So talking about England as "home" is merely a turn of phrase for me. Though I was at school there, naturally. For my wife, it's quite different, of course. She grew up in Sussex. Where do you come from, Ironside?'

'Coventry, sir.'

'Of course. How ridiculous of me. And you don't have to keep calling me sir.'

When they braked back outside the house, Captain Fairford said something over his shoulder to the *syce*, who leaped from the car and hurried off into the dusk, then turned to Sam.

'Well – it's marvellous: just what I was hoping for! I can hardly wait to find out all about it and take the wheel myself. Now—' He leaped energetically from the car and turned on his heel to say, 'We dine at seven-thirty, and you'll join us, of course. Consider yourself one of the family while you're here, eh? Now – let's get someone to show you your quarters.'

Sam made sure he was dressed and ready by seven-thirty. He'd brought his Sunday suit, thanks to Helen.

'They're bound to dress for dinner,' she'd said. 'You've got to look right. And there'll be church on Sundays.'

He felt pretty intimidated when he first went into the house. This was how the other half lived all right! Posh was hardly an adequate word to describe it. As for his quarters, he had never slept in a room like it before, although by their standards it was probably quite simple. There was a deep red carpet on the floor, a wide bed draped in mozzie netting and an array of dark, polished furniture and a long gilt-framed mirror, all of first-class quality. On the washstand stood a pitcher decorated with pink roses, all ready, full of warm water.

Before leaving the room he checked his appearance. The suit was quite run-of-the-mill and he wondered if he would measure up. Pulling his shoulders back he was at least reassured by his strong, manly stature. Keen as mustard, that was the impression people had. And he didn't come across as some office-*wallah*, that was for sure. Sam knew he was good-looking. Smooth dark brown hair, alert grey eyes, strong brows. And he knew he was good at his job. 'Cocky sod, isn't he?' he'd heard

52

himself described at the works. But he was going places – he knew it. And he wasn't going to be intimidated by the wealth of the Fairford mansion.

Opening the door, he jumped, startled by a small figure peering up at him outside. The corridor was rather dark and Sam was unnerved for a moment. It must be a girl, since she had long, dark hair and was wearing a white frock. And she had some sort of doll tucked under one arm. But she stood in a strange pose, knees and feet turned out and her face was ... well, not *normal*: it was partly the way she stared at him, not smiling or speaking, that was disturbing.

'Izzy? Isadora!' It was a native voice calling along the passage, high pitched and exasperated. 'Naughty girl, where are you? Come here, now!'

At that moment a mellow-sounding gong ran through the house and the male servant appeared to take Sam to dinner, shooing the child away.

'Who was that?' Sam asked, carefully.

'Mr and Mrs Fairford's daughter,' the man said. 'Her name is Isadora.'

'Is she ... well, all right?'

'She is a mongol, sir.' He spoke with a slight inclination of his head, as if to acknowledge this as a personal sorrow.

'I saw another child? How many are there?'

'Only Miss Isadora and Master Cosmo, Sahib. Miss Isadora stays with her *ayah* – Master Cosmo is undertaking his education with Miss Waters.'

Sam immediately thought of the dark-haired woman carrying the child. 'I see. And the boy, Cosmo. Is he ... ?'

The servant's face broke into a broad smile.

53

'Master Cosmo is perfectly all right. Oh yes, very much so, thanking God.'

The Fairfords were already in the dining room, standing each side of a long, shining table laid with silver and glass. A heavy chandelier cast a gentle pool of light on to the table, leaving the edges of the room in shadow. Sam knew he had not imagined that as he came in the two of them stopped talking abruptly. There'd been some disagreement, it was obvious. Sam was a married man, after all: he knew the sort of thing.

After a second's silence, they summoned smiles to their faces, but the atmosphere was strained. Captain Fairford seemed pleased to break away.

'Ironside! Found your way all right? Fancy a Scotch?'

'*Darling,*' Mrs Fairford reproached him. 'We haven't been introduced.' She had one of those pure, cut-glass voices which set Sam on edge to start with. And after all, wasn't it pretty obvious who he was?

'Sorry – remiss of me. Darling – this is Mr Ironside, the mechanic from Daimler. Ironside, this is my wife, Susan.'

She glided closer to shake his hand, and said, 'Yes – Mrs Fairford.' This sounded like a put-down to Sam, after her husband had used her Christian name. 'How d'you do?'

She was wearing a sapphire-blue dress which swept the floor, a long string of pearls swinging sinuously as she moved. In the dim light, Sam saw her as very pretty. Of course, she was a beautiful woman, with that slender, curving figure and the pale hair, swept up and decorated with tiny jewels which caught the light as she moved.

Her face had all the requirements of prettiness: wide blue eyes, even features, with a distinctive sharpness about them and a definite, smiling mouth. Her neck was long and slim, and the overall impression she made was striking. And yet, when she came up close, somehow the prettiness turned to something else, as if there was a wall around her built of defensive snobbery which drew the life from her features and, to his eyes, made her look pinched and calculating.

'So pleasant to meet you,' she purred, without it sounding so at all.

Her smile communicated no warmth and her eyes contained a subtle contempt which did not allow her gaze to meet Sam's for more than a second, in case, it seemed, she might be soiled by even fleeting contact with someone of inferior standing. Trade, of course, was all he was to her. She allowed her hand to touch just the tips of his fingers, then withdrew.

'How d'you do, Mrs Fairford?' Sam said, already knowing that he loathed the stuck-up bitch for looking at him like that. Or, more precisely, for refusing to see him at all.

'I hope you had a safe journey?' she asked, though her attention was turned to the table, which was laid for three. She straightened one of the place settings.

'On the whole,' Sam said, though he directed the answer at the captain, who was handing him a glass of Scotch. 'Though I must say, sea travel doesn't suit me completely.'

'Oh!' To his surprise, Mrs Fairford agreed fervently. 'Isn't it simply awful! I remember feeling so desperately ill on the journey out here! It almost puts one off the idea of going home to dear old England again, if that were not such a terrible thought!'

The two of them gestured towards the table, and as if some signal had been given, though if there was Sam never saw it, a cohort of servants, each dressed in a similar maroon and white livery, began to bring in the food: a tureen of soup, some wide, white dishes and a tray of bread.

Captain Fairford sat at the head of the table and Mrs Fairford and Sam were opposite each other. Mrs Fairford fretted at the servants about details of the meal – could they not have cut the bread more elegantly, and had they remembered to strain the soup properly? Two of them stood silently in the shadows by the wall as they ate. Sam wondered what on earth they should talk about. Had it been just himself and the captain, they could have talked all evening about the car. There was no stopping him on that subject! And it was clearly what the captain would have liked to discuss as well. But of course, that wasn't women's talk. So Sam kept the conversation light, not technical, talking about things which he thought would amuse.

'Tell me, Ironside,' the captain said, as they began on the soup. 'Surely there isn't still the same fierce opposition to the motor car in England now? While I was at Eton I seem to remember there were all sorts of protests going on – outrage about freedom of the roads, terrorizing of neighbourhoods and so on.'

'Well, yes – we haven't lost that yet,' Sam said, trying to get used to the strange, spicy flavour of the soup. 'There's the Highway Protection League, who'd like to ban the motor car altogether. With attitudes like that, no wonder the French and Germans have been quicker off the mark than us! They're always complaining about the dust and noise – and of course there are always those that will complain because they can't afford a motor, so it's sour grapes against anyone who can.'

'And all those with investments in the railway, of course,' Susan Fairford added. 'Like my dear father, who could never say a single good word about the motor car!'

She gave a genuine smile, seeming to relax for a moment, and Sam thawed towards her fractionally.

'I seem to remember they were hardly allowed to get up any speed at all,' Charles Fairford said.

'We've come on a bit since the early days of steam engines. Remember the early vehicles – only go at two miles an hour in town, and don't go out without a stoker and the fellow walking ahead with a red flag to warn everyone! At least we're allowed to get up to twenty miles an hour now . . .'

'Ah yes, thanks to Lord Montagu's bill.'

'A good Daimler customer,' Sam said. The conservative MP Lord Montagu had brought the Motor Car Act onto the statute book in 1903. Montagu was a Daimler driver and motor enthusiast. 'He's brought it home that we're here to stay,' Sam said. 'Even if there are still people jumping into ditches when they hear a motor coming round the bend!'

Charles Fairford laughed and his wife gave a faint smile.

'It's no easier here,' the captain said, chuckling. 'A fellow I know goes up to Mahabaleshwar in the hot season – that's a hill station down near Poona. The whole town is utterly hostile to the motor car and there are signs everywhere. He said his favourite is one that says, "Any motor car found in motion while travelling to its destination will be vigorously dealt with"! I mean, I ask you!'

As they were laughing, the servants came to remove the soup bowls and bring in the next course, which proved to be beef olives.

After this hiatus, Susan Fairford began on Sam, with a battery of questions between mouthfuls of beef and potatoes. She had evidently had enough of talking about motor cars.

'So where is it you come from exactly, Mr Ironside?'

'From Coventry.' He was about to add 'ma'am' but decided against it. He sipped his drink. The meat had a rather more fiery filling than he was used to.

'Ah, the industrial Midlands! Rather like Charles!' She gave a little laugh, as if the idea of Fairford and himself coming from anywhere remotely similar was too ridiculous for words. 'Charles's family have an estate in Warwickshire – Cranbourne – some miles from Rugby.'

'Not that it's anything much to do with me,' Captain Fairford added. He refilled Sam's glass with Scotch. He'd have to watch it and not get tight, Sam realized. He was pretty tired and he wasn't used to much in the way of spirits. A couple of pints of ale was more his style. These colonials all drank a great deal, he had heard, what with the heat and nothing much else doing.

'I spent school holidays up there,' the captain was saying, 'but apart from that, it's a foreign land to me – as I was telling you earlier.'

'And are you married?' Mrs Fairford continued. She was very direct in her questioning, as if she had some right to know everything.

'Yes, I am.'

'Children?'

'Our first child is expected in June.'

He thought he saw a flicker of some emotion cross

58

her face, but all she said was, 'How nice. I wonder whether it will be a girl or a boy.'

'I couldn't say.'

'No, of course not. How silly of me. And how old are you, Mr Ironside, if you don't mind me asking?'

'Darling!' Her husband reproached her.

'No, it's all right.' He already thought her rude and condescending and this made no difference. 'I'm just twenty-one.'

'And your wife . . . ?'

'Helen? She's twenty.'

She paused, finishing a mouthful.

'And have you always been a mechanic?'

'I've recently completed my apprenticeship with Daimler.' For a moment he was homesick for something familiar: the great machine shops at the works, the lathes turning. It was all part of him. 'I joined the firm at fourteen. So, yes, I suppose I have.'

'And your wife? Presumably she's not a mechanic?' She gave a silly little laugh. Sam just looked back at her. He wasn't going to let her get under his skin.

'Helen was a photographer – before we married, that is.'

That took her aback. 'How extraordinarily exciting! A photographer! However did that come about?'

Sam laid his soup spoon down for a moment. 'Well, she was taken on and trained. A local photographer – portraits and so on. Helen can develop the pictures, tint them and all the tricks. She knows her trade.' He felt proud of her then, his little woman, whom he had left behind in their modest house, beginning to show that she was carrying his child. He hadn't thought about her enough, he realized. Not for a newly married man.

Before Mrs Fairford could ask any more questions,

he said, 'I believe you have two children? Your daughter tried to pay me a visit earlier on.'

'Izzy?' Her voice was sharp. 'What do you mean?'

'Oh, she only peeped in, when the servant was by the door. Someone was calling her . . .'

'*Ayah*,' she sighed, pettishly. 'She just can't seem to keep control of the girl.'

Captain Fairford laid a hand gently on hers for a second. 'But where would we be without her, darling?'

'I know.' She looked up at Sam with a kind of defiance. 'You see, Isadora is a problem of a child. *Ayah* is the only one she really cares for . . .'

'Oh, nonsense,' the captain interrupted. 'Srimala, our *ayah*, is a jewel though, we have to admit. Had Isadora been like other children we would have brought out an English nanny for her, of course, before she went to school. Our son Cosmo has a nanny, a Miss Waters . . .' His brow creased. 'You know, darling, since Mr Ironside is here, we could have invited Miss Waters to dine with us as well. She might have been glad to meet a visitor from England.'

Susan Fairford's face tightened again suddenly and with a languid little laugh she said, 'Oh no – I really think her place is with the children, darling. After all, we don't want to be *outnumbered* by the lower orders, do we?'

Chapter Ten

Coventry, 1906

Helen's hair was the first thing Sam noticed about her. He saw her coming out of Timmins, the photographer's, which he passed on his way home from the Daimler works every day. Once he had plucked up the courage to speak to her, he sometimes walked her home.

The first time he touched her hair properly was last winter when they managed to find half an hour to themselves away from Mrs Gregory, Helen's mother. They were in the Gregorys' house, it was sleeting outside and they were in the back room by the fire. There was a knock on the door and Mrs Gregory was called out to a neighbour who was in some strife or other. Sam gave a great inner cheer at the thought of being able to be alone with Helen. There always seemed to be some obstacle to his being with her! There was that Laurie fellow from the Armstrong works who was forever hanging around her with his daft grin. Helen always laughed off the idea that she had any interest in Laurie.

'Oh, I've known him since we were knee-high,' she'd say. 'He's just old Laurie.'

But there was also the child and today, for once, she wasn't there either.

Mrs Gregory was a woman of good works, many would have said kindness itself. So upright, Sam sometimes thought sourly, that you could hang a lamp from her.

Although a widow herself, she had taken on the upbringing of her dead sister's child. Helen said that the sister had lived in Liverpool and had taken ill and died tragically young, leaving the baby girl, Emma, to a feckless husband who would never be able to care for her. So Ma Gregory stepped in. The child was a sweet enough little thing, but Helen had to take her turn in minding her and from Sam's point of view she was yet another obstacle to his getting anywhere near Helen. Today, though, Emma was round playing at a neighbour's house and his chance had come!

Mrs Gregory said with a meaningful look, 'I won't be long, you know. You might polish the brasses while I'm gone, if you're short of summat to do.' And she set out into the slushy Coventry street in her old brown hat and coat, her sinewy figure bent against the wind.

'Well, there's a miracle, anyway,' Sam said, shuffling closer along the settle towards Helen.

'Sam! You're awful. She'll get drenched out there, and Mrs Nightingale's been taken bad again.'

Helen turned to him, her creamy face dotted with toffee-coloured freckles, tawny eyes twinkling reproachfully while she tried not to look pleased that they were alone. Sam could think of nothing but his urgent desire to hold her.

'I want to kiss you, love,' he said, taking her hand. 'I've been sitting here bursting to kiss you all afternoon!'

'Oh, Sam!' she said again, as if he was a naughty schoolboy.

He felt like anything but a schoolboy. His feelings were much more manly than that! To give her a few token moments to pretend she was resisting him, he caught the end of a thick strand of her hair. She had washed it and was drying it by the fire. To the touch, it was deliciously thick and heavy.

'Caramels and cream, that's you,' he said. He tilted his head and lightly kissed the shadowy part of her neck beneath her ear. 'All sweet. That's my girl.'

She giggled and her face lit up. Helen was nineteen then, Sam twenty. She was so pretty and everyone liked her, though she was quiet and shy. It all felt right to Sam: Helen was the wife he was looking for, because he needed a wife. It was the right thing. He was going to be a successful and respectable professional man and such men had wives and lived in one of the new, nicely-kept-up villas at the edge of town.

And he thought he was in love. What else could these overpowering feelings mean? It was like an itch on him all the time, that powerful longing to know what it would be like to lie with her, to *have* her, even though he was scarcely sure what that meant. He could see why men said women were a torment. He'd sit beside her and they'd be talking, yet all the time, all he could think about was the way her frock pushed out, tightly covering her chest, a tantalizing swell that gave him an almost overwhelming hunger to reach out and touch.

He took Helen in his arms, seeing her smiling eyes turn solemn, and he had his kiss that day. Once a few months of little walks to the park and snatched kisses had passed, he asked her to marry him. He was at such a pitch by then, something had to shift. He had to lie with her and make her his or he was going to go mad. He knew he was a good prospect, with his apprenticeship. He wasn't sure that Mrs Gregory had taken to him, not *fondly*, but she had no good reason to object to him.

Their wedding night was the first time he saw her naked, though she didn't want him to.

After a nice mutton dinner in an old inn a few miles away, they went up to the old oak-beamed room which was their private haven at last. God knew, Sam didn't know what he expected exactly, but that night was a bitter disappointment. Almost as soon as they got through the door he went to take her in his arms, but she pushed him off, frowning.

'Just let me get ready, Sam!'

Stung, he stood watching her go to the door, saw her slip a little on the uneven floor and say, 'Oh, damn it!' as she disappeared out to the bathroom across the passage. He wanted her to *want* him. He told himself she was shy, and waited, taking his boots off and unbuttoning his shirt, hearing the splash of water, and Helen clearing her throat, then a long silence. He sat on the edge of the bed, beginning to wonder if she was all right or had perhaps been taken ill.

At last she came back in, wearing an enveloping white garment, her lovely hair brushed loose and hanging down her shoulders. Sam's heart leaped at the sight of her, seeing the rounded shape of her soft breasts pushing at the white stuff of her nightdress. Full of desire he went to her at once, to take her in his arms again, and found that she was trembling, and seemed close to tears.

'Helen, my lovely?'

Again, she pulled back.

'Hadn't you better get ready, Sam?'

'Ready for what? I am ready, love—' he managed to put his arms around her – 'I've been ready for you for months and months . . .'

Her face was buried in his chest. It was queer, and frustrating.

'Come on, love,' Sam said coaxingly, though he was getting more and more het up. 'I just want to be with you – for a bit of lovemaking. That's what married people do, you know that, don't you?'

She nodded and a tiny voice said, 'Yes' into his shirt.

'Let me look at you,' he said. Reluctantly she drew back and raised her face. The room was quite dark by now, lit by a single candle, and he could only just make out her features.

'What's the matter, dear?' He kept his voice very patient.

'I don't know what it is. Lovemaking, I mean.' She looked up then, like a little girl, ashamed. 'I don't know what we do.'

Her being so innocent like that made him want her all the more.

'Never mind,' he said. 'We'll find out somehow, together, won't we?' He looked lovingly into her eyes and said, 'I want to see you, Helen. See how lovely you are.'

'What d'you mean?' She sounded frightened.

He managed to talk her sweetly into lying down on the bed with him and once he started touching her round, soft body, she began to loosen up a bit and he did see her at last because, gently pulling her shift up high, she let him complete the marital act. She didn't put up any protest, but watched him, wide-eyed, and when he'd finished she made a little sound, of pleasure, he thought and hoped, and clasped her legs round him.

'Oh, Samuel,' she said, and he felt her breath on his ear. He was happier then. She'd get used to it, of course she would. It was always more difficult for a woman, he understood, and at least he didn't seem to have given her any pain.

Married life started with them living with Mrs Gregory. It was bad from the word go. Anything in the bedroom department felt impossible in her house, and it was difficult enough on their own: Helen just about tolerated the physical side of things. There was very little privacy, especially with the child about. Helen was far too patient with her, in Sam's view. After all, Emma was nothing to her really. But if the child came knocking on the door, Helen would say, 'I'll just let her in, just for a few minutes, poor little thing.' And bang would go their time together. He quickly began to think she did it on purpose to avoid him touching her. But he couldn't stop wanting it, and wanting her. He'd waited long enough and he was a passionate man.

As soon as he could, after a couple of months, he found a house. He had a decent wage now and he thought, We'll get out of Coventry, right away from Mrs G and all that stifling set-up. So they took out the rent on a place in Kenilworth. Helen was a bit upset at first as she'd never lived away from home. But she loved the village and the old castle and cleaner air, and she was such a kind girl that she soon made friends. She took a little job in the grocer's shop and got to know people that way. And they settled. They didn't find a great deal to say to one another, but they both worked hard, and got on with it.

That autumn, after they moved into the house, they

realized there was a baby on the way. Helen was poorly to begin with and went to the doctor.

'Dr Small says you shouldn't have relations of an "intimate" kind during the time a child is expected,' she told Sam.

This came as a blow to Sam. It was an important thing in life to him. He even wondered if the doctor had really said that and almost asked his mother if it was true, but shyness prevented him.

'You make it sound like something dirty,' he said resentfully. 'An animal thing.' She talked as if he was disgusting, like a hog. 'It's just the way men are and I don't see why I should have to be ashamed of it!'

'It won't be long,' Helen tried to soothe him. 'You'll just have to be a good boy, Sam – just until the babby arrives.'

And then, after Christmas, Sam was called into the offices at Daimler.

'We want you to go with a delivery,' he was told. 'One of the new models, to be shipped to Bombay and up to a place called Ambala. Big army station. All being well, you should be back end of March or so.'

God, he was excited! Seeing a bit of the world on the job! And the fact that the delivery out here came up while Helen was carrying the child seemed good timing. She could have some peace and he wouldn't be tempted by the feel of her close to him in the bed. She could rest, safe and cosy in the English winter, while he went off adventuring and slept under the Indian stars.

Chapter Eleven

Ambala, India, 1907

His first morning in Ambala, Sam woke to a tremendous racket of crows from the trees round the house. For a second, he thought the room was full of fog, then realized everything was shrouded in white because of the mozzie net round the bed. He'd got used to being on the ship and it was a shock finding himself in this new place, especially as he'd woken from a dream about Helen and expected to find her in the bed beside him. It was one of those times when he wanted her badly.

There was plenty to take his mind off it, though. So far as Charles Fairford was concerned, today was to be devoted to the Daimler, and he was looking forward to showing the Captain all he knew. And that wife of his would be well out of the way, Sam hoped, doing whatever it was such women did in India.

As soon as he set foot out of bed there came a knock on the door. It was only six in the morning, but when he opened up, there was a native chap standing out there with a tray of tea. My goodness, Sam thought, that's service for you. The man came in, very deferentially, and put the tray down. Beside the teapot was a plate on which were arranged several biscuits and two bananas.

'Sahib would like me to pour the tea?'

'Oh – yes, please! Er – is Captain Fairford up already?'

'Captain Sahib has gone for his morning ride.'

'Ah. I see. Thank you.'

Before his morning ablutions he sat to drink his tea in the cane chair by the window. It was rather misty out, all soft greens and greys. There were Indian voices coming from somewhere and he could just see a chap, thin as a railing like most natives, working with a rake in front of the trees. The sound of his coughing carried across the dew-soaked lawn.

Once he'd downed this rather meagre breakfast and dressed it was still early and all the action seemed to be going on outside, so he decided to slip out for a look around. It was then that he saw Lily Waters properly for the first time, though he didn't know her Christian name then.

He was strolling through the cool morning air smelling the mixed scents of a country that was not his own, along the drive to the gate, thinking to walk a little along the road. He had gone very little distance when he heard the sound of hooves behind him and, turning, saw the two women riding towards him. They made a lovely sight. Susan Fairford was in front, her pale hair just visible under her *topi*, riding elegantly side-saddle, the boy tucked in front of her with a rapturous expression on his face. And riding behind was the woman whom they called Miss Waters. Unlike her mistress she was not riding side-saddle, but astride the bay horse, clad in a modest, feminine blouse and jacket and pair of manly breeches. She was managing the animal with apparent confidence and obvious pleasure, a radiant smile playing round her lips.

'Good morning, Mr Ironside!' Susan Fairford greeted him. There was laughter in her voice and she seemed very different from last night. 'I trust you slept well?'

'Very, thank you,' he replied. He nodded at Miss Waters, touching his hat to them both.

'Good morning,' Miss Waters said, and her eyes seemed full of joy as she looked at him, then shyly away.

They passed on towards the stables and Sam watched, his eyes fixed on Miss Waters's curving form above the shining rump of the horse.

God, he found himself thinking. *What a woman.*

The sun was higher when he returned from his stroll, beginning to burn off the mist. Captain Fairford came round from the side of the bungalow where they'd left the car, striding along manfully, still dressed in riding gear, jodhpurs and puttees. While slender, he was a superbly athletic man. Sam pulled his shoulders back, feeling conscious that he had only ever once sat astride a horse and that an old farm nag, to boot. The safety bicycle had been more his sort of ride!

'Morning, Ironside!' The captain sounded very cheerful, now he was free from the domestic realm.

'Good morning,' Sam rubbed his hands together. 'Chillier morning than I expected!'

'Ah yes – winter nights are pretty cold here,' the captain said as they walked round to where the Daimler was parked. 'You've come at the right time, though – gets damnably hot later in the year. Actually, you'll catch the beginning of it. Come March, the temperature starts to creep up, and by May, June time, phoo! But you'll be long gone by then. Course, we get the extremes here on the northern plains. Anyway – got your breakfast all right?'

'Very nice, thank you, sir.'

'No need to "sir" me – I told you. So, if you're set, we can get cracking. Tell me about this car!'

That had Sam straight into his element, of course. The car was a 45 hp, one of the first new 1907 models, and Sam knew it was an excellent choice. So far as he was concerned, you wouldn't find a better on the market anywhere, and he had admired the captain just from his choice of motor without even meeting him!

'Right then . . .' He hesitated. 'Did you not want your groom to learn about the car too, sir?'

'Oh, there'll be plenty of opportunity to teach Arsalan. He's quick as anything. Just give me a once-over first.'

'Right you are, sir.' Sam was already enjoying himself. 'Well, let's start with the chassis. Of course, they're all built on a pressed steel frame now, not like the old models, you know, all flitch plate, channel steel and wood frames . . . This is a strong animal, this one.'

Animated, he pointed out all the special features, like the clearance between rear axle and side frames, *and*, 'Look here.' He ducked down at the back and beckoned to Charles Fairford to do the same. As they squatted side by side the odours of horse and sweat came off the captain, a pungent, manly combination. For a second, Sam found a powerful image of the women he had met earlier on flash into his mind. Miss Waters: as if she had been summoned by the primitive earthiness of smell. Bewildered, Sam banished her from his thoughts.

'D'you see the height of the floorline?' He was full of it now, rattling on at full speed! 'Well, if you look at any of the models that went before, the floor's been lowered considerably so it's easier to get into the seats – especially for the ladies, of course. Now, you might be thinking, well that's no good, because we'll be scraping the car's belly along the road at that rate.'

He looked round at Charles Fairford and saw he had his complete attention.

'Well, yes, so you would think . . .'

'Ah – well, this is the thing. Just take a look underneath her.'

As requested, Captain Fairford knelt and peered under the car. Sam noticed the sallow colour of his skin at the back of his neck, edged by his strong mahogany-coloured hair. From living out here, he thought. Never really goes white like the rest of us

'See? Good clearance off the road, isn't there?'

'Well, I don't have much to compare with . . . But it seems very good.'

'Lower frame, but more road clearance – so, how have we done it? By raising the engine higher up in the frame, that's how! The gearbox is lower because we reversed the position of the gearshaft and countershaft. *So* – the great thing is, you gain more stability *and* reduce the amount of dust raised off the road. Two things which will be of great importance out here. Quite a thing, wouldn't you say?'

The captain looked genuinely impressed. 'Splendid! Thoroughly splendid.'

They spent a very comfortable couple of hours, kneeling, prodding, peering into the engine, like two schoolboys with a Meccano set. Sam took him through every detail of the engine, cooling system, gears and the springing, which was another of Daimler's proudest developments: springs four feet long – marvellous! And he could see the captain was hooked.

'All I can say is, Captain, you've made an excellent choice,' Sam finished. It was ten o'clock by now, the sun was well up and the air pleasantly warm. A sweet smell of flowers drifted from the beds and pots.

'Well.' The captain straightened up. 'If Daimler's good enough for the king I assumed it would be for me. You've painted a damned fine picture of the workings – thank you, Ironside.'

'More than a pleasure, sir.'

'Fancy breakfast?'

'I thought I'd already had that.'

Charles Fairford laughed. He was a handsome so-and-so, Sam had to hand him that.

'Ah – that was just *chota hazri*, a sort of minor breakfast I take before my ride. It's about time for *bari hazri*. Breakfast major, let's say!'

As they stood there, there came a flurry of running feet and the boy, Cosmo, came tearing round from the back of the house.

'Pater! I want to see the car!'

Close behind, looking flustered, there she was again: Miss Waters, no longer in riding gear.

'I'm sorry, Captain Fairford!' She was blushing, though in her eyes Sam saw elements of mischief on the boy's behalf. 'He's been trying to get out here with you all morning. I couldn't hold him any longer.'

'Not at all,' the captain said easily. 'Of course he must see it! Come here, Cosmo, old chap!'

He swung the boy up into his arms, and into the driver's seat. Cosmo laughed with glee, jumping up and down on the seat, holding on to the steering wheel.

'Make it go, Pater! Make it go fast!'

'Not now, Cozzy. You just have a look for the moment. But we'll get Mr Ironside to take us for a spin later on, shall we?'

They all stood watching the boy for a few moments,

73

with all his four-year-old, full-hearted glee. Miss Waters's eyes were fixed on him with a rapt smile. But for a moment Sam saw her gaze turn towards him with frank curiosity. He looked back, giving a faint smile, but she fixed her eyes on the boy.

Captain Fairford turned to them.

'I don't know if you've met Miss Waters? She's Cosmo's nanny – doing a sterling job too, I might say. Miss Waters, this is Mr Ironside, from the Daimler Motor Company, who has provided us with this splendid machine.'

They turned to one another again and Sam extended his hand.

'How d'you do, Miss Waters?'

'Pleased to meet you, Mr Ironside.'

She gave him that shy, yet somehow vivacious, look. He had never seen eyes contain more energy and depth. Then she looked quickly away again. Her hand was small and soft and he shook it so carelessly then. He had touched her for the first time, simply as a social formality. Sam had no notion that morning of the extent to which, engraved on his future, would be the mark of his longing to touch her again.

Chapter Twelve

One afternoon, when he had not been in Ambala many days, Sam went for a stroll in the garden while he waited for Captain Fairford. The captain was obliged, naturally, to spend parts of each day working with his regiment on administration, parades and so forth. By three-thirty or so he was usually free, and Sam instructed him, and Arsalan, on the workings of the engine.

The hottest part of the day was rather like English summer, and when Sam approached the house, sweating a little in the afternoon sun, there was a commotion going on outside on the veranda. The two children were there with Mrs Fairford and Miss Waters. He lost his stride for a second, as he didn't relish seeing the captain's wife at any time. It was bad enough having to have dinner with her every night. However, the girl, Isadora seemed to be screaming blue murder, so they weren't taking any notice of him.

'*Ayah* – where is *Ayah*?' Susan Fairford's voice was shrill. 'Lily, fetch the wretched girl. Fetch her at once!'

But before Miss Waters had moved more than a step the *ayah* appeared.

'Oh, for goodness sake, take her indoors until she's quietened down. This is unbearable!'

The *ayah* led Isadora screaming into the house and Mrs Fairford flung herself down into one of the chairs.

She was dressed to go out, in a white, lace-trimmed dress and hat.

'Oh, it really is too much. Just when she was ready. That child will be the death of me. I can't bear it!'

Miss Waters was kneeling with her back to Sam, with Cosmo, whose shoelaces she appeared to be fastening, in front of her on a chair. But then Mrs Fairford caught sight of Sam.

'Mr Ironside.' She sat up, only just managing to regain her formal composure. In fact, she sounded annoyed at having another thing to contend with. 'You'll have to forgive us. We are just taking the children out to a party.'

'Not at all,' Sam said. 'Don't let me get in your way.'

'Do come and sit down,' she instructed, distractedly. 'Charles will be back at any moment.'

He went into the shade of the veranda and sat on one of the lounging chairs, with wooden arms long enough to rest one's legs on, though Sam kept his feet on the floor. He was not far from Miss Waters. She stood up, her attention fixed on the boy, who was looking the image of the perfect gentleman child in a sailor suit. Sam saw a faint smile on her lips, as if she was pleased with her handiwork. Not once did she turn and acknowledge him.

'Don't want my shoes on,' Cosmo was saying, petulantly.

'Oh glory – don't you start as well!' Mrs Fairford snapped, exasperated. 'You see, dressing Isadora to go out is the most *awful* ordeal. The child would run around naked all day if we let her. The moment we begin on petticoats and so forth, all hell breaks loose!'

Sam could hear her trying to make light of the problem, but there was a desperate note in her voice.

She had a printed card of some sort in her hand and was fanning herself with it and he noticed she looked pale and unwell.

'As ever, the only person who can make her see any sense is the *ayah*.'

'So what is her secret, do you think?' Sam asked. He didn't really give a damn what the answer was, but he was trying to be civil.

'Heaven knows,' she replied languidly. 'So long as she gets her out here with her party clothes on, I couldn't care less.'

But his question provoked a reaction from Miss Waters.

'The *ayah* sings to her,' she explained, quietly. 'She sings her into her clothes.'

'With her native mumbo-jumbo, no doubt,' Mrs Fairford snapped.

'She just sings about each item of clothing as they put it on,' Miss Waters said. 'And Izzy gets caught up in it, like a game. Srimala is rather clever like that.'

Her face was as calm and inscrutable as ever, but Sam saw a momentary light in her eyes as she looked down at Susan Fairford. *She can't stand the woman either*, was his first thought, because that was what he wanted to think. He felt a complicity with Miss Waters, since they were both bracketed together as the 'lower orders'. But immediately he saw that it was not that. There was something rather tender in her expression and he was puzzled. Sam wanted to catch her eye and smile, but she didn't look at him. The boy was swinging his feet vigorously, kicking the legs of his chair and she laid a hand on his shoulder to still him.

'Well, whatever she does, let's hope it doesn't take too long. I ordered the *tonga* for half past three. And –

oh, my goodness!' Susan Fairford leaped up. 'Have we the milk? Really, Lily, you should have reminded me.'

'Cook's doing it. He said he'd bring it.'

'Well, go round to the cookhouse and ask him to hurry. Quickly! Knowing him, he's probably only just lighting the fire! *Really*,' she exclaimed as Miss Waters obeyed. 'You have to do everything yourself if you want anything done properly. And really, one doesn't keep dogs to have to bark oneself, does one?'

'Indeed not,' Sam agreed, repelled by her attitude. He realized, to his surprise, that he had less respect for her than for the *syce*, Arsalan. Instructing him about the car, he found that the fellow had a mind like greased lightning; you only had to tell him anything once.

'One can't trust anyone else's servants to boil the milk properly, you see. They're all so lazy and heaven knows what we might all go down with. This country's full of filthy diseases. So we always take our own children's milk, to be quite sure.'

Miss Waters appeared then, holding two bottles of milk wrapped in tissue paper, and a moment later came the sound of hooves and a jingling bell as the *tonga* came along the drive, pulled by a scrawny pony. With magical timing, the *ayah* appeared with a tear-stained, but frilly-clad Isadora, and the three women and two children climbed on to the *tonga*. Cosmo perched on the seat facing the front, between his mother and Miss Waters, and the *ayah* took the girl at the back. It was Miss Waters who put her arm round the boy to steady him, though, and Sam found himself thinking, She is the one who looks as if she is his mother.

As the *tonga* moved off, Miss Waters glanced at him. Their eyes met, though he didn't think it intentional on her part. He felt she was sizing him up in some way.

But there was something in the look, a momentary nakedness in that usually closed face, which affected him. He sat and watched the *tonga* disappear past all the flowerpots along the Fairfords' drive and on to the road and found that he was staring for quite some time afterwards.

Chapter Thirteen

As March arrived it grew hotter. The *punkah-wallahs* began their work on the verandas, pulling fans to keep the rooms cool. And Charles Fairford decided that he was now enough of a driver to take the family out for a spin and a picnic tea. They readied the car at four, once tiffin was well digested.

The ladies appeared for the jaunt, erupting from the bungalow and across the veranda in a swirl of skirts, parasols, scarves and fidgeting children. But Sam's eye had only interest in one detail. Was *she* coming? He was not disappointed. With a leaping heart he saw her there behind her mistress.

'Are you ready for us, Charles?' Susan Fairford called. 'We can't keep Cozzy at bay any longer!' Isadora, it appeared, refused to get dressed and was staying behind with the *ayah*.

'Yes, darling – all ready.' He stood smiling, relaxed, one hand resting on the bonnet. He was wearing loose, dust-coloured clothing.

The women had dressed up for the occasion, Mrs Fairford in white, with a very wide-brimmed hat tied under her chin with diaphanous lengths of chiffon. She came sweeping across the drive, but Sam had no eyes for her. Miss Waters followed with Cosmo, who was skipping with excitement. She was dressed more or less as usual, in a long dark skirt and white blouse and a straw hat, of a more modest size than her mistress's, with a strip of soft brown cloth tied round it, forming a bow at the back. It suited her. God, she was a beautiful woman, Sam thought. He had to tear his gaze away so as not to stare. She seemed to have taken up occupation in his mind. It was her eyes which he kept seeing, especially when he lay under the mozzie net at night: those deep, brown eyes, sad in repose, but which could change in a second into dancing life. He ached to see her smile directed at him. And then, ashamed, he would think of Helen, waiting at home to give birth to his child. Good old Helen.

Cosmo broke free from her grasp at last and ran to his father.

'Hello there, old chap!' Captain Fairford laughed. 'Ready for the off?'

'Want to go now. Can we go fast, Pater? Can I drive it?'

To begin with, Sam sat up front beside Captain Fairford, and Mrs Fairford and Miss Waters sat behind with the boy on Miss Waters's lap, yelping with excitement.

Sam watched the captain as he released the brake and set off, steering the car through the gate to the road, face tense with concentration; Sam couldn't help a tinge of envy at the first-class competence of the man. He had everything it took: breeding and money, no struggle to work his way into the right position like the rest of the herd. Charles Fairford had told him that the two portraits hanging either side of the fireplace in the hall were of his father and grandfather, both astride their horses in full military regalia, both also in the 12th Royal Lancers, the same cavalry regiment as himself. His father had been born shortly before the Mutiny began in 1857, to a father who was killed by cannon fire during its suppression, at the Siege of Lucknow. You could hardly compare, Sam thought, his own father, a cycle engineer, and a grandfather who had been a shopkeeper. It didn't lift you so high up in the world's stakes. Yet he felt a stubborn pride in them as well. They had done well, according to their position.

Steering the car along the road was easy enough, except for the erratic traffic of Indian roads, natives scurrying here and there, pedlars, *dhobis* with huge bundles of washing, native children who ran away from the car but turned to wave from a safe distance, bicycles and *tongas*, dogs and cows.

They bowled along for a time, passing some of the military administrative quarters and the parade ground. The air was lovely, and mellow afternoon light shone through the trees edging the road. Sam began to relax. The driving was not going to present any problems, and if trouble of a mechanical nature arose, he knew he could deal with anything. In fact, he half hoped that something would. Cosmo was chattering constantly with the women behind, and Sam enjoyed the sensation of knowing that if he turned his head far enough to the right he could glimpse Lily. He heard her soft replies to the boy's questions.

'No, Cosmo,' he heard her say. 'You can't sit with Pater today. Your father needs to have the mechanic sitting there.'

Being called 'the mechanic' felt somehow chilling, but he reasoned that he and Miss Waters had barely exchanged more than a word. He was determined to change that.

'We'll be on the Grand Trunk Road soon!' the

captain said. 'It goes all the way from Calcutta, across here to Amritsar, Lahore – right up to the Khyber Pass.' Charles Fairford glanced at Sam quickly, then back to the road. 'We call it the "Long Walk". Have you read any Kipling?'

'No,' Sam admitted foolishly. He'd never been much of a reader.

'Read *Kim*. It's a marvellous yarn and he passes right through here. *Um*ballah, he calls it. He writes about the GT Road, says it's "a river of life such as exists nowhere else in the world". You'll see what he means in a moment.'

Once they had turned on to the wide road, elevated a little above the surrounding fields, they were among a busy stream of carts pulled by stoical-looking white bullocks; of horses, of men and women carrying pots and bundles, some of the men stick thin and strangely dressed, faces painted with white and coloured powders.

'Holy men,' the captain said. 'The road leads to Benares, one of the holiest places in India, on the Ganges.'

People working close to the edge of the fields looked up, their relative peace jarred by the roar of the engine. They passed one or two other cars also and waved at them.

No Daimlers, Sam noticed. A Wolseley and a De Dion – both fine models, of course, even if Daimler was the best. He was tuned in to how the car was running, almost as if it was part of his own body, and she was going well, especially now they were on a superior road. And once again, as with the railways, he thought, My goodness, what an achievement of the empire this is, this great road, stretching hundreds, if not thousands, of miles.

'We've done them a great service here!' he shouted to the captain.

'Who?' he frowned, keeping his eyes on the road.

'Our engineer boys – putting this great road in.'

The captain glanced round, seeming amused.

'We didn't build this, you know! It was here long before we arrived. It was built three hundred years ago, or more, by the emperor of the time – fellow called Sher Shah Suri. He wanted to connect up his own provinces. We've made a few improvements, of course, but it wasn't one of ours. There was plenty going on before we got here. British people so often forget that.'

This stung. Sam felt put in his place. But of course he *had* thought of it like that: India as a backward, primitive place that they were civilizing, with engineers and soldiers and missionaries; a blank sheet to be written upon by the British Empire.

He kept being challenged to see things with new eyes, and was beginning to realize why one could become captivated. The fields spread away on either side, flat and patched with varying shades of greens, dotted with mud huts, haystacks and trees and the movement of small, colourful figures, all dwarfed by the pale arc of the sky

'It all looks so big.'

'Takes getting used to,' the captain said. 'You've been bred on a small island! You should come to the mountains.'

'I'd like to,' Sam found himself saying, to his surprise.

He felt the women listening to their loud conversation from the back and hoped he hadn't made too much of a fool of himself.

Chapter Fourteen

They happened on a picnic spot by chance, a charming spot, a clearing shrouded by several gnarled old banyans with a great many of the vine-like shoots hanging from them.

'How lovely!' Sam heard Miss Waters exclaim. 'It feels almost like a church!'

But that Fairford woman had to go and sour the moment. The captain and Miss Waters were pulling out the things they had brought from the back: a modest hamper, a tarpaulin and rug, and Captain Fairford, gentlemanly as ever, began to help spread the tarpaulin on the dry mud. Susan Fairford stood by the car, adjusting her bonnet and complaining that they hadn't thought to bring chairs. Sam was by the car, giving it a look over to check all was well, and she looked across at him and said, 'It's very strange for us, you see, to be out without the *native* servants to do anything!'

That's telling you, Sam thought. God, the insufferable snobbery of the woman! It was bad enough in England, but it seemed fossilized here. One day it would all have to be knocked down, the whole blessed system, he thought furiously. He hurried over to help Miss Waters with the tarpaulin. She was just picking up a green woollen rug to spread over it.

'Let me help.' He spoke rather sharply, because he was still angry.

'Thank you.' She stood back, as if obeying an order, and he felt apologetic then, but said nothing.

'Miss Waters – Lily!' Mrs Fairford cried, shrilly. 'You must watch Cosmo – he's already right over there, and there might be snakes! Oh, hurry up, do!'

Miss Waters looked dismayed. The boy had already toddled off some distance away.

'Don't you worry – I'll go after him.' In moments, Sam was beside Cosmo.

'Hello, old chap,' he coaxed. 'We're going to have cakes and lemonade. And afterwards, you could help me drive the car a little way.'

Cosmo's face lit up. 'Me drive it? Can I? Oh, *can* I?'

'We'll have to ask your father,' Sam said. 'But if I say you can sit on my lap and have a go, I expect you can drive us back to the big road.'

He had Cosmo in the palm of his hand immediately, and warmed to the child for loving something he loved too. By the time they joined the others they were friends.

Both the Fairfords were standing a short distance from the rug. The captain was enjoying the view across the fields and smoking a cheroot. The smell of it wafted pleasantly on the breeze. Mrs Fairford stood, sipping from a cup, quite near her husband, Sam thought, as if she was still preserving her rank and not wanting to sit down with the rest of them. Miss Waters, though, was seated on the rug, unpacking cakes from the hamper. Sam saw his chance and took Cosmo to sit beside her.

'I'm going to drive the motor car!' Cosmo burst out.

The smile which she gave the boy was still on her face when she looked up at Sam and it was the first full, unreserved smile he'd seen her give. Her lovely, though sometimes melancholy, features lifted, the brown eyes shone. That was the moment, he knew later, when he fell, if that's what you could call it. More like being shot through the heart with no mercy or explanation.

'You seem to have a way with children, Mr Ironside.' The smile had faded.

'I'm not sure that's true.' He sat down beside her. 'I think this young one would do almost anything to be put behind the wheel of a motor!'

She looked astonished, but delighted as well. 'You really are going to let him take the wheel! But how?'

'Oh, I can guide him.' Sam eyed the Fairfords to see if they were moving closer, but they were standing a little apart from one another in the leafy shade. Like Helen and me, he thought, startled. Not ever really close. The thought came as a shock. But he did not want to think about that: he wanted more time to talk with Miss Waters alone. Cosmo settled happily beside her and she handed him a cup to drink from.

'How long have you been with the family?' he asked.

Immediately the words were out, he sensed a change in her, as if a veil, which had been lifted just a second, came down again. He did not feel she was unfriendly, but there was guardedness about the way she spoke which puzzled him. He tried to guess her age but it would have been hard to say. Perhaps like himself, just of age?

'I've been here almost two years,' she said, stroking Cosmo's head of curls. 'They wanted a European nanny for the children, but of course, with Isadora being the way she is, they have had to keep Srimala – the *ayah*. She's been so very good with Izzy. She looked after both of them for a time – and the baby . . .' She hesitated, then, to Sam's surprise, glanced round to see if they were overheard, then whispered, 'There was

87

another child. Two years after Izzy. She died at eight months. That's why Mrs Fairford is so ... particular. They think it was water, or some milk she was given. It makes her very nervous about what they eat and drink.' Sam could see this was a plea for Susan Fairford, as if she had seen his dislike and wanted to say, she's not so bad really. 'It has made her nervous about everything.'

'I suppose it would,' he said, looking back into her eyes. God, she was lovely, that was all he could think about. Being a man, and with such slim experience of these things then, he didn't appreciate the impact of such things: childbirth, the death of a baby, or what they can build or destroy between a man and woman.

'And you like it here?'

'Oh *yes!*' She looked up from arranging little cakes on a plate edged with flowers. The way her eyes moved, that flicker of the lashes, captivated him further. 'I *do*. I liked India straight away. And I've been able to do so many things – like being able to ride. I suppose you're riding with the captain? I've never seen you.'

'No,' Sam said ruefully. 'I'm afraid I don't. Truth is, I'm frightened to death of horses. What with those stamping hooves and whipping tails and tombstone teeth – and the way they throw their heads about!' She was laughing at him now, a surprisingly full-hearted gurgle which delighted him and spread a grin across his own face. 'As for climbing on the back of one, I'd rather lie down in the road in front of a motor car. At least they have brakes and you know they'll stop if you press your foot!'

'You would hope so.' She was still laughing. 'Unless the driver has taken very seriously against you!'

'How long will you stay, do you think?' he asked.

Her face clouded. 'I suppose, only until he goes.'

Fondly, she laid her hand on Cosmo's curls again. 'He'll go to England to school, you see. He's just four – they'll send him at five or six.'

As she said the last words, he was moved to see her eyes fill with tears and she looked down, busying herself with the delicate tea plates and knives. Just then, a young brown bullock appeared on the path, followed and goaded by a small boy trailing a stick in his hand. He came upon their gathering with astonishment, turning to stare as he passed. After a few moments the boy and cow disappeared behind the trees. Miss Waters gave a faint smile again.

'There will be nothing more for me to do here.' She sighed, looking in the direction of the young native child. 'Sometimes I think their children are better off than ours.' She nodded towards Cosmo, who was already tucking busily into a cake. 'They live with their families and stay with them. Most of them, anyway. Terrible things happen to some of them, of course. All the diseases and misfortunes of life here. But at least they don't send them away to live with strangers on the other side of the world when they're hardly old enough to dress themselves.'

'It does seem odd,' Sam agreed, hearing the anger in her voice, though until then he'd never thought about it, not having mixed much with that echelon of people. He would have liked to ask her more about herself before the Fairfords came to join them, but suddenly she said, 'You have come from Daimler? There are a good many motor manufacturers in Coventry, I believe?'

'Yes – why, do you know it?'

She hesitated, just for a second, then looked calmly back at him again.

'No. I don't know Coventry. I stayed, for a very short time, in Birmingham – for a lady where I worked.'

'Ah well – of course, there you've got the Wolseley, Siddley and the Austin,' Sam began enthusiastically. 'Plenty going on there.' He was about to start holding forth the way he could when anyone got him going on motors. But he wouldn't learn any more about Lily Waters by boring her half to death, would he?

'Where's your home then? I mean, in England.'

Looking down and smoothing out the rug, she said, 'Oh, I'm from Kent, originally. But I've moved around a little. My father was a clergyman, you see, so we had parishes in various different counties.'

'Had?'

'Both my parents passed away at all too young an age.' Unlike the plight of Cosmo, this statement did not seem to rouse any emotion in her. 'That is why it has been a pleasure to me to become part of another family. I'm afraid I am really rather alone in the world.'

'No brothers or sisters?'

'I had an elder brother, but he had a weak heart. He was dead at fifteen.'

'How sad.'

'Yes, sad,' she agreed, with such melancholy that it made the pistol wound in his heart throb again. He had a terrible desire to reach out and touch her hand.

'I say – this looks good!' The captain approached with boyish glee and rumpled Cosmo's hair. Sam supposed the boy must get very tired of that as everyone seemed to do it. His hair seemed to ask for rumpling. 'I see you've started tucking in already!'

'Pater, the mech— mech-an-ic man says I can drive the car!'

The captain winked at Sam. 'Good for you!' he said

to his son, then added, 'Better if he goes with you, I'd say, at this stage!'

'But you drove here like an expert,' Sam said truthfully.

Mrs Fairford was settling herself down in a disdainful way, as if sitting on the ground was a terrible trial.

'What a marvellous spot, eh?' the captain said.

It truly was. The evening air was delicious, the sun sending sidelong rays of orange-pink light through the trees. The shifting shadows of the banyan leaves and its strange, primeval shape fell over them. Beyond, they could looked out upon the green of the paddies and the dusky edge far, far in the distance where, but for a verdant scattering of trees, the warm, flat land met the sky with no obstacle between.

Cosmo got up and skipped about, happily full of cake and not seeming to want to run too far off. The warm evening light had a calming effect on all of them. A group of four young lads passed along the path and the captain called out a greeting. The boys looked frightened at first, before he greeted them in Hindustani. Sam didn't know what he said to them but they all started grinning away like mad and called something back and they went off, laughing and chattering together. They drank tea and Captain Fairford offered Sam one of the cheroots. Even Susan Fairford, once recovered from having to slum it on the ground, seemed to mellow into a more gentle person for the moment and Sam saw her genuinely pretty smile.

It was an evening he'd never forget. There was the motor there under the trees, all shipshape with no problems and looking splendid, and this soft, caressing air, his life of streets and factories and cramped dark houses all opening out into this unexpected and wondrous world.

And beside him, a woman who he scarcely knew, but whose face and voice, whose *being* utterly captivated him. She had got right under his skin. Perhaps he should have been more frightened. Or guilty. But all he could feel was a sense of expectation as if he was fully, abundantly alive.

Chapter Fifteen

Every moment of the day now he was alert to thinking about Lily Waters and whether he might see her. It was as if Helen did not exist. All he could see was this radiant, mysterious woman's face in his mind and know his craving to be near her. He was quietly in a constant state of maddening excitement.

Two days later, something out of the ordinary happened. They had all gone to bed and the dark house was making its usual creaking, scuttling noises. Sam had slept for a time when a great commotion broke out: the sound of crying, and women's voices raised in panic. Cursing the mozzie net, he climbed out quickly and dressed. Opening the door, he heard Susan Fairford shrieking orders to the servants. She sounded quite beside herself.

'Tell the cook to get the fire going to boil water – quickly, you fool! Send for Dr Fothergill!'

Wondering if he could be of help, Sam lit the candle and crossed the main hall to the other side of the house. The sound of fretful crying was coming from the boy's nursery, and he saw Lily Waters run from the room into the neighbouring one and emerge again in seconds carrying a white cloth. She wore a silky green robe, her hair fastened in two plaits and she looked younger like that, and so sweet, to his eyes, but she was obviously frantic.

'What's wrong?' He went to her. 'Is there anything I can do to help?'

'Of course!' Urgently, she caught hold of his arm. 'You can take us to the doctor's – please, will you? He's so slow and Cosmo's so very poorly!'

'Lily, do come!' Mrs Fairford called in a distraught voice from Cosmo's room. She came to the door, her pale hair loose on her shoulders. 'Have you found Arsalan?' She didn't seem to see Sam standing there.

'Mr Ironside is here,' Lily told her. 'He could take Cozzy straight to Dr Fothergill, in the motor.'

'Will it be all right with Captain Fairford?' Sam was saying, as Susan Fairford ran into the room and snatched her son out of his bed. Even in the dim light Sam could see that the child was running a high fever.

'It's of no consequence whether it is or not!' Mrs Fairford snapped. 'He's asleep. I believe he'd still be asleep if the house caved in! Take him – now! Lily, you take him!'

'I need to dress . . .'

'No, you don't! It's dark! Mr Ironside—' For another brief moment Sam saw Susan Fairford in a different light which softened him towards her a fraction. She looked like a young girl in her nightclothes, her hair loose, frightened and vulnerable. 'Please – can you take him safely?' She looked down desperately at her limp son and put her right hand to her mouth for a second, biting on her knuckles. 'Oh God, look at him! I'm so worried. I want him to see Dr Fothergill straight away. He knows us well . . . I don't want to lose him . . .' She began to sob.

'Of course,' Sam said, feeling sorry for her. And it sounded as if Lily Waters would be accompanying him. Would she? Oh God, *please*, his mind begged.

'Do go, quickly!'

Sam ran to fetch his jacket and by the time he got back to the hall, Lily Waters was waiting with Cosmo in her arms, wrapped in a sheet. Sam was surprised to see Susan Fairford wrapping a shawl round Lily's shoulders in an almost motherly gesture.

'I should come with you – but you're better with him. You'll be calm.'

'It's all right, Susan,' Miss Waters said. 'He'll be all right. Don't worry yourself.'

In those fleeting moments Sam took in with surprise the gentle intimacy between the two women.

'Oh, look after him!' Mrs Fairford came to the door, her voice cracking as the tears came again. 'Look after my little darling!'

'You know I will,' Miss Waters said tenderly as they stepped out into the night.

And then, apart from the sick little boy, Sam found himself alone with this woman whose presence had such a powerful effect on him.

The night was a little chill, but not uncomfortable, the sky an immense field of stars. As they moved round the side of the house the *chowkidar*, a stringy fellow with a cloth tied round his head, loomed in front of them and Miss Waters spoke to him immediately so that he nodded and backed away.

'You speak Hindustani?' Sam said, admiringly.

'I've been here for some time now. You pick it up.'

Sam got the Daimler started and jumped into the driver's seat. They set off, the road lit by the clear white light of the acetylene lamps.

'You know the way?'

'Of course,' she snapped. A moment later, thinking perhaps that she had been impolite, Lily said, 'He had a

95

fit, you see. I don't even know if we should be moving him, but Mrs Fairford was in such a panic and Dr Fothergill doesn't reckon to hurry himself too much if you send for him. Sometimes he doesn't ever arrive . . .'

'I'm surprised the captain didn't wake,' Sam said. There'd been enough racket, after all.

Lily's voice came back sharply. 'He's not there.'

'What d'you mean?' The captain had been at home for dinner.

'He goes out sometimes at night.' She almost snapped the words and Sam did not like to ask any more.

The doctor's house was a mile and a half away, and for the rest of the journey Lily Waters spoke only to give terse instructions. Apart from the occasional grizzling cry, Cosmo stayed ominously silent. Once when Sam glanced at them, he thought he saw the child's eyes open, but wasn't sure. He could feel Lily Waters's worry and tension beside him.

Dr Fothergill's bungalow was a simple white building close to the road.

'You stay sitting,' Sam said gently. 'At least until we've got an answer at the door.'

In the gloom he saw her give a faint smile which felt like a huge reward.

The house was all in darkness and as soon as Sam went near the front, the doctor's watchman leaped up and started nattering at him but of course Sam couldn't understand a word and knocked the door anyway. He expected to have to get through a battery of servants before reaching the doctor but, to his surprise, when the door swung open, there stood a very substantial white man with a bushy, grizzled beard, wearing a vast pair of pyjama trousers, his hairy chest and ample belly covered by nothing but a blanket draped round his shoulders.

With one hand he held an oil lamp and with the other he was rubbing his portly abdomen in a soothing manner.

'Yes?' he boomed. 'Who the devil are you?'

'I'm Captain Fairford's mechanic,' Sam blurted, foolishly.

'*What?* Charles Fairford? Well, what the blazes d'you want? Have you come to tinker with my motor car at one o'clock in the morning? What the devil's the matter with you?' A rather abrupt belch took the doctor by surprise as he finished speaking, followed by the groan of a man plagued by dismally acidic innards.

'Their boy's here with me in the car. He's been taken ill – they said he had a fit.'

'What – young Cosmo?' Reluctantly, he was all attention now. 'Well, speak up, man, do. You should have said before . . .' Pulling the blanket closer round him he held the lamp high and came down to the car.

'So, what's up with this young fellow? Bring him into the house, um?'

He led them into a kind of snuggery, arranged with the rudimentary carelessness of a bachelor, with the usual animal trophies on the walls and very basic furnishings: chair and table, a mess of belongings and papers, a pair of boots slung to one side, a rug thrown on the floor. There was a thick smell of stale tobacco smoke.

'Bit of a pickle,' Dr Fothergill said. 'Not meant for decent company. Put him down on here.'

He swept a few brass objects off the table, and with a laborious grunt picked up a rug from a chair and spread it on the top. Sam moved to help Miss Waters as she laid Cosmo's distressed little body down on the table. Cosmo stirred and moaned, without opening his eyes.

'What's up with you, young fellow?' Dr Fothergill was gentle with him, feeling the boy's head and limbs. 'Fever, obviously . . .' he mused. 'You say he had a fit?'

'He was restless tonight,' Lily Waters told him. 'His temperature went up very fast so I stayed with him. And suddenly he just went rigid, and his eyes were rolling. He was twitching and not himself at all. And Mrs Fairford was worried.' She looked up into the doctor's eyes and saw that they shared knowledge about Susan Fairford.

'Yes,' he sighed. 'I know, poor girl. Thinks she's cursed by nature – even when she's got a fine, healthy boy here.'

Dr Fothergill listened to Cosmo's chest with the stethoscope, asked a few more questions, and seemed satisfied.

'Well, Miss, er . . .'

'Waters.'

'Of course.' He was speaking very kindly now. 'Tell Susan he'll be quite all right if he just has plenty to drink and isn't kept wrapped up too warmly. Sometimes, if the temperature shoots up like that, they can have a bit of a turn. Febrile convulsions, we call it. There's nothing else wrong that I can see. But I'll call in tomorrow. Best thing for him now will be a nice ride home to bed in the breeze. Off you go, both of you.'

At the door, he stopped Sam, laying a weighty hand on his shoulder. 'And whose employ are you in?'

'The Daimler Motor Company, sir.'

'Ah – the royal carriages.' He chuckled. 'Trust Charles! Very good, very good! Well, goodnight to you! And don't overheat that child!'

Chapter Sixteen

Things felt quite different now that they knew Cosmo was not seriously ill.

'What a nice doctor,' Sam said, helping Lily Waters into the car, where she settled Cosmo on her lap.

'He is kind really, even if he seems crusty. I think he's rather fond of Sus— of Mrs Fairford.'

Sam shut her door and stood beside her. He was still wondering about her remarks about the captain, but did not want to ask more questions. 'And you are too. You seem to be a very good friend to her.'

'She's all right, really, underneath.' She looked up at him again, and in the dim light he just made out her smile. It made him lurch inside.

He climbed behind the wheel, taken aback to realize that his hands were shaking. Nobody had ever affected him like this before.

'D'you fancy a bit of a drive – cool the little chap down a bit more?' He released the brake, longing to drive for miles on end, just so that he could stay sitting beside her.

She laughed, which made him ridiculously happy. She seemed relaxed being alone with him. Of course, they were more of the same class, he thought. They didn't have to talk up or down to each other. But was it more? he longed to know. Did she feel the way he was feeling?

'You're a funny one, aren't you?' she said. 'Any excuse to be driving this car! But Mrs Fairford will be worried.'

'Just round the block – the main cantonment road,' he persuaded her. 'We can say it was doctor's orders – it was almost.'

'Goodness – I'm in my nightclothes. I don't think Dr Fothergill even noticed!'

'He was hardly in any position to, was he? He was in his as well!'

They both laughed then, and he eased the car forward.

'It's all right, Cozzy,' Lily soothed him. 'You sleep, little love – we'll be home soon.'

Sam headed away from the Fairfords' house.

'I hope you know the way round by now,' he said. 'Or we'll be lost.' Although that would have suited him perfectly, being lost for hours in this soft night, with a thin moon up and all the stars and this bewitching woman close beside him. She was here, actually here beside him! The very air felt charged and crackling with life.

'If you keep turning left we should be all right. We'll know we're near when we see the church.'

He drove slowly, realizing that he couldn't be sure who or what might loom up into the lights. People seemed to keep odd hours in India, up and on the roads day and night. And of course he wanted the journey to last, on and on so that he could see her face lit by the pink Indian dawn. He glanced round at her for a second, but then had to swerve when some scuttling creature tore across the road in front of the car.

'Damn it – what was that?' His heart was pounding.

She laughed. It was the first time he had ever heard

her laugh like that, a carefree, young woman's laughter and, hearing it, he knew he was completely lost to her.

'I think it was a mongoose!'

Further along he said, 'It's pretty warm tonight. I don't know if I could stand the summer here.'

'Yes, from April to June it's stifling,' she said. 'But we go to Simla. Mrs Fairford likes to get Isadora up to the hills early. She suffers terribly from heat. You've seen what she's like with clothes, even in the winter!'

'She's certainly a character,' Sam said carefully.

'Mrs Fairford is ashamed of her. Always ashamed. It seems such a pity – for both of them. But they rent a nice house up there and it's much more comfortable. And when you see the hills, you'll really love India.'

'I don't know that I shall see them!'

'Surely you must, while you're here?' she said seriously. 'The mountains are so grand, and the air is cool and there are lovely woods and flowers. You can walk for miles and it's not dusty and dirty.'

She was speaking more fluently now. It felt easy being with her. As she talked, though, without being so guarded, he heard an occasional lilt in her voice. She was very hard to place.

'Where're you from again – originally?' Again he glanced round in the dark. He cursed having to drive. He wanted just to sit and look at her. They'd already been quite a way round the block and time was running out. He would have loved to pretend to get them lost to give them more time, but the trouble was that before long he would not have been pretending and there was no telling where they might end up.

'I've lived in several places. I suppose I could say I'm from Kent.'

'It's a queer thing, but when you spoke earlier I

thought you sounded – well, more like me. Touch of the Midlands.'

There was a pause. When she spoke it was as if she had closed down on him again.

'I suppose I begin to sound like whoever I'm with. Some people are like that – they take on other people's way of talking.'

'Like those lizard creatures that change colour depending on what colour the branch is they're sitting on.'

From the corner of his eye, he saw her turn to look at him.

'A chameleon?' she said. 'Yes, just like that.'

He was bursting with questions, and with feeling too, but he could see that if he kept on asking her too much she would withdraw completely. She was not an open person. She told you just enough, but no more. They drove in silence for a few moments, seeing flashes of the trees beside the road in their lights and insects swimming towards them in the beams like tiny scraps of paper. Sam's mind was racing. Here he was, alone with this astonishing woman. What did she think of him? And – the thought came as a terrible reproach – did she know he was married? He had certainly never told her, but it was just possible that Mrs Fairford had. None of these things seemed to matter when he was so overwhelmed with need for her.

'Turn left here,' she said suddenly, breaking into his thoughts. A few moments later they turned into the Fairfords' drive and Sam parked in the usual place along the side of the house. He had no idea how long they had been out or what time it was. It felt like a very long time, but must not have been as much as an hour.

He switched off the engine, leaving them in a sudden

silence, the air full of aromatic night smells. He thought she would get up to leave immediately, but she still sat.

'He's got himself well settled,' she said, looking tenderly down at Cosmo. 'It seems a pity to move him. The ride seems to have calmed him down.'

Sam reached over and very gently stroked the boy's head. Cosmo still felt hot, but perhaps less than before. Seeing his gesture, Lily Waters looked up at him and smiled. Blood seemed to pound round Sam's body. There was an answer in that smile – he knew it!

'Lily,' he said, impetuously. 'May I call you Lily? At least while we're alone?'

'All right,' she looked down then, shyly. 'And what's your name?'

'Samuel – Sam, my pals call me.'

'Sam,' she said, in a considering way, and stared ahead towards the trees in the dark garden in a way which made her again completely mysterious to him.

But here was this moment. He might never find the chance to be alone with her again. He had to say something!

'We should go inside – Mrs Fairford will be worried,' Lily said. But still she didn't move.

Her left hand was cradling Cosmo's shoulder, keeping him pressed close to her, and Sam reached round and laid his over it, stroking it with all the ardour he felt, finding the courage to look into her eyes. She looked back at him, a wide-eyed, almost frightened look.

'You're such a beautiful woman,' he told her. He wanted to say everything, all that she made him feel, but he was no good with words. 'You just have . . .' He attempted. 'You have a strong effect on me.'

'Do I?' she whispered. And still she didn't look away.

He could feel the blood pumping round his veins as if there was a giant turbine inside him, as if he might burst, or boil over, without some release.

'Dear God,' he said, barely meaning to let the words escape. 'You're so lovely.'

Impetuously he leaned down and let his lips brush hers, and still she didn't move away. She made a tiny sound in her throat, which encouraged him and he kissed her, gently. She did not resist, and as he became more passionate he felt her respond until he was completely inflamed by her. He had to tear himself away, drawing back so as not to lose control.

'God, woman,' he said. 'I love you. Do you realize?'

She was looking up at him. 'I've never—' she began, then looked down at Cosmo in confusion. 'We must take him in.'

'Where can I see you? There's never anywhere to be alone here – always someone watching . . .'

Again she stared ahead with those dark, mysterious eyes, thinking.

'After tiffin, there's often a time when everyone sleeps. The veranda at the side is usually quiet.'

'Tomorrow?' he said. 'Today now, I suppose.' He could hardly stand the thought of being away from her for so long.

Meeting his eyes, she whispered, 'Yes, all right. At three.'

Chapter Seventeen

He was so afraid that she wouldn't come.

She had told him to wait on the back veranda, overlooking the wide lawn, edged by trees which spread fronds of shade along the edge of the grass. The lawn was beautifully cut: Sam had seen the *mali* out there guiding a young white bullock which pulled the heavy mowing machine, with leather mufflers on its hooves to stop them churning up the turf. The pots of plants edging the lawn looked tired in the heat. It was just after the hottest part of the day and even the insects moved sluggishly. Sam caught the scent of the eucalyptus tree close to the house.

The household was miraculously quiet, and Hassan, the *punkah* lad, was fast asleep on his back, the rope wrapped round the toes of his right foot but hanging limp. He looked in a state of delicious comfort and Sam certainly had no intention of disturbing him.

He sat on one of the cane chairs and tried to distract himself from his inner turmoil by watching two chipmunks darting about at the foot of the tree. He was well fed after today's tiffin of cold meat and potatoes with the fieriest of pickles, but he was not in the least ready for sleep. Not when every fibre of him was on full alert to hear *her* step coming towards him!

The chipmunks were replaced by three wrangling

crows, and then he heard the door open and nothing else after could steal his attention. His blood raced.

She came round the house on tiptoe, looking down at her feet almost as if there might be glass underfoot and he saw that this was out of shyness. He stood up to greet her and at last she met his eyes and gave a smile which sent vibrations through him.

'Shall we sit here?' he suggested.

'Yes' – she spoke very quietly. 'I don't know how long I'll be able to stay.'

Sam nodded towards the *punkah-wallah*. 'He's having a good rest, anyway.'

Lily smiled with real amusement. 'Yes – that's why it's taken me some time to get Cosmo to sleep. His room is stifling!' She selected a chair, carefully arranging the folds of her deep green skirt, but sat perched on the edge, obviously not at her ease.

'How is the boy today?'

'Still feverish, but no more alarms in the night. I've put an ice pack in the bed to keep him cool. But I think Dr Fothergill was right – there's nothing more to it than a fever of sorts.'

'Oh, well that *is* good news.'

'Yes.' She looked up for a second and gave him another faint smile, but then dropped her eyes again, seeming filled with confusion. There was a terrible silence in which both of them were at a loss. But then she seemed to collect herself. Looking across at him, she said, 'How long will you be staying with the Fairfords altogether?'

'It was envisaged that I'd be here for up to six weeks. The captain has taken to the driving and looking after the car like a duck to water, so I can't imagine it will be more.' Sam kept talking, out of his own nerves. 'Strictly speaking, we ought to make a longer trip since he is thinking of taking it on tour. It can be a problem here, you see – what the roads do to the tyres, for a start. The good roads, *pukka*, I suppose they'd say here, like the Grand Trunk Road – they're made of laterite. It's a metallic material, lots of iron in it, and if it breaks up – well, you've got trouble: knife-edged bits of road that slash the tyres to pieces. And of course another thing is all those bullock carts. Get a whole train of those going along a laterite road and you've got eight-inch ruts. It's not the rainy season now, but when it comes, the water washes the ruts out and Bob's your uncle – knife edges again! Your tyres go and your inner tubes . . . We need to get out there and try it all out a bit more. And that's only one thing . . .'

He was about to launch into a catalogue of other besetting problems of dust and accumulator leakage but caught himself in time. Why was he prattling on in this crazed fashion about something a woman would have not the least interest in?

'Sorry,' he said foolishly. 'I get a bit carried away when you get me on to cars.'

But she smiled then, seeming more comfortable.

'I've heard. Mrs Fairford says you're like an endlessly babbling stream on the subject. Oh!' She blushed deeply, putting her hand to her mouth. 'How terribly bad mannered of me to repeat that! I'm so sorry!'

'It's all right,' he laughed. 'I'm surprised she didn't say something even worse. I don't think she takes to me very much.'

The look on Lily's face and her lack of denial of this made him laugh more. He didn't need her to tell him of Susan Fairford's snobbish attitude to him!

'Tell you what,' he said impulsively. 'D'you fancy a spin now?'

'You can't, can you?' she looked alarmed. 'Just take the car out as you like?'

'Don't see why not.' He was all for getting to his feet. 'Just round the roads again, maybe?'

'No – really, I can't. I'm supposed to be keeping an eye on Cosmo. Today especially. I really should be in there now.'

'Of course.' Sam sat back. 'How silly of me.'

They sat for a few more moments, talking of day-to-day things about the household, laughing about the sour-faced Mussulman cook, but Sam was in an agony. Time felt as if it was rushing by so fast and he wanted to say things to her, loving, affectionate things, but he could not seem to begin. A few moments later he saw Hassan stirring in his sleep as if he might wake. How difficult it was to be alone!

Leaning forwards he spoke to her urgently. 'Last night, Lily – what I said to you. I meant it, you know. Every word. Ever since I've been here in Ambala I have noticed you and wanted to know you better. If I was here for longer it might be different, but there isn't much time . . .'

She looked pleased, or worried, or both. But her eyes told him: she wanted him too, he knew it! God, he was in a state. It was the very look of her. And it wasn't how it had felt with Helen (whom he kept trying not to think about). Lily had such a full, graceful figure, and my goodness he'd have loved to take her in his arms, but it wasn't the same animal sort of desire he'd had before bedding Helen. That was there too, of course, he couldn't deny it, but it was more like adoration. He wanted to kneel before her, have her take his head and rest it on her full breast.

Breathing in deeply, he said, 'I've never met anyone

like you before, Lily. You must think me very forward, rude, even, but you just ... You captivate me. I don't know what else to say ...'

She was watching him intently and her face showed confusion, as if there was a struggle going on, which he could not make sense of in this beautiful woman who was at once so bold and so shy.

'You're very kind,' she said, looking down into her lap, where her hands were tightly clasped. 'You really are, Mr ... Sam. I don't know what to say. Except that ...' And she looked very directly at him, her dark eyes intense. 'You don't want to know me. I don't have any background – nothing to offer ...'

What was this nonsense she was talking? It made him feel abundantly tender towards her.

'If you're not worth knowing,' he teased gently, 'then why have you come out here to see me?'

She sighed, seeming remote. 'I don't know. Because I wanted to ... Very much.'

Sam felt like a man meeting a roe deer at the edge of a clearing: that he must not move, hardly breathe, because it would leap back at his slightest twitch. He longed to reach out and take her hand, but he held back, full of respect for her and said gently, 'Well, I'm glad of that, at least.'

She was beginning to smile, and said, 'You're not like anyone I've ever ...' when there came a moaning cry from inside, and she leaped up, murmuring, 'Cosmo! I'm sorry – I must go!' and was away along the veranda.

Her cry roused young Hassan, who sat up blearily and began to pull on the *punkah*, trying to look as if he had been doing precisely that all the time.

Chapter Eighteen

Isadora was writhing on her bed, screaming and tearing at her red, flayed skin.

'*Ayah* – the calamine lotion. Where is it, you silly girl? Oh, Izzy, be quiet, for the love of God!' Susan Fairford was close to tears as she tried to quieten her flailing daughter. '*Stop* it, Isadora! Oh, Lily, what's going to become of her?' she wailed despairingly.

Lily fetched the jar of calamine lotion and handed it to Srimala. Every year Isadora suffered terribly from prickly heat as soon as the winter was over, and these distressing scenes had repeated themselves since she was very young. Lily knew it was the time Susan Fairford dreaded the most.

'It's all right,' Lily soothed her mistress. 'You know how it is – the lotion will help a little.'

'Oh God … If we could just get up to Simla, away from this godforsaken place …' Susan Fairford sank down on the nursery chair, putting her head in her hands.

'What is it?' Lily knelt down, looking up into her face. She knew Susan well, her despair over not being able to love Isadora, her grief for the little girl whose life had fluttered away in her arms when she was only eight months old, and her sense of never being a good enough mother to Cosmo. Haunting her also was the knowledge that whatever she did or said, once he was

110

five he would be torn away from her. Susan had, over time, allowed Lily to see her at her most emotionally raw – and, as well as the children, there was the pain of her marriage.

'I don't even know where he is!' she sobbed one night, in Lily's arms when Charles had disappeared again after dinner. He had also not visited her room for any intimate contact for a long time. Susan was a woman who hungered for love and for understanding, and weeks could go by without his ever requiring such union with her.

'Charles only married me because he knew it was the form to have a wife. I was really the only girl he knew,' she told Lily when she was a little calmer. 'My brother was at Eton with him – they educated Lewis, of course. They hadn't the funds for Audrey and me. I met Charles when I went to a prize-giving. The first time I saw him he was standing under a pink blossom tree and he looked like a god! I remember I thought he was very handsome and charming, but we hardly knew each other. And I suppose he just thought I was suitable. He was supposed to choose a wife from home and I was the first resort rather than the fishing fleet.'

The 'fishing fleet' consisted of girls who caught the steamers to India for the winter season in search of eligible men to marry, and the love-starved bachelors of the army and police, the trades and civil service were all expected to take their pick. The disappointed fisher girls would have to get back on a boat home at the end of the season, still single and without prospects.

'I don't know if he even likes me, quite honestly,' Susan told Lily despairingly that night.

'Of course he does,' Lily said. She was baffled by the whole situation. 'He's always so nice to you!'

'He's *polite* to me,' Susan retorted. 'Of course, we can both put on a good show. But other than that, he'd rather be in the mess, where he's got the men round him. He needed me to have children, of course. I was his brood mare. But now he's got the son he wanted, he hardly ever comes anywhere near me. And I feel so *useless*. Some days I just can't bear the thought of life going on and on like this . . .'

Lily knew now that so much of Susan Fairford's tense, angry manner arose through her unhappiness and that there was a lonely, girlish person inside. Today she seemed close to despair.

'I'm not much of a mother,' she said flatly, staring at her lap as Srimala struggled with Isadora. 'You'd think I could manage at least to get that part right, wouldn't you?'

'Oh, dear Susan,' Lily said, taking her hand. 'Cozzy, do come and see your mater and cheer her up.'

Cosmo approached, wide-eyed. He was really more used to Lily's company and was slightly in awe of his mother, but he did as Lily bade him and came and took Susan's hand.

'I don't feel well,' Susan admitted.

'You go and have a lie down,' Lily encouraged her.

'Oh, I get so weary with it all,' Susan said, dragging herself to her feet. 'This climate, all these sicknesses. I just ache to be at home so much I think sometimes I'll die of it.'

Lily took Cosmo out on the lawn. She had a big parasol and they sat in the shadow of the tamarind trees, but unlike Susan Fairford, she mostly didn't mind the heat.

She had taken some story books and Cosmo sat

beside her on a rug, looking at pictures of animals. Susan insisted that he learn the names of British birds and flowers, although he was surrounded by an almost completely different flora and fauna. He sat in the crook of her arm saying, 'That's a robin' or 'a blackbird', as if they were wildly exotic species from another world.

Lily listened with less than half her mind to Cosmo's reading. She had come outside because she knew that Sam might appear in the quiet time after tiffin and that sooner or later Cosmo would drift off into a nap and they might be alone. And more than anything she longed to be alone with Sam Ironside.

She had never met anyone like him before, and she had certainly never felt like this before. She could think of nothing else these days: of his intense gaze which seemed to burn into her each time they met. She had felt it even before he spoke to her, the way he watched her. She loved his strong, impatient walk, and his love of the Daimler and expertise when anything went wrong. She loved the fact that he was funny and kind. That night they had taken Cosmo to Dr Fothergill's, she had felt the electric atmosphere between them and found herself more and more affected by him. But she was afraid. Anyone else whom she had even come close to loving had died or disappeared. How could she let herself feel for this man? Yet, when he declared that he loved her, her whole heart and soul longed to answer. Someone loved her! This handsome, interesting man loved her – and she loved him back! Since that night nothing had been the same and, despite her fear, she had fallen more and more deeply in love.

Of course he soon appeared. He knew she would be there, and they could not keep away from each other.

'Motor-car man!' Cosmo enthused, seeing a movement at the side of the house.

'Motor car' had been one of his first words, very precisely pronounced.

'Oh yes!' Lily said, trying not to sound too excited as Sam strode towards them.

'Hello, young fellow!' He sat down on the rug beside them and, with mock formality, he doffed his hat and added, 'Afternoon, Miss Waters.'

'Good afternoon.' She tried to sound sober but could not stop the joyful smile which took full possession of her face. He was here, at last!

They sat talking in the quiet afternoon, but Cosmo was not going to be left out.

'Story! Story!' he demanded. He loved to hear any tales of motoring exploits.

'Oh, all right then,' Sam laughed. 'Let's see now. What about the Thousand Miles Trial, eh? That was a good one! You see, Cozzy, when new cars are built they have to be put through their paces to see how fast they can go and whether they can climb hills and so on. So there are all sorts of races and trials to test them. So to test a car over a thousand miles is a very big test!'

Cosmo listened, rapt. They knew he would only understand a fraction of what Sam was saying, but he listened with absolute attention.

'Just a few years ago – nineteen hundred it was – sixty-five motor cars and motorcycles all met in Hyde Park – that's in London, Cozzy. There were Napiers and MMCs and Daimlers, of course, and all the foreigners, De Dions, Panhards, Benz . . . They all set off to do a thousand miles – west to a big city called Bristol and then north to Birmingham, Manchester . . .' He smiled at Cosmo's fascinated expression. 'And there were all sorts of mishaps, I can tell you! One fellow had the brakes fail and d'you know how he stopped his car? It was a Daimler like your pa's, as well – and he ran it backwards into a wall! And there was another good story about a Daimler: a chap called Grahame-White bust up his steering gear by running into a ditch. So, you'll never guess what he did.'

Lily was laughing as Sam talked excitedly, as much with his hands as his voice.

'Go on, tell us!' Lily said.

'Well, he needed to steer the car somehow, so he stood on the step, stuck his foot out onto the front wheel and steered it all the way to Newcastle with his boot – fifty-two miles! And d'you know what?'

'What?' Cosmo breathed, utterly captivated.

'When he got there, the sole of his boot was completely worn through.'

'No!' Lily cried. 'That can't be true! Surely no one could do that?'

'True as I'm sitting here.' Their eyes met in mutual love and laughter and Lily felt herself turn weak with longing for him to hold her, for them to kiss and while away the whole afternoon together.

'More stories!' Cosmo insisted.

Sam laughed. 'No peace with children around, is there? I suppose I'll soon . . .' But he bit back the rest of what he had been about to say: that he would soon know what it was to have a child of his own.

Chapter Nineteen

Sam knew he was in love in a way he had never experienced before, as if every nerve in his body was alert – more than alert – on fire! And with it came a tenderness which took him by surprise, and a sense of vulnerability that he, cocky, ambitious Sam Ironside felt in this woman's presence. It was like nothing he had known before. It was exhilarating and rather frightening; above all, he knew he could not let it go.

He had made clear his feelings to Lily, or he hoped he had. He gave scarcely a thought to Helen and all that was waiting back in England. It was as if he had walked into another life so very far off and different that neither one had anything to do with the other. Every moment around the Fairfords' house was charged with excitement at the thought that he might see Lily and be able to speak to her. Through the days, like a miracle, ran a refrain in his head, *I love Lily Waters, my Lily, Lily, Lily...*

The next few times he saw her after their meeting on the veranda, she was with Cosmo, or Susan Fairford. One morning he met her with Srimala and the children out on the drive with nets and she said they were going out looking for butterflies. She was dressed in pale blue and looked at him from under her hat, her eyes full of dancing life.

'I only wish I could come with you,' he said, as they stood on the drive, out of hearing of the *ayah*.

Lily looked down for a moment, then back. 'So do I,' she said softly. And her gaze sent a spasm of intense longing through him.

'Where can I see you?' he said quickly. 'I can't bear not seeing you alone.'

She hesitated for a moment, and he thought he saw a struggle going on within her.

'Outside, at the back. Late – eleven o'clock. It's the only way. We'll just need to keep out of the watchman's way.'

There was a moon that night. Sam had dinner with the Fairfords then spent the evening in an itch of impatience. At last, when the house was quiet, he slipped out of the back door and stood under one of the trees at the back of the house in the night air. How he loved that smell, he realized, breathing in deeply. Dung smoke and vegetation and the rich smell of the country's earth. He had not expected this, that he would begin to love the place as well. India was changing him into a new man.

The door opened and he heard her coming out to join him. She stopped, in the darkness, uncertain.

'Over here, Lily . . .' He had been about to call her Miss Waters.

She came to him and for a moment they strained to see each other's faces through the darkness.

'Oh God, you're here,' he said. And they couldn't hold back then, but were in each other's arms immediately. He nuzzled her cheek, seeking out her warm, full lips, stroking her face, her hair, overwhelmed by the feel of her.

'Sam,' she whispered, when they drew back for a second. 'Sam.'

'I love you.' He kept saying it because it seemed the only thing to say. 'God, Lily, I love you.'

She was silent and he realized she was profoundly moved. 'Do you?' Her voice was full of wonder. 'Do you love me? No one – not one person has ever ... I've never ...' She stumbled over the words and he was touched by her difficulty. He saw her looking searchingly into his face. 'I don't know if I know how to love. But the way I feel, Sam, it's something I've never known before ... I love you, I think. Yes, I'm sure I do!'

'Oh, my Lily,' he said. 'Lily, my sweet darling ...' And all sorts of soft things spilled from his lips that he'd never said before because he had never felt like this before, so melted and overcome.

And she, though seeming frightened and unsure of it at first, responded, holding and stroking him as if there was a deep reservoir of love in her, never used, that she was pouring out over him.

'Meet me every night, my love,' he begged her, after they had stood talking in the darkness for a long time, so softly that they had not roused the elderly *chowkidar* from his doze on the veranda. 'I can't bear a day without being with you.'

'Of course I will,' she whispered back. 'Oh, Sam – I never, ever believed anything like this could happen to me. And now it has, I never want to let you go!'

That week was the happiest Lily had ever known, like an ecstatic dream. Since Sam Ironside had come into her life, she knew she was not the same person. She had

118

allowed herself to love and to be loved. When, in their meetings in the dark garden, Sam held her and kissed her, she felt she had been reborn. Everything was lit up about her life. India, the beauty of the garden, Cosmo and her work here: all appeared intensely beautiful because of him. Because of love.

She had never talked so much with anyone. After that first night they moved further from the house and found a spot to stand in under the trees, where they held each other close and kissed and talked – of their hopes and dreams, about the Fairfords and Lily's time in India. She teased Sam about his fear of horses.

'You should learn to ride while you're here, and come out with us!' she urged him. 'There's nothing to it!'

'Not on your life!' He seemed to enjoy her teasing, was prepared to laugh at himself over his ineptitude.

He told her about his family, his widowed mother, his brothers, Alfred and Harry, and his Coventry childhood. And she drank this in, hearing about a real family, something which she idealized as the height of human happiness. And she told him about Mrs Chappell and how she came to be her companion, and about all the grandchildren because they were the nearest thing she had to family. But the rest of her past, her vanished parents and her suffering at the hands of the Hornes, she had still locked firmly behind her.

Sam, longing to know her, would say, 'But your family, your mother and father – you must be able to tell me something about them?'

And she would divert him, kissing him playfully and saying, 'Oh, it's all very boring,' or change the subject, saying, 'There's nothing much to tell.' The truth was she knew so little about her own origins that she was a closed book even to herself. And she did not want to admit that they had abandoned her. It felt so shameful. That was all she knew of her parents – that they didn't want her. What did it matter now, anyway? It was the future she wanted to think about, and now she dared to dream that she might have some of the things which she had never allowed to hope for herself: family, marriage, her own children.

After that first meeting in the garden she sat by her dressing table and looked in the glass. Letting her hair down, she brushed its thick, wavy length over her shoulders, then twisted the skein of hair and pinned it up again, smiling to herself. Her eyes glowed back at her. Had her real mother had eyes like that? she wondered. But she dismissed the thought. What was the point in thinking about it? It was now she wanted to hold on to, the sight of Sam's loving face, his passion for her and the longing she felt for him.

'You're so beautiful,' Sam had kept saying to her in wonder. 'You're the most beautiful thing I've ever seen.'

And tonight, miraculous as it seemed, for the first time in her life she felt beautiful and loved and full of hope.

Chapter Twenty

That weekend, Captain Fairford invited Sam to the Guest Night at the Officers' Mess.

'It's the ladies' night,' the captain said. 'Not at all the form for them to go in any other time! I like to go, even though Susan's not keen. I thought you might find it jolly to come along as my guest instead.' Sam couldn't help noticing that he didn't sound disappointed by his wife's lack of enthusiasm.

Captain Fairford assured Sam that he would provide him with clothes for the occasion.

'We're much of a size, you and I, aren't we? I'll get my bearer to look you out the right sort of gear. It'll be very jolly – high jinks and so forth. You should enjoy yourself.'

By teatime on the Saturday, Sam found a very good quality dinner suit laid out on his bed, with a crisp white shirt, its collar and cuffs starched rigid by the expert *dhobi*, and the studs laid carefully with them. His boots had been polished until they shone like metal. Looking in the glass, he trimmed his moustache and combed back his hair. His mind strayed, as it did so often, to Lily Waters, only a few rooms away on the other side of the house, perhaps changing her clothes for dinner also. The most lovely and arousing of pictures came to mind.

'Ready, Ironside?' He heard the captain outside the door, sounding boyishly cheerful.

'Ready!' Sam called. He found he was looking forward to this, though full of nerves, of course, about how to conduct himself. He felt quite abashed to see the captain clad in full regimentals in blue with a red trim and insignia and gold frogging at the front, with knife-edge creases and all very impressive. But as ever, he treated Sam as an equal.

'We'll take a *tonga*,' the captain said as they left the house. 'I know you're a fine driver, but we don't want anything to go amiss with the car.'

Sam concluded from this that they were in for some heavy drinking. In the lights of the house which spilled out over the grass he saw the *tonga* waiting on the drive, its bony horse dozing with drooping head.

'Listen, Ironside,' the captain said as they clopped away into the dusk. 'I haven't filled you in on plans because I hadn't made up my mind. I'd like you to stick around for another few weeks. We've more to learn on the motor car, for a start. But shortly I'm going to transfer the family up to Simla, in the hills. Then we can go on tour – for a fortnight or so. Give the machine a good working over – our own reliability trial, if you like! And I can show you the country then. India isn't the cantonment. It's a queer, artificial life we lead here and you should see something else. Are you game?'

Sam was flattered and excited. If Captain Fairford required his presence here to put the car through its paces, then who was he to argue?

'Well – yes! That'd be marvellous!'

'Splendid. This is a terrific country. We'll take in all we can – just chaps together, eh?'

Sam realized as he said it that he hadn't been imagining his relief that Susan Fairford did not want to come to the dinner.

The Officers' Mess was not as grand as he had expected, and, like the buildings housing other ranks, it looked pretty jerry-built. As they walked in they were assailed by loud, male chatter and the air smelled of smoke and whisky. The crowded foyer inside had the usual array of game heads on the wall, as did the billiard room, which the captain showed him, to one side of the door. The other officers were also in full regimental dress, a sea of blue, red and gold, and he felt conspicuous in civvies.

Other officers greeted the captain with calls of, 'Evening to you, Fairford. Brought your man with you, I see?'

Waiters were circulating with trays of drinks and Sam found himself holding a Scotch. Immediately, a round-faced, ginger-headed chap appeared beside them, all smiles.

'Pelling – this is Ironside, my mechanic,' Captain Fairford said. 'He's teaching me more than a thing or two about the workings of my new Daimler – fine fellow.' He looked at Sam, who took a mouthful of Scotch, which proved to be harsh stuff. 'This is one of my counterparts – Captain Jim Pelling.'

'Evening – Ironside, did you say?' Pelling clicked his heels together. It was like a reflex with these people. Sam braced himself for condescension, but he could see straight away the fellow was halfway genuine, and not just one of those types who looked straight through you because he sees you as socially inferior. 'Wouldn't mind your skills, old chap. Marvellous. You'll have to take me for a spin, Fairford. My goodness, if I had the funds behind me I'd get myself a motor like a shot. Bombay's the place, I gather. That where yours came from?'

'I had it shipped in,' the captain said, modestly. 'Mr Ironside came with it, all the way.'

'I *say*,' Pelling laughed, without apparent envy. 'You're really rather a maharaja, aren't you, Fairford?'

Various bods came and went and before long the signal was given and they all trooped in for the meal in the mess, which looked just as ramshackle as the rest of the building, with long tables and benches and other oddments of furniture. There were the regimental colours hung over the mantelpiece and portraits of military bods all along the walls, gonged up to the nines.

'Commanding officers through the years,' the captain said, nodding at them as they took their place at the table.

There seemed to be a whole lot of protocol attached to where they sat. Sam held on to the general sense that along the table to his left were the superiors, majors and upwards, and the other side the lower ranks, senior subalterns and so on. Some of them looked flaming intimidating, but he was determined to keep calm and not look rattled.

The meal was an extraordinary affair, though in the end Sam only remembered the beginning of it because he was plied with more strong drink than ever in his life before. Later he could only recall the end of the evening as a blur of rapscallion chaos. The meal began with something called the 'first toast', which was, in fact, a sardine on a piece of soggy bread. There followed a small helping of tinned fish, and then a roasted joint with all the trimmings, all served by the liveried native waiters. All through, Sam found he was downing copious amounts of whisky and gin, to the point where he soon scarcely knew what he was eating or drinking in any case.

'There's a rule in the mess,' the captain instructed him, early on, 'that one mustn't mention any woman's name throughout the evening. If you do, the forfeit is buying a round of drinks! Course, it wouldn't be the end of the world, old chap, but it's a matter of red faces, you see!'

Sam realized that the captain was telling him that if he slipped up, he would foot the bill, but Sam was determined not to embarrass himself or the captain. What he did notice, was that although this was ladies' night, looking along the table, noisy with the sounds of clinking cutlery and glass, and raucous, male chatter, there were in fact remarkably few ladies present at all.

'Do the ladies not enjoy the evening?' he asked. 'There aren't many here.'

Charles Fairford gave a mischievous, boyish smile. 'I think they find it rather rowdy.'

By the time they embarked on a mountainous slab of suet pudding, Sam had sat surrounded by talk of polo games and pig-sticking exploits, all of which was growing more riotous as every half-hour passed. Every so often great bellows of laughter broke out round the table, and occasional bursts of singing, and the noise in general grew louder and louder. Sam was not able to join in the conversation a great deal but by then he didn't mind. In fact, he had had so much to drink that he didn't mind anything at all. He was floating somewhere in his own head, and this changed him too. It wasn't the first time he'd been tight, not by a long way, but large quantities of Scotch made him feel more enlarged and set free. It was something also to do with being away from England, from all kinds of narrowness and keeping yourself pressed in on all sides. England, from here, seemed to him a teatime world of aprons and cake knives and small sandwiches in shadowy, velveteen parlours, all of which stopped you expanding as a man. Here, in all this racket, breathing in a miasma of sweat and booze, he was with physical, manly men who had a place in the world that they were sure of. After the pudding they were served the 'second toast', which this time was a half a hardboiled egg on the same sort of soggy bread. By then all the room was an amiable haze and Sam sat revelling in his sense of inner expansion, of becoming the new man he knew he was supposed to be.

And they weren't done then, by a long way. As they were serving the final course, he saw the mess sergeant place three decanters on the table in front of the commanding officer, a thin, moustachioed fellow.

'The toast, in a moment,' the captain told him, leaning aside from a joke he had been sharing with his neighbour with great guffaws of laughter. 'They'll send round port, Madeira and marsala – take your pick.'

Sam stuck to port when the decanters were circulated and they stood, solemnly, many, including Sam, swaying a little.

'Let us drink to the health of the King Emperor, His Majesty, King Edward VII!' And the place was abuzz with 'Hear! hear!' and 'To His Majesty!', and then the commanding officer lit up a cigar and this, apparently, gave the signal that everyone else could do the same. Charles – as Sam thought of him now – lit a cheroot, and was turning to speak to him when everything was drowned out by the most appalling racket. In Sam's sozzled state it made him jump violently. It sounded as if the place was being attacked, whereas it was in fact the military band striking up.

This was where the evening faded into a dim, dreamlike memory. The sprinkling of ladies vanished somewhere and there was a great noise of furniture being moved in the anteroom and riotous laughter. He could remember flashes of it next morning, in his rotten, morning-after state. Never, in a backstreet brawl had he ever seen anything quite like the 'high jinks' in the mess of these officers of the crown that night. It was the most gloriously appalling behaviour he could remember seeing anywhere!

'Come along, Ironside.' Captain Fairford tugged on his arm. They were both tight as ticks already and Sam was swaying like a tree in a storm. 'Can't have you sitting on the sidelines, now, can we? You come and join in, old man – one of the crowd!'

There was some game called High Cockalorum which involved leapfrogging over other men's backs and throwing each other about in a way injurious both to them and to the remaining furniture. In the midst of it, Sam fell and jarred his elbow against something and later could recall yelping with pain. There were contests with pairs of chaps wrestling on the floor, and at some stage one was being thrown about in a blanket, and glass was breaking somewhere, and Sam could remember seeing two chairs smashed to matchwood and laughing until he was sick into an umbrella stand by the door and was too far gone even to feel embarrassed.

God, it was a lark! What he remembered was the *freedom* of it, and even in his drunken state, standing to one side of the room, heady with thinking, *This is what class and money can do.* Having a position. Doing what the hell you damn well liked, like these chaps, not being pressed down by petty, small-town proprieties. It looked a bigger life, and he wanted it. God, he ached with wanting it.

After that he could remember nothing at all until he

found himself draped over the back of a moving *tonga* with someone's arm holding him firmly on board as if he were a sack of coal, the night sky passing above, blurry with stars, though none of this felt especially odd. And he was singing, in ecstasy and crying, 'Lily, my beautiful Lily, oh, how I love you!' And then he lost consciousness.

Chapter Twenty-One

'Where's the motor-car man? Where is he?' Cosmo's voice rang along the corridors where the servants were scurrying about making preparations for the move to the hills.

They were due to set off the next day, and the passages were scattered chaotically with objects that would not fit into the zinc-lined trunks: tennis rackets, a saddle, a japanned tin bath. Susan Fairford was not the most organized of people and her *distrait* approach to life seemed to infect the servants. The heat was also very intense now and everyone was irritable.

Lily led Cosmo out to the garden, narrowly avoiding tripping over a bootjack which had been left by the door.

'I expect Mr Ironside is with your pater,' she said, trying to be patient, but the truth was she was even more impatient to know where Sam was than Cosmo. This was the last whole day in Ambala before they set off for Simla and Sam would go on tour with the captain, and she desperately needed to see him. So far, apart from Sam's declarations of love for her, they had not talked properly about the future. They were about to be torn apart and there was so little time!

For once the heat was really affecting her, since she was already tense and out of sorts and she found herself unable to be patient. Cosmo's constant questions and demands had brought her almost to screaming pitch and she decided to leave the nursery where Srimala was still trying to distract a fractious Izzy from her prickly heat rashes. Even moving through the house was a relief. Perhaps she'd meet him? Dear God, where was he? She was full of doubts. Was he doing this on purpose? Did he not care for her enough to come and find her?

The morning dragged cruelly. She took Cosmo to play ball in the garden until the heat became really unendurable and her clothes were soaked. Every second of not knowing when she might see Sam was a torture to her.

'Come – we'll go in and have *limbopani*,' she said wearily to Cosmo. Homemade lemonade was one of his favourite things, so he would not make a fuss.

Back in the nursery, she at last had news that explained Sam's absence from circulation. One of the other servants had been talking to Srimala.

'Mr Ironside is not feeling at all well today,' she told Lily.

'Oh?' Lily was immediately anxious and sorry for her doubting him. 'What's wrong – it's not serious?'

Srimala was smiling mischievously. 'He is recovering from his visit to the Officers' Mess with the captain last night.'

Lily rolled her eyes. What went on at the mess Guest Nights, and quite a few other nights also, was legendary.

'Ah – that explains it.' She felt loving and peeved at the same time. Just when they had so little time left and she was so longing to see him! How could he have been so silly as to get so tight that it took most of the next day to recover? Captain Fairford always seemed to be on parade the next day however much he had drunk!

'Oh.' Srimala turned to her. 'Mrs Fairford said she

would like a word with you – I think immediately. Leave Cosmo with me.'

Puzzled, Lily gave her face a quick wash and went along to Susan Fairford's sitting room. She very seldom sent for Lily in this way. Perhaps it was something to do with their transition to the hills tomorrow?

Pushing back strands of hair from her damp forehead, she knocked on the door and Susan called to her to come in. She was sitting at her writing desk, trying to augment the effect of the *punkah* by fanning herself with a thin volume of poetry which often served this purpose but which Lily had never actually seen her open and read.

'Shut the door, Lily.' Her face was pale and solemn, unusually so, as if she had bad news to impart. Lily frowned, beginning to feel nervous.

'Is there something wrong?' she asked.

Susan Fairford gestured to her to take the chair close to her, in quite a friendly way, and sat for a moment looking into her eyes.

'Lily – I know I'm your employer, but I think we have lived enough together to be frank with one another at times. Would you agree?'

'I think so,' Lily said rather hesitantly, though she often held back from being completely frank with Susan Fairford since she felt it was not her place.

'Well, I'm speaking to you this afternoon as a friend. Last night Charles took the mechanic, Mr Ironside, to the mess dinner, as I'm sure you know. There was no problem, nothing untoward, though of course they all had rather a lot to drink and Mr Ironside perhaps is less used to it than most of the regiment.'

She stopped and looked pityingly into Lily's face. Lily's insides turned, sickeningly. What was she going to say? It was obviously bad news. Had something happened to Sam – a terrible accident on the way home? Surely if that was the case she would have heard by now?

'I had not realized that you and Mr Ironside had formed an attachment. Is this true?'

Without dropping her gaze, Lily nodded proudly. 'Yes, it is.'

'We hadn't seen it, you see. Charles heard him, on the way home, singing your praises and his own feelings rather immoderately from the back of the *tonga*.' Seeing Lily begin to smile, she leaned forwards.

'Lily, my poor girl, don't throw your heart away on this man. For heaven's sake, I'm begging you!'

Lily felt her temper flare. What business was it of Susan Fairford to tell her what to feel! She may have been her employer, but this was private business.

'I can't just stay here with you forever!' she retorted fierily. 'I love him, and Cosmo will be gone soon and I shall have to make another life ...'

'But you can't make it with Mr Ironside!' Susan snapped the words out, trying to drum some sense into her. 'For God's sake, Lily. He hasn't even told you, has he? The man's already married – his wife's at home, expecting their first child ...'

She stopped, seeing the shock, as if from a slap, spread over Lily's face.

'Oh, my dear ... My poor girl ... I'm so sorry!' Susan leaned forwards and took Lily's hand which was turning cold, as if her blood supply had been cut off.

'If he is untrustworthy in this respect,' she said gently, 'then how would you ever be able to trust him in any way? Dear Lily, I'm not trying to be selfish about your future. I just couldn't bear to see you in the thrall of a man who can't even tell the truth about the most fundamental things of his life!'

The deep hurt on Lily's face was unmistakable and painful to see. She sat utterly still, unable to speak, as if she had been felled.

Chapter Twenty-Two

'How *could* you? How could you lie to me, tell me you love me, when all the time you've got a wife?'

Sobbing, she stood before Sam in his room late that afternoon. The day had passed in a swirl of pain. Lily could remember nothing of it. And still she had not seen him, until she could stand it no longer, and just ran to his part of the house and hammered on the door, not caring now who heard her.

Sam, though still looking seedy, was up and dressed. At her distraught accusation, she saw his face fall and become stony. He hurried over to shut the door, trying to take her hand to pull her closer.

'Don't touch me!' she stormed at him. 'How could you?' Her outburst ended with a wordless cry of anguish. Her hair was loosely tied, wild strands curling round her face and hers eyes were swollen with tears.

'God, Lily, my love, listen to me. Just listen to me, *please*!' Sam took both of her hands and almost shook her, trying to make her hear him. 'I know I should have told you. I *should*. But it didn't seem real, not while I was here with you. I've never been in love before, not like this, with you. God forgive me, I married Helen not knowing what it was to love a woman, really love . . .'

His face was distraught and she stared at him, wanting to believe, to hear something that would make everything all right so that she could forgive and love him again. All those times they had gazed at each other, all that she had seen in his eyes, it had to be real. She could not bear it all to have been pretence.

'I didn't know love was like this – that it could be like this,' he said helplessly. 'And we can't let it go, Lily. How can we, after this? I'll do anything; I'll stay here in India. Let's just be together, you and me, away from it all . . .'

Just for a moment she was drawn into his persuasion, his saying to her all the things she wanted to hear. How she longed for it all to be all right, to know she could be with him! But she heard Susan Fairford's words in her mind – how could she ever trust him after this, or have any future with him?

'What are you *talking* about?' she raged at him. 'You've lied to me and now you want to lie to your wife. How could I ever be with you if you can't tell the truth?'

She sank down on the bed, her head in her hands. 'I was all right until you came here.' She could not see the misery her words provoked. 'I was settled. I've never expected much of anything because I've never had much. I had a bad start. But I've liked it here – my work and Cosmo. I felt safe and that was all I wanted. And then you . . .' She raised her distraught face to him. 'I've never loved anyone before – not like that. And you've killed it. You've killed trust, and hope, and all my life here.'

'Lily, don't.' He knelt down beside her and she saw that he was weeping. The day before it would have moved her to the core, but now she felt a terrible coldness seeping through her.

'Don't come crying to me.' She pushed him away

and went to the door. 'What on earth do you expect from me now?' She stared at his bowed head, her eyes icy and hard. 'You've broken it – everything, Sam. Keep away from me. I hate you.'

Early the next morning, in the growing heat, the assortment of carts and *tongas* required to transport the family and their belongings to the railway station began to assemble outside the Fairford bungalow. The servants hurried back and forth with the trunks and bags and other assorted objects, and the family readied themselves.

Lily had packed for Cosmo and that morning she washed and dressed him, replying mechanically to his questions. Her heart was so heavy with distress she could hardly think straight. When she had left Sam yesterday, she was in a cold fury. This morning she felt numb, a dead person with no feeling at all. Would this be how it was now, she wondered, this deadness, forever? Was it not easier just to be like this, to feel nothing, risk nothing? She was used to that, after all. Only Mrs Chappell and Cosmo, and above all Sam, had opened up places of light and need in her which she scarcely knew of and now they had been forced back into darkness again like a cell door slamming.

She did not expect to see Sam Ironside again, did not know if she could bear it if he were to appear. She knew that he and the captain would leave on their tour the next day, once the household were safely out of their way. Surely he would not show his face while she was still here?

She led Cosmo out to their waiting *tonga* and the driver was lifting the little boy aboard when she heard a low, urgent voice behind her.

'Lily!' Sam had come running out from the house, not seeming to care who saw them together. His face looked bleached and sick. 'For God's sake, don't leave me like this, woman. I love you – don't you understand? I can't go on without you! I'm sorry for not telling you, but how could I? I fell in love with you almost the moment I saw you, and I'd never have got near you if you'd known about Helen, that I was married ...'

'Yes – but now I do,' Lily said. She could not let her heart soften even for a second, watching this man she loved in such distress. It was no good. He was married and that was how it was. There could be no argument about that.

She climbed up on to the *tonga* and put her arm around Cosmo.

'Lily, *please* – I'll divorce her. I'll do anything to be with you!'

'Drive!' she ordered the *tonga* driver. '*Chelo!*'

She sat up very straight as the pony trotted away pulling the *tonga* along the drive and out into the broad cantonment road, and she did not look back.

Chapter Twenty-Three

Coventry, 1907

Sam Ironside dismounted from his bicycle to push it through the front gate and along the side of the house. Already, something felt different about the day. He had taken off his canvas bag in which he took his dinner into the works and was going to the back door, when it was opened by Mrs Blewitt, their neighbour.

'Oh, Sam – you've come 'ome just right!' she cried, flustered. 'Things are getting going all right now. She must've started after you left this morning – you're about to be a father any minute!'

'What, today? Now?' Sam pulled off his cap, bewildered. He hadn't expected this. He was hungry and tired and suddenly it all seemed to be happening frighteningly quickly. He wanted to put it all off for another day.

'Look at you, all sixes and sevens!' Mrs Blewitt was in her forties, a motherly woman with five children of her own who seldom stopped talking to draw breath. 'I'll make you a cup of tea, Sam. Mrs Rodgers is here with her. She delivered two of mine. Helen's doing ever so well.'

Sam sat waiting in the back room. Helen had made it into a neat, cosy place, with a maroon velvet drape over

138

the mantel with jugs and horse brasses arranged on it, a pretty fire screen and their chairs facing each other by the fender. As he drank his tea, he could hear Mrs Rodgers moving about on the bare boards upstairs and her voice, speaking quietly and reassuringly to Helen. Every so often there came a moan or a long-drawn-out wail of pain, but not very loud. Good old Helen, he thought, she was never one to make a fuss. He felt out of place here in the middle of this women's business. He half wished he'd stayed later at the works where everything was familiar, then felt ashamed of this thought.

'I'm surprised you don't want a drop of summat stronger,' Mrs Blewitt joked, as she passed through the room. 'My Sid always had a few stiff ones while I was hard at it!'

Eventually, after several especially agonized sounds, they heard the rasping cry of a newborn and Sam was allowed upstairs. Helen was lying back, looking plump and pale, with her hair raked back from her forehead, a broad smile on her face.

'I feel as if I've been run down by a horse and carriage, Sam,' she said with a wan smile. 'But there she is, anyway.'

In a drawer, by the bed, Sam saw the little crumpled shape of his first child. Her face was puckered, and her eyes seemed to him rather oriental.

'Beautiful, isn't she?' Mrs Rodgers said. 'A proper little maid, you should be proud.'

'She's . . . lovely,' Sam stammered, staring in astonishment. He had never seen a newborn before and could scarcely connect her with himself.

'And your wife's done ever so well. A natural, you are, Mrs Ironside.'

'I don't know about that. At least it was quick.'

Mrs Rodgers looked down at her, folding a towel. 'Well, it's not your first, is it?' she prattled thoughtlessly. 'I saw the stretch marks on your belly from the last . . . Usually takes longer the first time, of course.'

It took Sam a moment to take in what she had said. Those shiny trails on her skin – he had never known it could be anything to do with that . . . He turned to look at Helen, seeing the horrified look of shock on her face, and her stricken eyes met his.

The next afternoon, instead of cycling home he went from the Daimler works to his mother's. She hadn't heard yet that she was a grandmother, but Sam had more than this news on his mind.

'Oh hello, Sam, boy! I've baked today – come in and have summat!' Mrs Ironside greeted him. 'Can't have you looking so peaky – you don't look right these days. That's what happens if you go off to foreign parts . . . Ooh' – she stopped, noticing his expression – 'you've got summat to tell me, haven't you?'

Sam smiled wanly. 'She's had a little girl, Mom. Born yesterday afternoon.'

'A girl! Oh, now that *is* a blessing!' His mother sank down on the old settle, beaming at him. Her cheeks were moist and pink from standing over the range. 'After all you boys I always longed for a girl to dress. Not that I'm not proud as punch of my boys . . . What weight is she, Sam, and what're you going to call her?'

Sam realized he had no idea how heavy the baby was. When Helen asked him about names he'd not even thought, and said, 'Lily.' It surprised him how it just slipped out like that.

'Not sure I like Lily all that much,' Helen said. 'Couldn't we call her Sarah or Ann – something *sensible*? Not like that actress.'

Sam agreed, though the king's mistress, Lily Langtry, had not been the Lily he had in mind.

'She'll be called Ann,' he said. And then, because he'd been in a fever over it at the works all day and couldn't keep it in any more, he burst out with, 'It wasn't her first – she's had a baby before and she never said!'

His mother's head whipped round. 'What on earth d'you mean, Sam?'

Suddenly he was close to tears, and he felt a proper fool and swallowed them down. He'd sat on the side of the bed last night when at last Mrs Rodgers and Mrs Blewitt had taken themselves off, and looked sternly into Helen's eyes.

'You'd better tell me what she meant.' He had been holding on to his anger, prepared for lies and deceit, prepared to find that his wife was someone quite other than he imagined. The first thing that came to mind was Laurie, that friend of hers who was always hanging about, and he was all set for righteous fury. But what she told him, crying heartbrokenly as she choked out the words, did something unexpected to him. He couldn't sort himself out over it. It had gone round and round in his head all day.

'I'm sorry, Sam. I'm so, so sorry for not telling you.' She struggled to sit up, wincing with pain. 'I was only young. I didn't know what was happening, and he . . . Well, I was fourteen, and it was when Auntie Lou asked me to stay out on the farm at Stivichall. It was one of the men on the farm . . . He just kept talking to me, all friendly like, and showed me the horses and then one day he just, well, he *jumped* on me . . . It was in the barn . . .' She stopped for a moment, weeping shamefully. Sam couldn't move to comfort her. He just sat, watching.

'He was so big and heavy and he hurt me, forced himself on me. Made me bleed . . .' She was sobbing. 'And I didn't have any thought of what might happen – not 'til months later and my belly was all swollen up. And Mom . . . Well, you know what she's like. Considering, she was very good to me and said she knew I was too young to know what was what and I could stay home, so . . .'

Sam's eyes widened as his mind raced. 'Emma! She's yours, isn't she?'

Face running with tears, Helen nodded. 'She doesn't know. She thinks she's my cousin – like they told you. From my auntie in Liverpool. She died just before Emma was born so Mom decided that was what she'd tell everyone. She's been very good to me, in her way. Some mothers would've washed their hands of me and put me out on the streets. And I thought if you knew, you'd think . . .' She began sobbing again. 'That I was dirty, second-hand goods and you wouldn't want me.'

Sam remembered their wedding night. He had thought all that hesitation was only shyness; her not having any idea what the marital act consisted of because she was so innocent. He knew now, and from how she had been since, that it was something very different. That to her it was associated with force and fear and she didn't like it, had never really liked it with him either, even though he had tried to tell himself it was getting better.

'Mrs Rodgers saw those marks on me, you know, the little snail trails, as you call them . . . I never dreamed she'd say anything, not blurt it out like that. I didn't want you to have to know.'

He had sat, numbly, as she told him. He knew he felt things but wasn't sure what they were. But now, here with his mother, he knew he felt let down, cheated, not just by her but by his marriage. It had all been a fake, with secrets and lies in the background. And that he hadn't known what love was until he met Lily Waters and now that was lost to him forever as well.

'You should've told me,' was all he said.

'Would you have married me?' She was so plaintive, her hair all rumpled now, like a little girl's. 'I wanted to marry you so much, Sam.'

'Yes, of course I would.' He forced himself to sound kind, and he wanted it to be true, but secretly he wasn't sure if it was.

When he had spilled out the story to his mother, she sat looking solemnly at him.

'Now, Sam,' she said emphatically. 'What you've got to do, boy, is stick by her and not let this make any difference. She was young – she wasn't the first this has happened to and she won't be the last. Heaven knows, it wasn't her fault, the poor little thing. She didn't do it to hurt your pride, my boy, and you're none the worse off, are you? You've made your vows and even if this has upset you, you've got a lovely new daughter – a family to look after. Now you take yourself home, Sam, and do your best. Life has its ups and downs like this, boy. And it'll all be the same in a hundred years.'

Cycling home along the Kenilworth Road that night in the mellow evening light, Sam's thoughts were in turmoil. It was June, and warm. He had a good cycle, a

Starley, Coventry-made, of course, and pushing down hard on the pedals was an outlet for the strong feelings surging through him. He rode like a fury, batting away the tickling midges that flew into his face. Soon, though, he realized that at this speed he would get home before he really wanted to and he stopped at the Grove, a fork in the road, where he dismounted and sat down in the shade of the trees.

'*Damn* it!' he erupted, banging his fist on the ground in fury. He was too het up to care that he startled a matronly looking woman who was walking past pushing a perambulator. 'Damn and *blast* it!'

It wasn't helped by the fact that sitting there in the Grove reminded him of that picnic with the Fairfords, in the stronger Indian light but also on a still evening like this one, when he had felt so full of hope and such a sense of expansion. And he had sat talking to Lily. God, how could he have sat there so casually when she was close to him? An ache spread right through him. What he wouldn't give for her to be here now.

Pushing his sleeves up, he lay back and looked up into the leafy branches above him. His thoughts rolled over those months in India. It had been like a book in two volumes. First there was Ambala and Lily, the extraordinary miracle of falling in love, he realized, for the first time in his life. But then their leaving for Simla, and the way it happened between them was still an agony to him. Her face, when she discovered that he was married, had snapped shut, enclosing all the pain he had given her, and he had felt completely helpless, and then she was gone, holding tightly to Cosmo, and he could not reach her.

After that he had spent more than two weeks on the road with Captain Fairford and Arsalan, and it was something he would never forget. The car had fared excellently, and they had rolled on through villages and towns, camped, and stayed in cheap lodgings, gone out shooting game, and gradually wound their way to the foothills of the Himalaya with their precarious terraced cultivation, and then higher up, among the bare peaks with their gigantic screes and icy green streams. Sam saw country of a grand scale and awesome wildness that he could never before have imagined. And he felt it change him, as if the shutters of his mind had been flung wide open to let in all the sights. He understood, humbly, that there were places and people very different from what he was used to. And the captain was like a different man. Away from the routines and domestic obligations of Ambala Cantonment, he seemed to come fully alive. He spoke in a more animated way, laughed more, and Sam could see that he was in his element. He wondered if the captain even liked being married and he wondered the same thing about himself.

One evening when they had camped out in the foothills, the three of them built a fire and were sitting round it in the chill darkness. Arsalan was a complete equal to them for the entire journey. Sam's respect for his capabilities and sheer likeableness grew by the day, and he sensed that of everyone he had seen the captain with, he was most comfortable with his *syce*.

'How long have you worked for the captain?' he asked Arsalan, who was squatting on his slim legs, prodding the fire with a stick.

But Charles Fairford answered, 'Oh, Arsalan and I go right back, don't we?' He made some joking comment in Hindustani and both men laughed. 'We grew up together, you see, Ironside. Arsalan's father was *syce* to mine; they each had sons within the same year, so we were playmates, and it went on from there. We've scarcely ever been apart, except when I was at school.'

Sam saw just how much Charles Fairford could never have anything like this close understanding with his nervy, Sussex-born wife.

He looked back upon that journey as sheer heaven, only marred by his aching heart over Lily, and the thought that he might never see her again. When he boarded the liner for home it had felt like being wound in like a kite, the string shorter and shorter as they approached England's shore. Now his life was contracted back between the walls of the factory and those of their little house in Kenilworth with Helen, who, for all her solid sweetness, could never ever arouse in him the feelings he had known with Lily. It felt all the crueller that now even the wife he had left behind was not quite who he had thought.

After a time he sat up, brushing himself down, and looked out soberly across the road. He thought about what his mother had said.

'Well, pal,' he murmured to himself. 'You'd better pull yourself together and knuckle down.' Immediately he thought of the one thing that did not seem to disappoint: the motor car. He was good at his work, he knew it, and it was satisfying. At least there was something he could pour himself into, heart and soul.

Climbing on to his cycle he pedalled on more soberly than before. He had a good job, and now a family. He had responsibilities. Fulfilling those was a way of showing he was a man. He rode home, thinking hard thoughts about life's limitations. He felt doors closing in his mind.

Chapter Twenty-Four

Mussoorie, India, 1909

The night train from Delhi rocked its way across the Dun valley towards the northern railhead at Dehra Dun, which nestled between the toes of the Himalayan foothills.

Lily was travelling during the July monsoon. The rain was tippling down outside as she looked out, in the grey dawn, at the soaked green paddies stretching into the distance. She saw families crouched together under pieces of sacking, under bridges and against haystacks, anywhere they could find shelter from the relentless rainfall. Droplets blew in gusts against the train windows and ran streaming from the roof, spattering down on to the oozing mud.

The rain had brought the summer temperatures down to a manageable balminess, and in the cool of early morning Lily even felt the need to pull her shawl round her. The other passengers in the ladies' compartment were still sleeping.

Yesterday, she had left Ambala and the Fairfords for the last time. The wrench of it was worse even than she had expected. Her heart was like a heavy stone and her eyes kept filling with tears every time she thought about Cosmo on his sea voyage to England, and Susan

Fairford's distraught face when she had kissed Lily goodbye, before the *tonga* pony trotted off, taking her out along the drive for the last time.

'*Chai!*' The insistent voice of a tea vendor rang along the corridor. '*Chai, garam chai!*'

Lily quickly wiped her eyes, fumbled in her purse for a few *annas* and opened the compartment door.

'Yes – one tea, please!'

The man poured a little cup of steaming tea into a clay cup and handed it to her. She thanked him with an inclination of her head and cupped the little pot of fiercely sweet liquor between her hands. That was how she felt, like a child needing comfort.

She had said goodbye to Cosmo a week ago. They had sent him before the summer vacation so that he could spend some weeks acclimatizing on the family estate in Warwickshire, before starting at his prep school in the Michaelmas term. Accompanying him on the long sea voyage was an elderly missionary lady called Miss Spurling, who was returning to England on furlough and had offered to make herself useful on the journey.

Parting with Cosmo was an agony. For several days she had been overwhelmed with grief, as if all the losses in her life so far culminated in this one. She had made Cosmo the centre and solace of her life, especially over the past two years after Sam. Sam Ironside: his name was engraved on her heart however much she tried to cast him out. Her love for him and his betrayal of her stayed deep and raw in her. It was only by turning all her attention and affection, her need, onto Cosmo that she had been able to survive and start to imagine a future.

For these two years she had watched Cosmo develop each day, from a child of four to one of nearly six, and he was her joy. His lively body slimmed down as he grew taller, and he became agile and already a promising horseman. His face was thinner now, but his blue eyes were always full of the loving trust that she had seen in him when he first arrived. And he loved Lily. Loved and trusted her as he did Srimala, both loving, female presences who were always there. And now they had all been snatched away from each other. Lily knew she would miss Srimala very much as well, since the girls had become such friends over the years. What made it even worse was Susan's lack of faith in Uncle William, Charles's brother in England.

'Charles calls him eccentric,' she told Lily bitterly. 'I'd say he was unhinged myself.'

'He won't be unkind, will he?' Lily asked anxiously.

'Not unkind. He'll probably just forget Cosmo's there most of the time, my poor little lamb. The house-keeper will be the one who looks after him and I gather she's kind enough.'

Sipping the last of the warm tea, Lily slid the window up wide enough to throw the little cup out onto the tracks, where it would sink back into dust. From her bag, she slipped her precious pictures. Before he was sent away, Susan Fairford had engaged a photographer to take several portraits of Cosmo – and one of Isadora, which seemed almost an afterthought. And at the end, Susan said generously, 'Perhaps you would like to pose for a portrait with Cosmo, Lily? It would be something for you to keep.'

Lily was touched. She was delighted to have the picture of Cosmo, but it was also the first picture she had ever seen of herself. The two of them had been photographed in a formal pose, with her sitting, her hair arranged prettily. Susan had fastened it up for her and pinned some small white flowers in it with little pearls at their centre. For the first time, Lily had taken out the seed pearls from Mrs Chappell's velvet-lined box and put them on.

'I say,' Susan had said admiringly, feeling their warm lustre. 'Lily, you are a beauty, you know. Now it really is time you stopped looking solemn and put a real smile on your lovely face.'

Startled, Lily smiled dutifully at her. Did Susan have any idea that she still grieved for Sam? She had managed a radiant smile in the photograph, dressed in her high-collared blouse and long, green skirt, with her beloved Cosmo standing at her knee. He wore a favourite sailor suit, his hair a cloud of pale curls. Despite the solemnity of the occasion, there was just the trace of an impishness in his face, with his raised, slanting brows. It captured him excellently and Lily adored the picture. Looking at it now, she smiled, her heart aching, and kissed his face.

'There, my little darling. Your Lily is thinking of you. Oh, I do hope you're all right, my little dear, and that Mrs Spurling is taking good care of you. And you know Lily will never leave you, darling. I'll be thinking of you and I'll write to you, always.' It was the only way she had been able to manage the separation, by making this pledge. She would be there, like his guardian angel, watching over him, if only from a distance.

She sighed, carefully stowing the picture back in her bag. They were coming into the town now and the other three women in the compartment were on the move.

'I say, Minnie,' one of them urged. 'Do hurry up. We're nearly into Dehra Dun.' She pronounced it 'Derra Doon'.

Lily looked out, her stomach clenching with nerves.

She was on the way to a new post in the hills, not as a nanny this time, but as housekeeper to a Dr McBride and his invalid wife. She had applied for the job because she had liked Simla when the family spent the summer up there, the town nestling precariously in the cool of the immense mountain landscape, and she knew she was going to like Mussoorie. When she heard about the job she thought, I'll go there. I don't want to go to another family, not yet. I couldn't ever replace Cosmo. This still felt like the right decision, but she found the change terribly hard, the thought of beginning again, having to make her way so alone in the world.

She straightened her back and positioned her feet together determinedly. How frightening could a middle-aged doctor and a sick woman be, after all? Breathing in deeply, as if to fill herself with courage, she waited until the train eased its way into the tranquil railhead at Dehra Dun.

The bus wheezed laboriously up the mountain road which snaked between the dark trees, all topped with thick swirls of cloud. The rain fell and fell and twice they had to stop while the earth from landslips was cleared from the side of the road. The bus was a very recent newcomer on these mountain tracks.

Lily had eaten a breakfast of poached eggs in the railway station at Dehra Dun and now her stomach turned queasily as they switched back and forth round the bends. As they climbed and climbed, though, and the rain stopped for a brief interval and there were shreds of sunlight, she caught her first glimpses of the hill station of Mussoorie and her spirits lifted excitedly.

It's lovely! she thought, wiping the condensation

from the window. She was filled with a sense of exaltation, immediately liking it even more than Simla. She saw Mussoorie's buildings scattered across the hillsides among the trees, the dark peaks of the foothills ringed with cloud, and she felt at home. She found herself sending up a prayer that she would like Dr McBride and his wife and that she could stay on and on here with them in this little paradise in the clouds. But it seemed too much to hope that she could have as happy a situation again as she had found with the Fairfords and she was full of nerves waiting to see her new home. It seemed a good omen, though, that the rain had stopped.

At last the bus jerked to a halt and Lily climbed down, and stood at a loss for a moment before an elderly bearer approached her, a lean man in a *dhoti* with a shawl wrapped round him.

In Hindi she told him what she needed and mentioned Dr McBride's name. Taking her bag, which he swung up on to the pad on his head, he beckoned to her and set off up the steep, narrow street through the town. The path was still running with water after the heavy shower and all the shop awnings were dripping and hanging with sparkling water droplets. Lily caught glimpses of the food stores, chemists and drapers of Mussoorie before they turned into a quieter side street where they had to edge round two cows which stood ruminatively obstructing the path. At the end of the street suddenly they were facing out over the mountain valley and he led her to a steep little flight of steps, from the top of which she could see over the roof of a large bungalow below.

'This Dr McBride house,' the bearer said, setting off down the steps with goat-like agility in his loose sandals.

Like most of the buildings in Mussoorie, as in Simla, the McBrides' house was perched on the edge of the mountainside with a sheer drop below it, looking out over a dark valley flecked with white flags of cloud. Across the valley was a similar hillside dotted with other yellow and white painted dwellings. At the back of the house Lily saw a tiny garden, with well-tended flower-beds. At first glance, the place looking promising.

'Come, Missy,' the bearer called her. Her young, pretty looks evidently did not qualify her as a memsahib.

A moment later, the door opened, and Lily first saw a very large, thin, curving grey dog, and behind it, she glimpsed Dr Ewan McBride.

Chapter Twenty-Five

'Miss Waters, I presume?'

Lily found herself facing a large, powerful-looking man. His body filled the doorway and the main impression she had of his face was of two stone-grey eyes and a thick, grizzled beard.

'It's all right' – he glanced down at the dog – 'this is Cameron. He won't hurt you. Wolfhounds are very gentle creatures.'

The dog did have mild-looking eyes and he seemed quite timid. She could very easily have been intimidated, however, by the imposing presence and deep-voiced Scottish accent of the doctor, but she was determined not to be overawed. She stood up, straight and self-possessed, and looked directly back at him.

'Yes, Dr McBride. I am Lily Waters. I take it you have been expecting me?'

'Expecting you?' He was suddenly irascible. 'We most certainly have! We've been expecting you for the past three days! ... Yes, yes ...' He paid the bearer off and the man trotted away, apparently satisfied. 'Come in, come in.'

'Well, I don't know why that would be,' Lily said, following him into the hall. There was a very large oil painting of a waterfall facing the front door. 'I said in my letter that I should be here on the eighteenth, and here I am.'

'So you are,' he admitted. He seemed like someone who was unused to ordinary conversation. It was strange to her after Charles Fairford's easy social manner. 'I had the fifteenth in mind. My mistake. We'll get you settled in your room, let you rest, and then we can talk about things, um? I expect you'd like some tea?'

'That would be very nice, thank you,' Lily said. She smiled, and Dr McBride attempted to smile back, which barely lifted the gloom from his face.

To her surprise, Dr McBride did not summon a servant to take her to her room, but picked up her bag and led her there himself. His portly frame blocked the light along the darkened corridor, so that she had only an impression of alternating surfaces underfoot, floorboards and rugs, and the dark shapes of pictures on the walls. He opened the door right at the end.

'There – this one's for you,' he said rather curtly. 'The tea'll be along in a few moments. Everything you need, I hope?'

Lily gasped when she went into her room. It was simple enough in itself: a wooden bed, with a rich red coverlet, its legs resting on a large bamboo mat, a small writing table and chair, an armchair and stool. Someone, to her surprise, had left a little jug of flowers on the table by the bed and she wondered who in this household would have added such a touch. But it was the view from the window which captivated her. Apart from one other house, nestling into the hillside to the left and a school below, all she could see was a wide panorama of the black mountain peaks, with puffs of white cloud hanging in the valleys between and gathered in heaped piles against the grey sky behind. Dark birds were wheeling across the white cloud. It was one of the most lovely sights she had ever seen. And this was to be the view she looked out on every day!

A shy servant girl brought her some tea and Lily sat on the chair by the window, unable to tear her eyes from the sight. Gradually the cloud thickened and the rain began to fall again until it was rattling hard on the roof. It felt cosy in the room, though it was a strange feeling sitting there wondering who else was in the house. She wondered if it was the young servant who had left her the flowers.

Soon she grew sleepy after the long hours of travel, and lay down on the bed, thinking about the doctor. He seemed a gruff, austere man and she knew she felt nervous of him, but he had not been unpleasant. Wondering what his wife might be like, she fell asleep.

Her first sight of Mrs McBride was later that evening.

The young girl who had brought her tea woke her and said haltingly that Dr McBride wanted her, if she was ready. Lily quickly washed her face and hands and followed her. She was struck by the fact that so far, this girl, who only looked about twelve, was the only servant she had seen. When asked, the girl told Lily her name was Prithvi.

'Thank you for the flowers,' Lily said.

'No, no,' the girl assured her at once. 'That was Miss Brown.'

With no further explanation she led Lily to Dr McBride's dimly lit study, where the walls were lined almost completely with shelves of books. Entering the room, she found him sitting at his desk, a curved pipe in his mouth and surrounded by a haze of sweet-smelling pipe smoke. Cameron the wolfhound was lying close to his feet. The room contained dark furniture, with thick rugs on the floor, and smelled of a combination of pipe smoke and damp dog.

'Ah, Miss Waters.' He stood up with a slight grunt and gestured at a chair in front of the desk. 'Do be seated.'

This was all rather unusual, Lily thought as she obeyed. In most households it was the mistress who dealt with the new staff, but Mrs McBride was evidently not well enough.

'I hope you're rested?' he asked, sinking back into his chair.

'Yes, thank you.' She sat looking demurely at him. She guessed his age to be about fifty. There was a silence and she wondered if she was expected to say more, but she was distracted suddenly by a loud squawk which came from somewhere behind Dr McBride's desk and a strange, chirpy voice said, 'Afternoon!' with a definite Scottish accent. Seeing her astonishment, Dr McBride smiled for the first time.

'Ah – now that's Mimi . . . Are you being a cheeky girl, now? Come – see . . .'

Lily moved to where she was bidden and found herself looking into the mischievous, beady eyes of a black, yellow-billed bird in a cage which stood on a table in a dark corner of the room.

'She's a mynah,' he told her. 'They like to mimic . . .'

'Afternoon!' the bird offered again, with such apparent spirit that Lily laughed.

'Yes, she's good company.' The doctor indicated that she should sit again. He seemed uncomfortable, glancing at her and away. Beneath his austere, clipped exterior, she saw, there was a shy man. She also sensed an odd intensity.

157

'I'd better tell you a little about us,' he began in his rumbling voice. 'You've come here as a sort of house-keeper, and that's the long and short of it really. Muriel, my wife, has been an invalid for some years now and she doesn't like to be fussed over by a whole gaggle of natives. She has a nurse, from Cambridge, and we have a cook – a Eurasian fellow, Stephen. Other than that, there's the little girl you saw who does some fetching and carrying and an older woman who comes in to clean. We get by, you see. But we felt another face was needed in the house to oversee everyone. The household has become somewhat chaotic and I'm too busy – patients to see to and so forth. Even a bit of cooking might be required – Stephen's family seem to suffer one crisis after another. Could you manage that?'

Lily was surprised by his rather humble expectations of his servants.

'I've done some cooking,' she volunteered. After all, she had looked after a family before she was ten years old – she could take on anything and master it, she knew that! But she wasn't going to tell Dr McBride such a thing. 'Though you'd have to let me know what you prefer. As for the rest, I'm sure I can help you.'

'Your references were exemplary. Done the job before, eh?'

'No, sir.' She looked into his eyes. 'I was a nanny before.'

'Ah.' He made a small coughing sound, glancing down for a moment. 'That is not a service that will be required here, I'm afraid. No, no, indeed. Anyway . . .' He stood up. 'Before we all dine you'd better come and meet my wife, and Miss Brown our nurse.'

Lily followed him along the corridor to one of the doors, on which he gave a tactful knock and opened it

158

only after invitation from a small sound from within. Inside, Lily saw that the room was a larger, grander version of hers, facing outwards with a sweeping view of the hills between the bronze-coloured curtains. In the monsoon gloom she saw the bed, quite close to the window, with a small form lying on it. She quailed inwardly at the sickroom atmosphere.

Standing beside the bed, stirring something into a glass, was a European woman whose age it would have been hard to guess, a task made the more difficult by a nurse's veil which hid her hair, leaving visible a homely face. She looked up warily at Dr McBride, as if she was afraid of being caught doing something wrong. Lily guessed the woman to be a few years older than herself, possibly as much as thirty.

'Ah, Nurse Brown – I've brought Miss Waters to meet Muriel. Miss Waters is our new housekeeper – she's come to help keep us all in order.'

'How d'you do?' she said to Lily, while busily continuing what she had been doing.

'How d'you do?' Lily replied politely. At this, a fleeting smile appeared on Miss Brown's face, and Lily felt a little more hopeful. She wondered whether to thank her for the flowers, but Miss Brown was looking away as if not welcoming more conversation.

'Muriel . . .' The doctor went gently to his wife's bedside, indicating to Lily that she should follow. 'How are you today, dear?'

Lily was horrified by the sight of Mrs McBride. She saw a tiny woman with faded auburn hair, her body in a state of extreme emaciation which made the blue eyes that looked up in greeting appear enormous in her face. She looked fragile and ill enough to snap if she was moved, but she suddenly gave a very sweet smile.

'I'm as you see, Ewan, dear. No better, no worse.'

He took her hand and perched beside her on the edge of the bed. 'Well, I'm glad no worse,' he told her. Lily watched the tender exchange between this huge, robust man and his sickly bird of a wife, feeling tears rise in her eyes.

'May I meet Miss Waters?' Muriel McBride asked faintly.

'Of course, my dear.' The doctor got up and made room for Lily to move forwards and take the bird-like hand that was held out to her. As she did so she heard the doctor say quietly to Miss Brown, 'Has she taken anything today?' And she replied, 'A little, Doctor. About like yesterday.'

Lily had never seen anyone quite so thin before. Muriel's McBride's forearms were shockingly wasted and her cheeks was sunken. Yet the eyes contained a life which seemed to beam up at Lily from this pinched-looking face.

'What a pretty girl you are,' Muriel McBride said. Like her husband, she spoke with a Scottish accent: her voice was high and thin but her tone was welcoming. She gazed at Lily for a moment, asked her name again, then said, 'And where have you come from, dear?'

'From Ambala,' Lily found herself smiling back. 'I was with an army family, but now their son has been sent home to school.'

'Ah yes, of course. And how long have you been in India, dear?'

'Four years, ma'am.'

'And you like it?'

'I do, very much.'

'Yes, I can see you do. I've liked it too. People find that hard to believe. They think it has finished me off.

But I love it. This is a wonderful town ... The mountains here ... Most beautiful ...' She trailed off, and Lily could see the nurse hovering as if waiting to end the conversation. She seemed very protective of her patient. Lily stepped back and Mrs McBride added, 'You are most welcome to our home, dear. I hope you will help look after Ewan, as I am unable to.' Then she gave a strange little smile and much more quietly, whispered, 'You'll be strong, dear, won't you?'

'Oh – yes, I hope so,' Lily said, not at all sure what this meant and feeling terribly sorry for the woman. What on earth had brought the poor thing to this terrible plight? She felt as if she had joined a very odd household.

Once they had left the room, Dr McBride commanded her, 'Come with me a moment.'

Lily followed him to the hall.

'Look, I need to tell you about your duties. After all, there isn't really anyone else to do it. Perhaps you'd care to dine with me this evening?'

To her surprise they dined in Dr McBride's study. It seemed that other than sleeping, he did almost everything else in this room. At the other end of the room from the desk were chairs and a card table which had been laid for the meal.

Seven-thirty found Lily sitting, after a wash and change of clothes, at table with Dr McBride, Cameron the hound under the table, being waited on by Prithvi, the young girl, who fetched and carried with great efficiency from the kitchen. Lily realized that she was older than she seemed, as old as eighteen, perhaps.

The food, consisting of a thin soup and some kind of

meat rissoles with barely cooked boiled potatoes, was rather poor, certainly nothing like as impressive as the food she had been used to at the Fairfords' residence, but she was very hungry by now and downed everything that was offered.

For a time they ate in silence. Even Mimi the mynah had gone quiet. Dr McBride sat hunched at the end of the table, eating with some intensity. At last he rested his knife and fork down and said, 'I know we don't run the household like many Europeans, with servants for every jot and tittle. It's not a money problem, you understand, it's just that Muriel feels safer without too many folk around in the house. You'll have to be a bit of a jack of all trades, sorting out the servants we do have, making sure they knuckle down, a bit of cleaning, bit of cooking, giving Nurse Brown a day off now and then. She won't like it, of course, letting someone else nurse Muriel. But there's nothing to nursing Muriel really – it's more a question of company, and making sure she eats a little.' Again he spoke of his wife very solicitously.

'How long has Mrs McBride been ill?' Lily ventured to ask.

'Ah, well now . . .' Dr McBride put his elbows on the table, clasping his hands, and stared at the little silver candelabra in the middle of the table. 'I'd say . . . It wasn't always anything like this bad, not until recently. Muriel is almost ten years my junior. She's forty-four . . .' Lily realized her guess of the doctor's age had been just about right. 'It's been coming on for quite a while. We never had children, you see. Couldn't seem to. And I suppose . . . Well, the beginning of it dates right back to then . . .'

Lily was disconcerted to be given such intimate detail, but the doctor seemed to want to speak.

'There's nothing wrong, you see – not medically.' He sat back, abandoning his watery dish of milk pudding, and lit his pipe. 'It's something that stems from the mind. Hard to understand.' He blew out a cloud of sweet-smelling smoke. 'In the past year she seems to have reached the point of no return. Nothing I seem to be able to do.' A tone of self-pity had crept into his voice. 'She has become like a child, utterly dependent. It does limit my life rather, I must say . . .' He looked appealingly at her then. 'It wasn't what I hoped for in marriage, I must admit . . .' There was a silence, then the dog stirred, making a small sound and the doctor seemed to recover himself.

'Sorry. My problems. Don't want to bore you with all that.'

'No, it's quite all right,' she said, feeling sorry. 'It must be very worrying.'

'Oh yes . . .' He sighed, wearily. 'Worrying – well, you get beyond worry as such. A doctor who can't heal his own wife. It's . . . Well, humiliating wouldn't be a strong enough word.'

'Heartbreaking?' Lily suggested.

Startled, he looked sharply at her. 'It's certainly that, Miss Waters. Oh yes. It's heartbreaking all right.'

Chapter Twenty-Six

Lily spent her first weeks in Mussoorie getting to know the place and people, and establishing her role in the McBride bungalow.

Her first task was to understand the working of the household and to get to meet the servants. She soon got to know Prithvi, who was seventeen and had had a life of hardship, her mother dying when she was young, leaving her to care for her sick father and two younger sisters. When her father died as well she lost hope of having any sort of dowry to marry and came to live with the McBrides. She was not educated as Srimala had been, by the Sisters in Ambala, and she seldom had much to say, but she was sweet and obliging and ready to accept instructions from Lily.

The cook, Stephen Owen, also presented little in the way of difficulty. Stephen was a very thin, anxious-looking man in his late thirties, whose hair was receding rapidly and who lived his life in a condition of spaniel-eyed anxiety. He invested everything, from his wife's evidently petulant demands to the over-boiling of an egg, with an air of tragic melodrama.

'I am not successful with junkets or blancmanges,' he told Lily woefully, the first morning they met. 'They are forever getting the better of me.' This was followed by a sigh which suggested that this was one of his life's deepest regrets.

He arrived late for work almost every day, always sprucely dressed in European clothes. Stephen's father had been an English engineer, he confided to Lily after a few days. Hubert Owen had fallen in love with a Punjabi girl who had been very pretty but not, Stephen said wistfully, of a very high caste. Nor had he been a man of honour: he abandoned the girl and Stephen grew up in Delhi in an orphanage for the illegitimate children of Anglo-Indian liaisons. He had done a series of jobs in service and had been working in the McBrides' long, thin kitchen for three years, during which, it seemed, his cooking had improved scarcely at all.

'The doctor is a man of great kindness and tolerance,' Stephen told Lily, stretching his eyes wide in his long, sensitive face. She could see that this was a plea for her to be the same.

'We'll get along very well, I'm sure,' she told him. 'But I expect there may have to be a bit of reorganization.'

That, in fact, was an understatement and she found herself surprised that the McBride house was functioning at all when she saw the chaotic state of the kitchen, the lack of any sort of order in Stephen's work, including a sheer lack of basic supplies. She knew she could get stuck in straight away and make things better, as well as helping to improve his cooking.

'The trouble is also Mrs Das,' Stephen admitted. 'She is coming and stealing things and I have never been able to stop her.'

Mrs Das was a very stout, dyspeptic widow who came in to clean for the McBrides and moved round the house muttering bad-temperedly, terrorizing Prithvi and letting out ragged-sounding belches so that it was almost impossible to be unaware of where she was at any time.

Her cleaning skills were also questionable and Lily wondered why they didn't find someone else, but realized that Dr McBride was probably easily satisfied in these areas and did not notice much so long as some sort of meal was placed before him at the right times of day.

'Are you sure she's stealing supplies?' Lily quizzed Stephen.

'Sure as eggs is eggs, Miss Lily,' he said earnestly. 'I have seen her with my very eyes.'

'Well, why didn't you stop her?'

Stephen's face dropped into a study of dismay. 'I did try. But she is a very bullying sort of lady.'

'I'll speak to her,' Lily said. And we'll get some locks put on the cupboards.'

Confronting Mrs Das produced nothing but sly smiles and slippery excuses, but the locks, to which Lily kept the keys, rendered Mrs Das daily more grumpy. Lily wondered whether Dr McBride was neglecting to pay his servants sufficiently, but when she checked, tactfully, with some other households in the area, the rupees they were taking home each week seemed generous in comparison with some.

She set to work cleaning and reorganizing the kitchen and took Stephen out to the bazaar to buy supplies, something she enjoyed so much that she said she would do it with him regularly.

'Oh yes, please, Miss Lily!' he said. She felt sorry for his hopeless air.

'And we'll learn to cook some new dishes, shall we?' she suggested.

By the time she had been there a month, the household was running much more smoothly and the meals had improved no end. The one member of the staff whom she took longer to get to know was Jane Brown, Muriel McBride's nurse. This was partly because at first she saw very little of her. Jane Brown's hours were spent mostly in the sickroom or in her own little room opposite, which faced out to the back and so did not share the spectacular view. So far as Lily could see, she had no other life apart from looking after her charge and going out to Christchurch for the Holy Communion service on Sunday mornings. Lily, on the other hand, was off out during any spare time she had, getting to know this beautiful hill town to which she had already given her heart.

When she did encounter Jane Brown, she seemed at first a very reserved person. It began when she came into the kitchen to heat up milk for Mrs McBride.

'I'll do it if you like,' Lily offered. The first time she had been scouring pans and her hands were covered in grimy soap, but she was truly willing to help.

'Oh no!' Miss Brown said. 'No need for that. *I* attend to Mrs McBride's needs.'

All right then, Lily thought, offended by her tone. I was only trying to be helpful.

She bent her head over the big pan she was scouring out. Miss Brown stood waiting for the milk and Lily could sense her watching.

'Well, you're not afraid of hard work, it seems,' Nurse Brown observed.

Lily looked up at her. In the brighter light of the kitchen the nurse seemed a little younger than Lily had guessed. She wore a long black skirt and white blouse with a high, plain collar, with a starched apron over the top. Her figure was sturdy and well proportioned and her face was kindly, but so far she was not very forthcoming.

'No – hard work has never put me off,' Lily agreed carefully.

'A good scrubbing's well overdue in this house.' Miss Brown nodded at the blackened pan Lily was working on, then said wryly, 'I'm surprised *he* hasn't finished us all off by now. Calling himself a cook – he can scarcely boil an egg without some mishap!'

'Yes,' Lily smiled. 'He is a bit accident prone.'

This seemed to break the ice a little and gradually Miss Brown came into the kitchen more and more when Lily was there.

'How is Mrs McBride today?' Lily would ask.

At first Jane Brown gave non-committal replies: 'Much the same,' or, 'One can't expect much, I'm afraid.'

One morning, however, when Lily had been there about three weeks, Jane Brown came in when Lily was just despatching Stephen to buy the daily supplies. The nurse was obviously agitated and once Stephen had left, the room seemed to be filled with her mood. Lily's thoughts were on the next job, sorting laundry for the *dhobi* man, but she took courage and said, 'Is something wrong? Mrs McBride – is she not progressing today?'

Miss Brown whisked round from staring at the pan of milk, a furious look on her face. 'Progressing?' Her voice was full of pent-up emotion. 'Do you seriously imagine that that poor woman is ever going to be well again, you silly?'

Lily was bewildered. She had not considered that Mrs McBride would not get better even after hearing the little she knew.

'Well, I don't know,' she said hesitantly. 'I don't really understand what is the matter with her. Dr

168

McBride said there was nothing wrong with her, not medically wrong. I'm sure that's what he said.'

'The woman's dying!' Miss Brown cried. 'Slowly, day by day, she's slipping away, and there's nothing any of us can do about it. And what's worse is, she can't do anything about it either!'

Lily stared at her. 'But why?'

'Because she won't *eat*.' A tear escaped and ran down Miss Brown's cheek. There was more life in her face, suddenly, than Lily had ever seen before, a kind of terrible passion. She poured out the ordeal of her daily work. 'This milk – she'll barely manage a sip or two, though I try and try. Have you any idea what it's like to watch over someone closely when they will *not live*? To watch them lose their hold on life and yet still be alive, day after agonizing day? She started starving herself years ago, a gradual thing at first, I think, and it became a habit, a state she couldn't get out of. And now her body knows nothing else. They've tried everything – mental doctors, all sorts of cures, but nothing works. And she's in decline much faster now, day by day, and I don't think she could take food even if she wanted to.' Miss Brown brushed her hands over her apron in a gesture of nervous distress and wiped her wet cheek. 'She was a nurse herself, you know, trained in Edinburgh.' Her tears flowed again and Lily sensed they had been stored up for a long time. 'Nothing works properly . . . Her body . . . It's like walking to Calvary with her every single day.' She put her face in her hands and for a moment gave way to her grief.

Lily felt deeply affected by what she was hearing. She had seen the starving poor in India, the scrawny beggars in Ambala, but she had never heard of anyone starving themselves to death deliberately. She was also moved by the sight of this reserved woman breaking down in front of her.

'How terrible,' she said, tears in her own eyes. She had been touched by the sight of Mrs McBride, even when she knew nothing. Now she found her plight deeply upsetting.

'Yes, well...' Miss Brown became brisk now, ashamed of her outburst. She wiped her eyes and poured the warm milk into a cup. 'Mustn't give way. Sorry about that.'

'But it's so very sad,' Lily said. 'You have a very difficult job.'

'Yes.' Miss Brown seemed pleased to hear this acknowledged. 'I do. A slow crucifixion, as I say. Such a life they used to have, I've heard, parties, the high life. He lives like a recluse now – they both do. It's a terrible thing. But one doesn't desert one's post. I certainly shan't leave her.'

Without another word she took the milk and left.

After that, Lily found herself thinking a good deal about Muriel McBride.

Whenever she could get out and have some time to herself, she went walking in between the monsoon showers, loving being outside with the immense mountain panorama spread out before her. The weather had a dramatic character all of its own, changing by the moment so that every time she looked out across the mountains there was something different to see. The clouds were constantly on the move. Sometimes the valleys were dotted with diaphanous white, at others filled with grey, boiling heaps of cloud and the rain would come down in an almost solid mass, followed by sunshine, when the colours leaped out from every rock and bush, the blue sky seemed a miracle and every leaf and flower gleamed with drops.

The main centres of Mussoorie were like two lively little towns, Kulri Bazaar and Library Chowk, joined by the Mall, a straight walkway cut along the mountainside. But there was another route between the two, the Camel's Back Road, which made a winding loop from a point not far from the McBride bungalow for roughly two miles to Library Chowk. It was Lily's very favourite walk, quiet and beautiful, the houses perched on the hill to her left and the dark conifers, the mountains and clouds to her right.

One afternoon, when the sun had broken through for a time, she was just about to set out when she met Dr McBride in the hall.

'Ah,' he said, in the rather austere way he usually spoke to her. 'Off out somewhere?'

'I usually go for a walk in the afternoon, sir,' Lily said. She already had her hat on.

'Splendid idea,' he said. 'Good for the constitution.'

The rain held off that afternoon. On a couple of occasions showers had begun when she was far from home and it was too late to go back, but this time she walked out into hazy sunshine. After some minutes the path took her past the Christian cemetery, its gated entrance like a small whitewashed church beside the path, the burial ground falling away down the hillside. Once or twice she had walked in there and read the names of the British dead who had given their lives to India and never returned home. It was such a peaceful place, the straight trunks of the deodars soaring above and the vivid green terraces of the hillside dotted with the gravestones and crosses of an English parish churchyard.

Two monkeys, ghostly grey with black faces, were perched on the fence. She paused at a cautious distance from them to look down. The air smelled fresh, damp and pine-scented. Today, as so often, her thoughts turned to Cosmo. She missed him with an ache that never left. Had he been here she would have helped him perch on the fence and they would have looked down together, he chattering about the monkeys, asking questions which she answered, in an endless conversation that had lasted through those years of his infancy and without which she still felt bereft. Every week without fail, she wrote him a letter, telling him little things she thought he would understand and be interested in and always sending her love, letting him know she was thinking of him. She knew she would tell him about these monkeys.

Looking out along the peaceful valley she thought how lovely it was here compared to the dusty heat and regimented streets of Ambala. She had wanted to come and forget everything, forget her past and the pain of her brief, but overwhelming experience of love for Sam Ironside. Against her will he still came often into her thoughts as she remembered and wondered painfully whether he ever thought about her.

'Oh, Sam,' she whispered to the quiet trees. 'Sometimes I just wish you were here.'

There had never been time to talk properly, to explain things. She had been so hurt by his deception that all she could think of was getting far away from him. It was still so painful when she thought about it now, even though at times she longed for the feelings of love and happiness that Sam had aroused in her.

But that was in the past: it had to be. And she wouldn't make that mistake again, she thought, walking slowly along the Camel's Back Road. Nothing was worth that amount of pain. And no man would ever again have her heart, open and ready to be hurt.

Chapter Twenty-Seven

A few days later Lily was about to set off for her afternoon walk again. Mrs Das had been particularly disgruntled since the cupboards were now locked up and she could not pilfer rice, sugar and other staples from the kitchen. She positively creaked with complaint, like an old cart.

'What *is* the matter, Mrs Das?' Lily was stung into asking, as the corpulent woman flicked her broom ineffectively round the hall, issuing a constant stream of mumbled invective.

'Nothing is matter,' Mrs Das pronounced resentfully. 'I am saying prayers.'

'Well, they sound very cross prayers,' Lily retorted. What with her and Stephen's endless family problems, it would be good to get out of the house.

She was just heading for the door when Dr McBride came out of his study with his dog.

'Are you going for your daily walk, Miss Waters?'

'Yes, sir.' She waited, uncertain if she was needed.

He came closer. 'Have you ever been up Gun Hill?' She knew where he meant because it was from that hill that the big gun fired every day to mark the hour of noon.

'No, Doctor, I haven't.' She did not meet his eyes. 'I usually take my walk along the Camel's Back Road.'

'There's a splendid view from up there,' Dr McBride

said. 'Not so good in the rains, of course – too much cloud. But they'll be over soon and in the winter, my goodness, you'll see how lovely it is up here. From the hill you can see the really high Himalaya.' He hesitated, then said awkwardly, 'Would you care for a stroll up there this afternoon? Cameron and I would benefit from the exercise.'

Lily was startled. She wanted to say no because she enjoyed her solitary walks which gave her time to think and dream, but it would have seemed rude.

'That would be very nice,' she replied, wondering that he didn't mind being seen out in the company of a maid.

'I'll bring my umbrella, in case,' the doctor said, putting on his hat, a comfortable tweed trilby. He opened the door for her and said, 'After you, Miss Waters.'

They passed through the lively streets of Kulri Bazaar, narrow and teeming with life. There were mixed smells of incense and coffee and frying eggs and the shops selling fruit and vegetables and medicines and bolts of colourful cloth. Lily loved to see the English nannies out with children, holding their hands as they dragged along, staring at the shop windows. She knew some of them by sight now and sometimes stopped to talk.

Dr McBride raised his hat to greet people, and he seemed to know very many of them.

'I can't get far without stopping for a conversation, I'm afraid,' the doctor said. 'It's always rather slow progress.'

'Well, you're a doctor,' Lily said, not being sure what else to reply.

Dr McBride said, 'So I am,' and let out a chuckle,

which surprised her as she'd never heard him laugh before and wasn't sure what was funny.

She saw that people responded to him with deference, but also that they felt sorry for him because his wife was so sick. But she also saw, to her surprise, that he seemed to be enjoying it all. She had imagined that he was a recluse by nature, when now he seemed rather sociable. A few people registered surprise at seeing her at his side, someone unknown to most of them, but as it had been his idea she did not feel disturbed by this.

They passed along the Mall, with its ornate railings edging the drop into the valley, and its big, wrought-iron lamps. There were rickshaws moving among the walkers, and vendors selling mangoes and roasted *dal*, and the sound of horses' hooves coming from behind. A group of riders passed, out for a pleasant ride. Suddenly Lily ached to ride a horse again.

'Now – here to the right, look,' the doctor said. 'This is where we begin the climb.'

A steeply sloping path zigzagged up and up so that the Mall receded below them and they were looking down on houses which had been above them before. Soon they passed the long snout of the gun which gave the hill its name. Lily found the climb easy as she was slender and agile. The doctor, however, had to take it more slowly, and stop on some of the bends to catch his breath. The dog, who was rather old, also loped along slowly.

'You're a fit young filly, I must say,' the doctor said, catching Lily up as she waited for him. Until now he had acted towards her with a distant courtesy, but now, in his look she realized that he was seeing her as a person, not just a servant.

176

'I have been used to being active,' she said, feeling her cheeks glowing with the exercise.

'How so?' he asked as they walked on together again.

'Well, until I came here I was looking after a small boy who had a good deal of energy. And we used to ride out every morning. They taught me to ride in Ambala.'

'Did they, indeed? Good sort of family?'

'Yes. Very good.' She told him a little about the Fairfords.

'Not sure the cantonment life would have suited me,' the doctor mused. 'Nor Muriel, for that matter. She was never much of a joiner – clubs, and so on. She only went out really to please me, you know, do her duty. She was always rather shy and unsure of herself. Still – all in the past that, anyway.'

He stopped himself as if he had said too much. Lily was not sure what to say: her quiet presence often seemed to encourage people to talk.

'I don't know anything about you, Miss Waters,' he said suddenly. 'Do tell me about yourself.'

Lily felt her usual uneasiness at being questioned. 'There isn't a great deal to know.'

But he persisted, so she gave him the story about her father being a clergyman and moving around a good deal.

'You must miss your family, being over here alone?'

'I have no living family,' she said. 'Or none that I am close to.' She looked down at her feet as she walked, hoping to discourage any more questions.

'So what brought you to India?'

'I wanted an adventure, I suppose. To see something of the world.'

'You're a courageous young woman,' he said. 'It

takes a certain sort of person to be able to launch out on their own like that. It's something I admire.'

'Thank you,' Lily said, startled at hearing him flatter her.

Round the next bend she saw that they were nearly at the top.

'Let's see now if any of those shy peaks are going to show themselves today.'

They stood side by side at the viewing point, looking out over what would have been a vista of peaks flanked by the lower foothills, had the whole expanse not been swathed in a thick blanket of white cloud.

'Oh dear, dear,' Dr McBride laughed. He seemed unexpectedly light-hearted and she was seeing a new side of him. 'I did say this wasn't the best time of year. But I hope you've enjoyed the climb. We'll have to come back in a few weeks when the rains are over.'

'It's been a lovely walk anyway,' Lily said. The climb had filled her with a sense of well-being.

'If you like,' Dr McBride said hesitantly, 'I could show you some other places around here. I don't suppose you've been able to go very far. And you appear to enjoy a walk.'

Lily was not really sure she wanted his company as it was more relaxing to be on her own. After all, why would he want to be out and about with his servant? But she always felt obliged to please people and she did feel flattered by his attention.

Blushing a little she said, 'Thank you, that would be very nice,' assuming that he was being polite too and would forget about it straight away.

*

But he did not forget. A few days later he asked her to accompany him. Now it was late in September the rains were drying up and the days were more pleasantly warm. Lily found that her grey walking skirt and cream blouse no longer felt oppressively hot, but quite comfortable, her wide-brimmed hat no longer quite so essential.

That afternoon they walked out to Landour, a village perched along the hillside outside Mussoorie. It was a pretty walk and Dr McBride named for her the medlar and tamarind trees and oaks and flowers growing along the path. He was very gentlemanly and correct and Lily relaxed a little. Of course, the man was lonely, she realized. He didn't mean any harm. He just wanted someone to go for a walk with as his wife could not give him her company.

'Look – a redstart!' He pointed as they were standing on a high path, looking down into the green valley. Lily caught a glimpse of the bird as it flashed past.

'Beautiful,' she said politely, though she had barely seen anything.

Dr McBride turned to her suddenly and smiled, the first spontaneous and joyful smile she had ever seen him give.

'There are some beautiful sights to be seen here, indeed,' he said, looking away into the distance again. 'I've shut myself away too much these past years, and almost forgotten. I have you to thank for reminding me, Miss Waters. I had given up hope of anything better.'

Lily gave a faint smile, unsure what to say. There was a silence, until Dr McBride said, 'Your name is Lily, I gather?'

'Yes, sir.' She looked down at her boots.

'My name is Ewan. You don't need to keep calling me Sir or Doctor, you know.'

Lily felt her heart begin to thump nervously harder. Why was Dr McBride being so familiar with her all of a sudden?

'Yes, I know your name,' she said, looking up at him. 'But I am one of your servants. It would not seem right for me to call you anything so informal.'

His eyes looked deeply into hers. 'Only perhaps when we're alone, Lily?'

And his voice held a pleading tone, but it was also a command that she knew she was not expected to refuse.

Chapter Twenty-Eight

Gradually Jane Brown became friendlier. Though she did not have a great deal of spare time as her life was very tied to Muriel McBride's, she invited Lily to her room one afternoon.

'I bought cakes,' she said unexpectedly. 'I thought we might have tea, if you'd like that?'

'Oh yes!' Lily said. 'I'd love to!' She was pleased by the warmth she saw in Jane Brown's eyes. Lily realized that Jane was shy and had needed time before she could issue such an invitation. For herself, she longed to have a friend to talk to. She so missed the companionship that had grown up between herself and Srimala and also with Susan Fairford.

Jane Brown's room surprised Lily. She had imagined her to be a rather austere person, but when she was admitted to the room opposite Muriel McBride's, she was greeted by a very colourful sight. The bed was swathed in a coverlet of red, yellow and blue paisley patterns and nearby on the wall was a silk hanging in iridescent blue and gold. On other walls were small paintings on silk depicting scenes from the Hindu religious stories, one small painting on ivory and along the shelf processed a number of wooden carved elephants arranged in decreasing size. Lily also saw some prints which looked Chinese and close to the bed, on the wall, hung a wooden cross. There was also quite a collection of books.

'How lovely!' Lily exclaimed. 'You've made it look so jolly!'

'I thought I might as well make a home of it,' Jane said. 'And I like a bit of colour around me. Do sit, Lily – that's the most comfortable.'

She indicated a low wooden chair whose arms ended in a scrolling curve of wood. Lily sat and watched as her new friend arranged cakes on a plate. She was not in uniform, and had on a skirt in deep, watery blues and it was the first time Lily had seen her without her nurse's veil. Her hair was a gingery brown and rather frizzy, and she had it tied loosely in a thick ponytail. She was not a pretty woman, but there was a kindness and intelligence to her face that drew Lily to her.

'Here we are – I've got a pot of tea already made,' she said, handing Lily a cup. 'Sugar? And do have one of these cakes. They really are rather good.'

She settled opposite Lily on the bed and the two of them ate the cream cakes and began to get to know one another.

'I was wondering where you came from by your exotic looks,' Jane Brown said, gazing at Lily's face. 'You do look wonderfully unusual.'

'Oh.' Lily smiled. 'I don't know. I've been told I'm like my mother, but she died when I was very young.'

She told Jane Brown a few details of her usual version of things, and then quickly asked her about herself. Jane seemed to see that Lily did not wish to be questioned and she talked quite fluently then about her own background. She had grown up in Cambridge, where her father was a professor of Chinese history.

'Actually, I spent my first six years in China,' she said, smiling as she tussled with a dab of cream which attached itself first to her lips and then her hand. 'Daddy was researching his book – look, I have a copy here.'

She reached over for a book from the shelf and showed Lily a thick, scholarly-looking work by an author called N. E. O. Brown.

'Goodness,' Lily said. 'That looks very clever.'

'Oh, don't imagine I've read the whole thing!' Jane Brown laughed. 'I never got involved in Daddy's work. But I suppose you do get used to living abroad – it gave me my wanderlust. So when I'd done my training I applied to come over here. I was in a nursing home in Calcutta for nearly two years and then I answered the doctor's advertisement. I liked the sound of the hills and I wanted a change. Goodness ... I say, that was *nice* ...' She put her cake plate down, wiping her lips on her handkerchief.

'Yes – I liked the sound of it up here too,' Lily said. She felt comfortable and well fed after the tea and cakes and she began to relax. She told her about Ambala and the Fairfords.

'I don't know that I'd like cantonment life,' Jane said. 'It all seems a bit claustrophobic to my mind. I get the impression there's a sense of shutting out the rest of the country as if it doesn't exist ... That's what they want, I suppose.' She shifted back on the bed, kicked her shoes off and tucked her feet up.

'Yes, it does feel like a world of its own in many ways,' Lily said. 'I must say, I prefer it here.'

'Course, everyone's haunted by the Mutiny,' Jane said. 'They don't say much about it but when you think of it, how can it go on? All of us over here.'

'What d'you mean?' Lily asked.

'Well, they don't want us here really, do they? We're foreigners, trespassers. It's all absurd in a way. And we know it really – what happened back in fifty-seven – if it happened once, the natives getting up and saying "no more", it can happen again. And it will one day. Don't you think?'

Lily thought about it, the strangeness of the British being in this country somehow. She thought of the cemetery on the side of the hill. 'Yes,' she said, feeling foolish that she did not have any strong opinions. 'I suppose you're right.'

Jane Brown poured them more tea and their talk turned to the household. Lily wanted to ask more about Muriel McBride, about what had happened to her, and Jane Brown, though not a gossip, obviously needed to relieve her own feelings. She reclined sideways on the bed, leaning on her elbow, her skirt spread over her legs and talked.

'Sometimes when I look at her when she's asleep, I just boil with rage that anyone should be in the state she's in. Everyone seems to be doing all they can, but I feel as if I come up against it every day – slap!' She clapped her hands together. 'Just like running into a wall. And sometimes I'm *so* angry with her I just want to shake her and say, "Live! *Just get on with it and live!* You've been given this life and look what you're doing with it, lying here as if you're in a tomb when you're still alive." She's the sweetest person, you know, but she can't do it. She's forgotten even to *want* to live.'

There was a silence in which Lily guessed she was trying not to weep, but when Jane Brown looked up she was dry-eyed.

'I have to get out sometimes or I think I'd go mad. I tend to walk very early in the morning, while she's still asleep. I quite often see the sun come up . . . Sometimes I just . . .' She pushed herself more upright again for a moment, her eyes searching Lily's face. 'I don't know . . . I have these doubts . . .'

'What about?' Lily asked.

'About *him*. The doctor.' She was obviously troubled but could not quite identify why. 'He's such a nice man, and I feel sorry for him. It's just that now and then, the way he comes into her room, things he says . . . I almost wonder if it's him . . .'

Lily frowned, leaning forwards. 'I'm sorry. I really don't . . .'

'No.' Jane lay down again. 'I don't understand what I mean either. It's more of an intuition. But' – she gabbled the words as if they needed to be said – 'it's almost as if he likes her being so ill. As if he likes feeling in command of it all . . .'

Lily sat back, shocked. 'But how could that be? Surely you can't make someone else ill?'

Jane Brown looked thoughtful, and shamefaced. 'No – you're probably right. I'm being fanciful. It's probably being alone with her too much, because it's all so strange and awful, and I start to imagine things.' She smiled, as if shaking the thoughts off. 'Let's talk about something more cheerful.'

Chapter Twenty-Nine

As the days passed, Lily found she saw more and more of Dr McBride. He seemed unable to leave her alone. Before, when he was not out attending to patients, the house had been very quiet with the doctor secluded in his study, but now Lily kept meeting him in the hall, the corridors, walking up and down as if he was going somewhere purposefully. But it soon became clear to her that he was looking for opportunities simply to be in her company.

There were more walks, and his behaviour was always reserved and very correct, he just seemed to want to be with her, until one day, the second time they went back to climb Gun Hill. They had reached the top, able to see the high, snowy peaks of the Himalaya now the monsoon clouds had cleared. Beyond the dark foothills rose the silent white peaks, the sun shining on them.

'Oh!' Lily was enraptured. She was still panting slightly from the climb, her cheeks glowing with good health. And she had never seen anything so mysteriously beautiful.

'I knew you'd feel like that!' Dr McBride said, and she felt him gazing intently at her face. She didn't turn to look back, but a moment later he clasped her hand, holding it in both of his. 'Oh, my dear girl, you really are so exotic – such a rare flower!'

Lily froze and Dr McBride swiftly let go of her hand.

'I'm sorry, my dear. I just ... But you really are lovely.'

'It's very kind of you, Dr McBride,' she said breathlessly. She did not know what to do: she mustn't offend him, she thought. She might lose her job and be sent away! She gave him a careful smile. 'I don't know what to say.'

'I know. I apologize.' Seeming embarrassed, he looked away at the sweeping mountains laid out before them, thoughtfully stroking his thick beard. 'Perhaps it's something to do with being up here. Some of the highest peaks in the world over there – Everest, of course. They call it the roof of the world, Lily ...' He turned back to her, then away. 'Oh, good God,' she heard him say. Then, with an effort, he said soberly, 'It won't happen again.'

As they walked back, she accompanying his long stride, he seemed restored and talked about the things they could see around them. Lily was relieved. How could he expect that she could feel anything for him? He was twice her age and a married man, and there was a great gulf between them when it came to class and upbringing. He was obviously lonely and suffering a temporary madness!

But that night, he sent for her and asked her, very formally, to have dinner with him. 'I dine alone night after night. It would be very pleasant to have some company. And especially –' he cleared his throat – 'if it were yours.'

As usual, he ate his evening meal in his study, and when Lily was admitted she found the small table near the window laid for two with candles burning on it. Her palms begin to perspire with nerves. But she told herself, He's lonely, he just wants some company, that's all.

'Come in, my dear, do come in.' He welcomed her at the door and once again she was intimidated by his sheer physical bulk. He was not a fat man, but built on a grand scale, and his large head and square, curling beard only increased his appearance of size.

'I'm so glad you have come, Lily. Come and sit down. Can I offer you a sherry?'

She realized then just how nervous he was of her as he ushered her to the table. On her side plate she found a single rose, deep red and still in bud.

'How lovely!' she cried, without thinking.

'For you.' He gazed at her solemnly. 'I saw it and thought of you. Your lovely face is like a mysterious, closed rose.'

'Oh, I don't think so.' She gave a slight giggle. The first sip of sherry, which she was not used to, was already going to her head. Other than the candlelit table, the rest of the room was in shadow and she felt as if she were somewhere strange and primitive, like a cave.

Dr McBride seated himself opposite her. 'Prithvi will bring us our meal in a moment, though I'm afraid it will not be much of a surprise to you. I expect you supervised Stephen in planning it?'

'Yes – we are to have mutton curry and a sweet rice mould,' she told him. 'And I think Stephen has done it all very well today.'

'I'm relieved to hear it,' Dr McBride laughed, sipping from his own glass of whisky. 'His cooking, so far, has been a little erratic. I'm not given to fussing about food, though. One has to eat to live, that's all. Though I must say, now and then it's good to tuck into something that has not been either charred or boiled to death.

188

Especially,' he leaned forwards, 'when one is in such delightful company.'

Again, Lily felt a sense of panic rise in her for a moment at what all this might mean. She put her sherry glass down, determined to keep a straight head.

A moment later Prithvi came in. She was wearing a shimmering pink sari, and waited on them with her usual demure shyness, keeping her eyes lowered and silently disappearing without any indication that she found it strange seeing Lily dining with the master.

'Can I treat you to a glass of wine?' Dr McBride asked. 'There's fresh *limbopani* as well, but I thought you might enjoy a drop of good French wine from the Rhone.'

'Oh no, thank you!' She felt rather swimmy already, from the sherry. 'I'd like lemonade, please.'

'As you please, my dear.'

They began to eat, and Dr McBride talked. Lily was glad that he did not expect much from her in the way of conversation. She took a mouthful of Stephen's curry and rice and found it to be very good, so she sat and enjoyed her meal while the doctor told her about his childhood in Edinburgh and how he had come to meet Muriel.

'It was a student prank, you see. Arthur's Seat in the dark – all that kind of foolishness.' Seeing her puzzled expression he explained that Arthur's Seat was an old volcano. 'It's in Holyrood Park, in Edinburgh, my dear. Anyway, of course I broke my ankle and when they took me to the infirmary, I met Muriel. I'd never seen her before even though I was training in the same hospital, so it all felt rather destined. Oh, she was lovely! You should have seen her – all that pale red hair, freckles and so much life in her face. Lord God . . .' He shook his head and she could see his emotions surfacing. 'How could I ever have imagined how she'd come to be ... Impossible. It's a torment watching her ...' He looked across at her, his expression pitiable, and she was touched. But she could also see that he wanted something from her and she was disturbed and flattered all at once.

'What is the matter with Mrs McBride, exactly?' she dared to ask.

'Nothing. And everything.' He sighed and sat back, holding his wine glass and unbuttoning his tweed jacket. He spoke with the creaking slowness of someone unaccustomed to talking about his personal life.

'Muriel and I couldn't have children. I know where the problem lies. Being a medical man and so on, I looked into it more thoroughly than most. There is nothing wrong with Muriel, as I've told her a thousand times. It's me. I'm infertile.' These last words came out awkwardly, as a confession of pain. 'Sometimes that's the way. So together we can't conceive. Of course, with another man she could bear a child, but Muriel is a most honourable woman and she loved me, loves me still, I do believe. But from then on, gradually, everything went wrong. We were only in our twenties when we married. Of course, the attempts at childbearing went on for a time, but then she started to eat less. It took time and no one noticed at first, until the weight began to fall off her. She spent her thirties eating like a bird. She was thin as a stick and her looks left her, I must say. She used to have a bloom to her and it just made her fade. Terrible to watch.' He took another sip of wine. Lily watched his face. She could feel herself being drawn in by him.

'I've never talked to anyone about it before,' he said.

190

'Or not in more than cold medical terms. It's something about you, Lily . . . I seem to be able to say things . . .' He gazed emotionally at her for a moment, then looked away.

'Muriel's condition is a sickness of the mind which makes people starve themselves of food, and it's very hard to understand. It's so life-denying, yet Muriel has always said she does not want to die. A year ago things became very bad and we reached the point you see us at now. I suggested we go home to Edinburgh, but Muriel begged me to let her stay here. She is afraid that they might force-feed her and she says if they did that she would hang herself. I've asked myself day and night for months whether there is anywhere else I could take her that would help. She's had help from the psychiatric doctor here – the physicians of the mind, Lily – but nothing seems to give her back the key to life and instead we have to exist in this living death, day after day . . .'

For a moment she thought he was going to weep, but he checked himself and wiped his hand emotionally over his eyes.

'For years now I've just closed in on myself. I love the woman – but she doesn't seem to love me, or herself, enough to nourish herself into life. Part of me has been dying with her. And then you come along, Lily, so alive and so beautiful, with your wonderful, living body and your face . . . God, the sight of your face. You've given me such joy, did you know? Just the sight of you each day has given me back my life again!'

'Has it?' Lily said. She felt more in command of herself now, and smiled at him. Perhaps that was all he wanted, she hoped, just to see her, if it made him feel better. 'If so, then I'm glad.'

'Glad isn't a strong enough word for what I feel, Lily.'

She jumped as he got to his feet and came round the table. He was becoming more and more passionate and he took her hand and held it to his lips.

'I adore you. I want to make you mine. I'm not just the crusty old doctor you've seen. There's far more to me than that, but it's been shut away more as every year goes by. I'd give anything for you, to be with you even a little of the time . . .'

Goodness, what was he asking her? Lily thought, panic-stricken. Was this respectable man asking her to become his mistress? Did he think she was some woman of easy virtue who would just do anything he asked? She was in turmoil, half wanting to pull her hand away, but not feeling she could because of the look of longing in his eyes, and the longing inside her which answered it.

'Lily—' He spoke urgently, words pouring from him. 'I know what I am saying to you is very shocking. But I'll lay my cards on the table. I am a quite wealthy man with a dying wife and no offspring to spend my money on. I have entombed myself in my house and my medical practice . . . I don't want to live like this any more. I'm asking you to help me find life again. I can give you so much, my dear . . . I worship you, I can make a queen of you . . . You would not lose respect, or not for long. I am very highly thought of in this town, and I am also much pitied. I have had many offers from women who feel sorry for me, but no one has ever been like you.' He paused for a moment, staring at her. 'Tell me what you want of me, darling one – you only have to ask.'

Something inside her responded to this. She was

alone in the world, with no hope of a real love or marriage, and he was offering an arrangement which she could see might be to her advantage. For the first time in her life Lily felt a real sense of strength. A voice in her answered, Why not? You have nothing to lose and a lot to gain. And amid all her calculations there was a simple longing to be loved and held and desired.

'There's one thing . . .' He sounded bashful now, looking down at his plate. 'I'm being very forward but I did say I wanted to lay my cards on the table. What I said about my inability to father a child – I know for certain that that is the case. I've performed certain tests . . . So if you were to agree to . . . to offer me love in every way possible there would be no issue. You need not trouble yourself about that.'

Lily had never heard anyone speak so directly, and felt a blush spread all over her body. She looked down, hoping that in the dim light he would not see.

'I feel a little overcome,' she said carefully. 'I wasn't expecting this. You are very kind.'

The doctor drew Lily to her feet and she obeyed. 'Please say yes, Lily. I don't think I could bear it if you turned me down.'

She made her decision in that split second. A yes to something she barely understood. Standing up, in the candlelight she allowed him to pull her close to him. He seemed so very large as he drew her against him and she was a little afraid, but she quelled her fears. She wanted things from life that she could barely name and this seemed to be a way she could get them.

'Oh, my dearest love,' he said breathlessly, and pulled her to him. A moment later she was wrapped in Ewan McBride's arms, his lips hot and ardent on hers.

Chapter Thirty

For a short time Lily thought Dr McBride was going to be satisfied with her company on the afternoon walks and an evening meal with a few kisses at the end of the evening. But as the days went by, he became more and more ardent until one evening, as Lily pulled away from him to leave his candlelit study, he said hurriedly, 'Let me come to you – tonight!'

Lily turned, hand on the door handle. 'What do you mean?'

Dr McBride was at her side again, taking her other hand. 'Let me lie with you, Lily, my darling! I'm burning for you – you can see.' A sweat had broken out on his forehead. 'I want to lie beside you and make you mine, my darling girl.'

'I've never been that kind of person,' Lily said. 'I don't ... know men.' She was trembling and for a moment she could not look at him, then she raised her eyes to see him watching her with a tender expression.

'I can see that.' He reached for her other hand and held both of hers in his, turning her to face him. She saw his face tighten with desire.

'Of course you're not, my dear. And I don't want you to think I'm treating you in a beastly way, that I have no care for you. God, Lily, I'd do anything for you. I shan't deflower you and discard you. I love you. I want to be with you and look after you.' He stared into her eyes. 'Go to your room, darling, and I'll come to you. My own is too close to Muriel. She mustn't hear anything.'

As if in a dream, she found herself obeying. Alone in her room, she lit two candles and sat on the edge of the bed. She could not seem to think properly. Nothing seemed quite real. Should she get undressed, or wait as she was?

There came a discreet knock and the doctor came inside without a word and softly closed the door. He came to her immediately, his breathing fast and heavy and took her in his arms.

'At last. Oh, at last, my dear little girl!'

Lily pressed against his large body, smelling him, sweat and tobacco and old wool, and felt his hands moving over her with increasing intimacy.

'Let's take some of these clothes off, my dear.'

He undressed her and she let him, passive as a doll, until she was standing naked and he was still fully clothed and she felt vulnerable and embarrassed. He knelt, suddenly, as if before an altar and said, 'Oh, my dear, you're so lovely.' Hungrily, he kissed her breasts, and Lily felt sensations pulse through her nipples as his tongue played over them. She felt confused. How could she feel pleasure in this when she had no love for this man?

'Lie on the bed – I must have you,' he ordered, and stood to undress himself, with great impatience, until she was confronted for the first time in her life by the sight of a naked man, fully aroused and kneeling over her. She found the sight of his body disturbing, the shadows round his belly and groin, his thick penis standing up, and she made a small sound of distress.

'Don't worry, my dear – I shall be gentle with you.

I'm not a monster. And remember, Lily, there will be no issue. There's no need to be afraid.'

But she could see that he was very aroused and he reached down so that she felt his fingers moving in the intimate parts between her legs and it was sore and made her gasp. He eased his fingers inside her and she lifted her body, moaning more from pain than pleasure, which excited him all the more.

'Oh, dear God, open up for me, Lily . . .' He moved urgently on top of her, pushing her legs apart and forcing his way into her so that she yelped at the burning pain it caused. The pain ebbed away but he felt so hard and strange moving in her, acutely excited by her. His bulk blocked out most of the light so that he was like a great shadow engulfing her and she was trapped under the weight of him as he groaned and thrust into her. It was soon over and he rolled to the side and took her passionately in his arms and to her surprise she found herself grateful for it. It was something new, to be held like that, as if she was loved and precious. Her chest began to ache, but she pushed any feelings away. It was no good thinking she could have any emotion about this. Look what had happened with Sam. She had been hurt almost beyond enduring and it was not going to happen again.

'Thank you,' Ewan McBride breathed into her hair. 'Thank you, my dearest love. Oh, you're mine now. My very own. You and I will have some times together, Lily, my love. Oh, we shall!'

Lily closed her eyes. She felt sore and stretched down below and all she could think, at that moment was, *I've survived it, then. It wasn't so bad.*

*

From then on, Dr McBride treated Lily as his lover. She dined with him every evening and he came to her room afterwards, almost nightly as well. He liked her to come to the study for dinner at exactly the same time every night and he was always waiting. One evening she was held up and a few minutes late and when she reached the doctor's study room he was standing just inside.

'Where have you been?' he demanded, and he seemed really worked up.

'Nowhere,' she said, puzzled. 'I just had to show Prithvi how to do something, that's all.

'Don't be late for me.' It was a mixture of plea and stern command. 'I don't like it. I can't stand it.'

So long as she did as he wanted, Lily saw this shy, unhappy man blossom in front of her eyes. This gave her a certain amount of satisfaction, that she could have such an effect on someone. And the doctor had quickly grown besotted with her, promising her all the things he would buy for her and places they would visit. He made her feel special, and adored, and Lily drank it in hungrily. Suddenly she felt powerful and excited. Sometimes she woke, alone in her bed, and wondered if she had dreamed the entire thing. How had this come about? And she did not know if it was a secret in the house. No one said anything, even Jane Brown, though they took tea together regularly and talked. Jane would be embarrassed to raise such a subject, of course, but Lily realized, too, that other than Prithvi, no one saw her very much with the doctor. Even so, she felt self-conscious.

One night, over dinner, she said, 'Ewan, whatever must the rest of the servants think, with me eating in here every night? Don't you worry about them telling your wife?'

The doctor sat back, lighting his pipe, looking contented and well fed.

'There's no need to worry, Lily. The only one who has any contact with Muriel is Jane Brown and she won't breathe a word even if she guesses. She'd be far too wary of upsetting her. She's a good woman, Jane is, if rather starchy. And you know,' he sat back, beaming at her across the table, 'apart from the question of Muriel, whom I obviously don't want to hurt, I find myself strangely indifferent to the idea of scandal. There's plenty of all sorts going on in Mussoorie, make no mistake. It's rather that kind of place. And too many people look for my help for them to condemn me. Blind eyes will be turned, you can be sure.' He reached across for her hand, speaking with great energy. 'I just want to *live*, Lily. God, I do. All this time, I feel as if I've been buried alive. And then you came along . . .' He smiled beatifically at her. 'Say I can come to you tonight, darling! Don't shut me out, will you?'

He had developed some fiction in his mind that Lily was the one who could decide whether to give or withhold her favours, when she felt now that in fact she had no choice.

Chapter Thirty-One

'Whoever's that?' Lily heard the gossip as she and Dr McBride swept in through the airy foyer of Mussoorie's Savoy Hotel. People didn't even trouble to lower their voices.

'It's that creature old McBride's been seen out and about with. Hadn't you heard? She's his housekeeper, I'm told, but my goodness, you can see what he sees in her! Fancy – you wouldn't have thought he had it in him, would you?'

'Well! You'd think he might be more discreet. Positively flaunting her! But she really is rather a looker, isn't she?'

The hotel was buzzing with one of the winter parties, walls festooned with green boughs, bows and baubles and the red glow of poinsettia leaves and holly, fires burning in the hearths, polished cutlery and glasses and crisp white cloths on tables laden with food and drink. Snow had fallen all across the hills outside, blanketing them in magical white and the mornings were bejewelled with icicles hanging from railings and roofs. The air was bitterly cold, breath streaming away white. On bright days the view across the hills was glittering clear, but when the fog came down, filling the valleys, everyone moved along the Mall and through the bazaars like spectres: *jhampanis* and women in saris, bearers with huge loads tied to their backs and mountain people in hats with ear-flaps appearing in silhouette out of the gloom.

It was warm and cosy inside the hotel, and loud with the sound of festive British chatter. Lily took off her wraps and shawls and they were whisked away by a smartly liveried servant.

'Come along, my dear,' Dr McBride said, taking Lily's arm. When they were out together he always seemed to want to be touching her, pulling her arm through his, or holding his hand in close contact with hers. He left no one in any doubt as to what their relationship was. And as they passed through the festive partygoers, soon finding themselves with glasses of sherry in their hands, he was greeted with cordiality but also a certain embarrassed reserve.

'Evening, McBride!' a short, whiskery man boomed at him. 'Nice to see you in circulation again, old man. Been a long time!'

'I say – Dr McBride!' This time a thin woman, with a harsh voice and inquisitive face. 'So glad to see you're still joining us, with your, er, friend! I don't believe we've been introduced?'

'This is Miss Lily Waters,' Dr McBride declared. He gave no other explanation. He knew they had been seen about together already and that the gossip was flying.

'Didn't I see the two of you at Kempty Falls a few weeks ago?' the woman shrilled. 'How very lovely it is there. So marvellous for an outing.' Lily had noticed, in all the time they had been out in public, that no one ever mentioned Muriel McBride, as if she and her condition were some kind of dirty and shameful secret.

'You may indeed have done,' Dr McBride agreed amiably. They had taken an afternoon out together to the waterfall, a beauty spot outside Mussoorie, in the glowing autumn sunshine, not long after Lily had become Dr McBride's lover. Since then they had gradually come to be seen out more and more in public.

'Lovely spot, isn't it?' the woman cooed to Lily. 'And I must congratulate you on your dress, my dear. What a marvellous design. You really are the belle of the ball tonight, I must say!'

Lily could hear the barbed tone of her voice, but she also knew that what the woman said was true. She had seen an entirely different side of the apparently austere doctor emerging. Ewan McBride liked to dress her himself, choosing the highest quality silks and velvets from stores in Mussoorie and Dehra Dun, even ordering items for her from emporia as far away as Bombay and Madras. He did have an eye for colour, and Lily discovered in herself a gift for adorning herself lavishly, flatteringly, which she had never realized before. Among her wardrobe she now had some of the most beautiful handiwork that India could offer, fashioned into European-style gowns: turquoise and gold silk from Benares, rich coloured mirror cloth from Rajasthan for a dress she had worn for the Hindu festival of Diwali – where the doctor had paraded her among the burning lights of scores of oil lamps and the firework display – Kashmiri embroidery and shawls, and dyed raw silks tailored by the best *dirzi* in the area.

Tonight she had on a long, sweeping gown in a rich cranberry and a delicate, cream, hand-embroidered pashmina. She had smoothed her hair up into a pleat and clipped tiny glass beads into it, rather as she had seen Susan Fairford wear hers, and put on Mrs Chappell's lovely brooch and seed pearls. The jewels glowed against her fresh skin. When she looked at herself in the glass she recognized that her pretty, rounded girlishness had matured into a feminine beauty which took even herself by surprise.

'Oh, my dear, you look quite out of this world.' Dr McBride seemed excited when he saw her. He stroked her cheek as if she were a marble statue. 'Oh, my Lily, you are so beautiful, my dearest child. You really have excelled yourself this time. Come now – are you ready?'

Lily realized that more and more people were starting to recognize her and that she and the doctor were becoming the talk of the town. As they went about the place some were scandalized, some kind, and some a mixture of the two. No one could fail to notice the doctor's transformation from a crusty old recluse to a cheerful socialite with the most beautiful and stylish woman in the room on his arm.

They were much less sure how to deal with Lily, though. As his consort, she smiled at the doctor's side, looking gorgeously attractive but being quiet and reserved. All her life she had never welcomed questions about her background or her past. She did not fit into a normal social mould in any case and now they were scandalizing such moulds by her acting blatantly as his mistress. The other women had to decide whether to be envious or to make a friend of her, but the doctor, it seemed, was indifferent.

'You don't need to worry,' he had said one evening as they rode along the moonlit Mall in a rickshaw on the way back from a party. In the distance Lily caught sight of the white peaks, lit by the moon. The doctor was in a relaxed mood after several whiskies. 'I've told you, I have high standing in the town and despite my outraging some of the more, let's say puritanical types, they'll just have to accept me. I've lived like a dead man long enough. And besides, I've attended most of them at their bedsides over the years and they know it. They're grateful. So you don't need to be afraid. Why don't you just tell them about yourself? Come to that, why don't you tell *me*, to start with?'

'Oh, Ewan.' She rested her gloved hand on his and smiled at him. 'I've told you – there's nothing to say of any note. I'm a vicar's daughter who became a nanny and came to India. That's all.'

'Well,' he chuckled. 'You don't *behave* much like a vicar's daughter, I must say. Or perhaps you do.' He nuzzled his face up close to hers, searching out her lips. 'Perhaps they're the naughtiest of the lot!'

After he had kissed her he drew back and in the dim light she saw his face harden. 'You're not *fast*, are you?' His tone was nasty. 'Giving favours to anyone who asks?'

'*No!*' she said, appalled. What on earth made him say that? 'I'm not. You know I'm not!'

'Well, I hope so. Let's keep it that way, hm?' Lily was chilled by the tone of his voice. Every so often he had these little bouts of jealousy over things he imagined she might be doing. They were all in his mind, but she was stung by the way he talked to her.

She stayed at his side throughout the evening, eating some of the Anglo-Indian mix of food: mutton and poached salmon accompanied by chicken pilau and pickles. Lily was the doctor's decoration: the conversations, the decisions about where in the room they moved or sat, were all his. Sometimes one of the young women who had decided to be friendly would come up and talk to her and Lily found she enjoyed the company, but if Ewan McBride decided to move she would have to cut short her conversation. She had to sit with people he wanted to be with, who were usually older, and she was often bored, but she told herself this was the price she had to pay. It was her job. She had a fine life, lovely clothes and status as a beautiful woman to be looked at. The doctor had told her to cut down on her work in the house, to preserve her energy and keep her hands smooth and soft. She was barely more than his mistress now. But at times she felt terribly lonely and went to the kitchen to talk to Stephen and Prithvi. If it was not for them and Jane Brown her life would have been really very solitary.

She followed the doctor round the room, exchanging pleasantries. The party included some singing of Christmas carols round the piano, led by a plump woman in a crimson dress who was an accomplished player and good at jollying everyone along. The doctor steered Lily into the carousing huddle just as 'I Saw Three Ships' was coming to a lusty end with clapping and cries of, 'Encore!' and 'Marvellous. I say, it does make one long for home!' There was a moment of confusion during which someone pushed in and positioned himself somehow between Lily and the doctor, who had to step aside for politeness sake.

'How about "Good King Wenceslas"?' the pianist cried, and everyone joined in enthusiastically, except Lily, who had no idea of the words. She stood among the crowd, the air laced with smoke and whisky fumes, pretending to mouth the carol and hoping no one would notice. But someone did.

'Would one of these be any help?' a voice said close to her ear, and she turned to see a fair-haired young man in a well-cut suit smilingly offering her a sheet with some of the words on it and little drawings of bells and holly printed in the corners.

'Oh – thank you!' she said, startled. 'Is it so obvious I don't know it?'

'Oh no, not at all,' he assured her. 'I suppose I'm just rather good at lip-reading, that's all! What you're mouthing doesn't seem to correspond all that well. Nothing to worry about, though!'

He laughed so merrily that Lily could only join in as the group launched into, '*Hither, page, and stand by me . . .*' 'Thank you – I don't happen to know this one.'

She saw a puzzled expression come into his eyes, but he refrained from further comment at this odd gap in her education. One of so many, Lily thought. She had been skivvying for the Horne family instead of going to school.

'I'm Johnny Barstow,' he said, holding out his hand.

Lily shook hands, and as she did so, saw the doctor's gaze swivel towards them.

'Lily Waters.'

They were almost having to shout above the singing and he drew her aside a little. She saw that he was well built and very sprucely dressed. His jacket fitted beautifully.

'I've seen you about town, I'm sure,' Johnny said. 'Where do you live?'

'Kulri – near the end of Camel's Back.'

'Ah yes – a fine spot.' He was sipping from a glass of something dark and warm and saw her looking. 'Punch – have you not had some? Here – I'll snaffle you a glass.'

The two of them moved over to where a waiter was ladling out the hot punch and he handed her a glass. Lily sipped it and found it strong and fruity. It made her cough and Johnny laughed.

'Not used to that either, eh? Are you long in India?'

She told him a small amount about her time there, about Ambala.

'Ah yes – good old Umbala,' he said, pronouncing it the old way. 'Funny that – I spent a short time there. I'm an engineer – based at Meerut now, though I'm not army. I'm with the railways. But I always like to get up to our lovely Mussoorie whenever I can. Much better than stuffy old Simla. D'you know the place?'

'Yes,' Lily said, glad she knew something for once. 'We used to summer there, from Ambala.'

'Course, yes. Well, I like it here much better. Very jolly. Tell me – where are you from back home?'

Again, the questions, always questions, Lily thought. How inquisitive people were about each other! She did what she had always done and made up a story.

'Kent,' she said firmly. She wasn't sure why she had fixed so firmly on this version of events. After all, she had only been to Kent once, for her interview with Susan Fairford's sister, but it had felt a respectable place, far from Birmingham's industrial grime and her real childhood.

'How very nice – Garden of England,' Johnny smiled. 'I'm from Essex as a matter of fact. It's splendid to meet you, Lily. I should like to get to know you a great deal better.'

Lily decided she liked Johnny Barstow.

'I expect you've made a lot of friends here in Mussoorie?' he was asking, but she was saved from answering by the carol coming to an end and a sozzled cheer going up from the singers. In a second, Dr Mc-Bride was at her side.

'Lily?' His tone was civil, but commanding. 'I think it might be time for us to go home, don't you?'

Lily was a bit disappointed. 'Well, if you think . . .

I was just talking to Mr Barstow here. This is Johnny Barstow,' she introduced him. 'Dr McBride.'

'I think I could have managed to introduce myself,' Dr McBride snapped. It was only then that Lily realized he was trembling with barely controlled emotion.

'Good to meet you, Doctor,' Johnny said, holding his hand out. He had not noticed McBride's furious state. 'I was wondering if our friend would fancy a walk one day, out to Happy Valley perhaps? I'm sure I could arrange a chaperone?'

'I don't think that will be possible,' the doctor snapped. 'We need to be going now. Good evening to you.' He left Johnny Barstow staring after them, ushering Lily towards the door, his hand on her back. Lily just managed to shoot Johnny a regretful smile as they left. She had enjoyed talking with someone of her own age and thought him rather fun. She couldn't understand why the doctor had acted so jealously and hustled her away. Soon they were dressed again in their warm hats and shawls for the ride home. It was snowing lightly outside.

No sooner had the *jhampani* begun to haul the rickshaw away through the snow than the doctor began speaking in tones of icy fury.

'I can't imagine what you thought you were doing in there, young lady!' he spat at her. 'Flaunting yourself like that in so unbecoming a way, I was embarrassed to witness it!'

Lily felt as if she had been slapped. Whatever was he talking about? Up until now, Ewan McBride had been possessive of her, it was true, and he liked to dress her and say where they would go and when, but she had never experienced a reaction like this before.

'I'm sorry,' she gasped, careful not to enrage him any

further. She remembered what Mr Horne had been like. You had to calm them down, men who were like that. 'I don't think I was flaunting myself, dear, I was just having a polite little conversation.'

'*Dear?*' He said mockingly. 'Calling me *dear* now, are we? Oh, we are the biddable little miss when it suits, aren't we? When it comes to being taken out and about and having the best finery to wear. You certainly know how to use a man, don't you, Lily? How to play with my heart?'

Lily felt disorientated and a little scared. Whatever had come over him?

'I'm sorry,' she said contritely, even though she didn't really know what she was supposed to be sorry about. 'I don't really understand what I've done to offend you, Ewan, dear. But I apologize from the bottom of my heart. There's no need for you to be like this, really there isn't.'

'Isn't there?' His jealous rage was not over yet. 'How do I know I can trust you? I can't be sure you're not going to give yourself to every holidaying officer in town, can I? Not after tonight, the way I saw you carrying on. After all, you're cheap enough to give yourself to me, aren't you? Parading about like a lady when in truth you're nothing but a little whore.'

Lily felt a rage rise up in her so strong that she wanted to slap his face at such an accusation. My God, the injustice of it, after the pressure he'd put her under! But she also felt cheap. Was that it, she was really a cheap whore? Whatever the case, if she lost her temper all would be undone. She took a long, slow breath, soft handfuls of her shawl clenched in her hands and said calmly, 'Ewan, you really have made a mistake. The young man in there only handed me a carol sheet and was fetching me a drink. We had scarcely said more than a few words to each other. And if you think I would throw away all your love and care for me, and mine for you in such a brief time, then you really are jumping to conclusions and giving yourself pain for nothing.'

By the time they got home she had talked him round and he was in a fever of shame and contrition for his outburst.

'Let me come to you tonight,' he breathed, as soon as they were inside the house. 'I've got to have you. To make things right again.'

He made love to her that night in a hurried, frantic way, and when he climaxed he fell on her, weeping.

'I didn't mean it, Lily, my love,' he sobbed, close to her ear. 'I'm sorry. I didn't mean to say those things. It's just that I love you so much. I worship you, my darling, my princess ... I couldn't bear to lose you. And seeing you with a younger man – it makes me feel wild, jealous ...'

He begged her to let him stay all night with her and soon he was sleeping beside her, his limbs and sex limp after the drink and exertion. Lily held up the candle before she blew it out and looked down at his wide, bearded face. It was almost a handsome face, with a grandeur to it. Lily tried to decide what she felt for him. Did she love him, could she? But there was no warm feeling in her, only detachment and a crumb of pity. She had seen him in a frightening new light that night and felt very uneasy, despite his tears and apologies. Perhaps it was the drink, she thought. But he drank most nights and this had never happened before.

Blowing out the candle she lay down to sleep as the snow fell gently outside, blanketing the roof. She felt very alone and a little frightened.

Chapter Thirty-Two

The winter passed in a whirl of social events. Lily found herself at the centre of British Mussoorie's wealthy social life of parties, evenings of singing, dancing and of plays. She even acted in one, persuaded by some of women who were most friendly to her. She did not have many lines, and was dressed in Japanese costume which the other women told her suited her.

'Just right for you, Lily, when you're so silent and *mysterious*! *Do* tell more about yourself. We're all so keen to know you.'

But Lily smiled and blushingly gave her usual reply, that there was nothing very much to tell and she wasn't at all interesting.

There were many late nights in the colourful, warm rooms of hotels and Mussoorie mansions, among the chattering socialites, the colourful gowns and shawls of the women, smoke from the cheroots and pipes of the men, plenty of drink flowing and the aroma of cardamom and cumin from dishes of rice and chicken, the silent servants. Lily learned to drink just a little but never too much. The evenings ended with the late-night rickshaw journeys back along the Mall in the moonlight, and this became, as time passed, the occasion when Dr McBride let loose the recriminations he had been storing up all evening. After the jolly farewells to other guests as they all piled into their rickshaws, Lily and the doctor would perch side by side on the narrow seat, a blanket wrapped round their knees and for a brief time there would be silence. Then, explosively, he would begin. The last time it was, 'I saw you rubbing yourself up against that Barstow lout again. You really do have to go out of your way to make an exhibition of yourself, don't you?' His voice came down on her like a hammer. He never looked at her during these outbursts, but stared icily ahead of him.

As usual, when he started, Lily felt herself go cold and detached inside. Any small beginnings of tenderness for him, the idea that she might even learn to love this man, had been frozen out of her when his jealous behaviour began the night she first met Johnny Barstow. She had had very little to do with Johnny but the doctor behaved as if she was in some way closely involved with Johnny and was trying to provoke him. All she wanted, in her few conversations with Johnny, was friendship with someone closer to her own age. And in any case, Johnny would be gone soon, back to Meerut.

'Your behaviour disgusts me.' The doctor ground out the words. 'I've given you everything, and look at the way you just hurl it back at me. No gratitude or loyalty! But what can you expect from a cheap street girl. That's what you are, isn't it? A cheap bitch who'll go with anyone for her own gain, to get what she wants . . .'

'But Ewan, I haven't *done* anything,' Lily protested as calmly as she could. She had learned not to let herself feel anything. 'And you know I haven't really. Why do you keep accusing me like this?' She tried to humour him, to bring him out of this black mood. You know you only get upset when you start like this. Don't do it – just take my hand and we'll be friends again.'

'Don't touch me!' he roared at her. 'Your filthy hand you've touched *him* with!'

'But I never . . .'

'I didn't ask you to argue with me! You're my servant – you will not speak to me like that!'

His voice boomed along the street. He was slipping out of control and Lily was sure the other rickshaw riders along the Mall must hear them. She sank into silence. It was no good arguing. Why did he imagine all these things about her? Was he mad? But she found now that she didn't care what he imagined. She just wanted to keep him calm so that he didn't hurt her. What would come next was becoming familiar. She would go silently to her room, where he would follow, sometimes still angry, sometimes already full of remorse. Tonight when he appeared, his face in the candlelight looked distraught.

'Lily, my love, my darling!' He sounded almost like a child. 'Oh God, I'm so sorry. I don't know why I said those things – I wasn't myself. I must have had too much to drink. Oh, my little girl, don't look at me like that. Let me love you – come here, let me have you, my darling.'

He was urgently aroused and Lily, indifferently, let him take her while she lay looking at the ceiling waiting for it to be over. At first his lovemaking had given her a certain amount of pleasure. Now she had no feeling or openness to him. She let him use her and that was that. And soon he came with an emotional cry and murmured, 'Oh, my little love. Things are well again now. They are, aren't they?' And he sank into sleep.

*

During those winter months, while the town was covered in snow, Muriel McBride still clung somehow to her fragile life, shut away from view. The doctor visited her solicitously at his usual times during the day and occasionally Lily saw her and heard reports through Jane Brown.

Though she and Jane were still friends, Lily felt very distant from her. She had been pulled more and more into Dr McBride's orbit, and he was demanding of her time. And while she did see Jane and spent some cosy times drinking tea in one or other of their rooms, Lily knew there were a great many things she could not speak to Jane about. She wondered what Jane Brown thought of her. It must, she assumed, be very obvious what her position had become in the household, but the young nurse never said a word about it.

One afternoon when Jane invited her in, Lily felt she really must say something.

'Cold, isn't it?' Jane remarked as she let Lily into her colourful room. She had a fire burning in the grate. 'I'll be glad when the snow goes now. Would you like tea?'

'Yes, please,' Lily said.

As ever, they talked about day-to-day things for a time, but when there was a short silence, Lily said, flushing, 'I know you must disapprove.'

Jane raised one of her thick eyebrows. In her calm voice, she said, 'Of what, exactly, Lily?'

'Of me . . . Of this . . . Of my . . .' She wrestled for the words. 'The way Dr McBride . . . behaves towards me.'

Jane Brown looked steadily at her as if considering what to say. Then she looked away and stared into the fire. She was quiet for some time and Lily began to regret speaking. At last, in her quiet way, Jane Brown said, 'What Dr McBride does is not my affair. All I'd say to you, Lily, is be careful. He seems to be in a rather . . . excitable state.'

Lily looked at Jane Brown's solid, quiet figure. *What do you mean?* she was longing to ask. But she could see that Jane Brown was not prepared to say any more.

More and more, it seemed that Ewan McBride could not bear to let Lily out of his sight. On the evenings when they were not going out to some social event, he would demand that she dine with him. In the secluded study, once Prithvi had served them their meal, he talked to her as they ate. He poured out all his memories of his Scottish childhood spent in Currie, about his younger brother Duncan who had drowned in a river. Sometimes he wept as he talked about his school, the church they attended, his father's humiliation there when his mother was caught in a liaison with a man from the town who was not a churchgoer and who already had a wife. Lily listened, night after night, to his talk, to memories and rage and sorrow. She was relieved that he did not ask her to lay out her past. But she also came to see that he didn't need to know about her, not as she really was. He needed her to be a blank, a mirror for him, to give him back everything he needed.

Sometimes he sat beside her just staring at her, stroking her thick, chestnut hair as if she was a statue he had acquired.

'You're the most beautiful thing I've ever seen,' he said and sometimes tears would come into his eyes. 'I just want to be with you always, Lily – to look at you, to know you're mine,' he kept saying. 'Don't ever leave me, will you? I think I'd go mad. I know I would.'

Before, when he stroked her like that and gazed at her, it had made her feel flattered and admired. Now, though, she felt empty. Sometimes it seemed as if he didn't see her at all, but instead something he had created in his own mind.

The evenings invariably ended in her bed and she lay awake long after he had fallen asleep, looking up into the darkness in lonely silence.

Still, she reasoned, she had had worse times in her life. And she could not seem to see out from it any more. She couldn't imagine anything else.

Chapter Thirty-Three

The Mussoorie snows melted at last, the sun grew warmer and delicate flowers appeared in abundant, pale sprays down the hillsides. However, while spring had arrived, the doctor's moods had darkened.

One morning, when icy streams and waterfalls were rushing the last of the mountain snows down the steep slopes, Lily walked along, drinking in the sight of the hillside glittering green after all the snow. Birds called and fluttered among the branches and all nature seemed to smile, reawakened. The air felt warm and hopeful and Lily took in deep breaths, freeing herself from the constrained feeling she now had all the time in the house. She thought of the mighty sweep of the mountain range on whose hem she was walking, its giant ripple of the earth's crust extending across to Kashmir, Nepal, Tibet, the awesome white wilderness she had heard of so often, and it gave her a sense of exhilarating freedom. She realized, as she moved even faster, almost wanting to break into a run, just how much this winter she had become a puppet who had to dance all the time to a tune played by the doctor. And for these precious moments she could be free of it, could regain a sense of herself. These times made it bearable, standing out on the sunny Mussoorie hillside, when she felt free and young again, and as she made her way back into the house she was smiling.

He was standing in a dark corner of the hall. She saw the dog Cameron before she saw him, coming to greet her out of the shadows.

'And where exactly have you been, missy?'

Lily jumped, laying a hand over her thumping heart. 'I . . . I've been out for a little walk.' She used the low, taming voice she had learned to use with Ewan McBride when he was like this. 'It's so lovely now spring's coming.'

He approached her, and she could see he was tense with rage. 'You went out, alone, without asking me?'

Lily could hear Mrs Das moving about further along the corridor, but the doctor seemed too overwrought to care who heard him.

'I'm sorry, dear,' she said softly. 'But you weren't here. It doesn't do any harm, going out to take the air for a few minutes, surely?'

'Who did you meet?' His hands gripped her shoulders and he brought his face close up to hers, breathing his tobacco breath in her face. She could see where the hairs of his beard entered his skin. 'You're going out to meet someone, aren't you? Behaving like a little whore again. *Tell* me!' He squeezed her so hard that she yelped. Here again were all the accusations he was forever throwing at her. She breathed in deeply, quelling her urge to shout at him, *Of course I'm not meeting other people! How do you expect me to when you keep me here like a prisoner!* But she must not shout: it would be a disaster.

'My dear, I . . .'

'Your *dear*!' She thought for a moment he was going to slap her. His nostrils were flaring, his breath fast and shallow. 'You little hypocrite. You don't care for me! You're just after everything you can squeeze out of me while you torture my heart with your wanton behaviour, running after other men, younger men, to make me feel old and of no value to you. That's all you can think about isn't it – showing yourself off to other men while I rot here, all alone . . .'

Very quickly his rages sank him into misery, so that sometimes he wept in her arms, full of remorse and self-pity.

'Shall we go into your study so that the servants don't hear?' Lily suggested and took his hand. 'Come along, dear.' She led him like a child. 'Everything will be all right.'

As they walked along the corridor she calculated that the most dangerous moments were over. He had begun to hit her, just once or twice. Both times he had caught her on the arm, where the bruises did not show, but she was afraid of worse and constantly alert for his more violent moods. And she knew how to pacify him. It was an instinct deep in her from her years with Mr Horne, from trying to be whatever other people needed her to be. Once they were in the study with the door shut, he started to weep in earnest, sinking down on his chair beside the desk.

'Oh God, one day I'm going to hurt you, Lily. I don't know what comes over me!' She tried to quiet him, her hands on his shoulders, looking down at the thinning crescents of hair at the top of his head. She saw that her hands were bonier than they used to be.

'I'm not a violent man – never have been. It's something you do to me. You're like a demon – you've possessed me, body and soul, woman! I can't bear to think of you with anyone else. It would tear me apart – do you understand?' He turned to face her, full of anxiety. 'I don't mean to hurt you, my dear. I wouldn't harm you for the world. But when I think of you leaving me, of you in another man's arms, it's as if I'm blinded ... Can you forgive me?'

'Of course,' Lily said, mechanically. She tried to make her voice warm and forgiving, though she felt nothing.

'Do you, my dear – really?' Now he was almost like a child.

'Come – sit on my lap, my sweet, and give your foolish old man a kiss.'

Lily slid round on to his lap and he pulled her close, hands moving greedily on her body. Over his shoulder she looked out at the sunlight slanting over the hills, her mind out on the paths and tracks bright with flowers. Dr McBride was already highly aroused and Lily knew she was not going to get away with just a quick embrace to put things right for him. His hard penis was pressing against her and his breathing was fast and urgent.

'God, woman, I need you!' His breath was hot on her neck and he began fumbling to unfasten his clothes. He gestured towards her and she knew he meant her to remove her underclothes and she obeyed, knowing she must be quick or she would summon another of his rages.

He beckoned to her to straddle him, and he groaned and sighed as he found release and afterwards he clung to her.

'Don't ever go away from me, my Lily,' he murmured. 'Don't ever leave me.'

Chapter Thirty-Four

There was a period, in the February, when Muriel McBride revived for a time and was able to sit up. Lily saw the transformation in Jane Brown as well, a lightness and sense of hope, that she was not necessarily party to an inexorable and tragic slide downwards to death. Lily saw her smile more, and she even became rather humorous in her dry way.

'Mrs McBride would like to see you,' she said to Lily one afternoon when they were in the kitchen again. 'That is, of course, if you're not too busy.'

Lily could see the twinkle in Jane Brown's eye.

'I think I could manage to fit it in,' Lily quipped. 'But why on earth does she want to see me?'

'Oh, I expect she'd just like a change from looking at me all day long.'

Both of them laughed, and exchanged an unusually fond look. Whatever Jane Brown knew or thought, Lily realized, she was not one to sit in judgement.

'I'll come and see her today,' she promised.

She went to the sickroom and found Muriel McBride propped up on pillows, looking out at the sunlit view. As Lily came in, she smiled. There was a strange down of fair hair on her cheeks and her skeletal form seemed thin enough to let the light through. She didn't look any more substantial, but she did seem to have a fraction more energy.

'Come and sit by me, Lily,' she said in her reedy voice. She raised one of her stick-like arms to gesture to a chair and Lily saw the blue veins under her skin.

Lily obeyed. Jane Brown hovered in the background tidying up and Lily liked her being there. The room was light this afternoon, seeming more cheerful, and Lily felt her own spirits lift. She only occasionally realized how much the sad presence of this sick woman dampened the atmosphere of the house.

They talked a little about Muriel's health, though she seemed hardly to acknowledge that she was ill. It was almost like something separate from her that she had no interest in.

'I'm quite all right really,' she said, closing down Lily's enquiries. 'Nothing much to say about it. I must say, Lily, you are looking rather thin and tired. Are you all right?'

'Yes, perfectly, thank you,' Lily said, though Mrs McBride was not the first person to comment on her loss of weight. 'I feel very well.'

She tried to think of a few things to say about her work, even though Dr McBride no longer liked to think of her as employed as housekeeper any more. And she said how lovely it was outside now the weather was changing. It was a friendly conversation, but after a time she saw Muriel McBride still looking rather intently at her with her huge blue eyes.

'I wanted to say something to you, Lily.' She paused and Lily could feel Jane Brown listening somewhere behind her. 'Just to mention that my husband is a man who can tend to run to extremes. Over the years I have seen a number of people affected by it. Just be careful.' These last words were spoken very sadly. Then she looked up, sharply. 'By that I don't want you to think I mean myself. What I have done, I have done to myself. I can't help it, not now. But it's no fault of Ewan's. You, though, Lily – you don't have to stay here. You are free.'

For some reason the words brought tears to Lily's eyes. She did not understand why and she looked down for a moment in confusion, her cheeks burning.

After that, they talked about ordinary things again.

You are free. The words stayed with her, like birds fluttering in her head. She did not feel free, not at all. Every part of her day was hedged in by Ewan McBride, by his need to parade her in public in her finery, his demand for her in bed, and by his rages if he thought she was running out of his control, until she felt like a prisoner in the house. One day, when he was out on his rounds, Lily was about to slip out for a walk when Jane Brown came out of the sickroom, looked hurriedly back and forth and beckoned Lily to her. In a low, urgent whisper, she said, 'Lily, I feel terrible saying this, but he's told me not to let you go out.'

Lily, who had been buttoning her blue velvet coat in readiness for a walk, gaped in disbelief. 'Dr McBride? But he hasn't said anything to me.'

'He says he doesn't want you going out unless you're accompanied by either me or himself. He knows perfectly well that I'm not free to accompany you any-way . . .' The words were left unspoken. In other words Lily was not allowed out at all without the doctor.

'But I *have* to go out. I can't just stay in here all day!'

'Yes, I know,' Jane Brown said, her eyes troubled. 'But I'm just warning you. I didn't see you go.'

Lily went out anyway, slipping quietly along to her favourite spot along the Camel's Back Road, but she felt very shaken. More and more often she had reason to feel afraid of Ewan McBride. For the first time she thought seriously about leaving, but the idea of having to start in yet another strange place was so wearying, just when she had made friends here and felt, at least in some ways, secure.

So far he had not found out about her morning walks and they were her one piece of real freedom. She could settle for this, she decided, at least for the moment. She had grown to love Mussoorie very much, seeing its beauty in all the seasons.

One day, she thought, I'll get out of here, but not yet. What she was not prepared for was a change that was approaching even as she stood looking out over the valley that day, one which would turn her life upside down all over again.

Lily was in her room that morning, and as it happened she was writing a letter to Cosmo. He wrote to her, very occasionally now, telling her about rugby and cricket and about boys whose faces she would never know. Though she tried to tell herself that Cosmo had not grown into a stranger, in sad moments she wondered if she would even recognize him now he was almost seven. Of course she would, she told herself. She kept the photograph of herself taken with him on her dressing table.

She heard, distantly, the knock at the front of the house but ignored it. Mrs Das or Prithvi could deal with it and she took no notice of the voices in the distance. But in a moment there was a tap on her door.

'Miss Lily?' It was Prithvi, standing outside with her usual air of apology. 'There is a man,' she said. 'He is asking for you.'

Lily frowned. No one ever came calling at the house for her. She did not have that sort of social life.

'Well who is it, Prithvi?'

'I do not know, Miss Lily. But he is asking for you by name.'

She walked along to the hall and saw a man standing, looking down at his feet as she approached, hat in hand. Hearing her step he looked up, and it was only then she knew him. Her walking stopped, abruptly.

'Lily? It *is* you.' His voice was gentle, wondering.

There again, with no warning: Sam Ironside.

Chapter Thirty-Five

'Oh Lord, why are you here?' she heard herself say.

Sam stepped towards her. He looked just the same, as if he had never been away. The three years since she last saw him evaporated and in those seconds she wanted to pour out all the things she had never been able to say to him, but it was impossible. Her chest felt tight, as if she'd been running.

'Lily?' He stood before her, seeming unable to say any more either, his eyes searching her face. And then he retreated into formality. 'I hope you don't mind my calling.'

'We must get away from here.' It was the first thing she could think of. She could not let Dr McBride come home and find her here talking to another man, let alone one who meant so much to her.

'Well, if that's what you'd like,' Sam said, startled by the urgency in her voice. 'Whatever's convenient.'

'We must go – quickly . . .' Frantic, she snatched up her coat and hat and hurriedly put them on, words tumbling from her lips. 'We'll go along the Camel's Back Road. I walk there often and it's fairly quiet. He won't come there but we must be back by midday . . .'

She saw Sam looking strangely at her and when she'd led him, half running, up the steps out of the garden and turned right along the path, he stopped her, putting a hand on her arm, in a way which felt so familiar she almost wanted to weep.

'Lily, what's the matter? You seem in such a state – all nerves, and so pale and thin! Not like before. What are you so frightened about?'

It was only then that she felt how true that was, how overwrought was her constant state living with the McBrides and how frightened she was of the doctor. But she couldn't begin to put this into words.

'I'm not in an easy situation here in some ways,' she said abruptly. She still felt they were too near the house and she wanted to stop him asking difficult questions. 'Let's walk on. Why are you here? To deliver another motor car?'

'Yes – to the Fairfords again. He wanted the latest model . . . The thing is, they're here, Lily. Staying in a house about a mile away. It was all rather sudden. I asked after you, of course, and they said you were up here. And it was Mrs Fairford – she suggested that they come here instead of going to Simla. I don't think she's all that keen on Simla and she wanted a change, and she said she'd like to see you. She's very taken with the way you've kept up the contact with young Cosmo all this time. I rather think she misses you.'

'Yes, I hear from her now and then,' Lily said. 'I missed her when I first came here, and Cosmo, of course, but I haven't missed Ambala and the canton-ment life much. You can see why they all want to get away from it.'

'It seems very nice here.' Sam looked across at the scene unfolding to their right from the Camel's Back Road. 'This is a beautiful place. My goodness, it is.'

They walked for a moment in silence. Lily was wearing a skirt in dark red wool. She became acutely aware of everything: the movement of her skirt, the sounds of their boots on the path, of the astonishing fact of Sam here beside her after all this time, his left hand at his side, so close, and of the huge, longing ache which rose in her which she knew she must suppress.

'How is your wife?' she asked, sharply.

'She's well, thank you. Yes, going along all right.'

'And children?' She didn't look at him, but ahead, at the gateway to the cemetery which they were approaching, with its monsoon-stained paint.

'Yes. We have two daughters, Ann and Nancy.' Sam's tone was stiff, as if somehow he did not want to give her the information.

'How old?' She wanted to drill him, to make him suffer, yet she knew it would be herself who suffered the most from hearing about his family.

'Ann is two and a half, Nancy just over a year.' He did not look at her, but peered at the plaque inside the cemetery gatehouse: *MDCCCXXVIII – I am the Resurrection and the Life.*

'And do they look like you?' She glanced at him then, those familiar, intent eyes, the dark moustache. How close she had once been to every detail of him. A kind of tremor went through her, remembering the feel of his body as they had held each other. *Stop it*, she raged at herself. *It should never have happened.* They were passing the grounds of the cemetery on their right and both of them instinctively walked towards the fence and leaned on it.

'Ann does, yes. Nancy favours her mother.' They looked down at the stone crosses and angels among the tall conifers, sunlight shining between the branches and white flowers scattered like stars in the grass.

'And what does her mother look like?' Lily was

relentless. She knew she was being hostile, but she couldn't manage the hurt she felt any other way.

'She's ... Well, her hair is sort of, I suppose you'd call it toffee-coloured...' He was tremendously uncomfortable, she could see. For a moment he stared ahead of him, tapping one hand on the fence in an agitated way. Then abruptly he turned to her.

'Lily, for God's sake – I had to come and see you. Don't keep on like this!'

'Like what? I'm asking about your family, that's all. The family you somehow didn't think to tell me about the last time you were here.'

She didn't meet his eyes. A lump had come up in her throat which made it hard to speak and her cheeks were aflame. How humiliating to show this emotion, all the feelings that had erupted back up in her that she hoped she had long ago laid to rest.

'I know,' Sam said wretchedly. The long pent-up words poured out of him. 'It was wrong of me – utterly wrong. But I was in love with you, Lily ... So in love in a way I'd never been before – and never have been in my life apart from with you. You bring out feelings in me which no one else ... I *had* to get to know you, had to love you. If I'd told you then you would never have had anything to do with me, would you? It would have been terrible ...'

'And it's been terrible ever since!' It came out in an anguished wail, and she found she was overtaken by sobs, quite unable to hold back. She put her hands over her face, her shoulders shaking. 'Oh God, Sam, I wish I'd never met you so I didn't know how it was possible to feel ...'

'Oh, Lily ... Lily, my sweet love ...'

She moved her hands away from her cheeks, which

were running with tears, and saw the anguish on his face.

'My lovely Lily. I just . . . I didn't know what to do, to say . . . You were so angry and I knew I'd done wrong. When you left the house in the *tonga* that day I felt as if I was being torn apart . . .' He seemed about to weep too, but controlled himself.

'I married Helen because I thought I loved her. I've tried to be true. I've been a good husband in every other way – we don't go short. We have our children, our house . . .' He stopped and drew in a deep breath. 'And not a day goes by when I don't think of you, Lily. I told myself it would wear off, that I'd forget – you know, knuckle down, get on with my work . . . But it's been like that ever since I left, and I try . . . The thought of you is like an *ache* that I can never seem to lose.' Daring to move closer, he put his hand on her shoulder and said helplessly, 'You're the woman I love. But . . . in another way it's all wrong! I'm married, responsibilities . . . I just don't know what to do. I just love you – that's all I know.'

'Oh, Sam!' Lily felt her hurt and anger melt away in the face of his sadness and her heart was filled with tenderness. She drank in the sight of him, so full of sorrow and so lovely to her. 'I was so hurt, so sure you'd deceived me just to play with me, as if I was a little diversion while you were away from home. And I didn't want to believe that because I felt so much for you. But you were married – what was I to think?'

'I don't know.' He took his cap off and rubbed his head as if to try and order his thoughts. 'You couldn't have thought any different. How could you know whether to trust me? And why should you have trusted me when I wasn't telling you the truth?' He replaced his hat and looked into her eyes. 'I'm so sorry. You have my heart, Lily. But even now . . .'

'You're still married,' she finished for him, soberly.

'But, my God, I don't *want* to be, not to her.' There was great sadness and regret in his voice. 'Seeing you again . . . Oh, my love, you're really here . . .'

He was looking down at her, seeming about to kiss her when a giggling group of Indian girls from one of the local schools came past, dressed in red and navy-blue uniforms. Lily and Sam turned and looked down over the cemetery again until the children had moved on.

'I mustn't be long,' Lily said, remembering with a jolt of panic. For those moments Dr McBride had seemed like another life. But here she was and he was horribly real.

'You seem so nervous. What's wrong?' Sam was concerned.

'Nothing.' How could she say what her status was in the McBride household? A servant-cum-mistress, to be controlled and used? For that was the truth of it and she saw now how she had let herself slide down and down into it. 'It's just that they're very particular about punctuality.'

He was staring at her, as if he could still scarcely believe she was here. 'God, girl . . .'

'How long are you staying?' she asked. Suddenly she was excited. It would be lovely to see the Fairfords as well! She would hear more of Cosmo.

'I'll be here for two weeks. I expect Mrs Fairford and Isadora will be staying during the heat. That'll be nice for you, won't it? They said to ask you to call in as soon as you can. Can you get away? You have time off, I take it.'

Lily's mind was working fast. The one thing the doctor must not find out on any account was that she was meeting Sam. But she knew that if she said the Fairford family were here in Mussoorie and she would be visiting Mrs Fairford, that would be just about acceptable, unless he was in an especially difficult or demanding mood, when nothing she did except giving him her full and slavish attention would do.

'Oh yes – of course I'll come! I'd like to see Mrs Fairford very much.'

'And me . . . ?'

'Oh, Sam.' Her eyes were full of pain as she looked up at him. 'Have you come to break my heart all over again?'

With great solemnity he said, 'No, Lily. No. I've come to be with the woman I love, and have loved ever since I saw her.'

And uncaring of who might be watching, he took her in his arms and kissed her passionately.

Chapter Thirty-Six

Lily lay awake much of that night. The doctor had left her alone, to her enormous relief, but she felt as if her heart had been broken open and her emotions were raw and strong. Sam Ironside loved her and she loved him, and she was so full of tremulous joy, as well as fear and disquiet about what that might mean, that she could hardly bear even to lie down. All she could think of was his face, his words of love to her. Her body was full of restless energy and in the small hours she got up and walked around the room trying to quiet herself.

The most immediate worry was how she was going to see anything of Sam without the doctor finding out. The very thought of her anywhere near another man would send him into a jealous rage.

And then a miracle happened. Before he went out to his surgery the next morning, Dr McBride said, 'I've had a wire from an old friend, Duncan McCluskie – he trained with me in Edinburgh. He's doing a spot of work in Patna for a few months and he's coming up to pay a visit. He'll be arriving at about tiffin time. So things will be different for a few days, Lily. I shan't be able to spend as much time with you, I'm afraid. You'll have to find ways to amuse yourself.'

Lily felt her eyes widen and had to suppress a grin of astonished delight. She seized her chance immediately.

'I'm sorry to hear that,' she said, trying to look sober

and talking in the quiet, careful way she always used with him now. 'But perhaps it's a happy chance. You see, I heard yesterday that the family I worked for in Ambala are staying here in Mussoorie and I was going to ask you if I might visit and spend some time with them.' She couched the request very humbly. 'Would that be all right, while you have a visitor yourself?'

'This is Captain Fairford's family, I take it?' he asked. There was an edge of suspicion but he seemed in a good humour. 'Who will be there, d'you suppose?'

'So far as I know, just the captain and his wife and daughter and a handful of servants,' Lily said. 'And I should very much like to see Mrs Fairford and Isadora, their daughter. I spent a lot of time with them, you see.'

Dr McBride seemed reassured. He came and gave her a fatherly pat on the shoulder, then kissed her on the lips, forcing his tongue into her mouth. 'That sounds like a nice little holiday for you, my dear, to spend time with your old mistress. And you deserve a little break. You'll be here at nights, of course, if I need you.'

'Of course,' Lily agreed, her heart soaring with excitement. She could hardly believe how easily he seemed to accept the thought of her going out, and realized it was because he saw no threat to his control. 'Things will be just as normal, dear.'

When it came to meeting Sam again later that morning, as she had arranged to do, Lily was full of misgiving. She felt shy of meeting him, as if they would have to break the ice again.

She wore a favourite dress stitched in raw silk of kingfisher blue and a blue hat to match. The costume looked very striking set against her sultry colouring and she saw Sam react to the sight of her. He was waiting just where she had asked him to, at the corner of the road leading up into Kulri Bazaar. There was a strong smell of frying onions and spices in the spring air and she breathed in happily, catching sight of Sam standing, looking rather self-conscious on the corner, beside a cow with sharp horns that was trying to nibble his sleeve.

'I'm glad you've come to rescue me – I think she has taken too much of a shine to me altogether!'

Lily laughed, as the cow moved away with an affronted slouch.

'God, Lily—' Sam looked at her closely then, seeming awed. 'You're so beautiful. You look astonishing.'

Lily felt herself light up at the sight of him. Her eyes met his, and the bustle of the streets around them seemed to disappear. All she could see was him and she was filled with a soaring happiness.

'I can't believe you're here,' she said, feeling her voice catch. 'I keep thinking you'll just disappear again.'

'I've got ten whole days. The captain said we might as well do the necessary with the car while he was in the hills. It's good for putting her through her paces up here.' He paused, then said, 'Are you free to come up to the house?'

As she walked beside him towards the Mall, Lily kept stealing glances at him. *He's here. Sam's really here, walking beside me.* It was a miracle.

The bungalow which the Fairfords had rented nestled into the side of Gun Hill, along a path off the main one up to the top. Lily climbed up the familiar, steep slope, and what joy to have Sam beside her, not Ewan McBride with Cameron plodding along behind! It was quiet this morning, and they passed very few other walkers.

'I've walked up here so many times,' she said, pausing to catch her breath and looking across at the valley, the green hills with a scattering of houses tucked between the trees. 'I never once thought I'd walk up here with you.'

'I know. It's heaven.' He turned to her and took her hand, lifting it to his lips to kiss it. She saw that he was moved, and it brought tears to her eyes.

'I've tried my best with Helen, my very best, but she's not you, Lily. I've tried not to let myself see it, or feel it. I just keep on, work hard every day, don't think about anything deeply. Then, before Christmas, they told me I was doing another delivery to Ambala and it brought it all rushing back, brought *you* back, stronger than ever. I didn't know if you were there any more, but I knew I couldn't come back to India and not try to find out, to see you again if you were here.'

She listened, moved, all the hurt of the past years forgotten.

'When you left, I think I hated you,' she said. 'You lied to me – or at least you didn't tell me all the truth. I'd never loved anyone – not the way I did you. And do still.'

His eyes registered her words. He glanced around to see that they were alone before leaning down, intensely serious, and kissing her, pulling her close. After a time he drew back, smiling down at her.

'I've got the motor parked in a garage up at the other end.' Sam pointed to the Library end of the Mall. 'I think I might be able to take it out one day. We could go somewhere, just us together. Who's going to worry about all the rules up here?'

Lily's immediate thought was the doctor. How would she ever get away for the day? She decided she really didn't care; she'd find a way.

'That sounds like heaven,' she said, as they climbed the path at the front of the Fairfords' yellow holiday bungalow, outside which there were neat flower beds and a wooden sign by the path which said 'Zinnias'.

Srimala, Isadora's *ayah*, opened the door. She seemed just the same, and with a cry of delight she flung her arms round Lily's neck.

'Oh, Miss Lily! I am so happy to see you again!' She stood back in the doorway, wiping tears of joy from her eyes and looked Lily up and down. 'I have missed you very much. I wish you were still with us! But you are looking so very lean and tired – not like the Lily we knew before. Are you sick?'

'No,' Lily laughed. She felt more relaxed now than she had in weeks. 'I am quite well, really I am.'

They were in the hall, a sparsely decorated space with two cane chairs and a table and a coloured rug on the floor. Just then Susan Fairford appeared, her expression set into its customary cool formality which made her seem very distant. Lily felt chilled by it and said politely, 'How do you do, Mrs Fairford?'

'Lily—' Susan Fairford was about to hold out her hand as she would to an acquaintance, but as she came closer her face softened and she smiled prettily. 'It's so very nice to see you again,' she said, and leaned to kiss Lily on the cheek. Then, to Lily's surprise, briefly, she put her arms round her and when she drew back there were tears in her eyes. She wiped them away hurriedly. 'We have missed you, my dear. All of us.'

Lily felt her eyes fill as well. Even when she left Ambala, Susan Fairford had scarcely shown any emotion. Lily had told herself that she was only a servant and of course her leaving would mean nothing.

But now she saw how much feeling Susan Fairford had been holding back at the time and it touched her.

'We'll order some tea and sit out, shall we?' Susan Fairford suggested. 'It's such a good day. I say, how marvellous you look, Lily – what an extraordinary dress.'

Srimala vanished with a regretful smile and Lily reminded herself that she must go and see her later.

'We're all very casual here,' Susan Fairford said, leading them out to the veranda. 'You find us in our holiday mood.'

It was an apology for the simplicity of the house, which was certainly a far less sumptuous dwelling than they were used to in Ambala. There were more cane chairs out on the veranda, which faced over a small rectangle of garden edged by flower beds with roses and phlox and snapdragons and was, at this hour, in the shade. The three of them settled round a table and soon one of the servants, whom Lily recognized and greeted with pleasure, brought out tea and biscuits and a Victoria sandwich cake filled with jam.

'Ah – that looks very nice,' Sam said. 'The air up here seems to give me an appetite.'

'Well, let's carry on,' Susan Fairford said. 'Charles has taken Isadora out to have a pony ride. She is absolutely mad on horses now – quite different from how she used to be. We ride out with her every day now, and she could not do without it here. Mind you, neither can Charles!' She laughed, pouring the tea. 'I think you'll find our Izzy changed a little, Lily. Wouldn't you agree, Mr Ironside?'

'Yes,' Sam said, accepting a slice of the cake with enthusiasm. 'She's older, obviously. But much calmer than I remember.'

'Of course, you were quite a horsewoman yourself, Lily!' Susan said, handing her a cup of tea.

'Yes,' Lily sighed. 'But there's not much chance here.'

'But there are the pony rides! Surely you could go out very occasionally at least?'

Lily was seized by a sudden great hunger to ride. She had not mounted a horse for a long time, but now the memory of those beautiful mornings riding out on the Punjab plains came vividly back to her and she sighed. How could she explain that her freedom here was curtailed not just by her being a servant but by her master's obsessive moods and whims?

'Perhaps we could go for a ride?' She looked round teasingly at Sam who made a face. She had not forgotten his fear of horses.

'I think I'll stick to the motor,' he said ruefully. 'You can go much further in it.'

'So how is life here treating you, Lily?' Susan Fairford said over the rim of her teacup. She looked relaxed, in a pale pink cotton dress. Lily could see that Sam was more at ease with her than he had been on the first visit, and indeed Susan did seem less tense and forbidding.

'Very well, thank you,' Lily said, carefully. 'I'm employed as a sort of housekeeper. The doctor's wife is an invalid. They're all very kind, and of course I love the town. But do tell me – what news is there of Cosmo?' Though she had occasional letters from him they told her very little.

'Oh!' Susan Fairford rolled her eyes humorously, but then she looked pained. 'You might well ask. It seems he is turning into a rebel – he's been in no end of trouble.'

'*Has* he?' Lily cried. This was not the sweet, biddable Cosmo she remembered! 'What's the matter?'

'Well, so far as I can gather, it's mostly just lack of discipline, and any sort of attention in lessons . . .'

'But he used to be so good!' Lily protested.

'I know.' Susan Fairford took a sip of tea, looking upset. 'He was evidently had up for stealing something off another boy recently as well. Nothing very big, I don't think, but they take that sort of thing very seriously there and of course he was caned. Charles's brother got to hear about it and wrote to us.' She looked at Lily with stricken eyes. 'My poor boy. I feel so far away from him, and there doesn't seem to be anything I can do. I'm so grateful that you still keep in touch, Lily dear. We heard that he still receives letters from you.'

'Oh yes – I'll never forget our little man,' she said. Once more she saw her old mistress looking close to tears and realized just how great a toll the separation was taking on her.

'Our little man . . .' Susan Fairford echoed, bitterly. 'Yes, this is how it happens here, that a child spends more time with strangers, or servants, than with his own mother.' She caught herself out then. 'Still – that's how it is, I suppose.'

They spent a happy hour reminiscing about Lily's time in Ambala and Susan gave her news of people she had known, and other children. Later on they heard the front door open and voices.

'Charles?' Susan called. 'Come out here – Lily Waters is here!'

A moment later Charles Fairford appeared, almost seeming to bound out of the bungalow door. He looked a little heavier to Lily, slightly more thickset, but very strong and healthy. He was beaming broadly.

'How very nice to see you!' he cried, and it sounded genuine.

Lily stood up, smiling, and they shook hands.

'You know, we're really up here because of you?' the captain said. 'Everyone wanted to come and see you, and I thought Sam here should see Mussoorie . . .'

'*So* much nicer than stuffy old Simla,' Susan said.

'I hope you'll be able to come on a few jaunts with us while we're here,' the captain continued. 'How's it suiting you?'

'Very well . . .' Lily began, but she then caught sight of Isadora, who walked out confidently on to the veranda carrying a riding crop and switching it at the air behind her as if she was still on a mount. She was taller, and though her long dark hair was just as messy as ever, she seemed calmer and more self-possessed.

'D'you remember Lily?' her father said gently.

Isadora stared hard at Lily and then, to all their surprise, walked up and planted a kiss on her cheek, saying, 'Lily. She's a friend.'

'Oh – thank you!' Lily exclaimed, deeply touched. She hadn't expected Isadora to remember her.

'There you are, you see,' Sam said. 'No one forgets you, Lily.'

And Lily saw Susan Fairford turn to look at them both, sharply, with a slight frown on her face.

Chapter Thirty-Seven

The week turned out to be more wonderful than Lily could ever have imagined.

When she returned home that afternoon, Dr McCluskie had arrived as promised and seemed to have put Ewan McBride in an exceptionally good mood. Duncan McCluskie was a slim, mild-mannered man. On first sight his blue eyes seemed to hold a melancholy seriousness, but this changed, when he smiled, into an impish cheerfulness as he shook Lily's hand.

'Miss Waters!' His Scottish accent was like crisp mountain ice. 'How nice to make your acquaintance.'

'How d'you do?' Lily said, deciding he looked reasonably pleasant. She had no idea of what Dr McBride had told his friend about her, but assumed he had told him that she was the housekeeper. But then Dr McBride said, 'Dr McCluskie will be staying in the middle room, and we'll be dining together. I hope you'll join us one evening, Lily?'

'Yes, Doctor,' she said, obediently, though she felt a blush spread all over her, and she was sure she saw a sudden sharp look of curiosity come into Dr McCluskie's eyes. What on earth must he think! Housekeepers did not dine with the master of the house! She knew Ewan McBride wanted to show her off as his prize as he did in the town. But she told herself it was not important. He would be gone soon, back to Patna, and she would never see him again, whatever he thought. And the fact that he was here meant she could get out to see Sam and that was all that mattered.

There were several jaunts with the Fairfords. Charles Fairford appeared more relaxed than Lily ever remembered seeing him before. He was obviously delighted with his new model of Daimler and, she saw, was enjoying Sam's company again. He had not brought his *syce* Arsalan with him, and when she asked about him Susan Fairford told her that the groom's wife was very ill with a fever and he had not been able to leave her.

What took Lily by surprise was the difference in the way Susan Fairford treated her. Whereas before, when in her employ, Lily had been a servant, although one to whom Susan Fairford often turned for company and in times of distress and loneliness, now they were no longer mistress and servant, and she treated her more like a friend. The first time the five of them set off for a picnic in the car, the two women sat at the back with Isadora, and Lily felt like Susan Fairford's confidante. She talked about some of the other women in Ambala and what was happening in their lives far more openly than she would have done before. After a time she turned to look at Lily, with a little frown.

'Here am I, rattling on about people. You know' – she considered for a moment – 'you've changed, Lily. I mean, look at that marvellous gown you're wearing. It's quite lovely. You've become a good deal more *sophisticated*. Yes, that's it. You're more like one of us. That's why my tongue's running away.'

'Thank you,' Lily said, choosing not to regard this as rude. She knew what Susan Fairford meant, of course. After all these months of acting as a social companion for Dr McBride, she not only had a wardrobe full of beautiful clothes, including the powder-blue woollen outfit she was wearing today, but she had become used to mixing with the socialites of British Mussoorie, who had come to be more accepting of her now the first gossip had died down. For much of that time she had been quietly observing their ways, but she had gradually assumed some of those and become more confident and at home.

That day they drove out of Mussoorie and found a beautiful place to stop and picnic at the foot of a high waterfall. As the captain drove the car along the snaking road up and down the hills, the high ridges afforded them awe-inspiring views across to the white peaks, and the air was crisp and fresh and gave a great feeling of freedom and expansion. Lily had never been out this far before and she breathed in deeply, feeling her spirits soar with the air rushing against her cheeks, the blue ribbons of her hat streaming behind her, and this family, of whom she had become more fond than she realized, here with her and wanting to see her. Most miraculous of all, seated in front of her, exchanging remarks with Captain Fairford over the noise of the engine, was Sam Ironside. She felt full of powerful, melting emotion at the sight of him. *This is now*, she kept saying to herself, *and he's here, he's really, really here.* The feelings were so overpowering that she could not caution herself about his wife or think of anything but how much she loved him. She had to restrain herself from reaching out to stroke Sam's slender neck, with its dark, tapering hairline.

They parked at some distance from the falls and walked along a fern-lined path to find a place to sit and eat their picnic. Isadora had to be cajoled along with descriptions of the tumbling water.

'But I want to go for a ride,' she kept insisting.

Captain Fairford took her hand. 'We'll go riding later, I promise, Izzy, when we get back. We'll always go riding, you and I, won't we? But come and see the falling water. It's very exciting.'

And the falls were beautiful, tumbling down from the rocks in an abundance of meltwater, arced with rainbows in the sunlight. Nearby, all was vivid green, the rocks speckled with ferns and flowers, and they spread the picnic rug in the fronded shade of the deodars. Lily and Susan laid out the food from the hampers. There was the usual sumptuous Fairford assortment of fare: spiced fritters, cold chicken, a game pie and sandwiches filled with egg and mango chutney and anchovy and watercress. There were walnut pickles and cheese and biscuits. To follow there were fruits and jam tarts, chocolates and a fruit cake, and there was a bottle of champagne with a bucket of ice and crystal glasses and lemon and mango juices, which were Isadora's favourites.

For a time the two men leaned over the car, in earnest discussion, while Izzy skipped about, released from the confines of the car and enchanted by the sight and sound of the falling water.

'She seems so happy now,' Lily said as Izzy floated past, dreamily shredding a piece of green plant in her hands. The two women sat luxuriating in the beauty of the place and each other's company.

'Yes.' Susan looked up with a smile. 'I've tried to spend more time with her. She has been badly done by – by me, I mean. I was ashamed of her, I admit. And I didn't know how to manage her at all. But I've tried, very hard . . .' She looked sadly into the far distance for a moment. 'I don't have children easily. I suppose I'd have liked more babies, but not in this beastly country which snatches them away from you so cruelly. But Izzy is all I have here now – she won't leave me, you see. We won't have to send her away. Srimala's helped me to understand her better. I owe that girl a great deal and I think we'll need her for as long as she's prepared to stay. I suppose she'll marry one day, though I must say she's not showing much sign of it so far.' Susan eyed her daughter thoughtfully as Isadora squatted to bend over something that had caught her interest.

'She's older, of course. She doesn't get agitated quite so often – not when it comes to dressing and so on. It all used to be such a battle – every last thing. You remember, of course.' Lily could see that things had changed and she felt a great admiration for Susan Fairford. She still seemed nervy, not happy exactly, but a little more settled in herself.

'After all,' she said, self-mockingly, 'if you can't even get along with your own children it does seem a pretty poor show.'

There came a sudden burst of laughter from the men, both throwing their heads back, and Lily saw Susan watching them in wistful amusement.

'That's where he's always been happiest, of course. Not with me.' And she lowered her head as if she had said too much and arranged the linen napkins in a starched white fan on the rug.

Lily didn't need to ask what she meant and saw that Susan did not want to be asked.

'And our little Cosmo?' she said gently. 'When will you be able to see him again?'

Susan didn't answer for a moment. When she looked up her eyes were very sad.

'He stays every holidays with Charles's elder brother,

on the estate. Charles says it will be good for him, let him get to know England, the English countryside and so on. After all, he looks set to inherit the place. Charles did the same, of course – but then he wasn't alone; he had his brother and there were more relatives around then. Now there's only William . . .' She frowned. Lily realized she was battling tears. 'The man's . . . I don't know, unhinged in some way, I'm sure of it. He's most peculiar. Quite harmless, I would think, but – that's what I can't stand, you see . . .' Her eyes filled. 'There's my poor little Cosmo, every holiday in that great pile of a place with Uncle William, who's mad as a hatter, and the servants . . . No one to love him . . . And no other children except some of the servants' boys who are rough and older than Cosmo, and from what I gather he spends all possible time with them, when he's not wandering about alone. I'm sure they're a ruinous influence, but . . .' She was trying not to get worked up, but Lily could see she was fighting her sobs as she spoke. 'Charles keeps insisting that it will all be terribly good for him and character-building, and that it will stand him in good stead for the army – you know, the rough and tumble and mixing with all sorts . . . I really don't know . . .' She wiped her eyes. 'Sometimes I just can't bear it, not seeing him, having no say at all in what happens to my beautiful little boy. They're turning him into a stranger! He's become so naughty and rough and dishonest and he never used to be like that at all, did he, Lily?'

Lily found what she was hearing very sad and disquieting and her heart ached for Cosmo. But she wanted to try and be reassuring.

'No, of course not. He was always sweet and well behaved when he was little. But boys do go in for a lot more rough and tumble as they get older, don't they? After all, they don't stay tiny and sweet all their lives. Perhaps Captain Fairford is right. Cosmo's education must be rather like he had himself?'

'Yes, it is, exactly like. And that's what makes me wonder if he'll be like Charles . . .' She bit off her words and looked down, a flush appearing on her face. Visibly pulling herself together and wiping her eyes as the men were approaching for tiffin, she said in a different, sober voice, 'And, of course, this is the way of things. One must do one's duty.'

By the time Sam and the captain reached them she was a model of composure.

'My – this looks a good spread,' Charles Fairford said, rubbing his hands together. 'I've worked up quite an appetite even without my morning ride. I say, Susan, I could get jolly fond of this place. What do you think? A little more relaxed than dear old Simla, eh?'

'Yes, much more,' she agreed demurely, 'though I do rather miss our dear house in Simla.'

'But no motors allowed in Simla!' the captain said. 'That's no damn good, is it, Ironside?' As Sam sat down, the captain pointed at the rocks on each side of the falls. 'Fancy climbing up there after tiffin, Ironside?'

But Sam's eyes were fixed on Lily. He looked handsome and invigorated by the fresh air and sunshine, and he was smiling at her so hungrily, so attentively. She looked into his lovely face and for a moment they might have been alone.

'Ironside?'

'Ah – yes. A climb? That sounds a fine idea,' Sam agreed with absent-minded politeness.

The afternoon passed blissfully. The sky was a deep blue and they sat half in the shade of the tall trees, the sound of the white, rushing falls constantly with them, eating their sumptuous picnic. Everything tasted wonderful and Lily sipped the cool champagne, feeling herself growing even more relaxed and muzzy. She felt she was in heaven, in this place with Sam nearby, able to look at him, talk with him whenever she wanted to. She was just drinking in his presence and she could see that he was doing the same. She hummed with happiness like an instrument that had found the right note and could only keep playing it.

And Sam seemed in such happy form. He entertained them with more of his motor-racing stories, which the captain always seemed to be keen to hear and laughed unrestrainedly as he listened to the thrills and spills of attempts at a round-the-world car race.

'And when they got halfway across Russia – Zust, the Italian car, that is – first of all they almost drowned by driving on to what they thought was dry land and finding it was a swamp. And they had to botch together a new crankshaft bearing – and what did they have for the job? Well—' Sam chuckled gleefully – 'some bits of mud and wood and a handful of bullets in a tin which had had cough sweets in it, and that's how they made do! And then, to cap it all, when they finally got to Omsk, they were arrested – they didn't get to Paris for another two months!'

'But *why* on earth?' Susan Fairford was enjoying the story as well. Lily saw Sam cast a surprised glance in her direction.

'They thought they were spies, because they tried to send a cable in Italian. And when they did get to France, long after everyone else, they claimed that they were the winners because everyone else had cheated!'

'Oh really, that's too much!' Charles Fairford

laughed. 'I've heard of some rum carry-on during the reliability trials out of Bombay,' he said, chuckling at Sam's latest tall story. 'But that takes the biscuit, it really does!'

'Ah well, that's not the end of it.' Sam was enjoying himself, the corners of his eyes creasing with laughter. 'After the race, the Zust car was taken back to England – and it was caught up in a fire at a railway station and burned to billy-oh!'

'No – you're having us on, Ironside!'

'I'm not. It's true as I'm sitting here!'

'What a fellow you are,' Captain Fairford said. Lily could see that he genuinely enjoyed Sam's company. After all, the two of them had travelled together and it had created a bond. And she sat in the glow of Sam's presence, feeling that she had never been so happy before.

Chapter Thirty-Eight

'You're starting to get more roses in your cheeks, Lily,' Susan Fairford remarked a couple of days later as they sat looking out over a breathtaking view of peaks and piled clouds, the sun slanting along the steep green valley. For all the outings and trips the Fairfords took that week, they sent invitation to Lily. Taking the Daimler some way out of town, they drank in the beauty of the Himalayan countryside and picnicked surrounded by its icy streams, its trees and flowers.

The men had gone off for a stroll to keep Isadora happy and the two women were sitting after tiffin, relaxing together. 'You looked really pale and under the weather when we first arrived.'

Lily smiled. She *was* feeling better, but the smile was also one of fondness towards Susan Fairford. Remembering the tense, snobbish woman she had first met in Ambala, she could see what a softening there had been. She knew Sam was still not sure about Susan Fairford. She was less relaxed when he was present, of course, and he tended to read class superiority into everything she said and be needled by it, but Lily had grown closer to her and to respect the struggles of her life. Just because the family had money and class, she knew, it did not always mean happiness.

'Yes – all this lovely fresh air. And your picnics. The

McBrides' food is much more basic, though I've done my best to make it at least more tasty.'

'I'm sure you have – you're very capable.' Susan Fairford looked at Lily closely, with a slight frown. 'And, of course, even more lovely to look at than I remembered.'

Lily blushed under this close scrutiny.

'But I worry for you,' her old mistress went on. 'It's him, isn't it – Sam Ironside – who's put the colour in your cheeks?'

Lily looked down, not meeting her eyes, her blush deepening, but she said nothing, hoping Susan could not see her confusion.

'Lily?' Susan persisted gently. 'Oh dear, I do remember you were both a little involved with each other last time he was here, but all that was such a time ago and it must be over now, surely?'

Lily found the courage to look up into Susan's blue eyes and nodded. 'Oh yes,' she said lightly. 'Completely.'

'You were so quiet, so miserable afterwards. I didn't realize, of course. But Lily – he still is married!'

'I know,' Lily said, even more brightly. 'There's nothing to worry about, really!'

'Well, I do hope so!' Susan said urgently. 'I'm going to speak very frankly, Lily: if there was anything between you, you'd have to get over it, both of you. I'd feel so responsible for throwing you together again. You'll only be in a dreadfully unhappy and shameful situation, Lily, dear! I can see he is far from indifferent to you and men can use one terribly falsely! After all, he can't leave a wife and children, can he? So there's no place for you – none at all. And certainly not without scandal and heartbreak.'

251

Lily hated to lie when she knew Susan was trying to protect her, but she simply could not bear to let Sam go again or to admit to the obstacles in the way of their being together.

'It's all right, I assure you,' she said, looking Susan directly in the eye. 'I'm very touched by your concern, but there's nothing between myself and Sam Ironside. That was all over years ago. I feel quite calm and indifferent about seeing him again.'

'Well,' Susan said. 'I'm immensely relieved to hear it.'

There were brief times when she was alone with Sam, or almost, walking ahead of the Fairfords, or behind, on the way to or from a picnic. And they talked in low, urgent voices. Lily was now aware that they were being watched. That day, after Susan's warning, they stepped ahead along the path.

'She told me to keep away from you,' Lily murmured.

'Does she know?' Sam's voice was tense.

'She guessed. It's not surprising really, is it? She guessed last time as well. I mean look at us now. It must be very obvious. I told her she had nothing to worry about . . .' For the first time she allowed reality to wash cold over the situation. Turning to him, she said, 'Sam, I don't know what to think. Whatever are we going to do?'

Sam stepped round a rock in the path, his face very serious. 'God, I want to see you alone, Lily. To spend time with you somewhere so that we can talk properly.'

Lily felt just as desperate. It was wonderful to see Sam every day, but they had had so little time alone, and the days were rushing past. Only five remained, and he would be snatched away from her again. Until now she had barely allowed herself to think about it.

'But how can we? Everyone is so determined to chaperone us.'

'One evening? Could you get out, d'you think?'

'Not tonight. I have to dine with Dr McBride and his guest. Perhaps tomorrow?'

'Tomorrow,' Sam said. 'Without fail.'

Soon after breakfast that morning, Ewan McBride had ordered her presence for dinner in the evening.

'Make sure you wear something especially nice, won't you, Lily? Perhaps one of your more exotic gowns. Would you like me to come and choose for you?'

Lily felt her hackles rise at the way he had to control everything, and realized that that was new. Before, she had simply grown used to it. But she knew the way to handle him.

'Perhaps the mirror gown?' she suggested compliantly. It was a very striking dress, stitched from rich pink, blue and peacock-green cloth from Rajasthan, with circles of mirror glass embroidered into the skirt and sleeves. Light shimmered and danced off it and it always produced gasps of admiration when she had appeared in it at parties. She often wore it with a strip of raw green mirrored silk wrapped round her smoothly coiffured hair.

'Oh yes, I think so,' Dr McBride almost purred. She could see that she was to be shown off as a trophy to Dr McCluskie. The thought of dining with the two men made her recoil. She knew she would feel the usual

253

sense of being unreal, not herself, like the china doll that Ewan McBride required her to be.

Stephen, the cook, was in a tizzy because the advent of a guest was so unusual.

'There is going to be a misadventure,' he wailed to Lily, who, on return from the picnic with the Fairfords, decided she had better help.

'But everything is going perfectly well,' she told him. 'Look, you've already done nearly all of it.' They were to have a roast duck with trimmings, and apple pie, and Stephen always got himself worked up about pastry. Even Prithvi seemed in a bit of a state, though she only had to serve the food. The household was simply not used to visitors.

By seven-thirty Lily had dressed herself, with a little help from Prithvi with the hooks and eyes, and put her hair up, wrapping the bandanna round it, and applied a thin line of kohl round her lids. Turning her head from side to side she realized that she looked very exotic. The doctor would be pleased. It was her habit to try and please him. It made her life peaceful. Tonight, though, her own spirit was strong in her and she felt a great flare of anger. Who did he think he was, some sort of puppet master, to have her dancing to his every tune?

'You may think you've got me on a string,' she whispered to her reflection, 'but not for much longer, Doctor. Because I love Sam Ironside and he loves me. And you have no power over that.'

And walking tall, haughtily, she went to the doctor's study and rapped on the door.

'Ah Lily, my dear!' Dr McBride said, throwing open the door to enable her to make a triumphal entry, and in so doing made Lily see that Dr McCluskie knew exactly what was her position in the household, and that she was there to be displayed as if part of a harem. She felt deeply shamed and angry, but she knew that coldly, quietly, she would play her part, for the moment.

'I say, how splendid!' Dr McCluskie leaped to his feet. 'What a very beautiful addition you are to the room, Miss Waters.' Unlike the last time she had seen Dr McCluskie, when he had appeared very gentlemanly, this time she sensed a lascivious edge to his speech which repelled her.

'Good evening, Dr McCluskie,' she said coolly, as they shook hands. She saw by the blush rising from his collar that this bashful bachelor was strongly affected by her presence.

Dr McBride handed her a glass of sweet sherry and Lily sipped it, feeling its syrupy warmth in her throat.

'From what part do you hail?' Dr McCluskie asked, and Lily, feeling the usual dread of questions, trotted out her usual version of events very briefly, before quickly diverting the conversation on to himself, a subject on which he appeared ready to elaborate at some length. As Dr McBride ushered them to the table, Dr McCluskie was telling Lily that much of his work from Patna involved travelling the villages, where he lived for weeks at a time, scarcely ever seeing another white face except those of missionaries in the field.

'It can make a man very hungry for a sight or sound of home,' he said, almost apologetically. 'And tonight is a veritable feast.'

Lily smiled faintly. She saw Dr McBride frowning, but Dr McCluskie, who suddenly seemed to have come to life, began to regale Lily with stories of medical oddities he had encountered in his work in remote villages, and as Prithvi carried in the soup, he was in the midst of a descriptive parade of goitres and tumours and birth defects hideous enough to turn the stomach.

'The whole of the foot was infested with white ants,' he said enthusiastically, as Prithvi fled from the room.

'D'you think, Duncan, we could manage to find a less picturesque line of conversation in front of the ladies?' Dr McBride requested in irritation. 'After all, even some medical men are not used to the rigours of rural India.'

'How utterly remiss of me,' Duncan McCluskie said, raising his glass to Lily. There was a twinkle in his eyes, but whereas before he had seemed placid, now there was a hard edge to him, something mocking. He was already well gone for drink. Both men were drinking whisky. 'Ewan and I go back a long way together – and we medical men, you know, we grow accustomed to talking about things which are not usually aired in polite society. My humble apologies, Miss Waters.'

Lily inclined her head graciously. She wasn't having him thinking that she was so easily shocked. 'Not at all. It was most interesting. I haven't had the privilege of visiting the more remote parts of the country.'

'Ah – no place for a lady, that I can tell you,' Dr McCluskie said, and another stream of reminiscences began.

They finished their soup and Prithvi came in, looking terrified, with the duck, which turned out to be excellently done. As they ate the two men exchanged stories and memories of student years in Edinburgh and their work since and Lily became their captive audience, though she was in any case oblivious to most of it, her mind wandering longingly to Sam. From what she did hear, the more they drank, the more competitive the storytelling became, each man trying to cap the other's experiences. Dr McCluskie had worked in some of the poorest parts of Glasgow before arriving in India and he was a fund of extraordinary tales which Dr McBride, who had been in Mussoorie for years, simply could not match.

'I'm sure Miss Waters doesn't want to hear about all this,' he said more than once, leaning forward to replenish Dr McCluskie's glass.

'Ah, but I must just tell you this one,' Duncan McCluskie insisted, and launched into a story about a family he had been involved with in Glasgow with thirteen children and almost every degree of ill health and misfortune that could be imagined. Listening to him talking about the lives of this poor family made Lily very uncomfortable. Little do they know, she thought, that I come from a place not so different. The Horne girls had left her in no ignorance of the fact that she was a poor foundling whose parents had deserted her. She felt a shudder go through her at all that she might have become. Better to put up with Ewan McBride's maulings than be poor like that!

But she was also becoming more aware of the strained atmosphere between the two men and especially when Duncan McCluskie said to her, 'Perhaps you'd like to come with me on one of my jaunts into the countryside, Miss Waters? I'm sure you'd find it highly educational.'

Dr McBride let out a sudden gust of laughter, but Lily could tell there was a dangerous edge to it.

'Really, Duncan – you are a card. Can you imagine this Lily-flower here out in the squalor of the villages?'

'Oh – I rather think Miss Waters has more to her than meets the eye,' Duncan McCluskie said, looking deep into Lily's eyes, before she lowered her gaze. The conversation was making her feel increasingly uncomfortable, these men acting so competitively over her. Fortunately Prithvi came in again then to clear away the plates and bring in the hot apple pie.

'I say – you've done us proud here!' Duncan McCluskie said. 'I haven't enjoyed a splendid meal like this in a very long time!'

'That's also thanks to our Miss Waters here. She has taken responsibility for organizing the household and making us fully shipshape.'

'Well, it's time someone took you to task, if you won't employ the normal number of servants like anyone else, McBride!'

'I don't need servants – I just need Lily here,' the doctor replied unguardedly. In his half-drunken state he gave her a soulful stare, like a lecherous spaniel. Lily felt more and more uncomfortable, and as soon as the pie was eaten she got up quickly from the table.

'I'll leave you gentlemen to your coffee now,' she said.

The two men lurched to their feet in surprise. 'No, Lily – don't leave us yet,' Dr McBride said. Lily knew it was an order, but she decided to treat it as a request.

'It's kind of you, but I'm very tired and I'm sure you would like more time to talk alone. Goodnight, Dr McCluskie. It has been most enjoyable.'

He took her hand in his clammy one and held it for seconds longer than necessary, staring into her eyes.

'Goodnight, Miss Waters. I'm charmed. Utterly charmed.'

At last she was free to leave the room.

*

If he knocked on the door she didn't hear it. The first thing she became aware of was a light in the room and she sat up, pulsing with shock. She had been deeply asleep, but now there was a figure standing by her bed, holding a candle and she knew immediately from his slender build that it was not Dr McBride.

'No need to be frightened,' he whispered. He lifted the mosquito net and sat down on the bed. Lily could see that Duncan McCluskie was very much the worse for drink. His eyes looked glazed and strange.

'What are you doing here?' She was torn between outrage and fear. It must be the small hours and he had seen fit just to wander in here! What was she, some woman of the streets that everyone could use on a whim? But he was a strong-looking man, with a wild look in his eye at this moment and she was frightened of what he might do. Setting the mosquito net alight with the candle seemed a distinct possibility, quite apart from anything else. She eased herself away from him, in readiness to slide off the other side of the bed.

'Don't pretend you don't know, you beautiful, teasing whore.' His voice was low and urgent. 'Flaunting yourself at me like that all evening. This is what you do for him, isn't it? So you can do it for me. That's what you want, isn't it? I can see you looking at me . . . Well, I'm ready for you.'

Without even putting the candle down he lunged at her, grabbing her round the shoulders with his left hand and forcing his lips to hers while he held the candle with the other, perilously close to her hair. Lily struggled, panic-stricken, and managed to get her legs on to the floor the other side of the bed. She struggled away from him, fighting her way out from under the mosquito net.

'For God's sake – you'll set the place alight! Get that candle away from me. How *dare* you come in here and behave like this?'

But he was not easily deterred. He reached over to put the candle down on the washstand and stood up to fling the mosquito net over the wooden frame before lunging at her.

'Don't go all prissy on me. I know you're his mistress. It's obvious. If you go about dressed up like a bitch on heat, what do you expect? I haven't had a woman in months and it's no way for a man to live. I want you, Lily, and I'm going to have you. By God, if you can give yourself to that old dog, you can give yourself to me too ...'

He seized hold of her, pressing himself against her with frantic urgency, pushing his tongue in her mouth, his hands groping at her breasts. He took hold of her shoulders and tried to force her down on to the bed. Lily found her mind working faster than she had ever known it. Knowing how drunk he was, she leaned her weight against him. Duncan McCluskie took this as being the response he wanted.

'That's it ...' He breathed whisky fumes into her face. 'I knew you wanted it. Get on the bed, lie down so I can have you ...'

Lily drew back as if she was about to obey, but then stepped fast towards him again and shoved him as hard as she could. For a moment the doctor wavered, then toppled over backwards on to the bed.

'You scheming bitch!' he growled.

'Get out,' Lily hissed, standing over him. 'Or I'll wake the whole house. Is that what you want? How *dare* you come and behave in this disgusting way? Now you get up and get out of my room!'

260

He sat up, groggily, seeming stunned, as if coming to his senses.

'All right, I'll go – I'm sorry.' He got up off the bed. 'Don't say anything, will you? I'm sorry – it's just been so long . . . I got it wrong . . .'

Lily opened the door without another word and waited for him to leave.

'You won't tell Ewan?'

Lily had no intention of telling Ewan McBride because she knew far better than Duncan McCluskie what his jealous anger was like. But she said stiffly, 'So long as it doesn't happen again.'

Chapter Thirty-Nine

Lily did not see Dr McCluskie the next morning, but what had happened in the night and the way she had stood up for herself made her feel stronger. In any case, her mind was full of thoughts of Sam.

She spent a pleasant teatime hour at Zinnias with Susan and Srimala, playing with Isadora, and in a snatched moment, she and Sam arranged to meet at the beginning of the Camel's Back that night.

Lily ate her dinner alone. After last night's events she had wondered how Dr McCluskie would be able to face her, and her only sighting of the two men was that evening. As Lily was standing in the hall exchanging a few words with Jane Brown, the doctors came in out of the dusk. Lily saw a shade of emotion pass across Dr McCluskie's face, a reflex of extreme embarrassment, which was then converted into a superior contempt.

'Good evening, Miss Waters,' he said coldly.

She nodded. 'Mr McCluskie.' It had not been deliberate, omitting to call him 'doctor' but she saw the insult register with him.

However, she spent most of the evening fretting in her room about whether she would be able to leave the house without anyone seeing. She thought about trying to climb out of the window, but, like so many Mussoorie houses, it was built clinging to the edge of the hillside and outside, apart from a narrow ledge, was nothing but a steep drop into darkness. She would have to get through the house as best she could.

At five to eleven her heart was beating so fast she could hardly bear it. She had been pacing the room trying to find an outlet for all her pent-up energy, and at last she opened the door of her room very quietly and crept out into the corridor. She had even left the pillows in her bed to look like her sleeping shape. As she crept along the corridor she heard the two doctors' voices in Dr McBride's study, could smell whisky and pipe smoke and hear their drink-laced laughter. They would be carrying on like that for hours to come. She went to the front door and slipped out into the mild, sweet-scented darkness.

Her steps sounded loud out in the street and she realized that she was never out at night unaccompanied and was unused to the deep darkness, lit only by a crescent moon.

'Lily?' His voice came from the shadows and her whole being leaped with happiness at the sound.

'Sam!'

He caught her immediately in his arms and they clung to each other, at last alone and able to express their feelings.

'God, girl, I love you,' he said into her neck. 'I love you so much.'

'And I love you. Oh, Sam, what are we going to do?'

She wanted to pour out all her fears, but this was not the time to talk and for those moments all they wanted was to stand in each other's arms. But then they heard whistling, and footsteps coming from the Camel's Back Road, and they stepped apart.

'Come on – the car's parked below the Kulri Bazaar. We'll get out of town.'

'*Can* we?' Lily was amazed. 'Surely we can't just take it?'

'Lily.' His voice came out of the darkness. 'This is something that doesn't happen except once in a lifetime. And terribly soon I'll have to be gone – back on the ship. What could be the harm?'

'I can't believe it – us just being able to be on our own!'

'All week it's been all I've been able to think about. Come on.' He reached for her.

They walked hand in hand through the winding bazaar, all shut up for the night now, and down, past poor native houses, hearing the sounds of families crowded inside, the cry of an infant, voices, a man singing. And all around, the smells of dung fires, incense and spiced food. Lily breathed in the smells of India, and everything was made lovely because Sam was walking beside her, holding her.

The car was parked in a low building which looked and smelled like a stables. When Sam cranked up the engine the noise seemed to explode into the quiet, and he jumped in and released the brake, switching on the bright headlights.

'Right – we'll find a spot just for us.'

She couldn't see much as they drove along except for moving shadows, aware sometimes of the tall trees above, and of their delicious smell, and of the switching bends in the road. They didn't speak much, not then. Sometimes, as he drove, Sam reached across and touched her hand, pressing it gently.

'You're here – you're really here!' she said once, full of love, drinking in the wonder of his presence.

At last he stopped in what appeared to be the edge of a little clearing and as the engine died the silence expanded round them, broken by the high squeak of some woodland creature. The thin moon looked down on them through the trees which moved gently in the breeze.

'We've been here before – d'you remember?' he said. 'The picnic a few days back.'

'Have we? I couldn't tell on the way.'

'The one with the little stream running between the trees. Where Isadora got her clothes sopping wet.'

'Oh yes!' she laughed. 'Yes, of course I remember!'

Sam got out of the car and was foraging in the back for something.

'I've got a surprise for you. Come on. We'll make it nice.'

She could see very little, but followed him over the soft woodland earth and to the place he seemed to have in mind and she heard a small clanking sound as he put something on the ground.

'I've got wood and paper, matches, a lamp – even tea and cake,' he said. 'We'll have a nice little fire and make it cosy. And there's a rug in the car. I'll just nip and get it.'

'Don't leave me here!' Lily said, alarmed. 'I'm coming with you!'

Sam laughed. 'Well, I'd better bring the bag back with me as well, or we might never find it again.'

Holding hands, giggling like two children, they hurried back through the trees to the motor car to collect the rug.

'Like babes in the wood,' Sam said.

'Isn't there supposed to be a gingerbread house?'

'No.' He thought about it. 'I think that's a different story – I couldn't be sure, though!'

In their clearing he laid the fire and got it burning,

and the wood caught gradually, the flames building and glowing in the night, sending off their warm light and dancing shadows. Lily busied herself spreading the rug on the ground, feeling that although they were outside, with no shelter and the most basic of provisions, she had never before experienced such a sense of luxury. She unpacked the bag, the bottles of tea and bananas and slabs of cake wrapped in waxed paper.

'How completely wonderful!' she said, amazed by the careful preparations he had made.

'I picked up quite a bit camping with the captain,' he said. 'I don't think there are too many animals up here to worry about, but they don't like fire anyway.'

She watched it burning, and glowed with happiness herself, smiling at him in the orange light.

Once everything was ready they sat together on the rug, faces and hands warmed by the flames. In the firelight Sam turned to her.

'Lily, I'm so sorry about last time – that I wasn't straight with you from the beginning. I'm not a liar, not as a rule, only I was so keen to get to know you, so set on you, I knew if I said anything about home and Helen ... Well, I wouldn't stand a chance, and I just ... See, even now, I can talk to you the way I can't to anyone else ...'

'It's all right.' She looked into his eyes. 'It was terrible then. Truly, it was. You broke my heart, Sam. And your wife expecting a child – all of it ... I never thought I'd get over it.'

'I never got over you,' he said with great seriousness.

'Even now—' She hated saying it, but it had to be brought out. 'You've children, Sam – your girls.'

Sam stared gravely into the fire and let out a long sigh. 'Children are a blessing but sometimes ... I suppose it's the responsibility, the burden of it, at times. Being a father, I mean. And I wanted to do it well – take care of them. They're lovely, of course – pretty little things. I could never not take responsibility for them, Lily. But my God, I can't go on the way I am. Not while you exist somewhere. I feel as if everything stops when I'm not with you. As if you're what I'm made for.'

Moved, she reached up and kissed his cheek. 'And you're the same for me. You're the only man I've ever loved and it never went away, Sam, even though you did.'

'It's so strange,' he said slowly. 'Because although I love you, I don't know much about you. You were always a mystery. And you know a bit about me – Coventry, cars and Helen, that's my life. Tell me about you, Lily – will you?'

Immediately she felt the old reflex of shame for the past which made her want to hide everything, even from him. Here he was, a man she felt so much for and even so, she found it so difficult. But his eyes looked down into hers with intense love and he leaned down and lightly kissed her lips. And as well as the shame, she found herself full of an ache, a longing to talk and share with him who she was and where she had come from and feel accepted for it instead of having to pretend to be someone she wasn't. And the longing drove her to speak.

'I don't know much about my background,' she began, her heart beating fiercely. It felt like opening a room which had been locked for many years and being afraid of what might be inside. For the first time in her life she started to talk about the things Mary Horne had told her, about them finding her in the street in

Birmingham, alone in the cold outside a dismal slum dwelling, and about the things she could remember, living with the Hornes, and Mrs Chappell.

'I thought I'd never get over it when she died,' she said, sitting wrapped in Sam's arms, looking into the fire as she spoke. 'I thought she was the only person in the world who would ever care for me, and when she'd gone I had no one else. I wanted to get out and start again, to go somewhere new, so that's when I came out to work for the Fairfords. And there was Cosmo – my beautiful little Cosmo . . .'

Leaning against Sam, warm and cherished, Lily found to her surprise that she wanted to cry, and the tears started coming even though she tried to stop them. She rested her head on his chest, quietly shaken by sobs.

Sam stroked her head. 'What's the matter?' he asked, gently.

When she could speak, Lily drew back and looked up at him wet-cheeked, and seeing his face bronzed and gentle in the firelight, gazing down at her so lovingly, more tears came.

'I've never known this. Not being held like this.'

'Oh, Lily, my love . . .' he said, moved by her and her story. He drew her even closer to him again, his hand on her head, rocking her. For a time they sat quietly, hearing the crackle and spit of the fire, and the breeze gently moving the trees. It felt like sitting in a cave, the light a halo around them, and only darkness beyond. Lily felt warm and loved and alive in a way she never had before. She couldn't say to Sam that although she had been clasped in Dr McBride's arms night after night, it had never felt like this. It had been not love, but being used, and this difference, the longing it answered, filled her with emotion. She felt Sam gently

268

kissing the top of her head and she turned and looked up at him with serious eyes.

'I've got to go home,' he said at last. 'My passage is booked. The works will be waiting for me to come back . . . But I'll . . .' He was struggling with his emotions. 'Lily, I can't be away from you again. We've got to be together. I'll go and . . . finish things, somehow. There's Helen, and the work, and then . . .'

'I'll come home,' Lily said. 'It's no good, you coming out here, is it? What would you do? And your daughters . . .'

'But we'd have to move away. Somewhere where no one knows us . . . I'd send Helen money . . .'

'We'd have to find somewhere . . .'

It all seemed so momentous, so shocking and terrible and wonderful a decision to be having to make that neither of them could take it in or think clearly. Only then had it become fully clear that they had to be together, at all costs, but how on earth?

'I *have* to be with you,' Sam said in the end, holding her tightly. 'I don't know how, not yet, but it's the only thing I've ever known or been so sure about. Whatever it takes, Lily, I've got to get back to you.'

'I can't bear the thought of you going away,' she said, gazing into his eyes. 'I wish we could just go now, keep moving on, and be together, just you and me.'

Sam smiled fondly. 'I think the captain might have something to say if we just make off with his motor car.'

'We'll go in a *tonga* then!'

'And live on air for the rest of our days?' He squeezed her lovingly. 'My Lily, I want to keep you better than that. I want you to be happy and comfortable.'

She looked up at him in wonder. No one had ever told her such things before, or looked at her with such love in their eyes. Even Mrs Chappell's concern for her was a pale shadow of this.

'I love you, Sam,' she said. 'I want to be with you – always.'

She could scarcely believe it was her saying these words. Sam got up for a moment to put more wood on the fire and it blazed brightly, creating more leaping shadows around them.

'Here – let's have the tea before it's cold,' he said. They sipped from the little tin cup, sharing it, and ate the fruit cake he had brought, and then snuggled together on the rug in the heat of the fire, a coat rolled up under their heads.

'D'you think there's anyone else around?' Lily said. It felt as if they were the only people ever to breathe this clear mountain air.

'I doubt it. There were some huts but they were a way away.'

'Tell me about Helen,' she said

He leaned up on his elbow and looked down into her face. 'What about her?'

'Well, you know – what's she like? Is she anything like me?'

'Lily – no one is like you.'

'You must have liked her or why would you marry her?'

Sam lay back and stared up at the starlit sky. He sighed.

'We've been married for four years. Seems like an eternity. She's all right, Helen is. A good sort, and she's a good mother – you know, kind-hearted and steady. She seems to know what to do for them, without anyone telling her, which must be nature, I suppose. That side of it's all right – the children. But when it comes to me she doesn't want me, not really. I think she married the wrong man, and she knows it. She's got a friend, a chap called Laurie. She should have married him.' He stopped and sighed for a second.

'When you first meet someone, and you're young, you don't know anything, do you? You just think, This must be it, because it's happening and you feel *something* – a lot of it just the body when you come down to it – and you think this is *it*. This is love and how it's meant to be. But you don't know how much more it can be. We don't do anything much for each other, Helen and me. We don't light each other up, never have. And I didn't know there *was* lighting up, not like this, until I met you.'

Leaning up on his elbow, he reached down to kiss her and she responded passionately.

'Oh God, girl . . .' He looked down at her, face full of a wistful hunger. 'It's no good. You're my woman and that's how it is. I've tried and tried, but I can't go back now.'

Wide-eyed she looked up at him, moved by the strength of his desire for her.

'Don't go back,' she whispered. 'Please don't leave me again, ever.'

He kissed her forehead, stroking away strands of her hair. 'I shan't leave you, girl. You're mine.'

It came so naturally, their lovemaking. Lily had gone through the motions so many times with Dr McBride, sometimes feeling her body respond a little, in spite of itself, but never her mind. She had never before responded to a man, or opened her whole self, to anyone. Sam's hands moving over her, his face as he touched her body, gave her feelings she had never had before. The sight of his body as they removed some of their clothes moved her, instead of repelling her the way Ewan McBride's portly frame did.

'God, you're so beautiful,' Sam said, gazing on her as they knelt together, their skin rosy in the firelight. His eyes were full of desire for her, and all she longed for was to hold him close and stroke his hair, his back, to pour all her pent-up affections on to him.

'Come here, love,' he said, and they wrapped their arms round each other and she was overcome by sensations, her fingers caressing his back, the supple skin over hard muscle, the long, powerful spine, and his lips first on her lips, then seeking out her breasts, filling her whole body with sensations of longing and then his urgent request for her to lie back on the rug, her head pillowed as he lay over her, looking down into her eyes.

Sam's desire for her and the loving way he stroked her and entered her filled her with tenderness and longing for him and she felt as if this, not the mechanical way she had fulfilled the doctor's demands, was the first time she had ever made love with a man. This first time was so passionate, so intense that it happened urgently and quickly. But they lay together then, close and warm, pulling the rug round them.

'I never knew it could be like this,' Sam said, looking deeply into her eyes. 'I had no idea. God, Lily, I love you so much.'

'Don't leave me, Sam,' she whispered again, fearfully. 'I love you.'

'I won't.' His breath was warm on her ear. 'Even when I'm gone, I shall be here with you, because you're part of me. We belong together.'

'We'll be together – we *will*,' she murmured, tenderly

kissing his cheek, her hands caressing his warm chest and belly. They lay there, pressed close together in the firelight, among the smell of the pines, until they slept, two tiny figures amid the great Himalaya, where the dark flank of the mountain reached up to greet the star-bright sky.

Chapter Forty

Lily woke first. There was already a fringe of light along the eastern sky and she felt the cool breeze on her face, smelled the trees, the dampness of the dew-soaked ground and knew, even before her waking mind confirmed it, that everything was changed. The sight of Sam's upper arm beside her in the dawn light, his slender features and dark moustache gave her a great surge of happiness. He was here, they were together, and however damp and stiff with cold, now the fire was long dead, this was the only place on earth she wanted to be.

'Sam . . . Sam, my lovely . . .'

His eyes opened and after a second's bewilderment, a smile of wonder spread across his face.

'Oh, Lily!' His lips searched immediately for hers. 'I thought I'd dreamed you!' He held her as if she was the most precious thing on earth and she lay with her head on his chest, hearing the confident beat of his heart.

'Lord,' he said suddenly. 'We'd better get back! The sun's coming up!'

Tearing themselves away from one another they carried the rug and picnic things through the heavy dew to the car, only then noticing how cold they were, pulling the rug across their laps to drive back through the dawn. The sun was coating the mountain ridges with pink and gold as they set off, and as they came into

Mussoorie, hurrying back to Kulri and the parking place, the higgledy-piggledy mountain town was bathed in a bronze dawn light. Sam steered the Daimler into the shed and her engine sputtered into quietness.

'There.' Sam turned, smiling at her, though the thought of having to part again was unbearable. 'Will the McBride household be up by now?'

'No – but it won't be long.' She was fluttery with nerves, but also didn't care what happened now. She had Sam, they were together, and nothing else mattered.

'Come round to the bungalow later – can you?' He put his arm round her, in the dark shelter, and they gazed into each other's eyes. Sam kissed her tenderly. 'I don't think I can stand more than a few hours without you, my lovely.'

'I'll come – of course I'll come,' she said. 'Nothing can stop me being with you.'

When she left him, warm with his kisses, it felt like being physically torn away, but strengthened by the knowledge that she would see him again in only a few hours she hurried up the hill to the bungalow. Alone, panic filled her. It must be after five in the morning – would everyone still be asleep? Prithvi started work very early, but at least she could rely on her not to make any trouble.

She had left the front door unlocked and when she turned the iron handle it opened silently. Catching her breath she stepped into the dark hall expecting the doctor, or at least Cameron the dog, who might bark and give her away. Seeing there was no one around, she closed the door quietly behind her.

'And where exactly have you been?'

He must have been waiting there silently in the passage, because when she turned again she was no longer alone. Dr McBride's form seemed to fill the whole doorway. In the gloom she could make out only the outline of his features, but the tone of his voice told her all she needed to know. He was seething with a rage only barely controlled.

'I've just been out for a little walk,' she gabbled brightly. 'I woke early and the light was so lovely I thought I'd go out and watch the dawn – like Miss Brown does. I used to get up very early in Ambala and ride out with Mrs Fairford and it reminded me of how beautiful the early light is—'

'You lying little bitch!' He strode over to her and seized her shoulders. Lily gasped with shock at the enraged force of him. 'You haven't been in your bed all night so don't play the little innocent with me! I went to you last night and you weren't there. You were with *him*, weren't you? Tell me, you overheated little whore!' He shook her terrifyingly hard.

'With who?'

'With that goat McCluskie, of course! Did you go to his room? Couldn't control yourself? Or some little tryst somewhere? My God, after all I've done for you you'd think you could behave in a trustworthy manner, but oh no, one male visitor to the house and I have to watch you every second.' Again, he shook her so abruptly that her head throbbed and she felt tearful. She was tired, and this came with the shock of a slap after Sam's loving embrace. 'Tell me – admit it! And where is he? Where's that bastard gone off to?'

'I've no idea,' Lily gasped, confused. 'I haven't seen Dr McCluskie – not since yesterday morning, I swear to you.' In her fright she grasped the fact that the only way she was going to calm him down was by appeasement. She could see the anguish mixed with his rage and she spoke to that. Taking courage, she laid her hands on his shoulders.

'Ewan, dear . . .' He went to shake her off but she persevered. 'No, listen, please – I need to tell you something. I didn't want to tell you, to upset you or your guest, but it seems I must now.'

He stared at her, face full of hostility, but he was listening.

'Two nights ago Dr McCluskie came to my room and attempted to have . . . relations with me. He was the worse for drink and rather unpleasant, but I managed to make him leave without anything happening. It was all quite horrible and obviously made facing him again very difficult. But I can assure you, Ewan, dear, that nothing happened, I made sure of it, and that I have no interest in such a boor of a man who could approach me in such a way. He's not like you, dear, not gentle and manly. He behaved like a coward and I hoped never to see him again . . .'

'The cad!' Ewan McBride was still breathing heavily, but she could see he believed her and his fury was not directed at her for the moment.

'And I really have no idea at all where he is now,' she said. 'Let's not worry about him, dear.'

She thought she had talked him round, but then his mood switched again, eyes narrowing, his breath quickening in agitation.

'That may be so,' he said. 'But you must have led him on in some way. I know you, the way you prey on men, I've seen you. And where have you been? You can't just shift the blame to McCluskie. You've been with him, or some other man – I know it, I can *smell* it on you!'

He was winding his temper up again and she became

frightened that he was going to hit her. Even in his rage, on this occasion he did not raise his voice above a venomous hiss: it wouldn't do to have anyone hear. He seized hold of her even harder, grabbing her wrists, and pulled her along the corridor.

'An end to this – I'm not having it. You're going to learn how to behave like a lady, the way I've taught you!'

'Ewan – stop it! You're hurting me – please, don't!'

'Inside – and don't think you're coming out until I say so!' Dr McBride threw open the door of Lily's room and forced her in, shoving her so hard that she stumbled and fell half across the bed. For a second she was stunned, but then she found herself full of explosive rage.

'Don't you push me like that!' she shouted as he disappeared. 'Don't you dare treat me like that!' She ran to the door and went furiously to open it but he was holding the handle the other side and she could not turn it.

'Settle down, you little wild cat.' She could only just hear him, sounding smug and powerful, through the thick wood. 'You're not coming out – not until I say so.'

'You can't keep me in here,' Lily spat at the door. There was no lock so how did he think he was going to stop her getting out? 'I'm not your chattel to push around. I'll come out whenever I like!'

'Oh, that's what you think, my pretty little tiger. We'll soon see to it that you don't come out of there except with my express permission.'

'I'm not staying here!' With a supreme effort she quietened her tone, though the anger she felt with him, the filthy old sod, almost choked her. After her night with Sam, after all Sam meant to her and had made her feel, the thought of Ewan McBride and the way she had serviced him sickened her. Never again was she going to let any man treat her like that!

'Ewan – you're being a bit harsh.' She spoke calmly, seductively. 'I told you, I haven't been with any other man. What man would there be, for goodness' sake, when I never see anyone? Just come in here and we'll talk about it. I'll make you feel better.'

'Don't you come that one.' He still had a firm hold on the door and she heard him shouting for Prithvi, whose voice Lily heard a moment later. Dr McBride issued some abrupt order to her in Hindustani and she was gone again.

A quarter of an hour passed while Lily pleaded, struggling every now and then with the handle, and the doctor held the door fast. She heard a voice outside and thought, Surely Jane must be back from her walk now? But she realized it was Stephen.

'Miss Waters has been taken ill,' she heard the doctor say. There came a murmured reply from Stephen and that was all.

Soon she heard another voice, male and native. There was a clink of tools being put down, then a drill. In a moment Lily realized, to her horror, what was happening.

'No!' she screamed through the door. 'You can't! You can't just lock me in here! For God's sake, this is too much, Ewan – let me out! Oh, please, let me out!'

She was sobbing now as he held the door cruelly closed and she could hear bolts being screwed into the door, one top, one bottom, and finally the rasp of them as they were pushed home.

'There!' Ewan McBride called to her. 'Now you're mine all right, my Lily. And don't you forget it!'

And then the footsteps went away and it was all quiet.

Chapter Forty-One

Lily sank down on the edge of the bed, trying to take in what Ewan McBride had done.

He couldn't really mean it! She had known the doctor wanted to have her in his control but she had never dreamed he would go as far as this. Surely he'd let her stew for an hour or so and then come and let her out? She'd still be able to get to Sam this afternoon if she was patient. And if he didn't come and release her, she'd find a way out, of course she would!

At first she was full of hope, almost light-hearted and still not believing. She crept to the door and turned the handle.

'Oh no you don't, Lily, my love. Don't think you're going to get away with it.'

She sprang back, heart pounding. Lord above, was he still out there, guarding her? The house was quiet and she had assumed he had gone away to begin on breakfast and work as on a normal day, when all the time he had been waiting, silently, outside her door. For the first time she felt a cold plunge of fear. Surely, sooner or later he'd have to go and attend to his patients?

In stockinged feet she tiptoed to the window and looked out over the majestic grey hills bathed in early-morning sunshine. In the yard of the school below the children were doing their morning drill and she could hear the slap of their feet as they ran round and the gong beating time. Below the window was the steep drop. What if she really needed to get out, if the doctor kept her in here all afternoon? The mood he was in made her realize that she had no idea what he might do. What if she couldn't see Sam? The thought was too terrible. No – she was going to find a way out.

She thought about knotting the bed sheets. If she tied the sheets to the window frame, would she be able to climb down? But she knew the back of the house. There was nowhere to climb down to, only the drop many feet to the shrubbery surrounding the schoolyard. She prowled the room. What other way out was there? It did not take long to realize that there was only the door and the window. Other than that the room was completely sealed. Suddenly tired, chilly, she sat on the bed again. She'd find a way, she told herself. She was not going to let him defeat her! What she must do was wait until he must surely have to go away and get someone else to let her out. Prithvi would help her, of course she would. In the meantime she would wait quietly. A nap would pass the time. Lying down on the bed, weary from a night with so little sleep, she cuddled her pillow, longing for Sam.

It was half past ten when she woke, cold and low with an insistent ache in her bladder. At least there was a chamber pot in the room, and she was able to relieve herself, but this did not help with the fact that she was now hungry and needed breakfast. The buoyancy of her mood earlier had completely gone and she sat hugging herself, feeling chilly and desperate. Did he want her to beg, was that it? Would he let her out if she went and pleaded pitifully? She hated the thought of having to grovel to him, but she was already humiliated by being locked up in here. She saw everything very starkly now. This was simply an extension of the humiliating way he had used her all along. And why had she let him? In exchange for pretty dresses and security and, if she was honest, for the sense of feminine power it had given her. She felt disgusted with herself. But that time was no more. All that mattered now was that she get out and be able to be with Sam for these precious hours before they were parted again, and Ewan McBride was not going to stop her!

'Ewan – are you still there?' She held her ear against the door, trying to sense his presence. There was no reply. Once again she tried the handle, straining vainly and with increasingly frantic impatience against the bolts, but the door was well and truly secured. There was no reply from outside.

Lily felt a surge of hope. If he'd gone out on his rounds, surely she could get someone else in the house to let her out?

'Help!' she shouted. 'Can someone help me? Prithvi, *Prithvi* – are you there? Mrs Das? Is there anyone there? Let me out, please!'

She shouted until she was hoarse and then stopped to listen, but there was still no response. The doctor really had gone, she realized, and it sounded almost as if everyone else in the house had as well. Her shouting was completely in vain.

'Oh, please, *please* . . .' she finished in a whisper, sinking to her knees by the door. The tears came then, at being locked in and left here, so powerless. She curled up, rocking herself until the emotion had exhausted itself, then got up, draggingly, and went to the bed where she lay down again. She told herself to be calm.

The morning was only half gone. It was hours before she was due to meet Sam and the doctor would come back at tiffin time, calmer and seeing sense. He would have to make sure she was fed at some time, and then, somehow, she would make sure she got out. She *had* to!

Lying on the bed, she strained her ears to hear the sounds of the house. Distantly she heard doors open and close, but no one came near. There was no sound of Mrs Das sweeping, or Prithvi humming. They must have been told to keep away. She lay thinking longingly of Sam. The minutes dragged past with appalling slowness: eleven o'clock, twelve. The gun boomed across from Gun Hill signalling midday. Lily sat up, driven to an agony of impatience. Was Dr McBride intending to starve her to death? Surely someone would come now?

But another half-hour passed, and nothing. She was very thirsty and there was nothing to drink except the remains of some water in her pitcher for washing. She hesitated to drink it. It might make her ill – but her health had been exceptionally good since she had been India. She poured water into the glass on the washstand and drank deeply, then used a little more of the water to have a wash. After this purposeful activity it was almost one o'clock. All she could think of was that in two hours she must set out to go to the Fairfords' house and meet Sam.

At one o'clock she heard the bolts being drawn back and she leaped up from the bed, hoping desperately to see Prithvi, bringing tiffin for her, and she could beg her for help and everything would be all right. She could hurry down the road to Sam, even if too early.

'Glad to see me, are you?' the doctor said.

His voice was low, full of a controlled triumph. He

was carrying a tray on which there was a small pot of tea, a plate of bread and butter and a boiled egg with a white shell. Balancing it on one hand he closed the door, then put the tray down on the small table near the window. In that split second Lily thought of running for the door, getting it open again, but then he had turned to her and it was too late. He saw the direction of her glance.

'You don't want to be running away, do you now, Lily, dear?' He spoke sweetly, affording himself the pleasure of being kindly since he knew he had the upper hand. Making sure he was between the door and Lily, he came towards her until he was intimately close, looking down into her eyes, laying his hands heavily on her shoulders. Lily controlled herself so that she did not recoil. She knew that he was in a state beyond anything she had seen before and that it was vital for her to behave calmly. She'd do anything she could to get herself out of this situation and regain her freedom.

'Why would you want to run away from me?' He sounded genuinely wounded now. 'I've done so much for you, my Lily. I've fed and clothed you, loved you, given you a good life. You're my little Lily and I don't understand why you'd want to go running after other men like Duncan McCluskie. What has Duncan to charm you?'

'Nothing, Ewan.' She looked up earnestly at him. That at least was true. She found Duncan McCluskie even more repellent than Ewan McBride. 'You've made a mistake, really you have. I don't know why you've let this idea grow in your mind when you know I've always been here when you've needed me. You mustn't get so upset about things that are only your imagination and nothing else.'

'You mean I'm yours – that I mean something to you?' Suddenly he sounded pathetic.

'*Yes.*' She forced as much sweet sincerity into her voice as she could muster. 'Of *course* you do. You've always been so kind and generous to me, dear, and I shall always be so grateful to you.' She stood on tiptoe and kissed his cheek. 'I'm your little Lily, aren't I? No one else's.'

The doctor stared down at her in silence and she thought for a second she had won him over, but then his eyes narrowed.

'You're a wily young minx, aren't you?'

'Whatever d'you mean?' she asked, in a tone of injured innocence.

'Where . . . did . . . you . . . go?' As he said each word he squeezed her shoulders painfully hard as if trying to wring the truth out of her. 'You came in this morning with the look of a lover, Lily. I'm no fool – you can't hide it from me. And I'm not going to let you out of here until I get the truth.'

'You're hurting me!' Lily felt like crying but she wasn't going to break down in front of him. 'I've told you, I went for a walk, that's all. The dawn was lovely, and . . .'

'You little liar!' He slapped her hard round the face, his own contorting with rage. Lily cried out. The sting of it was very sharp and she felt a jarring all along her jaw. 'You stand there, lying to me grossly, wantonly, like that! I thought if I could get out of you a sweet word of truth and apology I might think about letting you out some time today. But I can see I was fooling myself. You won't be going anywhere – not today, not ever, if you don't learn to stop lying and tell me the truth!'

Dr McBride gave her a contemptuous shove which sent Lily backwards so that she almost fell on to the bed, and he slammed out of the room. She heard the bolts being rammed furiously into place and his footsteps fading along the passage.

Lily sank to her knees by the bed and buried her face in the covers. How was she ever going to get out of here to see Sam? Her whole being was full of urgency, the need to fly to him. It was now the only thing that mattered. And the doctor seemed to be almost unhinged with jealousy and suspicion. Would she even get out of here today? She buried her head in the covers and sobbed with rage and frustration.

Chapter Forty-Two

After her meal, Lily's spirits recovered for a time. She felt more optimistic. Of course he couldn't keep her here! As soon as his own tiffin was over he'd come and insist that she accompany him on one of their walks. At least then she would be out of the house.

Desperate plans hatched in her mind. She would set off with McBride and somehow give him the slip as they passed through the bazaar. Or she would simply run away from him, straight to Zinnias and Sam!

But as the minutes passed, the clock ticking loudly and ringing out the quarter hours, and there was no sound of footsteps out in the passage, once more she was full of desperation. Half past one, two o'clock. The school below on the hill went quiet. How the minutes dragged as she alternately sat and then paced the room, able to think only about Sam expecting her, looking out for her. Two-thirty came and went and when the time arrived when she should have been setting off she was in an agony of need. He would be waiting for her and think she had decided to let him down!

For the first time she lost control of herself. Weeping, she hammered on the door, bruising her fists as she raged at it.

'Let me out! Someone come and get me out, please! Oh, please don't leave me in here any more! Prithvi? Jane? Help me!'

Still no one came. There was only silence from the house. Three o'clock. Sam would be waiting. She knew that kind of expectation he would be feeling, the way she felt every time she waited to see him. And she would not come. The next two hours passed in an agony as she thought of the Fairfords' bungalow, imagining what was happening there and what Sam might be feeling and thinking of her. If only she could get a note delivered to him, but there was no one she could ask! Once more she wept helplessly.

By the late afternoon, as the sunlight faded to coppery pink, she had sunk into a state of lassitude. She had eaten very little that day, she had only been able to relieve herself in the chamber pot, which badly needed emptying, and any hopes for the day had been dashed. She thought about all the violent things she would like to do to Dr McBride. Sam was leaving for Bombay to catch his ship in two days and she had already missed a precious afternoon with him, thanks to the doctor! All she could think of now was seeing Sam before he left.

All night her thoughts span with anxiety. Surely the doctor would come to his senses and let her out in the morning? How was he explaining her absence to the rest of the household? But this was a worry. The title 'doctor' commanded such power! He could give them some trumped-up explanation for her absence and no one would even question it, possibly even Jane Brown. Lily felt panic rise in her. What if Dr McBride had really lost his senses and was planning to keep her here for as long as he liked, to play with her?

The pink dawn brought a new sense of hope and balance. Of course he'd let her out! He came to her with a tray of breakfast, having neglected to give her dinner the night before. Scrambled eggs and toast and a banana fortified her, but he barely spoke, despite her pleas to him to forgive her and let her go, to tell her what he planned to do. Once more the door was closed and the bolts slammed into place.

The day passed in an agony of uncertainty. Lily sat, half in a trance, or paced the room, losing all sense of time. When the doctor next came in, soon after four o'clock, she had a plan.

'Ewan,' she said, very gently as he put the tray of tea down. 'I wonder if you would allow me to do something. As you know, the Fairfords, my employers in Ambala, are here in Mussoorie, but they'll be leaving tomorrow. You've been so kind and generous in letting me spend some time with them but I wonder now if they won't be thinking me awfully rude for just disappearing without a word. I wondered if I might just go out to see them, perhaps, to say goodbye? Their holiday is almost over and they'll be going back. Might I, d'you think, just walk out along towards Gun Hill for a little while?'

He eyed her, as if considering her proposal seriously, and then, as if to a small child, said, 'We'll see. Let's just see how you behave yourself until then, shall we?'

This gave her a chink of light, of hope, and she dared to ask, 'I don't suppose there has been any message for me, has there? A note, perhaps?'

He poured her tea and handed her the cup. She saw that the soft skin under his eyes looked more puckered than usual with tiredness.

'And who might that be from, Lily?' He spoke with that teasing, ominous tone again and she could hear how suspicious he was.

'From the Fairfords, of course,' Lily said brightly.

'Mrs Fairford has been very kind to me and she was expecting to see me yesterday afternoon. She's the sort of person who might worry – she might even come to the house to enquire . . .'

'No. Nothing has come for you,' he said, going to the door.

'Doctor – the chamber pot needs emptying, badly!' she blurted.

Silently and with distaste, he took it and brought it back empty. Then, abruptly, he left the room again.

The rest of the day passed. At times, Lily grew severely agitated and then at others, simply flat and hopeless. She tried to sleep as much as possible, to pass the time so that she could avoid the agony of feelings that came upon her. Sam was leaving tomorrow. She had not seen him and he had evidently not attempted to contact her. Surely the doctor would have challenged her over it triumphantly if any note had arrived? She could hardly bear to imagine what Sam must think of her. That she had been playing with him and had deserted him? And why had he not come to see her? She racked her brains desperately for a way she could get out to see him tomorrow.

What if, when the doctor came in with a tray of tea, she could throw it over him and escape while he was standing, scalded and shocked? The next time he came in she was almost on the brink of doing it, trembling at the thought, but she could not quite find the nerve. She thought of writing a note for Prithvi or Jane Brown and slipping it under the door, but of course that was no good. The doctor would most likely find it when he next came to bring her food. Again and again she opened the window and stared down, desperately trying to see if there was any ledge, any staging point big enough that she might lower herself down on to it, hoping every time that she had perhaps missed something. Each time all she could see was the sheer drop down the side of the house and the monkeys' playground of the trees and roofs below in the valley, and she knew that to try and climb down would almost certainly lead to her death. There were moments when even that seemed preferable to staying a prisoner here.

The morning of the day Sam was due to leave, she was awake before dawn. She left the bed and as she did so many times in the day, turned the handle of the door, pushing on it and hoping, vainly. Once again the bolts were fastened. There was no way out. That was the moment when she decided that whatever it took, she was going to get past Ewan McBride, even if she had to scald him or knock him unconscious to do so.

Dressing herself in readiness, she waited as the light changed from an uncertain haze of grey to the strong colours of morning. It was a beautiful day, the mountains touched with gold, and tiny wisps of cloud strewn across the valleys. Lily sat on the bed and breathed in deeply, watching the light change, thinking how many times she had seen that sight.

I won't be here soon to see it, she told herself. She had no fixed idea of what was going to happen, except that she felt strong and desperate and somehow she was going to get out of there and never return. How could she stay with Dr McBride now? She would go and find Sam, travel with him, run away with him and somehow beg a passage on the boat back to England . . . In those moments anything seemed possible. She was full of a vibrating energy. All she had to do was to wait for him to come and she would spring at him. Whatever she had to do, she would be free, and she would go to Sam, be with Sam forever . . .

But he did not come. He brought her no breakfast, not even a cup of tea. He must, surely, come with tiffin, she reasoned, beside herself with anxiety. Was he punishing her in some new way? And if so, for what? Hadn't she been punished enough? When the hour of tiffin came and went she became frantic again. Sam would be leaving on an evening train from Dehra Dun. If she didn't leave the house by mid-afternoon there was going to be no chance of seeing him. He would be gone, thinking the very worst of her, and she'd never see him again. Desperately, she hammered on the door, weeping and begging to be let out.

No one came. The day crawled agonizingly past and by the late afternoon she knew with a dull numbness of despair that she had missed him. Sam Ironside would be gone, with the Fairfords, driving away from her down the twisting mountain roads and bearing in his heart feelings of utter betrayal and anger towards her. Perhaps he would think she had been playing with him, that this was her revenge for his leaving her last time. He would be angry that she had not kept her promises to come. And she ached for his suffering. But then she felt angry and betrayed herself. Why had he not come to the house to find her? Not moved heaven and earth to make sure he saw her? All she had now were the torn ends of unanswered questions and she felt a terrible despair. All the future held was life without him, without love or happiness, and it was a future in which she had no interest. Now he had gone for certain, she scarcely cared whether McBride let her out of the room or not. She had nothing to leave for.

She lay on her bed, facing the wall.

Chapter Forty-Three

The days turned into a week, then two weeks.

No one came near her except Dr McBride, who sometimes brought her food at the normal times, and sometimes not. She realized that this was a calculated means of keeping her in uncertainty. Now and then he brought her a jug of fresh water for washing, emptied her chamber pot and even, once, brought fresh sheets for her bed.

'Why does no one else come and see me?' Lily asked him soon after Sam had left. 'Where do they think I am?'

'So far as they're concerned, you have a fever, a highly infectious one, from which they need to keep their distance,' the doctor told her, genially. He seemed happy now, as if convinced Lily's spirit had surrendered to him. She no longer put up much of a fight about anything. Now she knew that Sam was gone, that he had not even tried to contact her before leaving again forever, nothing else seemed to matter. She lay for hour after hour, feeling she had no energy to care about anything. Occasionally she would rouse herself to eat, or wash herself, or to sit by the window, looking out over the mountains and hearing the distant children's voices from the school. Every so often, almost absent-mindedly and without hope, she tried the door. But it never gave.

'How long are you going to keep me here?' she asked one day.

'Until you're better,' he said, sitting by her bed and taking her hand. 'You're not very well, are you, my little one?'

Lily sighed. It was true, she didn't feel well. Certainly not the robust health she was used to. She found it hard to eat much and her innards felt sluggish. She had so little energy that sometimes it was hard to rouse herself from the bed.

'Perhaps if I had some fresh air and exercise I'd feel better,' she said.

'Oh, I don't think that would be a good idea,' he said, concerned. 'You mustn't do anything to weaken yourself further, Lily, my dear. We want you back in the best of health as soon as possible, don't we?' He was speaking to her in the wheedling, childlike voice that he had started to use with her all the time.

Lily felt a chill go through her suddenly. Where had she heard that before? In Muriel McBride's bedroom, the day the doctor had come in and sat beside her with such tender concern, looking down in to his wife's eyes as if she was the most important person on earth. Lily stared back at him, at his heavy form leaning over her, and big soulful eyes, full of the same concern. Inside her, there came a surge of revival. Somehow, she saw, the doctor had made Muriel McBride the way she was and now he was starting on her. He *wanted* her to be ill! She felt herself flood with energy.

Calmly she said, 'You're right, of course, Ewan. I do think I'm not myself at the moment. Perhaps the best thing I can do is sleep for an hour or two.'

'Very wise, my darling,' he said, patting her shoulder. 'And I'll sit with you while you sleep. I love to watch you.'

Lily tried not to let her alarm show. 'There's no

need,' she said, forcing a rueful smile on to her face. 'In fact, if you were here I should want to stay awake and be with you. So it might be said you wouldn't be doing your patient much good! Why don't you go and see your wife? She must be missing you.'

'As long as you promise you'll rest, Lily, darling. I don't want you coming to any harm, ever.'

'Of course I shall.' She lay back obediently, as if ready for sleep and he left the room, casting a look back at her as he did so, as if checking on her.

Lily lay still until his footsteps had receded along the passage. Only then, she realized, she had been holding her breath.

From then on she continued to act her part as the feeble invalid, but now, instead of allowing herself to slip into the poorly stupor which Dr McBride seemed to encourage, Lily's mind was working constantly on plans for escape. Her frustration and anger returned multiplied since her renewed determination did not make it any easier to actually find a way out of the room. Then, one afternoon, she heard a timid little tap on the door and leaped up from the bed.

'Miss Lily?'

'Is that you, Prithvi?' Lily ran to the door.

'Yes. Are you sick, Miss Lily? Dr McBride said you are very sick and must not be disturbed. He said we must not come near. But I was feeling so sorry for you and he has gone out. I came to see if there is anything you need.'

'Prithvi, I'm not sick, I'm all right!' Lily cried. She was trembling wtih excitement. At last, a way out! 'Open the door, will you! He won't let me come out. Just pull the bolts back, Prithvi, please!'

There was a pause.

'The doctor is saying that we must not open the door. That you are not to be let out under any circumstance whatsoever.'

'But I'm not ill!' Lily pleaded desperately. 'He just wants me to be, to keep me here, but I'm perfectly all right, honestly. He's the one who's not well!' As she said this, thinking of the controlled face the doctor showed to the rest of the world, she realized how crazed it sounded. 'Oh, please just let me out and you'll see – just for a moment!'

She knew how timid Prithvi was, how she could never seem to take any decision without authority from someone else, and already her hope was fading.

'I cannot disobey the doctor's orders,' Prithvi's soft voice came from behind the door. 'I am sorry, Miss Lily. But I hope you will be better soon. I must go now. He will be coming back soon.'

'Prithvi, no – don't go!' But it was too late. It seemed so long since Lily had seen anyone, a friendly face she could trust, that she sank to her knees, sobbing. How was she ever to get out if everyone thought she was crazy and wouldn't believe anything she said? Curled up, she wept for a time, feeling defeated. She got up to lie on the bed, but then stopped herself. She often fell asleep in the day, as if to escape from the long, dreary hours, but it stopped her from sleeping at night and if she was sleepless the nights seemed even longer than the days.

Instead she calmed herself and sat at her table, taking a piece of writing paper.

'Dear Cosmo . . .' The idea of writing to him strengthened her. She had been disturbed by all the news she had heard of him from Susan Fairford. What had happened to the sweet little chap she had known in Ambala, to turn him into the ungovernable boy the school was seeing? It made her sad, yet she could sense, somehow, his unhappiness, however little he said in his occasional scrawled notes to her. How he must have loathed England, the cold, grey days, after the brilliance of India, shut behind the dark school walls. And with no family, no Lily or Srimala to give him love and affection. Her heart ached for him and the ache in her today reached out to him. In her grief, he seemed to be the only person she had left. She wanted to send her reassurance to him even if she had no idea whether the letter would ever be posted. Surely the doctor would not deny her that?

'I am still here in Mussoorie, in the hills,' she wrote, 'and it is very pretty here. You would like it. Not long ago your mother and father were staying here with Isadora and Srimala and some of the servants. I expect they told you. Isadora has learned to ride really quite well. Your father has another new Daimler and the same man who brought the first one came again to deliver it to him. Sam Ironside. You were very small last time he came but perhaps you remember that too?'

She stopped, sucking the end of her pen and gazing out over the hills, seeing nothing. All she could see, with a stab of terrible longing, over and over again, was Sam's face that night when they had lain by the fire, the intense love in his eyes. And now, what did he feel or think of her. She wanted to write, *He's the man I love . . . and now I've lost him, lost him forever . . .*

She found a few other cheerful things to say to Cosmo, telling him she hoped he was working hard at his lessons and that he must try and be obedient and not get into trouble again.

'I hope you remember me, Cozzy, and that I'll see you again one day,' she finished. 'This letter comes with much love from your friend, Lily.'

In her neatest copperplate she addressed the envelope to his prep school. Writing the letter steadied her. She must be patient if she was going to get out of here. Sooner or later, her chance would come. He couldn't keep her locked up here forever.

Dr McBride agreed to post Lily's letter to Cosmo without any obstacle, but still more days passed and Lily had to hold on very hard to her hope of escape. Many times in the day she opened the windows and stood breathing in the fresh mountain air, stretching her body to keep supple and strong.

She tried to keep the day and night separate, but often sleep did not come at night. One night, when she had been in the room for three and a half weeks, she was particularly restless and unable to settle. The house was very quiet, something scuttling in the roof above her head, but otherwise, silence. She lost track of the time, but the silence almost seemed to make a sound of its own.

Lying on her back, she was aware that she felt slightly unwell, suddenly rather queasy.

I mustn't give in to this, she thought. Any sign of illness worried her, as if it meant that she was surrendering to Dr McBride's attempts to sicken her. I'm not ill, I'm perfectly well and I shall not let him make me ill ... But the feeling did not go away. Lily plumped the pillow under her head and turned to lie on her side, closing her eyes. She must sleep, that would see it off.

A moment later, she heard a sound and her eyes

snapped open, her heart banging hard. There was a sound outside the door. Someone was out there!

She sat up in the total darkness, listening with every fibre of her being. She wanted to light the candle but she was listening too intensely to move. She held her breath. No, she was not imagining it – someone was easing back the bolts, slowly, carefully, not the rough way the doctor did it, but softly, so as not to be discovered. The top bolt was eased free, then the bottom.

Lily leaped off the bed as the door opened, letting in a warm glow of candlelight. Standing in the doorway in her nightdress was Jane Brown.

'Lily?' She came hurriedly into the room and shut the door, turning to look at Lily with stern, troubled eyes. 'Are you all right? We hear you have been very unwell.'

'No!' Lily went to her, grasping her arm urgently. 'Please, for God's sake, you've got to help me. He's had me locked up in here and I don't know why! I'm not ill – I never have been ill!'

Jane Brown's eyes searched her face. 'No, I can see. Mrs McBride sent me, to tell you the truth. She was quite sure you weren't ill either.'

Chapter Forty-Four

'Miss Waters, are we awake?'

The brisk tap on the door was followed by the appearance of a white-veiled head. Lily's eyes opened and she sat up groggily. Her bewilderment was plain in her face. Where was she? This small, bare room, the iron bedstead, the work-worn but bright-eyed face staring down at her. Of course, the convent!

'Oh – good morning!' Hurriedly she swung her legs over the side of the bed and felt a lurch of nausea as she did so.

'Slept through the bell again – you are exhausted, aren't you, dear!' Sister Fidelis commented. 'I suppose the last few days can't have been easy for you. But you should be down at breakfast, and the laundry won't wait, you know!'

'I don't usually sleep so heavily,' Lily apologized, pulling her nightdress closed at the neck. She felt uncomfortably aware of her full-breasted body compared with Sister Fidelis's, slim in its chaste attire. 'I'm most terribly sorry. I really will try to do better.'

'Not to worry!' Sister Fidelis almost sang, making to depart again. 'Just get yourself up and ready as fast as you can. There's water in the jug.' She turned at the door and peered at Lily. 'Are you all right, dear?'

'Yes!' Lily fibbed. She felt dangerously close to being sick but didn't want to be any more trouble.

'Perfectly, thank you, Sister. I'll be down in a few minutes.'

'Right-oh.'

Immediately she'd gone, Lily ran to retch over the wash bowl and then sank groaning on the bed. She sipped some water, wondering at how deeply she'd been asleep when all around, from outside, came the sounds of the girls occupying St James's School. This was one of Mussoorie's many educational institutions and was run by Church of England sisters originally from an order in Oxfordshire, most of whom spoke in beautifully modulated English and gave off an air of cultured sensitivity, however mundane the tasks with which they were presented. The convent and school sat perched high above the valleys, with breathtaking views from almost every room.

Lily closed her eyes for a moment and breathed in deeply. She felt better now, but what on earth was the matter with her? Sister Fidelis must be right, she realized. She was in a state of nerves after all that had happened over the past weeks. It was only now beginning to hit her how extreme and bizarre Dr McBride's behaviour towards her had been.

That night, when Jane Brown released her from the room where she had been imprisoned for almost a month, she took Lily's hand and led her like a child down the creaking stairs to her own quarters, where she locked the door behind them and hurried to light the lamp. Both of them then stood and smiled, exhaling with relief, then Lily, completely overwrought, burst into tears and was taken into Jane's comforting, shawl-clad arms.

'Oh, thank you for letting me out. I was beginning to think no one would ever come. He's kept me locked in there all this time – he's mad, I swear it . . .' She sobbed for a moment, then drew back. 'I expect I smell terrible . . .'

'Not at all,' Jane Brown said kindly. 'Are you all right, Lily?' Her eyes were wide with concern.

'Yes. I am now. He just . . .' Her tears came again. She realized how lonely and frightened and humiliated she had been.

'We had no idea – not at first,' Jane Brown said, taking Lily to the chair. 'He told us you were ill, something really contagious, but then when it went on and on. And he was so peculiar about it, his behaviour . . . The man's an absolute menace . . .'

The two women talked for a long time, through the night, sitting wrapped up in shawls and blankets near the unlit fire. Jane Brown described her increasing suspicion towards Dr McBride.

'I'd leave tomorrow, if it weren't that I feel for *her*.' She nodded her head towards Muriel McBride's room next door. 'It's taken me a long time to work it out. He's always so gentle, so solicitous towards her. And whatever she's done, she's done it to herself, there's no doubt. But it's *because* of him, I know it!' Her voice grew passionate. 'He's *caused* it somehow – he helped her to destroy herself and it's so tragic to watch. She's even admitted it to me, in a sort of way. But she's too far gone now to do anything about it.' Jane wiped her eyes, wearily.

'She did warn me about you, to take care of you, I mean – several times, now I come to think about it.' Her face darkened. 'She must have sensed something. The man wants locking up himself, but what can we do? He's such a smooth-talker, so well thought of. Mind you . . .' She hesitated, blushing as she looked across at Lily. There was a hint of a smile on her lips.

'What is it?' Lily asked.

'You should have seen him with that other doctor who was here, McCluskie. Two nights before he went back to Patna or wherever it was, he went missing – all night.'

'Yes – he thought McCluskie was with me,' Lily said candidly, and saw Jane Brown look really embarrassed. She realized then that even if the nurse had guessed perfectly well the full extent of Ewan McBride's uses for her, she was certainly not used to talking about such things. 'Where was he, then?' she asked.

'In a brothel.' She brought out the words rather harshly, as if determined not to be coy. 'They had a very loud argument about it when McCluskie came sloping back in the morning. Dr McBride couldn't seem to control himself at all. You could hear him all over the house.' Lily realized she, too, had heard the argument in the distance. 'That's the only time I've ever known the doctor let rip like that. He always likes to be so in command.'

There was a pause, then Jane Brown looked across at Lily with a sad puzzlement in her eyes.

'Why have you let him use you like this, Lily? You seem such a strong person.'

It was Lily's turn to blush, a deep sense of shame seeming to swamp her. How could she explain that in some way she felt this was what she deserved? But for the first time ever she tried to be frank with this woman who had rescued her.

'I don't know. I suppose he gave me a good job, security. My own background was rather poor, you see. I'd never been wanted by anyone much, or taken out and about like that before, and it didn't seem too high a price, not then. I sort of slipped into it without meaning to and couldn't get out again. I suppose that sounds terrible to you.'

When she looked up she saw Jane looking at her with real pity in her eyes.

'Not terrible. Just sad. We must get you away from here, Lily. Even Muriel has asked me to get you away from here. I know where you can go – at least for the short term.'

Before dawn, Jane Brown dressed and they crept back to Lily's room, where she also pulled some clothes on and packed a small bag of belongings before the two of them quietly let themselves out into the dark street.

'It's a good distance,' Jane Brown said. 'Over towards Happy Valley. We'll have to wake one of the *jhampanis* when we get further away from here. But I should be able to get back in good time. Fidelis and I went to school together – only she was called Rosamund then.'

They found a rickshaw to take them some of the way, and climbed the last mile on foot up to St James's, where Jane Brown knocked loudly on the heavy convent door. At last a sleepy looking *chowkidar* appeared and Jane Brown asked for Sister Fidelis.

'Please tell her Miss Brown is here, and it is an emergency.'

Lily stood feeling very nervous at the idea of rousing the nuns in this awesome-looking place at this time in the morning, but Sister Fidelis appeared, already dressed and carrying an oil lamp, in the light of which she looked remarkably cheerful.

'Miss Waters urgently needs a discreet place to stay,' Jane Brown told her. Lily blushed, suspecting that Sister Fidelis would immediately jump to the conclusion that she was carrying an illegitimate baby. But the woman's expression did not change, nor did she ask any questions.

'Come in,' she said, with a welcoming sweep of her arm. 'Are you capable of helping with the laundry, d'you think?'

'I'm sure I am,' Lily said.

'Just wait there a moment.' Sister Fidelis indicated a stiff-backed chair and Lily obediently sat down. She felt suddenly very safe. Sister Fidelis and Jane Brown talked in low voices outside, then Jane came in. Lily stood up.

'I must go back.' Jane Brown looked deep into Lily's eyes. 'You'll be all right here, for a while. They'll find you some work. Then you can look for a new appointment somewhere.'

'Thank you so much,' Lily breathed. She felt tearful, as if that night she had discovered a true friend, then lost her again.

'Let me know how you get on. Sister Fidelis can pass a message on to me.'

Tears in her eyes, she held out her arms and embraced Lily. 'I'll miss you, I truly shall. But you'll find something better, dear, I know you will. Just be careful of yourself, won't you?' And with a kiss on Lily's cheek she moved away, leaving Lily still trying to thank her, and disappeared out of the convent door into the waning night.

Sister Fidelis, Lily was to learn, was a continuous ball of energy who ran the school and convent dispensaries and filled in anywhere else she was required on the domestic front. She handed Lily over to a Sister Rosemary, a plump, cheerful woman of about forty who was in charge of the laundry, an immense room with a high, vaulted ceiling at the very back of the convent, where the nuns' habits and clothing of the girls who boarded were all laundered.

'We could just send everything to the *dhobi*,' she told Lily. 'But we think it's a good training for some of our girls – and for the young native girls who come in to work here. Some have gone on to work in some quite distinguished families. Now – what we could do with is some help with ironing. You know how?'

'Yes, of course,' Lily said.

'No of course about it,' Sister Rosemary retorted. 'Let me tell you, there are plenty of young maids in this town who don't know one end of a flat iron from another.'

The laundry room was warmed by a huge range at one end, on which several irons were heating at once, and close to which was a large, square table padded and draped in singe-marked sheets. At the far end were the washtubs, where a number of native girls were pounding away with dollies in the steamy heat. They looked curiously at Lily as she passed but did not say anything, though one girl gave a sweet smile. They all seemed to have great respect for Sister Rosemary. Above their heads, clothing hung on drying racks hoisted up near the ceiling, and there were three poles which reached up to the ceiling, each with arms extending out like tree branches, also with items drying on them.

'We have to dry everything in here during the monsoon, but there is a yard out at the back. Most of the bigger things are out on lines at this time of year. Now,' Sister Rosemary added briskly, 'let's get you started. I'll show you what's needed with these. They've all been starched already.'

Lily found that her days in the convent were spent quite pleasantly, ironing, often with one or two others, usually native girls of about fourteen years of age, who were respectful and friendly to her, and the day was punctuated by the bell summoning the pupils in and out of their lessons, and by services in the simple chapel. Lily was expected to keep the hours with them, going into the chapel early in the morning, and midday and in the evening.

She didn't mind any of this. Though she had never been exposed to religion she found the life a peaceful haven, and liked the flowers and whitewashed walls of the chapel. But as the days went by, the most difficult problem became her getting up in time in the morning. More and more she found herself burdened by an overwhelming sense of exhaustion, which would come over her when she was standing at the ironing table in the oppressive heat. One day she fainted, coming round to find that she had banged her head, and that she was sitting on a chair with her head forced down between her knees. She sat up groggily to find Sister Rosemary standing over her, along with a small crowd of the laundry workers.

'Back to work!' Sister Rosemary urged, clapping her hands and the other girls scattered. Narrowing her eyes appraisingly, she said in a low voice, 'I think you'd better come outside.'

Humbly, Lily obeyed. In the yard, strung with washing which flapped gently in the hillside breeze, Sister Rosemary faced her in her black habit, which somehow looked more severe in the open air. 'It seems you're not very well. Can you tell me what's the matter?'

'I don't know, Sister,' Lily said miserably. 'When I first arrived I just thought I had an acid stomach. I'd been in a bit of a state, you see. But it hasn't gone away. I don't feel well at all sometimes . . .'

'Especially in the mornings?' Sister Rosemary enquired coldly. 'Hence your frequent absence from morning prayer?'

Lily nodded miserably. There was a pause, Lily sensed, of disbelief.

'Well, don't you realize what this might mean? Is there any possibility that you are expecting a child?'

The question was so shaming it felt like being slapped. Lily felt a thick blush spread through her cheeks. Her mind was reeling. Surely it couldn't be? Dr McBride had assured her he was infertile and she had been with him months with no outcome like this. The only other thing was ... It had truly not occurred to her until then, so ignorant was she of women's ways. That night with Sam! Surely it couldn't be from that. You couldn't find yourself expecting after one night, could you? Surely that wasn't possible! But her confused expression must have spoken volumes to Sister Rosemary.

'I see.' She spoke gravely, and Lily could hear the deep disapproval in her tone. 'Well, we weren't told about this, but of course Fidelis has been wondering ... This changes things, certainly.' She spoke with cool detachment. 'You'll have to stay here for a time, live discreetly. We can see if we can find a home for the child – otherwise it'll have to go to an orphanage. Once it's over and done with, you'll be able to apply for another post.' Her eyes seemed to bore into Lily. 'You foolish girl. What a state to get yourself into. I wouldn't go expecting any sympathy. Now go back to work, while you still can.'

Chapter Forty-Five

Lily spent the next few days in a state of shock and anguish. A child! How could she be expecting a child!

She continued with the struggle of getting up and working in the laundry, but her mind was completely elsewhere. A child – and it had to be Sam's! All the pain she had been trying to shut out over the past strange weeks came crashing in on her, all the agony of her unanswered questions about Sam. What had he thought that day when she did not come to the Fairfords? Had he tried to contact her? He must have been hurt and angry. Had he sailed back to England possibly hating her for rejecting him and letting him down, perhaps thinking only the worst of her? She had no address for him, and how could she contact him now when she was in this state? The hard truth of the matter hit her with a crushing force. How could she trust Sam either? He had come to her as a married man, on the other side of the world from his family. Had he used her for his own entertainment? What would his reaction be if she ever told him she was carrying his child? Might he simply laugh at her naivety and walk away, back to Helen and his settled, respectable life?

Pain and anger surged round in her constantly, leaving her exhausted. Yet, at times, especially when she lay at night in the narrow convent bed, she would call to mind Sam's face, his absorbed, loving expression as he had gazed on her, and she wept with longing at the thought. How could she doubt him? He loved her, she knew it! She was the one who had hurt him and let him down, and she ached for him to be here with her, to pour out to him all that had happened. When morning came, though, and she woke sick and feeling as if she had not even slept, all the doubts crowded in again, accompanied by hard and disquieting certainties: that she was disgraced and carrying a child, that there was no love for her and little help and that, once again, as she had been so often, she was utterly alone.

She worked mechanically in the laundry, at least grateful for the shelter offered her by the nuns. She knew that they were aware of her state and most of them left her alone, unsure what to say to her. But the one person who was kind was Sister Fidelis. Now and again she would come up and sit in Lily's room and talk to her. Often she regaled her with stories about her own life and about the order.

'Oh, it was quite a feat getting everything established up here, of course. It was eighty-seven we started up here. The sisters in the early days arrived on bullock carts – you can imagine how long that must have taken, can't you?'

Then, after a few stories, she might say suddenly, 'Now, Lily, don't fret too much. We'll make sure you're all right. And something will come up for you. God always provides – you'll see. Would you like Jane to come and see you?'

Lily shook her head. In one way she would very much have liked to see Jane Brown, but she was too ashamed to face anyone else. 'I just want to be alone,' she said.

As the days passed, punctuated by the bell-ringing

routine of the school, and May arrived, the heat increased, though of course it was a pale shadow of the blistering scorch of the plains. Mussoorie was bathed in sunshine and filling up fast with summer visitors from Delhi and the Punjab. And after a few more weeks had passed, Lily also began to feel better. What was more concerning now was that, instead of feeling ill, she was beginning to notice the swelling of her abdomen. The idea of there being a baby in there didn't seem real at all and she felt no sense of fellow feeling for it. There were no women around her whom she could confide in, or who had had experience of child-birth, and all she could feel was ignorant and very frightened, despite Sister Fidelis's assurances that every-thing would be all right. All she could wonder was what was to become of her.

Within a few days, however, Sister Fidelis came bounc-ing into the laundry room in the middle of the morning. Lily, feeling much better now, was able to stand and do the ironing without any sickness or faintness and she was ironing one of the sisters' robust black habits.

'Lily!' Sister Fidelis hailed her in bubbly tones. She was a woman incapable of formality, it seemed, and had never called Lily 'Miss Waters' the way Sister Rosemary insisted on doing. 'Could you come outside with me for a moment?'

Once more, Lily found herself in the drying yard among the lines of washing.

'I have come to offer you an opportunity to go home – if that's what you would like.'

Lily stared stupidly at her. 'Home – what d'you mean?' For a horrible moment she thought Sister Fidelis meant to the McBride house, that the doctor had come looking for her and softened the nuns with his charms.

'To England, of course! Where else would home be, dear?' Sister Fidelis chuckled heartily.

'What . . .' Lily stuttered. 'What d'you mean?'

'A paid passage home on the P&O is what I mean. There's a family called the Bartletts who come up to Mussoorie regularly every summer and they worship with us. They donate sums of money and so forth.' She waved a hand as if this was of little consequence. 'All very good. Their son is almost six years old and they feel it's high time he was back home at school. Mrs Bartlett happened to mention to me this morning that they're very concerned at how late they've left it and how they want to make sure he is safely accompanied. Well, I thought to myself, Lily has worked with children! What could be more fortunate! All you have to do is accompany young Bartlett – the boy's name is Eustace – on the P&O and deliver him to Mrs Bartlett's sister in Leamington Spa. And then you're free to go. How does that sound?'

'But . . .' Lily was almost too astonished to speak. 'That would mean leaving India!' It was India that felt like home now.

'Well, yes, naturally!' Sister Fidelis laughed at her utter confusion. 'You weren't thinking of staying here forever, were you?'

'I don't know,' Lily admitted. 'I suppose I *hadn't* thought. I've always liked it here . . .'

'Well – think about it now,' Sister Fidelis said briskly. 'I told Mrs Bartlett I had someone in mind, but that I'd have to ask around. I can let her know your reply tomorrow.'

Lily was thrown into complete turmoil for the rest

of the day. She stood moving the heavy flat iron over sheets and starched wimples without even seeing them.

Leave India! She had taken to the country straight away, had thrived here, and thought to stay, but now everything was different. If she had her child adopted, of course, she could apply for another post as a nanny and start again, closing the door on the past, pretending. That was the most tempting solution. It was what she had done so far. But now life had thrown this choice in her way. If she went back to England, would she see Sam? Immediately she knew the answer to that. It was impossible. He was there with his family and that was where he had chosen to return to. Common sense whispered in her ear, compounding her doubts. If he had known she was carrying a child, might he not have deserted her anyway? That was the way men behaved, wasn't it? But somehow, even though she couldn't make sense of all her feelings, she was drawn to going home. She would be near him, at least, in the same country. And she could get a new post with glowing references from the Fairfords. It would be a new start, not in a foreign land this time, but back where she had come from. She knew, with suddenly clarity, that it was what she must do.

That evening, she told Sister Fidelis that she would accompany Eustace Bartlett on his sea journey home to England.

Chapter Forty-Six

Birmingham, 1911

Lily knelt over the pail of filthy water, gasping as the pains tore through her back and abdomen. The scrubbing brush hit the floor with a clatter. Though she could see her breath in the freezing air, she broke out in a sweat. Droplets of it ran down inside her frock. Then she felt a rush of wetness between her legs and realized her underclothes were soaked through. All morning these outbreaks of agony had been coming and going.

'Oh!' she breathed, shakily as the pain died away at last. 'Oh God, help me, somebody.' Looking down the ill-lit corridor, she could see no other human face, only the great expanse of floor which it was her job to scrub, as it had been ever since she came to the home. 'Home' certainly did not feel like the right name for the Bethel Home, two miles from the middle of Birmingham, which took in unmarried mothers. It had been a place of dread even before she got here, that and the gory stories of childbirth she had heard from the women in the bedstead factory where she had worked out the last months before her confinement. Their talk had frightened her terribly.

For a moment she slumped over the bucket, resting her head on her arms, too weary to care about the rank smell of the water.

'I should've gone to the workhouse,' she whispered to herself. They might even have been kinder there, she thought, than these so-called Christian Evangelical ladies who ran Bethel.

A door opened somewhere along the corridor and she was half aware of brisk, clicking footsteps.

'What do you think you are *doing*?' Lily heard, in scandalized tones. It was the one she disliked the most, a long-nosed, zealous woman who they referred to as Sister Leigh. She had a pale, waxen face, brown hair taken back severely under her black uniform bonnet, and a thin figure on which her long black frock hung unbecomingly loose.

'Your job is to scrub the floor, you know that, Waters.' She spoke with a harsh Lancashire accent.

Lily raised her head, straining to see the woman's angular form in the poor light. For a moment her eyes were clouded.

'It's idleness that lets the Devil in. Don't let me find you idling again. Get to work.'

Lily's eyes cleared. She focused on the woman's shiny black boots, loathing her with a passion, with all her self-righteous judgements, her certainty of her own rectitude. It was humiliating to have to beg her, but things had become desperate.

'I'm in pain. The baby – I think it's on the way.'

'Nonsense, you look perfectly all right to me. You're not due yet. I know you girls – not that you are a girl, Waters, which makes you even more of a disgrace – any excuse not to do a full day of wholesome work. No thought of the condition of your souls, any of you.' She folded her arms. 'You deserve to burn.'

As she spoke, Lily was gripped by another racking pain. She seized the sides of the pail and pressed down, crying out as the great muscular clasp of her abdomen pressed tighter until she was panting and moaning. In the midst of her distress she became aware of Sister Leigh's lips urgently whispering words close to her ear.

'Does it hurt? Does it tear and rend you? It should hurt, sister, and it should rend, because only through the time of trial, through suffering and repentance, will you find the light of Christ in the darkness of your sin and wantonness. Pray for suffering, to be put harshly to the test . . .'

Lily gave a loud cry at the height of her pain, feeling as if she was being torn in two.

'That's it, feel your punishment for sin, feel it hard . . . Did he do it to you hard, hard inside you? Did he? Did it burn . . .? You'll burn, Waters, for your depravity, you'll burn in the everlasting fires . . .'

'For God's sake, help me!' Lily cried, when she had more command of herself. 'It's coming. Help me!'

Sister Leigh straightened up abruptly and came to her senses. 'Always such a fuss, you women,' she snapped. 'You should deliver the fruits of your fornication in silence, not with all this carry-on. Get up. Your time has come, and you deserve to suffer.'

She grabbed Lily's upper arm and hauled her to her feet.

Standing on Leamington Spa railway station all those months ago, once she had delivered Eustace Bartlett to his relatives, Lily had felt utterly alone. Eustace was a most obnoxious child and she was overjoyed to be rid of him, but now was the first time she really confronted the question she had been avoiding: what could she do next when she had nowhere and no one to go to? Her solitariness in the world and the precariousness of her situation overcame her. For a moment she thought about how near to Coventry she was, to Sam, but she pushed the thought angrily away. She had got this far without him. She had to manage her life alone. But amid the passengers and movement of luggage, the cars and carts coming and going, she felt like a tiny dot, invisible to everyone else and impossibly small.

As she stood, fearfully looking around her, the station tannoy announced the next train north to Birmingham. It was not somewhere she had ever thought she would return to, but at least she knew it a little and she ached for something familiar. She had hurriedly picked up her holdall and made her way to the Birmingham train.

The home, to the east side of Birmingham, had space for twenty women at a time. When Lily walked in through the forbidding front door she had vowed to do what she always did in a new situation: keep herself to herself, not answer questions or give anything away.

It was a terrible trial being back in England, in this drizzly, soot-begrimed city with its filthy streets and pale, threadbare people, but the home was even more of a shock. The girls were all expected to wear the same clothes: coarse grey frocks, baggy as sacks, to accommodate their swollen bodies, and their hair tied in a regulation plait down their backs. They were housed in bleak, splintery-floored dormitories of six or seven beds. At first Lily loathed the idea of sharing with such rough women after all she had been used to, and the lack of privacy. But she quickly saw that most of the girls in the home were so very much younger than herself. At twenty-eight she was almost old enough to be mother to some of them. And far from being nosy, most of them were desperate to find a listening ear to pour out their own woes and stories to. Lily had a bed in the corner, away from the window which looked across on to the frontage of a sheet-metal works, and next to her was a poor, malnourished-looking girl called Rachel, whose belly was the only rounded thing about her otherwise wasted form.

'It was my dad done it,' she whispered to Lily on the second night. 'He and my mom threw me out and told me to go to the workhouse. So I come 'ere instead. But they're cruel 'ard 'ere, that they are. Sometimes I wish I'd gone and finished myself in the cut.'

Lily listened, her sense of horror increasing even more when she learned that Rachel was only fifteen. After Rachel had fallen asleep she lay looking up into the dark. For the first time in a long while she allowed herself to think of Sam, and she ached with longing and sadness. But, she thought, if she had had nothing else in her life she had had those days with him, that night, and those looks of love, or what she had thought was love. It seemed Rachel's life was over when it had barely even begun, ruined by her father's incestuous attention.

As she got to know some of the other girls better she discovered how young many of them were and how sad their stories. Most of them had been taken advantage of in their naive innocence. Only one, Madge, was older, and at twenty-five had been deserted by the man who promised to marry her. Lily found that the younger girls looked to her, and over those days before the baby started coming she had tried to encourage them and be kind to them. Some of them seemed to have had so little warmth or kindness in their lives.

But now she was in one of the two delivery rooms down in the cellar of the big house and there was no one to show warmth or kindness to her. Sister Leigh half dragged her down the stairs, barely allowing her to stop as the pains came over her again. She tore away from the woman's needling fingers and knelt, groaning, on the stone stairs.

'Come along. Stop all this ungodly noise,' Sister Leigh scolded, pulling at her shoulder. She gave Lily a hard slap round the face. 'This is nothing you haven't brought on yourself so you'll have to put up with it.'

Lily threw her off. Nothing would induce her to move in the middle of this terrible agony. At last Sister Leigh led her down into the stone-floored room which contained a sink, a trolley laid out with various implements and a high, flat bed covered by a sheet up against the wall. There was a gaslight hanging from the ceiling close to the bed, which Sister Leigh lit resentfully.

'Loosen your clothes and get up there,' she ordered. 'Someone will come to you.'

She stood watching, arms folded, as Lily removed her sodden bloomers and petticoat and unfastened the buttons on her dress. Lily wanted to ask what was going to happen, longed for some sort of reassurance, but she wasn't going begging to this granite-faced, sanctimonious woman and she held her tongue.

'Get up on the bed and stay there,' Sister Leigh snapped. She turned abruptly and left the room.

What seemed like a very long time passed. Lily lay on the hard bed. There was no pillow and only the grey wall for company. Every few moments there came a terrible onslaught of pain, burning through her, pressing down on her like a weight. Each time she curled convulsively on her side, gasping and sobbing. Once she bent up so abruptly that she banged her head on the wall. She wanted to get off the bed and each time the agony stopped she thought about getting up but never seemed to be able to raise the energy. She had no idea how long had passed but the pains were coming more and more frequently.

'Oh God!' she cried out at the height of one of the worst contractions. 'God, help me, help me!'

'You might well ask God's help,' a voice said. 'He's certainly the only one who can really help you now.'

The woman standing over her was a plump, blunt-faced person, but she did not speak with the vicious unkindness of Sister Leigh, more a matter-of-fact indifference to Lily's pain. She had on a huge white apron over her black dress, and a white nurse's veil.

'Lie on your back,' she ordered. 'It's more seemly and I want to examine you. Legs up and apart!'

To Lily's horror she realized the woman was inserting her fingers up inside her, but she was determined not to cry out and humiliate herself further.

'You're nearly there,' the woman pronounced. 'It'll be here within the hour, I'd say.'

Even in these last days, with the baby kicking vigorously inside her, Lily had shut from her thoughts the reality that there was a living being inside her that was part of her. She did not want to know, could not let herself take in what that might mean. She certainly would not let herself begin to love it, because unless she got rid of it, pretended that it, and Sam, had never happened, she would have no life. She would be condemned to a life of shame and disgrace, trying to bring up a bastard child on her own, pretending she was a widow or one of the tricks such women had to play to live with any ease in society. And now she was too overtaken by the sheer ordeal of birthing to give any thought to the outcome.

Time swam by. She had no idea how long had passed.

Her whole existence was strung between the pains which seemed to arrive so close together that she was riding a sea of agony. She writhed, wanting to get up, to be on her knees, on her side, but each time she tried to move the woman in black forced her down.

'Get on your back! I'm not having you moving about. It's bad for the baby.'

Eventually the pains became overwhelming. Lily leaned back on her elbows, her legs apart and felt the enormous press of the child's head bearing down out of her. She thought she might split right in two. Screams issued from her mouth. In the midst of it there came a sharp slap round her face.

'Be quiet! How dare you make all that noise?'

It seemed to go on forever.

'Push!' the woman commanded her. 'Breathe and push, push it out!'

'I can't,' Lily cried, hoarsely. It felt impossible. She was completely exhausted. There had been no rest in this 'home'. Only work and more work.

Finally, bearing down with every fibre of her being, she managed to deliver the baby's head, and a few moments later she felt the slither of the body. She lay back, finished, panting. *That's it*, was all she could think. *It's over!*

Then, into the silence came the cry, a cracked, desolate sound which seemed to seize her at the centre of her being and draw her towards it. She leaned up on her elbow again to see the nurse unceremoniously wrapping the child in a length of white cloth. All she caught a glimpse of was dark hair. Sam's hair, she thought, filled with a terrible ache.

'Let me see . . .' Lily begged. 'Oh, please, bring it here . . .'

'It's no good. You're not keeping her, are you?'

'No, but . . .'

'Then it's no good. You'll have to feed her, but you're not to see her now. Won't do you any good. You must accept it. She'll soon be gone – and if you've got any sense, so will you, a gentlewoman like you.'

She took the baby from the room and Lily was left alone, hearing again and again in her head that rending, newborn cry, a sound which she knew would stay with her forever.

There was a nursing room, a place of mixed joy and desolation, where the new mothers were expected to go and feed their infants. The occasions of feeds were strictly timed and no extra time was allowed for holding or playing with the babies.

'No good getting a feel for her when you're giving her up.' Sister Jenkins, who was in charge of the nursing room, was a hearty but heartless person who treated both mothers and babies with utter lack of feeling. Lily watched her sometimes, her pink, brawny face bent over one of the young mothers, waiting to snatch the infant from them the second they had finished their allotted time at the breast.

Lily secretly called her little girl Victoria after the old queen. The home didn't allow the giving of names.

'They'll be given a name,' she was told. 'By their new families.'

The first time she saw the little one, once she had been cleaned up after the birth, was in the nursing room. Sister Jenkins carried her in from the nursery next door.

'Now – here you are. Undo your gown.' She had been issued with a thick, rough frock; the front crossed over her chest, with special ties so that it could be loosened for feeding. Lily was so fixed on seeing the child that she forgot to obey.

'I said undo your gown!' Sister Jenkins snapped. Lily found that her breasts were seeping a clear liquid. 'Now – take her and latch her to the breast.'

Lily held out her arms. She stared and stared at the tiny, perfect form that was handed to her. Tears welled up in her eyes and ran down her cheeks. Oh, she was Sam's child all right! She had thick tufts of dark hair and his sallow complexion.

'It's no good looking,' Sister Jenkins bossed her, trying to manoeuvre the baby on her arms to turn her to the breast.

'It's all right.' Lily drew back. 'I'll do it.'

She wanted to scream at the woman to go away. *Don't touch my baby, you cold, heartless woman! Leave me with her. Leave us in peace!* But she knew it was no good. It would only get her into trouble.

The feeling of the child's mouth on her nipple was strange and powerful and she sat wincing at it and the pains it caused in her stomach. Sister Jenkins sat watching her like a hawk and Lily kept her head down, trying to hide the overpowering rush of emotion which filled her. Here was this tiny being, sucking at her breast, so small and so dependent on her. And she was the first person Lily had ever known who was truly hers, who belonged to her. She felt stripped naked by the emotion, by the need she had for this little child. She would look down at her, wrung with tenderness, wanting to hold her in her arms forever.

What if she were to keep her? The idea ran round and round in her head. But she thought of going out again, alone, to the streets. All she had to her name was the payment from Eustace's family, the small remnant of her wages from the factory and Mrs Chappell's jewellery. What could she possibly give her baby? She would be so much better off with a family who could give her a good life. She forced herself to close down any such thoughts in her mind.

Victoria, she thought, looking down at her, willing both herself and the little girl to be strong. It was a strong name, and she would need to be victorious. She stroked her finger gently over the tiny, warm cheek.

'Right – that's long enough,' Sister Jenkins would decree, peering at the fob watch pinned to her ample chest.

Lily felt as if little Victoria was being torn from her as Sister Jenkins took her briskly away. How could she do the work she did, Lily wondered, when there was all this love and grief in front of her, all the powerful instincts of new mothers? She saw that Sister Jenkins had killed all such feelings in herself. And as she left the nursing room that evening, after Victoria's first feed, Lily knew that to survive losing her, she was going to have to do the same.

It was a freezing day in February when she stepped out through the forbidding front door of the home, dressed once more in her own clothes, holdall in her hand, head down against the bitter wind.

In her head were her instructions: the train to Euston, the directions to her new place of work, where, with Susan Fairford's glowing references, she had obtained a new post as nanny to two young girls at a respectable west London address.

Her figure had soon recovered. She was as rounded

and curvaceous as before, and walked with a healthy step, boots clicking along the cobbles. Looking up, she crossed the road, hurrying out of the path of a coalman's dray. She was wearing new clothes, bought with her payment from Eustace's people, a smart green dress, a new black coat and hat, and in every way she looked like a beautiful young woman setting out to embark on a new life. It was only her eyes that gave away her state, the pain locked in her heart. As she looked along the street, working out her route to the railway station, there was a deep sadness, a hardness which had not been there before, which covered up her grief, her bereavement, which she could not let herself feel.

Holding her head high, and with a determined step, she walked quickly away.

Chapter Forty-Seven

France, March 1918

'Oh God, here we go!'

Sam's hands tightened automatically on the truck's steering wheel. His convoy had just set off as the bugle sounded across the wide expanse of hospital huts to summon the nurses for emergency duty. Already they could hear the planes. Should he stop and turn back?

A small convoy of them had been ordered to drive desperately needed supplies to the casualty clearing station at Armentières. The raids had been coming night after night now the stalemate along the front had been broken by the German assault. Things were bad, very bad. The reception huts in the hospital were flooded with wounded, Allied and German, the place was like a scene from hell and all of them knew the war was hanging by a thread. The Germans were coming closer – they had reached Amiens.

Gripping the wheel, Sam eased his shoulders up towards his ears for a moment, a movement which had become so habitual that he no longer noticed it. His body had been forever taut during the three years he'd been in France; now it was pulled tense enough to snap. It was as if, in this endless hell of war, there was nothing but fear and exhaustion, no other state.

'Where are you buggers, then?' He leaned forward to try and see the droning threat in the darkness. He could hear nothing now, over the roar of their own truck engines. The Boche would be after the Étaples railway, which ran between the wide settlement of the hospital and supply depot and the sand dunes of the coast. Ambulance trains moved relentlessly along the tracks day and night, bringing the wounded from the Front, and it was the main artery along which the supplies to service General Haig's vast army were carried from the base depot. Shell that, and others like Calais and Boulogne, and they would paralyse the Allied supply lines. Just what they wanted, of course, Sam thought grimly. His mind slid round the fear: *And they'll win the war, and then what? What will happen?* But he buried the thought immediately.

He fixed his gaze on the lights of the lorry behind him. Bert, the driver, had leaned from the cab before they set off and called chirpily through his Woodbine, 'Don't lose sight of me, Ironside – no kipping on the job!' Act as if nothing was happening, that was Bert. That was all of them, come to think of it. Close down: don't think.

And you had to use every grain of strength to stay on the road. These rural routes were being grossly overused, bottlenecked with the traffic servicing the vast army, the roaring lorries and ammunition wagons, the horses and carts, the files of khaki-clad men. The area was already low-lying and marshy and the combination of spring rains and constant churning by wheels and hooves and feet had turned the roads into a quagmire of liquid mud, filling the deep holes and ruts. He began the usual lurching trial of strength which driving in these conditions involved, fixing his mind on it, trying not to think of anything beyond . . .

He didn't hear it coming. Afterwards he knew it was a shell, that it had landed in the mist-filled pasture close by, that it had hurled his lorry over on to its side. But all he knew then was instant blackness.

For a long time he passed in and out of consciousness. When he surfaced, groggily, he knew he was lying somewhere hard, that his face felt stretched and tight, he didn't know whether with caked mud or blood or both, that there was something strange about his left eye, that there were pains all round his body and that he was shaking. He was aware of a dimly lit place, of groaning cries, of a ghastly stench. And then he dipped under again into the darkness.

He was aware of being moved, much later, lifted higher on to a bed; of an atmosphere of chaos, and light in his face.

'I don't think there's much wrong, despite the look of him,' a man's voice said. 'He'll lose the eye, that's all. Not urgent – leave him till later, Nurse.'

'What d'you mean?' Sam tried to say. His mouth tasted metallic, of blood, and nothing sensible came out.

A woman's voice came next and with his good eye he caught a glimpse of her in the dim light of the oil lamp: the VAD uniform, a white veil, her face pale and thin beneath, dark circles under the eyes. And she understood what he was asking

'You've got an eyeful of glass and a lot of bruising. But you seem to be all right otherwise. You've been very lucky. I'll come back to you later ... Too many others to see to ...'

He drifted again, but each time he surfaced, his mind snagged on something. *You've been very lucky ... Too many others to see to . . .* Something familiar. That voice, prim and well spoken. He knew that voice from somewhere.

'Water . . . A drink . . .' His mouth was parched, foul-tasting.

His head was lifted and he sipped water. God, water was lovely. He just wanted to keep lapping it, more and more, but the cup was taken away.

Sam opened his good eye. It was that nurse again.

'What time is it?' he said hoarsely.

'Why?' Her voice was flat and exhausted. 'Does it make any difference?' Then her natural good manners took over. 'I suppose it's five in the morning, or so.'

'Thanks. Am I going to be blind?'

'Can't you see out of that one either?' She came a little closer. Yes, he could see out of his right eye, and he knew then. She had changed a good deal. Had it not been for the voice he wouldn't have known her. But with the voice he was sure now. What on earth was she doing here? Would she remember him?

'I'm going to see if I can get some of the glass out of your eye,' she was saying. 'Before another convoy arrives and we're swamped again.' She seemed about to move away, perhaps to fetch instruments, but somehow he couldn't bear it.

'Aren't you . . . I mean . . . I know you, I think . . .' he said, confusedly. He was stunned, disorientated by seeing her again, here of all places.

'No.' Her voice was brimful of sadness. 'I'm sure you don't. I'm not your mother, or your sister, dear. But I'll look after you, all the same, as if I were.' The utter sweetness with which she spoke brought a lump to his throat.

'But you're Mrs Fairford – aren't you?' As he said it he even wondered himself if he was hallucinating. 'Captain Fairford's wife – Ambala Cantonment?'

With only his one blurred eye he could still make out the change in her face. There was shock, and then she began to tremble. He thought she would weep.

'I seem to recognize you as well . . .' Her voice was high and tremulous, just in control. 'I'm not imagining what you're saying, am I?' She put a hand to her forehead. 'Sometimes I start to doubt myself . . . I'm so very tired . . .'

'No – it's all right. I'm Sam Ironside – remember? From Daimler. I brought your husband his cars.'

He saw her staring hard at him. Even now he felt himself tense, waiting for the response he remembered in her when they first met, the class superiority, her cool snobbishness. Her words came out haltingly, the recognition sinking in.

'Your face – you've so much blood on it I can hardly tell . . . Ironside . . . Of course, Charles's driver . . . We had picnics with the children, and Charles . . . Oh!' The last was an uncontrollable cry. 'Oh God!' She put her hands over her face, her shoulders shaking. 'I'm so sorry . . . Oh, forgive me . . .'

For a few anguished moments, Susan Fairford stood sobbing at the side of his bed.

As the dawn light increased through the windows of the hut, she bent over him, the lamp hanging from a hook near her head, and assessed his injuries again. She was quite collected now. He was covered in blood, she told him, because of a large number of cuts from small glass splinters, which had made his injuries seem far more serious on first sight. Sam realized the tightness in his cheeks was because of the dried blood. His eye was the only thing more seriously damaged and he knew he was one of the most fortunate blokes in there. Even losing an eye was as nothing compared with what some of them were going through.

'There's a bit of a lull,' Susan Fairford said. 'Let's see what I can do.'

And she began to try and remove some of the glass. Her only equipment was a small pair of tweezers. As yet, though, there was no pain, or very little, only a numbness, a feeling that his eye had been punched rather than pierced. As she worked, with great care, he did begin to feel the sharpness in his eye and he winced.

'Sorry,' she said, frowning with concentration. 'It's difficult. I can't see terribly well.'

'Am I going to lose it?'

'Hard to say as yet.'

With his good eye, Sam took the opportunity to study her and it helped take his mind off the discomfort of the operation. In the morning light he was very struck by the change in her. He knew he would not immediately have recognized her had she just walked past in the ordinary way of things. With her hair covered by her VAD veil, her face was uncrowned by its pale, curling prettiness and was thinner than he remembered, and sagging with exhaustion. She didn't look tense any more, or at least not in the way he remembered, her seeming to push other people away as if they might contaminate her. Instead, as well as a deep tiredness, he saw something quieter and more vulnerable.

'How is everyone?' he asked. 'The family, Captain Fairford, young Cosmo?'

She had just drawn back with something pinched in the end of the tweezers which she disposed of into a kidney dish.

'Nasty big piece there,' she murmured. Then, staring down in the direction of Sam's chest, she braced herself to say, 'Charles was killed – in 1915, at Neuve Chapelle. I was told he was shot. Isadora died the year before the war. Heart failure, at thirteen. And my dear Cosmo – well, he's fifteen now . . .'

'Oh God,' Sam said. There had been so many deaths, yet this one, of the fit, energetic captain he had known in India, seemed impossible and utterly tragic. 'You poor woman.'

He hadn't expected to say that, not to her. It seemed too presumptuous and intimate, but that was what came out and he was surprised at himself. Once more her face was gripped by a terrible spasm of grief.

'They say he was very brave,' she said heartbrokenly. 'And I know this should matter, should compensate in some way. But it's not true, of course, it doesn't. Nothing does. And now we look as if we'll lose the war as well, after all of it . . .' There was a pause. 'He never loved me, you know, not as I loved him, but . . . All I want . . . I just want him alive . . .' With a convulsive movement she reached into her pocket for a handkerchief. 'Selfish of me, I know, but that's how it is.'

'There can't be a grieving wife who doesn't feel the same,' Sam said, moved. But even as he said it, he thought, Would Helen feel it? Would she? Would he?

Susan Fairford wiped her eyes and set to work with the tweezers again. 'I'm sorry. I'm very tired. And I must get on before I'm called away.'

'How is Cosmo?' Sam asked. 'He was to go to Eton, wasn't he?'

She sighed. 'He was expelled from Eton. He nearly burned his house down – and it was not an accident. They weren't having any more of him. His housemaster said some terrible things about him. He's now in another establishment in Hertfordshire – Charles's brother's paying. Cosmo loathes it there, but what can I do? It was what Charles wanted for him, an education like his. I only pray to God the war will be over before he takes it into his head to join up. He's so reckless and he'd have no qualms about lying about his age. I've seen younger than him in here.'

'Yes,' Sam agreed. Boys as young as fourteen were fighting on the Western Front.

Delicately she fished several more tiny pieces of glass from his eye. He winced, trying not to cry out.

'Sorry . . .' She frowned with concentration. Once she had eased the eye a little, she said, 'Mr Ironside, you have a family? I'm afraid I can't remember.'

'I do. Three daughters. The last time we met I think we only had Ann and Nancy. Now there's Ruth as well.'

'Of course!' Susan stopped to look at him again. 'Mussoorie! My memory is so bad, I don't know what's happened to me! We were there with Lily – and Izzy was riding horses with Charles every moment she could . . . Oh, if I'd known . . .'

The memory was so sharp for Sam, so painful. Lily Waters. God, what he had felt for that woman! And she had played with him: let him down. The burn of it had never left him. It had made him ill for a time after. When he got home, and was so thin and sad and withdrawn, Helen had thought it was some disease he'd picked up in India.

His tone chill, he asked, 'And what news of Miss Waters?'

'Oh, I believe she's doing well – with a family in London. She's invaluable to them, I believe. And she's been so good to Cosmo – never forgotten him. She writes to him and so on.' Another sigh. 'Sometimes I feel she's more like a mother to him than I am. But I'm grateful, I suppose. At the moment. I had to come out here, you see – to be near Charles, close to where . . . I had to *do* something. We had gone home at the beginning of the war . . . I knew I'd go mad staying with my people in Sussex. At home all everyone complains about are the shortages – food, servants and so on, and living on their nerves waiting to hear bad news all the time. You feel stuck, *suffocated*. And of course I wasn't used to England, after all that time away. At least here you can be of use.'

Sam could see now why she had changed, her face scoured by grief.

'I think,' she said, peering into his injured eye, 'that I have taken out everything I can by this method. Not very satisfactory, I agree, but we'll just have to wait and see. I'll bandage you up – then I must go and see to someone else.'

'I'm very grateful,' Sam said, feeling a distance between them again. He didn't know where he was with this woman, though she had moved him in her sadness. The war changed everything, and she seemed a softer person, whom he began to like, though things like class could quickly rear their head again.

But she looked down at him, and amid the exhaustion, there was something kind and genuine.

'It's so good to see a familiar face,' she said. 'In all this madness.'

Chapter Forty-Eight

Brooklands Racetrack, Surrey, 1922

'All right, Ironside? Marks? Have a good ride down?'

Sam saw a cheery, familiar face through the crowd soon after he and his friend Loz Marks arrived at Brooklands, walking stiffly, cheeks air-burned after the long morning's ride from Birmingham. On their way across to the track, Sam bought a race programme from one of the eager young volunteers who sold them, spending the day moving among the excited crowds in order to be close to the racing. Lucky lads, Sam thought. Had he lived close when he was young he'd have done just the same.

Resentfully, he tried to recall the name of the man who had attached himself to them and it came to him: Jack Pye, someone he had known at Daimler before the war. Sam groaned inwardly.

'There're going to be some marvellous outings today. Count Zborowski's Chitty 1's lapping later – highlight of the day for me, of course,' the man was saying. Sam was barely listening. He found Jack Pye irritating, with his chubby, drinker's complexion and his obsession with high society bods, collecting them the way some people did with loco numbers. The bloke was like a flaming walking encyclopaedia of toffs. Course, he was going on about Chitty 1 because she was built by a count's son, not because he really cared about the engineering involved, Sam thought sourly. He knew he had grown sour about a lot of things these days. God, life was a weary business compared to when he was young! The one thing that lifted his spirits was being somewhere like this, anywhere to do with motors, without it being spoilt by some boring sod like Jack Pye. He moved away, morosely, and left Loz to deal with him.

Sam drank in the sight of the race ground, breathing in the clean air laced with cigarette smoke and exhaust fumes, hearing the motors roaring and the excited social chatter all about them. In the distance he could see the steep curve of the track, crowds of spectators in the middle. There was a race about to begin and the roaring of engines thrilled him. Brooklands attracted enthusiastic crowds for every event and the Whitsun bank holiday meeting seemed to mark the real beginning of summer, and visitors sprawled on the grass, luxuriating in the spring sunshine. High society people came from all over the region with sumptuous picnic hampers, the women in splendid gowns and feathered hats, men in sharply tailored clothes and cravats. Some removed the seats from their motors and sat on them to eat their picnics and sip champagne. These were the ones Jack Pye was inexplicably interested in. Then there were the more ordinary types, eager for a day out, coming into Weybridge on the train, or turning up on motorcycles and sidecars, or pushbikes – and there were the real motor enthusiasts with know-how, like Sam and Loz.

Sam kept one hand in his pocket holding his handkerchief and brought it out every so often to dab his watering left eye. The bright light made it worse. He cursed under his breath as a teardrop escaped and began to roll down his cheek.

'Damned thing!' Then he was ashamed. He'd come all through the war with only some minor scars on his body and that dodgy eye. Some of the glass was still in there and its vision was not good but he didn't have much to complain about.

'Family all right, Ironside?' Jack Pye was at his side again, persisting in talking to him. 'How many children've you got now?'

'Four,' Sam said, resigned to conversation. 'All girls.' He wasn't going to mention Joe. They never did mention Joe, of course. Not at home. And Helen's mother had never said a word afterwards. His own mother had tried to bring it up once or twice but Sam had changed the subject. No good digging it up. It was as if Joe had never been, yet his presence, the ghost of his two-month visit into their lives, lay between himself and Helen more emphatically than any living person.

'Blimey – a houseful of women!' Jack Pye chortled. You must be glad to get out of there, pal!'

Sam laughed it off. *Yes, I am*, he could have said. But it was too close to the truth to joke about. He dreaded going home these days, to the resentment which seemed to be Helen's constant expression. He knew that under it her heart ached with grief for Joe, and for Laurie, who was lost somewhere on the Somme, but she could not show it. She had become a hard, discontented woman and all he saw was her anger and disappointment with him.

He had thought a new start would make things better after the war, leaving Daimler, going to live in Birmingham. Racing had been part of the attraction there, of course, the races Austin had taken part in before the

338

war. They'd been one of the very few British entrants in the Grand Prix as early as 1908. And he'd struck lucky, been one of the handful of engineers taken on by the Austin works out at Longbridge. Business was still hanging by a thread, of course, with the slump, but Sam knew he couldn't have gone back to Daimler and taken up his old life as if nothing had happened. It had been bad enough back in '07, after India, trying to settle back into a life that seemed so shrunken and dull after Ambala and all the travelling he'd done with the captain; after Lily. The thought of her sent a spasm of pain through him, as it always did. After the war there was too much change amid the claustrophobic dullness: too many blokes missing from the neighbourhood, and too much change inside him. No, he'd had to move on or he'd have gone mad. He told Helen, 'I can't stay here.' He never gave her a choice. That was another thing she held against him, uprooting her from her friends, miles from her mother. All his fault, of course and she never let him forget it. She'd never liked Birmingham.

He and Loz managed to shed Jack Pye and cut across quickly towards the track. Along the railings there stood the bookies in top hats taking bets at their stalls. A woman stood close to one of them with a male friend, giggling uncontrollably. Sam saw with distaste that she had bad teeth.

'You going in for a flutter, Sam?' Loz asked.

'No,' he snapped. No point in wasting money.

'All right, I only asked,' Loz said.

The first race was about to begin. It was a small car handicap race and the two of them stood loudly discussing the entrants among the excited crowd, as the expectant roaring of the engines grew louder and louder despite the silencers on the cars. One was a 20 hp Austin, a sports model. God, Sam would have liked to be part of the Austin race team, but he hadn't managed to wangle it yet. At least there was some hope of that, more than of he and Loz building their own 'Special', one of the cars put together privately by amateurs for racing. Loz was forever on about it. Old Loz was a dreamer, pie in the sky.

Sam stood breathing in the scent of exhaust fumes, his eyes fixed on the track. This was the only place where he could almost feel happy. Brooklands was the only track for car racing in the country – the first in the world of its kind. The three and a quarter mile outer track had been built in under nine months and there was a purpose-built test hill for putting the cars through their paces on a steep gradient. All around the grounds were a hive of activity also, sheds divided into work-shops where cars were maintained and developed, giving off that engine-oil smell which was the breath of life to Sam. Of course, there were areas fenced off where you could only go if you were an Automobile Racing Club member and he had not reached that hallowed position. Like almost everything else, he couldn't afford it, in this land fit for heroes. The members had their own separate bridge over the track for viewing, as well as a clubhouse, and Sam's usual resentment of the upper classes stirred in him when he thought about it. But that was not something he was going to let spoil his day. He looked round and grinned at Loz.

'We'll be here,' Loz shouted to him, his snub-nosed face beaming with enthusiasm. 'One of these days we'll be racing our own!'

'You're a one,' Sam shouted back. 'Not a hope!'

'Course we will!' Loz was forever optimistic.

'What're we going to use for capital, eh? Potato peelings?'

Sam had met Loz soon after moving to the Austin works, in the machine shop where they started Sam off and where Loz had recently completed his own apprenticeship. The two of them sparked off each other, both mad keen on motors and Loz especially on racing. When Sam was moved out to the works test track which ran round the perimeter of the factory site, the two of them stayed friends. Helen and Loz's wife Mary also got on well. In fact, Mary had been a saving grace. Helen tended to keep herself to herself and be even more miserable and defeated otherwise. Loz and Mary were both cheerful types and had two young sons. Loz was forever on about building a Special with Sam. But they both knew that just getting hold of an old racing car and trying to rebuild and maintain it was fraught with problems, even for amateurs as skilled as themselves.

'Go down that road and all you've got is something out of date before you know it,' Sam said. 'It'd give you nothing but problems.'

Their dream was to try something other enthusiasts were doing since the war – building aero-engines into an old chassis. The thought of all the extra power it gave to the vehicle was heady.

'We know all there is to know, don't we?' Loz had said enthusiastically one evening a couple of months ago when the two of them were ensconced in the corner of a Northfield pub on the Bristol Road, not far from where they both lived. 'All we need's a place to get going ...'

'And money,' Sam said gloomily. 'It's way beyond us, Loz, on our own, you know it is. It's not just

341

building the thing – there's the maintenance and fuel and getting it to the track meetings. It'd cripple us before we'd even got started.'

What was the good of even talking about it? As a qualified engineer he was on a respectable salary, but he was a father of four. It wasn't the same for Loz, with only two to bring up and a wife who was happy. Sam was only three years older than his pal, but sometimes he felt like a burdened old man in comparison, and his funds seemed to disappear down the drain.

Loz took a long swig of his favourite M&B ale, of which he could drink prodigious amounts without any apparent effect other than an increase in his already chirpy optimism.

'We'd manage,' Loz grinned. 'What's got into you, Sam? I thought you were all for it. I mean, we're a good prospect, not like some. We've got our own tools – we know what we're looking for and how to do it, given the chance. Come on, mate – are you for it? I'm game if you are.'

Unfortunately Loz's sparkling optimism was not always rewarded by events and they were no nearer to doing anything except dreaming. Coming to Brooklands, however, was a great opportunity to see other Specials go through their paces on the racetrack, and find out who was using what engines and which parts, as well as to drink in the excitement of the atmosphere.

The day seemed to fly past as Sam and Loz watched the races from the stands. There were the more serious contests, and others to amuse the spectators, like the Old Crocks race. Nearly all of it was utterly absorbing to them, watching the cars from the various big manufacturing stables like Austin and Vauxhall, but above all the privately built Specials which gave them endless amounts to chew over each time – which chassis, which engine, and all the engineering detail that followed from them.

In the afternoon there was a flurry of added excitement over Count Zborowski's motor Chitty Chitty Bang Bang, setting out to beat his own lap record, running on a Maybach airship motor which had been used in Zeppelins. At last year's Easter meeting it had been the star of the show, winning two races and coming second in another. Zborowski had built a second model called Chitty 2 with a Benz aeroplane engine. Loz and Sam took a keen interest in them.

'They drove it right into the Sahara at the beginning of the year,' Sam said wistfully. Never, ever, had he forgotten the sense of freedom and adventure of being out on the road in India with Captain Fairford in the Daimler. He still remembered those weeks in India as the most exciting of his life.

As Chitty 1, with her long, pointed nose, roared round the track at dizzying speed, Sam found himself baying with the rest of the crowd massed along the track, shouting himself hoarse for Zborowski's car to go faster, faster, to exceed what had been possible before. That was the thing about this game, Sam thought, fizzing with excitement. There was always progress, a sense of new possibility. How desperately he needed to feel that when his home life was so stuck, so deadening!

'She's really cutting a hole in the wind!' Loz yelled at Sam, his fist clenched in the air with excitement.

'She is – must be a record-breaker!' Sam could feel himself lit up, as he so seldom was in his life these days. It was only cars and racing that could ever get him truly excited now and give him a sense of adventure. He could feel his pulse racing, his spirits lifting and a delighted grin spreading across his face. Soon it was announced over the tannoy that Chitty Bang Bang 1 had just achieved her fastest ever lap of 113.45 miles per hour.

'God,' Sam said, awed. He looked round at Loz and both their faces were suddenly serious.

'We've got to do it!' Loz said. 'We've got the know-how. We've got to put together something as good as that!'

Sam was on fire as well – thank God! At least he could be on fire about something! He knew, suddenly, that that was where all the energy and passion of his life could now be directed.

The two of them strolled across the grass in a frenzy, talking non-stop amid the milling crowds. Sam was oblivious to them for a time, lost in his vision of what he and Loz might create with their skill and sense of adventure. Hang the money! They'd do it somehow. They had to! He gave an actual groan when he saw Jack Pye hoving into view again, his fat face pink with excitement.

'Did you see her go! What a thing! I bet the count's pleased as punch!'

Sam and Loz were looking for a spot to sit down and open their flask of tea and it seemed inevitable that they were now stuck with Jack Pye again. They walked on together, Sam keeping his distance a little, and it was when he at last glanced ahead that he saw the young man, just a few yards away from them. He often thought later, with a chill, that had he not just looked up then, none of what happened next might have happened.

But he did look up, and saw a very tall, startlingly handsome young man walking towards him with blue eyes, which seemed to hold a defiant arrogance, and a head of wavy, very thick blond hair. He cut such a figure that it would have been difficult not to stare: he was so obviously moneyed, and conscious of his own wealth and good breeding. He exuded confidence and superiority. And Sam recognized him, somehow, yet he was sure he had never seen him before. He was walking just ahead of a couple who were strolling along in a leisurely fashion, the woman holding the hand of a little ginger-haired boy. The young man seemed impatient as if they were all holding him up.

Sam took in the couple: a tall, thin man in his forties dressed in a beautifully tailored navy coat and holding a rolled umbrella, although the day had turned out so fine. Apart from his clothing he was not very distinctive. He had brown wavy hair, was gentle-featured and, Sam sensed, shy. Resting her arm in the crook of his, was a strikingly beautiful woman. At first all he noticed was the bold flair of her clothing, the crimson velvet skirt, an impression of dark, flowing material at the top, almost as if she were an exotic bird with her feathers moving behind her, and a crimson cloche hat, with a dark band and a black feather tucked in jauntily at one side. The women Sam encountered usually had neither the wealth nor the daring to dress with this kind of panache. Certainly Helen didn't. He was captivated by the sight. And then in those few seconds, beneath the brim of the hat he saw the face, the dark, flashing eyes, and he knew her immediately, with a physical shock, and he was rooted to the spot. He knew it was her, with his whole being, and while he stood, stunned, beside him the tedious Jack continued his endless commentary to Loz.

'Now there's a bit of all right – classy, eh? That's

Piers Larstonbury, carrying her on his arm, the lucky bloke! You don't know who Piers Larstonbury is? The architect – oh, he's got a name for himself in London all right – worth a pretty penny! And that's Cosmo Fairford walking ahead there – another family with a pile of loot stashed away – up our way, Warwickshire, although he's a bit of a waster, by all accounts. Any road, Piers Larstonbury...' He repeated the name almost as if it was holy, then lowered his voice portentously. *'That's his boy, but that dame he's with certainly isn't his wife!'*

'Come on, Sam,' Loz said impatiently. 'What's up with you?' They had been walking along towards the paddock surrounding the clubhouse, which was where the society types mingled.

Sam had to remind himself to move his feet. He could not begin to explain what was up with him. Jack might not have known the woman's name, but he knew all right. He had thought all that was over, that he had burned her out of him and that he could even have met her again and not felt anything. But even after all this time, in only a second he had known that that beautiful, mysterious woman was Lily Waters, the woman with whom he had spent the happiest, most intense days ever in his life, who had betrayed him so badly that he had thought at one time that he might never recover. And there she was, moving further and further away, taking with her the answer to the question, *Why, Lily, why did you do that to me?*

He knew in that split second that whatever happened, however much of a fool he might be about to make of himself, he *must* speak to her, submit, if necessary, to her scorn and rejection, to set himself free of her. And if he didn't hurry they'd be in the paddock where only

BARC members were allowed, and he would be shut out.

'I'll just be a minute,' he said to Loz distractedly. 'You and Jack go ahead . . . There's just something . . .'

Leaving a baffled Loz staring and calling after him, he turned back and tore towards the racetrack.

Chapter Forty-Nine

For a moment he thought he had lost them.

He ran faster, not caring what anyone thought, colliding at one point with a man in a loud checked sports jacket.

'Sorry!' Sam shouted to the man's curses.

Had it not been for the crimson of Lily's skirt and the child's bright ginger hair he might have had more difficulty in keeping sight of them. He realized that the four of them were almost at the paddock railings and he hurtled towards them. Only as he came really close did he question his sanity. What in heaven's name was he going to say? Suddenly it all felt like a crazed dream. And he could not just let her pass out of his life again, not without speaking to her.

Cosmo was now lagging, apparently sulkily, behind the others and Sam caught up with him first.

'Excuse me!' He blundered into speech before he could lose his nerve.

Cosmo Fairford's penetrating blue gaze was turned on Sam. He must be nineteen years old by now and what an immensely striking fellow he was, with that god-like combination of looks and breeding! Sam felt all his usual class resentments surfacing again, made worse by the fact that the expression in Cosmo Fairford's eyes was cold and supercilious.

'Yes?' The tone was clipped, as if words cost him dearly.

'Are you Cosmo Fairford?'

Cosmo stopped, with an air of dealing with a tiresome tradesman who it would be easier to humour and get shot of quickly.

'I am.'

Sam was not going to defer to him. He held out his hand.

'Samuel Ironside. You won't remember me, but we met when you were a young 'un. I sold your father a car – stayed with you in Ambala.'

The handshake was instinctively, but languidly, returned. 'I see,' Cosmo said. 'I'm afraid I don't—'

'No, well of course you wouldn't,' Sam interrupted him hurriedly. The tiny boy with blond curls who bounced up and down on the seat of the Daimler back then would not have the faintest idea who he was. That child who Sam had first seen cradled in Lily's arms ... This man he had grown into, Sam thought, was more cold and superior than even his mother had been.

He saw then, in the corner of his eye, that the rest of the party had turned to look for Cosmo and were walking towards them: Piers Larstonbury with Lily on his arm. Sam turned to them, marvelling that he could achieve such cool composure when he was burning, trembling inside.

'Good afternoon.' Piers Larstonbury's tone was enquiring, his voice quiet. It was plummy, of course, but not with that hectoring bellow adopted by many of his class.

'Good afternoon.' Sam decided to speak out with confidence. 'I just stopped to speak to Mr Fairford. I once delivered a car to his father in India.'

'How splendid!' Piers Larstonbury said. Sam felt himself relax a fraction. He could tell he was in the presence of a true gentleman, one who would treat everyone with courtesy no matter what their walk of life. 'And by which company are you employed, if I may ask?'

'Well, at the time I was with Daimler,' Sam said. 'This was a good while ago – before the war. I'm one of the Austin's engineers now, at Longbridge.'

He had the man's attention: he was genuinely interested, Sam could see.

'And your name is?'

'Samuel Ironside.' He spoke very clearly and only then, he looked at Lily.

There was no pretence. In that moment, he felt strangely proud of her. She was not one of these upper-class misses with their feelings buried under deep layers of social propriety, the sort who might now stare icily at him, or turn away, affecting indifference. She was a real woman, that was how he remembered her. *His woman*, he thought, and now he saw that her gaze was fixed on him, utterly, deeply as if there was nothing else to be seen. He remembered with a terrible pang those dark eyes fixed on him with longing and devotion, where now he could see questioning and pain and, not far below the quiet surface, a quivering restraint of emotions.

'A pleasure to meet you,' Piers Larstonbury was saying. 'I must say, Daimler have made some fine motors, very fine. I have yet to experience driving an Austin. But I'm sure I should like to.'

'The Twenty and Twelve have been highly success-ful,' Sam said. He did feel a personal pride in the models the company had developed since the war. 'What do

you drive?' Piers Larstonbury somehow indicated that
he should walk with them and he found himself drawn
along in front of Cosmo, Lily and the boy.

'A Daimler, in actual fact – a rather old model now.
But I must admit to enjoying a Morgan as well. Damn
fine cars. I'm not highly knowledgeable at all. It's
Cosmo who's the expert there. He's very keen to race –
very keen indeed. He's trying to find his way into it.'

As they strolled along the edge of the paddock, Sam
told Piers Larstonbury about the new model of Austin
being developed at the works – something more afford-
able for the ordinary driver. And then he found himself
talking about Chitty 1 and Specials and somehow Sam
announced that he was in the process of building one
himself.

'How absolutely marvellous! Are you a driver
yourself?'

'Not a racing driver,' Sam said.

Piers Larstonbury actually stopped, gazing at him.
Sam realized the man was not just being polite, he really
did not know much about motoring. He was just a
social day tripper, one of the ones who went to the
Henley Regatta or racing at Ascot for the social scene,
and Sam saw that he was eager to learn and prepared to
listen with real attention.

'Course,' Piers Larstonbury said, 'a chap like you
with all the expertise – it's ideal! I must say, I rather
envy you. All rather new to me, this, you see. I've not
come to Brooklands before. I came because . . .' He said
no more but the tiny tilt of his head towards Lily and
Cosmo gave some explanation. Jack Pye had insisted
that Lily was not Piers Larstonbury's wife. So what was
between them? Did Lily love him? Sam tried to stop

himself speculating. He had seen nothing in Lily's eyes which spoke of love for the man, but perhaps that was what he wanted to believe ...

They had reached the railings round the paddock. Inside, there were a number of cars parked and clusters of members were standing talking.

'I do wish you luck with your vehicle,' Piers Larstonbury said. 'It sounds immensely exciting.'

Sam knew he had given a misleading picture of the situation, but he was still taken aback to hear Piers Larstonbury speak as if the car was already half built. He could hardly admit now that there was no Special – that he had no money and nowhere to work.

'Well – we're definitely going for an aero-engine – chain-driven chassis, of course – a Mercedes.' He found all their dreams pouring out passionately. 'High gear ratios – we can sort that out with countershaft sprockets. It'd be fantastic to be able to test it on the hill climb here ... My God,' he finished, 'she's going to be good when we've finished. The likes of Chitty 1 will have to look out!'

'Marvellous.' Piers Larstonbury was looking at him intently. Sam could see he had impressed the man with his know-how and enthusiasm, and he turned to include the others in the conversation.

'Cosmo – Mr Ironside here is in the process of building a Special himself – on a Mercedes chassis. I imagine you have ambitions to race her here when she's finished?'

'Oh yes, of course,' Sam said, still full of conviction. Of course that was what they were going to do!

He could see Cosmo Fairford looking at him with a new respect which he found gratifying. But now he was also face to face with Lily again.

'Cosmo is far more knowledgeable on the subject than I. A devotee, one might say. And a demon driver.'

'Well,' Sam said, attempting to overcome his instinctive dislike of Cosmo. 'From what I remember you started very young. Your father had you at the wheel from about the age of four!'

'Yes,' Lily added suddenly. 'And for ever after.'

Piers Larstonbury looked from one to the other of them in puzzlement. Sam's and Lily's eyes met and held each other's gaze steadily, somehow defiantly.

'You two have met before!'

'Yes.' Lily was in command now, cool and detached as any upper-class mistress of the drawing room. 'We have, briefly. A very long time ago.'

Sam felt her words like ice poured into him. They seemed loaded with cruel indifference. And he realized, foolishly, that they were waiting for him to leave. They could see he was not a BARC member and they wanted their tea. Sam felt small and deflated, like a small boy with his nose pressed up against a sweet-shop window. He had been a little diversion in their day of entertainment and now he was holding them up.

'My colleagues are waiting for me over the other side,' he said brusquely. 'I just wanted a quick word with Mr Fairford here – for old times' sake.' He raised his cap with careful courtesy.

'Well, it's been a delight to meet you Mr, er, Ironside,' Piers Larstonbury said, returning the salute. 'And I wish you every success.'

And it was time for Sam to take his leave. It was over. And nothing had even begun.

Chapter Fifty

'Damn,' Sam railed to himself, walking away. 'Damn and blast it! And damn *them*!'

He felt like slamming his hat down on the ground, he was so frustrated and humiliated. He had not managed a single proper word with Lily. Unable to stop himself, he turned back at least to watch her walk away, to have a final glimpse of her.

His eyes caught hers, just as she had also turned to look back over her shoulder. Neither of them could pretend they were not looking for the other, and he saw Lily hesitate. She paused to say something to Piers Larstonbury, then turned back, leaving the boy, to hurry towards Sam.

He saw that she was even more beautiful than he remembered. Her face had matured and there was a more chiselled curve to her cheekbones. She seemed more sophisticated and poised, more formidable. The sight of her utterly captivated him. They stood feet apart, in silence, for some moments. He looked into her eyes but her expression was guarded, frightened even. At last, as she said nothing, he could not hold back.

'I saw you – earlier. I knew it was you.' Looking very directly at her he said, 'I'd know you anywhere, Lily.'

There was a moment, a flicker of vulnerability, but then she said coolly, 'Major Larstonbury felt that he had been very remiss in not inviting you to be our guest for tea in the clubhouse.'

So Larstonbury was a major as well, Sam thought. Course, he would be. Officer class and all that.

'I have people waiting,' Sam said with dignity. 'They'll already be wondering where I am.'

Her eyes widened. 'Family?' He was glad she asked, that the question mattered to her.

'No. Just a couple of pals.'

She seemed to decide something, and stepped closer, speaking fast and urgently.

'Sam, you can help – please. I know you can. We've got to do something for Cosmo – set him on the right path. He's been so unhappy. School has been a disaster for him and the family made him go into the bank and he *loathes* it. I'm so very worried for him. Everything has gone wrong for him ... Losing his father the way he did – and Isadora. The one thing he wants to do is race – he's good, *really* good. He drives on the estate, but he's had such bad luck. Please, Sam – come back and talk about it with us. At least join us for tea.'

There was such appeal in her eyes and voice, such passion in her concern for Cosmo that Sam knew he was already being drawn in. For her, not for Cosmo: he'd do anything to be near her. But he had to be honest with her now. He didn't want to make a complete fool of himself.

'You must understand – we're not far on at all,' he said. 'I may have misled Major Larstonbury. You see, we have no money to begin.'

Lily shook her head dismissively. 'Oh, money! Money's not a problem for these people.'

It was that which decided him. The way she spoke of them, distancing herself from Piers Larstonbury's upper-class sort in a way which put her on Sam's side. For all her learned sophistication it was a class alliance. She looked intensely into his eyes. 'If you need money, you're in the right place. And they need you. Come and have tea, Sam. You won't regret it.'

And so he walked into something he had never expected, not in his most fanciful of dreams.

The clubhouse was an airy-looking pavilion, sporting a low turret and a veranda round the sides, with the atmosphere of a seaside resort. They were served tea round a small table in a wide room full of the genteel sounds of conversation and laughter and teaspoons clinking against china and the sweet scents of cake and strawberry jam. Piers Larstonbury behaved with utter courtesy, apologizing to Sam for his oversight in not inviting him the first time.

'Miss Waters is so much better at these things than I,' he said. And he shot a look at Lily which revealed, quite nakedly, his feelings.

He adores her, Sam saw. He watched carefully to try and make sense of it all. Did she feel the same?

'Not at all,' Sam said carefully.

'This is my son, Hubert,' Piers Glastonbury said. The little boy, whom Sam guessed to be about five, had just taken a huge mouthful of jam sponge and he stared round-eyed at Sam, who gave him a smile.

There was a silence and Sam took a sip of tea, then turned to Cosmo. He could swallow his dislike of the fellow for Lily.

'I gather you're keen to race? What have you done so far?'

Cosmo came to life then. 'I've driven always – on my

uncle's estate. He's had a few motors, mostly saloon models, of course, but I've hammered those round the track. A couple of friends bring their motors – we have all sorts going round there. One or two Austins, a Mercedes, a Weigel . . .'

Sam frowned. 'You mean you've got a circuit?'

'Oh yes!' Cosmo said proudly and for a second Sam caught a glimpse of the eager young boy. 'I mean, not like here, of course, not banked and all that, but a track Uncle's let me carve out round the grounds. He's plenty of space, after all. There's even rather a good hill for testing uphill speeds . . .'

Sam began to feel a real glimmer of excitement. He didn't like Cosmo, but he could see the passion in him, the real hunger for motors and driving which gave him a sense of kinship. And surely the boy must have some of his father's qualities?

'Why not have a go building your own, then?' he asked. 'Plenty of people give it a go.'

Cosmo's face fell, became almost sulky. 'No idea where to begin, old man. I've had a few thoughts, but I've no expertise and none of my friends are in that line. They sent me to work in a bank . . .' he finished in disgust.

While he was speaking, Sam noticed that Lily and Piers Larstonbury were quietly conferring beside them and he saw, with a dart of deep jealousy, that she had laid her hand on his forearm and was looking into his eyes. Piers Larstonbury gave her a smile of intimate adoration, then he looked at Sam.

'She's a great persuader, this young woman. Tell me, Mr Ironside. Where do most of these vehicles, these Specials, come to be built?'

'Anywhere anyone gets the chance,' Sam said. 'At the

back of workshops, in old barns and sheds – I've even heard of one or two being pieced together in people's bedrooms. Course, there are also the workshops here.' He sighed, not realizing how much longing there was in his voice. 'This would be the dream place to do it. There are all those workshops away from the track with all sorts going on in them, and you'd be breathing the air in this place, with the company reps on hand for parts and right by the track and the test hill. A lot of these are company-owned, of course, most of the big firms have sheds here. Most amateurs can only dream of anything like that. They'll work at it every spare moment they've got, hardly sleeping, hardly doing anything else to get it built, get it right. But they'll still be in the shed at the bottom of the garden until what they build is successful. Then, with any luck, they can live on their winnings!'

Piers Larstonbury smiled at his wistful passion. Sam saw him exchange a glance with Lily. Her eyes burned with feeling and she gave the slightest, persuasive nod. Cosmo seemed unaware what was passing between them and sat eating cake, sunk back into his usual sulkiness.

'Mr Ironside.' Piers Larstonbury became business-like, pushing his tea plate to one side and reaching into his breast pocket for a fountain pen and a small note-book. 'I have a proposal to make to you.'

Chapter Fifty-One

Lily sat beside Piers Larstonbury in the front of the Daimler. Little Hubert was so exhausted that he was asleep with his head on Lily's lap before they had even left the race ground. Even so, Lily kept her head bent low, stroking his hair to hide the tumult of feeling going on inside her. Sam . . . *Oh God, seeing Sam again* . . .

After a while she looked out of the window, but it was not the trees and fields of Surrey she was seeing but Sam's face, the way he had looked at her, searching her eyes in pain and bewilderment. Why should *he* be in pain when he had hurt her so badly? She gripped the edge of the seat until her left hand ached. All the agony of those years, of Sam, the baby, she had locked away deep in herself.

Don't ever look back, she had told herself. *Forget. Don't ever think, don't expect anything from life, not of love, of having a real life of your own. Just take what you can wherever you can.* She had never expected to see him again, but suddenly there he had stood, those deep grey eyes staring into hers, filling her with an agonized sorrow and anger and longing. She had loved him – God how she had loved him. And their child, little Victoria. All of it came back, searing through her.

'Are you all right, my darling?' Piers Larstonbury asked.

'Yes – thank you. Just a little tired.' Lily managed a

calm voice. 'I think I might have a little doze if you don't mind.'

'Of course, my dear. You rest. It's been a demanding day.'

She was not in the least sleepy but closing her eyes would give her refuge. Before doing so she turned to look at his gentle face, frowning slightly as he steered the motor car. He was a good man, she knew that. An unlikely looking man to have been a soldier, like so many who were thrown into it, but all she had ever heard of him was praise for his complete dedication to his men and his kindly way with them. He had had a reputation for it. And he was utterly besotted with her. But although at times she appreciated his kindness, her gaze held no returning passion. He was another man she allowed to use her. It had become her way of surviving.

Laying her head back, she thought instead of the young person who had been her one enduring passion. She felt a surge of satisfaction. At last today she had managed to achieve something for Cosmo, to please him, set him on the road to a life he really wanted. The thrill of seeing his face when Piers and Sam had shook hands on their agreement to let him race was reward enough. It had been she who had engineered that exchange, who had taken Piers's hand and looked deeply into his eyes, knowing that in those rare moments, when he thought she was truly responding to him, she could ask of him almost anything. Major Piers Larstonbury was an unhappily married man and Lily, as he told her endlessly, was the true light of his life.

'I just don't know what I'd do if you were to leave,' he told her sometimes. 'My darling Lily, I simply couldn't bear it.'

And she remembered almost the same words on Sam's lips, and those of Ewan McBride and Harold Arkwright, in whose household she had worked briefly when she first came back to England: those same old words, she thought, quite empty of meaning, and in the end, so cruel. Never ever would she believe anyone again who said those words to her. But she knew Cosmo would not leave her. He depended on her in a way he had never been able to do with his mother. She had been the one who had held him in her arms for so many days of his childhood. She had written to him faithfully at school, she had been the one to visit him during the war when Susan Fairford was in France, trying to bury her own grief in her work as a VAD. Lily knew Cosmo needed her, even though he was so often rude and disagreeable. And just occasionally she was repaid by him becoming sweet and vulnerable, his buying her bunches of flowers and apologizing for his behaviour.

'You're the only one who's ever really bothered about me, Lily,' he'd say despondently, looking wretched in a way that melted her heart. 'You've been like a mother and sister to me in one.'

Yes, he was her boy. She needed no one else and she would do anything in her power to help him. That was her mission in life, other than her own survival: her devotion to Cosmo. Anything else that might truly have been hers had been cruelly snatched away.

Piers Larstonbury was simply a means to an end. She had gone to his house to earn her living and as the months passed he had become more and more obsessed with her, as men always seemed to. And in her need to earn a living, and seeing his wealth as an opportunity, she had given in to him, becoming his lover, allowing him to quench his loneliness with her. She would not admit to her own loneliness. Her heart was cold and closed now, since Ewan McBride and above all since little Victoria. She was untouchable – and that was how she had intended to remain, and had done. Until today, when Sam Ironside stood in front of her and looked into her eyes, and she was torn open again.

Chapter Fifty-Two

Once she had stepped out of the Bethel Home that day, leaving Birmingham for London, knowing that she would never see her baby Victoria again, Lily had vowed that she would not look back. If she did, she would not be able to go on.

She had secured her job with the Arkwrights, in a comfortable home in Islington. Harold and Letitia Arkwright had three small daughters. Letitia Arkwright informed Lily on her arrival that the last nanny had 'got herself into trouble' and had to depart. She was a thin, wrung-out-looking woman even though still only in her twenties, who looked perpetually anxious, screwing up her face as she spoke as if the sun was too bright, even though they were in a darkened room.

'I must be sure of having someone of good character this time,' she said.

Lily, who had no desire to go near another man ever again, had no difficulty in reassuring her.

A month passed and she and the three girls, who were not too difficult a challenge, all got used to each other. But long after that, things went quickly to the bad when Harold Arkwright started on her. It began with long, lingering stares from his mud-coloured eyes when he met her on the stairs or when she presented the girls to their parents in the evening. Lily soon realized the cause of the last nanny's 'trouble', though poor Letitia Arkwright seemed not to have recognized the rabid womanizer she was married to, even though his attempts at seduction happened quite blatantly under her own roof. Harold Arkwright owned a number of successful millinery businesses in different quarters of London. He also displayed a shrewd ability for making money on stock and shares and the family were certainly comfortable, if not extravagantly, wealthy. He was a short, stocky man with very thick, black hair, an impressive moustache and an air of urgent muscular energy which contrasted rather pitifully with his wife. Letitia spent most of her evenings reclining on the couch exhausted, reading a novel and not inviting company. Harold, as soon as he came home from attending to business, began to spend his evenings in pursuit of Lily. Though she slept in the nursery she had her own tiny sitting room, very simple, with just a couple of easy chairs and a small table, and an old Turkey rug partly covering the dark floorboards. Over the little leaded fireplace was a shadowy oil painting of chrysanthemums. Mr Arkwright started appearing there in the evenings, tapping discreetly on the door. At first she didn't feel she could refuse to open it.

'You are the most beautiful thing I've ever seen,' he would murmur, hovering on the threshold. Bolder, he would then come in and close the door. 'God, what a woman you are, Miss Waters. Come here, my dear. Come and sit beside me.'

'No – I really must go and see if Lizzie has settled,' Lily would say, or some similar excuse, and flee to the nursery. She became frightened and did not answer the door, pushing a chair up against it. Harold Arkwright took to mooning about outside the door. At first he was hesitant, polite. Then, as his ardour for her grew, it became extreme.

Lily endured several very lonely, desperate weeks at the Arkwrights. Though she never once succumbed to Harold Arkwright's advances, she felt under continual sexual threat. Once only he pushed his way into her room one night, begging her to let him lie with her, but she threatened to scream and wake up the children and call his wife. He seemed surprised and very offended at her resistance to him. He never tried it again although she went to bed with a chair pushed under the nursery door handle. But she was not sleeping well, and was jumpy day and night. It felt like revisiting a nightmare.

Though she scarcely knew it, she was not very well. She was still in a raw state after all the grief and shocks she had endured. Also, she was not used to England, to the grey drabness of the city streets after the loveliness of Mussoorie, and she did not know another soul in the place to call a friend.

Worst of all, here she was once again being pursued in this gross way. Why did men behave like this to her? Was she giving them some abnormal signal which she did not recognize? She felt lost and contaminated, and at times like those she could believe all the cruel accusations those religious women had made in the Bethel Home, that she was dirty and shameful. Sometimes she looked in the yellow tinted mirror in the nursery and even though her same wide, dark eyes looked back at her, her strong brows and thick, waving hair, she could barely recognize who she saw. At night she lay in bed and wept until she was so tired that sleep had to come.

At the height of her desperation, one evening, while Harold Arkwright patrolled the carpeted corridor outside the nursery, she sat on a cork-seated stool in the children's bathroom beside the nursery. It was quiet, except for a persistent drip from one of the bath taps, and for the first time she allowed herself to think, to remember.

In the dark winter gloom she often pined for India. Taking leave of it had been so painful and made all the more fraught because she had had the dreadful Eustace in her care. Unless actually asleep he couldn't sit still for more than a few moments at a time and he fidgeted ceaselessly. He needed constant entertaining and, whether entertained or not, was rude and aggressive. The train journey to Bombay had entailed some of the most exhausting and trying hours she had ever experienced. She sat sweating by the window of the train as they chugged for endless hours south-west to the coast, intermittently trying to engage Eustace in games of 'I Spy' or noughts and crosses, or in his story books. It was only when he was actually asleep, in the afternoon, that she had enough time really to look out and think about her own farewell to India, and in doing so, she ached with sadness.

Five years she had been in this country, but England now felt a lifetime away. She thought about all her time with the Fairfords, and with a shudder the strange, dream-like months with the McBride household, yet all amid the loveliness of Mussoorie which had stolen her heart. She thought of Sam with an agonized longing which never left her. But, she reasoned, if he had really loved her and wanted her, he would surely have found some way to let her know. Had things been different, had Sam not changed her, opened her to her feelings, she could have made her life in India. But what would have become of her? She might have floated from post to post in the houses of British families whom she might admire or despise, but she would always be a servant, forever a foreigner, an old maid growing scrawny and strange. And now she was carrying a child and only difficulty and disgrace could follow. She had no fellow feeling, then, for the infant. There was no sign of it except sickness and exhaustion and all she could think of was that she had to be rid of it. She had to survive and struggle to find a new life. Staring out at the endless skies and plains of India, she felt her own aloneness and a surge of determination. She would go back to England; she would not let herself fall prey to maternal feelings – that would lead her only to disaster. She was going to survive and make something of herself, no matter what it took.

But when the P&O steamer pulled majestically away from the port at Bombay, Lily found tears pouring down her face. The hotchpotch of streets of the city, the ghats and hills all faded as they moved away on the deep green water, until the coast with its smells and sounds was lost to her, its colours only a line of blurred umber in the distance.

It all felt like a dream now: India, Birmingham, the bedstead factory. She could have found more genteel work, but she wanted something anonymous, where she'd be one of a crowd, and could disappear again almost without comment. These frightening, lonely months of waiting were something she just had to get through. She took a cheap room with a Miss Spencer, who, while haughty in manner, was also clearly very particular about cleanliness. Lily could not bear the thought of anything less, after all the lovely houses she had lived in. When she went back alone at night to her little attic, her legs and back aching dreadfully, her hands burning sore from handling wire all day, at least it was to an atmosphere of order and cleanliness even though it was poor. Even so, the musty smell of these houses, their dampness, the odour of boiled cabbage and potatoes spoke to her of a familiar poverty and meanness, so that sometimes when her eyes were closed she could believe she was back in Mrs Horne's house, with Ann and Effie about to torment her the moment she moved.

Lily lay on her back and stared despairingly at the crack running along the dingy ceiling.

Dear God, she thought. *What on earth am I doing back here?* All she had tried to be, and here she was, a fallen woman carrying the child of a man who she thought had loved her, but who had left her with no message, or hope of seeing him again. And now she was back where she started in the squalid Birmingham streets. But she pushed these thoughts away. She would not think. She would not feel. If she did, she would go mad.

She allowed herself, now, to remember the horror of the home, and to think of Victoria. Supposing she worked hard and earned herself enough means to try and get Victoria back ... ? Abruptly she stopped this fantasy, leaning against the edge of the bath, shaken by racking sobs. It was far too late. Victoria had been taken away for adoption. They had told her this and at the time Lily had been pleased at the chance of a home for her instead of knowing that she would just be handed over to the orphanage. But that meant Victoria was even more completely lost to her. She couldn't go snatching her from her home even if she could find her. There was no use in thinking about it. Victoria was better off with a family who could give her a proper life. She must think no more about it and look to the future.

She let herself weep for a time, then dried her eyes, back in the present with the drip-drip of the tap. What on earth am I reduced to? she thought. Spending my evening hiding in the bathroom from Harold Arkwright? This was madness. She got up, resolved to find another post where she could feel safe.

Such a haven presented itself with a Mrs Jessop and her two little girls, whom Lily had cared for all through the war in a house in Surbiton. Mr Jessop was away for most of the war and Lily found a female household in which to pass the shortages and endless bad news of those years. Daisy Jessop was a kindly, timid, rather dull woman who, unlike some, did not flourish when her husband was away but came to rely more and more on Lily. She became very fond of the two girls, Cissy and Margaret, and Mrs Jessop kept her on longer really than her help was required and after Mr Jessop had returned, looking ill, but otherwise unharmed. But Lily started to feel as if her life was slipping past in this quiet, suburban life, and that there must be more on offer, even for someone like her.

Chapter Fifty-Three

The Larstonburys' house in Hampstead, an imposing brick mansion of four storeys close to the heath, impressed Lily immediately.

When she arrived in June 1921 the walled garden behind was a feast of colour with pots of tobacco plants and daisies and geraniums, the white pom-poms of guelder roses and mauve clusters of wisteria blossoms hanging from the back wall of the house.

Inside, the big, light rooms were richly furnished to exotic taste, with large mirrors giving a sense of space and light, the rich colours of Persian rugs and elegant furniture gleaming with care and smelling of beeswax.

Lily, loving children as she did, became very quickly fond of the two Larstonbury infants, Hubert, aged five, and little Christabel, who was two. Virginia Larstonbury, a willowy, intellectual redhead who spent much of her day buried in books, had named her daughter after the suffragette Christabel Pankhurst. Virginia had also come from a moneyed family. She had a taste for hangings and drapes in rich, eastern colours and Lily felt at home with the silken touches of India, the echoes of Benares and Rajasthan that she saw about the house.

She did not dislike Virginia Larstonbury exactly, but she found her intimidating. Virginia was a woman of 'interests', the chief one apparently being 'theosophy', and she attended a great many meetings, some of them held in the front parlour of the house in the evenings, when a strangely dressed, intense collection of people arrived and sat talking for hours on end. Virginia was twenty-nine, and, as Lily discovered, fifteen years younger than her husband. She was also not his first wife. Piers Larstonbury had been married and widowed before the war, leaving him with his first two children, Elspeth, now seventeen, and Guy, fifteen, who only appeared from their boarding schools in the holidays. Guy, Lily gathered from the servants, was a sensitive, artistic soul rather like his father. Elspeth, on the other hand, was a firebrand who resented Virginia and had an explosive relationship with her.

Hubert was pale, with Virginia's colouring and wide, rabbity blue eyes. He was very delicate and sweet-natured, prone to being set upon by other more robust boys, and Lily felt protective towards him. Though he was not as heart-meltingly beautiful as Cosmo had been, she found him easy to deal with, a child who responded easily to affection. Christabel was more solid, dark-haired like her father, but with a much more temperamental nature than her brother. She was, however, a particular favourite of Virginia's mother, Lady Marston, who adored girls and had very little time for boys, so on the day Lily took Hubert to Brooklands, Christabel was with her grandmother in South Kensington.

Virginia Larstonbury, beautiful in a languid way, with her tresses of straight red hair and pale, freckled skin, was a woman of moods and strong tempers.

'I don't believe in the difference between human beings,' she proclaimed one day from the couch, looking up from her book. Lily caught sight of the book's title: *Married Love* by someone called Marie Stopes. 'We are all equals, no matter what our state in life, and should be treated as such. Do you not agree, Lily?'

Do you mean we *are*, or we *ought to be*? Lily wanted to ask. But she usually found it better to appear to agree with people, so just said quietly, 'Oh yes, I'm sure you're right.'

However, Virginia Larstonbury's ideals of equality did not seem to extend as far as her servants, some of whom she treated arrogantly. And she was sure she was right about almost everything, which was one of the things that made Lily begin to pity Major Larstonbury, wondering why he allowed his wife to speak to him so contemptuously. After all, he was an architect with a successful practice in town, but because he did not share her lofty notions she sometimes treated him as if he never had a thought in his head.

'Oh, it's no good talking to *you*, Piers,' Lily sometimes heard her say. Yet she seemed to like Lily, who was nine years older than her, and who was genuinely fond of the children.

'I don't know how you do it,' Virginia often said, on her rare visits to the nursery. She would throw herself languidly into the cane chair and pick up Christabel to swamp her with a cuddle.

'Hubert never behaves as well as that for me. Oh, but I just couldn't spend all day with them, much as I adore the little darlings. It would drive me quite frantic! One must have a place for learning, for cultivation of the inner life. Or perhaps it's not necessary for everyone. Some of us are very sensitive to *life*. Are you sensitive to life, would you say, Lily? After all – you're very *pretty*,' she finished, rather inconsistently.

'I don't really know,' Lily said, blushing because she really did not know how to conduct such a conversation. 'Not like you, I don't suppose.' Although in some ways she thought Virginia Larstonbury was very *in*sensitive, especially when it came to her husband and children. Almost anything else seemed to matter more, most of the time.

Piers Larstonbury had not behaved to Lily the way most men in her life had – far from it. Months of her employment in his household went by before he did more than pass the time of day with her. He worked a great deal and was not much in the house, but when he was at home, he was always very well-mannered to his wife, however irritable and impatient she could be with him.

For the first five months of Lily's time in Hampstead she scarcely saw the master of the house, except during those after-tea visits each evening with Hubert and Christabel into the cosy drawing room, and even then her task was only to take the children down, well cleaned and dressed for their parents, and to fetch them away again at the appointed time. Her main exchanges with Piers Larstonbury consisted of 'Good evening', 'Goodnight', and little more. He seemed to her a pleasant man, very good mannered, in particular to Virginia, a man who treated his servants with respect and his children with affection during the brief times he was with them. Other than that she had little impression of him, except from some of the servants like Lottie, the tweeny, who always said he was 'ever so nice. Much nicer than *her*.'

That winter, though, Lily had an unexpected visit from Piers Larstonbury in the nursery. It was a miserable November night, bitter outside, with drizzling rain and the wind whipping meanly along the London streets. The children were not well. As the afternoon darkened early into evening, first Christabel and then Hubert began to complain of sore throats and to run a high temperature. It was not long before they both obviously needed to be put to bed and to miss the evening visit to their parents. Lily sent a message down with Lottie to say that the children were ill.

'Lor',' Lottie said, with a frightened face. 'I hope it ain't that influenza! Any rate, *she's* not in, for a start, so I don't know as anyone'll come.'

The thought of the Spanish influenza made Lily even more worried. So many people had died from it and there seemed to be no cure. The fever took a grip on both children quickly. Lily only managed to snatch a quick bite to eat and spent the evening wiping the two feverish infants down with a cool flannel, as she had done for Cosmo when he was poorly in India.

At eight o'clock or so, when she was sitting on Christabel's bed, stroking the child's forehead and worrying about whether they should call the doctor, there came a discreet tap on the door.

'Come in!' Lily called softly. Startled, she saw the master of the house in the dim light of the doorway.

'May I come in?' He spoke softly, thinking the children were asleep.

Hubert was lying in a twitching slumber, but Christabel cried 'Daddy!' and immediately tried to sit up.

'No, Christabel – lie down!' Lily quietened her.

Piers Larstonbury came over to his daughter's bed and stood looking down as she lay with her teddy bear beside her. Lily was touched by the look of tenderness on his face.

'I thought I'd pop up and see my little dears. I don't

like to think of them being ill and Virginia's gone out. I hope I am not causing a disruption?'

'Of course not,' Lily said shyly. She felt a little overwhelmed by his presence so close to her but glad of someone to share her worries with. 'I was wondering whether we need to call the doctor. I'm worried it might be influenza.'

Piers Larstonbury adjusted the tails of his jacket out of the way and sat down on the edge of the bed, opposite Lily.

'Hello, Chrissie. How're you feeling, dear?'

'Feel poorly,' Christabel said.

'Oh dear, well we can't have that, can we? Do we need a special fairy to come and make you feel better?'

He laid his hand across the little girl's head and gently felt around her neck and throat with his long fingers. Christabel winced as he touched her throat.

'Is it sore, darling? Perhaps you're right, Miss Waters. Don't you worry. I'll drive round and ask for Dr Marchant.'

He returned within the hour with the doctor, a very small, serious man who decreed that the children needed to be kept cool and for the fever to 'come to a head'.

'They're two fine, strong children – they'll be right as rain in a few days,' he said, looking at his fob watch as if in a great hurry. Lily thought he could have taken a little bit more trouble, but of course you wouldn't dream of arguing with a doctor.

The two men disappeared and Lily was about to ready herself for bed, when to her astonishment, Piers Larstonbury came back into the nursery.

'I just thought I'd pop up again and say goodnight,' he said softly. Once again he sat himself down, this time

375

on Hubert's bed. Hubert stirred and gave a miserable little moan. 'Poor little things. I thought Dr Marchant was a bit short with us, didn't you?'

'Well, yes,' Lily agreed shyly. She thought how kind Major Larstonbury was. 'He did seem to have other things on his mind.'

Piers Larstonbury looked across at her and smiled suddenly. She had the impression that he had suddenly seen her really as a person, not just a servant.

'How long have you been here now, Miss Waters?'

'Almost six months, sir.'

'And where were you before?'

'Not too far away.' She told him about her post with Mrs Jessop through the war, but did not mention the Arkwrights. 'Before that, I worked in India.'

'Did you, by jove!' He turned fully to look at her. 'Well, you've seen more of the world than I have. I must say, it's a country I'd be most interested to visit. Did you like it there?'

'Very much.' As she sat down on the chair close to the bed, memories flashed across her mind, lovely ones of the Fairfords, Cosmo and the horses. And then followed the wave of pain and longing which came with thoughts of India: Mussoorie and Sam. 'But I thought really I should return to this country at some stage. I did notice that people who had been there for a very long time found it terribly difficult to come back.'

'Yes – I'm sure you're right,' Piers Larstonbury said. 'How very wise.'

There was a pause, during which he looked into her face in a somehow troubled way and she realized that she liked him. She had seen him in a new light that night, realized how much he loved his children, and that he had also come back up here because he was lonely. He lingered, talking of this and that, asking her things about the children, about herself. Soon he had been there almost an hour, seeming to forget the time. At last he stretched and looked round at the clock.

'Goodness me!' He leaped up. 'It's almost half past ten! I suppose Virginia will be home from her meeting any moment. I'm so sorry to have kept you.'

'Not at all!' Lily had been surprised how much she had enjoyed it. She had, as ever, not given too much away about herself, but it was a pleasure to sit and talk to someone. Her job could be a very lonely one.

'Well – goodnight, Miss Waters. I hope the children are not too restless in the small hours.'

'We'll all get on all right,' Lily said.

Before leaving the room he gave her a sweet, grateful smile.

Chapter Fifty-Four

He fell in love with her during the grey chill of that winter.

Piers Larstonbury was not like other men Lily had met and at first she did not recognize his growing devotion to her. She did notice that he was about the house more, and thought the children's illness, from which both of them recovered well within a week, had drawn him close to them and he wanted simply to spend more time with them. Sometimes he came to the nursery and sat quietly looking at a story book with Hubert. But every so often his gentle voice reading the story would become halting and Lily might look up and find his gaze resting on her as she played with Christabel and her doll on the floor.

If she met him anywhere in the house he made a point of speaking to her now, when before he had seemed absent or almost unaware that she existed. And gradually she saw in his eyes something she did recognize: the deep, helpless stare of a man who had become strongly affected by her.

She first realized it at Christmas. There was a very festive atmosphere in the house. Virginia Larstonbury was lavishly hospitable and liked the house to be decked out with a tree and boughs of greenery and holly, streamers and candles and vases of winter blooms. The children were very excited. Piers's two older children,

Elspeth and Guy, were home for the holidays. They did not see a great deal of Guy, who spent much time either visiting his friends or in his room at the top of the house, where he painted in watercolours. Elspeth, however, was much in evidence, particularly in her explosive rows with Virginia. She was small in stature, with long, mousy hair, and looked as if she should be gentle and timid, but she was in fact highly temperamental, especially in the presence of her stepmother.

'I don't know why I bother coming back at all sometimes!' Lily heard Elspeth storming at Virginia one afternoon. Lily and Lottie the maid met on the stairs in the middle of this particular spat as raised voices came from the drawing room. 'When you treat me like some kind of *servant*. You don't want me here! I feel like Cinderella in my own home!'

'Oh, don't talk such utter nonsense, you ridiculous girl!' they heard Virginia snap at her. 'You really are the end, making everything into such a drama, when I'm doing all I can for you – and you making me into some kind of witch in a fairy story.'

'Well, sometimes you are just like a witch!' Elspeth shrieked. '*Just* like! You don't really care – not about Daddy or anyone. You only care about those queer people at your coven, or whatever it is you do . . .'

As Virginia exploded in outrage, Lottie raised her eyebrows comically at Lily. 'I don't know where she gets it from,' Lottie said. 'Miss Elspeth, I mean. They say her mother was the gentlest woman you could meet . . .'

Lily had learned that Piers Larstonbury's marriage before the war had lasted until Cecily Larstonbury died after a long illness in 1912. The couple's children had been brought up by a succession of mother substitutes against whom Elspeth had evidently perfected her skills in verbal combat. Lily kept out of Elspeth's way as much as possible. So far as she was concerned, her job was with Hubert and Christabel and no one else.

The house was full of visitors over the Christmas period, people from various branches of the family, and the children were sleepless with excitement for several nights before. The evening before Christmas Eve there was a party, the house lit up, music and comings and goings, loud laughter and chatter until very late. Lily stayed in the nursery trying to distract the children into sleep. On Christmas Eve there was another row about who would be going to church. Virginia did not hold with Church of England religion any more. Piers Larstonbury, who was more conventional, wanted to go to the midnight Eucharist. Elspeth, it appeared, was also prepared to go, chiefly in order to fall out with Virginia about it, and the evening was punctuated by bad-tempered outbursts between the two women.

In the midst of all this, Lily, having just got the children to sleep, heard a tap on the nursery door. With Christabel's little frock that she had been folding still in her hand, she tiptoed to the door.

'May I come in?' he whispered. Piers Larstonbury was always very polite, almost as if he found Lily intimidating.

Hesitating, she said, 'The children are already asleep,' but she stepped back to let him in.

'I thought they might be by now.'

She closed the door and went to lay Christabel's dress on the little white wicker chair in the corner. Close by, on a table, a dim light was burning.

'Actually, it was you I wanted to speak to.'

From his breast pocket his brought out a small

package and held it out to her, though she stood across the room from him.

'This is for you – a little Christmas gift.'

Lily felt a sense of panic rise in her. She knew that all the servants in the house would be given small gifts in the morning – but all together, by Virginia, not like this.

'Please,' he said, seeing her hesitation. 'Take it. It's just a token, but when I saw it I knew it would suit you.'

Lily was full of confusion, but also of curiosity to see what he had thought would suit her. She took the slender, tissue-wrapped gift from him, her fingers trembling, aware of him watching her intently.

Within the folds of tissue lay a silver object, studded with turquoise stones. Lily gasped.

'Oh – it's so beautiful!' Then, foolishly, 'Is it a hairslide?'

Piers Larstonbury lifted it from the paper. 'Perhaps I can show you. Your hair looks marvellous like that – so modern.'

Just two weeks earlier she had had her hair cut much shorter, into a fashionable pageboy level with her ear lobes. Piers Larstonbury stood on her right and drew the silver slide in past her temple. For a second it felt cold against her scalp.

'Perfect.' His voice was quiet, somehow awed. 'I knew it would be. It's perfect.'

Lily put her hand up and felt it. The clip was so beautiful – she knew somehow without him telling her that it was silver, that he had bought her something expensive and beautiful – and she had no idea what to do next.

'Thank you,' she said, her cheeks burning as she turned to him. 'It's lovely. I don't know why you . . .'

'No – you don't, do you?' They were standing close and his gaze was fixed intently on her. 'You don't know, you don't see – that's one of the things which makes you so extraordinary, my beautiful Lily. You're so lovely, so innocent, somehow.'

Her heart began pounding with panic. *Oh God, no, not this again.* Not another man ... What he saw as innocence was really the fact that she was closed to people, to men especially. She had built a rampart round herself so that she need never feel pain again – or thought she had.

'You've no idea what I feel for you, have you, you lovely, lovely woman?'

From this reserved, gentle man the words began to pour out. He was worked up, his face tight with emotions, 'You captivate me, Lily. You're so very beautiful, so gentle ... I feel as if you've given me life back again ... Your presence in the house has made the difference to everything ... I need to see you, to keep looking at you ...'

She stood under his words as if they were a shower of rain, not knowing what else to do. She knew that she had no feelings of this kind for Piers Larstonbury, but his words filled her with yearning to feel herself loved and to be able to love after these long, lonely years. And they also made her afraid and suspicious, because she knew that men's words of love meant nothing and she must not give way to them.

At last he stopped, and stood looking down at her. 'I couldn't hold back from telling you how I feel any longer. You're all I think about. I'd forgotten it was possible to feel like this, to love like this.' He laid his hands on her shoulders, looking at her with burning longing. 'Oh, Lily, let me kiss you, please do!'

'Major Larstonbury . . .' She struggled for words, and in the difficulty of it all felt anger rising in her. He had given her a gift as a bribe, something to force her to give into him! 'We are in your house, under the same roof as your wife, and your children are asleep here . . .' She waved her hand towards the sleeping children's beds.

'I'm sorry . . .' He lowered his hands to his sides abjectly. 'I've offended you. I've been clumsy and foolish. I'm just so much in love with you, so overwhelmed.'

Lily stood, looking at him. She could hear Ewan McBride: *I love you, I need you, Lily* . . . And Harold Arkwright and Sam. *Samuel Ironside.* She was filled with a bitterness of pain that she had not allowed for a long time. It seemed to rise up behind her throat. Men betrayed, they took what they wanted, without a care for your feelings. Men were liars.

Her expression seemed to freeze him.

'I'll go,' he said, to her astonishment. 'I'm sorry. I've been clumsy . . . A fool.'

Full of anger and of a longing regret, she watched him leave the nursery.

Chapter Fifty-Five

During the excitement of Christmas, she saw very little of him. He was there, in the parlour, standing in the background on Christmas morning when Virginia and Elspeth, in the shelter of a temporary festive truce, distributed little gifts to the servants. Lily received a little case of fine-quality writing paper and envelopes. She wondered who Virginia Larstonbury imagined she might have to write to, but she thanked her politely. She felt Piers Larstonbury watching her but she did not look at him.

He kept away from her for days, and she thought that that was the end of it. Then, gradually, as if nothing had happened, he made excuses to be near her again, to spend time with the children, even accompanying her to Hampstead Heath one Sunday afternoon when she took them out. He behaved with absolute decorum on all occasions and was also very attentive to his children.

'I scarcely saw my own father, growing up,' he said, as they strolled across the winter heath. Lily was pushing Christabel in a little carriage while Hubert trotted happily alongside his father holding his hand, awed by the treat of his being with them. 'He died without me knowing him.' He talked about his school, about having been sent away to board at the age of five.

'It was why Cecily, my first wife, and I decided to send Guy so much later, when he was ten. She was so attached to him, she didn't want him to go at all, but it's the thing to do, of course. Boarding school makes a man of you. Certainly helps you fit in when you're thrown into the army.' As he spoke he didn't sound altogether convinced. 'But I do think they go too young: it breaks some bond with the parents which you can never quite mend again.'

'Yes, I think you're right,' Lily said, thinking of Cosmo. 'Sometimes children seem to be more attached to their nanny than their parents.'

'Exactly so.' He smiled down at her. 'Which is why I want to be with them some of the time. I wasn't with Elspeth and Guy enough. Guy's remote from me, really.'

'Will you send Hubert away?'

'Perhaps.' He sounded miserable suddenly. 'I don't know. That will depend partly on Virginia. She rather favours boarding. I suppose she's not really very maternal. Not like you. You're marvellous with children.'

Lily blushed. 'I suppose I've always felt at home with them.'

She felt more relaxed with him that afternoon, though she could hardly forget his outburst of those weeks ago. And as they walked home along the smart London street, though, she realized she had not had such a long conversation with anyone in a long time, and he didn't speak to her like a servant. As they neared the house again, he said, very politely, 'It's been a real pleasure, this walk, Miss Waters. I've enjoyed our time together a great deal.'

She had to admit to herself that she had enjoyed it too. Above all, it was his kindness which drew her in. But all the time, in his attention she felt an unspoken pressure. Although he was behaving like a gentleman, she knew the strength of his feelings for her and that they had not gone away. She had already become very fond of Hubert and Christabel: supposing she kept refusing to give in to their father's desires and he got rid of her? It was a terribly painful thought. Each time she left a family, the separation from the children almost broke her heart. She was living under his roof and he was being so kind to her. Somehow, as the days passed, it seemed impossible not to repay him by giving him what he wanted.

It happened the first time when Virginia was away, staying with her sister in Hampshire. Very occasionally she took the children with her to be looked after by the sister's nanny, but more often she went alone, in her colourful, drifty clothes, leaving the two infants in Lily's care, seeming content not to see them for days at a time.

She made such a visit in the last week of January, saying she 'simply couldn't bear London and this filthy weather any longer', and after a flurry of case-packing, disappeared in a cab to Paddington without saying when she would be back.

Lily barely noticed when Virginia was not there and the day passed much as usual, trying to keep the children occupied in cold, rainy weather.

But he came to her that night, late in the evening. It was as if she could predict what would happen, that he would come knocking softly on the door of her room, the way Ewan McBride used to come, and Harold Arkwright tried to, as if this was what she was destined for. She was proud of herself for not giving in to Harold Arkwright, whom she found detestable, but this was different. When she heard the soft knocking she was already in her long flannel nightdress, her hair brushed.

She found her thoughts very cold and collected as she pulled round her the red silk dressing gown which Virginia had handed on to her, with a dragon across the back. The situation felt at once very familiar, yet far removed from her as if happening to somebody else.

'Lily?' He stood in the dimly lit passage. In the daytime he called her 'Miss Waters'.

Lily said nothing. She stood looking up at him.

'You know why I'm here.' His tone was soft, almost humble. 'Will you let me in?'

Dreamily she stood back to let him step past her and closed the door, turning to face him.

'I don't want to force myself on you,' he said straightforwardly. His hands were in his trouser pockets. 'I'm not that sort of man and I think you know I'm not. It's just that what I feel for you is so overpowering. I see you day after day and I long for you. I think you know Virginia and I don't have a … an intimate marriage. Sometimes I don't think she has much regard for me at all. And you …' He took his hands from his pockets, making a gesture which somehow encompassed her. 'You arrived in this house and at first I scarcely noticed. It seems incredible to me now. This astonishing, beautiful woman, with something …' He looked at her with his head on one side. 'Something sad in her, which moves me …'

As he spoke, to her astonishment, she felt a lump rise in her throat and the beginning of tears. She did not know what he had seen in her, nor did she really know what there was to be seen, but it felt a miracle that anyone had tried to see and understand. She lowered her gaze, embarrassed by her emotion.

'Lily?' He came to her and put his hands softly on her shoulders, then, as she did not resist, drew her into his arms. It was as if something broke open in her then, something quite unexpected and long dammed up, his gentle concern reducing her to sobs which shook her whole body, seeming to come from somewhere so deep in her that she was silent for long seconds at a time before they broke over her.

'Oh, my girl,' he said, so lovingly that it made her weep all the more, feeling held, somehow like a child, and being treated kindly. It brought out a deep tenderness in him.

'Oh, darling, little darling,' he said, stroking her hair, and as she grew calmer, he drew her to the bed. 'Come – lie down and let me embrace you ...' When she was calmer he looked seriously into her face. 'I would marry you, d'you know that? I want you to know, Lily. If I could see a way ... I feel so very strongly about you.'

She stared back at him, astonished. But he scarcely knew her at all! How could he be so sure? She thought men very strange.

The comforting turned to lovemaking, and she surrendered to him, to being held and cared for. As they lay together he lifted himself on to his elbow, his gentle face looking down at her. 'I shan't leave you with a child,' he told her, adding with a faint smile, 'I have a way to stop it. Of course, Virginia has educated me very thoroughly about this with all her talk about women needing control over their fertility.'

His fingers teased open the front of her nightgown, pulling back the soft cotton until he could see her breasts. He gave a low moan of pleasure and began to lick her nipples, his eyes closed, seeming to lose himself in her. Lily felt flickers of pleasure go through her, knew she was beginning to respond to him, her body seeming to spread and open at his touch, yet her mind was quite detached.

He rolled on to her, needing urgently to be inside her, and he moved in her with absolute pleasure and absorption.

'Oh God,' he gasped, breathless, 'Lily, oh, my Lily . . .' And after a number of urgent movements he climaxed in her with a sob, holding her very tight and close as if she were the most precious thing in the world.

Lily held him as he recovered his breath in her arms, feeling the comforting warmth of him, his hair close to her cheek. She liked the smell of him, a mixture of sweat and something sweet and exotic. Staring up at the shadowy ceiling she knew she was held in the arms of a nice man, a kind enough one for her to have let herself weep. But could she love him? She did not believe so, but in those moments she wished that she could.

Chapter Fifty-Six

At first, Lily had never considered that Piers Larston-bury might be able to help Cosmo.

He conducted his affair with Lily with absolute discretion, so that she was certain no one else knew what was going on. He was very cautious about coming to her at night, choosing times when Virginia was away or when it was so late that she was asleep, so their time together was limited.

The winter passed and Virginia was as preoccupied as ever, going out to her theosophy meetings, lunching with her friends, exploding over political disappointments.

'They've turned down votes for women in the United States!' Lily heard her voice expostulating from somewhere in the house one morning. 'And I thought they were supposed to be an *enlightened* country!' Virginia had been a suffragette in her younger days, marching for the vote before it was granted to women in 1918.

'I suppose that was when I fell in love with her,' Piers told Lily. 'She was so full of conviction, so *fiery*, and of course so lovely to look at as well.' He sighed with great melancholy. 'The trouble is, I'm not sure women like that are meant for marriage.'

'I don't want to hurt her feelings,' he said one night as they lay together. He stroked Lily's back. With a pang, it reminded her of Sam. 'I just need you, Lily, my darling. You came and took me by surprise.'

It was that night that she decided to tell him about Cosmo. Piers had somehow managed to bring a tray of tea up to her room in the small hours, waking her because he longed for her so much and Lily laughed at the picture he painted of him creeping about down in the kitchen once the maids were asleep.

'Anything for you, my darling,' he twinkled at her. Often he sat just staring at her adoringly, as if he could not drink in the sight of her enough. 'Hell, high water ... Anything for my love!'

Lily smiled in what she hoped was a proper acknowledgement of his words.

'My goodness.' He sat holding his teacup, eyes fixed on her. 'You're such a mysterious woman. I never have any idea what's really going on in your beautiful head. It makes you even more attractive, darling.' He leaned forward and kissed her lips, lingering over it. He drew back and asked, 'And where did you go today?'

It had been Lily's day off, a break she was allowed every fortnight.

'I went to meet a friend.' She hesitated, frowning. Cosmo had worried her that day, more than ever before. 'I say friend – he was the boy I looked after in India – Cosmo Fairford. He's grown up now, of course, and working for Lloyds Bank. I can hardly believe he's already nineteen, and so very handsome, towering above me!'

'Fairford ...' Piers mused. 'Is he one of the Warwickshire Fairfords?'

'Yes – his uncle oversees the estate. His father Charles stayed on in India – in the army. He was killed in the war. Cosmo came here to school, of course.'

'Oh, well I'm sure he's thriving,' Piers said lightly. She could tell he was not really interested, but listening because he felt he had to. He put his empty teacup down and sat beside her, stroking her. This was always the beginning of lovemaking, the warm movement of his hand on her shoulders, her neck, before his fingers found their way inside her nightdress, seeking out her breasts.

'I'm not sure.' She could not keep the worry from her voice. She wanted him to hear what she was saying, not go off into the trance of lovemaking without taking notice of her worries. Intimate relations had narrowed the social gap between them and she wanted to make this demand on him. 'It's not really what Cozzy's cut out for at all. He's always been rather more of an outdoors sort of boy. I wish I knew how to help him.'

Piers rested his hand on her collarbone, looking down into her eyes and said, 'Tell me more about him.'

She had met Cosmo in the Lyons Corner House in Oxford Street that afternoon. They sat at a table close to one of the grand marbled columns, not too close to the orchestra, and she drank in the sight of him. He was even more handsome than the last time she had seen him. His hair had remained thick and blond, his eyes were a vivid blue, gazing coldly from above a nose which had developed to become prominent and aquiline. Lily was full of pride at the sight of him, though he had come rather more casually dressed than she would have liked, attired as if for summer in white flannels, a grey jacket and rather foppish bow tie. But she passed no comment as she was so pleased and grateful to see him, and his mood was already sombre and off-hand. She felt she must humour him, until he softened and became her boy again.

'Now, let me buy you tea,' he said expansively. He seemed to be putting on a rather lord of the manor attitude which Lily found touching and sad because he also seemed to her so young. He ordered a huge tea of scones and cakes, far more than was really needed, and they sat talking while the orchestra played jaunty waltzes and mazurkas.

'How are you enjoying the work – any better than last time I saw you?' Lily ventured. She saw him about once a month now they were both in London.

Cosmo was spreading copious amounts of butter on a piece of fruit tea bread.

'Oh, it's not so bad,' he said airily. Then he stilled the knife and looked up at her. His face fell into something less posed. 'Actually, I loathe it. Every damned minute of it, to tell you the truth. It's like being buried alive.'

'But you were so fortunate to be taken on,' Lily said encouragingly. She said no more but both of them knew she was talking about his disastrous school record. Lloyds seemed a great career to her. 'And I'm sure you'll be marvellous at it.'

'You know I loathe being stuck indoors all day,' he said, biting ravenously into the tea bread.

'But you could have stayed on the estate, surely?'

'What with Uncle William, that crazed old fool? God in heaven, I've had a lifetime's worth of him, I can tell you. The only reason I go there at all is that it's the only place I can drive. He hardly knows what's going on on the estate any more and he certainly doesn't take any notice of what I do. But I don't want to be running the blasted place. When my turn comes I'll pay a man to do it. I want to be *driving*, Lily – motor racing! That's my thing. I *know* it! If I could just get someone to take me seriously, get a break . . .'

Lily watched him sadly. She wondered how good a driver he really was. And no wonder nobody would take a risk on him with a record like his. When he was twenty-one, perhaps he might have the wealth to buy himself into whatever he desired, but at the moment he did not have the connections or personality to get where he wanted. She knew he put people off by his manner and her heart ached for him when she thought how sweet and trusting he had been as a boy. She watched sadly as she saw him take a little hip flask from his pocket and steal a drink out of it, even while they were taking tea.

'Cosmo,' she reproached him. 'Is that really necessary?'

'Oh, don't *you* start,' he snapped, really unpleasant for a moment and she immediately had to appease him.

'I expect things'll work out: they have a manner of turning out in ways you don't expect,' she said lamely. What else could she say? 'How's your mother? Have you heard from her?'

'Oh, I suppose she's about somewhere,' Cosmo said bitterly. 'I had a birthday letter from her, that's all.'

Perhaps you're not nice enough to her when you do see her, Lily thought. Perhaps you drive her away.

She and Susan were in contact occasionally, short notes which mainly exchanged news of Cosmo. Susan was now living down on the south coast and did not disclose much about her life to Lily. However, she had once mentioned her encounter with Sam Ironside when she was a VAD in 1918 and the thought made Lily ache. There was nothing else she could do except hope that meant that he had safely survived the remainder of the war.

Sitting here with Cosmo, though, she also felt a pang

of possessive pride that once again she was the one seeing him, mothering him, not Susan. She needed Cosmo to need her, for her to be special to him.

But when she parted from him she felt uneasy. He was unhappy, felt thwarted by his work in the bank, which he had in fact chosen to do himself, even though he always made out he had been forced into it. Why had he gone to do the very thing he was going to dislike so much? she wondered. He had succumbed to the pressures of his class and family, it was true, but it seemed more than that. There was a vein of perverse self-destruction in him that she could sense and which worried her deeply.

As the weeks passed, she mentioned Cosmo to Piers Larstonbury quite regularly. She did not tell him that Cosmo had been expelled from Eton, or about any of the other troubles. She painted a picture of an admirable, if frustrated young man who was trying to make his way in the world.

As Piers fell more and more deeply in love with her, he seemed prepared to do anything for her.

'Perhaps we could meet somehow – you and I and Cosmo?' she suggested. It was Cosmo who talked about Brooklands, about how he loved going there. He haunted the racetrack as often as he could. Lily did not think Piers knew much about cars, but she had heard him say many times that he was interested in widening his life, in finding out about new things.

'It's as if I've narrowed things down so that I barely do anything except work,' he said. 'I feel younger with you, Lily. I don't know much about the motor car, but maybe we could find a way to go without it being a problem. I know – we could take Hubert. He might be very taken with it all!'

And so, come the Whit holiday, when she had been Piers Larstonbury's mistress for four months, she found herself at Brooklands with Piers and Cosmo – and Sam Ironside.

Chapter Fifty-Seven

Sam returned to Birmingham from Brooklands that evening after the Whitsun meeting, feeling set on fire.

After the long ride back to Northfield in the dark, once he had dropped Loz off, he had a feeling of bottomless energy, as if he had just been reborn. As he pushed his motorcycle round to the back of the house he knew that whatever happened, there was no going back. In those few hours, everything had changed.

Helen was standing in the back room, heating a pan on the range. She looked a little hunched, her long hair tucked in the back of her checked dressing gown. Her hair was still a caramel colour, but thinner and less abundant now. Her face looked thin and sallow. He realized again with a shock that she was younger than Lily Waters. As he stood at the back door he was able to watch her for a second before she saw him, and he had a bewildering sense of her being utterly strange to him. Although she was the mother of his four daughters, it was as if he did not know who she was and never had. He found it disturbing and reassuring at the same time, as if he knew he did not belong to her, and was sure now that he did not want to and had never truly wanted to.

'You've made good time,' she said, glancing at him, while her attention was still half on the simmering milk. He knew she was resentful of the way he could just take off for the day and she couldn't, even if in truth she did not want to go anywhere herself.

'Yes,' he said, pulling his jacket off. The room felt warm and cosy after the buffeting night air. 'It was a good run.' He flung the jacket over a chair. On the table there was a teapot with a crocheted green and yellow cosy which Helen's mom had given them, and the last of a loaf, lying face down on the board next to the bread knife. There was also a bowl of sugar with a few crumbs in.

'Want some cocoa? Or tea?'

'Stick the kettle on, will you? I'll make the tea.'

She silently did as he asked and brought her own cup of cocoa and spooned sugar into it, tutting.

'Girls've made a mess of the sugar again. I've told 'em and told 'em.'

And then she gave him a long, penetrating look.

'What's up with you?' she said.

He did tell her, but not then. He had to get used to the idea, of all that Major Larstonbury had said that afternoon.

'I am, as I have said, an outsider to the motor trade and motor racing,' the major said. 'However, thanks to ... circumstances' – once more his eye rested on Lily for a second – 'I can see myself becoming quite an enthusiast. Today has been an eye-opener: you've impressed me, Ironside. So – I'm prepared to make available whatever funds are needed to keep you for, let's say a year. I'll rent you the work space to build your motor car and you will have a free hand in all technical aspects, which I know very little about. You will, I know, do the job to the very best of your ability.

398

There is only one condition I would ask of you: that once you are ready to enter your vehicle in track races, your driver will be' – he gestured – 'Cosmo Fairford.'

Cosmo sat up straight and looked utterly astonished. Sam could not take in what he had just heard either. He looked at Lily, who was watching him, her eyes aglow. Sam stuttered into questions. What did Captain Larstonbury mean – where was he to work? Who with? Did he seriously mean simply to hand over the project to him, trusting a man whom he had met only this afternoon?

'It sounds to me as if the best place you could possibly work is here, at Brooklands,' Piers Larstonbury said. 'If that would be acceptable. And you mentioned that you already have colleagues who are ready to work on developing the vehicle with you? I am offering myself as your patron. My own instincts and those of Miss Waters, who clearly thinks highly of you, point in the direction of a very fruitful partnership. I realize this may mean some personal sacrifices for you and your family. Perhaps you'd like a little time to think about it?'

'No!' Sam was mentally rushing ahead. He could not think straight about the details. He only knew he was being made the most astounding, once-in-a-lifetime offer and all his instincts told him to grab it! He could scarcely take it all in and felt like dancing about on the tables.

'I'd be delighted to accept,' he said as soberly as he could manage. 'Thank you, Major Larstonbury.' All his class niggles were forgotten now. What a great man the major was! 'We'll build a marvellous Special. We won't let you down.'

There were hand shakings and the writing down of addresses in Piers Larstonbury's artistic hand, and he assured Sam that he would make arrangements for him as soon as possible. He would even write a letter to request leave of absence for him from the Austin works. Sam felt as if his fairy godmother had arrived and he was in a daze as they stood up to go. And then he knew he had to part from Lily.

He was beside her as she walked from the clubhouse, holding the boy's hand again. Cosmo, full of life now, was talking animatedly to Piers Larstonbury.

'Lily – this was your doing, wasn't it?'

She turned and looked at him and he could not read her expression. It was triumphant yet amused, as if she were celebrating her own sense of power.

'He'd do anything for me,' she said softly, looking down at the ground.

Sam leaned close to her, with a desperate impulse. 'I've got to see you.'

Lily raised her eyes. 'I expect we shall meet, through all this.' And her gaze left him again.

Hope leaped inside him at what he thought he saw in her eyes. She was still his woman – deep down they both knew it. But there was not time to say anything else. He took his leave of the party, and watched them depart towards their car, and it was only then, once he was alone, that the full impact of what had happened had hit him. He was going to work at Brooklands and build a Special!

'Loz! Where the hell are you? He's never going to believe this ... He's going to think I've been on the bottle all afternoon ...'

Leaping and fizzing with excitement he pulled his hat off and tore across the ground to find his friend.

*

He told Helen, straight out with it, a few days later, after the wire had arrived from Piers Larstonbury, and after he had sorted things out with the Austin.

That had been like a dream as well, going to the old man and telling him what he wanted to do. Herbert Austin stood looking at him in silence for a few moments, considering the situation. Sam knew he was in a strong position. He had been taken on at the Austin as a promising engineer in the years when things were very lean. During the Depression which hit the industry after the war heaps of men had lost their jobs. Who could afford to buy cars then? Come 1919, Austin had had to lay out to re-equip the works for peacetime production and that had set them back; they were installing automated machines to speed production, but the first model, the 3.6-litre Austin Twenty, trying to do something like Ford, had not really taken off. It was too big and clumsy. By last year some of them were doing stints at the works with no wages – Austin was broke. Sam was one of the ones who stuck it out. It had been a hell of a time – living on air almost, Helen keeping on at him to leave and go back to Coventry, and they were still recovering. He didn't really know why he'd stayed – bloody-mindedness mostly. And Austin had promised him a job for life if he wanted it after that. He knew Herbert Austin felt a debt of gratitude to the engineers who stuck by him. They were the ones who had saved the company in its darkest hour.

'I had a cable from this Major Larstonbury,' Herbert Austin said.

Sam stood while Austin sat behind his desk, its surface littered with drawings from the company draughtsmen. There was great excitement at the moment

– the new model, known as the Austin Seven, about to be launched. Some thought it was misguided, but Sam was in favour of a car the ordinary man could afford – he might stand a chance himself! He felt a pang of regret.

Austin slipped the end of his pen in his mouth for a moment, then withdrew it. 'He's talking about your being released from us for a year. And he's going to meet your wages?'

'So he says,' Sam said. 'And Loz ... Lawrence Marks.'

'Hmph,' Herbert Austin said. There was a pause, which seemed to imply that the man must have more money than sense, but then he said, 'You wanted to be in the company's racing team, I seem to remember.'

'Oh yes,' Sam said. 'I'd've liked to. There hasn't been an opening.'

'I should have found you one, shouldn't I?' A little smile played on Herbert Austin's rather austere features. 'Then I shouldn't have had to let one of my finest engineers go taking off. You'll come back?'

It was a more of a statement than a question.

'Oh yes. I've a wife and four children.'

'This Piers Larstonbury – is he an engineer?'

'An architect, I believe. He doesn't know much about motors at all.'

'Hmph,' Herbert Austin said again. 'Well, well. I suppose you'll have to do it. Don't you go beating us, though.'

And a moment later Sam was leaving Austin's office, feeling as if he had grown wings. Later, he and Loz sat in the pub and grinned at each other for a long moment before they erupted into yells of delighted laughter. They were going to Brooklands! They had been given the chance of a lifetime, to build their own Special and race it – and the old man had more or less given his blessing!

They downed a pint each at high speed. Loz's round, boyish face was pink and alight with glee.

'By crikey, Sam – we're going to do it! We're going to build the best bloody Special that's ever gone round Brooklands!' Then he put his glass down slowly on the table and his face sobered rapidly. 'Christ – what's Mary going to say?'

Mary Marks evidently had quite a bit to say at the idea of her husband taking off to go down and 'play racing cars' at Brooklands. But Mary and Loz were good pals and Mary had only two children, and two sisters near. In the end she was also proud and grudgingly pleased for Loz even though she desperately didn't want him to be away so much.

Helen was a different matter. As he came out with it, blunt and direct because he couldn't think of another way of doing it, Sam saw her face close up, as if he had frozen something deep in her. But he could do no other, he knew that. The opportunity was irresistible to him. And under and within it also, running like a deep, subterranean river of new life, was the thought of Lily. He tried not to think of Lily, keeping his mind on the practical things, the cars and engineering, his head swarming with ideas and plans. But in quiet moments, in bed at night beside Helen's resentful sleeping form, or at odd moments of the day, the memory of her came to him overwhelmingly. However much she had hurt him, he knew she felt something for him. Her eyes had given it away just in those seconds when they met, and the pull of her now was far too strong. He was going south, could only go south to do the things he burned to do – and to be near her.

'You're leaving me,' Helen stated.

He told her the day he saw Herbert Austin, that teatime. He was astonished by the way she just plunged in like that, as if she could see it all so clearly.

'Don't talk daft!' he said. 'It's for a year – overall. But I'll be back up to see you!'

This was said with a kind of guilty optimism. He knew he probably wouldn't come often. He had been careful to tell her straight away that there would be money – the equivalent of his wages. She wouldn't go short, so she needn't worry on that score. When the wire of confirmation had come through to him so promptly and to Herbert Austin, he knew the man was not fooling him. And he also knew that Lily was behind it. Of course, Lily wanted to get that Fairford boy on to the track. That was part of the deal. But was it not more than that? Was it not seeing him again that had spurred her to use her influence over Piers Larstonbury? He did not think she was in love with the man, though it was hard to tell. A pang of jealous suspicion filled him at the thought. But she had said she would see him . . . She wanted to see him.

Over those days Helen rocked between resentment, anger and a pathetic sadness. She had lost him and she knew it. And she was full of rage and grief and at times begged and begged him not to go.

'But I'll be back – very soon,' he assured her. 'It's a great chance – old man Austin even thinks so. I'm doing this for all of us – for the girls and you . . .'

'You don't love me – you never have,' she said one evening, perched in utter misery by the range.

And he knew with terrible clarity in that moment that what she said was true. But he said, 'Don't talk daft. You're my wife, aren't you?'

She looked across at him, with tear-stained cheeks.

'But you're still going, aren't you? Whatever I say?'

Quietly, able to do no other, he said, 'Yes, love. I am.'

Chapter Fifty-Eight

July 1922

'So—' Sam stood up from where he had been bending over the open engine as Loz rushed into the shed – 'are we on?'

Loz's hair was standing on end from his habit of running his oily hands through it. Like Sam, he was dressed in an old boiler suit smeared with oil and there was a good helping of it on his face, which was otherwise pink and beaming with excitement.

'Yep – Shelsley Walsh, Saturday! We'll be ready by then, easy!'

Sam grinned, flexing his stiff back. He wiped his left eye, which was watering badly this morning, then gave the car's bodywork a fond pat. She'd held up well on the test hill here at Brooklands. It was a specially built incline where the motor cars could be put through their paces on a gradient as steep as one in four in parts. But now it was time for a new challenge.

'Better send a wire to the major. I expect he'll want to be there.'

And if the major came all the way over to Shelsley, and Cosmo Fairford, surely *she* might come too. The thought made Sam ache.

They had been installed at Brooklands for five weeks

now and he hadn't seen Lily or heard from her. Piers Larstonbury, who seemed to have been infected by huge enthusiasm for the project he had taken on, had been down to visit for four out of five of the weekends since they began. He had learned very fast, soaking up information and learning from their expertise. Sam saw that the man was genuinely humble and lacking in arrogance. He treated Loz and Sam as equals and Sam soon came very much to respect and like Major Larstonbury.

During those earliest days, while the two of them tried to decide on the key specifications for the motor, the major had perched on an upturned crate in the shed listening to all the animated conversations about the ratio between power and weight so that it would be as fast as possible but still hold the road, how rigid the structure should be, what size the brakes. Every so often he asked questions.

'Thing is,' Sam explained enthusiastically, 'we need to keep the frontal area down – the cross section. The size of hole it makes in the wind, in other words. Smaller it is, faster she'll go.'

'Won't that engine – all that power – just destabilize the whole structure?' Piers Larstonbury asked. They had got hold of a Mercedes chain-driven chassis and an airship engine. It had worked for Count Zborowski, they reasoned. All the power in that engine!

'No – that's the beauty of it.' Loz was fizzing with enthusiasm. 'You can put a much more powerful engine in without too much problem. Course, the crankshaft speed is so low in an engine that size that you have to up the gear ratios no end, but it's easy enough.'

Piers Larstonbury joined in hours of conversations and watched Sam and Loz chewing over all the figures and alternatives of what they might do. They saw their patron become quite boyish and excited about what he had taken on and the skill of the men carrying it out.

'That's really thoroughly splendid!' he would say and often he gave a happy laugh as he said it.

And the weekdays Sam and Loz spent in a blissful state, something Sam celebrated in himself several times a day, when he thought how grindingly different everything would have been if he had never met the major. Even if he and Loz had ever got together enough money to begin building a motor, which was very doubtful, they would have been incredibly lucky to have found anywhere that touched this in terms of a place to build it. And they would have been at it after a day's toil at the Austin, squatting about in some cramped place God only knew where, on dark evenings when they were hardly able to see, and every hour they could spend of their weekends with their wives nagging them to stop. But at Brooklands they had their own shed in a row of others, amid the buzzing hive of activity round the racetrack, and they could absorb themselves totally in their passion with monkish single-mindedness.

Race days were only a small part of what went on at Brooklands. Cars were designed, built, tested, rejigged ... Some chaps went through a great to-do about covering up the engines of the cars they were working on if anyone came close, as if guarding highly innovative secrets. But mostly Brooklands felt like a college or university. They met engineers from all over the place, talked, shared problems and ideas, all endlessly fascinated by the same challenges and triumphs of the motor car. And they could spend all day there, sunshine pouring in through the windows on to the cluttered space: the plentiful supply of tools which Major Larstonbury had ensured they were provided with hung all round the walls, and the smells of metal and rubber and oil, meant Sam felt he had found paradise.

'I'll let the major know,' Loz said. He paused, about to go out of the door again. 'Sam – are you sure about that Fairford bloke?'

Cosmo was to undertake his first drive at Shelsley Walsh. Previously they had only seen him on runs round the test track at Brooklands. Loz had taken an instant dislike to Cosmo Fairford. Sam knew it was partly that he was of the class Loz was forever making fun of and he just wasn't comfortable with him. But it was more than that: Loz didn't trust him. He hadn't said outright, but Sam could tell.

'He's a good driver by the look of him,' Sam said. 'We'll give him a try.'

Loz stared at him for a moment as if trying to work something out. *Why are you risking our precious motor to this toff who you've only seen drive a handful of times?* Then he went out again.

Sam stood, hands on waist, watching him through the window as he walked away. There was a slight frown on his face. Loz was right. They hadn't fully got the measure of Cosmo Fairford – they were taking a risk. But they needed a driver. Neither of them was up to it, not at race speeds, and Loz hadn't suggested anyone better, had he? He was not prepared to explain his reasoning to Loz. *Lily loved Cosmo.* And he knew that this was why he and Loz were here at all, because Lily Waters had such influence over Piers Larstonbury, because the major was in love with her. Cosmo was part of the arrangement whether they liked it or not and Sam hoped to God he was as skilled a driver as he claimed to be. He found Cosmo petulant, and arrogant, but none of that mattered so long as he could hold that motor through the wind and take her as fast as she'd go! And out of a sense of loyalty and respect for Cosmo's father, Captain Fairford, and the child he remembered Cosmo to have been, and of gratitude for those weeks in Ambala, he was prepared to give him a chance. And because of Lily. Of course because of Lily.

Sam and Loz motored to Worcestershire separately from the major and Cosmo, towing their racing Special on a trailer. Like most of the racing cars she had been given a name – Piers Larstonbury had insisted that she be called the Heath Flyer, as befitted a vehicle which he had had fantasies of racing round Hampstead Heath.

They set off very early, and after pulling into the race ground at Shelsley Walsh in the late morning, soon found Cosmo Fairford's Morgan and the major's Daimler parked up side by side, evidently having not long arrived themselves. As he braked and shut off the engine, Sam's heart gave a lurch to see that climbing out from the Daimler's passenger seat was Lily.

'You coming?' Loz said impatiently, as Sam stayed at the wheel, staring across at her.

'Yes, all right, just give me a minute,' he said absently.

Loz tutted and went round to unhitch the trailer. Sam sat drinking in the sight of Lily. He just couldn't stop looking at her: she was so beautiful, with those remarkable, sultry looks, her clothes stylish and elegant and all a deep plum-red, except for the white band round her cloche hat. As he gazed at her, she called out lightly to Piers Larstonbury, obviously reminding him that he had forgotten something, and jealousy flared in him.

'God, she's lovely . . .' he murmured, seeing her

cherry lips turned up in a gentle smile. He longed with a deep ache just to be able to go over and speak to her in the easy, loving way they had once shared. For her to smile at him, for everything between them to be as it had been for those enchanting days in India, as it should always have continued to be. The hurt which came at the end of those days stabbed at him again like an unhealed scar. She had hurt him, and at times he wanted to hurt her too.

His eye was caught by movements around Cosmo Fairford's sporty vehicle. There seemed to be someone with Cosmo in the car, but Cosmo climbed out first, from the driver's seat. He even managed to do that with a kind of swagger, Sam thought, watching Cosmo smooth back his wayward blond hair. If it wasn't for Lily's obvious devotion to the lad, Sam could have developed a serious dislike for him, even though he had to concede, he was a damned fine driver. He had proved that on some of the latest test runs at Brooklands, and even Loz had had to agree. *You'd better do all right today, Sonny Jim*, he thought, staring fiercely at Cosmo. *You'd better not mess up with this baby of ours . . .*

Then he saw the other figure emerge from the Morgan. It took Sam a few seconds to recognize Susan Fairford. She was dressed to the nines in a fashionable, pale green outfit which shimmered in the sunlight. She wore a green cloche hat jauntily tilted on her head and looked every bit the society lady. Sam thought of her that night in France in the last spring of the war, thin and exhausted, yet somehow more real, much more likeable when the class barrier had come down. He wondered sourly whether she would even give him the time of day now.

Composing himself, he climbed out of the car and,

catching up with Loz, went over to greet the rest of their party.

'Ah – Ironside!' Somehow Piers Larstonbury always treated Sam as the senior of the two of them. Sam was not sure if Loz resented this, but if so he didn't show it. 'So – here you are! Journey go all right?'

'Very well,' Sam said. 'All in one piece and ready to go. Are you fit, Fairford?' He always spoke jauntily to Cosmo. He wasn't going to treat him with any kind of deference.

'Oh yes,' Cosmo said. 'Raring to go.'

Sam saw suddenly that the lad was almost tremulous with nerves and he felt for him. He knew he had to prove himself.

'Mother,' Cosmo turned to Susan who was coming up beside him. 'This is Sam Ironside – the chief mechanic. I don't suppose you remember him from Ambala, do you? Says he delivered a car . . . ?'

Sam braced himself for Susan's chill offhandedness. When he looked at her, though, to his surprise, he saw a genuine, warm smile in her china blue eyes and she held her hand out.

'Of course I remember, Cosmo. Mr Ironside and I have met more recently than that.' She explained, briefly, and Sam saw that she was proud of her months as a VAD. She peered at him with a kind of professional concern. There was still the cut-glass voice of course, but in every other way she seemed to have thawed and her manner was more genuine. 'My goodness, you were lucky not to lose the sight in that eye. How is it?'

'Not too bad, thank you,' Sam said. 'Plays me up a bit, but at least I can see out of it.'

'Were you in until the end?' she asked. 'You had other wounds.'

'Nothing too serious. Yes – I made it to the end.' And he returned her smile.

'And you have given my son the chance he's been craving for a very long time. We're all most grateful.'

'He's a skilled driver,' Sam said carefully.

'Is he?' Seeing her more closely now, Sam realized how anxious she was, and how nervous for Cosmo. 'We do all hope so.' Turning, she said, 'Perhaps you remember Miss Waters – surely you do? She was Cosmo's nanny and she has been a true friend to him.'

Sam was struck by the warmth in her voice, the note of real gratitude.

'Lily – you remember Mr Ironside? He came with that Daimler for Charles?'

Lily had been standing beside Cosmo, her arm in his, smiling proudly up at him as Sam praised his driving.

'Yes, I remember,' Lily said, quite composed. She loosened Cosmo's arm and for a second her hand was in Sam's. 'How d'you do?'

And then she withdrew and a moment later they all moved apart and he had to see to the car. Sam found that the blood was thundering round his body.

I must speak to her soon, he thought, speak to her properly, or I'm going to go mad.

Chapter Fifty-Nine

'Oh goodness, I do hope he'll be all right,' Susan Fairford said. 'I don't know if I can bear to watch!' She had a handkerchief in one hand, gripped to her.

'Of course he will,' Lily said, but her stomach was also knotted up in apprehension at the thought of Cosmo hurtling into view in the Heath Flyer, which Sam and Loz had thrown such passion and energy into building. Supposing it was all a disaster; supposing he crashed the car – ruined it! Lily sensed that Sam did not have a high opinion of Cosmo. He had had to let him drive since it was part of the arrangement if he was to have the patronage of Piers Larstonbury, but imagine what his reaction would be!

Oh, Cosmo, darling, please be careful, her mind called out to him, but she tried to look calm.

They were behind the barrier at the lower S bend of the Shelsley Walsh track, amid the excited atmosphere. Although a lot of hill tests were still done on the public roads, officially there was a speed limit of twenty miles per hour, which put events like this on the wrong side of the law. Shelsley was a private ground, however, the track twisting through beautiful green, hilly countryside. Shelsley was famous for its 1,000-yard steep climb, a stamina challenge for all kinds of motor car.

All day, since they arrived, the air had been full of excitement and the screech and roar of the motors being put through their paces up the hill. Lily and Susan had spent the time together, and it had been a good chance for them to re-establish their friendship while the men were caught up in all the motoring activity.

Susan was now living alone on the south coast outside Eastbourne, and Lily worried for her. She had only once been down to visit Susan, who had seemed very pleased to see her, but that had been almost a year ago, soon after Lily went to work for the Larstonburys. The two of them had walked on the beach on a warm, early summer afternoon and Lily was struck by how much Susan seemed to need her to be there. She put it down to the war and all the bereavements Susan had suffered, and that she was someone who knew Susan's past. Though she had confided in Lily in Ambala, it had been out of desperation, since there was no one else. Now she seemed a sad, more humble woman altogether, and one who was clearly living a lonely life. She evidently saw a few people for bridge afternoons, but no one to whom she could really feel close, and she met Cosmo only occasionally.

When Lily left to catch the train, Susan almost begged, 'Oh do come again, won't you, please?'

Lily had intended to, but weeks had passed and now she was so much in demand from Piers Larstonbury during any of her time off duty that somehow she had never visited again. She was pleased to see, though, that today Susan had dressed up and looked younger and attractive again.

As they had passed the afternoon together waiting for Cosmo's event, Susan poured out her worries about him.

'I can't seem to get near him at all – he's so sullen with me. And he throws himself into such rages. I'm

415

sure he drinks far too much ... I can't bear to see my boy like that, but he won't listen to me – does he listen to you, Lily?'

Lily smiled, sadly. 'Not so far as I can see. But I know how much he loathes it at the bank. I so much hope that this chance to drive will give him a new lease of life ...'

From far in the distance came a ripple of sound. Susan's eyes widened.

'He's off! Oh, dear God, please let him be all right!'

They stood amid the excited crowd on the bank behind the track, straining their ears to hear the sound of the engine approaching. Lily pictured Cosmo, face tensed with concentration, eyes narrowed, jaw clenched so that his chin jutted, alive in every nerve. And she thought of Sam who was never far from her mind. She knew she would be seeing him later and her nerves were so jangled at the thought that she could barely stand still. There was the pull of him, the overpowering need to see him and the fear and anger that went with it, and sooner or later she knew she wasn't going to be able to avoid it any longer.

At last they heard the car and within a moment it rounded the bend at the bottom of the S, its slim, streamlined shape coursing fast up the slope with what seemed astonishing speed. It was over in a few seconds, and they could not see Cosmo's face, only his head and hunched shoulders, and the car swung along towards the top of the S in the track and was gone with a receding roar.

'Oh, dear God,' Susan Fairford breathed.

'He looks marvellous,' Lily said, full of pride for him.

'Let's just pray he gets through ... He's so impulsive

– erratic, somehow . . . We must go and join them at the end!'

Lily hesitated. Being here with Susan, away from the men, she could avoid it all: Piers Larstonbury's gentle face, his eyes always following her with a besotted, admiring gaze, and Sam, who she knew would be trying to catch her eye, trying to draw her in. Somehow she always seemed to be trapped by the gaze of men. And with Sam Ironside it was all so much more disturbing, frightening, since he was the one man for whom she had ever felt anything real.

Chapter Sixty

That evening they all put up in an inn called the Pack Horse in a nearby village, where a sturdy feast of meat pies, mashed potatoes and gravy, with plenty of the local ale, turned into a triumphant celebration. The car had not only held up but made a very respectable time on the 1,000-yard hill and Cosmo had shown that he could handle her beautifully.

There were nine of them seated round a long table in a low-ceilinged room. At the head of the table Piers Larstonbury presided, with Cosmo and Lily on each side of him. Lily found herself seated beside Mary Marks, Loz's wife, whose two boys were beside her and Loz at the other end of the table, with Sam beside him. Susan sat between Cosmo and Sam.

Piers Larstonbury was obviously enjoying the homely food after Virginia's eccentric fare. He lifted his glass of ale and smiled warmly at Cosmo and then down the table towards Sam and Loz, his mechanics.

'Well!' He raised his well-spoken voice. 'I'd say today was a great triumph and a marvellous beginning. I congratulate you all – and thank you all. You've done me proud.'

'Oh, there are still plenty of improvements we can make!' Loz called along the table. His face was rubicund with beer and excitement and Lily could see he was immensely proud to be able to show off his prowess in front of his wife and sons.

'We'll beat Frazer-Nash yet!' Sam joined in excitedly. 'You just wait and see!'

'Oh yes – we certainly shall!' Cosmo's voice was louder than everyone else's.

Captain Archie Frazer-Nash, in his little two-cylinder car, was winning more events than any other driver. He was certainly setting the standard.

'Well, I sincerely hope so – and believe so too, after today!' Piers Larstonbury said.

Lily was astonished to see the difference in him since they had left London. She was used to seeing him as the sober, rather browbeaten husband of Virginia Larstonbury, someone quiet, dutiful and industrious who lived a genteel and cultured Hampstead life. But the racetrack and the company of a different kind of man seemed to have brought out something lively and boyish in him. She saw that he looked animated and happy in a way she had only ever glimpsed before when he was alone with her.

Beside him, Cosmo was smiling and excited as well, though as the evening passed she watched anxiously as he drank more and more. *Stop now*, she kept thinking as Cosmo grew more red-faced and loud. *Don't spoil everything.* She had no idea whether Sam and the others realized how much Cosmo was drinking. She raised her eyebrows warningly at Cosmo several times across the table, but he chose to ignore her as if she was of no consequence, and she felt slighted by it.

It was impossible for her to relax and simply enjoy the evening. Having Piers, Sam and Cosmo there all at once was overwhelming. She wondered what everyone guessed about her relationship with Piers Larstonbury.

It must have been obvious that she was his mistress. She told herself she didn't care. After all, she had done all this before, hadn't she, and what ever came of it? The British social classes of Mussoorie knew what she was to Dr Ewan McBride, but what could they do? Accept or reject her – it was all the same to her, she thought. No one here was in a position to question anything about Piers Larstonbury. But Sam – what did he think? All evening she avoided his eye, but every so often she looked along the table, surprised to see how much time he spent in conversation with Susan Fairford. She knew he had not liked Susan while they were in Ambala, had been quite scathing about her, where now they seemed to be talking easily, almost affectionately. She took the chance to watch Sam while his attention was elsewhere. He did not seem to have changed, she thought. He was still the slender, serious-eyed man she remembered, still with that quiet intensity about him which had drawn her to him in the first place, yet which would suddenly break open into a burst of spontaneous, twinkling laughter, lighting him up with mischief and warmth. She did not see him laugh like that this evening, even though there were glimpses of it in his smiles at Susan or Loz. And she noticed that every so often he took his handkerchief out and wiped his left eye which seemed to be troubling him. She thought she had also noticed a slight limp. So many young men limped these days. Every so often, as she talked to Loz's wife, Mary, beside her, she felt Sam's gaze fixed on her. It made her tremble inside and she did not look back.

She was glad of the company of Mary Marks, who was a homely, cheerful woman with a pink, round face rather like her husband's, and a broad smile. She clearly felt a bit out of her depth in the present company and in her nervousness became very talkative, in between turning to her boys to admonish them to sit still, be quiet or eat up. Lily smiled encouragingly at the boys. They were in fact very well behaved, perhaps a bit overawed by the occasion, and they seemed nice lads.

'I never thought my Loz would get involved with something like this,' Mary chattered to Lily, soon after they sat down. 'I mean, he's only a mechanic, just very ordinary, in a factory, like, and I've never been out of Birmingham before. It's all very new to me.'

Lily, to her own surprise, since she never usually told anyone anything, found herself saying, 'In actual fact, I come from Birmingham myself. I was born there.'

'Really – were you?' Mary's brow furrowed. 'You don't sound like it – if you don't mind me saying,' she added anxiously. 'Which part?'

Lily hesitated, her usual habits of secrecy pressing in on her. But what did it matter if she was honest with this kindly woman?

'Well, I worked in Hall Green for a good many years. But I was born in Sparkbrook, I believe.'

'Sparkbrook – are you sure?' Mary blushed in confusion at having sounded so surprised. 'I mean, I don't mean to be rude, but it's a bit rough round there. Perhaps your family went up in the world after . . . ?' Realizing she was being rather forward she faltered into silence, blushing even more.

'Yes.' Lily closed down the conversation. 'We did soon move away.' She told Mary that she had worked for Susan Fairford and knew Cosmo as a child.

'Oh, I see.' Mary said, but clearly she didn't see and didn't ask any more questions. Instead she spent a good

421

deal of the rest of the evening chattering about her two boys, a subject she never tired of. But it was a relief to Lily.

Several times during the meal, Piers Larstonbury, who was talking with Cosmo, reached for her hand under the table and whispered, 'All right, my love?'

She smiled, and once, glancing at Cosmo, whispered, 'Please – don't let him drink too much . . .'

She was so happy for Cosmo, that the day had been a success. It was all she dreamed for him, her boy, but she worried for him constantly. There was something in him that felt dangerous, and she wanted to take him to her and protect him the way she had when he was very small. Of course, he would never let her.

The men were all in high, celebratory spirits and as the evening wore on, Lily felt she might drown in Mary Marks's chatter and she began to feel very drowsy.

'I'm going to slip out to the ladies' cloakroom,' she whispered to Mary, and smiling at Piers she slipped from the room. In the little privy out at the back she sat on the wooden seat and rested her head in her hands for a moment. Her head was muzzy after drinking ale and now she was in private, her emotions began to course through her. She found she was shaky and close to tears. Sitting so close to Sam all evening was a torment which filled her with longing for a past she knew she could never recapture, and seeing him opened up raw feelings of grief and anger. If only he'd never come into her life again! She had had those few sweet days with him and then he had caused her nothing but agony and distress.

Angry and close to tears, she washed her hands and dried them on the old piece of towelling hanging on a nail, but they were still damp and she waved them gently in the air as she emerged from the privy into the warm gloom, lit only by light shining through the curtains at the back of the inn.

'Lily?'

His voice: she knew it immediately, and froze like a trapped animal. She saw his slender figure emerge from the shadows and he was beside her.

'Lily . . .'

She did not speak, could not.

'Please – I want to talk to you. We've got to talk properly and there's never any time or place to do it. We never had the chance.'

Her silence made him falter.

'God, woman, I'll never understand you. I thought you loved me – the way you acted, the way you looked at me . . .'

Lily felt a pressure inside her of rage and hurt and tears which strangled the words in her throat. *I did love you, I did, I do!* She lowered her head, full of panic, forcing herself to be a fortress. *Don't let him in. He'll hurt you again and again . . .*

'Leave me alone, Sam,' she managed to say in a low, calm voice. 'I don't want to be disturbed. There's nothing we can say to each other. It's all too long ago – past history. I don't want to dig it up.'

'I see.' His voice was low at first, but it grew louder as he let out his hurt resentment. 'Well, if that's how it is. I just thought you might want to tell me who that woman was in Mussoorie who told me she loved me, who promised to meet me and who never damn well turned up or bothered to explain or apologize and who *I loved*, damn it! Who I've never been able to forget since, who I see all over again and she's as cold as a fish and won't even speak to me. God, I've been a proper fool!'

He backed away from her, still talking.

'Love! Huh – there's no such thing, is there? All this time there was me thinking I'd had something, but that wasn't real either, you were just pretending and playing with me until you had a better offer, no doubt. Some classy toff you could sponge off and mess about with his feelings as well. Piers Larstonbury loves you, did you know? It's written all over him, poor sod. Well, good luck to him – and you. I hope you get what you want, Lily – damn you!'

And he was gone, back into the public house with a slam of the back door, leaving her shocked and trembling in the darkness.

Chapter Sixty-One

'Darling – what a wonderful evening! I had to come and at least say goodnight.'

Piers slipped into her room without invitation. He had arranged for them to have separate rooms, trying to be discreet, even if in other respects he was not in the least careful about letting people know she was his mistress.

'But you're not undressed yet! Are you all right, my dear?'

With genuine concern he came and sat beside her on the pink flowery eiderdown. Lily had no idea how long she had been sitting there after she came up from her encounter with Sam. She knew she should have gone back to the table, but she simply could not face it.

'Are you unwell?' Piers's slim hand caressed her forehead and Lily suddenly felt like crying. She did feel almost unwell, but she knew there was nothing wrong but an eruption of shock and grief which she could not explain.

'My dear, you don't look yourself. Is there anything I can do?'

Lily forced herself to look brightly at him. 'No – thank you,' she said quietly. 'I was just having a few moments of quiet. It's been such a busy day.'

Piers smiled, his delicate features lighting up boyishly. A lock of his light brown hair lay across his forehead.

'Hasn't it just! My goodness – truly splendid. I've had my doubts about that Fairford fellow, but he handled the motor marvellously today. And didn't she go once he got her up to speed! I say, it's all awfully jolly. And I have you to thank, darling. I feel as if I've been given a whole new life – with the motor racing, and you . . .' His face softened as he turned to her. 'Above all, you, my dear. You've made my life so very happy.'

He drew her to him and kissed her, laying his hand over her left breast with a sigh of pleasure. For a second Lily wanted to resist, to ask him to leave her alone when she felt so raw and sad. But then, as he kissed her, she felt a surge of defiance, an angry passion. Damn Sam Ironside, damn him! Why was she still letting herself tangle her emotions with him when he could come to her and rant at her the way he had without ever truly asking her for the truth or for her side of it? And when, whatever he had felt, she had had to bear and lose his child and had suffered so much more! When all the time, here was this man who did love her and was so very kind to her. As Piers Larstonbury began making love to her, she responded with an angry vigour which he interpreted as passion.

'Oh, my darling!' He drew back and looked into her eyes, moved. 'My fiery girl – you are truly extra-ordinary.'

He stood up and gently helped her to her feet, removing her diaphanous blouse until she stood in her skirt and camisole. Reverently, Piers lifted the little white garment over her head.

'My God, you're so splendid . . .'

She watched his face, his seeming to fall into a trance as he caressed her breasts and saw him with a certain tenderness. He was kind, good to her. Was that not enough?

He managed to contain himself enough to maintain his natural politeness.

'May I, my dearest? May I stay with you tonight?'

In answer, Lily unfastened her skirt and let it drop to the floor, then pulled back the covers and got into the bed, sitting looking up at him.

'Oh God,' he sighed. 'Those eyes. You beautiful, beautiful girl.'

Lily watched him hurriedly undress until he stood naked, his thin, pale body, for which she always had to overcome a certain revulsion before she could let him touch her. As he came to lie down beside her, she closed her eyes for a second, preparing herself.

'Come to me, my love,' he said with reverence, holding out his arms.

His lovemaking was always gentle, never rough or anything but kindly, yet it left her somehow untouched. As his hands moved over her body, stroking her smooth skin, she kissed the soft flesh of his neck, longing to respond without having to pretend, to be moved by more than his kindness to her.

Tonight she felt choked, as if she was so full to the brim with emotion she could not contain it, after Sam's angry words and all the turbulent feelings she had been pushing down in herself all day. As Piers lay on top of her, moving inside her, speaking gentle endearments to her, without knowing it was going to happen, she began to cry. Soon she could not control it and she was shaking with emotion.

Feeling her moving under him excited Piers further and he thrust into her harder and faster, so aroused that he did not notice at first that she was weeping. It was only after he had cried out as he reached his climax and lay panting on top of her that she began to cry aloud, the sobs tearing out of her, beyond anything she could quieten or even understand. She wept as if for a heart broken long ago, sobbing and mewling like a small child and she could not help herself.

'Lily – oh, Lily, my love, what is it?' Piers leaped up, disturbed by the violence of her crying, his face full of concern. But she could not answer, could only cling to him and weep all the more, feeling she had gone right down into a dark place which she would take time to come back from. Her eyes squeezed tightly closed as she clung to him, wanting to be held tightly herself.

And he did hold her, not knowing what else to do. 'There, there,' he whispered, as if to a small child. 'It's all right, my darling, it's all right.'

When she was calmer he said anxiously, 'Did I hurt you? I should hate to hurt you.'

'No, you didn't, it's not that.' Lily felt suddenly overwhelmed with tiredness.

'Then, for goodness sake, what is it? You sounded in such distress!'

Lily couldn't begin to explain, even to herself, about feelings that seemed to come from somewhere so long ago, from a time when she was tiny and couldn't remember. And she certainly couldn't explain about Sam.

'Just let me sleep,' she murmured.

Piers held her close to him and stroked her hair. 'Yes, my darling, you sleep.'

The last thing she felt was his kiss on her cheek.

Chapter Sixty-Two

Sam stormed back into the Pack Horse after his tirade at Lily, quivering with fury. The passage, where he stood for a time to calm himself, smelled of stale beer and cigarette smoke. A burst of laughter came through a door which opened and closed nearby. His rage soon drained away into misery.

What have I done? Oh God, why on earth did I speak to her like that? All these weeks he'd waited to be able to talk to her and when he did, all he had managed was to insult her. Why would she want to have anything to do with him now, after that? The thought was unbearable. He considered going back out to try again, to pour out the words of hurt and longing and adoration he felt for her, but then her rejection of him ignited his fury again. She had betrayed him in India, and she would only betray him again!

Defiant once more, he went back to the room where they had dined to find that the meal had broken up. Loz and Mary were just shepherding their sons up to bed.

'Night, Sam,' Loz said, pink-cheeked. 'S'been a great day.'

Sam said his goodnights to Loz and Mary. He saw that Cosmo was being helped to his feet by Piers Larstonbury, and was evidently the worse for drink.

Silly sod, Sam thought savagely. *Given every bloody*

chance in the world and look at the state of him. Cosmo seemed to him like a child, spoilt and petulant. But he could handle a motor all right, there was no denying that. It was as if it was in the blood.

Piers and Cosmo disappeared after their goodnights and the one person left in the room, looking unsure what to do, was Susan Fairford.

Sam was reluctant to go up to bed. He couldn't stand the thought of lying there, full of grief and jealousy as he thought of Lily with Piers Larstonbury. He wanted some company and sensed that Susan did as well.

'Would you like a nightcap?'

Susan gave a faint smile, looking relieved. 'That would be very pleasant. I don't feel quite ready to turn in.'

He fetched them each a small brandy, enjoying the sight of the warm-coloured liquid in the globular glasses. The two of them sat at one end of the long table. Somehow, since the war there was an ease between them.

'He did well today,' Sam said.

'Yes.' She smiled, knowing he meant Cosmo, and he could see the pride and relief, though there was always sadness just behind her social face. Sam felt a twinge of tenderness for her.

'He wants you all to go and stay at Cranbourne, you know, and put the motor through its paces there. I suppose he's always wanted someone to play with up there!' She smiled sadly. 'He has all his toys, but no playmates.'

There was a pause, while Susan sat leaning forwards, turning her glass round and round on the table.

'I do so worry about him.' She frowned. 'He's had so little family – and no father now. Charles would have taken him in hand, been able to show him what to do, had he lived. But Cosmo was so anti everything – the army, India ... I mean, he says he was incredibly homesick for India when we first sent him to school, and then it wore off. Of course, he hadn't lived in India since he was five: he certainly didn't want to go back and join the army there like Charles.' She looked up at Sam with tears in her eyes. 'You know, I don't think Cosmo has ever known what it *means* to be happy.'

Sam looked into her pretty, tired face. 'Have you?'

'*Yes* ... Well ...' She hesitated, considering. I've never really thought ... But yes, I have known happiness. When Charles and I were first married. I loved him, you see – far more than he loved me, I realize ...'

Sam thought of the Charles Fairford he had seen on the open roads of India, the adventurer, always seeking the distant horizon, and so very happy in the company of men, and he saw that to correct her would be an untruth, and she would know it to be.

'I did like India at first. It was an adventure and, of course, Charles was so wealthy and so well thought of. And he was always kind to me. It was one of his great qualities. That's something I realize, from the war, I suppose: even with all the awfulness of things, there is a lot of kindness in the world.'

Her face crumpled for a moment, but she held back her tears. Sam resisted an impulse to lay his hand on her shoulder, to give comfort.

'I was married at eighteen and I was truly happy for, let's say, two years. I had gone up in the world: my family are in trade, you see, not like the marvellous Fairfords. But my people sent my brother to Eton and that's how I met Charles, at prize-givings and concerts and so on. Lewis, my brother, and Charles were good friends. They were in the cricket team. Anyway, that's how it happened. I suppose I was just a reasonably suitable, jolly sort of girl . . .'

'And very pretty,' Sam interrupted.

Susan blushed girlishly for a moment. 'Yes, well that always helps. Anyway, Charles's family wanted him to marry so I was sent out after he'd gone to Meerut. I wasn't part of the fishing fleet – we were already engaged, from a distance.'

She took a sip of brandy. 'We were married in Meerut, and at first I found it all exciting. You know what India's like. In some ways we had it so easy out there, our life of luxury. It was rotten for the young BORs* who weren't married – dreadfully lonely. We used to have some of them round for tea and so on. But of course there's all the social life, and the colour and it's all so exotic and different. And I was madly in love with Charles. I thought he was the most amazing man I'd ever met. And he was, I suppose. But then we had Isadora. I felt dreadfully ill through most of the pregnancy and then she was . . . Well, you remember how she was . . . And it was as if everything went bad on me. I started to loathe the place. I was afraid, I suppose, as if India had cursed me in some way. Even when Cozzy arrived and he was so lovely I couldn't rid myself of a feeling of doom and dread, all the time, that something simply awful would happen to him. Very foolish really. But . . .' Another sip of her drink. 'In the end perhaps not entirely misplaced.'

'You've had a very sad time,' Sam observed. She seemed so different now, from the frosty young woman he had known in Ambala.

* British Other Ranks.

'And you?' She turned to look at him and gave a faint smile. 'How odd, that we should be here like this.'

'My life's been all right,' Sam said. He thought guiltily of Helen, of little Joe. His heart ached. There must be more to love, to life. And he knew there was, but it was cut off from him. He thought of Lily, of what he had said to her and for a second he almost felt like weeping. God, he thought, it's been a long day. I'm more tired than I realized.

He felt he should say something. There was an atmosphere of intimacy between them and he did not want to lose it.

'I suppose the war changed everything,' he said.

Susan nodded gravely. He knew what losses she had endured. 'Yes, everything's shifted somehow. We are not who we were before.'

They were sitting close together and she smiled wistfully into his face.

Without knowing he was going to do it, Sam leaned forward and kissed her. At first he kissed her cheek, but she held his gaze, her face turned up to him, and in the privacy of the quiet back room he kissed her on the lips, holding her slender frame briefly in his arms. He felt her gently kiss him back.

When he drew back, there were tears in her eyes.

'I long to love again,' she said. 'To feel something beautiful and true.'

To his surprise, Sam felt a lump rise in his throat, and he nodded.

Chapter Sixty-Three

'Of course you must come – I wouldn't dream of going without you, darling!'

For several days now, Lily and Piers Larstonbury had been discussing the invitation from Cosmo to go and stay at the Cranbourne estate. This time it was very late, a hot August night, with a night breeze stirring the lacy curtains, and they were once more lying together in Lily's bed.

'But what about Virginia . . .' Lily protested, as she so often did.

'Virginia is scarcely ever here,' Piers said, adding bitterly, 'do you seriously think Virginia ever concerns herself with what I do?'

Lily had realized some time ago that Virginia Larstonbury had taken a lover herself and was completely preoccupied, what with that and with her strange spiritual friends. Lily had seen a burly fellow with a beard and colourful, dashing clothes arrive at the house on several occasions and realized that all the hours they spent shut away together upstairs did not consist of praying or whatever it was theosophists did. But she did not know whether Piers knew about his wife's infidelity. Virginia would appear in the evenings looking pink and sated and unusually good-tempered.

'Oh, my little darlings, come and play with your mama!' she would greet Hubert and Christabel, flinging her arms round them extravagantly and playing with them for much longer than the normal time allotted. With her long red hair hanging loose, kneeling on the floor with the children pretending to be a witch or a bear, since she was good at pretend games, she looked like a large child herself and Lily could feel almost affectionate towards her. She often wondered whether Virginia had any idea of Piers's affair with her. Certainly she never showed the least sign of it and he was ever discreet. Lily had come to realize just how deep was Virginia's indifference to her husband, so perhaps even if she had known she would not much have cared.

'What about the children?' Lily said.

'Bring them as well,' Piers said. He laid his hand on her stomach, stroking her. 'Oh, my beauty, how lovely you are.'

'Could we bring them? It would do them good to be out in the country.'

Piers raised himself on one elbow and looked down at her seriously.

'You are more of a mother to them than Virginia ever has been.'

'I'm very fond of them.' It was true, she was fond of timid, sweet-natured little Hubert and fiery Christabel and had become attached to them.

'We can motor up on Saturday morning, have an early start. And Ironside and Marks are coming with our Flyer with her brand-new engine!' Piers immediately sounded keen and boyish as he always did when he talked about the car.

Lily's heart thumped painfully hard for a moment. Sam would be there! She longed to go and see her beloved Cosmo, to look at the estate where he had spent so much of his boyhood and to be out in the country with the children, but if Sam was to be there too … However much she made herself angry with him, it didn't make it any better. Seeing him filled her with so many emotions, most of them painful.

'I should stay behind,' she tried to suggest. 'I'll be in the way – me and the children.'

'Not at all! I want you by my side. I know none of them say anything because they're too polite and so on – and they can't do without me, of course – but they must all realize what you mean to me by now. It's one place we can go and feel comfortable, not worry about what people think. What is it, darling? You look anxious.'

She stared past him, up at the ceiling. It was her own fault that she and Sam kept being thrown together like this. She had made it happen, hadn't she? And she also knew that, as so often in her life, when she had occupied this strange social territory, somewhere between servant and confidante as she now did again with Piers Larston-bury, that in the end she never had any choice but to do as she was asked.

Forcing her lips into a smile, she said, 'Nothing, dear. I'm quite all right. Of course we'll go.' It was for Cosmo, all of it, wasn't it? If there was one thing she could do it was to see him set on a path to success. Of course – it was all for Cosmo.

They were up at dawn, carrying the children out to the car into a hazy morning which promised to turn into the hottest of August days. The journey reminded Lily of taking Eustace Bartlett to his people in Leamington Spa and she wondered how he was getting on. What a handful he had been! She looked fondly down at Hubert beside her. No child had ever replaced Cosmo in her affections, but she did have a very soft spot for little Hubert.

When, amid the rolling Warwickshire countryside, they turned off the road into the gates of Cranbourne House, Piers and Lily exclaimed with astonishment.

'My goodness me!' Piers Larstonbury cried. 'I wasn't expecting it to be as imposing as this! Young Fairford has always given the impression of it all being a rather crumbling, unmanageable sort of place that's descending into chaos.'

'It's absolutely beautiful,' Lily said, feeling a great swell of pride. All this would be Cosmo's one day since his Uncle William was unmarried. To think her boy would be the master of a place like this!

The house, at the end of a curving drive, was a four-square and symmetrically proportioned brick Regency manor, its grand front door flanked by white columns. In front of the house Lily saw a garden laid out with rose bushes and small shrubs and flowers.

'What a lovely *parterre*!' Piers exclaimed.

Lily smiled. 'Yes, isn't it.' She had never heard the word *parterre* before. The shaped grass cut round the flowers reminded her of a doily.

'And what a house – no wonder young Fairford was keen for me to see it!'

But Hubert was jumping with excitement for another reason. 'Look!' he cried, leaning across Lily's lap to see better. 'Aeroplane – an aeroplane!'

In the distance, on a bright sward of grass, was an aeroplane, tilted to one side and white and delicate as a resting insect.

'Is it going to fly?' Hubert was asking, when from round the side of the house they saw Cosmo appear with a slow, languorous walk, dressed in white flannel trousers and a red and white checked shirt. His golden hair fell, curling over one eye, and he tossed his head back and raised an arm in greeting, squinting in the bright sunlight.

As Piers braked in front of the house, Cosmo leaned down to the window and Lily beamed with joy at the sight of him. He was so lovely, so tall and handsome!

'Well, you've made good time,' he drawled, not looking at Lily and she felt a stab of rejection. It was as if he could never acknowledge her properly or show how much he needed her, especially if there was any other company about. But she knew it was just his way.

'Hello, Cosmo, dear,' she said.

'Oh, hello, Lily,' he said offhandedly. 'I'll get our man to show you all where your quarters are. There's an attic where you can go with the children. Mother wired to say she's on her way up. And you must come and meet Uncle William.'

William Fairford was about as different from his young brother Charles as it would have been possible to imagine. Lily and Piers were introduced to a short, rotund man dressed in very tightly fitting tweeds, his belly thrusting out dangerously hard at the buttons of his waistcoat. He had a red, jowly face and a great many whiskers protruding from his nose and ears. From under a tweed hat he looked at them with narrowed, sludgy-coloured eyes and said, 'Hmmm. I didn't know there were going to be children. Cosmo – you must inform Mrs Rainbow at once. *She* likes children. And don't think I want to know anything about anything because I don't. Good day to you!' He touched the brim of his cap and sauntered off, tapping the floor with a silver-topped walking cane. 'See you at dinner time!' he called over his shoulder.

Lily watched him in astonishment. Was this really the man Cosmo had spent all his school holidays cared for, or rather ignored, by? He seemed most peculiar and certainly not interested in anyone else around him. How could he be Charles Fairford's brother? But then Susan Fairford had told her that he had suffered with his nerves as a young man, that he had taken after his peculiar uncle. She still felt indignant on Cosmo's behalf and exchanged a look with Piers. But then they heard a woman's voice approaching, talking non-stop before she had even come into view.

'. . . there's a room up to the right and you'll find it's very comfortable and I don't know how many of you there are and of course we're not used to visitors here, him being the way he is and no one ever tells me a thing, of course, not a thing . . . Hello, dears – oh, and little ones as well! He never said there'd be children coming! Oh, my word. Well, that's a treat for us!'

All this from a very stout woman as she appeared panting in the doorway. She wore an enormous white apron and a startled expression in her watery grey eyes.

'Deary me, it's a warm one today!' Her cheeks were very red and she was fanning herself with one hand. 'I'm Mrs Rainbow and no doubt Cosmo hasn't done the first thing to make you comfortable, let alone *him*.' She flicked her head in the direction of the departed Uncle William, not even trying to disguise her exasperation.

Within moments they were being shown into rooms where the beds had been made up most efficiently and Mrs Rainbow swiftly settled them in.

'I've six of my own, all grown and gone now,' she said wistfully. 'And my Herb passed on six years ago ... Time of your life when your children are young – you never get it back.' For a moment she looked watery and woeful, but then beamed at Hubert, and Christabel, who was lying on her bed kicking her chubby legs in the air. 'Oh, and look at you two. Oh, I'm going to like having you here!'

Lily had been given a room at the opposite end of the house to Piers Larstonbury, a relief as she was glad of a break from his attentions, but she tried to look disappointed when he mentioned it later.

'Never mind, my love, I'll be with you!' he whispered to her, and she gave him a smile.

'Has Mrs Rainbow been here for a long time?' Lily asked Cosmo when they joined him downstairs in the drawing room, from where there came a strong smell of coffee. On a silver tray were laid a coffee pot and cups and a plate of biscuits and iced cakes decorated with diamonds of angelica.

'No – only five or six years,' Cosmo said, eyeing Hubert and Christabel as they stormed the corridors at high speed in ecstasy at being released from the car. Cosmo looked a bit irritated, but Lily sensed that he also envied them. 'Before that, when I was at school, it was Mrs Saxsby, and she was an *ogre*.'

'Oh yes,' Lily laughed at the face he pulled. 'I remember now. You wrote about her.'

'Mrs Rainbow will love you being here,' Cosmo said. He nodded at the cakes. 'She likes feeding people. That's why Uncle's so stout. Oh!' He looked out, roused by the engine and sound of gravel crunching outside. 'Here's Ironside!'

Lily found every nerve in her body suddenly on

alert, her heart pounding. Any moment, once again, she would have to greet Sam! And now she knew what he thought of her, his anger and disgust with her. Oh, why had she let Piers talk her into coming here?

They all went out into the sunshine from the cool of the house, to find Sam and Loz pulling up outside, the streamlined silver body of the Heath Flyer looking magnificent on the trailer behind the car. Both Sam and Loz were obviously hot, but they grinned broadly at the sign of the reception party. Cosmo ran forward to meet them, excited as a child.

And amid all the greetings, Lily stood to one side with the children while Sam worked his way through the handshakes. Mrs Rainbow had appeared again and was exclaiming over the car, and her mouth ran away with her when she saw Sam as well.

'Ooh, aren't you a good-looking one!' she said and Lily saw Sam's smile in reply.

'I'm glad somebody thinks so,' he quipped.

At last, very formally, he came forward to shake Lily's hand.

'How d'you do, Miss Waters?' he said, his voice cooler than if she had been a stranger he had never met before.

And while, for the seconds his hand was in hers, she couldn't help remembering how that same hand had moved lovingly over her bare skin and, aching for the tenderness of it, she said equally coolly, 'Good morning, Mr Ironside.'

Chapter Sixty-Four

While Sam and Loz took the motor from the trailer and made some adjustments to her, Cosmo said he would give Piers, Lily and the children a tour of the estate in Uncle William's spacious Morris Cowley.

'That's awfully kind of you, old chap,' Piers said, 'but I think I'd like to stay and watch our Flyer being unloaded. I'm most intrigued by the whole thing and I haven't managed to get down to Brooklands to see her in progress nearly as much as I'd hoped lately. And I can be here to greet your mother when she arrives. Why don't you take Lily? She's very keen to see your home.'

Lily sat in the front beside Cosmo, awed by the sheer size of the estate, which seemed to go on and on across the Warwickshire countryside. She felt so proud sitting next to him, looking at the fields of wheat turning golden in the August sunlight, the gardens and farm cottages and the orchards to one side of the house. What Cosmo most wanted to show her, however, was the driving circuit. The dusty track snaked round a wide area at the far end of the estate, cutting along the side of a hill on a sharp incline.

'My goodness!' Lily said as he took her along it at high speed. 'This is steep – oh, do slow down a bit, Cozzy. You're frightening the children!' Hubert was clinging to her skirt, his hands clenched into fists.

'You have to go fast to keep up the momentum,' Cosmo retorted, not slowing down at all. 'Like the track at Brooklands – remember the slope on that?'

'Yes,' Lily said sharply, 'but we're not racing now.'

She had expected that alone with her, Cosmo might soften and become his more boyish self, the sweet Cosmo who she loved. But he seemed even more on edge.

'You've been doing so well,' she said trying to appease him. 'I'm so very proud of you.'

Since the event at Shelsley Walsh, Cosmo had entered various events at Brooklands and come home in a very respectable time – in one case, in second place. He was riding high and very pleased with himself at the time, but now he seemed morose and unsure.

Lily watched him as he drove, his expression grim with concentration. He looked forbidding. His face, which she had thought of as distinguished, with its Grecian nose, now seemed hard, his forehead more enlarged as he grew older. In fact, she recognized with a shock that in profile he looked very slightly like his Uncle William. She had never connected Cosmo with this part of the family before. William Fairford was an unbalanced, melancholic fellow. Surely Cosmo was not taking after him?

'Darling,' she said softly, trying to reach the Cosmo who would respond to her. 'You're doing so awfully well.'

'Oh, don't mumsy me, Lily,' Cosmo snapped. 'I'm not your little boy any more.'

Lily tried not to show how much he had hurt her. She was also trying not to notice how fast he was still driving. She held Hubert's hand, reassuring him.

'All right. But you are doing so very well.'

'We'll see, won't we?' he said grimly.

After that she was silent, trying to understand him, and why, when he was surrounded by so much wealth and now he was doing all the things he had always wanted to and doing them so well, his mood seemed to have such an edge of despair.

Once they got back, Susan Fairford had arrived and she greeted Lily affectionately.

Mrs Rainbow had set out an impressive meal of cheeses and cold meats and pickle on the long, gleaming dining table and Lily felt the weight of silver cutlery in her hands. There was a silver tureen of creamy watercress soup and they all ate ravenously. The men all stuck together, talking motor cars and aeroplanes, and she heard Cosmo promise to take the others up in it over the weekend. Lily stayed at the other end of the table from Sam and the others, but she was acutely aware of his presence as he sat talking with Piers Larstonbury. She could see from the tensed hunch of his shoulders that he was not entirely comfortable in these surroundings. Sam had always had a chip on his shoulder about wealthy people. *Toffs*, she could hear him saying. Another thing they had had in common, not being sure where they fitted in. His eyes met hers along the table, just once, a deep look when he thought she was not aware, but as soon as her gaze met his he looked away.

She spent the afternoon with Susan Fairford, who was very tired, and the children, who had a nap and then were taken off for some of the afternoon by Mrs Rainbow, who seemed to be on pins to get her hands on them.

The two women sat in an exquisitely decorated sitting room which Susan said was barely ever used. The room looked out to the flower garden at the side of the house through long glass doors edged with cream muslin curtains, delicately embroidered with pink and gold flowers. Susan eased the doors open and they sat on comfortable chintz-covered chairs on either side of a marble fireplace, enjoying the faint breeze in an otherwise baking afternoon. Susan kicked off her shoes and at her invitation, Lily did the same, stretching out in the chair and luxuriating in the feel of the thick Chinese rug under her stockinged toes.

They talked idly in the heat, dozing for a while, and at four o'clock Mrs Rainbow brought in a tray of tea, accompanied by Hubert and Christabel, both looking unmistakably floury.

'Look what we made!'

Hubert was proudly holding a plate of jam tarts.

'Oh, how delicious, dear!' Lily cried, smiling at the child's proud face. 'Thank you so much, Mrs Rainbow.'

'Shall I take them out to the garden for a while?' Mrs Rainbow said.

'Well – yes, if you'd like to!' Lily was delighted.

'Ooh – it's a treat. Come along, 'ubert, Christabel! I've got summat to show you.'

Susan smiled wistfully after her. 'She misses her brood.' Then, suddenly, she said, 'Sam Ironside has come a long way since he first arrived in India, hasn't he?'

Startled to hear his name mentioned, Lily found herself blushing.

'Yes,' she agreed, trying to sound neutral. 'I suppose he has.'

'I realize I know so very little about him. I suppose I never cared to ask before.'

Lily could not think of anything safe to say in reply. In the pause which followed, they heard a dove calling from the roof in the hot, sleepy afternoon, accompanied by the distant hum of an engine.

'He was rather sweet on you at one time, wasn't he?' Susan rearranged the skirt of her pretty floral dress. 'I suppose that's all over with by now?'

'Oh – yes,' Lily said lightly.

'And he's not really in the same class as the major, is he?'

Lily blushed, full of confusion. Her relations with Sam Ironside and Piers Larstonbury were both things she felt quite unable to talk about, but as she sought desperately to think of a way of changing the subject, Susan raised a finger and said, 'What's that noise?'

The sound was growing louder and the two of them got up and went to the doors. The scent of honeysuckle and lavender wafted from the warm garden. Against the mellow stone nearby grew a profusion of sweet-smelling yellow climbing roses.

Susan, looking a thin, girlish figure, put a hand to her forehead and squinted upwards.

'Oh Lord – it's Cosmo. He must be taking someone up. Oh dear, I do so worry about him . . . He can fly as well as he can drive, but all the same . . .'

Shading her eyes, Lily looked up into the soaring blue and saw the tiny white plane scratching its way across. Who had Cosmo taken up? Sam? . . . *tell me who that woman was in Mussoorie who told me she loved me* . . . His words throbbed through her.

'They all love machines so much, don't they?' Susan said. 'Come along – let's go and see them land.'

They hurried, shoeless, following the plane with their eyes, out towards the wide hayfield at some distance from the house, where they found Mrs Rainbow and the children all staring upwards at the circling plane. Sam and Loz were nowhere to be seen.

As they reached the place where the children were standing, the plane landed bumpily in one corner of the field and Cosmo and Piers Larstonbury opened up the cockpit, Piers laughing with pleasure. Lily had never seen him so animated.

'My word, it's just astonishing!' he cried, leaping down, running unguardedly to her and flinging his arms round her. 'Darling, it's the most astounding experience!'

Lily looked across to see Susan watching, and knew that whatever Susan had been guessing, she had now had her thoughts confirmed.

Chapter Sixty-Five

By the end of the afternoon, Lily was wishing she had never come to Cranbourne House.

She had wanted to see Cosmo's home, his inheritance, but being near to Sam was a torment. She felt raw and sad, and that she had been wrong in rejecting his attempt to talk to her. But now it felt too late. Sam simply behaved as if she wasn't there.

'I think I'll have an early night,' she told Piers Larstonbury that evening, after Mrs Rainbow had served them a sumptuous meal of roast pork and a huge syrup pudding. Uncle William, it appeared, liked the best of solid, traditional food and nothing fancy, although he did not eat with them but took all his meals on his own.

Piers was about to join the other men in the smoking room and Lily caught him before he disappeared across the panelled hall.

'All right, my dear,' he said, mellowed with drink and the plentiful food. Moving closer to her, he whispered, 'I'll come to you later, darling one.'

Lily nodded, but kept her eyes cast down.

She lay in her bedroom at the top of the house. The children were in the next room, which had once been the nursery, Mrs Rainbow had told her. The window was open but it was stiflingly hot. She had nothing on but her bloomers and a camisole, but it still felt stuffy and unbearable. For a while she managed to doze, but then woke with a start, drenched in perspiration. Sitting up, she looked out at the dark garden. The house was quiet. She hoped that Piers had been well plied with brandy so that he had gone to his room and fallen fast asleep. Please, she thought, don't let him come in here tonight! All she wanted was to be alone.

The night air smelled delicious and she leaned out of the casement window for a while, the air cooling her. Her room was at the back of the house, facing over the lawn, edged with trees. She could smell the sweet scent of cut grass where the men had been scything that evening.

Lighting a candle, she moved restlessly about the room. On the floor to the left of the window was a small wooden trunk and out of curiosity she lifted the lid, wondering if it contained more toys for Hubert and Christabel to entertain themselves with.

The box smelled strongly of wood polish and camphor. On the top, inside, there was a limp rag doll, not a girl doll, but one made to resemble a soldier, with a helmet and faded scarlet jacket. The face had fierce, staring eyes drawn on in ink and a curling moustache of black wool. She thought it didn't look a very comforting sort of toy. Surely it had not been Cosmo's? She did not remember ever having seen it before.

Underneath there were various little boxes and she opened the top one, which was wooden and full of tin soldiers rather like the rag doll soldier. So there were toys! The next was a box made of faded white card decorated with a painted garland of mauve flowers. Inside, she found a collection of old letters, the paper yellowed and barely holding together on some of the folds. Carefully she picked up the top letter and opened it, seeing a short, blotchy note in childish handwriting, with several crossings out. It was addressed from his prep school and dated December 1887.

Dear Mother and Father,
I am doing very well and I hope you are to. I have got better from my cold and also the chilblains on my toes are not hurting eny more. It is still very cold. We are learning to play rugby. Please write and tell me more about Haroon's pups and about Arsalan.
We are singing carols and getting ready for Chrismas.
I hope you have a happy and holy Chrismas.
Your loving son,
Charles

There was a large collection of other similar notes, dated over several years, and as Lily read them, seeing the handwriting mature gradually, her eyes filled with tears.

'I felt sick for weeks when they sent me to England,' Cosmo had once told her. 'It was that sort of misery that makes you feel as if you have a stone inside you. I thought about running away constantly. But how do you run away all the way back to India?'

The letters from Cosmo's father, from a homesick little six-year-old, far away from his parents, his friends and pets, seemed to say so much by saying so little, the ache of it seeping between the lines. She felt very tender towards both father and son. And now Charles Fairford, the rather courtly man she remembered, who seemed happier on a horse out in the Indian countryside than anywhere else, had been laid to rest on the battlefields of France.

Closing the chest, she looked at the garden and was filled with a longing to be out in the night air. Slipping her dressing gown round her and her shoes on, she looked in to check that Hubert and Christabel were sleeping soundly, then crept out and down the long flights of stairs. Remembering her way to the little sitting room where she had sat with Susan that afternoon, she let herself out through the glass doors and into the warm, caressing air.

The sense of freedom exhilarated her and in the relative cool outside she felt full of life and energy. Following the path round to the back, she felt the brush of lavender against her nightdress, and smelled its scent mingled with roses, then the smell of the grass as she moved across the lawn and stopped to look back at the house. She could not see a light on in any of the rooms. A little bubble of laughter rose in her and she turned and ran lightly across the soft green expanse, feeling she might run and never stop. It felt exciting and free to be out so late.

At the far end of the long lawn the grass was longer near the trees and she stopped and looked back again. It was a slightly hazy night, but a half moon was visible through a chiffon of cloud. Its faint light showed the lines of the house. She thought she had never been anywhere more beautiful, not since India, and in the warm night she half expected to smell the dung fires and dry earth and scented oils of the Indian darkness. She thought of those sad little children sent away from home, aching for India in the darkness of English winter nights. Cosmo, she realized, knew as little as herself about family life, or how it felt to be loved and secure.

It did not cross her mind to be afraid to move into the deeper darkness of the trees and she wandered into the longer grass, feeling it tickling her calves. The arching branches above felt benign, like an embrace. She reached out and trailed her hand along one of the tree trunks.

It was then she realized she was not alone. She heard a sound which she knew was a human voice, even though she heard no words. It came from her left and she turned her head to hear better, her heart bumping harder, although she was not afraid so much as curious. As soon as she heard the voice again she knew whose it was, and her heartbeat accelerated even more. Something deep in her would have recognized Sam's voice almost anywhere. But who was he talking to? She crept towards the sound.

Almost immediately she heard a long sighing noise, this time from a woman. Lily's mind raced. Susan – it had to be Susan Fairford!

'You've had a very thin time of it,' she heard Sam say.

Lily realized she was quite close to them and she froze, straining to hear, her emotions a mixture of painful jealousy and a kind of triumph. Wasn't it just like Sam Ironside to be declaring his love for her one day then snuggling up to someone else the next – while he still had a wife at home?

'I'm hardly unique in that,' Susan said.

Lily strained to hear. The low, intimate tone to their voices told her that this was more than just a night-time stroll.

'You must have found me very standoffish when we first met,' Susan was saying.

There came a low laugh from Sam. 'I did rather, I'm afraid. But not now.'

'No. I have changed. The war changed me – changed everything. I suppose I was rather insufferable. I was afraid, somehow. I always had the feeling that I was about to be found out in some way. You know – let the side down.'

'Oh, I don't suppose you ever did that.'

There was a silence, then Susan Fairford said, 'Oh, Sam, you've been very kind to me.'

Lily held her breath.

'You lovely, beautiful woman,' she heard Sam say ardently. 'God, I never thought I'd be holding you in my arms. Not in a million years.'

'Dear Sam . . .'

And then there was a silence in which Lily guessed they were kissing, and there came a faint sound, like a sigh of pleasure from Susan.

Unable to bear hearing any more and terribly afraid that they would hear and realize she was there, Lily crept away through the trees, full of a chaos of emotions. The wide lawn, the smell of grass in the night no longer seemed enchanted but soured.

She clenched her fists, almost bursting with anger and jealousy. *You told him to leave you alone!* she raged at herself. *What do you expect him to do? You don't want him, you know you don't. He's let you down badly enough already. Keep away from him!*

But the pain was almost overwhelming. Hurrying along the lavender-scented path and into the house she was fighting her storm of tears which were only released when she got back to her room. She lay face down on the bed letting the sobs of grief and jealousy and longing begin to break out of her. She knew, with terrible helplessness, how much she loved Sam Ironside, how

453

precious the memory of their love was to her. And when she had been given another chance and he had tried to approach her, she had pushed him away. How he must despise her! And now it was too late. He had given his heart to someone else.

Chapter Sixty-Six

The thought of facing them the next morning was terrible. Lily had had no sleep that night and her reflection in the glass was pale and strained.

'I'll stay with Mrs Rainbow and keep the children out of the way,' she told Susan.

There had been much talk of more flying and of putting the Heath Flyer through her paces on the track and Lily knew that at least Sam would be completely absorbed in that.

'Won't you come out and see Cosmo drive?' Susan said. 'Surely the children could come out as well.' She looked at Lily more closely. 'Are you feeling all right? You don't look terribly well.'

'I just seem to be feeling the heat,' Lily said. 'Nothing to worry about.'

Lily spent much of the day with Mrs Rainbow and Christabel, glad of the woman's cheerful company and to be able to do household tasks rather than be out with all the men and the complications of her heart. She felt overwhelmed with mourning for her love of Sam and did not want Piers Larstonbury anywhere near her, although, to her shame, she knew he genuinely loved her. All this time she had been pretending and the one person she had ever truly loved, whose child she had given life to, she had let slip through her hands through cowardice and pride. Seldom had she spent such a bitter few hours.

She was out in the walled garden with Christabel and Mrs Rainbow when they heard the shouting.

Earlier, Cosmo had swept above them, twice, in the little plane.

'Look at that,' Mrs Rainbow tutted, squinting up as the plane disappeared above the house. 'Nearly shaving the roof. That boy's a case, he truly is.'

When the plane did not reappear they realized that the men were out at the track. And that was the direction from which the estate men came running.

Mrs Rainbow heard the shouts.

'Summat's amiss,' she said to Lily, going to the back door of the kitchen where they had been making tea. 'That's Tim and Bernard.'

'Quick!' Lily heard a deep voice shouting. 'Fetch us a blanket. There's been an accident – Master Cosmo!'

Lily filled with cold dread.

'We need to bring 'im in!'

'But there's a stretcher – remember?' Mrs Rainbow had her wits about her. 'In the outhouse – over there.'

'So there is – come on, Tim!'

Lily picked up Christabel, who was eating a jam tart, and she and Mrs Rainbow followed them. The men had hauled the old khaki stretcher and poles out of the shed and taken off again along the track. Neither Mrs Rainbow nor Lily could move as fast as them and they were soon left behind. But Lily still ran faster than she could ever have expected carrying the little girl. The track was almost a mile away, along the edge of a wheat field, and in the distance they could see the hill rising up with the track cut into the edge of it.

'Oh, my Lord, I can't keep this up,' Mrs Rainbow said, bent over and puce in the face. But Lily ran on, Christabel clinging stickily to her.

She saw the wreck of the car before making out who was who, the men all gathered round, the silence as she drew nearer. The Flyer was upside down and she could see it was in a dreadful mess. She saw Sam bend over Cosmo, who was lying on the stretcher, then straighten up and say something to Piers Larstonbury, shaking his head. She thought her heart would burst. She could not see Susan, and how was Cosmo? *Oh, dear God, let him be all right. Don't let him be hurt, don't let him be dead!*

'What's happened?' she shouted. 'Cosmo – is he all right?'

She saw Susan then, behind Sam, squatting down beside the stretcher by the crumpled silver wreckage of the car. Sam's face turned towards her, and Loz's. Both of them looked stunned and grim.

And then, on the stretcher she saw Cosmo struggling to sit up and her whole being leaped with relief.

'Cosmo!' It was as if she was the only person who could speak. Everyone else was shocked into silence. Lily put Christabel down and tore across to him.

'I'm all right,' Cosmo snapped furiously. He had a great discoloured bump on the side of his head. He sat with his knees slightly bent, arms hanging limply and he was shaking uncontrollably.

'What happened?' She turned wildly to Sam.

Sam shrugged, not seeming to trust himself to speak.

Loz was less reserved. 'The stupid bugger turned the

car over, that's what. And look at it – weeks of work and he goes and wrecks it . . .' He punched the air in miserable frustration and stormed off. Lily could see he was fighting tears of anger and disappointment.

'Never mind,' Piers Larstonbury was saying soothingly. 'We can get her fixed – improve her, even. Thank heavens you're all right, Cosmo.'

Susan turned to Lily with a stricken expression. 'He was going too fast – far too fast. Oh, darling, why did you have to . . . ?' She was stroking Cosmo's hair as if he were a small child and he shook her off and got groggily to his feet.

'It was an accident,' he shouted, furiously. 'I didn't mean to turn it over. D'you think I meant to make a mess of it? Now just bloody well leave me alone, all of you.'

'You should come back to the house and get some attention, Master Cosmo,' Bernard, the older of the two men, said. He seemed to be the only one Cosmo would listen to. 'Come along now.'

Cosmo was swaying and clearly faint and he agreed then to get back on the stretcher and for the men to carry him to the house. As they set off along the border of the field, Piers came and in front of everyone put his arm protectively round Lily's shoulders. Lily was so caught up in Cosmo, in the simple relief that he was alive, that she burst into tears. Susan put her hands over her face.

'Oh, dear God,' she wept. 'Oh, my boy.'

And through her tears, Lily saw Sam go to her and take her by the arm to lead her back to the house. She stood, with Piers's arm round her, watching them go.

*

458

The doctor was called out to Cosmo, and he was pronounced to have severe bruising to the head and three cracked ribs.

'You obviously have the good fortune of a cat,' the doctor said. 'That's certainly one of your lives crossed off the list, young man.'

After the initial shock, having seen the crushed state of the car, it began to sink into everyone just how lucky Cosmo had been.

'A quite astonishing escape,' Piers said as they sat at teatime, eating Mrs Rainbow's fruit scones.

Lily felt sick, terribly anxious about Cosmo and finding the presence of Susan and Sam almost unbearable. Sam avoided her eyes, talking to anyone but her, and Lily had to struggle with her sense of betrayal by Susan. But she had told Sam to leave her alone, hadn't she? What else was he supposed to think?

Now the weekend was almost over, they were all making preparations to leave, and Lily knew she had to see Cosmo. She asked Mrs Rainbow to show her to his room at the other end of the house. Lily was taken aback by the bleakness of the place, furnished with only the bed, a chair and a chest of drawers on the bare, polished boards. She had expected a room littered with the remains of a childhood spent here, whereas it looked more like the sort of cell one might expect for a monk. But then, she reminded herself, Cosmo was not here permanently and never had been. He had never belonged here.

Cosmo was stretched out in bed looking very pale and limp. His bright hair was plastered to his temples, the bruising was beginning to come out on his face and he was obviously in a lot of pain from his ribs.

'Hello, dear.' She moved some of the clothing from

the chair beside the bed, and sat down. 'How are you, Cozzy?'

His eyes were half open and he seemed very sleepy.

'My ribs . . . Hellish . . . Hurts to breathe . . .'

Lily reached out to caress his forehead and Cosmo flinched, giving a gasp which made him moan with pain.

'Don't!'

'Sorry, dear – you know I'd never hurt you. I was trying to make you feel better.' Frowning, she looked at the swollen lump on the left of his forehead, then, unable to help it, burst out with, 'Oh, Cozzy! How could you be so silly and reckless? Think what might have happened! You could have hurt yourself so dreadfully – and you're lucky not to be dead.'

Cosmo's eyes opened wide suddenly, and in bursts of pained speech he said, 'Am I? Ironside . . . I've let him down. All of them. I'm no good to anyone . . .'

'Cozzy!' Anguished by his suffering she went to stroke him again but he turned his head away.

'Don't baby me!'

'I'm sorry, dear. But I hate to see you like this. Don't take everything so badly! It was an accident. You've done everything so well up until now – remember all the other times? All the successes you've had? Don't let this one cloud everything else.'

'But I've wrecked the car! Completely smashed it! Ironside and Marks will never forgive me.'

Lily thought of the expression of utter fury she had seen on Loz Marks's face and was filled with a sense of dread for Cosmo. Perhaps Piers would want to find another driver.

'It'll be all right, darling,' she said, wanting to pour her love over him as she had always done, to make him feel better. 'I'll talk to Piers – we'll see that it's all right.'

460

'Oh God!' Cosmo cried, with such force she thought he was about to launch himself off the bed. 'Can't you stop interfering, Lily? Everything has to come from you, doesn't it? You can't let me do one thing for myself. You swamp me and make me feel completely useless. Oh, just leave me alone, woman. I'm useless to everyone – just let me face the fact on my own!'

He turned away from her and Lily could see that there was nothing she could say to bring him back to her. She stood up, knowing that he was in one of his dramatic moods, but she was very hurt nevertheless.

'Well, I hope you feel better soon,' she said, trying to keep her pain and anger from her voice. 'Next time I see you perhaps you'll be feeling a little more forthcoming – and grateful for everything that's been done for you.'

Cosmo did not respond or open his eyes, and angry as she was with him, she was frightened by the expression of utter wretchedness on his face.

Chapter Sixty-Seven

'We've got to get shot of him – he's a drunk and a fool and there's no telling what he'll do next!'

There was silence. The two of them were in the work shed at Brooklands and Sam was bent over the engine of the Heath Flyer.

'Sam!'

Sam straightened up, his expression grim. They had come back from Cranbourne the day before, very late, and he knew Loz had been working up to this.

'You know I'm right. You're all pandering to that spoilt brat because you're afraid to say no. He's no good – he's a bloody menace. That Larstonbury fellow can afford to hire any driver he wants, we've built him a bloody good motor and here we are risking it with that *halfwit* Fairford, who can't get through a morning without sucking at a Scotch bottle like a ... a *baby*. Christ, what a shower! I've never seen anything so ridiculous. And you just take it all. "Yes, Major Larstonbury, no, Major Larstonbury, three bags full, Major Larstonbury."'

'No, I don't!' Sam's temper began to flare now. 'But he's the one with the money. If he pulls out on us we've nothing!'

Sam found he was shouting. He knew this was only part of the story, but he couldn't put into words the confusion of emotions he felt. He had to put up with

Cosmo because of the money, it was true, but if he had gone to Piers Larstonbury and suggested they take on a different driver, he knew Piers would listen, even despite the fact the man was clearly helping Cosmo to please Lily. But there was also his old loyalty to Cosmo's father Charles, to the new, tender emotions he felt towards Susan Fairford, and because ... Lily, there was always Lily, and her devotion to Cosmo – and because he felt as if he was going to explode with all the conflict and muddle inside him. He was still haunted by the wail he had heard Lily let out when she saw Cosmo lying on the stretcher. Her anguish had pierced deep into his heart and his first impulse had been to run and take her in his arms.

They had brought the car back on the trailer to Brooklands with full encouragement from Piers Larstonbury to get her roadworthy again.

'D'you think you'll be ready by the September meeting?' he asked. 'She's in a dreadful mess, I can see.'

'Oh, I think so,' Sam said. It was terrible to see the Flyer in that crushed state but already he was making mental notes of what needed doing. The bodywork would need replacing completely. Cosmo had taken the curve of the hill far too fast, showing off, of course. She'd turned over and rolled. God alone knew how Cosmo had got out with barely a scratch. Must've had the patron saint of drunkards on his side, Sam thought bitterly. Types like that always seemed to get out of trouble and inflict it on everyone else.

He had known Loz would explode sooner or later, and this was only the first of an increasing number of rows that started with Loz over Cosmo. The arrival of Cosmo a week later, still wincing in pain from his ribs, infuriated Loz even more.

'He's a liability,' he ranted to Sam after Cosmo had come into the shed to see the work on the car, the unmistakable aroma of Scotch hanging round him like a mist. 'We've given him a chance and he was all right to start with, I grant you. But he's shown his true colours now. He's hardly ever bloody sober! For God's sake, Sam, we've only got this year and we'll be back to square one if we don't get somewhere with this. In fact . . .' He wiped his oily hands on a rag and flung it over on to the bench. 'I'm wondering whether I want anything more to do with it!'

Sam knew that Loz was in a different position from him. He had no emotional entanglements with this project and he was also missing Mary and his boys.

'Well, you make up your bloody mind whether you're staying or going,' Sam said, 'and stop keeping on.'

He was furious himself. He didn't want to fall out with his old friend Loz. He didn't want Cosmo Fairford as his driver. But without Cosmo there might be no Piers Larstonbury, no car . . . And, still such a strong factor, yet one which he could hardly admit, no Lily.

Chapter Sixty-Eight

'They're ready! It's time for the off!'

Once again Lily stood in the crowd of spectators beside Susan Fairford, but this time they were at Brooklands for the September race meeting. The Heath Flyer, newly restored, was entered in the first handicap race.

Lily thought of Sam down beside the finishing straight with Piers and Loz, of all the passion they had poured into the Flyer. And Cosmo was in the driver's seat. *Oh, keep him calm – let him drive his very best. At his best he's so brilliant, has so much nerve and skill . . .*

'How did he seem this morning?' Susan had come up from the south coast, arriving late so that she had not seen Cosmo before he was marshalled for the race. Lily could see that Susan was even more nervous than she was. She tried to push from her mind what she had heard between Susan and Sam at Cranbourne last month, all her hurt and jealousy. After all, had she not pushed Sam away?

'Oh, he was in fine form,' Lily said. 'Absolutely full of beans. Talking nineteen to the dozen.' In fact, she had not seen Cosmo so talkative or full of energy for a very long time. 'He said he felt ready, and his ribs are healed now.'

Once again Susan was chewing at her fingers, her blue eyes troubled. 'I'll be so glad when all this is over.'

There was a roar in the distance from the crowd,

accompanied immediately by the acceleration of all the engines as the race began. Lily and Susan craned their necks to see the cars approach in a loud, buzzing mass like a swarm of giant bees.

'There he is – oh, Lord God!' Susan gasped. 'Oh, Cozzy, be careful!'

Lily found herself holding her breath as the scattering of cars roared past them along the alarming tilt of the steep Brooklands track. The Flyer looked like a sleek silver teardrop whizzing past, so fast that she could not catch a proper glimpse of Cosmo's face under his leather flying helmet, but only his shape, braced as he grasped the wheel of the rushing car, and then they were gone round the bend, the buzzing roar fading.

'Imagine how it would be without the silencers!' Lily said, rubbing her ears. Silencers were compulsory at Brooklands races.

'Oh, this is awful,' Susan said tremulously. 'I worry so about him. He'll kill himself doing it, I'm sure he will. So many of them have . . .' She craned her neck looking along the track, head topped by a snug green hat, just showing the ends of her pale hair. Lily saw she had lately had her hair cut like her own, in a neat bob.

With each lap they relaxed fractionally. It felt as if Cosmo was in command, was holding on well among the other vehicles, many of them company-built ones.

'There's the Austin,' Lily pointed as they rushed past. She was about to say how pleased Sam would be to beat them on lap times, but she decided not to mention Sam.

Round and round they sped, burning along the tilted outer circuit of track. By the end of the race two cars had had to drop out with mechanical troubles but otherwise all went well and during the last lap Lily found herself almost shaking with relief. He had done it – and he had done it well!

There was another swell of sound from the crowd as the cars tore along the finishing straight and at last the air quietened to a lull, filled with excited chatter and the bookies calling out from their stalls along the track.

'Oh – I feel as if I've just lived a hundred years!' Susan said, shakily.

Lily felt drained as well.

'Sometimes I think it's worse watching than doing it,' she laughed. She wondered how Sam was feeling. Was he pleased with the result?

They did not get to the men until some time later, when they had agreed to meet for lunch, and they could immediately see that everyone was in glowing form. Piers was the first person they saw, waiting for them at the edge of the paddock as they had agreed so that they could come in as his guests for the meal. He beamed as he saw them approaching.

'What a morning, eh?' he cried, his pale, rather donnish face crinkled with enthusiasm. 'Your son has done us proud, Mrs Fairford. We're all delighted. A very respectable lap time – averaged 83.7 miles per hour! He was in marvellous form – come along and join us all for luncheon! Over here.' He indicated their picnic spot on the grass. 'As you see, we're dining *al fresco*!'

For the first time in a long time, as Lily sat down on the warm rug, she saw Sam turn to her and smile, a smile which she realized may not have been particularly directed at her, but somehow also encompassed her in the jubilation of the moment. Those seconds lifted her even more than Cosmo's success and she smiled back happily. For those few seconds his eyes rested on her face and they were caught in each other's gaze.

'Oh, well done, my darling! What a marvellous morning you've had!' Susan went to kiss Cosmo on the top of the head, and for once he did not react with resentment. He was very flushed in the face, eyes bright, and seemed high-wired and taut with success.

They had a light luncheon of cold meats and salad and a crisp white wine and the men all talked excitedly.

'What about going for a land speed record?' Cosmo said. His voice seemed raised a little too loudly. Lily could sense the vibrations of excitement coming from him. He was electric with it, though his moods seem to shift from moment to moment. 'We could go to Pendine Sands – I could take her faster than today if we were on the flat. She can go like the wind . . .'

'What's the current record?' Piers Larstonbury asked.

'It's a hundred and thirty-three point seven over the mile,' Sam said. 'That was here – back in May. Fellow called Guinness.'

'Well, what do you think, Ironside?'

Lily watched as Sam considered the idea, his face serious. In that moment, watching him, she knew he would always affect her by his presence.

'It'd certainly be interesting to try. I doubt she's up to that. It'd test our ratios all right – a new engine possibly . . .'

He and Loz began a technical conversation about what might be needed for more speed, to which Piers listened avidly. Cosmo ate his plateful of food ravenously.

'That's right,' Susan said to him. 'You need to keep your strength up for this afternoon.'

The Flyer had been entered, daringly, for one of the International Class races, competing against models from all over the world.

'I'm flying, Mater,' Cosmo told her, fizzily. 'You wait and see. There's nothing can stop me.'

'Here we go!' Susan cried. All eyes were turned in the same direction and once again the posse of cars came careering round the bend into view at frightening speed. The Heath Flyer was there among them, in the middle, and the two women gasped with relief.

'Go on, Cosmo – drive her!' Susan yelled, in a way quite out of character. 'Go on, go on!'

'He's doing fine!' Lily shouted in excitement.

There was a lull as they waited for the next lap. Cosmo was so full of it he would probably have overtaken a few of them by the time they next saw him. The first cars appeared, screaming their way round the track. Lily narrowed her eyes. Where was the Flyer? To her surprise, Cosmo had slipped back a little, was not holding his own as they might have expected.

'Oh dear!' Susan said.

There seemed nothing else to say and they watched dismally, waiting and hoping that during the next lap he would pick up and overtake.

But the next lap brought an even more worrying picture. As the cars spun round into view there was not a sign of Cosmo, not at first.

'He must be in trouble,' Lily said. 'Perhaps the engine's packed up . . .'

But then, there he was, second from the back, and by the next lap he was trailing way behind everyone else, to the point where there rose a joking kind of jeer from the crowd, seeing Cosmo moving along the track at an apparently leisurely speed.

'That one's out for a Sunday afternoon pleasure

cruise!' a man joked near then, and everyone around laughed. 'Looks as if he's dozed off at the wheel!'

Anguished, Lily strained her eyes to try and see Cosmo. He looked quite composed, very still as he drove, but he was losing speed all the time, the car following a more and more erratic course along the track.

'Looks as if he's had a few as well,' the man next to them suggested. 'Well, that's a bit of a joke – look at that!'

By the time the lap came round again, they stood on tiptoe, straining to see if he was trailing in their wake, but this time there was no sign of Cosmo at all.

'Dear God,' Susan said uneasily. 'Something's gone badly wrong this time. Oh, I do hope he's all right . . .'

'He could be anywhere,' Lily said miserably.

Not knowing what else to do, they waited among the crowd, willing Cosmo to appear. The race still had a couple more laps to go and they heard them coming round again, roaring and then receding, and still no Flyer. Then, moments later, Susan cried, 'Oh, look – there!'

On the near side of the track at the very bottom of the slope they caught sight of the silver gleam of Flyer's bodywork. Moving closer they saw that she had ground to a standstill alongside the bottom edge of the track.

'She looks all right!' Lily said, from the little she could see as they pushed their way across to her. The crowd close to the edge were all peering over at her, talking, speculating and calling out to Cosmo.

Looking down over the barrier, Lily saw that the car was slewed sideways into it, and all they could see was the back of Cosmo's head, encased in brown leather, as he sat, slumped unconscious, over the wheel.

Chapter Sixty-Nine

Once the race was finished and the car could be dragged to safety from the track, Cosmo remained slumped over the wheel and did not surface until they had reached a place to stop at the side of the finishing straight.

Piers, Sam and Loz gathered round, then hurried beside the motor as it was trailed along. Lily and Susan went tearing down to them. There was another great to-do going on, as one car had smashed through the railings on the finishing straight and hit a spectator, but they were far too worried about Cosmo to take in fully what had happened or that a good number of people were staring at them.

Cosmo came round, fighting furiously.

'Get off me, woman!' he bawled at Susan. 'Stop fussing over me! Oh, God in heaven . . .'

As he tried to get up and leave the car he seemed overcome by dizziness and sat quickly back down again, looking sick and drained.

Lily was frightened by the sight of Cosmo's flushed face and glazed look. She realized, though, that she had seen him like this before, that perhaps there had been something terribly wrong for a long time and that he had not told them.

'He looks terribly ill,' Susan said, white with worry.

'Just let me go to bed,' Cosmo was saying, his voice full of aggression.

'The doctor'll come,' Sam said, 'but he's seeing to the other smash . . .'

Eventually the doctor appeared, a serious-faced young man.

'Get these people away from me!' Cosmo roared.

'Perhaps you could all stand back and let me examine Mr Fairford,' the doctor said quietly. He measured Cosmo's blood pressure, apparently asking questions. Lily could see Cosmo's face, serious but mutinous. After some time the doctor stood up abruptly and walked over to them, his black bag in hand.

'You're his party?' His voice was curt. 'I should take him back to wherever you're staying and let him rest. There's no point in troubling the hospital.'

'But what's wrong?' Susan asked.

'Nothing that I can remedy,' the doctor snapped. 'You'd better ask him that yourself. Are you his . . . ?'

'Mother.' Susan's brow was crinkled with dismay. 'I don't understand, Doctor. Is he seriously ill?'

'No, he's not. I can't discuss a patient's symptoms when he has expressly asked me not to. Just put him to bed and quiz him yourself. He's a lucky man. That race could have been fatal for him or for several others.'

'Oh yes,' Cosmo shouted from where he was now sitting on the ground, his back against a front wheel of the Flyer. 'Aren't I always the lucky one?'

They all travelled back to the Pack Horse, the cosy public house where they had rooms once more, and Sam and Loz made sure Cosmo was put to bed. Lily's room was next to his, and she told them she would keep a lookout to see that he was all right. Cosmo said he wanted to sleep, but when she looked into the room, she saw him moving restlessly, looking flushed and uncomfortable. His bed was positioned under a low, sloping roof and she was worried that he might hit his head on the beam.

Daring to go closer, she sat beside him, placing her cool palm on his forehead. He looked so young and helpless suddenly and she wanted to mother him as she had when he was tiny.

'Darling Cozzy,' she whispered. 'What is the matter with you, my love?'

Cosmo opened his eyes, which filled with tears suddenly at the sight of her.

'Oh, what is it, dear?' Lily was really dismayed. It was so seldom that he showed any gentle emotions these days.

'I've disgraced us all . . .' He turned his head restlessly. 'I feel so rotten . . . I can't help it, Lily, believe me. I've tried . . . I've tried so hard . . .'

'Tried to do what, darling?' She took his hand, which felt very hot and dry, and leaned over to look down into his eyes.

Cosmo stared at her, and the tears began to run down his cheeks.

'Oh, Lily, you're the only one . . . You're the only one I've ever been able to turn to. You've been so loyal, so patient with me . . . I've let everyone down.'

'No, darling, of course you haven't!' She caressed his hand, as if trying to warm him and thaw the icy coldness of his self-loathing. 'You did marvellously this morning. I know Sam and Piers were absolutely delighted with the time you made. It can't always go right. You know you can do it, and no one's angry with you – you were just taken poorly. It'll be all right next time. Here, love, you look so hot – have a drink of water.'

He lifted his head to accept the glass of water, and she wiped his eyes with her handkerchief, feeling such great tenderness for him.

'You sleep a bit more, dear. I expect you'll wake feeling calmer.'

Once more she stroked his head and he stared up at her. Afterwards, she always blamed herself for not recognizing the utter desperation in his eyes.

'How is he? Shall I go up?' Susan half got to her feet when Lily went downstairs to find her. 'I looked in earlier but he seemed to be asleep. I could take him up his food.'

It was almost time for the evening meal and the smell of roasting beef filled the lower rooms and corridors.

Lily was touched by the way Susan deferred to her over Cosmo, as if she still felt that Lily had a better understanding of how to deal with him.

'He's upset,' she said, sitting beside Susan at a table. 'About the race, I mean. He feels in the doghouse.'

'Well, it was a shame, but if you're ill, you're ill.' Susan put away her leather writing case. Lily couldn't help wondering who she could be writing to. Susan had few people left in the world now, but for her elderly mother and her sister. 'Does he want food?' she asked.

'Perhaps a bit later,' Lily suggested. She did not think it a good moment for Susan to go up there and talk to Cosmo.

The men soon came down and they all ate a good dinner of roast beef. Though there was a subdued atmosphere round the table, Piers rallied them.

'Come along now, do cheer up. We had a marvellous result this morning – quite a cause for celebration! Let's raise a glass to our Flyer and to many more successes! Don't you agree, Ironside?

Sam raised his glass. 'The Heath Flyer. Onwards and upwards.'

Lily wondered what he thought, but he seemed surprisingly calm, almost detached from the situation, and she suddenly realized he was a man of great patience, whereas Loz was sitting at the table with a thunderous expression. Lily's eyes met Sam's. Both of them knew what Loz thought of Cosmo, and how angry and resentful he was about this afternoon's race.

'Well, I'm with you for as long as it takes,' Piers Larstonbury said happily. 'This has been a great adventure for me, thanks to your skill, the two of you.' And he raised his glass again, face breaking into a boyish smile. 'There'll be setbacks, of course, but it's all part of the process – eh, Marks?'

Looking at Piers, sitting there drinking beer with them all in his well-cut clothing, and seeing his kind, courteous way of trying to cheer them all, Lily felt a burst of great gratitude and affection for him. He was a good man, she thought. Such a good man, and she knew he would leave his wife for her in a moment, so devoted was he to her, if she ever showed any inclination to ask. She longed, in that moment, for his goodness to be enough.

'We'd better organize some food for Cozzy,' Susan said as the meal ended. 'I'm sure they'll do a tray or something. Lily, perhaps you'd better take it to him.'

Sam leaned gently towards her. 'Perhaps I should go up as well. I haven't had a chance for a chat with him and I'd like to stop him tearing himself up about it. I know what he's like.'

'All right,' Susan said gratefully.

475

Sam followed Lily up the stairs with the tray of beef and delicious treacle tart and she was conscious of his presence behind her all the way up. Despite these occasional meetings in the company of others they were still very awkward with each other, as if the air between them vibrated with unspoken emotions that they could not seem to begin on.

'I think it will help if you to talk to him,' she whispered outside Cosmo's room. 'He looks up to you a lot. And he was feeling very wretched about what happened today.'

'He shouldn't,' Sam said. 'It's all part of it. He was taken bad, that's all there is to it.'

Lily gave him a faint smile and went into her own room, whispering, 'Good luck!'

She heard Sam's voice speaking quietly from next door as she folded her clothes away on to the chair and looked for her night things, and she hoped Sam would be able to make a difference to Cosmo's state of mind. Poor Cozzy, he did get so cast down. So often he still seemed like a little boy to her, except that the saddest thing was that he had somehow seemed more happy and complete when he was four than ever he did now.

She was about to undress when she heard a tapping on the door, soft but insistent. Sam was outside, his face very grave. For a second he hesitated, then, inclining his head towards the next-door room, he said, 'I think you'd better come.'

To her astonishment he took her hand, leading her into Cosmo's room where he carefully closed the door.

'Prepare yourself, dear,' he said to her tenderly, and his face was terribly concerned.

'Cozzy?' Wild with dread, she ran to the bed. He was lying just as she had left him, eyes closed, seemingly asleep. The only thing she saw as different was the glass of water which he had somehow tipped over. Then she saw other things: the paper crumpled in one hand, the white dusting of powder on his upper lip, the blueness of both his lips and the stillness of him that was beyond waking. All these things she took in during those seconds which shook inside her like an earthquake invisible to anyone else.

She reached out, trembling, to touch Cosmo's neck, feeling for a pulse of life and hope, but there was nothing. Looking up, her fingertips still pressed to his lifeless flesh, her eyes met Sam's.

'What's happened? Oh my God, Sam, what's he done?'

Sam looked to Cosmo, then helplessly back at her again. There seemed nothing to say.

Chapter Seventy

'Cocaine hydrochloride?' You mean to say that my son has been . . . inhaling this . . . this powder like some sort of *poet*?'

They were gathered with the doctor and a policeman in the back room of the Pack Horse. Susan, in her shock and grief, had retreated back into the glassy, commanding woman Sam remembered so disliking in Ambala. She sat up very straight, hands clasped in her lap, giving off an air of superior frostiness. Loz and Piers stood tactfully nearby, as did the owner of the public house, who kept repeating that there had never been a death at the Pack Horse before, not while he was landlord.

'I'm afraid to say, Mrs Fairford,' the doctor said, 'that your son appears to have quite a lengthy history of drug addiction, judging by the condition of him.'

They were all frozen with shock and as yet Susan was too forbidding to accept comfort. Lily stood next to Sam, who seemed suddenly to be always at her side. She was also too shocked yet to weep. The doctor said that Cosmo must have known that he was taking a huge overdose of cocaine, that he had taken his own life, and she knew that she must have been the last person to speak to him. The memory of Cosmo's face suddenly made her tremble so that she thought her legs might give way. She groped for a chair and found Sam's arm holding her up.

'Thank you,' she whispered, sinking down on to a wooden bench. She looked up at him and then her eyes filled with tears.

Cosmo's funeral was held ten days later at the church at Lapsley, the village closest to the Cranbourne estate. There had been an inquest, which confirmed that Cosmo had died by his own hand.

There were not many at the funeral. Susan's mother and sister came, as well as Uncle William and some of the estate workers. Lily saw Bernard and Tim there, in their best Sunday suits. Piers Larstonbury drove up with Lily, and Sam came on his own. Loz, he said, regretted that he could not be there: he was needed in Birmingham with his family. Uncle William, no doubt through the prompting of Mrs Rainbow, had invited all who needed to, to sleep overnight at Cranbourne House.

They all stood in the village church amid the smells of old hymn books and candlewax and sang 'Abide with Me' and 'Lead Us, Heavenly Father, Lead Us'. Lily wept, unable to help herself as she thought of Cosmo's life, of his little face as she knew him in India, the eager, loving little boy he had been and all that he had become. Piers stood beside her, gently touching her arm at times when her tearfulness overwhelmed her. He understood that her loss of Cosmo in this tragic way was like losing her own son.

Susan, between her mother and sister, was dry-eyed and brittle, determined, as she said, not to 'lay all my emotions out in public'. She stood very straight, in her black coat and a wide-brimmed hat with a feather trailing gracefully down to the side, and elegant, high-heeled shoes. No one could get close to her: she had closed off from them all.

She's burying the last remaining member of her family, Lily thought. And the memory came to her of them all that day in Mussoorie when they picnicked under the deodars amid the sweeping mountain peaks with their waterfalls and meadows of flowers, when Isadora had been in love with horses and Charles and Susan seemed relaxed together and Cosmo ... But of course by then the circle had already been broken. Cosmo had been sent away: banished from the family, as it had always felt to him. Her eyes filled with tears again. The poor little mite, she thought. He had never really recovered from that.

Piers held her arm as they processed out of the church after the coffin. Cosmo was to be buried on the estate, close to the track where he had so loved to drive. Lily and Piers walked behind Susan and her family and Lily knew Sam and some of the other men were walking behind her. She knew with great clarity then that she needed to be walking on Sam's arm, that that was what was right and that nothing else ever had been or ever would be.

Once they had left the church she turned, looking for Sam with a sudden desperate need, but he had peeled off and was some distance away among the old graves, as if he needed to be alone. He stood looking across at the elms bordering the field beyond the churchyard, a slender, lonely figure in his dark overcoat, and in that glimpse, amid the desperate sorrow of the day which had somehow made everything clear, Lily knew how much she loved him. She longed to go to him, to pour out everything she felt to him.

Instead she walked obediently on Piers's arm to the

convoy of cars which would follow the black-plumed horses carrying Cosmo's body to its resting place at the edge of the fields where he had reluctantly spent so much of his boyhood.

Chapter Seventy-One

It was only once she was in the privacy of her room at Cranbourne that Susan allowed her grief to surface, and then it seemed to come over her with the impact of a heavy blow. Lily was with her as she wept, becoming utterly distraught, and in the end Lily was frightened by the force it. Not knowing what else to do, she went to Mrs Rainbow.

'I've been with her for an hour or more,' she said shakily, 'and she's more and more hysterical.'

'I'll send out for the doctor,' the housekeeper said. 'I expect 'e'll give her a little summat to sedate her.'

Whatever it was they gave Susan worked very effectively and by nine o'clock that evening she was in a deep sleep. Waiting by her bedside, Lily felt waves of exhaustion rolling over her, but she was not sleepy. She felt as if she needed hours to unwind and to think before she could relax enough.

Once she was certain Susan would not stir for some time, she crept from the room, closing the door very softly. She had barely got any distance away when she met Piers in the passage and realized that he had been on his way to her room. Immediately she felt resentful and hemmed in. Poor Piers, how kind and thoughtful he was! But just at present she ached to be alone in order to let the great void of Cosmo's death open within her. She did not want Piers's sexual advances, however much they were dressed up as offering comfort.

'Darling,' he said gently. 'Oh, my poor little girl, what a tragic time it has been. Come to me, my love.'

He went to take her in his arms in his kindly way but Lily, though not wanting to hurt him, found she simply could not bear it.

'Piers.' She stood her ground, resisting him. 'Dear, would you mind letting me be alone for a time, please? It's been such a terrible day.'

'Let me come with you, darling girl. I won't talk, I'll just be beside you . . .'

'No!' she said, more adamantly than she really meant to. Trying to soften the message she said, 'No, Piers. Do go and get some rest. It's been a very tiring day, but I do just need some time alone tonight. Please don't worry about me.'

'Of course, my dear.' She could not tell if his feelings were hurt. He was always so courteous. He kissed her and she watched him go towards his room, turning to raise a hand in affectionate parting to her.

Lily slipped down the stairs and let herself out into the enclosed garden at the side of the house. It was still warm and that lovely space between the walls seemed to distil the early autumn scents: the velvet sweetness of the last roses on the darkening air mixed with the more pungent smells from the herb garden. It was the time of night when the light is so uncertain that she began to imagine she was seeing shapes moving the other side of the garden, then realized that the dark, moving shadow she had seen was a tabby cat which lived in the wake of Mrs Rainbow, and it came up and miaowed at her.

'I haven't anything for you,' she said, bending to stroke it. 'It isn't any use carrying on at me like that.'

She left the walled part of the garden, remembering the loveliness of the smooth expanse of lawn beyond, its scent and the sense of space and freedom it gave her. For the time being her emotion was spent. The day had focused so intensely on Cosmo, on loss and tragedy, that now it was as if her mind had closed down and she could not think, or feel, any more about it. She felt scoured out and blank, needing simply to be quiet and be cradled by the gentle greenness of the place. She bent down and unbuttoned her shoes, slipping them off to feel the cool grass between her toes.

As she walked she saw another shadow moving where the edge of the lawn met the long grass and margin of trees. This time it was far too big to be a cat and she assumed it was one of the gardeners. She prepared herself to say a polite goodnight, but in a moment she knew who it was and that he had seen her.

'Lily?'

Sam stepped forward a few paces, then waited as she moved towards him. The memory of hearing him, here in the clearing with Susan, hardened her towards him, made her try to hold aloof from her need of him. Would this be another fight? she wondered. Another time when they just could not say what needed to be said? She stood barely more than a yard away, hardly able to see his expression.

'Last time we were here,' she said, hardly knowing what would come from her lips, 'I heard you down here with Susan. You were kissing her, were you not?'

There was a silence in which the gaze of each of them met somewhere in the dark space between them.

'Lily . . .' His voice was low and she knew immediately that now nothing would be hidden. 'You can't have forgotten. Please tell me you haven't. I don't know why you decided not to meet me in Mussoorie. I've wondered and agonized about it ever since, about your silence, even after I wrote and wrote. It was so cruel, so impossible to understand . . .'

'You wrote?' she burst out. 'You never wrote! I never heard a word from you. And I was . . .' She stumbled over how to explain about Ewan McBride and the crazed strangeness of those weeks.

'My employer wouldn't let me out. I couldn't get to you, I didn't hear from you . . . I thought you had left without saying goodbye, without trying . . .'

'But you never came! Not a word! I sent notes to the house – nothing back! What was I supposed to think? Lily . . .' He moved closer, but she stepped back, still terribly afraid of him.

'What about your wife? And what about Susan? What *were* you doing out here that night, Sam?'

'Oh God, Lily . . .' Sam made a despairing sound. 'Susan was . . . We just . . . I don't know. We were both lonely, taking comfort in each other for a few moments. It was no more than that. I like her – I never thought I'd say that, for a start! And I feel for her. She's had a rough ride. But we don't want each other, not really – you must know that! I'm not her sort – wrong sort of class altogether. When we came across each other in France, in that hospital, after the captain had been killed, it sort of ironed things out, made us more equal, and I liked her better . . . But that night here – it was just a thing of the moment . . .'

'And your wife?'

Sam sighed. 'I married Helen when we were far too young. Even back then I knew I'd made a dreadful

485

mistake, that first time in Ambala, when I'd met you . . .
I didn't know, not before then, what it could be like. I
got married, thinking that was the done thing, and soon
there was a baby on the way. But that second time, in
the hills – God help me, if you'd turned up that night, I
would have left her and stayed with you. I'm not proud
of that, but that was how it was – how it is. You're the
one, Lily. There's never been anyone anything like you
– nothing's touched it. That week in Mussoorie . . .' He
paused, shaking his head.

'God, woman, I was ill when I got home to England,
just being without you, thinking I'd never see you again
and never understanding why you . . . I suppose I was
pining for you. I was thin as a railing . . .' He looked up
at her. 'But you weren't there, you didn't want me.
You'd made that clear enough. And I had to go on and
do the decent thing for Helen and find other things to
occupy me – to *console* me . . .'

Lily stood quite still, letting the wonder of his words
sink into her.

'What about Piers?' he said miserably. 'He's married
as well.'

'They're only married under the law,' Lily said.
'There doesn't seem to be anything else left.'

'He's a thoroughly decent man, Lily, and a wealthy
one. Do you love him?'

'No,' she said simply. 'I don't.'

He waited a long interval for her to find words, until
at last she spoke into the darkness.

'Sam, I've been and I've done a lot of things I'm
ashamed of. I've been what people – what men,
especially – have wanted me to be. You've probably
heard things about me which must disgust you. I've
been Piers's mistress – for a living, yes, for money when

486

you come down to it, almost like a woman of the streets only more respectable, of course – because I couldn't seem to find any other way to be. I forced myself not to remember you and how it was in Ambala and in Mussoorie because I didn't think I could ever have that again, not with anyone. It frightens me even saying anything now . . . And after you'd gone . . . Oh, Sam . . .'

As the memories came she started to weep, but he did not dare move forward to touch her yet.

'You left me your child . . . When you left I was . . . I was . . .' The sobs interrupted. 'I was expecting and I didn't know what to do. I knew you didn't want me. I went to the nuns on the mountain . . .'

She told him then, about the laundry and the Bethel Home and about walking out that winter morning and shutting away any thoughts of their baby, of closing her heart down and training it to be a cool, calculating place where there were exchanges and bartering of services but no love. As she talked she realized gradually that he was weeping as well.

'Our child,' he said, wiping his eyes. 'Was it a boy or a girl?'

'A little girl,' Lily told him. 'I called her Victoria.'

The tears came then, a crying like none she had ever managed for the grief of Mussoorie, for Victoria, or now for Cosmo, the pain of it all tearing at her inside until she was on her knees, felled by it. Moments later she realized that Sam had come to kneel beside her, holding her head close to his warm chest, saying soft, loving words of comfort while he cried with her.

When she was a little calmer they stood up and held each other close, not speaking for a long time, as the darkness thickened and a night bird shrieked somewhere in the distance. And his body felt so familiar, so lovely against her and she breathed in the smell of him. Their lips found each other's and she remembered the feel of his kisses and the tears ran down her cheeks again at the joy of the memory.

'God,' Sam said, awed, 'I've found you again. Lily – my Lily.' He looked down into her eyes. 'I thought life was going to be the same now until I died, or Helen did. That there'd be nothing, no love. Nothing real that I could call mine.'

'And I thought I'd always look after other people's children, their houses and marriages – that I'd never have my own.' She gazed seriously at him. 'I love you, Sam and I always loved you and I wanted to come to you that afternoon, I honestly did, and I couldn't … I'll explain to you properly what happened, but I want to know that you believe me.'

'I do,' he said seriously. 'And I always wanted to. I didn't want to doubt you but I didn't know what else to think. Oh, Lily – there's no one like you, my dearest love. No one in this world.'

They stayed in the garden a long time, walking arm in arm round the margin of the lawn, Lily carrying her shoes in one hand, beginning to tell each other what had happened in these years of separation and all that they had felt and done. Sam told her about Joe, the words pouring out.

'We managed to rub along until he happened to us, Helen and me and the girls. I had my work, of course, kept busy and tried to keep on the straight and narrow. And then Joe came … when he died, well, that was truly the end of it. Helen and I just couldn't seem to get on after that, not even on the surface, the way we'd managed before …' He gave a deep sigh. 'You keep telling yourself things will be all right. They have to be because you're married, children, responsibility, and that's that. And I do feel responsible – I'll see she's all right. But, oh God, Lily . . .'

He stopped to hold her, kiss her again and she closed her eyes, her head pressed to his chest. She loved this man, how she loved him! It was such a relief, a miracle to know she had not imagined it, all those years ago, that she could love like this and be loved in return.

The moon was high in the sky when they crept up to Lily's room, arms round each other, the stair carpet feeling dry and rough under her feet after the night grass. They knew without saying anything that they could not be separated tonight, or ever again, and closed the door of her room behind them with a sigh of relief and a feeling of complete rightness. They had found each other again.

Chapter Seventy-Two

Bombay, India, 1924

Lily sat on the veranda at the back of the bungalow, smiling across the garden at the sight of a slim Indian girl dressed in a deep crimson sari, leading a little European boy across the shady strip of grass between the flower beds. The boy's grey eyes were fixed solemnly on his feet as he accompanied his *ayah* with his first tottering steps.

'I will sit here for half an hour or so, Lakshmi,' Lily called to the girl. She always made a point of calling her by her name, not just *ayah*, the way so many of the British women did in that imperious way. 'I shall take a little while to write my letter, and then he can come to me.'

'Yes, Memsahib.' The girl smiled shyly. She seemed almost always on the point of giggling whenever addressed, showing a row of strong, widely spaced teeth, and Lily liked her for her happy disposition.

She sat looking out for a moment, watching a clutter of crows wrangling around the birdbath, a little stone pool of water which the *mali* kept topped up. Somewhere nearby there were parrots in the trees. It was very hot and for a few moments Lily sat fanning herself with a few sheets of writing paper before opening the ink bottle and settling down to write.

14 Napier Road,
Bombay

May 10th, 1924

Dear Susan,

It was such a pleasure to receive your postcard telling us the likely day of your arrival. I am so happy at the thought of you coming to the hills with us and your being here. Though the people around here are pleasant enough, I shall so enjoy having a real friend and I'm longing for you to see our darling little Edward again. He will no doubt have grown up a lot since we left – I can scarcely believe we celebrated his first birthday three days ago!

So, we are settling in. We have an airy bungalow, which is very simply furnished and suits our needs perfectly well, and the cook is a good deal better tempered than some! Sam's agenting job for the Austin Company has worked out well so far. Imports are increasing like anything, of course, and, more importantly, he can also work more at what he really loves – dealing with the actual motor cars. He's such a good mechanic that now the word has got round he is much in demand and is happy as anything, off here and there and is already talking about entering the reliability trials here later in the year for the Motor Union of Western India. They have to drive to Mahableshwar and back, and you know Sam – if there's one thing he loves it's being out on the road! Last week we were invited out to one of the villages and while we were there, a man went round with a tom-tom and gathered a crowd together for a lecture on hookworm disease. I didn't understand the local language, but the lecturer used lantern pictures and the effect was very vivid.

As for my Edward – well, I could write pages. He seems to have settled well and I feel very much at home being back here myself. Back to the old mixed feelings of affection and exasperation towards the place! With a child now myself, though, I am anxious about all the illnesses he might pick up and am a bit more jumpy – I know I don't need to explain to you. But so far Edward has kept remarkably well, and even though the great summer heat has arrived, he still seems very happy and lively. He has half adopted a mongoose which lives at the bottom of the garden, and calls it Oose!

I shall leave all else to catch up on once you arrive – and look forward to it with great happiness. We shall come to meet you as soon as we hear!

Wishing you a safe and pleasant voyage and so looking forward to see you.

My love and good wishes,
Lily

Chapter Seventy-Three

Mussoorie, India, 1924

'We should be able to see the mountains today – although it's hard to tell with this cloud,' Lily said.

She and Susan were toiling up the steep path to Gun Hill, both dressed in light frocks, for although they were in the mountains it was still the hottest time of the year. The monsoon rains were due to arrive at any time.

'Phew – I need to get in better condition,' Susan said, pausing on the path, close to a small Hindu shrine which had been cut into the rock since they were last here, containing a small, stumpy Siva *lingam* draped with marigolds.

'Does it upset you, being here?' Lily asked anxiously. They were not all that far from Zinnias, the house Susan and Charles Fairford had rented for those weeks in 1910.

Susan smiled wistfully, wiping her forehead with her handkerchief. Her face, if anything, was even more attractive now she was older. Though more lined, it was more giving, not like the closed young woman she had been.

'Not upset, no. It feels very strange, and brings it all back . . . So much of it, especially before the war, feels so very long ago. And, of course, we weren't here with Cozzy . . .'

Her eyes filled and she looked away. Lily felt her own throat ache with tears. There was no need for either of them to say any more.

They walked on and reached the top, catching a sight of the great peaks of Banderpunch, Pithwara and the Gangotri in bright sunlight, though a pall of deep mauve cloud was massing to obscure its light. They were buffeted by sudden powerful gusts of wind.

'It's changing fast,' Lily said, shading her eyes. 'The rain's coming.'

'It's astonishing, isn't it?' Susan said. She sighed. 'I so loathed living here, yet it's wonderful to be back.'

She had docked in Bombay the week before, while the plains were gripped by the great heat, and travelled with Lily, Sam and little Edward, the *ayah* and servants, first by rail to Dehra Dun, then road, up to this simple bungalow in Mussoorie.

After a silence, while they watched the cloud edge its way over, blanketing the high Himalaya, Susan turned to her.

'It must be strange for you too?'

'Yes – it is a little bit,' Lily said.

Lily had never told Susan all that had happened to her in Mussoorie, not about the way she had let Ewan McBride use her, or about little Victoria. It felt too private and shameful. Sam was the only person she had told, or would ever tell about all that. The first afternoon after they arrived in Mussoorie, she slipped out while the others were resting, delighting in being in the lovely mountain town again, but with a mission that she wanted to fulfil on her own. She suddenly felt very uncomfortable, wondering if there were people still living here who would remember her, and she pulled the brim of her straw hat well down.

She walked towards the beginning of the Camel's Back Road feeling more and more on edge as the McBrides' bungalow came into view. Her heart pounded at the recollection of how she had had to escape with Jane Brown that night, of the desperation of those days imprisoned inside. The house did not look the same, though. It was painted yellow now, and there were many more pots of flowers in the front garden. She sensed already this was no longer a house belonging to Dr McBride. They must have gone.

Even so, she did not have the courage to knock at that door. Instead, she called at the next house, where she was greeted by a young, slender servant who cocked his head in an enquiring way.

'This bungalow next door,' she pointed, 'whose house is it?'

'That is house of Mr Jenkins,' he said.

'Ah. Not Dr McBride, then?'

This was met with another small inclination of the head. He probably knew nothing about the former occupants, Lily thought, but in case, she asked, 'Where is Dr McBride?'

'He is dead, long time,' the young man said. 'Wife die, then he die soon after.'

Lily was surprised. 'You knew him?'

He nodded. 'I have been here a long time.'

Lily dimly remembered a child of the servants who worked in this house when she was here before and guessed this must be the same boy.

'Thank you.' She smiled at him. 'You have been very helpful.'

She walked away, feeling released. She could walk the streets of the town without coming face to face with the doctor. That part of her past would not come back to pursue her. She revelled in being back, walking the sloping streets, seeing the houses perched along the edge of the hills, all the school children, the bazaars and the awesome sights of the mountains which met her at every turn. It was like a homecoming.

'You seem so very happy,' Susan said, as they walked back down the path. It became easier to talk about personal things, out here in the hills.

'Yes.' Lily darted a smile at her. 'I am. Very. Even though things are irregular. I don't know if we'll ever be able to marry properly . . .'

'People assume you're married, I suppose?' Susan instinctively lowered her voice, even though there was no one else around. The sky was fast turning a threatening, inky colour and they walked faster.

'Yes,' Lily said. 'There might be a divorce. Helen, Sam's wife, is not keen and we'll have to wait for a time. And of course we're a family.' She blushed. 'I'm not young, and I'd still like one more child . . .' For Susan, the old Susan, the whole situation would have seemed a deep disgrace. But Susan had suffered and changed. And, Lily realized, she and Sam were of the same spirit: they were adventurers. He longed to escape from what he felt to be stifling suburban life, and Lily was happy outside social convention so long as she could be with him and with her boy. So much in her life had been irregular right from the start, far more than Susan really knew, that she simply lived with it and rejoiced in finding love.

'No one has said anything to us,' she said with a wry smile. 'But you are not staying in a house that is in the least respectable!'

'Oh,' Susan smiled wanly. 'I think I can learn to live with it.'

'And you? Tell me more about him.' 'Him' was someone who had been given a faint but increasing mention in Susan's letters.

'Well, he's gentle and kind, not wealthy but comfortable enough. His name is Edmund Reardon and he's an antiquarian bookseller, in Brighton . . .' She looked at Lily and laughed wholeheartedly. 'You see, I should really rather like a quiet suburban life, dear, just for a change. I've had more than enough of loss and change and shifting from place to place carrying my garden about in flowerpots!'

'And is he a bachelor?'

'A widower,' Susan said. Lily could hear the affection in her voice as she talked about him. 'He's ten years my senior and his wife died of TB, very sadly – not so very long after they were married. There's one grown-up son. And Edmund is just utterly, utterly sweet, Lily . . .' She looked bashfully at her friend and both of them laughed.

Lily dared to say, 'You know, there was a time when I thought you might find some happiness with the major – Piers Larstonbury.'

'Oh no! Nice fellow, of course, but even if I'd been keen, I don't think he'll ever leave that dreadful wife of his, even if she does run rings round him. And now he and Mr Marks and the rest of the team are so embroiled at Brooklands building all these motors, I should never have seen anything of him anyway!'

Lily wondered whether Susan was right, whether Piers would in the end have ever left Virginia for her. All she could feel for him now, though, was a tender gratitude for his sorrow and generosity when she told him her true feelings for Sam.

'I can't keep you here if your heart is somewhere else,' he said, his face pale with shock and hurt. 'But I shall never forget you, Lily. You're a beautiful woman and he's the luckiest man alive.' He was a gentleman, Piers Larstonbury, a kind and rather lonely one.

Susan was telling Lily about her gentle courtship with Edmund Reardon when the first drops began to come down. They were close to the bottom of the zigzag path from Gun Hill and the sky was creaking with thunder, the first drops seeming like the overspill from a vast store of water just waiting to release itself.

'Oh, here it comes!' Lily cried. It was impossible not to feel a sense of exaltation at the beginning of the monsoon, so that the thought of a drenching was glorious after all the dust and heat. As they hurried along the Mall, the vendors were quickly pulling scraps of tarpaulin over their wares and everyone who had somewhere to go was running for cover, putting up umbrellas as they did so.

And then down it came, the water seeming to gush from the sky in a great, hissing, splashing fall of giant drops which were soon bouncing from awnings and roofs, pouring out from the end of guttering, forming a stream which ran down the sloping streets. Children ran out in it, laughing and catching handfuls of water, the cows took cover under overhanging roofs and everyone seemed to be smiling and shrieking and running or just standing, turning their faces up to catch its cool rush on their cheeks and letting it soak all through their clothing. By the time Lily and Susan reached the gate of the bungalow they were wading, ankle-deep in water.

'Wait for me!' Sam was striding along the road, laughing as water streamed down his hair.

Lily opened the door and ushered Susan inside as Sam reached them, gasping.

'I was looking for you, dear – where've you been?'

'Gun Hill . . .'

She was about to step into the house after Susan, but he caught her hand and they stood for a moment in the little front garden with their hands linked, letting the rain come down and down over them, drinking it in like flowers and loving it.

'That's my girl – God, I love you, Lily . . .' His smiling eyes met hers and he pulled her close and kissed and kissed her in the rain.

For a time, that evening, the great force of the rainstorm had passed and there was a calm lull before a gathering of the next. The air felt washed and clear, and full of the new smell of soaked earth and all the plants and trees looked washed and vivid.

Lily, Sam and Susan sat on the veranda, sipping whisky and water after their evening meal. Edward was settled in bed and as they enjoyed the calm of the evening, comfortable in wicker chairs, every so often, Lily felt Sam take her hand privately, between their chairs, and hold it, giving it a loving squeeze.

A deep quietness seemed to fill the valley. From far away an occasional cry, human or animal, broke into the silence, a peace which had also come upon the three of them. The sun sank behind the dark peaks far over to their left and every now and then they saw the black outlines of birds wheeling against the changing colours as the newly washed sky altered with the sun's retiring. It passed through white-gold to orange and pink, the mountains edged with purple shadows which sank into the smoke-grey of dusk, and they could just distinguish the outline of the peaks. Still they sat on without lighting candles, not wanting to break into the gradual eclipse of the day but let things be, watching the darkness gather, until the hour when there are no more edges to the land, and sky and rock are one.

FOR MORE ON

ANNIE MURRAY

sign up to receive our

SAGA WRITER NEWSLETTER

Packed with **features, competitions, authors'
and readers' letters** and **news of exclusive events,**
it's a 'must-read' for every Annie Murray fan!

Simply fill in your details below and tick to confirm that you would
like to receive saga-related news and promotions and return to us at
Pan Macmillan, Saga Newsletter, 20 New Wharf Road, London, N1 9RR.

NAME _____

ADDRESS _____

_____ POSTCODE_____

EMAIL _____

☐ *I would like to receive saga-related news and promotions (please tick)*

*You can unsubscribe at any time in writing or through our website where you can also see
our privacy policy which explains how we will store and use your data.*